The Wheel of Time®

By Robert Jordan

New Spring: The Novel
The Eye of the World
The Great Hunt
The Dragon Reborn
The Shadow Rising
The Fires of Heaven
Lord of Chaos
A Crown of Swords
The Path of Daggers
Winter's Heart
Crossroads of Twilight
Knife of Dreams

By Robert Jordan and Brandon Sanderson

The Gathering Storm
Towers of Midnight
A Memory of Light

By Robert Jordan and Teresa Patterson

The World of Robert Jordan's The Wheel of Time

By Robert Jordan, Harriet McDougal, Alan Romanczuk, and Maria Simons

The Wheel of Time Companion

TOWERS
OF
MIDNIGHT

ROBERT JORDAN
AND
BRANDON SANDERSON

A TOM DOHERTY ASSOCIATES BOOK
NEW YORK

This is a work of fiction. All of the characters, organizations, and events portrayed in this novel are either products of the authors' imaginations or are used fictitiously.

TOWERS OF MIDNIGHT

Copyright © 2010 by Bandersnatch Group, Inc.

Excerpt from *Memory of Light* copyright © 2012 by Bandersnatch Group, Inc.

The phrase "The Wheel of Time" and the snake-wheel symbol are trademarks of Bandersnatch Group, Inc.

All rights reserved.

Maps by Ellisa Mitchell
Interior illustrations by Matthew C. Nielsen and Ellisa Mitchell

A Tor Book
Published by Tom Doherty Associates
120 Broadway
New York, NY 10271

www.tor-forge.com

Tor® is a registered trademark of Macmillan Publishing Group, LLC.

ISBN 978-1-250-25261-6

Our books may be purchased in bulk for promotional, educational, or business use. Please contact your local bookseller or the Macmillan Corporate and Premium Sales Department at 1-800-221-7945, extension 5442, or by email at MacmillanSpecialMarkets@macmillan.com.

First Edition: 2010
First Premium Mass Market Edition: 2020

Printed in the United States of America

0 9 8 7 6 5 4 3 2

For Jason Denzel, Melissa Craib, Bob Kluttz, Jennifer Liang, Linda Taglieri, Matt Hatch, Leigh Butler, Mike Mackert, and all those readers who over the years have made The Wheel of Time part of their lives, and in doing so have made the lives of others better.

Contents

It soon became obvious, even within the *stedding*, that the Pattern was growing frail. The sky darkened. Our dead appeared, standing in rings outside the borders of the *stedding*, looking in. Most troublingly, trees fell ill, and no song would heal them.

It was in this time of sorrows that I stepped up to the Great Stump. At first, I was forbidden, but my mother, Covril, demanded I have my chance. I do not know what sparked her change of heart, as she herself had argued quite decisively for the opposing side. My hands shook. I would be the last speaker, and most seemed to have already made up their minds to open the Book of Translation. They considered me an afterthought.

And I knew that unless I spoke true, humanity would be left alone to face the Shadow. In that moment, my nervousness fled. I felt only a stillness, a calm sense of purpose. I opened my mouth, and I began to speak.

—from *The Dragon Reborn*, by Loial, son of Arent son of Halan, of Stedding Shangtai

The Wheel of Time

the Dead Sea

Aile Dashar

Aryth Ocean

North

Bandar Eban

RIVER DHAGON

ARAD DOMAN

RIVER ARINELLE

Katar

Falme

Toman Head

Almoth Plain

Taerst Suar Tork wood

Baerlon

THE TWO RIVERS

Emonds Field

Tanchico

Aryth Ocean

RIVER ANDAHAR

TARABON

Jehannah GE

Elmora

Amador

AMADICIA

the Shadow Coast

RIVER SHAKIA

Tremalking

Windbiter's Finger

Ebou D

Qaim

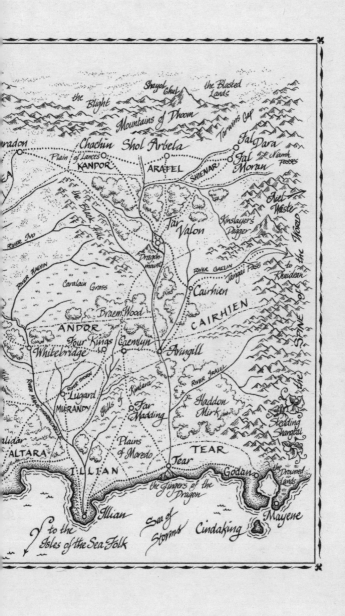

PROLOGUE

Distinctions

M andarb's hooves beat a familiar rhythm on broken ground as Lan Mandragoran rode toward his death. The dry air made his throat rough, and the earth was sprinkled white with crystals of salt that precipitated from below. Distant red rock formations loomed to the north, where sickness stained them. Blight marks, a creeping dark lichen.

He continued riding east, parallel to the Blight. This was still Saldaea, where his wife had deposited him, only narrowly keeping her promise to take him to the Borderlands. It had stretched before him for a long time, this road. He'd turned away from it twenty years ago, agreeing to follow Moiraine, but he'd always known he would return. This was what it meant to bear the name of his fathers, the sword on his hip, and the *hadori* on his head.

This rocky section of northern Saldaea was known as the Proska Flats. It was a grim place to ride; not a plant grew on it. The wind blew from the north, carrying with it a foul stench. Like that of a deep, sweltering mire bloated with corpses. The sky overhead stormed dark, brooding.

That woman, Lan thought, shaking his head. How quickly Nynaeve had learned to talk, and think, like an Aes Sedai. Riding to his death didn't pain him, but knowing she feared for him . . . that did hurt. Very badly.

He hadn't seen another person in days. The Saldaeans had fortifications to the south, but the land here was scarred with broken ravines that made it difficult for Trollocs to assault; they preferred attacking near Maradon.

That was no reason to relax, however. One should never

relax, this close to the Blight. He noted a hilltop; that would be a good place for a scout's post. He made certain to watch it for any sign of movement. He rode around a depression in the ground, just in case it held waiting ambushers. He kept his hand on his bow. Once he traveled a little farther eastward, he'd cut down into Saldaea and cross Kandor on its good roadways. Then—

Some gravel rolled down a hillside nearby.

Lan carefully slid an arrow from the quiver tied to Mandarb's saddle. Where had the sound come from? *To the right,* he decided. Southward. The hillside there; someone was approaching from behind it.

Lan did not stop Mandarb. If the hoofbeats changed, it would give warning. He quietly raised the bow, feeling the sweat of his fingers inside his fawn-hide gloves. He nocked the arrow and pulled carefully, raising it to his cheek, breathing in its scent. Goose feathers, resin.

A figure walked around the southern hillside. The man froze, an old, shaggy-maned packhorse walking around beside him and continuing on ahead. It stopped only when the rope at its neck grew taut.

The man wore a laced tan shirt and dusty breeches. He had a sword at his waist, and his arms were thick and strong, but he didn't look threatening. In fact, he seemed faintly familiar.

"Lord Mandragoran!" the man said, hastening forward, pulling his horse after. "I've found you at last. I assumed you'd be traveling the Kremer Road!"

Lan lowered his bow and stopped Mandarb. "Do I know you?"

"I brought supplies, my Lord!" The man had black hair and tanned skin. Borderlander stock, probably. He continued forward, overeager, yanking on the overloaded packhorse's rope with a thick-fingered hand. "I figured that you wouldn't have enough food. Tents—four of them, just in case—some water too. Feed for the horses. And—"

"Who *are* you?" Lan barked. "And how do you know who I am?"

The man drew up sharply. "I'm Bulen, my Lord. From Kandor?"

From Kandor . . . Lan remembered a gangly young messenger boy. With surprise, he saw the resemblance. "*Bulen?* That was twenty years ago, man!"

"I know, Lord Mandragoran. But when word spread in the palace that the Golden Crane was raised, I knew what I had to do. I've learned the sword well, my Lord. I've come to ride with you and—"

"The word of my travel has spread to *Aesdaishar?*"

"Yes, my Lord. El'Nynaeve, she came to us, you see. Told us what you'd done. Others are gathering, but I left first. Knew you'd need supplies."

Burn that woman, Lan thought. And she'd made him *swear* that he would accept those who wished to ride with him! Well, if she could play games with the truth, then so could he. Lan had said he'd take anyone who wished to *ride* with him. This man was not mounted. Therefore, Lan could refuse him. A petty distinction, but twenty years with Aes Sedai had taught him a few things about how to watch one's words.

"Go back to Aesdaishar," Lan said. "Tell them that my wife was wrong, and I have *not* raised the Golden Crane."

"But—"

"I don't need you, son. Away with you." Lan's heels nudged Mandarb into a walk, and he passed the man standing on the road. For a few moments, Lan thought that his order would be obeyed, though the evasion of his oath pricked at his conscience.

"My father was Malkieri," Bulen said from behind.

Lan continued on.

"He died when I was five," Bulen called. "He married a Kandori woman. They both fell to bandits. I don't remember much of them. Only something my father told me: that someday, we would fight for the Golden Crane. All I have of him is this."

Lan couldn't help but look back as Mandarb continued to walk away. Bulen held up a thin strap of leather, the *hadori,* worn on the head of a Malkieri sworn to fight the Shadow.

"I would wear the *hadori* of my father," Bulen called, voice growing louder. "But I have nobody to ask if I may. That is the tradition, is it not? Someone has to give me the right to don it. Well, I would fight the Shadow all my days."

He looked down at the *hadori*, then back up again and yelled, "I would stand against the darkness, al'Lan Mandragoran! Will you tell me I cannot?"

"Go to the Dragon Reborn," Lan called to him. "Or to your queen's army. Either of them will take you."

"And you? You will ride all the way to the Seven Towers without supplies?"

"I'll forage."

"Pardon me, my Lord, but have you *seen* the land these days? The Blight creeps farther and farther south. Nothing grows, even in once-fertile lands. Game is scarce."

Lan hesitated. He reined Mandarb in.

"All those years ago," Bulen called, walking forward, his packhorse walking behind him. "I hardly knew who you were, though I know you lost someone dear to you among us. I've spent years cursing myself for not serving you better. I swore that I would stand with you someday." He walked up beside Lan. "I ask you because I have no father. May I wear the *hadori* and fight at your side, al'Lan Mandragoran? My King?"

Lan breathed out slowly, stilling his emotions. *Nynaeve, when next I see you . . .* But he would not see her again. He tried not to dwell upon that.

He *had* made an oath. Aes Sedai wiggled around their promises, but did that give him the same right? No. A man was his honor. He could not deny Bulen.

"We ride anonymously," Lan said. "We do *not* raise the Golden Crane. You tell nobody who I am."

"Yes, my Lord," Bulen said.

"Then wear that *hadori* with pride," Lan said. "Too few keep to the old ways. And yes, you may join me."

Lan nudged Mandarb into motion, Bulen following on foot. And the one became two.

Perrin slammed his hammer against the red-hot length of iron. Sparks sprayed into the air like incandescent insects. Sweat beaded on his face.

Some people found the clang of metal against metal grating. Not Perrin. That sound was soothing. He raised the hammer and slammed it down.

Sparks. Flying chips of light that bounced off his leather

vest and his apron. With each strike, the walls of the room—
sturdy leatherleaf wood—*fuzzed,* responding to the beats of
metal on metal. He was dreaming, though he wasn't in the
wolf dream. He knew this, though he didn't know *how* he
knew.

The windows were dark; the only light was that of the
deep red fire burning on his right. Two bars of iron sim-
mered in the coals, waiting their turn at the forge. Perrin
slammed the hammer down again.

This was peace. This was *home.*

He was making something important. So very important.
It was a piece of something larger. The first step to creating
something was to figure out its parts. Master Luhhan had
taught Perrin that on his first day at the forge. You couldn't
make a spade without understanding how the handle fit to
the blade. You couldn't make a hinge without knowing how
the two leaves moved with the pin. You couldn't even make
a nail without knowing its parts: head, shaft, point.

Understand the pieces, Perrin.

A wolf lay in the corner of the room. It was large and
grizzled, fur the color of a pale gray river stone, and scarred
from a lifetime of battles and hunts. The wolf laid its head
on its paws, watching Perrin. That was natural. Of *course*
there was a wolf in the corner. Why wouldn't there be? It
was Hopper.

Perrin worked, enjoying the deep, burning heat of the
forge, the feel of the sweat trailing down his arms, the scent
of the fire. He shaped the length of iron, one blow for every
second beat of his heart. The metal never grew cool, but
instead retained its malleable red-yellow.

What am I making? Perrin picked up the length of glowing iron with his tongs. The air warped around it.

Pound, pound, pound, Hopper sent, communicating in
images and scents. *Like a pup jumping at butterflies.*

Hopper didn't see the point of reshaping metal, and found
it amusing that men did such things. To a wolf, a thing was
what it was. Why go through so much effort to change it
into something else?

Perrin set the length of iron aside. It cooled immediately,
fading from yellow, to orange, to crimson, to a dull black.
Perrin had pounded it into a misshapen nugget, perhaps the
size of two fists. Master Luhhan would be ashamed to see

such shoddy work. Perrin needed to discover what he was
making soon, before his master returned.

No. That was wrong. The dream shook, and the walls
grew misty.

I'm not an apprentice. Perrin raised a thick-gloved hand
to his head. *I'm not in the Two Rivers any longer. I'm a
man, a married man.*

Perrin grabbed the lump of unshaped iron with his
tongs, thrusting it down on the anvil. It flared to life with
heat. *Everything is still wrong.* Perrin smashed his hammer down. *It should all be better now! But it isn't. It seems
worse somehow.*

He continued pounding. He hated those rumors that the
men in camp whispered about him. Perrin had been sick
and Berelain had cared for him. That was the end of it. But
still those whispers continued.

He slammed his hammer down over and over. Sparks
flew in the air like splashes of water, far too many to come
from one length of iron. He gave one final strike, then
breathed in and out.

The lump hadn't changed. Perrin growled and grabbed
the tongs, setting the lump aside and taking a fresh bar
from the coals. He *had* to finish this piece. It was so important. But what was he making?

He started pounding. *I need to spend time with Faile,
to figure things out, remove the awkwardness between us.
But there's no time!* Those Light-blinded fools around him
couldn't take care of themselves. Nobody in the Two Rivers
ever needed a lord before.

He worked for a time, then held up the second chunk of
iron. It cooled, turning into a misshapen, flattened length
about as long as his forearm. Another shoddy piece. He set
it aside.

If you are unhappy, Hopper sent, *take your she and
leave. If you do not wish to lead the pack, another will.*
The wolf's sending came as images of running across open
fields, stalks of grain brushing along his snout. An open
sky, a cool breeze, a thrill and lust for adventure. The scents
of new rain, of wild pastures.

Perrin reached his tongs into the coals for the final bar of
iron. It burned a distant, dangerous yellow. "I can't leave."
He held the bar up toward the wolf. "It would mean giving

in to being a wolf. It would mean losing myself. I won't do that."

He held the near-molten steel between them, and Hopper watched it, yellow pinpricks of light reflecting in the wolf's eyes. This dream was so odd. In the past, Perrin's ordinary dreams and the wolf dream had been separate. What did this blending mean?

Perrin was afraid. He'd come to a precarious truce with the wolf inside of him. Growing too close to the wolves was dangerous, but that hadn't prevented his turning to them when seeking Faile. Anything for Faile. In doing so, Perrin had nearly gone mad, and had even tried to kill Hopper.

Perrin wasn't nearly as in control as he'd assumed. The wolf within him could still reign.

Hopper yawned, letting his tongue loll. He smelled of sweet amusement.

"This is not funny." Perrin set the final bar aside without working on it. It cooled, taking on the shape of a thin rectangle, not unlike the beginnings of a hinge.

Problems are not amusing, Young Bull, Hopper agreed. *But you are climbing back and forth over the same wall. Come. Let us run.*

Wolves lived in the moment; though they remembered the past and seemed to have an odd sense for the future, they didn't worry about either. Not as men did. Wolves ran free, chasing the winds. To join them would be to ignore pain, sorrow and frustration. To be free . . .

That freedom would cost Perrin too much. He'd lose Faile, would lose his very *self*. He didn't want to be a wolf. He wanted to be a man. "Is there a way to reverse what has happened to me?"

Reverse? Hopper cocked his head. To go backward was not a way of wolves.

"Can I . . ." Perrin struggled to explain. "Can I run so far that the wolves cannot hear me?"

Hopper seemed confused. No. "Confused" did not convey the pained sendings that came from Hopper. Nothingness, the scent of rotting meat, wolves howling in agony. Being cut off was not a thing Hopper could conceive.

Perrin's mind grew fuzzy. Why had he stopped forging? He had to finish. Master Luhhan would be disappointed! Those lumps were terrible. He should hide them. Create something else, show he *was* capable. He *could* forge. Couldn't he?

A hissing came from beside him. Perrin turned, surprised to see that one of the quenching barrels beside the hearth was boiling. *Of course,* he thought. *The first pieces I finished. I dropped them in there.*

Suddenly anxious, Perrin grabbed his tongs and reached into the turbulent water, steam engulfing his face. He found something at the bottom and brought it out with his tongs: a chunk of white-hot metal.

The glow faded. The chunk was actually a small steel figurine in the shape of a tall, thin man with a sword tied to his back. Each line on the figure was detailed, the ruffles of the shirt, the leather bands on the hilt of the tiny sword. But the face was distorted, the mouth open in a twisted scream.

Aram, Perrin thought. *His name was Aram.*

Perrin couldn't show *this* to Master Luhhan! Why had he created such a thing?

The figurine's mouth opened farther, screaming soundlessly. Perrin cried out, dropping it from the tongs and jumping back. The figurine fell to the wood floor and shattered.

Why do you think so much about that one? Hopper yawned a wide-jawed wolf yawn, tongue curling. *It is common that a young pup challenges the pack leader. He was foolish, and you defeated him.*

"No," Perrin whispered. "It is not common for humans. Not for friends."

The wall of the forge suddenly melted away, becoming smoke. It felt natural for that to happen. Outside, Perrin saw an open, daylit street. A city with broken-windowed shops.

"Malden," Perrin said.

A smoky, translucent image of himself stood outside. The image wore no coat; his bare arms bulged with muscles. He kept his beard short, but it made him look older, more intense. Did Perrin really look *that* imposing? A squat fortress of a man with golden eyes that seemed to glow, carrying a gleaming half-moon axe as large as a man's head.

There was something wrong about that axe. Perrin stepped out of the smithy, passing through the shadowy version of himself. When he did, he became that image, axe heavy in his hand, work clothes vanishing and battle gear replacing it.

He took off running. Yes, this *was* Malden. There were Aiel in the streets. He'd lived this battle, though he was much calmer this time. Before, he'd been lost in the thrill of fighting and of seeking Faile. He stopped in the street. "This is wrong. I carried my hammer into Malden. I threw the axe away."

A horn or a hoof, Young Bull, does it matter which one you use to hunt? Hopper was sitting in the sunlit street beside him.

"Yes. It matters. It does to me."

And yet you use them the same way.

A pair of Shaido Aiel appeared around a corner. They were watching something to the left, something Perrin couldn't see. He ran to attack them.

He sheared through the chin of one, then swung the spike on the axe into the chest of the other. It was a brutal, terrible attack, and all three of them ended on the ground. It took several stabs from the spike to kill the second Shaido.

Perrin stood up. He did remember killing those two Aiel, though he had done it with hammer and knife. He didn't regret their deaths. Sometimes a man needed to fight, and that was that. Death was terrible, but that didn't stop it from being necessary. In fact, it had been wonderful to clash with the Aiel. He'd felt like a wolf on the hunt.

When Perrin fought, he came close to becoming someone else. And that was dangerous.

He looked accusingly at Hopper, who lounged on a street corner. "Why are you making me dream this?"

Making you? Hopper asked. *This is not my dream, Young Bull. Do you see my jaws on your neck, forcing you to think it?*

Perrin's axe streamed with blood. He knew what was coming next. He turned. From behind, Aram approached, murder in his eyes. Half of the former Tinker's face was coated in blood, and it dripped from his chin, staining his red-striped coat.

Aram swung his sword for Perrin's neck, the steel hissing in the air. Perrin stepped back. He refused to fight the boy again.

The shadowy version of himself split off, leaving the real Perrin in his blacksmith's clothing. The shadow exchanged blows with Aram. *The Prophet explained it to me . . . You're*

*really Shadowspawn. . . . I have to rescue the Lady Faile
from you. . . .*

The shadowy Perrin changed, suddenly, into a wolf. It
leaped, fur nearly as dark as that of a Shadowbrother, and
ripped out Aram's throat.

"No! It didn't happen like that!"

It is a dream, Hopper sent.

"But I didn't kill him," Perrin protested. "Some Aiel shot
him with arrows right before. . . ."

Right before Aram would have killed Perrin.

The horn, the hoof, or the tooth, Hopper sent, turning
and ambling toward a building. Its wall vanished, revealing
Master Luhhan's smithy inside. *Does it matter? The dead
are dead. Two-legs do not come here, not usually, once
they die. I do not know where it is that they go.*

Perrin looked down at Aram's body. "I should have taken
that fool sword from him the moment he picked it up. I
should have sent him back to his family."

Does not a cub deserve his fangs? Hopper asked, genuinely confused. *Why would you pull them?*

"It is a thing of men," Perrin said.

*Things of two-legs, of men. Always, it is a thing of men to
you. What of things of wolves?*

"I am not a wolf."

Hopper entered the forge, and Perrin reluctantly followed.
The barrel was still boiling. The wall returned, and Perrin
was once again wearing his leather vest and apron, holding
his tongs.

He stepped over and pulled out another figurine. This
one was in the shape of Tod al'Caar. As it cooled, Perrin
found that the face wasn't distorted like Aram's, though the
lower half of the figurine was unformed, still a block of
metal. The figurine continued to glow, faintly reddish, after
Perrin set it down on the floor. He thrust his tongs back into
the water and pulled free a figure of Jori Congar, then one
of Azi al'Thone.

Perrin went to the bubbling barrel time and time again,
pulling out figurine after figurine. After the way of dreams,
fetching them all took both a brief second and what seemed
like hours. When he finished, hundreds of figurines stood
on the floor facing him. Watching. Each steel figure was

lit with a tiny fire inside, as if waiting to feel the forger's hammer.

But figurines like this wouldn't be forged; they'd be cast. "What does it mean?" Perrin sat down on a stool.

Mean? Hopper opened his mouth in a wolf laugh. *It means there are many little men on the floor, none of which you can eat. Your kind is too fond of rocks and what is inside of them.*

The figurines seemed accusing. Around them lay the broken shards of Aram. Those pieces seemed to be growing larger. The shattered hands began working, clawing on the ground. The shards all became little hands, climbing toward Perrin, reaching for him.

Perrin gasped, leaping to his feet. He heard laughter in the distance, ringing closer, shaking the building. Hopper jumped, slamming into him. And then . . .

Perrin started awake. He was back in his tent, in the field where they'd been camped for a few days now. They'd run across a bubble of evil the week before that had caused angry red, oily serpents to wiggle from the ground all through camp. Several hundred were sick from their bites; Aes Sedai Healing had been enough to keep most of them alive, but not restore them completely.

Faile slept beside Perrin, peaceful. Outside, one of his men tapped a post to count off the hour. Three taps. Still hours until dawn.

Perrin's heart pounded softly, and he raised a hand to his bare chest. He half-expected an army of tiny metal hands to crawl out from beneath his bedroll.

Eventually, he forced his eyes closed and tried to relax. This time, sleep was very elusive.

Graendal sipped at her wine, which glistened in a goblet trimmed with a web of silver around the sides. The goblet had been crafted with drops of blood caught in a ring pattern within the crystal. Frozen forever, tiny bubbles of brilliant red.

"We should be *doing* something," Aran'gar said, lounging on the chaise and eyeing one of Graendal's pets with a predatory hunger as he passed. "I don't know how you stand it, staying so far from important events, like some scholar holed up in a dusty corner."

Graendal arched an eyebrow. A scholar? In some dusty *corner*? Natrin's Barrow was modest compared to some palaces she had known, during the previous Age, but it was hardly a hovel. The furnishings were fine, the walls bearing an arching pattern of thick, dark hardwoods, the marble of the floor sparkling with inlaid chips of mother-of-pearl and gold.

Aran'gar was just trying to provoke her. Graendal put the irritation out of her mind. The fire burned low in the hearth, but the pair of doors—leading out onto a fortified walkway three stories in the air—was open, letting in a crisp mountain breeze. She rarely left a window or door open to the outside, but today she liked the contrast: warmth from one side, a cool breeze from the other.

Life was about *feeling*. Touches on your skin, both passionate and icy. Anything other than the normal, the average, the lukewarm.

"Are you listening to me?" Aran'gar asked.

"I always listen," Graendal said, setting aside her goblet as she sat on her own chaise. She wore a golden, enveloping dress, sheer but buttoned to the neck. What marvelous fashions these Domani had, ideal for teasing while revealing.

"I *loathe* being so removed from things," Aran'gar continued. "This Age is exciting. Primitive people can be so interesting." The voluptuous, ivory-skinned woman arched her back, stretching arms toward the wall. "We're missing all of the excitement."

"Excitement is best viewed from a distance," Graendal said. "I would think you'd understand that."

Aran'gar fell silent. The Great Lord had not been pleased with her for losing control of Egwene al'Vere.

"Well," Aran'gar said, standing. "If that is your thought on it, I will seek more interesting evening sport."

Her voice was cool; perhaps their alliance was wearing thin. In that case, it was time for reinforcement. Graendal opened herself and accepted the Great Lord's dominance of her, feeling the thrilling ecstasy of his power, his passion, his very *substance*. It was so much more intoxicating than the One Power, this raging torrent of fire.

It threatened to overwhelm and consume her, and despite

being filled with the True Power, she could channel only a thin trickle of it. A gift to her from Moridin. No, from the Great Lord. Best not to begin associating those two in her mind. For now, Moridin was Nae'blis. For now only.

Graendal wove a ribbon of Air. Working with the True Power was similar, yet not identical, to working with the One Power. A weave of the True Power would often function in a slightly different way, or have an unanticipated side effect. And there were some weaves that could *only* be crafted by the True Power.

The Great Lord's essence forced the Pattern, straining it and leaving it scarred. Even something the Creator had designed to be eternal could be unraveled using the Great Lord's energies. It bespoke an eternal truth—something as close to being sacred as Graendal was willing to accept. Whatever the Creator could build, the Great Lord could destroy.

She snaked her ribbon of Air through the room toward Aran'gar. The other Chosen had stepped out onto the balcony; Graendal forbade the creation of gateways inside, lest they damage her pets or her furnishings. Graendal lifted the ribbon of Air up to Aran'gar's cheek and caressed it delicately.

Aran'gar froze. She turned, suspicious, but it took only a moment for her eyes to open wide. She wouldn't have felt the goose bumps on her arms to indicate Graendal was channeling. The True Power gave no hint, no sign. Male or female, no one could see or sense the weaves—not unless he or she had been granted the privilege of channeling the True Power.

"What?" the woman asked. "How? Moridin is—"

"Nae'blis," Graendal said. "Yes. But once the Great Lord's favor in this regard was not confined to the Nae'blis." She continued to caress Aran'gar's cheek, and the woman flushed.

Aran'gar, like the other Chosen, lusted for the True Power while fearing it at the same time—dangerous, pleasurable, seductive. When Graendal withdrew her line of Air, Aran'gar stepped back into the room and returned to her chaise, then sent one of Graendal's pets to fetch her toy Aes Sedai. Lust still burned Aran'gar's cheeks; likely she would use Delana to distract herself. Aran'gar seemed to find it amusing to force the homely Aes Sedai into subservience.

Delana arrived moments later; she always remained nearby. The Shienaran woman was pale-haired and stout, with thick limbs. Graendal's lips turned down. Such an unpretty thing. Not like Aran'gar herself. She'd have made an ideal pet. Maybe someday Graendal would have the chance to make her into one.

Aran'gar and Delana began to exchange affections on the chaise. Aran'gar was insatiable, a fact Graendal had exploited on numerous occasions, the lure of the True Power being only the latest. Of course, Graendal enjoyed pleasures herself, but she made certain that people thought she was far more self-indulgent than she was. If you knew what people expected you to be, you could use those expectations. It—

Graendal froze as an alarm went off in her ears, the sound of crashing waves beating against one another. Aran'gar continued her pleasures; she couldn't hear the sound. The weave was very specific, placed where her servants could trip it to give her warning.

Graendal climbed to her feet, strolling around the side of the room, giving no indication of urgency. At the door, she sent a few of her pets in to help distract Aran'gar. Best to discover the scope of the problem before involving her.

Graendal walked down a hallway hung with golden chandeliers and ornamented with mirrors. She was halfway down a stairwell when Garumand—the captain of her palace guard—came bustling up. He was Saldaean, a distant cousin of the Queen, and wore a thick mustache on his lean, handsome face. Compulsion had made him utterly loyal, of course.

"Great Lady," he said, panting. "A man has been captured approaching the palace. My men recognize him as a minor lord from Bandar Eban, a member of House Ramshalan."

Graendal frowned, then waved for Garumand to follow as she made her way to one of her audience chambers—a small, windowless room decorated in crimson. She wove a ward against eavesdropping, then sent Garumand to bring the intruder.

Soon, he returned with some guards and a Domani man dressed in bright greens and blues, a beauty mark shaped like a bell on his cheek. His neat, short beard was tied with tiny bells, and they jingled as the guards shoved him forward. He brushed off his arms, glaring at the soldiers, and straightened his ruffled shirt. "Am I to understand that I have been delivered to—"

He cut off with a choking sound as Graendal wrapped him in weaves of Air and dug into his mind. He stuttered, eyes growing unfocused.

"I am Piqor Ramshalan," he said in a monotone. "I have been sent by the Dragon Reborn to seek an alliance with the merchant family residing in this fortification. As I am smarter and more clever than al'Thor, he needs me to build alliances for him. He is particularly afraid of those living in this palace, which I find ridiculous, since it is distant and unimportant.

"Obviously, the Dragon Reborn is a weak man. I believe that by gaining his confidence, I can be chosen as the next King of Arad Doman. I wish for you to make an alliance with me, not with him, and will promise you favors once I am king. I d—"

Graendal waved a hand and he cut off in midword. She folded her arms, hairs bristling as she shivered.

The Dragon Reborn had found her.

He had sent a distraction for her.

He thought he could manipulate her.

She instantly wove a gateway to one of her most secure hiding places. Cool air wafted in from an area of the world where it was morning, not early evening. Best to be careful. Best to flee. And yet . . .

She hesitated. *He must know pain . . . he must know frustration . . . he must know anguish. Bring these to him. You will be rewarded.*

Aran'gar had fled from her place among Aes Sedai, foolishly allowing herself to be sensed channeling *saidin*. She still bore punishment for her failure. If Graendal left now—discarding a chance to twist al'Thor about himself—would she be similarly punished?

"What is this?" Aran'gar's voice asked outside. "Let me through, you fools. Graendal? What are you doing?"

Graendal hissed softly, then closed the gateway and composed herself. She nodded for Aran'gar to be allowed into the room. The lithe woman stepped up to the doorway, eyeing—and assessing—Ramshalan. Graendal shouldn't have sent the pets to her; the move had likely made her suspicious.

"Al'Thor has found me," Graendal said curtly. "He sent this one to make an 'alliance' with me, but did not tell him who I was. Al'Thor likely wants me to think that this man stumbled upon me accidentally."

Aran'gar pursed her lips. "So you'll flee? Run from the center of excitement again?"

"This, from you?"

"I was surrounded by enemies. Flight was my only option." It sounded like a practiced line.

Words like those were a challenge. Aran'gar would serve *her*. Perhaps . . . "Does that Aes Sedai of yours know Compulsion?"

Aran'gar shrugged. "She's been trained in it. She's passably skilled."

"Fetch her."

Aran'gar raised an eyebrow, but nodded in deference, disappearing to run the errand herself—probably to gain time to think. Graendal sent a servant for one of her dove cages. They arrived with the bird before Aran'gar was back, and Graendal carefully wove the True Power—once again thrilling in the rush of holding it—and crafted a complex weave of Spirit. Could she remember how to do this? It had been so long.

She overlaid the weave on the bird's mind. Her vision seemed to *snap*. In a moment, she could see two images in front of her—the world as she saw it and a shadowed version of what the bird saw. If she focused, she could turn her attention to one or the other.

It made her mind hurt. The vision of a bird was entirely different from that of a human being: She could see a much larger field, and the colors were so vivid as to be nearly blinding, but the view was blurry, and she had trouble judging distance.

She tucked the bird's sight into the back of her head. A dove would be unobtrusive, but using one was more difficult than a raven or a rat, the Great Lord's own favored eyes. The weave worked better on those than it did other animals. Though, most vermin that watched for the Great Lord had to report back before he knew what they'd seen. Why that was, she was not certain—the intricacies of the

True Power's special weaves never had made much sense to her. Not as much as they had to Aginor, at least.

Aran'gar returned with her Aes Sedai, who was looking increasingly timid these days. She curtsied low to Graendal, then remained in a subservient posture. Graendal carefully removed her Compulsion from Ramshalan, leaving him dazed and disoriented.

"What is it you wish me to do, Great One?" Delana asked, glancing at Aran'gar and then back at Graendal.

"Compulsion," Graendal said. "As intricate and as complex as you can make it."

"What do you wish it to do, Great Lady?"

"Leave him able to act like himself," Graendal said. "But remove all memory of events here. Replace them with a memory of talking to a merchant family and securing their alliance. Add a few other random requirements on him, whatever occurs to you."

Delana frowned, but she had learned not to question the Chosen. Graendal folded her arms and tapped one finger as she watched the Aes Sedai work. She felt increasingly nervous. Al'Thor knew where she was. Would he attack? No, he wouldn't harm women. That particular failing was an important one. It meant she had time to respond. Didn't she?

How had he managed to trace her to this palace? She had covered herself *perfectly*. The only minions she'd let out of her sight were under Compulsion so heavy that it would kill them to remove it. Could it be that the Aes Sedai he kept with him—Nynaeve, the woman gifted in Healing—had been able to undermine and read Graendal's weaves?

Graendal needed time, and she needed to discover what al'Thor knew. If Nynaeve al'Meara had the skill needed to read Compulsions, that was dangerous. Graendal needed to lay him a false trail, delay him—hence her requirement that Delana create a thick Compulsion with strange provisions in it.

Bring him agony. Graendal could do that.

"You next," she said to Aran'gar once Delana had finished. "Something convoluted. I want al'Thor and his Aes Sedai to find the touch of a man on the mind." That would confuse them further.

Aran'gar shrugged, but focused as if laying down a thick

and complex Compulsion on the unfortunate Ramshalan's mind. He was *somewhat* pretty. Did al'Thor assume she'd want him for one of her pets? Did he even remember enough of being Lews Therin to know that about her? Her reports on how much of his old life he remembered were contradictory, but he seemed to be recalling more and more. That was what worried her. Lews Therin could have tracked her to this palace, perhaps. She'd never expected that al'Thor would be able to do the same.

Aran'gar finished.

"Now," Graendal said, releasing her weaves of Air and speaking to Ramshalan, "return and tell the Dragon Reborn of your success here."

Ramshalan blinked, shaking his head. "I . . . Yes, my Lady. Yes, I believe the ties we made today will be extremely beneficial to both of us." He smiled. Weak-minded fool. "Perhaps we should dine and drink to our success, Lady Basene? It has been a wearying trip to see you, and I—"

"Go," Graendal said coldly.

"Very well. You will be rewarded when I am king!"

Her guards led him away, and he began whistling with a self-satisfied air. Graendal sat down and closed her eyes; several of her soldiers stepped over to guard her, their boots soft on the thick rug.

She looked through the dove's eyes, accustoming herself to its strange way of seeing. At her order, a servant picked it up and carried it to a window in the hallway outside the room. The bird hopped onto the windowsill. Graendal gave it a soft nudge to go forward; she wasn't practiced enough to take control completely. Flying was far more difficult than it looked.

The dove flapped out of the window. The sun was lowering behind the mountains, outlining them in angry red and orange, and the lake below fell into a deep, shadowy blue-black. The view was thrilling but nauseating as the dove soared up into the air and landed on one of the towers.

Ramshalan eventually walked out of the gates below. Graendal nudged the dove and it leaped off the tower, plunging toward the ground. Graendal gritted her teeth at the stomach-churning descent, the palace stoneworks becoming a blur. The dove leveled out and flapped after

Ramshalan. He seemed to be grumbling to himself, though she could make out only rudimentary sounds through the dove's unfamiliar earholes.

She followed him for some time through the darkening woods. An owl would have been better, but she didn't have one captive. She chided herself for that. The dove flew from branch to branch. The forest floor was a messy tangle of underbrush and fallen pine needles. She found that distinctly unpleasant.

There was light up ahead. It was faint, but the dove's eyes could easily pick out light and shadow, motion and stillness. She nudged it to investigate, leaving Ramshalan.

The light was coming from a gateway in the middle of a clear patch, spilling forth a warm glow. There were figures standing before it. One of them was al'Thor.

Graendal felt instant panic. He *was* here. Looking down over the ridge, toward her. Darkness within! She hadn't known for certain if he'd be here in person, or if Ramshalan would travel through a gateway to give his report. What game was al'Thor playing? She landed her dove on a branch. Aran'gar was complaining and asking Graendal what she was seeing. She'd seen the dove, and would know what Graendal was up to.

Graendal concentrated harder. The Dragon Reborn, the man who had once been Lews Therin Telamon. He *knew* where she was. He had once hated her deeply; how much *did* he remember? Did he recall her murder of Yanet?

Al'Thor's tame Aiel brought Ramshalan forward, and Nynaeve inspected him. Yes, that Nynaeve did seem to be able to read Compulsion. She knew what to look for, at least. She would have to die; al'Thor relied upon her; her death would bring him pain. And after her, al'Thor's dark-haired lover.

Graendal nudged the dove down onto a lower branch. What would al'Thor do? Graendal's instincts said he wouldn't dare move, not until he unraveled her plot. He acted the same now as he had during her Age; he liked to plan, to spend time building to a crescendo of an assault.

She frowned. What was he saying? She strained, trying to make sense of the sounds. Cursed bird's earholes—the voices sounded like croaks. *Callandor?* Why was he talking about *Callandor*? And a box . . .

Something burst alight in his hand. The access key. Graendal gasped. He'd brought *that* with him? It was nearly as bad as balefire.

Suddenly she understood. She'd been played.

Cold, terrified, she released the dove and snapped her eyes open. She was still sitting in the small, windowless room, Aran'gar leaning beside the doorway with arms folded.

Al'Thor had sent Ramshalan in, *expecting* him to be captured, expecting him to have Compulsion placed on him. Ramshalan's only purpose was to give al'Thor confirmation that Graendal was in the tower.

Light! How clever he's become.

She released the True Power and embraced less-wonderful *saidar*. Quickly! She was so unsettled that her embrace nearly failed. She was sweating.

Go. She had to go.

She opened a new gateway. Aran'gar turned, staring through the walls in the direction of al'Thor. "So much power! What is he doing?"

Aran'gar. She and Delana had made the weaves of Compulsion.

Al'Thor must think Graendal dead. If he destroyed the place and those Compulsions remained, al'Thor would know that he'd missed and that Graendal lived.

Graendal formed two shields and slammed them into place, one for Aran'gar, one for Delana. The women gasped. Graendal tied off the weaves and bound the two in Air.

"Graendal?" Aran'gar said, voice panicked. "What are you—"

It was coming. Graendal leaped for the gateway, rolling through it, tumbling and ripping her dress on a branch. A blinding light rose behind her. She struggled to dismiss the gateway, and caught one glimpse of the horrified Aran'gar before everything behind was consumed in beautiful, pure whiteness.

The gateway vanished, leaving Graendal in darkness.

She lay, heart beating at a terrible speed, nearly blinded by the glare. She'd made the quickest gateway she could, one that led only a short distance away. She lay in the dirty underbrush atop a ridge behind the palace.

A wave of *wrongness* washed over her, a warping in

the air, the Pattern itself rippling. A balescream, it was called—a moment when creation itself howled in pain.

She breathed in and out, trembling. But she had to see. She had to know. She rose to her feet, left ankle twisted. She hobbled to the treeline and looked down.

Natrin's Barrow—the entire palace—was gone. Burned out of the Pattern. She couldn't see al'Thor on his distant ridge, but she knew where he was.

"You," she growled. "You have become *far* more dangerous than I assumed."

Hundreds of beautiful men and women, the finest she'd gathered, gone. Her stronghold, dozens of items of Power, her greatest ally among the Chosen. Gone. This was a disaster.

No, she thought. *I live.* She'd anticipated him, if only by a few moments. Now he would think she was dead.

She was suddenly the safest she'd been since escaping the Great Lord's prison. Except, of course, that she'd just caused the death of one of the Chosen. The Great Lord would not be pleased.

She limped away from the ridge, already planning her next move. This would have to be handled very, very carefully.

Galad Damodred, Lord Captain Commander of the Children of the Light, yanked his booted foot free of the ankle-deep mud with a slurping sound.

Bitemes buzzed in the muggy air. The stench of mud and stagnant water threatened to gag him with each breath as he led his horse to drier ground on the path. Behind him trudged a long, twisting column four men wide, each one as muddied, sweaty and weary as he was.

They were on the border of Ghealdan and Altara, in a swampy wetland where the oaks and spicewoods had given way to laurels and spidery cypress, their gnarled roots spread like spindly fingers. The stinking air was hot—despite the shade and cloud cover—and thick. It was like breathing in a foul soup. Galad steamed beneath his breastplate and mail, his conical helmet hanging from his saddle, his skin itching from the grime and salty sweat.

Miserable though it was, this route was the best way.

Asunawa would not anticipate it. Galad wiped his brow with the back of his hand and tried to walk with head high for the benefit of those who followed him. Seven thousand men, Children who had chosen him rather than the Seanchan invaders.

Dull green moss hung from the branches, drooping like shreds of flesh from rotting corpses. Here and there the sickly grays and greens were relieved by a bright burst of tiny pink or violet flowers clustering around trickling streams. Their sudden color was unexpected, as if someone had sprinkled drops of paint on the ground.

It was strange to find beauty in this place. Could he find the Light in his own situation as well? He feared it would not be so easy.

He tugged Stout forward. He could hear worried conversations from behind, punctuated by the occasional curse. This place, with its stench and biting insects, would try the best of men. Those who followed Galad were unnerved by the place the world was becoming. A world where the sky was constantly clouded black, where good men died to strange twistings of the Pattern, and where Valda—the Lord Captain Commander before Galad—had turned out to be a murderer and a rapist.

Galad shook his head. The Last Battle would soon come.

A clinking of chain mail announced someone moving up the line. Galad glanced over his shoulder as Dain Bornhald arrived, saluted, and fell into place beside him. "Damodred," Dain said softly, their boots squishing in mud, "perhaps we should turn back."

"Backward leads only to the past," Galad said, scanning the pathway ahead. "I have thought about this much, Child Bornhald. This sky, the wasting of the land, the way the dead walk . . . There is no longer time to find allies and fight against the Seanchan. We must march to the Last Battle."

"But this swamp," Bornhald said, glancing to the side as a large serpent slid through the underbrush. "Our maps say we should have been out of it by now."

"Then surely we are near the edge."

"Perhaps," Dain said, a trail of sweat running from his brow down the side of his lean face, which twitched. Fortunately, he'd run out of brandy a few days back. "Unless the map is in error."

Galad didn't respond. Once-good maps were proving faulty these days. Open fields would turn to broken hills, villages would vanish, pastures would be arable one day, then suddenly overgrown with vines and fungus. The swamp could indeed have spread.

"The men are exhausted," Bornhald said. "They're good men—you know they are. But they are starting to complain." He winced, as if anticipating a reprimand from Galad.

Perhaps once he would have given one. The Children should bear their afflictions with pride. However, memories of lessons Morgase had taught—lessons he hadn't understood in his youth—were nagging at him. Lead by example. Require strength, but first show it.

Galad nodded. They were nearing a dry clearing. "Gather the men. I will speak to those at the front. Have my words recorded, then passed to those behind."

Bornhald looked perplexed, but did as commanded. Galad stepped off to the side, climbing up a small hill. He placed his hand on the hilt of his sword, inspecting his men as the companies at the front gathered around. They stood with slouched postures, legs muddied. Hands flailed at bitemes or scratched at collars.

"We are Children of the Light," Galad announced, once they were gathered. "These are the darkest days of men. Days when hope is weak, days when death reigns. But it is on the deepest nights when light is most glorious. During the day, a brilliant beacon can appear weak. But when all other lights fail, it will guide!

"*We* are that beacon. This mire is an affliction. But we are the Children of the Light, and our afflictions are our strength. We are hunted by those who should love us, and other pathways lead to our graves. And so we will go forward. For those we must protect, for the Last Battle, for the Light!

"Where is the victory of this swamp? I refuse to feel its bite, for I am *proud*. Proud to live in these days, proud to be part of what is to come. All the lives that came before us in this Age looked forward to our day, the day when men will be tested. Let others bemoan their fate. Let others cry and wail. We will not, for we will face this test with heads held high. And we will let it *prove* us strong!"

Not a long speech; he did not wish to extend their time in

the swamp overly much. Still, it seemed to do its duty. The men's backs straightened, and they nodded. Men who had been chosen to do so wrote down the words, and moved back to read them to those who had not been able to hear.

When the troop continued forward, the men's footsteps no longer dragged, their postures were no longer slumped. Galad remained on his hillside, taking a few reports, letting the men see him as they passed.

When the last of the seven thousand had gone by, Galad noted a small group waiting at the base of the hill. Child Jaret Byar stood with them, looking up at Galad, sunken eyes alight with zeal. He was gaunt, with a narrow face.

"Child Byar," Galad said, walking down from the hill-side.

"It was a good speech, my Lord Captain Commander," Byar said fervently. "The Last Battle. Yes, it *is* time to go to it."

"It is our burden," Galad said. "And our duty."

"We will ride northward," Byar said. "Men will come to us, and we will grow. An enormous force of the Children, tens of thousands. *Hundreds* of thousands. We will wash over the land. Maybe we will have enough men to cast down the White Tower and the witches, rather than needing to ally with them."

Galad shook his head. "We will need the Aes Sedai, Child Byar. The Shadow will have Dreadlords, Myrddraal, *Forsaken.*"

"Yes, I suppose." Byar seemed reluctant. Well, he'd seemed reluctant about the idea before, but he *had* agreed to it.

"Our road is difficult, Child Byar, but the Children of the Light will be leaders at the Last Battle."

Valda's misdeeds had tarnished the entire order. More than that, Galad was increasingly convinced that Asunawa had played a large role in the mistreatment and death of his stepmother. That meant the High Inquisitor himself was corrupt.

Doing what was right was the most important thing in life. It required any sacrifice. At this time, the right thing to do was flee. Galad could not face Asunawa; the High Inquisitor was backed by the Seanchan. Besides, the Last Battle was more important.

Galad stepped swiftly, walking through the muck back

toward the front of the line of Children. They traveled light, with few pack animals, and his men wore their armor—their mounts were laden with food and supplies.

At the front, Galad found Trom speaking with a few men who wore leathers and brown cloaks, not white tabards and steel caps. Their scouts. Trom nodded to him in respect; the Lord Captain was one of Galad's most trusted men. "Scouts say there's a small issue ahead, my Lord Captain Commander," Trom said.

"What issue?"

"It would be best to show it to you directly, sir," said Child Barlett, the leader of the scouts.

Galad nodded him forward. Ahead, the swampy forest seemed to be thinning. Thank the Light—did that mean they were nearly free?

No. As Galad arrived, he found several other scouts looking out at a dead forest. Most trees in the swamp bore leaves, though sickly ones, but those ahead were skeletal and ashen, as if burned. There was some kind of sickly white lichen or moss growing over everything. The tree trunks looked emaciated.

Water flooded this area, a wide but shallow river with a very slow current. It had swallowed the bases of many of the trees, and fallen tree limbs broke the dirty brown water like arms reaching toward the sky.

"There are corpses, my Lord Captain Commander," one of the scouts said, gesturing upriver. "Floating down. Looks like the remnants of a distant battle."

"Is this river on our maps?" Galad asked.

One by one, the scouts shook their heads.

Galad set his jaw. "Can this be forded?"

"It's shallow, my Lord Captain Commander," Child Barlett said. "But we'll have to watch for hidden depths."

Galad reached out to a tree beside him and broke free a long branch, the wood snapping loudly. "I will go first. Have the men remove their armor and cloaks."

The orders went down the line, and Galad took off his armor and wrapped it in his cloak, then tied it to his back. He hiked up his trousers as far as he could, then stepped down the gentle bank and plowed forward into the murky water. The sharply cold spring runoff made him tense. His boots sank inches into the sandy bottom, filling with water, stirring up swirls of mud. Stout made a louder splash as he stepped into the water behind.

It wasn't too difficult to walk in; the water only came up to his knees. He used his stick to find the best footing. Those skeletal, dying trees were unnerving. They didn't seem to be rotting, and now that he was closer, he could better see the ash-gray fuzz among the lichen that coated their trunks and branches.

The Children behind splashed loudly as more and more of them entered the wide stream. Nearby, bulbous forms floated down the river to catch upon rocks. Some were the corpses of men, but many were larger. *Mules,* he realized, catching a better look at a snout. *Dozens of them.* They'd been dead for some time, judging by the bloat.

Likely a village upstream had been attacked for its food. This wasn't the first group of dead they'd found.

He reached the other side of the river, then climbed out. As he unrolled his trouser legs and donned his armor and cloak, he felt his shoulder aching from the blows Valda had given him. His thigh still stung, too.

He turned and continued down the game trail northward, leading the way as other Children reached the bank. He longed to ride Stout, but he dared not. Though they were out of the river, the ground was still damp, uneven, and pocked with hidden sinkholes. If he rode, he could easily cost Stout a broken leg and himself a broken crown.

So he and his men walked, surrounded by those gray trees, sweating in the miserable heat. He longed for a good bath.

Eventually, Trom jogged up the line to him. "All men are across safely." He checked the sky. "Burn those clouds. I can never tell what time it is."

"Four hours past midday," Galad said.

"You're certain?"

"Yes."

"Weren't we to stop at midday to discuss our next step?" That meeting was to have taken place once they got through the swamp.

"For now, we have few choices," Galad said. "I will lead the men northward to Andor."

"The Children have met . . . hostility there."

"I have some secluded land up in the northwest. I will

not be turned away there, regardless of who controls the throne."

Light send that Elayne held the Lion Throne. Light send that she had escaped the tangles of the Aes Sedai, though he feared the worst. There were many who would use her as a pawn, al'Thor not the least of them. She was headstrong, and that could make her easy to manipulate.

"We'll need supplies," Trom said. "Forage is difficult, and more and more villages are empty."

Galad nodded. A legitimate concern.

"It's a good plan, though," Trom said, then lowered his voice. "I'll admit, Damodred, I worried that you'd refuse leadership."

"I could not. To abandon the Children now, after killing their leader, would be wrong."

Trom smiled. "It's as simple as that to you, isn't it?"

"It should be as simple as that to anyone." Galad *had* to rise to the station he had been given. He had no other option. "The Last Battle comes and the Children of the Light will fight. Even if we have to make alliances with the Dragon Reborn himself, we *will* fight."

For some time, Galad hadn't been certain about al'Thor. Certainly the Dragon Reborn would have to fight at the Last Battle. But was that man al'Thor, or was he a puppet of the Tower, and not the true Dragon Reborn? That sky was too dark, the land too broken. Al'Thor *must* be the Dragon Reborn. That didn't mean, of course, that he wasn't also a puppet of the Aes Sedai.

Soon they passed beyond the skeletal gray trees, reaching ones that were more ordinary. These still had yellowed leaves, too many dead branches. But that was better than the fuzz.

About an hour later, Galad noted Child Barlett returning. The scout was a lean man, scarred on one cheek. Galad held up a hand as the man approached. "What word?"

Barlett saluted with arm to chest. "The swamp dries out and the trees thin in about one mile, my Lord Captain Commander. The field beyond is open and empty, the way clear to the north."

Light be thanked! Galad thought. He nodded to Barlett, and the man hurried back through the trees.

Galad glanced back at the line of men. They were

muddied, sweaty, and fatigued. But still, they were a grand sight, their armor replaced, their faces determined. They had followed him through this pit of a swamp. They were good men.

"Pass the word to the other Lords Captain, Trom," Galad said. "Have them send word to their legions. We'll be out of this in under an hour."

The older man smiled, looking as relieved as Galad felt. Galad continued onward, jaw set against the pain of his leg. The cut was well bound, and there was little danger of further damage. It was painful, but pain could be dealt with.

Finally free of this bog! He would need to plot their next course carefully, staying away from any towns, major roads, or estates held by influential lords. He ran through the maps in his head—maps memorized before his tenth nameday.

He was thus engaged when the yellow canopy thinned, clouded sunlight peeking between branches. Soon he caught sight of Barlett waiting at the edge of the line of trees. The forest ended abruptly, almost as neat as a line on a map.

Galad sighed in relief, relishing the thought of being out in the open again. He stepped from the trees. Only then did an enormous force of troops begin to appear, climbing over a rise directly to his right.

Armor clanged, horses whinnying, as thousands of soldiers lined up atop the rise. Some were Children in their plate and mail, with conical helms shined to perfection. Their pristine tabards and cloaks shone, sunbursts glittering at the breasts, lances raised in ranks. The larger number were foot soldiers, not wearing the white of the Children, but instead simple brown leathers. Amadicians, likely provided by the Seanchan. Many had bows.

Galad stumbled back, hand going to his sword. But he knew, immediately, that he had been trapped. Not a few of the Children wore clothing adorned with the crook of the Hand of the Light—the Questioners. If ordinary Children were a flame to burn away evil, the Questioners were a raging bonfire.

Galad did a quick count. Three to four thousand Children and at least another six to eight thousand foot, half of those with bows. Ten thousand fresh troops. His heart sank.

Trom, Bornhald and Byar hastened out of the forest behind Galad along with a group of other Children. Trom cursed softly.

"So," Galad said, turning to the scout, Barlett, "you are a traitor?"

"You are the traitor, Child Damodred," the scout replied, face hard.

"Yes," Galad said, "I suppose it could be perceived that way." This march through the swamp had been suggested by his scouts. Galad could see now; it had been a delaying tactic, a way for Asunawa to get ahead of Galad. The march had also left Galad's men tired while Asunawa's force was fresh and ready for battle.

A sword scraped in its sheath.

Galad immediately raised a hand without turning. "Peace, Child Byar." Byar would have been the one to reach for his weapon, probably to strike down Barlett.

Perhaps something of this could be salvaged. Galad made his decision swiftly. "Child Byar and Child Bornhald, you are with me. Trom, you and the other Lords Captain bring our men out in ranks onto the field."

A large cluster of men near the front of Asunawa's force was riding forward, down the hillside. Many wore the crook of the Questioners. They could have sprung their ambush and killed Galad's group quickly. Instead, they sent down a group to parley. That was a good sign.

Galad mounted, suppressing a wince for his wounded leg. Byar and Bornhald mounted as well, and they followed him onto the field, hoofbeats muffled by the thick, yellowed grass. Asunawa himself was among the group approaching. He had thick, graying eyebrows and was so thin as to appear a doll made of sticks, with fabric stretched across them to imitate skin.

Asunawa was not smiling. He rarely did.

Galad pulled his horse up before the High Inquisitor. Asunawa was surrounded by a small guard of his Questioners, but was also accompanied by five Lords Captain, each of whom Galad had met with—or served under—during his short time in the Children.

Asunawa leaned forward in his saddle, sunken eyes narrowing. "Your rebels form ranks. Tell them to stand down or my archers will loose."

"Surely you would not ignore the rules of formal engagement?" Galad said. "You would draw arrows upon men as they form ranks? Where is your honor?"

"Darkfriends deserve no honor," Asunawa snapped. "Nor do they deserve pity."

"You name us Darkfriends then?" Galad asked, turning his mount slightly. "All seven thousand Children who were under Valda's command? Men your soldiers have served with, eaten with, known and fought beside? Men you yourself watched over not two months ago?"

Asunawa hesitated. Naming seven thousand of the Children as Darkfriends would be ridiculous—it would mean that two out of three remaining Children had gone to the Shadow.

"No," Asunawa said. "Perhaps they are simply . . . misguided. Even a good man can stray down shadowed paths if his leaders are Darkfriends."

"I am no Darkfriend." Galad met Asunawa's eyes.

"Submit to my questioning and prove it."

"The Lord Captain Commander submits himself to no one," Galad said. "Under the Light, I order *you* to stand down."

Asunawa laughed. "Child, we hold a knife to your throat! This is *your* chance to surrender!"

"Golever," Galad said, looking at the Lord Captain at Asunawa's left. Golever was a lanky, bearded man, as hard as they came—but he was also fair. "Tell me, do the Children of the Light surrender?"

Golever shook his head. "We do not. The Light will prove us victorious."

"And if we face superior odds?" Galad asked.

"We fight on."

"If we are tired and sore?"

"The Light will protect us," Golever said. "And if it is our time to die, then so be it. Let us take as many enemies with us as we may."

Galad turned back to Asunawa. "You see that I am in a predicament. To fight is to let you name us Darkfriends, but to surrender is to deny our oaths. By my honor as the Lord Captain Commander, I can accept neither option."

Asunawa's expression darkened. "You are *not* the Lord Captain Commander. He is dead."

"By my hand," Galad said, unsheathing his weapon, holding it forward so that the herons gleamed in the light. "And I hold his sword. Do you deny that you yourself watched me face Valda in fair combat, as prescribed by law?"

"As by the law, perhaps," Asunawa said. "But I would not call that fight fair. You drew on the powers of Shadow; I saw you standing in darkness despite the daylight, and I saw the Dragon's Fang sprout on your forehead. Valda never had a chance."

"Harnesh," Galad said, turning to the Lord Captain to the right of Asunawa. He was a short man, bald, missing one ear from fighting Dragonsworn. "Tell me. Is the Shadow stronger than the Light?"

"Of course not," the man said, spitting to the side.

"If the Lord Captain Commander's cause had been honorable, would he have fallen to me in a battle under the Light? If I were a Darkfriend, could I have slain the Lord Captain Commander himself?"

Harnesh didn't answer, but Galad could almost see the thoughts in his head. The Shadow might display strength at times, but the Light always revealed and destroyed it. It was possible for the Lord Captain Commander to fall to a Darkfriend—it was possible for any man to fall. But in a duel before the other Children? A duel for honor, under the Light?

"Sometimes the Shadow displays cunning and strength," Asunawa cut in before Galad could continue to question. "At times, good men die."

"You all know what Valda did," Galad said. "My mother is dead. Is there an argument against my right to challenge him?"

"You have no rights as a Darkfriend! I will parley no more with you, murderer." Asunawa waved a hand, and several of his Questioners drew swords. Immediately, Galad's companions did the same. Behind, he could hear his weary forces hastily closing their ranks.

"What will happen to us, Asunawa, if Child fights Child?" Galad asked softly. "I will not surrender, and I would not attack you, but perhaps we can reunite. Not as enemies, but as brothers separated for a time."

"I will never associate with Darkfriends," Asunawa said, though he sounded hesitant. He watched Galad's men. Asunawa would win a battle, but if Galad's men stood their ground, it would be a costly victory. Both sides would lose thousands.

"I will submit to you," Galad said. "On certain terms."

"No!" Bornhald said from behind, but Galad raised a hand, silencing him.

"What terms would those be?" Asunawa asked.

"You swear—before the Light and the Lords Captain here with you—that you will not harm, question, or otherwise condemn the men who followed me. They were only doing what they thought was right."

Asunawa's eyes narrowed, his lips forming a straight line.

"That includes my companions here," Galad said, nodding to Byar and Bornhald. "Every man, Asunawa. They must *never* know questioning."

"You cannot hinder the Hand of the Light in such a way! This would give them free rein to seek the Shadow!"

"And is it only fear of Questioning that keeps us in the Light, Asunawa?" Galad asked. "Are not the Children valiant and true?"

Asunawa fell silent. Galad closed his eyes, feeling the weight of leadership. Each moment he stalled increased the bargaining position for his men. He opened his eyes. "The Last Battle comes, Asunawa. We haven't time for squabbling. The Dragon Reborn walks the land."

"Heresy!" Asunawa said.

"Yes," Galad said. "And truth as well."

Asunawa ground his teeth, but seemed to be considering the offer.

"Galad," Bornhald said softly. "Don't do this. We can fight. The Light will protect us!"

"If we fight, we will kill good men, Child Bornhald," Galad said, without turning. "Each stroke of our swords will be a blow for the Dark One. The Children are the only true foundation that this world has left. We are needed. If my life is what is demanded to bring unity, then so be it. You would do the same, I believe." He met Asunawa's eyes.

"Take him," Asunawa snapped, looking dissatisfied. "And tell the legions to stand down. Inform them that I have taken the false Lord Captain Commander into custody, and will Question him to determine the extent of his crimes." He hesitated. "But also pass the word that those who followed him are not to be punished or Questioned." Asunawa spun his horse and rode away.

Galad turned his sword and handed it out to Bornhald. "Return to our men; tell them what happened here, and do *not* let them fight or try to rescue me. That is an order."

Bornhald met his eyes, then slowly took the sword. At last, he saluted. "Yes, my Lord Captain Commander."

As soon as they turned to ride away, rough hands grabbed Galad and pulled him from Stout's saddle. He hit the ground with a grunt, his bad shoulder throwing a spike of agony across his chest. He tried to climb to his feet, but several Questioners dismounted and knocked him down again.

One forced Galad to the ground, a boot on his back, and Galad heard the metallic rasp of a knife being unsheathed. They cut his armor and clothing free.

"You will not wear the uniform of a Child of the Light, Darkfriend," a Questioner said in his ear.

"I am *not* a Darkfriend," Galad said, face pressed to the grassy earth. "I will never speak that lie. I walk in the Light."

That earned him a kick to the side, then another, and another. He curled up, grunting. But the blows continued to fall.

Finally, the darkness took him.

The creature that had once been Padan Fain walked down the side of a hill. The brown weeds grew in broken patches, like the scrub on the chin of a beggar.

The sky was black. A tempest. He liked that, though he hated the one who caused it.

Hatred. It was the proof that he still lived, the one emotion left. The only emotion. It was all that there could be.

Consuming. Thrilling. Beautiful. Warming. Violent. Hatred. Wonderful. It was the storm that gave him strength, the purpose that drove him. Al'Thor would die. By his hand. And perhaps after that, the Dark One. Wonderful . . .

The creature that had been Padan Fain fingered his beautiful dagger, feeling the ridges of the designs in the fine golden wire that wrapped its hilt. A large ruby capped the end of its hilt, and he carried the weapon unsheathed in

his right hand so that the blade extended between his first
two fingers. The sides of those fingers had been cut a dozen
times over.

Blood dripped from the tip of the dagger down onto
the weeds. Crimson spots to cheer him. Red below, black
above. Perfect. Did his hatred cause that storm? It must be
so. Yes.

The drops of blood fell alongside spots of darkness that
appeared on dead leaves and stems as he moved farther
north into the Blight.

He was mad. That was good. When you accepted madness into yourself—embraced it and drank it in as if it were
sunlight or water or the air itself—it became another part
of you. Like a hand or an eye. You could see by madness.
You could hold things with madness. It was wonderful.
Liberating.

He was finally free.

The creature that had been Mordeth reached the bottom
of the hill and did not look back at the large, purplish mass
that he'd left atop it. Worms were very messy to kill the
right way, but some things needed to be done the right way.
It was the principle of the thing.

Mist had begun to trail him, creeping up from the
ground. Was that mist his madness, or was it his hatred? It
was so familiar. It twisted around his ankles and licked at
his heels.

Something peeked around a hillside nearby, then ducked
back. Worms died loudly. Worms did *everything* loudly. A
pack of Worms could destroy an entire legion. When you
heard them, you went the other way, quickly. But then, it
could be advantageous to send scouts to go judge the direction of the pack, lest you continue on and run across it again
elsewhere.

So the creature that had been Padan Fain was not surprised when he rounded the hillside and found a nervous
group of Trollocs there, a Myrddraal guiding them.

He smiled. *My friends.* It had been too long.

It took a moment for their brutish brains to come to the
obvious—but false—conclusion: If a man was wandering
around, then Worms *couldn't* be near. Those would have
smelled his blood and come for him. Worms preferred humans over Trollocs. That made sense. The creature that had

been Mordeth had tasted both, and Trolloc flesh had little
to recommend it.

The Trollocs tore forward in a mismatched pack: feathers, beaks, claws, teeth, tusks. The creature that had been
Fain stood still, mist licking his unshod feet. How wonderful! At the very back of the group, the Myrddraal hesitated, its eyeless gaze fixed on him. Perhaps it sensed that
something was terribly, terribly wrong. And right, of course.
You couldn't be one without the other. That wouldn't make
sense.

The creature that had been Mordeth—he would need a
new name soon—smiled deeply.

The Myrddraal turned to run away.

The mist struck.

It rolled over the Trollocs, moving quickly, like the tentacles of a leviathan in the Aryth Ocean. Lengths of it
snapped forward through Trolloc chests. One long rope
whipped above their heads, then shot forward in a blur, taking
the Fade in the neck.

The Trollocs screamed, dropping, spasming. Their hair
fell out in patches, and their skin began to *boil*. Blisters and
cysts. When those popped, they left craterlike pocks in the
Shadowspawn skin, like bubbles on the surface of metal
that cooled too quickly.

The creature that had been Padan Fain opened his mouth
in glee, closing his eyes to the tumultuous black sky and raising his face, lips parted, enjoying his feast. After it passed,
he sighed, holding his dagger tighter—cutting his flesh.

Red below, black above. Red and black, red and black, so
much red and black. Wonderful.

He walked on through the Blight.

The corrupted Trollocs climbed to their feet behind him,
lurching into motion, spittle dropping from their lips. Their
eyes had grown sluggish and dull, but when he desired it,
they would respond with a frenzied battle lust that would
surpass what they had known in life.

He left the Myrddraal. It would not rise, as rumors said
they did. His touch now brought instant death to one of its
kind. Pity. He had a few nails he might have otherwise put
to good use.

Perhaps he should get some gloves. But if he did, he
couldn't cut his hand. What a problem.

No matter. Onward. The time had come to kill al'Thor.

It saddened him that the hunt must end. But there was no longer a reason for a hunt. You didn't hunt something when you knew *exactly* where it was going to be. You merely showed up to meet it.

Like an old friend. A dear, beloved old friend that you were going to stab through the eye, open up at the gut and consume by handfuls while drinking his blood. That was the proper way to treat friends.

It was an honor.

Malenarin Rai shuffled through supply reports. That blasted shutter on the window behind his desk snapped and blew open again, letting in the damp heat of the Blight.

Despite ten years serving as commander of Heeth Tower, he hadn't grown accustomed to the heat in the highlands. Damp. Muggy, the air often full of rotting scents.

The whistling wind rattled the wooden shutter. He rose, walking over to pull it shut, then twisted a bit of twine around its handle to keep it closed.

He walked back to his desk, looking over the roster of newly arrived soldiers. Each name had a specialty beside it—up here, every soldier had to fill two or more duties. Skill at binding wounds. Swift feet for running messages. A keen eye with a bow. The ability to make the same old mush taste like new mush. Malenarin always asked specifically for men in the last group. Any cook who could make soldiers eager to come to mess was worth his weight in gold.

Malenarin set aside his current report, weighing it down with the lead-filled Trolloc horn he kept for the purpose. The next sheet in his stack was a letter from a man named Barriga, a merchant who was bringing his caravan to the tower to trade. Malenarin smiled; he was a soldier first, but he wore the three silver chains across his chest that marked him as a master merchant. While his tower received many of its supplies directly from the Queen, no Kandori commander was denied the opportunity to barter with merchants.

If he was lucky, he'd be able to get this outlander merchant drunk at the bargaining table. Malenarin had forced more than one merchant into a year of military service as penance for entering bargains he could not keep. A year of training with the Queen's forces often did plump foreign merchants a great deal of good.

He set that sheet beneath the Trolloc horn, then hesitated as he saw the last item for his attention at the bottom of the stack. It was a reminder from his steward. Keemlin, his eldest son, was approaching his fourteenth nameday. As if Malenarin could forget about that! He needed no reminder.

He smiled, setting the Trolloc horn on the note, in case that shutter broke open again. He'd slain the Trolloc who had borne that horn himself. Then he walked over to the side of his office and opened his battered oak trunk. Among the other effects inside was a cloth-wrapped sword, the brown scabbard kept well oiled and maintained, but faded with time. His father's sword.

In three days, he would give it to Keemlin. A boy became a man on his fourteenth nameday, the day he was given his first sword and became responsible for himself. Keemlin had worked hard to learn his forms under the harshest trainers Malenarin could provide. Soon his son would become a man. How quickly the years passed.

Taking a proud breath, Malenarin closed the trunk, then rose and left his office for his daily rounds. The tower housed two hundred and fifty soldiers, a bastion of defense that watched the Blight.

To have a duty was to have pride—just as to bear a burden was to gain strength. Watching the Blight was his duty and his strength, and it was particularly important these days, with the strange storm to the north, and with the Queen and much of the Kandori army having marched to seek the Dragon Reborn. He pulled the door to his office closed, then threw the hidden latch that barred it on the other side. It was one of several such doors in the hallway; an enemy storming the tower wouldn't know which one opened onto the stairwell upward. In this way, a small office could function as part of the tower defense.

He walked to the stairwell. These top levels were not accessible from the ground level—the entire bottom forty feet of the tower was a trap. An enemy who entered at the ground floor and climbed up three flights of garrison quarters would discover no way up to the fourth floor. The only way to go to the fourth level was to climb a narrow, collapsible ramp on the outside of the tower that led from the second level up to the fourth. Running on it left attackers fully exposed to arrows from above. Then, once some of them were up but others not, the Kandori would collapse the ramp, dividing the enemy force and leaving those above to be killed as they tried to find the interior stairwells.

Malenarin climbed at a brisk pace. Periodic slits to the sides of the steps looked down on the stairs beneath, and would allow archers to fire on invaders. When he was about halfway to the top, he heard hasty footfalls coming down. A second later, Jargen—sergeant of the watch—rounded the bend. Like most Kandori, Jargen wore a forked beard; his black hair was dusted with gray.

Jargen had joined the Blightwatch the day after his fourteenth nameday. He wore a cord looped around the shoulder of his brown uniform; it bore a knot for each Trolloc he'd killed. There had to be approaching fifty knots in the thing by now.

Jargen saluted with arm to breast, then lowered his hand to rest on his sword, a sign of respect for his commander. In many countries, holding the weapon like that would be an insult, but Southerners were known to be peevish and ill-tempered. Couldn't they see that it was an honor to hold your sword and imply you found your commander a worthy threat?

"My Lord," Jargen said, voice gruff. "A flash from Rena Tower."

"What?" Malenarin asked. The two fell into step, trotting up the stairwell.

"It was distinct, sir," Jargen said. "Saw it myself, I did. Only a flash, but it *was* there."

"Did they send a correction?"

"They may have by now. I ran to fetch you first."

If there had been more news, Jargen would have shared it, so Malenarin did not waste breath pressing him. Shortly, they stepped up onto the top of the tower, which held an enormous mechanism of mirrors and lamps. With the apparatus, the tower could send messages to the east or west—where other towers lined the Blight—or southward, along a line of towers that ran to the Aesdaishar Palace in Chachin.

The vast, undulating Kandori highlands spread out from his tower. Some of the southern hills were still lightly laced with morning fog. That land to the south, free of this un-

natural heat, would soon grow green, and Kandori herdsmen would climb to the high pastures to graze their sheep.

Northward lay the Blight. Malenarin had read of days
when the Blight had barely been visible from this tower.
Now it ran nearly to the base of the stonework. Rena Tower
was northwest as well. Its commander—Lord Niach of
House Okatomo—was a distant cousin and a good friend.
He would not have sent a flash without reason, and would
send a retraction if it had been an accident.

"Any further word?" Malenarin asked.

The soldiers on watch shook their heads. Jargen tapped
his foot, and Malenarin folded his arms to wait for a correction.

Nothing came. Rena Tower stood within the Blight these
days, as it was farther north than Heeth Tower. Its position
within the Blight was normally not an issue. Even the most
fearsome creatures of the Blight knew not to attack a Kandori tower.

No correction came. Not a glimmer. "Send a message to
Rena," Malenarin said. "Ask if their flash was a mistake.
Then ask Farmay Tower if they have noticed anything
strange."

Jargen set the men to work, but gave Malenarin a flat
glance, as if to ask, "You think I haven't done that already?"

That meant messages had been sent, but there was no
word back. Wind blew across the tower top, creaking the
steel of the mirror apparatus as his men sent another series of flashes. That wind was humid. Far too hot. Malenarin glanced upward, toward where that same black storm
boiled and rolled. It seemed to have settled down.

That struck him as very discomforting.

"Flash a message backward," Malenarin said, "toward
the inland towers. Tell them what we saw; tell them to be
ready in case of trouble."

The men set to work.

"Sergeant," Malenarin said, "who is next on the messenger roster?"

The tower force included a small group of boys who were
excellent riders. Lightweight, they could go on fast horses
should a commander decide to bypass the mirrors. Mirror
light was fast, but it could be seen by one's enemies. Besides, if the line of towers was broken—or if the apparatus

was damaged—they would need a means to get word to the capital.

"Next on the roster . . ." Jargen said, checking a list nailed to the inside of the door onto the rooftop. "It would be Keemlin, my Lord."

Keemlin. His Keemlin.

Malenarin glanced to the northwest, toward the silent tower that had flashed so ominously. "Bring me word if there is a *hint* of response from the other towers," Malenarin said to the soldiers. "Jargen, come with me."

The two of them hurried down the stairs. "We need to send a messenger southward," Malenarin said, then hesitated. "No. No, we need to send several messengers. Double up. Just in case the towers fall." He began moving again.

The two of them left the stairwell and entered Malenarin's office. He grabbed his best quill off the rack on his wall. That blasted shutter was blowing and rattling again; the papers on his desk rustled as he pulled out a fresh sheet of paper.

Rena and Farmay not responding to flash messages. Possibly overrun or severely hampered. Be advised. Heeth will stand.

He folded the paper, holding it up to Jargen. The man took it with a leathery hand, read it over, then grunted. "Two copies, then?"

"Three," Malenarin said. "Mobilize the archers and send them to the roof. Tell them danger may come from above."

If he wasn't merely jumping at shadows—if the towers to either side of Heeth had fallen so quickly—then so could those to the south. And if *he'd* been the one making an assault, he'd have done anything he could to sneak around and take out one of the southern towers first. That was the best way to make sure no messages got back to the capital.

Jargen saluted, fist to chest, then withdrew. The message would be sent immediately: three times on legs of horseflesh, once on legs of light. Malenarin let himself feel a hint of relief that his son was one of those riding to safety. There was no dishonor in that; the messages needed to be delivered, and Keemlin was next on the roster.

Malenarin glanced out his window. It faced north, toward

the Blight. Every commander's office did that. The bubbling storm, with its silvery clouds. Sometimes they looked like straight geometric shapes. He had listened well to passing merchants. Troubled times were coming. The Queen would not have gone south to seek a false Dragon, no matter how cunning or influential he might be. She believed.

It was time for Tarmon Gai'don. And looking out into that storm, Malenarin thought he could see to the very edge of time itself. An edge that was not far distant. In fact, it seemed to be growing darker. And there was a darkness beneath it, on the ground northward.

That darkness was advancing.

Malenarin dashed out of the room, racing up the steps to the roof, where the wind swept against men pushing and moving mirrors.

"Was the message sent to the south?" he demanded.

"Yes, sir," Lieutenant Landalin said. He'd been roused to take command of the tower's top. "No reply yet."

Malenarin glanced down, and picked out three riders breaking away from the tower at full speed. The messengers were off. They would stop at Barklan if it wasn't being attacked. The captain there would send them on southward, just in case. And if Barklan didn't stand, the boys would continue on, all the way to the capital if needed.

Malenarin turned back to the storm. That advancing darkness had him on edge. It was coming.

"Raise the hoardings," he ordered Landalin. "Bring up the store hitchings and empty the cellars. Have the loaders gather all of the arrows and set up stations for resupplying the archers, and put archers at every choke point, kill slit and window. Start the firepots and have men ready to drop the outer ramps. Prepare for a siege."

As Landalin barked orders, men rushed away. Malenarin heard boots scrape stone behind him, and he glanced over his shoulder. Was that Jargen back again?

No. It was a youth of nearly fourteen summers, too young for a beard, his dark hair disheveled, his face streaming with sweat caused—presumably—by a run up seven levels of the tower.

Keemlin. Malenarin felt a stab of fear, instantly replaced with anger. "Soldier! You were to ride with a message!"

Keemlin bit his lip. "Well, sir," he said. "Tian, four places down from me. He is five, maybe ten pounds lighter than I. It makes a big difference, sir. He rides a lot faster, and I figured this would be an important message. So I asked for him to be sent in my place."

Malenarin frowned. Soldiers moved around them, rushing down the stairs or gathering with bows at the rim of the tower. The wind howled outside and thunder began to sound softly—yet insistently.

Keemlin met his eyes. "Tian's mother, Lady Yabeth, has lost four sons to the Blight," he said, softly enough that only Malenarin could hear. "Tian's the only one she has left. If one of us has a shot at getting out, sir, I figured it should be him."

Malenarin held his son's eyes. The boy understood what was coming. Light help him, but he understood. And he'd sent another away in his place.

"Kralle," Malenarin barked, glancing toward one of the soldiers passing by.

"Yes, my Lord Commander?"

"Run down to my office," Malenarin said. "There is a sword in my oaken trunk. Fetch it for me."

The man saluted, obeying.

"Father?" Keemlin said. "My nameday isn't for three days."

Malenarin waited with arms behind his back. His most important task at the moment was to be seen in command, to reassure his troops. Kralle returned with the sword; its worn scabbard bore the image of the oak set aflame. The symbol of House Rai.

"Father. . . ." Keemlin repeated. "I—"

"This weapon is offered to a boy when he becomes a man," Malenarin said. "It seems it is too late in coming, son. For I see a man standing before me." He held the weapon forward in his right hand. Around the tower top, soldiers turned toward him: the archers with bows ready, the soldiers who operated the mirrors, the duty watchmen. As Borderlanders, each and every one of them would have been given his sword on his fourteenth nameday. Each one had felt the catch in the chest, the wonderful feeling of coming of age. It had happened to each of them, but that did not make this occasion any less special.

Keemlin went down on one knee.

"Why do you draw your sword?" Malenarin asked, voice loud so that every man atop the tower would hear.

"In defense of my honor, my family, or my homeland," Keemlin replied.

"How long do you fight?"

"Until my last breath joins the northern winds."

"When do you stop watching?"

"Never," Keemlin whispered.

"Speak it louder!"

"Never!"

"Once this sword is drawn, you become a warrior, always with it near you in preparation to fight the Shadow. Will you draw this blade and join us, as a man?"

Keemlin looked up, then took the hilt in a firm grip and pulled the weapon free.

"Rise as a man, my son!" Malenarin declared.

Keemlin stood, holding the weapon aloft, the bright blade reflecting the diffuse sunlight. The men atop the tower cheered.

It was no shame to find tears in one's eyes at such a moment. Malenarin blinked them free, then knelt down, buckling the sword belt at his son's waist. The men continued to cheer and yell, and he knew it was not only for his son. They yelled in defiance of the Shadow. For a moment, their voices rang louder than the thunder.

Malenarin stood, laying a hand on his son's shoulder as the boy slid his sword into its sheath. Together they turned to face the oncoming Shadow.

"There!" one of the archers said, pointing upward. "There's something in the clouds!"

"Draghkar!" another one said.

The unnatural clouds were close now, and the shade they cast could no longer hide the undulating horde of Trollocs beneath. Something flew out from the sky, but a dozen of his archers let loose. The creature screamed and fell, dark wings flapping awkwardly.

Jargen pushed his way through to Malenarin. "My Lord," Jargen said, shooting a glance at Keemlin, "the boy should be below."

"Not a boy any longer," Malenarin said with pride. "A man. What is your report?"

"All is prepared." Jargen glanced over the wall, eyeing

the oncoming Trollocs as evenly as if he were inspecting a
stable of horses. "They will not find this tree an easy one
to fell."

Malenarin nodded. Keemlin's shoulder was tense. That
sea of Trollocs seemed endless. Against this foe, the tower
would eventually fall. The Trollocs would keep coming,
wave after wave.

But every man atop that tower knew his duty. They'd kill
Shadowspawn as long as they could, hoping to buy enough
time for the messages to do some good.

Malenarin was a man of the Borderlands, same as his
father, same as his son beside him. They knew their task.
You held until you were relieved.

That's all there was to it.

CHAPTER
I

Apples First

T he Wheel of Time turns, and Ages come and pass,
leaving memories that become legend. Legend
fades to myth, and even myth is long forgotten
when the Age that gave it birth comes again. In one Age,
called the Third Age by some, an Age yet to come, an Age
long past, a wind rose above the misty peaks of Imfaral.
The wind was not the beginning. There are neither beginnings nor endings to the turning of the Wheel of Time. But
it was *a* beginning.

Crisp and light, the wind danced across fields of new
mountain grass stiff with frost. That frost lingered past
first light, sheltered by the omnipresent clouds that hung
like a death mask high above. It had been weeks since
those clouds had budged, and the wan, yellowed grass
showed it.

The wind churned morning mist, moving southward,
chilling a small pride of *torm*. They reclined on a flat, lichen-
stained granite shelf, waiting to bask in morning sunlight
that would not arrive. The wind poured over the shelf, racing
down a hillside of scraggly mura trees, with ropelike bark
and green tufts of thick, needlelike leaves atop them.

At the base of the foothills, the wind turned eastward,
passing an open plain kept free of trees and scrub by the
soldier's axe. The killing field surrounded thirteen fortresses, tall and cut entirely from unpolished black marble,
their blocks left rough-hewn to give them a primal feeling
of unformed strength. These were towers meant for war.
By tradition they were unoccupied. How long that would

last—how long tradition itself would be remembered in a continent in chaos—remained to be seen.

The wind continued eastward, and soon it was playing with the masts of half-burned ships at the docks of Takisrom. Out into the Sleeping Bay, it passed the attackers: enormous greatships with sails painted blood red. They sailed southward, their grisly work done.

The wind blew onto land again, past smoldering towns and villages, open plains filled with troops and docks fat with warships. Smoke, war calls and banners flew above dying grass and beneath a dockmaster's gloomy sky.

Men did not whisper that this might be the end of times. They yelled it. The Fields of Peace were aflame, the Tower of Ravens was broken as prophesied and a murderer openly ruled in Seandar. This was a time to lift one's sword and choose a side, then spill blood to give a final color to the dying land.

The wind howled eastward over the famed Emerald Cliffs and coursed out over the ocean. Behind, smoke seemed to rise from the entire continent of Seanchan.

For hours, the wind blew—making what would have been called tradewinds in another Age—twisting between whitecaps and dark, mysterious waves. Eventually, the wind encountered another continent, this one quiet, like a man holding his breath before the headsman's axe fell.

By the time the wind reached the enormous, broken-peaked mountain known as Dragonmount, it had lost much of its strength. It passed around the base of the mountain, then through a large orchard of apple trees, lit by early-afternoon sunlight. The once-green leaves had faded to yellow.

The wind passed by a low wooden fence, tied at its joints with tan linen twine. Two figures stood there: a youth and a somber man in his later years. The older man wore a pair of worn brown trousers and a loose white shirt with wooden buttons. His face was so furrowed with wrinkles that it seemed kin to the bark of the trees.

Almen Bunt didn't know a lot about orchards. Oh, he had planted a few trees back on his farm in Andor. Who didn't have a tree or two to fill in space on the dinner table? He'd planted a pair of walnut trees on the day he'd married

Adrinne. It had felt good to have her trees there, outside his
window, after she'd died.

Running an orchard was something else entirely. There
were nearly three hundred trees in this field. It was his
sister's orchard; he was visiting while his sons managed
his farm near Carysford.

In his shirt pocket, Almen carried a letter from his sons.
A desperate letter, pleading for help, but he couldn't go to
them. He was needed here. Besides, it was a good time for
him to be out of Andor. He was a Queen's man. There had
been times, recently, when being a Queen's man could get
someone into as much trouble as having one too many cows
in his pasture.

"What do we do, Almen?" Adim asked. "Those trees,
they . . . Well, it *ain't* supposed to happen like this." The
boy of thirteen had golden hair from his father's side.

Almen rubbed his chin, scratching at a patch of whiskers
he'd missed during shaving. Hahn, Adim's older brother,
approached them. The lad had carved Almen a set of
wooden teeth as an arrival gift earlier in the spring. Wondrous things, held together by wires, with gaps for the few
remaining teeth he had. But if he chewed too hard, they'd
go all out of shape.

The rows of trees were straight and perfectly spaced.
Graeger—Almen's brother-in-law—always *had* been meticulous. But he was dead now, which was why Almen had
come. The neat rows of trees continued on for spans and
spans, carefully pruned, fertilized, and watered.

And during the night, every single one of them had shed
their fruit. Tiny apples, barely as large as a man's thumb.
Thousands of them. They'd shriveled during the night, then
fallen. An entire crop, gone.

"I don't know what to say, lads," Almen finally admitted.

"You, at a loss for words?" Hahn said. Adim's brother
had darker coloring, like his mother, and was tall for his
fifteen years. "Uncle, you usually have as much to say as a
gleeman who's been at the brandy for half the night!" Hahn
liked to maintain a strong front for his brother, now that he
was the man of the family. But sometimes it was good to be
worried.

And Almen was worried. *Very* worried.

"We barely have a week's grain left," Adim said softly. "And what we've got, we got by promises on the crop. Nobody will give us anything, now. Nobody *has* anything."

The orchard was one of the largest producers in the region; half the men in the village worked it during one stage or another. They were depending on it. They *needed* it. With so much food going bad, with their stores used up during the unnatural winter . . .

And then there was the incident that had killed Graeger. The man had walked around a corner over in Negin Bridge and vanished. When people went looking, all they found was a twisted, leafless tree with a gray-white trunk that smelled of sulphur.

The Dragon's Fang had been scrawled on a few doors that night. People were more and more nervous. Once, Almen would have named them all fools, jumping at shadows and seeing bloody Trollocs under every cobblestone.

Now . . . well, now he wasn't so sure. He glanced eastward, toward Tar Valon. Could the witches be to blame for the failed crop? He hated being so close to their nest, but Alysa needed the help.

They'd chopped down that tree and burned it. You could still smell brimstone in the square.

"Uncle?" Hahn said, sounding uncomfortable. "What . . . what do we do?"

"I . . ." What *did* they do? "Burn me, but we should all go to Caemlyn. I'm sure the new Queen has everything cleared up there by now. We can get me settled right by the law. Who ever heard of such a thing, gaining a price on your head for speaking out in favor of the Queen?" He realized he was rambling. The boys kept looking at him.

"No," Almen continued. "Burn me, boys, but that's wrong. We can't go. We need to keep on working. This isn't any worse than when I lost my entire millet field to a late frost twenty years back. We'll get through this, right as Light we will."

The trees themselves looked fine. Not an insect bite on them, leaves a little yellowed, but still good. Sure, the spring buds had come late, and the apples had grown slowly. But they *had* been growing.

"Hahn," Almen found himself saying. "You know your

father's felling axe has those chips on it? Why don't you go about getting it sharpened? Adim, go fetch Uso and Moor and their carts. We'll sort through those fallen apples and see if any aren't rotted too badly. Maybe the pigs will take them." At least they still had two. But there'd been no piglets this spring.

The youths hesitated.

"Go on now," Almen said. "No use dallying because we've had a setback."

The lads hastened off, obedient. Idle hands made idle minds. Some work would keep them from thinking about what was to come.

There was no helping that for him. He leaned down on the fence, feeling the rough grooves of the unsanded planks under his arms. That wind tugged at the tails of his shirt again; Adrinne had always forced him to tuck it in, but now that she was gone, he . . . well, he never had liked wearing it that way.

He tucked the shirt in anyway.

The air smelled wrong somehow. Stale, like the air inside a city. Flies were starting to buzz around the shriveled bits that had once been apples.

Almen had lived a long time. He'd never kept count; Adrinne had done that for him. It wasn't important. He knew he'd seen a lot of years, and that was that.

He'd seen insects attack a crop; he'd seen plants lost to flood, to drought, or to negligence. But in all his years, he'd *never* seen anything like this. This was something evil. The village was already starving. They didn't talk about it, not when the children or youths were around. The adults quietly gave what they had to the young and to women who were nursing. But the cows were going dry, the stores spoiling, the crops dying.

The letter in his pocket said his own farm had been set upon by passing mercenaries. They hadn't harmed anyone, but they'd taken every scrap of food. His sons survived only by digging half-grown potatoes from the crop and boiling them. They found nineteen out of every twenty rotting in the ground, inexplicably full of worms despite green growth above.

Dozens of nearby villages were suffering the same way.

No food to be had. Tar Valon itself was having trouble feeding its people.

Staring down those neat, perfect rows of useless apple trees, Almen felt the crushing weight of it. Of trying to remain positive. Of seeing all his sister had worked for fail and rot. These apples . . . they were supposed to have saved the village, and his sons.

His stomach rumbled. It did that a lot lately.

This is it then, isn't it? he thought, eyes toward the too-yellow grass below. *The fight just ended.*

Almen slumped down, feeling a weight on his shoulders. *Adrinne,* he thought. There had been a time when he'd been quick to laugh, quick to talk. Now he felt worn, like a post that had been sanded and sanded and sanded until only a sliver was left. Maybe it was time to let go.

He felt something on his neck. Warmth.

He hesitated, then turned weary eyes toward the sky. Sunlight bathed his face. He gaped; it seemed so long since he'd seen pure sunlight. It shone down through a large break in the clouds, comforting, like the warmth of an oven baking a loaf of Adrinne's thick sourdough bread.

Almen stood, raising a hand to shade his eyes. He took a deep, long breath, and smelled . . . apple blossoms? He spun with a start.

The apple trees were flowering.

That was plain ridiculous. He rubbed his eyes, but that didn't dispel the image. They were blooming, all of them, white flowers breaking out between the leaves. The flies buzzed into the air and zipped away on the wind. The dark bits of apple on the ground *melted* away, like wax before a flame. In seconds, there was nothing left of them, not even juice. The ground had absorbed them.

What was happening? Apple trees didn't blossom twice. Was he going mad?

Footsteps sounded softly on the path that ran past the orchard. Almen spun to find a tall young man walking down out of the foothills. He had deep red hair and he wore ragged clothing: a brown cloak with loose sleeves and a simple white linen shirt beneath. The trousers were finer, black with a delicate embroidery of gold at the cuff.

"Ho, stranger," Almen said, raising a hand, not knowing what else to say, not even sure if he'd seen what he thought he'd seen. "Did you . . . did you get lost up in the foothills?"

The man stopped, turning sharply. He seemed surprised to find Almen there. With a start, Almen realized the man's left arm ended in a stump.

The stranger looked about, then breathed in deeply. "No. I'm not lost. Finally. It feels like a great long time since I've understood the path before me."

Almen scratched the side of his face. Burn him, there was another patch he'd missed shaving. His hand had been shaking so much that he might as well have skipped the razor entirely. "Not lost? Son, that pathway only leads up the slopes of Dragonmount. The area's been hunted clean, if you were hoping to find some game. There's nothing back there of use."

"I wouldn't say that," the stranger said, glancing over his shoulder. "There are always things of use around, if you look closely enough. You can't stare at them too long. To learn but not be overwhelmed, that is the balance."

Almen folded his arms. The man's words . . . it seemed they were having two different conversations. Perhaps the lad wasn't right in the head. There was something about the man, though. The way he stood, the way those eyes of his stared with such calm intensity. Almen felt like standing up and dusting off his shirt to make himself more presentable.

"Do I know you?" Almen asked. Something about the young man was familiar.

"Yes," the lad said. Then he nodded toward the orchard. "Gather your people and collect those apples. They'll be needed in the days to come."

"The apples?" Almen said, turning. "But—" He froze. The trees were burgeoning with new, ripe red apples. The blossoms he'd seen earlier had fallen free, and blanketed the ground in white, like snow.

Those apples seemed to shine. Not just dozens of them on each tree, but hundreds. More than a tree should hold, each one perfectly ripe.

"I *am* going mad," Almen said, turning back to the man.

"It's not you who is mad, friend," the stranger said. "But the entire world. Gather those apples quickly. My presence will hold him off for a time, I think, and whatever you take now should be safe from his touch."

That voice . . . Those eyes, like gray gemstones cut and set in his face. "I *do* know you," Almen said, remembering an odd pair of youths he had given a lift in his cart years ago. "Light! You're him, aren't you? The one they're talking about?"

The man looked back at Almen. Meeting those eyes, Almen felt a strange sense of peace. "It is likely," the man said. "Men are often speaking of me." He smiled, then turned and continued on his way down the path.

"Wait," Almen said, raising a hand toward the man who could only be the Dragon Reborn. "Where are you going?"

The man looked back with a faint grimace. "To do something I've been putting off. I doubt she will be pleased by what I tell her."

Almen lowered his hand, watching as the stranger strode away, down a pathway between two fenced orchards, trees laden with blood-red apples. Almen thought—for a moment—he could see something around the man. A lightness to the air, warped and bent.

Almen watched the man until he vanished, then dashed toward Alysa's house. The old pain in his hip was gone, and he felt as if he could run a dozen leagues. Halfway to the house, he met Adim and the two workers coming to the orchard. They regarded him with concerned eyes as he pulled to a halt.

Unable to speak, Almen turned and pointed back at the orchards. The apples were red specks, dotting the green like freckles.

"What's that?" Uso asked, rubbing his long face. Moor squinted, then began running toward the orchard.

"Gather everyone," Almen said, winded. "*Everyone* from the village, from the villages nearby, people passing on Shyman's road. Everyone. Get them here to gather and pick."

"Pick what?" Adim asked with a frown.

"Apples," Almen said. "What else bloody grows on apple trees! Listen, we need every one of those apples picked before the day ends. You hear me? Go! Spread the word! There's a harvest after all!"

They ran off to look, of course. It was hard to blame them for that. Almen continued on, and as he did, he noticed for the first time that the grass around him seemed greener, healthier.

He looked eastward. Almen felt a *pull* inside of him. Something was tugging him softly in the direction the stranger had gone.

Apples first, he thought. Then . . . well, then he'd see.

CHAPTER
2

Questions of Leadership

Thunder rumbled above, soft and menacing like the growl of a distant beast. Perrin turned his eyes toward the sky. A few days ago, the pervasive cloud cover had turned black, darkening like the advent of a horrible storm. But rain had come only in spurts.

Another rumble shook the air. There was no lightning. Perrin patted Stayer on the neck; the horse smelled skittish—prickly, sweaty. The horse wasn't the only one. That scent hung above his enormous force of troops and refugees as they tramped across the muddy ground. That force created a thunder of its own, footsteps, hoofbeats, wagon wheels turning, men and women calling.

They had nearly reached the Jehannah Road. Originally, Perrin had planned to cross that and continue on northward, toward Andor. But he'd lost a great deal of time to the sickness that had struck his camp—both Asha'man had nearly died. Then this thick mud had slowed them even further. All told, it had been over a month since they'd left Malden, and they'd traveled only as far as Perrin had originally hoped to go in a week.

Perrin put his hand into his coat pocket, feeling at the small blacksmith's puzzle there. They'd found it in Malden, and he'd taken to fiddling with it. So far, he hadn't figured out how to get the pieces apart. It was as complex a puzzle as he'd ever seen.

There was no sign of Master Gill or the people Perrin had sent on ahead with supplies. Grady had managed a few small gateways ahead to send scouts to find them, but they had returned without news. Perrin was beginning to worry about them.

"My Lord?" a man asked. He stood beside Perrin's horse. Turne was a lanky fellow with curly red hair and a beard he tied off with leather cords. He carried a warrior's axe in a loop at his belt, a wicked thing with a spike at the back.

"We can't pay you much," Perrin said. "Your men don't have horses?"

"No, my Lord," Turne said, glancing at his dozen companions. "Jarr had one. We ate it a few weeks back." Turne smelled unwashed and dirty, and above those scents was an odd staleness. Had the man's emotions gone numb? "If you don't mind, my Lord. Wages can wait. If you have food . . . well, that will be enough for now."

I should turn them away, Perrin thought. *We already have too many mouths to feed.* Light, he was supposed to be getting *rid* of people. But these fellows looked handy with their weapons, and if he turned them away, they'd no doubt turn to pillaging.

"Go walk down the line," Perrin said. "Find a man named Tam al'Thor—he's a sturdy fellow, dressed like a farmer. Anyone should be able to point you in his direction. Tell him you spoke to Perrin, and I said to take you on for meals."

The dirty men relaxed, and their lanky leader actually smelled grateful. Grateful! Sell-swords—maybe bandits— grateful to be taken on only for meals. That was the state of the world.

"Tell me, my Lord," Turne said as his group began to hike down the line of refugees. "Do you really have food?"

"We do," Perrin said. "I just said so."

"And it doesn't spoil after a night left alone?"

"Course it doesn't," Perrin said sternly. "Not if you keep it right." Some of their grain might have weevils in it, but it was edible. The man seemed to find that incredible, as if Perrin had said his wagons would soon sprout wings and fly off for the mountains.

"Go on now," Perrin said. "And make sure to tell your men that we run a tight camp. No fighting, no stealing. If I get a whiff of you making trouble, you'll be out on your ears."

"Yes, my Lord," Turne said, then hastened off to join his men. He smelled sincere. Tam wasn't going to be pleased to have another batch of mercenaries to watch over, but the Shaido were still out there somewhere. Most of them seemed to have turned eastward. But with how slowly Perrin's force had been traveling, he was worried the Aiel might change their minds and come back for him.

He nudged Stayer forward, flanked by a pair of Two Rivers men. Now that Aram was gone, the Two Rivers men had—unfortunately—taken it upon themselves to provide Perrin with bodyguards. Today's annoyances were Wil al'Seen and Reed Soalen. Perrin had tried chewing out the men about it. But they insisted, and he had bigger worries to bother him, not the least of which were his strange dreams. Haunting visions of working the forges and being unable to create anything of worth.

Put them out of your mind, he told himself, riding up the long column, al'Seen and Soalen keeping up. *You have nightmares enough while awake. Deal with those first.*

The meadow around him was open, though the grass was yellowing, and he noticed with displeasure several large swaths of dead wildflowers, rotting. The spring rains had turned most areas like this into mud traps. Moving so many refugees was slow, even discounting the bubble of evil and the mud. Everything took longer than he expected, including getting out of Malden.

The force kicked up mud as it marched; most of the refugees' trousers and skirts were covered with it, and the air was thick with its sticky scent. Perrin neared the front of their line, passing riders in red breastplates, lances held high, their helms like rimmed pots. The Winged Guards of Mayene. Lord Gallenne rode at their front, red-plumed helm held at his side. His bearing was formal enough that you might think he was riding in a parade, but his single eye was keen as he scanned the countryside. He was a good soldier. There were a lot of good soldiers in this force, though sometimes it was tough as bending a horseshoe to keep their hands from one another's throats.

"Lord Perrin!" a voice shouted. Arganda, First Captain of Ghealdan, pushed through the Mayener lines riding a tall roan gelding. His troops rode in a wide column beside the Mayeners—ever since Alliandre's return, Arganda had been set on equal treatment. He'd complained that the Winged Guards often rode in front. Rather than spur further arguments, Perrin had ordered their columns to ride side by side.

"Was that *another* batch of mercenaries?" Arganda demanded, pulling his horse up beside Perrin.

"A small band," Perrin said. "Probably once the guard of some local city's lord."

"Deserters." Arganda spat to the side. "You should have sent for me. My queen would want them strung up! Don't forget that we're in Ghealdan now."

"Your queen is my liegewoman," Perrin said as they reached the front of the column. "We're not stringing anyone up unless we have proof of their crimes. Once everyone is safely back where they belong, you can start sorting through the sell-swords and see if you can charge any of them. Until then, they're just hungry men looking for someone to follow."

Arganda smelled frustrated. Perrin had gained a few weeks of goodwill from him and Gallenne following the successful assault on Malden, but old divisions were resurfacing in the endless mud, under a sky full of tumbling thunderheads.

"Don't worry yourself," Perrin said. "I have men watching over the newcomers." He also had them watching the refugees. Some were so docile that they would hardly go to the privy without being instructed to do so; others kept looking over their shoulders, as if expecting Shaido to spring from the distant line of oaks and sweetgum trees at any moment. People who smelled that terrified could be trouble, and the various factions of his camp *already* walked as if trudging through itchweed.

"You may send someone to talk to the newcomers, Arganda," Perrin said. "Talk *only*. Find out where they're from, learn whether they did serve a lord, see if they can add anything to the maps." They didn't have any good maps of the area, and had been forced to have the Ghealdanin men—Arganda included—draw some from memory.

Arganda rode off, and Perrin moved to the front of the column. Being in charge did have its nice moments; up here, the smells of unwashed bodies and pungent mud weren't nearly so strong. Ahead, he could finally see the Jehannah

Road like a long strap of leather cutting through the highland plains, running in a northwestern direction.

Perrin rode, lost in thought for a time. Eventually, they reached the roadway. The mud didn't look as bad on the road as it had in the meadows—though if it were like any other road Perrin had traveled on, it would have its mires and washed-out sections. As he reached it, he noticed Gaul approaching. The Aiel had been off scouting ahead, and as Perrin's horse stepped up onto the road, he noticed that someone was riding behind Gaul up toward them.

It was Fennel, one of the farriers that Perrin had sent ahead with Master Gill and the others. Perrin felt a wash of relief to see him, but it was followed by worry. Where were the others?

"Lord Perrin!" the man said, riding up. Gaul stepped to the side. Fennel was a wide-shouldered man, and carried a long-handled workman's axe strapped to his back. He smelled of relief. "Praise the Light. I thought you'd never get here. Your man says the rescue worked?"

"It did, Fennel," Perrin said, frowning. "Where are the others?"

"They went on ahead, my Lord," Fennel said, bowing from horseback. "I volunteered to stay behind, for when you caught up. We needed to explain, you see."

"Explain?"

"The rest turned toward Lugard," Fennel explained. "Along the road."

"What?" Perrin said, frustrated. "I gave them orders to continue northward!"

"My Lord," Fennel said, looking abashed. "We met travelers coming from that way; said that mud made the roads to the north almost completely impassable for wagons or carts. Master Gill decided that heading to Caemlyn through Lugard would be the best way to follow your orders. Sorry, my Lord. That's why one of us had to stay behind."

Light! No wonder the scouts hadn't found Gill and the others. They'd gone in the wrong direction. Well, after slogging through mud for weeks himself—sometimes having to stop and wait out storms—Perrin couldn't blame them for deciding to take the road. That didn't stop him from feeling frustrated.

"How far behind are we?" Perrin asked.

"I've been here five days, my Lord."

So Gill and the others had been slowed too. Well, that was something, at least.

"Go get yourself something to eat, Fennel," Perrin said. "And thank you for staying behind to let me know what happened. It was a brave thing you did, waiting alone for so long."

"Somebody had to do it, my Lord." He hesitated. "Most feared you hadn't . . . well, that things had gone wrong, my Lord. You see, we figured you'd be faster than us, since we had those carts. But from the look of things here, you decided to bring the entire town with you!"

It wasn't far from the truth, unfortunately. He waved Fennel on.

"I found him about an hour along the road," Gaul said softly. "Beside a hill that would make an excellent camp. Well watered, with a good view of the surrounding area."

Perrin nodded. They'd have to decide what to do—wait until Grady and Neald could make large gateways, follow along after Master Gill and the others on foot, or send most people northward and send only a few toward Lugard. Regardless of the decision, it would be good to camp for the day and sort through things. "Pass the word to the others, if you will," Perrin said to Gaul. "We'll hike down the road to the place you found, then discuss what to do next. And ask some of the Maidens if they'd scout along the road in the other direction to make sure we're not going to be surprised by anyone moving up the road behind us."

Gaul nodded and moved off to pass the word. Perrin remained sitting atop Stayer, thinking. He had half a mind to send Arganda and Alliandre off to the northwest right now, setting on a path to Jehannah. But the Maidens had picked out some Shaido scouts watching his army. Those were probably there to make sure Perrin wasn't a threat, but they made him uneasy. These were dangerous times.

It was best to keep Alliandre and her people with him for now, both for her safety and his own, at least until Grady and Neald recovered. The snakebites from the bubble of evil had affected the two of them and Masuri—the only one of the Aes Sedai who had been bitten—worse than the others.

Still, Grady was starting to look hale again. Soon he'd

be able to make a gateway large enough to move the army through. Then Perrin could send Alliandre and the Two Rivers men home. He himself could Travel back to Rand, pretend to make up—most people would still think that he and Rand had parted ways angrily—and then finally be rid of Berelain and her Winged Guards. Everything could go back to the way it should be.

Light send it all went that easily. He shook his head, dispelling the swirling colors and visions that appeared to his eyes whenever he thought of Rand.

Nearby, Berelain and her force were marching out onto the road, looking very pleased to reach some solid footing. The beautiful dark-haired woman wore a fine green dress and a belt of firedrops. Her neckline was discomfortingly low. He'd started relying on her during Faile's absence, once she'd stopped treating him like a prize boar to be hunted and skinned.

Faile was back now, and it appeared his truce with Berelain was over. As usual, Annoura rode near her, though she didn't spend the time chatting with Berelain as she once had. Perrin never had figured out why she'd been meeting with the Prophet. Probably never would, considering what had happened to Masema. A day out of Malden, Perrin's scouts had run across a group of corpses that had been killed with arrows and robbed of their shoes, belts, and any valuables. Though ravens had gotten the eyes, Perrin had smelled Masema's scent through the rot.

The Prophet was dead, killed by bandits. Well, perhaps that was a fitting end for him, but Perrin still felt he'd failed. Rand had wanted Masema brought to him. The colors swirled again.

Either way, it *was* time for Perrin to return to Rand. The colors swirled, showing Rand standing in front of a building with a burned front, staring westward. Perrin banished the image.

His duty was done, the Prophet seen to, Alliandre's allegiance secure. Only, Perrin felt as if something were still very wrong. He fingered the blacksmith's puzzle in his pocket. *To understand something . . . you have to figure out its parts . . .*

He smelled Faile before she reached him, heard her horse on the soft earth. "So, Gill turned toward Lugard?" she asked, stopping beside him.

He nodded.

"That may have been wise. Perhaps we should turn that way too. Were those more sell-swords who joined us?"

"Yes."

"We must have picked up five thousand people these last few weeks," she said thoughtfully. "Perhaps more. Odd, in this desolate landscape."

She was beautiful, with her raven hair and strong features—a good Saldaean nose set between two tilted eyes. She was dressed for riding in deep wine red. He loved her dearly, and praised the Light that he'd gotten her back. Why did he feel so awkward around her now?

"You're troubled, my husband," she noted. She understood him so well, it was almost as if she could read scents. It seemed to be a thing of women, though. Berelain could do it too.

"We've gathered too many people," he said with a grunt. "I should start turning them away."

"I suspect they'd find their way back to our force anyway."

"Why should they? I could leave orders."

"You can't give orders to the Pattern itself, my husband." She glanced over at the column of people as they moved onto the road.

"What do—" He cut off, catching her meaning. "You think this is me? Being *ta'veren*?"

"Every stop along our trip, you've gained more followers," Faile said. "Despite our losses against the Aiel, we came out of Malden with a stronger force than when we started. Haven't you found it odd that so many of the former *gai'shain* are taking to Tam's training with weapons?"

"They were beaten down so long," Perrin said. "They want to stop that from happening again."

"And so coopers learn the sword," Faile said, "and find they have a talent for it. Masons who never thought of fighting back against the Shaido now train with the quarterstaff. Sell-swords and armsmen flock to us."

"It's coincidence."

"Coincidence?" She sounded amused. "With a *ta'veren* at the army's head?"

She was right, and as he fell silent, he could smell her satisfaction at winning the argument. He didn't think of it as an argument, but she'd see it as one. If anything, she'd be mad that he hadn't raised his voice.

"This is all going to end in a few days, Faile," he said. "Once we have gateways again, I'll send these people to their proper places. I'm not gathering an army. I'm helping some refugees to get home." The last thing he needed was *more* people calling him "my Lord" and bowing and scraping.

"We shall see," she said.

"Faile." He sighed and lowered his voice. "A man's got to see a thing for what it is. No sense in calling a buckle a hinge or calling a nail a horseshoe. I've told you; I'm not a good leader. I proved that."

"That's not how I see it."

He gripped the blacksmith's puzzle in his pocket. They'd discussed this during the weeks since Malden, but she *refused* to see sense. "The camp was a mess while you were gone, Faile! I've told you how Arganda and the Maidens nearly killed one another. And Aram—Masema corrupted him right under my nose. The Aes Sedai played at games I can't guess, and the Two Rivers men . . . you see how they look at me with shame in their eyes."

Faile's scent spiked with anger when he said that, and she turned sharply toward Berelain.

"It's not her fault," Perrin said. "If I'd been able to think of it, I'd have stopped the rumors dead. But I didn't. Now I've got to sleep in the bed I made for myself. Light! What is a man if his own neighbors don't think well of him? I'm no lord, Faile, and that's that. I've proven it soundly."

"Odd," she said. "But I've been speaking to the others, and they tell a different story. They say that you kept Arganda contained and put out flare-ups in camp. Then there's the alliance with the Seanchan; the more I learn of that, the more impressed I am. You acted decisively in a time of great uncertainty, you focused everyone's efforts, and you accomplished the impossible in taking Malden. *Those* are the actions of a leader."

"Faile . . ." he said, suppressing a growl. Why wouldn't she listen? When she'd been a captive, nothing had mattered to him but recovering her. *Nothing.* It didn't matter who had needed his help, or what orders he'd been given. Tarmon Gai'don itself could have started, and he'd have ignored it in order to find Faile.

He realized now how dangerous his actions had been. Trouble was, he'd take those same actions again. He didn't regret what he'd done, not for a moment. A leader couldn't be like that.

He never should have let them raise that wolfhead banner in the first place. Now that he'd completed his tasks, now that Faile was back, it was time to put all of that foolishness behind him. Perrin was a blacksmith. It didn't matter what Faile dressed him in, or what titles people gave him. You couldn't make a drawknife into a horseshoe by painting it, or by calling it something different.

He turned to the side, where Jori Congar rode before the column, that blasted red wolfhead banner flapping proudly from a pole taller than a cavalryman's lance. Perrin opened his mouth to shout for him to take it down, but Faile spoke suddenly.

"Yes, indeed," she said, musingly. "I've been thinking on this for the last few weeks, and—odd though it seems—I believe my captivity may have been precisely what we needed. Both of us."

What? Perrin turned to her, smelling her thoughtfulness. She *believed* what she'd said.

"Now," Faile said, "we need to speak of—"

"Scouts returning," he said, perhaps more abruptly than he intended. "Aiel up ahead."

Faile glanced as he pointed, but of course she couldn't see anything yet. She knew of his eyes, though. She was one of the few who did.

The call went up as others noticed the three figures in *cadin'sor* approaching alongside the road, the ones Perrin had sent to scout. Two Maidens hurried for the Wise Ones and one loped up to Perrin.

"There is something beside the road, Perrin Aybara," the woman said. She smelled concerned. That was a dangerous sign. "It is something that you will wish to see."

Galad woke to the sound of a tent flap rustling. Sharp pains burned at his side where he had been repeatedly kicked; they matched the duller aches on his shoulder, left arm, and thigh where he'd been wounded by Valda. His pounding headache was almost strong enough to drown out all else.

He groaned, rolling onto his back. All was dark around him, but pinprick lights shone in the sky. Stars? It had been overcast for so long.

No . . . something was wrong about them. His head pulsed with pain, and he blinked tears from the corners of his eyes. Those stars looked so faint, so distant. They made no familiar patterns. Where could Asunawa have taken him that the very stars were different?

As his mind cleared, he began to make out his surroundings. This was a heavy sleeping tent, constructed to be dark during the daylight hours. The lights above weren't stars at all, but sunlight through the occasional pinholes of wear in the canvas.

He was still naked, and with tentative fingers he determined that there was dried blood on his face. It had come from a long gash in his forehead. If he didn't wash it soon, infection was likely. He lay on his back, breathing in and out with care. If he took in too much air at once, his side screamed.

Galad did not fear death or pain. He had made the right choices. It was unfortunate that he'd needed to leave the Questioners in charge; they were controlled by the Seanchan. However, there had been no other option, not after he'd walked into Asunawa's hands.

Galad felt no anger at the scouts who had betrayed him. The Questioners were a valid source of authority in the Children, and their lies had no doubt been convincing. No, the one he was angry at was Asunawa, who took what was true and muddied it. There were many who did that in the world, but the Children should be *different*.

Soon the Questioners would come for him, and then the true price for saving his men would be exacted with their hooks and knives. He had been aware of that price when he'd made his decision. In a way, he had won, for he had manipulated the situation best.

The other way to ensure his victory was to hold to the truth under their questioning. To deny being a Darkfriend with his final breath. It would be difficult, but it would be right.

He forced himself to sit up, expecting—and weathering—the dizziness and nausea. He felt around. His legs were chained together, and that chain was locked to a spike that had been driven deep into the earth, piercing the rough canvas tent bottom.

He tried yanking it free, just in case. He pulled so hard that his muscles failed him and he nearly passed out. Once he had recovered, he crawled to the side of the tent. His chains gave him enough room to reach the flaps. He took one of the cloth ties—used to hold the flaps up when they were opened—and spat on it. Then, methodically, he wiped the grime and blood from his face.

The cleaning gave him a goal, kept him moving and stopped him from thinking about the pain. He carefully scrubbed the crusted blood from his cheek and nose. It was difficult; his mouth was dry. He bit down on his tongue to get saliva. The strips were not canvas, but a lighter material. They smelled of dust.

He spat on a fresh section, then worked the spittle into the cloth. The wound to his head, the dirt on his face . . . these things were marks of victory for the Questioners. He would not leave them. He would go into their tortures with a clean face.

He heard shouts outside. Men preparing to break down the camp. Would that delay their questioning? He doubted it. Striking camp could take hours. Galad continued cleaning, soiling the lengths of both straps, using the work as a kind of ritual, a rhythmic pattern to give him a focus for meditation. His headache withdrew, the pains of his body becoming less significant.

He would not run. Even if he could escape, fleeing would invalidate his bargain with Asunawa. But he *would* face his enemies with self-respect.

As he finished, he heard voices outside the tent. They were coming for him. He scrabbled quietly back to the stake in the ground. Taking a deep breath despite the pain, he rolled onto his knees. Then he took the top of the iron spike in his left hand and pushed, heaving himself to his feet.

He wobbled, then steadied himself, standing up all the way. His pains were nothing, now. He had felt insect bites that were worse. He put his feet wide in a warrior's stance, his hands held before himself with his wrists crossed. He opened his eyes, back straight, staring at the tent flaps. It wasn't the cloak, the uniform, the heraldry, or the sword that made a man. It was the way he held himself.

The flaps rustled, then drew open. The outside light was brilliant to Galad's eyes, but he did not blink. He did not flinch.

Silhouettes moved against an overcast sky. They hesitated, backlit. He could tell they were surprised to see him standing there.

"Light!" one exclaimed. "Damodred, how is it that you're awake?" Unexpectedly, the voice was familiar.

"Trom?" Galad asked, his voice ragged.

Men spilled into the room. As his eyes adjusted, Galad made out stocky Trom, along with Bornhald and Byar. Trom fumbled with a set of keys.

"Stop!" Galad said. "I gave orders to you three. Bornhald, there is blood on your cloak! I commanded you *not* to try to free me!"

"Your men obeyed your orders, Damodred," a new voice said. Galad looked up to see three men entering the room: Berab Golever, tall and bearded; Alaabar Harnesh, his bald, shadowed head missing its left ear; Brandel Vordarian, a blond hulk of a man from Galad's native Andor. All three were Lords Captain, all three had stood with Asunawa.

"What is this?" Galad asked them.

Harnesh opened a sack and dumped something bulbous to the ground in front of Galad. A head.

Asunawa's.

All three men drew swords and knelt before him, the points of their weapons stabbing the canvas. Trom unlocked the manacles at Galad's feet.

"I see," Galad said. "You have turned your swords on fellow Children."

"What would you have had us do?" Brandel asked, looking up from his kneeling position.

Galad shook his head. "I do not know. Perhaps you are right; I should not chide you on this choice. It may have been the only one you could have made. But why did you change your minds?"

"We have lost two Lords Captain Commander in under half a year," Harnesh said in a gruff voice. "The Fortress of the Light has become a playground for the Seanchan. The world is in chaos."

"And yet," Golever said, "Asunawa marched us all the way out here to have us battle our fellow Children. It was

not right, Damodred. We all saw how you presented yourself, we all saw how *you* stopped us from killing one another. Faced with that, and with the High Inquisitor naming
as Darkfriend a man we all know to be honorable . . . Well,
how could we *not* turn against him?"

Galad nodded. "You accept me as Lord Captain Commander?"

The three men bowed their heads. "All the Lords Captain
are for you," Golever said. "We were forced to kill a third of
those who wore the red shepherd's crook of the Hand of the
Light. Some others united with us; some tried to flee. The
Amadicians did not interfere, and many have said they'd
rather join with us than return to the Seanchan. We have the
other Amadicians—and the Questioners who tried to run—
held at swordpoint."

"Let free those who wish to leave," Galad said. "They
may return to their families and their masters. By the time
they reach the Seanchan, we will be beyond their grasp."

The men nodded.

"I accept your allegiance," Galad said. "Gather the other
Lords Captain and fetch me supply reports. Strike camp.
We march for Andor."

None of them asked whether he needed rest, though Trom
did look worried. Galad accepted the white robe a Child
brought to him, and then sat in a hastily supplied chair
as another—Child Candeiar, a man expert in wounds—
entered to inspect his injuries.

Galad didn't feel wise or strong enough to bear the title
he did. But the Children had made their decision.

The Light would protect them for it.

CHAPTER
3

The Amyrlin's Anger

Egwene floated in blackness. She was without form, lacking shape or body. The thoughts, imaginings, worries, hopes, and ideas of all the world extended into eternity around her.

This was the place between dreams and the waking world, a blackness pinpricked with thousands upon thousands of distinct lights, each more focused and intense than the stars of the skies. They were dreams, and she could look in on them, but did not. The ones she wanted to see were warded, and most of the others were mysteries to her.

There *was* one dream she longed to slip into. She restrained herself. Though her feelings for Gawyn were still strong, her opinion of him was muddled recently. Getting lost in his dreams would not help.

She turned about, looking through the expanse. Recently, she'd started coming here to float and think. The dreams of all the people here—some from her world, some from shadows of it—reminded her why she fought. She must never forget that there was an entire world outside the White Tower's walls. The purpose of Aes Sedai was to serve that world.

Time passed as she lay bathed in the light of dreams. Eventually, she willed herself to move, and located a dream she recognized—though she wasn't certain how she did it. The dream swept up toward her, filling her vision.

She pressed her will against the dream and sent a thought into it. *Nynaeve. It is time to stop avoiding me. There is work to be done, and I have news for you. Meet me in two*

nights in the Hall of the Tower. If you do not come, I will
be forced to take measures. Your dalliance threatens us all.

The dream seemed to shudder, and Egwene pulled back
as it vanished. She'd already spoken to Elayne. Those two
were loose threads; they needed to be truly raised to the
shawl, with the oaths administered.

Beyond that, Egwene needed information from Nynaeve.
Hopefully, the threat mixed with a promise of news would
bring her. And that news *was* important. The White Tower
finally unified, the Amyrlin Seat secure, Elaida captured by
the Seanchan.

Pinprick dreams streaked around Egwene. She considered trying to contact the Wise Ones, but decided against it.
How should she deal with them? The first thing was to keep
them from thinking they were being "dealt with." Her plan
for them was not yet firm.

She let herself slip back into her body, content to spend
the rest of the night with her own dreams. Here, she couldn't
keep thoughts of Gawyn from visiting her, nor did she want
to. She stepped into her dream, and into his embrace. They
stood in a small stone-walled room shaped like her study in
the Tower, yet decorated like the common room of her father's inn. Gawyn was dressed in sturdy Two Rivers wool-
ens and did not wear his sword. A more simple life: It could
not be hers, but she could dream . . .

Everything shook. The room of past and present seemed
to shatter, shredding into swirling smoke. Egwene stepped
back, gasping, as Gawyn ripped apart as if made of sand.
All was dust around her, and thirteen black towers rose in
the distance beneath a tarlike sky.

One fell, and then another, crashing to the ground. As
they did, the ones that remained grew taller and taller. The
ground shook as several more towers fell. Another tower
shook and cracked, collapsing most of the way to the
ground—but then, it recovered and grew tallest of all.

At the end of the quake, six towers remained, looming
above her. Egwene had fallen to the ground, which had
become soft earth covered in withered leaves. The vision
changed. She was looking down at a nest. In it, a group of
fledgling eagles screeched toward the sky for their mother.
One of the eaglets *uncoiled*, and it wasn't an eagle at all, but

a serpent. It began to strike at the fledglings one at a time, swallowing them whole. The eaglets simply continued to stare into the sky, pretending that the serpent was their sibling as it devoured them.

The vision changed. She saw an enormous sphere made of the finest crystal. It sparkled in the light of twenty-three enormous stars, shining down on it where it sat on a dark hilltop. There were cracks in it, and it was being held together by ropes.

There was Rand, walking up the hillside, holding a woodsman's axe. He reached the top and hefted the axe, then swung at the ropes one at a time, chopping them free. The last one parted, and the sphere began to break apart, the beautiful globe falling in pieces. Rand shook his head.

Egwene gasped, came awake, and sat upright. She was in her rooms in the White Tower. The bedchamber was nearly empty—she'd had Elaida's things removed, but hadn't completely furnished it again. She had only a washstand, a rug of thick-woven brown fibers, and a bed with posts and drapes. The window shutters were closed; morning sunlight peeked through.

She breathed in and out. Rarely did dreams unsettle her as much as this one had.

Calming herself, she reached down to the side of her bed, picking up the leather-bound book she kept there to record her dreams. The middle of the three this night was the clearest to her. She *felt* the meaning of it, interpreting it as she sometimes could. The serpent was one of the Forsaken, hidden in the White Tower, pretending to be Aes Sedai. Egwene had suspected this was the case—Verin had said she believed it so.

Mesaana was still in the White Tower. But how did she imitate an Aes Sedai? Every sister had resworn the oaths. Apparently Mesaana could defeat the Oath Rod. As Egwene carefully recorded the dreams, she thought about the towers, looming, threatening to destroy her, and she knew some of the meaning there too.

If Egwene did not find Mesaana and stop her, something terrible would happen. It could mean the fall of the White Tower, perhaps the victory of the Dark One. Dreams were not Foretellings—they didn't show what *would* happen, but what *could*.

Light, she thought, finishing her record. *As if I didn't have enough to worry about.*

Egwene rose to call her maids, but a knock at the door interrupted her. Curious, she walked across the thick rug—wearing only her nightgown—and opened the door enough to see Silviana standing in the antechamber. Square-featured and dressed in red, she had her hair up in its typical bun, and her red Keeper's stole over her shoulders.

"Mother," the woman said, her voice tense. "I apologize for waking you."

"I wasn't asleep," Egwene said. "What is it? What has happened?"

"He's *here*, Mother. At the White Tower."

"Who?"

"The Dragon Reborn. He's asking to see you."

"Well, this is a pot of fisherman's stew made only with the heads," Siuan said as she stalked through a hallway of the White Tower. "How did he get through the city without anyone seeing him?"

High Captain Chubain winced.

As well he should, Siuan thought. The raven-haired man wore the uniform of the Tower Guard, a white tabard over his mail emblazoned with the Flame of Tar Valon. He walked with a hand on his sword. There had been some talk that he might be replaced as High Captain now that Bryne was in Tar Valon, but Egwene had followed Siuan's advice not to do so. Bryne didn't want to be High Captain, and he would be needed as a field general for the Last Battle.

Bryne was out with his men; finding quarters and food for fifty thousand troops was proving to be near impossible. She'd sent him word, and could feel him getting closer. Stern block of wood though the man was, Siuan felt that his stability would have been nice to have near her right now. The Dragon Reborn? *Inside* Tar Valon?

"It's not really that surprising he got so far, Siuan," Saerin said. The olive-skinned Brown had been with Siuan when they'd seen the captain racing by, pale-faced. Saerin had white at her temples, some measure of age as an Aes Sedai, and had a scar on one cheek, the origin of which Siuan hadn't been able to pry out of her.

"There are hundreds of refugees pouring into the city each day," Saerin continued, "and any man with half an inclination to fight is being sent for recruitment into the Tower Guard. It's no wonder nobody stopped al'Thor."

Chubain nodded. "He was at the Sunset Gate before anyone questioned him. And then he just . . . well, he just said he was the Dragon Reborn, and that he wanted to see the Amyrlin. Didn't yell it out or anything, said it calm as spring rain."

The hallways of the Tower were busy, though most of the women didn't seem to know what they were to do, darting this way and that like fish in a net.

Stop that, Siuan thought. *He's come into our seat of power. He's the one caught in the net.*

"What is his game, do you think?" Saerin asked.

"Burn me if I know," Siuan replied. "He's bound to be mostly insane by now. Maybe he's frightened, and has come to turn himself in."

"I doubt that."

"As do I," Siuan said grudgingly. During these last few days, she'd found—to her amazement—that she *liked* Saerin. As Amyrlin, Siuan hadn't had time for friendships; it had been too important to play the Ajahs off one another. She'd thought Saerin obstinate and frustrating. Now that they weren't butting heads so often, she found those attributes appealing.

"Maybe he heard that Elaida was gone," Siuan said, "and thought that he would be safe here, with an old friend on the Amyrlin Seat."

"That doesn't match what I've read of the boy," Saerin replied. "Reports call him mistrustful and erratic, with a demanding temper and an insistence on avoiding Aes Sedai."

That was what Siuan had heard as well, though it had been two years since she'd seen the boy. In fact, the last time he'd stood before her, she'd been the Amyrlin and he'd been a simple sheepherder. Most of what she knew of him since then had come through the Blue Ajah's eyes-and-ears. It took a great deal of skill to separate speculation from truth, but most agreed about al'Thor. Temperamental, distrustful, arrogant. *Light burn Elaida!* Siuan thought. *If not for her, we'd have had him safely in Aes Sedai care long ago.*

They climbed down three spiraling ramps and entered another of the White Tower's white-walled hallways, moving toward the Hall of the Tower. If the Amyrlin was going to receive the Dragon Reborn, then she'd do it there. Two twisting turns later—past mirrored stand-lamps and stately tapestries—they entered one last hallway and froze.

The floor tiles here were the color of blood. That wasn't right. The ones here should have been white and yellow. These glistened, as if wet.

Chubain inhaled sharply, hand going to his sword hilt. Saerin raised an eyebrow. Siuan was tempted to barrel onward, but these places where the Dark One had touched the world could be dangerous. She might find herself sinking through the floor, or being attacked by the tapestries.

The two Aes Sedai turned and walked the other way. Chubain lingered for a moment, then hurried after. It was easy to read the tension in his face. First the Seanchan, and now the Dragon Reborn himself, come to assault the Tower on his watch.

As they passed through the hallways, they met other sisters flowing in the same direction. Most of them wore their shawls. One might have argued that was because of the news of the day, but the truth was that many still held to their distrust of other Ajahs. Another reason to curse Elaida. Egwene had been working hard to reforge the Tower, but one couldn't mend years' worth of broken nets in one month.

They finally arrived at the Hall of the Tower. Sisters clustered in the wide hallway outside, divided by Ajah. Chubain hurried to speak with his guards at the door, and Saerin entered the Hall proper, where she could wait with the other Sitters. Siuan remained standing with the dozens outside.

Things were changing. Egwene had a new Keeper to replace Sheriam. The choice of Silviana made a great deal of sense—the woman was known to have a level head, for a Red, and choosing her had helped forge the two halves of the Tower back together. But Siuan had harbored a small hope that she herself would be chosen. Now Egwene had so many demands on her time—and was becoming so capable on her own—that she was relying on Siuan less and less.

That was a good thing. But it was also infuriating.

The familiar hallways, the scent of freshly washed stone, the echoing of footsteps . . . When last she'd been in this place, she'd commanded it. No longer.

She had no mind to climb her way into prominence again. The Last Battle was upon them; she didn't want to spend her time dealing with the squabbles of the Blue Ajah as they reintegrated into the Tower. She wanted to do what she'd set out to do, all those years before with Moiraine. Shepherd the Dragon Reborn to the Last Battle.

Through the bond, she felt Bryne arrive before he spoke. "Now, there's a concerned face," he said, piercing the hallway's dozens of hushed conversations as he walked up behind her.

Siuan turned to him. He was stately and remarkably calm—particularly for a man who had been betrayed by Morgase Trakand, then sucked into Aes Sedai politics, then told he was going to be leading his troops on the front lines of the Last Battle. But that was Bryne. Serene to a fault. He soothed her worries just by being there.

"You came faster than I'd assumed you'd be able to," she said. "And I do *not* have a 'concerned face,' Gareth Bryne. I'm Aes Sedai. My very nature is to be in control of myself and my surroundings."

"Yes," he said. "And yet, the more time I spend around the Aes Sedai, the more I wonder about that. Are they in control of their emotions? Or do those emotions just never change? If one is *always* concerned, one will always look the same."

She eyed him. "Fool man."

He smiled, turning to look through the hallway full of Aes Sedai and Warders. "I was already returning to the Tower with a report when your messenger found me. Thank you."

"You're welcome," she said gruffly.

"They're nervous," he said. "I don't think I've ever seen the Aes Sedai like this."

"Well, can you blame us?" she snapped.

He looked at her, then raised a hand to her shoulder. His strong, callused fingers brushed her neck. "What is wrong?"

She took a deep breath, glancing to the side as Egwene

finally arrived, walking toward the Hall in conversation with Silviana. As usual, the somber Gawyn Trakand lurked behind like a distant shadow. Unacknowledged by Egwene, not bonded as her Warder, yet not cast from the Tower either. He'd spent the nights since the reunification guarding Egwene's doors, despite the fact that it angered her.

As Egwene neared the entrance to the Hall, sisters stepped back and made way, some reluctantly, others reverently. She'd brought the Tower to its knees from the inside, while being beaten every day and doused with so much forkroot she could barely light a candle with the Power. So young. Yet what was age to Aes Sedai?

"I always thought I would be the one in there," Siuan said softly, just for Bryne. "That I would receive him, guide him. *I* was the one who was to be sitting in that chair."

Bryne's grip tightened. "Siuan, I . . ."

"Oh, don't be like that," she growled, looking at him. "I don't regret a thing."

He frowned.

"It's for the best," Siuan said, though it twisted her insides in knots to admit it. "For all her tyranny and foolishness, it is *good* that Elaida removed me, because that is what led us to Egwene. She'll do better than I could have. It's hard to swallow—I did well as Amyrlin, but I couldn't do *that*. Lead by presence instead of force, uniting instead of dividing. And so, I'm *glad* that Egwene is receiving him."

Bryne smiled, and he squeezed her shoulder fondly.

"What?" she asked.

"I'm proud of you."

She rolled her eyes. "Bah. That sentimentality of yours is going to drown me one of these days."

"You can't hide your goodness from me, Siuan Sanche. I see your heart."

"You are *such* a buffoon."

"Regardless. You brought us here, Siuan. Whatever heights that girl climbs to, she'll do it because *you* carved the steps for her."

"Yes, then handed the chisel to Elaida." Siuan glanced toward Egwene, who stood inside the doorway into the Hall. The young Amyrlin glanced over the women gathered outside, and nodded in greeting to Siuan. Maybe even a little in respect.

"She's what we need now," Bryne said, "but you're what we needed then. You did well, Siuan. She knows it, and the Tower knows it."

That felt very good to hear. "Well. Did you see him when you came in?"

"Yes," Bryne said. "He's standing below, watched over by at least a hundred Warders and twenty-six sisters—two full circles. Undoubtedly he's shielded, but all twenty-six women seemed in a near panic. Nobody dares touch him or bind him."

"So long as he's shielded, it shouldn't matter. Did he look frightened? Haughty? Angry?"

"None of that."

"Well, what *did* he look like, then?"

"Honestly, Siuan? He looked like an Aes Sedai."

Siuan snapped her jaw closed. Was he taunting her again? No, the general seemed serious. But what did he mean?

Egwene entered the Hall, and then a white-dressed novice went scuttling away, tailed by two of Chubain's soldiers. Egwene had sent for the Dragon. Bryne remained with his hand on Siuan's shoulder, standing just behind her in the hallway. Siuan forced herself to be calm.

Eventually, she saw motion at the end of the hallway. Around her, sisters began to glow as they embraced the Source. Siuan resisted that mark of insecurity.

Soon a procession approached, Warders walking in a square around a tall figure in a worn brown cloak, twenty-six Aes Sedai following behind. The figure inside glowed to her eyes. She had the Talent of seeing *ta'veren*, and al'Thor was one of the most powerful of those to ever live.

She forced herself to ignore the glow, looking at al'Thor himself. It appeared that the boy had become a man. All hints of youthful softness were gone, replaced with hard lines. He'd lost the unconsciously slumped posture that many young men adopted, particularly the tall ones. Instead he embraced his height as a man should, walking with command. Siuan had seen false Dragons during her time as Amyrlin. Odd, how much this man should look like them. It was—

She froze as he met her eyes. There was something indefinable about them, a weight, an age. As though the man behind them was seeing through the light of a thousand lives compounded in one. His face *did* look like that of an Aes Sedai. Those eyes, at least, had agelessness.

The Dragon Reborn raised his right hand—his left arm was folded behind his back—and halted the procession. "If you please," he said to the Warders, stepping through them.

The Warders, shocked, let him pass; the Dragon's soft voice made them step away. They should have known better. Al'Thor walked up to Siuan, and she steeled herself. He was unarmed and shielded. He couldn't harm her. Still, Bryne stepped up to her side and lowered his hand to his sword.

"Peace, Gareth Bryne," al'Thor said. "I will do no harm. You've let her bond you, I assume? Curious. Elayne will be interested to hear of that. And Siuan Sanche. You've changed since we last met."

"Change comes to all of us as the Wheel turns."

"An Aes Sedai answer for certain." Al'Thor smiled. A relaxed, soft smile. That surprised her. "I wonder if I will ever grow accustomed to those. You once took an arrow for me. Did I thank you for that?"

"I didn't do it intentionally, as I recall," she said dryly.

"You have my thanks nonetheless." He turned toward the door to the Hall of the Tower. "What kind of Amyrlin is she?"

Why ask me? He couldn't know of the closeness between Siuan and Egwene. "She's an incredible one," Siuan said. "One of the greatest we've had, for all the fact that she's only held the Seat a short time."

He smiled again. "I should have expected nothing less. Strange, but I feel that seeing her again will hurt, though that is one wound that has well and truly healed. I can still remember the pain of it, I suppose."

Light, but this man was making a muddle of her expectations! The White Tower was a place that should have unnerved any man who could channel, Dragon Reborn or not. Yet he didn't seem worried in the least.

She opened her mouth, but was cut off as an Aes Sedai pushed through the group. Tiana?

The woman pulled something out of her sleeve and proffered it to Rand. A small letter with a red seal. "This is for you," she said. Her voice sounded tense, and her fingers trembled, though the tremble was so faint that most would have missed it. Siuan had learned to look for signs of emotion in Aes Sedai, however.

Al'Thor raised an eyebrow, then reached over and took it. "What is it?"

"I promised to deliver it," Tiana said. "I would have said no, but I never thought you'd actually come to . . . I mean . . ." She cut herself off, closing her mouth. Then she withdrew into the crowd.

Al'Thor slipped the note into his pocket without reading it. "Do your best to calm Egwene when I am done," he said to Siuan. Then he took a deep breath and strode forward, ignoring his guards. They hastened after him, the Warders looking sheepish, but nobody dared touch him as he strode between the doors and into the Hall of the Tower.

Hairs bristled on Egwene's arms as Rand came into the room, unaccompanied. Aes Sedai outside crowded around the doorway, trying to look as if they were not gawking. Silviana glanced at Egwene. Should this meeting be Sealed to the Hall?

No, Egwene thought. *They need to see me confront him. Light, but I don't feel ready for this.*

There was no helping it. She steeled herself, repeating in her head the same words she'd been going over all morning. This was not Rand al'Thor, friend of her childhood, the man she'd assumed that she'd one day marry. Rand al'Thor she could be lenient with, but leniency here could bring about the end of the world.

No. This man was the Dragon Reborn. The most dangerous man ever to draw breath. Tall, much more confident than she ever remembered him being. He wore simple clothing.

He walked directly into the center of the Hall, his Warder guards remaining outside. He stopped in the center of the Flame on the floor, surrounded by Sitters in their seats.

"Egwene," Rand said, voice echoing in the chamber. He nodded to her, as if in respect. "You have done your part, I see. The Amyrlin's stole fits you well."

From what she had heard of Rand recently, she had not

anticipated such calm in him. Perhaps it was the calm of the criminal who had finally given himself up.

Was that how she thought of him? As a criminal? He had done acts that certainly seemed criminal; he had destroyed, he had conquered. When she'd last spent any length of time with Rand, they had traveled through the Aiel Waste. He had become a hard man during those months, and she saw that hardness in him still. But there was something else, something deeper.

"What has happened to you?" she found herself asking as she leaned forward on the Amyrlin Seat.

"I was broken," Rand said, hands behind his back. "And then, remarkably, I was reforged. I think he almost had me, Egwene. It was Cadsuane who set me to fixing it, though she did so by accident. Still, I shall have to lift her exile, I suspect."

He spoke differently. There was a formality to his words that she didn't recognize. In another man, she would have assumed a cultured, educated background. But Rand didn't have that. Could tutors have trained him so quickly?

"Why have you come before the Amyrlin Seat?" she asked. "Have you come to make a petition, or have you come to surrender yourself to the White Tower's guidance?"

He studied her, hands still behind his back. Just behind him, thirteen sisters quietly filed into the Hall, the glow of *saidar* around them as they maintained his shield.

Rand didn't seem to care about that. He studied the room, looking at the various Sitters. His eyes lingered on the seats of Reds, two of which were empty. Pevara and Javindhra hadn't yet returned from their unknown mission. Only Barasine—newly chosen to replace Duhara—was in attendance. To her credit, she met Rand's eyes evenly.

"I've hated you before," Rand said, turning back to Egwene. "I've felt a lot of emotions, in recent months. It seems that from the very moment Moiraine came to the Two Rivers, I've been struggling to avoid Aes Sedai strings of control. And yet, I allowed other strings—more dangerous strings—to wrap around me unseen.

"It occurs to me that I've been trying too hard. I worried that if I listened to you, you'd control me. It wasn't a desire for independence that drove me, but a fear of irrelevance. A fear that the acts I accomplished would be yours, and not my own." He hesitated. "I should have wished for such a convenient set of backs upon which to heap the blame for my crimes."

Egwene frowned. The Dragon Reborn had come to the White Tower to engage in idle philosophy? Perhaps he *had* gone mad. "Rand," Egwene said, softening her tone. "I'm going to have some sisters talk to you to decide if there is anything . . . wrong with you. Please try to understand."

Once they knew more about his state, they could decide what to do with him. The Dragon Reborn did need freedom to do as the prophecies said he would, but could they simply let him roam away, now that they had him?

Rand smiled. "Oh, I *do* understand, Egwene. And I am sorry to deny you, but I have too much to do. People starve because of me, others live in terror of what I have done. A friend rides to his death without allies. There is so little time to do what I must."

"Rand," Egwene said, "we have to make sure."

He nodded, as if in understanding. "This is the part I regret. I did not wish to come into your center of power, which you have achieved so well, and defy you. But it cannot be helped. You must know what my plans are so that you can prepare.

"The last time I tried to seal the Bore, I was forced to do it without the help of the women. That was part of what led to disaster, though they may have been wise to deny me their strength. Well, blame must be spread evenly, but I will not make the same mistakes a second time. I believe that *saidin* and *saidar* must both be used. I don't have the answers yet."

Egwene leaned forward, studying him. There didn't seem to be madness in his eyes. She knew those eyes. She knew Rand.

Light, she thought. *I'm wrong. I* can't *think of him only as the Dragon Reborn. I'm here for a reason. He's here for a reason. To me, he must be Rand. Because Rand can be trusted, while the Dragon Reborn must be feared.*

"Which are you?" she whispered unconsciously.

He heard. "I am both, Egwene. I remember him. Lews Therin. I can see his entire life, every desperate moment. I see it like a dream, but a clear dream. My own dream. It's part of me."

The words were those of a madman, but they were spoken evenly. She looked at him, and remembered the youth that he had been. The earnest young man. Not solemn like Perrin, but not wild like Mat. Solid, straightforward. The type of man you could trust with anything.

Even the fate of the world.

"In one month's time," Rand said, "I'm going to travel to Shayol Ghul and break the last remaining seals on the Dark One's prison. I want your help."

Break the seals? She saw the image from her dream, Rand hacking at the ropes that bound the crystalline globe. "Rand, no," she said.

"I'm going to need you, all of you," he continued. "I hope to the Light that this time, you will give me your support. I want you to meet with me on the day before I go to Shayol Ghul. And then . . . well, then we will discuss my terms."

"Your terms?" Egwene demanded.

"You will see," he said, turning as if to leave.

"Rand al'Thor!" she said, rising. "You will *not* turn your back on the Amyrlin Seat!"

He froze, then turned back toward her.

"You can't break the seals," Egwene said. "That would risk letting the Dark One free."

"A risk we must take. Clear away the rubble. The Bore must be opened fully again before it can be sealed."

"We must talk about this," she said. "Plan."

"That is why I came to you. To let you plan."

He seemed amused. Light! She sat back down, angry. That bullheadedness of his was just like that of his father. "There are things we must speak of, Rand. Not just this, but other things—the sisters your men have bonded not the least among them."

"We can speak of that when we next meet."

She frowned at him.

"And so here we come to it," Rand said. He bowed to her—a shallow bow, almost more a tip of the head. "Egwene al'Vere, Watcher of the Seals, Flame of Tar Valon, may I have your permission to withdraw?"

He asked it so politely. She couldn't tell if he was mocking her or not. She met his eyes. *Don't make me do anything I would regret,* his expression seemed to say.

Could she really confine him here? After what she'd said to Elaida about him needing to be free?

"I will not let you break the seals," she said. "That is madness."

"Then meet with me at the place known as the Field of Merrilor, just to the north. We will talk before I go to Shayol Ghul. For now, I do not want to defy you, Egwene. But I *must* go."

Neither of them looked away. The others in the room seemed not to breathe. The chamber was still enough for Egwene to hear the faint breeze making the rose window groan in its lead.

"Very well," Egwene said. "But this is not ended, Rand."

"There are no endings, Egwene," he replied, then nodded to her and turned to walk from the Hall. Light! He was missing his left hand! How had that happened?

The sisters and Warders reluctantly parted for him. Egwene raised a hand to her head, feeling dizzy.

"Light!" Silviana said. "How could you think during that, Mother?"

"What?" Egwene looked about the Hall. Many of the Sitters were slumping visibly in their seats.

"Something gripped my heart," Barasine said, raising a hand to her breast, "squeezing it tight. I didn't dare speak."

"I *tried* to speak," Yukiri said. "My mouth wouldn't move."

"*Ta'veren*," Saerin said. "But an effect as strong as that . . . I felt that it would *crush* me from the inside."

"How did you resist it, Mother?" Silviana asked.

Egwene frowned. She hadn't felt that way. Perhaps because she thought of him as Rand. "We need to discuss his words. The Hall of the Tower will reconvene in one hour's time for discussion." *That* conversation would be Sealed to the Hall. "And someone follow to make sure he really leaves."

"Gareth Bryne is doing so," Chubain said from outside.

The Sitters pulled themselves to their feet, shaken. Silviana leaned down. "You're right, Mother. He can't be allowed to break the seals. But what are we to do? If you won't hold him captive . . ."

"I doubt we could have held him," Egwene said. "There's

something about him. I . . . I had the sense he could have broken that shield without a struggle."

"Then how? How do we stop him?"

"We need allies," Egwene said. She took a deep breath. "He might be persuaded by people that he trusts." Or he might be forced to change his mind if confronted by a large enough group united to stop him.

It was now *more* vital that she speak with Elayne and Nynaeve.

CHAPTER
4

The Pattern Groans

What is it?" Perrin asked, trying to ignore the sharp scent of rotting meat. He couldn't see any corpses, but by his nose, the ground should be littered with them.

He stood with an advance group at the side of the Jehannah Road, looking northward across a rolling plain with few trees. The grass was brown and yellow, as in other places, but it grew darker farther away from the road, as if infected with some disease.

"I've seen this before," Seonid said. The diminutive, pale-skinned Aes Sedai stooped at the edge of the road, turning the leaf of a small weed over in her fingers. She wore green wool, fine but unornamented, her only jewelry her Great Serpent ring.

Thunder rumbled softly above. Six Wise Ones stood behind Seonid, arms folded, faces unreadable. Perrin hadn't considered telling the Wise Ones—or their two Aes Sedai apprentices—to stay behind. He was probably lucky they let *him* accompany *them*.

"Yes," Nevarin said, bracelets clattering as she knelt and took the leaf from Seonid. "I visited the Blight once as a girl; my father felt it important for me to see. This looks like what I saw there."

Perrin had been to the Blight only once, but the look of those dark specks was indeed distinctive. A redjay fluttered down to one of the distant trees and began picking at branches and leaves, but found nothing of interest and took wing again.

The disturbing thing was, the plants here seemed better

than many they'd passed along the way. Covered with spots, but alive, even thriving.

Light, Perrin thought, taking the leaf as Nevarin handed it to him. It smelled of decay. *What kind of world is it where the Blight is the* good *alternative?*

"Mori circled the entire patch," Nevarin said, nodding to a Maiden standing nearby. "It grows darker near the center. She could not see what was there."

Perrin nudged Stayer down off the road. Faile followed; she didn't smell the least bit afraid, though Perrin's Two Rivers armsmen hesitated.

"Lord Perrin?" Wil called.

"It's probably not dangerous," Perrin said. "Animals still move in and out of it." The Blight was dangerous because of what lived there. And if those beasts had somehow come southward, they needed to know. The Aiel strode after him without comment. And since Faile had joined him, Berelain had to as well, Annoura and Gallenne trailing her. Blessedly, Alliandre had agreed to remain behind, in charge of the camp and refugees while Perrin was away.

The horses were already skittish, and the surroundings didn't help their moods any. Perrin breathed through his mouth to dampen the stench of rot and death. The ground was wet here too—if only those clouds would pass so they could get some good sunlight to dry the soil—and the horses' footing was treacherous, so they took their time. Most of the meadow was covered in grass, clover and small weeds, and the farther they rode, the more pervasive the dark spots became. Within minutes, many of the plants were more brown than they were green or yellow.

Eventually they came to a small dale nestled amid three hillsides. Perrin pulled Stayer to a halt; the others bunched up around him. There was a strange village here. The buildings were huts built from an odd type of wood, like large reeds, and the roofs were thatch—but thatch built from enormous leaves, as wide as two man's palms.

There were no plants here, only a very sandy soil. Perrin slid free of the saddle and stooped down to feel it, rubbing the gritty stuff between his fingers. He looked at the others. They smelled confused.

He cautiously led Stayer forward into the center of the village. The Blight was radiating from this point, but the village itself showed no touch of it. Maidens scattered forward, veils in place, Sulin at their head. They did a quick inspection of the huts, signing to one another with quick gestures, then returned.

"Nobody?" Faile asked.

"No," Sulin said, cautiously lowering her veil. "This place is deserted."

"Who would build a village like this," Perrin asked, "in Ghealdan of all places?"

"It wasn't built here," Masuri said.

Perrin turned toward the slender Aes Sedai.

"This village is not native to this area," Masuri said. "The wood is unlike anything I've seen before."

"The Pattern groans," Berelain said softly. "The dead walking, the odd deaths. In cities, rooms vanish and food spoils."

Perrin scratched his chin, remembering a day when his axe had tried to kill him. If entire villages were vanishing and appearing in other places, if the Blight was growing out of rifts where the Pattern was fraying . . . Light! How bad were things becoming?

"Burn the village," he said, turning. "Use the One Power. Scour as many of the tainted plants as you can. Maybe we can keep it from spreading. We'll move the army to that camp an hour away, and will stay there tomorrow if you need more time."

For once, neither the Wise Ones nor the Aes Sedai voiced so much as a sniff of complaint at the direct order.

Hunt with us, brother.

Perrin found himself in the wolf dream. He vaguely remembered sitting drowsily by the dwindling light of an open lamp, a single flame shivering on its tip, waiting to hear a report from those dealing with the strange village. He had been reading a copy of *The Travels of Jain Farstrider* that Gaul had found among the salvage from Malden.

Now Perrin lay on his back in the middle of a large field with grass as tall as a man's waist. He gazed up, grass brushing his cheeks and arms as it shivered in the wind. In the sky, that same storm brewed, here as in the waking world. More violent here.

Staring up at it—his vision framed by the stalks of brown and green grass and stems of wild millet—he could almost *feel* the storm growing closer. As if it was crawling down out of the sky to engulf him.

Young Bull! Come! Come hunt!

The voice was that of a wolf. Perrin by instinct knew that she was called Oak Dancer, named for the way she had scampered between saplings as a whelp. There were others, too. Whisperer. Morninglight. Sparks. Boundless. A good dozen wolves called to him, some living wolves who slept, others the *spirits* of wolves who had died.

They called to him with a mixture of scents and images and sounds. The smell of a spring buck, pocking the earth with its leaps. Fallen leaves crumbling beneath running wolves. The growls of victory, the thrill of a pack running together.

The invitations awakened something deep within him, the wolf he tried to keep locked away. But a wolf could not be locked up for long. It either escaped or it died; it would not stand captivity. He longed to leap to his feet and send his joyous acceptance, losing himself in the pack. He was Young Bull, and he was welcome here.

"No!" Perrin said, sitting up, holding his head. "I will *not* lose myself in you."

Hopper sat in the grass to his right. The large gray wolf regarded Perrin, golden eyes unblinking, reflecting flashes of lightning from above. The grass came up to Hopper's neck.

Perrin lowered a hand from his head. The air was *heavy*, full of humidity, and it smelled of rain. Above the scent of the weather and that of the dry field, he could smell Hopper's patience.

You are invited, Young Bull, Hopper sent.

"I can't hunt with you," Perrin explained. "Hopper, we spoke of this. I'm losing myself. When I go into battle, I become enraged. Like a wolf."

Like a wolf? Hopper sent. *Young Bull, you are a wolf. And a man. Come hunt.*

"I *told* you I can't! I will not let this consume me." He thought of a young man with golden eyes, locked in a cage, all humanity gone from him. His name had been Noam—Perrin had seen him in a village called Jarra.

Light, Perrin thought. *That's not far from here.* Or at least not far from where his body slumbered in the real world. Jarra was in Ghealdan. An odd coincidence.

With a ta'veren *nearby, there are no coincidences.*

He frowned, rising and scanning the landscape. Moiraine had told Perrin there was nothing human left inside of Noam. That was what awaited a wolfbrother if he let himself be completely consumed by the wolf.

"I must learn to control this, or I must banish the wolf from me," Perrin said. "There is no time left for compromise, Hopper."

Hopper smelled dissatisfied. He didn't like what he'd called a human tendency to wish to control things.

Come, Hopper sent, standing up in the grass. *Hunt.*

"I—"

Come learn, Hopper sent, frustrated. *The Last Hunt comes.*

Hopper's sendings included the image of a young pup making his first kill. That and a worry for the future—a normally unwolflike attribute. The Last Hunt brought change.

Perrin hesitated. In a previous visit to the wolf dream, Perrin had demanded that Hopper train him to master the place. Very inappropriate for a young wolf—a kind of challenge to the elder's seniority—but this was a response. Hopper had come to teach, but he would do it as a wolf taught.

"I'm sorry," Perrin said. "I will hunt with you—but I must not lose myself."

These things you think, Hopper sent, displeased. *How can you think such images of nothing?* The response was accompanied by images of blankness—an empty sky, a den with nobody in it, a barren field. *You are Young Bull. You will always be Young Bull. How can you lose Young Bull? Look down, and you will see his paws beneath. Bite, and his teeth will kill. There is no losing this.*

"It is a thing of humans."

The same empty words over and over, Hopper sent.

Perrin took a deep breath, sucking in and releasing the too-wet air. "Very well," he said, hammer and knife appearing in his hands. "Let's go."

You hunt game with your hooves? An image of a bull ignoring its horns and trying to leap onto the back of a deer and stomp it to the ground.

"You're right." Perrin was suddenly holding a good Two Rivers longbow. He wasn't as good a shot as Jondyn Barran or Rand, but he could hold his own.

Hopper sent a bull spitting at a deer. Perrin growled, sending back a wolf's claws shooting from its paws and striking a deer at a distance, but this only seemed to amuse Hopper further. Despite his annoyance, Perrin had to admit that it was a rather ridiculous image.

The wolf sent the image to the others, causing them to howl in amusement, though most of them seemed to prefer the bull jumping up and down on the deer. Perrin growled, chasing after Hopper toward the distant woods, where the other wolves waited.

As he ran, the grasses seemed to grow more dense. They held him back, like snarled forest undergrowth. Hopper soon outpaced him.

Run, Young Bull!

I'm trying, Perrin sent back.

Not as you have before!

Perrin continued to push his way through the grass. This strange place, this wonderful world where wolves ran, could be intoxicating. And dangerous. Hopper had warned Perrin of that more than once.

Dangers for tomorrow. Ignore them for now, Hopper sent, growing more distant. *Worry is for two-legs.*

I can't ignore my problems! Perrin thought back.

Yet you often do, Hopper sent.

It struck true—more true, perhaps, than the wolf knew. Perrin burst into a clearing and pulled to a halt. There, lying on the ground, were the three chunks of metal he'd forged in his earlier dream. The large lump the size of two fists, the flattened rod, the thin rectangle. The rectangle glowed faintly yellow-red, singeing the short grass around it.

The lumps vanished immediately, though the simmering rectangle left a burned spot. Perrin looked up, searching for the wolves. Ahead of him, in the sky above the trees ahead, a large hole of blackness opened up. He could not tell how far it was away, and it seemed to dominate all he could see while being distant at the same time.

Mat stood there. He was fighting against himself, a dozen different men wearing his face, all dressed in different types of fine clothing. Mat spun his spear, and never saw the shadowy figure creeping behind him, bearing a bloody knife.

"Mat!" Perrin cried, but he knew it was meaningless. This thing he was seeing, it was some kind of dream or vision of the future. It had been some time since he'd seen one of these. He'd almost begun to think they would stop coming.

He turned away and another darkness opened in the sky. He saw sheep, suddenly, running in a flock toward the woods. Wolves chased them, and a terrible beast waited in the woods, unseen. He was there, in that dream, he sensed. But who was he chasing, and why? Something looked wrong with those wolves.

A third darkness, to the side. Faile, Grady, Elyas, Gaul . . . all walked toward a cliff, followed by thousands of others.

The vision closed. Hopper suddenly shot back through the air, landing beside Perrin, skidding to a stop. The wolf wouldn't have seen the holes; they had never appeared to his eyes. Instead, he regarded the burned patch with disdain and sent the image of Perrin, unkempt and bleary-eyed, his beard and hair untrimmed and his clothing disheveled. Perrin remembered the time; it had been during the early days of Faile's captivity.

Had he really looked that bad? Light, but he seemed ragged. Almost like a beggar. Or . . . like Noam.

"Stop trying to confuse me!" Perrin said. "I became that way because I was dedicated to finding Faile, not because I was giving in to the wolves!"

The newest pups always blame the elders of the pack. Hopper bounded through the grasses again.

What did that mean? The scents and images confused him. Growling, Perrin charged forward, leaving the clearing and reentering the grasses. Once again the stalks resisted him. It was like fighting against a current. Hopper shot on ahead.

"Burn you, wait for me!" Perrin yelled.

If we wait, we lose the prey. Run, Young Bull!

Perrin gritted his teeth. Hopper was a speck in the distance now, almost to the trees. Perrin wanted to think on those visions, but there wasn't time. If he lost Hopper, he knew that he would not see him again this night. *Fine,* he thought with resignation.

The land lurched around him, grasses speeding by in a flash. It was as if Perrin had leaped a hundred paces in one step. He stepped again, shooting forward. He left a faint blur behind him.

The grasses parted for him. The wind blew in his face with a comfortable roar. That primal wolf inside of him sparked to wakefulness. Perrin reached the woods and slowed. Each step now took him a jump of only about ten feet. The other wolves were there, and they formed up and ran with him, excited.

Two feet, Young Bull? Oak Dancer asked. She was a youthful female, her pelt so light as to be almost white, with a streak of black running along her right side.

He didn't answer, though he did allow himself to run with them through the trees. What had seemed like a small stand had become an expansive forest. Perrin moved past trunks and ferns, barely feeling the ground beneath his feet.

This was the way to run. Powerful. Energetic. He loped over fallen logs, his jumps taking him so high that his hair brushed the bottoms of the branches. He landed smoothly. The forest was his. It belonged to him, and he understood it.

His worries began to melt away. He allowed himself to accept things as they were, not as what he feared they might become. These wolves were his brothers and sisters. A running wolf in the real world was a masterwork of balance and control. Here—where the rules of nature bent to their will—they were far more. Wolves bounded to the sides and leaped off trees, nothing holding them to the ground. Some actually took to the branches, soaring from limb to limb.

It was exhilarating. Had he ever felt so alive? So much a part of the world around him, yet master of it at the same time? The rough, regal leatherleafs were interspersed with yew and the occasional ornamented spicewood in full bloom. He threw himself into the air as he passed one of these, the wind of his passing pulling a storm of crimson blossoms from the branches. They surged around him in a swirling blur, caught in the currents, cradling him in their sweet scent.

The wolves began to howl. To men, one howl was like another. To Perrin, each was distinct. These were the howls of pleasure, the initiation of a hunt.

Wait. This is what I feared! I cannot let myself be trapped. I am a man, not a wolf.

At that moment, however, he caught scent of a stag. A mighty animal, worthy prey. It had passed this way recently.

Perrin tried to restrain himself, but anticipation proved too strong. He tore off down the game trail after the scent. The wolves, including Hopper, did not race ahead of him. They ran with him, their scents pleased as they let him take the lead.

He was the herald, the point, the tip of the attack. The hunt roared behind him. It was as if he led the crashing waves of the ocean itself. But he was also holding them back.

I cannot make them slow for me, Perrin thought.

And then he was on all fours, his bow tossed aside and forgotten, his hands and legs becoming paws. Those behind him howled anew at the glory of it. Young Bull had truly joined them.

The stag was ahead. Young Bull picked it out through the trees; it was a brilliant white, with a rack of at least twenty-six points, the winter felt worn away. And it was enormous, larger than a horse. The stag turned, looking sharply at the pack. It met Young Bull's eyes, and he smelled its alarm. Then, with a powerful surge of its hind legs—flanks taut with muscles—the stag leaped off the trail.

Young Bull howled his challenge, racing through the underbrush in pursuit. The great white stag bounded on, each leap taking it twenty paces. It never hit a branch or lost its footing, despite the treacherous forest floor coated with slick moss.

Young Bull followed with precision, placing his paws where hooves had fallen just moments before, matching each stride exactly. He could hear the stag panting, could see the sweat foaming on its coat, could smell its fear.

But no. Young Bull would *not* accept the inferior victory of running his prey to exhaustion. He would taste the blood of the throat, pumping full force from a healthy heart. He would best his prey in its prime.

He began to vary his leaps, not following the stag's exact path. He needed to be ahead, not follow! The stag's scent grew more alarmed. That drove Young Bull to greater speed. The stag bolted to the right, and Young Bull leaped, hitting an upright tree trunk with all four paws and pushing himself sideways to change directions. His turn gained him a fraction of a heartbeat.

Soon he was bounding a single breath behind the stag, each leap bringing him within inches of its hooves. He howled, and his brothers and sisters replied from just behind. This hunt was all of them. As one.

But Young Bull led.

His howl became a growl of triumph as the stag turned again. The chance had come! Young Bull leaped over a log and seized the stag's neck in his jaws. He could taste the sweat, the fur, the warm blood beneath pooling around his fangs. His weight threw the stag to the ground. As they rolled, Young Bull kept his grip, forcing the stag to the forest floor, its skin laced scarlet with blood.

The wolves howled in victory, and he let go for a moment, intending to bite at the front of the neck and kill. There was nothing else. The forest was gone. The howls faded. There was only the kill. The sweet kill.

A form crashed into him, throwing him back into the brush. Young Bull shook his head, dazed, snarling. Another wolf had stopped him. Hopper! Why?

The stag bounded to its feet, and then bounded off through the forest again. Young Bull howled in fury and rage, preparing to run after it. Again Hopper leaped, throwing his weight against Young Bull.

If it dies here, it dies the last death, Hopper sent. *This hunt is done, Young Bull. We will hunt another time.*

Young Bull nearly turned to attack Hopper. But no. He had tried that once, and it had been a mistake. He was not a wolf. He—

Perrin lay on the ground, tasting blood that was not his own, exhaling deeply, his face dripping with sweat. He pushed himself to his knees, then sat down, panting, shaking from that beautiful, *terrifying* hunt.

The other wolves sat down, but they did not speak. Hopper lay beside Perrin, setting his grizzled head on aged paws.

"That," Perrin finally said, "is what I fear."

No, you do not fear it, Hopper sent.

"You're telling me what I feel?"

You do not smell afraid, Hopper sent.

Perrin lay back, staring up at the branches above, twigs

and leaves crumpling beneath him. His heart thumped from the chase. "I worry about it, then."

Worry is not the same as fear, Hopper sent. *Why say one and feel the other? Worry, worry, worry. It is all that you do.*

"No. I also kill. If you're going to teach me to master the wolf dream, it's going to happen like this?"

Yes.

Perrin looked to the side. The stag's blood had spilled on a dry log, darkness seeping into the wood. Learning this way would push him to the very edge of becoming a wolf.

But he had been avoiding this issue for too long, making horseshoes in the forge while leaving the most difficult and demanding pieces alone, untouched. He relied on the powers of scent he'd been given, reaching out to wolves when he needed them—but otherwise he'd ignored them.

You couldn't make a thing until you understood its parts. He wouldn't know how to deal with—or reject—the wolf inside him until he understood the wolf dream.

"Very well," Perrin said. "So be it."

Galad cantered Stout through the camp. On all sides, Children erected tents and dug firepits, preparing for the night. His men marched almost until nightfall each day, then arose early in the morning. The sooner they reached Andor, the better.

Those Light-cursed swamps were behind them; now they traveled over open grasslands. Perhaps it would have been faster to cut east and catch one of the great highways to the north, but that wouldn't be safe. Best to stay away from the movements of the Dragon Reborn's armies and the Seanchan. The Light would shine upon the Children, but more than one valiant hero had died within that Light. If there was no danger of death, there could be no bravery, but Galad would rather have the Light shine on him while he continued to draw breath.

They had camped near the Jehannah Road and would cross it on the morrow to continue north. He had sent a patrol to watch the road. He wanted to know what kind of traffic the highway was drawing, and he was in particular need of supplies.

Galad continued on his rounds through camp, accompanied by a handful of mounted attendants, ignoring the aches of his various wounds. The camp was orderly and neat. The tents were grouped by legion, then set up forming concentric rings with no straight pathways. That was intended to confuse and slow attackers.

A section of the camp lay empty near the middle. A hole in the formation where the Questioners had once set up their tents. He had ordered the Questioners spread out, two assigned to each company. If the Questioners were not set apart from the others, perhaps they would feel more kinship with the other Children. Galad made a note to himself to draw up a new camp layout, eliminating that hole.

Galad and his companions continued through the camp. He rode to be seen, and men saluted as he passed. He remembered well the words that Gareth Bryne had once said: Most of the time, a general's most important function was not to make decisions, but to remind men that someone *would* make decisions.

"My Lord Captain Commander," said one of his companions. Brandel Vordarian. He was an older man, eldest of the Lords Captain who served under Galad. "I wish you would reconsider sending this missive."

Vordarian rode directly beside Galad, with Trom on his other side. Lords Captain Golever and Harnesh rode behind, within earshot, and Bornhald followed, acting as Galad's bodyguard for the day.

"The letter must be sent," Galad said.

"It seems foolhardy, my Lord Captain Commander," Vordarian continued. Clean-shaven, with silver washing his golden hair, the Andoran was an enormous square of a man. Galad was vaguely familiar with Vordarian's family, minor nobles who had been involved in his mother's court.

Only a fool refused to listen to advice from those older and wiser than himself. But only a fool took all of the advice given him.

"Perhaps foolhardy," Galad replied. "But it is the right thing to do." The letter was addressed to the remaining Questioners and Children under the control of the Seanchan; there would be some who had not come with Asunawa. In the letter, Galad explained what had happened, and commanded them to report to him as soon as possible. It was unlikely any would come, but the others had a right to know what had happened.

Lord Vordarian sighed, then made way as Harnesh rode up beside Galad. The bald man scratched absently at the scar tissue where his left ear had been. "Enough about this letter, Vordarian. The way you go on about it tries my patience." From Galad's observation, there were many things that tried the Murandian's patience.

"You have other matters you wish to discuss, I assume?" Galad nodded to a pair of Children cutting logs, who stopped their work to salute him.

"You told Child Bornhald, Child Byar, and others that you plan to ally us with the witches of Tar Valon!"

Galad nodded. "I understand that the notion might be troubling, but if you consider, you will see that it is the only right decision."

"But the witches are evil!"

"Perhaps," Galad said. Once, he might have denied that. But listening to the other Children, and considering what those at Tar Valon had done to his sister, was making him think he might be too soft on the Aes Sedai. "However, Lord Harnesh, if they are evil, they are insignificant when compared to the Dark One. The Last Battle comes. Do you deny this?"

Harnesh and the others looked up at the sky. That dreary overcast had stretched for weeks now. The day before, another man had fallen to a strange illness where beetles had come from his mouth as he coughed. Their food stores were diminishing as more and more was found spoiled.

"No, I do not deny it," Harnesh muttered.

"Then you should rejoice," Galad said, "for the way is clear. We must fight at the Last Battle. Our leadership there may show the way of Light to many who have spurned us. But if it does not, we will fight regardless, for it is our duty. Do you deny this, Lord Captain?"

"Again, no. But the witches, my Lord Captain Commander?"

Galad shook his head. "I can think of no way around it. We need allies. Look about you, Lord Harnesh. How many Children do we have? Even with recent recruits, we are under twenty thousand. Our fortress has been taken. We are without succor or allegiance, and the great nations of the world revile us. No, don't deny it! You know that it is true."

Galad met the eyes of those around him, and one by one they nodded.

"The Questioners are at fault," Harnesh muttered.

"Part of the blame is theirs," Galad agreed. "But it is also because those who would do evil look with disgust and resentment upon those who stand for what is right."

The others nodded.

"We must tread carefully," Galad said. "In the past, the boldness—and perhaps overeagerness—of the Children has alienated those who should have been our allies. My mother always said that a victory of diplomacy did not come when everyone got what they wanted—that made everyone assume they'd gotten the better of her, which encouraged more extravagant demands. The trick is not to satisfy everyone, but to leave everyone feeling they reached the best possible result. They must be satisfied enough to do as you wish, yet dissatisfied enough to know that you bested them."

"And what does this have to do with us?" Golever said from behind. "We follow no queen or king."

"Yes," Galad said, "and that frightens monarchs. I grew up in the court of Andor. I know how my mother regarded the Children. In every dealing with them, she either grew frustrated or decided that she had to suppress them absolutely. We cannot afford either reaction! The monarchs of these lands must *respect* us, not hate us."

"Darkfriends," Harnesh muttered.

"My mother was *no* Darkfriend," Galad said quietly.

Harnesh flushed. "Excepting her, of course."

"You speak like a Questioner," Galad said. "Suspecting everyone who opposes us of being a Darkfriend. Many of them *are* influenced by the Shadow, but I doubt that it is conscious. That is where the Hand of the Light went wrong. The Questioners often could not tell the difference between a hardened Darkfriend, a person who was being influenced by Darkfriends, and a person who simply disagreed with the Children."

"So what do we do?" Vordarian asked. "We bow to the whims of monarchs?"

"I don't yet know what to do," Galad confessed. "I will

think on it. The right course will come to me. We cannot become lapdogs to kings and queens. And yet, think of what we could achieve inside of a nation's boundaries if we could act without needing an entire legion to intimidate that nation's ruler."

The others nodded at this, thoughtful.

"My Lord Captain Commander!" a voice called.

Galad turned to see Byar on his white stallion cantering toward them. The horse had belonged to Asunawa; Galad had refused it, preferring his own bay. Galad pulled his group to a halt as the gaunt-faced Byar neared, his white tabard pristine. Byar wasn't the most likable of men in the camp, but he had proven to be loyal.

Byar was *not*, however, supposed to be in the camp.

"I set you watching Jehannah Road, Child Byar," Galad said firmly. "That duty was not to end for a good four hours yet."

Byar saluted as he pulled up. "My Lord Captain Commander. We captured a suspicious group of travelers on the road. What would you have us do with them?"

"You *captured* them?" Galad asked. "I sent you to watch the road, not take prisoners."

"My Lord Captain Commander," Byar said. "How are we to know the character of those passing unless we speak with them? You wanted us to watch for Darkfriends."

Galad sighed. "I wanted you to watch for troop movements or merchants we could approach, Child Byar."

"These Darkfriends have supplies," Byar said. "I think they might be merchants."

Galad sighed. Nobody could deny Byar's dedication—he'd ridden with Galad to face Valda when it could have meant the end of his career. And yet there was such a thing as being *too* zealous.

The thin officer looked troubled. Well, Galad's instructions hadn't been precise enough. He would have to remember that in the future, particularly with Byar. "Peace," Galad said, "you did no wrong, Child Byar. How many of these prisoners are there?"

"Dozens, my Lord Captain Commander." Byar looked relieved. "Come."

He turned his mount to lead the way. Already, cook fires were springing up in the pits, the scent of burning tinder rising in the air. Galad caught slices of conversation as he rode past the soldiers. What would the Seanchan do with those Children who had remained behind? Was it really the Dragon Reborn who had conquered Illian and Tear, or some false Dragon? There was talk of a gigantic stone from the sky having struck the earth far to the north in Andor, destroying an entire city and leaving a crater.

The talk among the men revealed their worries. They should have understood that worry served no useful function. None could know the weaving of the Wheel.

Byar's captives turned out to be a group of people with a surprisingly large number of heavily laden carts, perhaps a hundred or more. The people clustered together around their carts, regarding the Children with hostility. Galad frowned, doing a quick inspection.

"That's quite a caravan," Bornhald said softly at his side. "Merchants?"

"No," Galad said softly. "That's travel furniture—notice the pegs on the sides, so they can be carried in pieces. Sacks of barley for horses. Those are farrier's tools wrapped in canvas at the back of that cart to the right. See the hammers peeking out?"

"Light!" Bornhald whispered. He saw it too. These were the camp followers of an army of substantial size. But where were the soldiers?

"Be ready to separate them," Galad told Bornhald, dismounting. He walked up to the lead cart. The man driving it had a thick figure and a ruddy face, with hair that had been arranged in a very poor attempt at hiding his increasing baldness. He nervously worked a brown felt hat in his hands; a pair of gloves was tucked into the belt of his stout jacket. Galad could see no weapons on him.

Beside the cart stood two others, much younger. One was a bulky, muscular type with the look of a fighter—but not a soldier—who could be some trouble. A pretty woman clutched his arm, biting her lower lip.

The man in the cart gave a start upon seeing Galad. *Ah,* Galad thought, *so he knows enough to recognize Morgase's stepson.*

"So, travelers," Galad said carefully. "My man says you told him that you are merchants?"

"Yes, good Lord," said the driver.

"I know little of this area. Are you familiar with it?"

"Not much, sir," the driver said, wringing that hat in his hands. "We are actually far from home ourselves. I am Basel Gill, of Caemlyn. I have come south seeking business with a merchant in Ebou Dar. But these Seanchan invaders have left me unable to do my trade."

He seemed very nervous. At least he hadn't lied about where he was from. "And what was this merchant's name?" Galad asked.

"Why, Falin Deborsha, my Lord," Gill said. "Are you familiar with Ebou Dar?"

"I have been there," Galad said calmly. "This is quite a caravan you have. Interesting collection of wares."

"We have heard that there are armies mobilizing here in the south, my Lord. I purchased many of these supplies from a mercenary troop who was disbanding, and thought I could sell them down here. Perhaps your own army has need of camp furniture? We have tents, mobile smithy equipment, everything that soldiers could use."

Clever, Galad thought. Galad might have accepted the lie, but the "merchant" had too many cooks, washwomen, and farriers with him, and not nearly enough guards for so valuable a caravan.

"I see," Galad said. "Well, it happens that I *do* have need of supplies. Particularly food."

"Alas, my Lord," the man said. "Our food cannot be spared. Anything else I will sell, but the food I have promised by messenger to someone in Lugard."

"I will pay more."

"I made a promise, my good Lord," the man said. "I could not break it, regardless of the price."

"I see." Galad waved to Bornhald. The soldier gave commands, and Children in white tabards moved forward, weapons out.

"What . . . what are you doing?" Gill asked.

"Separating your people," Galad said. "We'll talk to each of them alone and see if their stories match. I worry that you might have been . . . unforthcoming with us. After all, what it *seems* like to me is that you are the camp followers of a large army. If that is the case, then I would very much like to know whose army it is, not to mention where it is."

Gill's forehead started to sweat as Galad's soldiers efficiently separated the captives. Galad waited for a time watching Gill. Eventually Bornhald and Byar came jogging up to him, hands on their swords.

"My Lord Captain Commander," Bornhald said urgently.

Galad turned away from Gill. "Yes?"

"We may have a situation here," Bornhald said. His face was flushed with anger. Beside him, Byar's eyes were wide, almost frenzied. "Some of the prisoners have talked. It's as you feared. A large army is nearby. They've skirmished with Aiel—those fellows over there in the white robes are actually Aiel themselves."

"And?"

Byar spat to the side. "Have you ever heard of a man called Perrin Goldeneyes?"

"No. Should I have?"

"Yes," Bornhald said. "He killed my father."

CHAPTER
5

Writings

Gawyn hastened down the hallways of the White Tower, booted feet thumping on a deep blue rug atop crimson and white floor tiles. Mirrored stand-lamps reflected light, each like a sentry along the way.

Sleete walked quickly beside him. Despite the lamps' illumination, Sleete's face seemed half-shrouded in shadow. Perhaps it was the two-day stubble on his jaw—an oddity for a Warder—or the long hair, clean but unshorn. Or maybe it was his features. Uneven, like an unfinished drawing, with sharp lines, a cleft in his chin, a hook to his once-broken nose, cheekbones that jutted out.

He had the lithe motions of a Warder, but with a more primal feel than most. Rather than the huntsman moving through the woods, he was the silent, shadow-bound predator that prey never saw until the teeth were flashing.

They reached an intersection where several of Chubain's guards stood watch down one of the halls. They had swords at their sides and wore white tabards emblazoned with the Flame of Tar Valon. One held up a hand.

"I'm allowed in," Gawyn said. "The Amyrlin—"

"The sisters aren't done yet," the guard replied, hostile.

Gawyn ground his teeth, but there was nothing to be done about it. He and Sleete stepped back and waited until—finally—three Aes Sedai walked out of a guarded room. They looked troubled. They strode away, followed by a pair of soldiers carrying something wrapped in a white cloth. The body.

Finally, the two guards reluctantly stepped aside and let Gawyn and Sleete pass. They hurried down the hallway and entered a small reading room. Gawyn hesitated beside the door, glancing back down the hallway. He could see some Accepted peeking around a corner, whispering.

This murder made four sisters killed. Egwene had her hands full trying to keep the Ajahs from turning back to their mistrust of one another. She'd warned everyone to be alert, and told sisters not to go about alone. The Black Ajah knew the White Tower well, their members having lived here for years. With gateways, they could slip into the hallways and commit murder.

At least, that was the official explanation for the deaths. Gawyn wasn't so certain. He ducked into the room, Sleete following.

Chubain himself was there. The handsome man glanced at Gawyn, lips turning down. "Lord Trakand."

"Captain," Gawyn replied, surveying the room. It was about three paces square, with a single desk set against the far wall and an unlit coal-burning brazier. A bronze stand-lamp burned in the corner, and a circular rug filled nearly the entire floor. That rug was stained with a dark liquid beneath the desk.

"Do you really think you'll find anything the sisters did not, Trakand?" Chubain asked, folding his arms.

"I'm looking for different things," Gawyn said, going forward. He knelt down to inspect the rug.

Chubain sniffed, then walked into the hallway. The Tower Guard would watch over the area until servants had come to clean it. Gawyn had a few minutes.

Sleete stepped up to one of the guards just inside the doorway. They weren't as antagonistic toward him as they tended to be toward Gawyn. He still hadn't figured out why they were like that with him.

"She was alone?" Sleete asked the man in his gravelly voice.

"Yes," the guard said, shaking his head. "Shouldn't have ignored the Amyrlin's advice."

"Who was she?"

"Kateri Nepvue, of the White Ajah. A sister for twenty years."

Gawyn grunted as he continued to crawl across the floor, inspecting the rug. Four sisters from four different Ajahs. Two had supported Egwene, one had supported Elaida, and one had been neutral, only recently returned. All had been killed on different levels of the Tower during different times of day.

It certainly did *seem* like the work of the Black Ajah. They weren't looking for specific targets, just convenient ones. But it felt wrong to him. Why not Travel into the sisters' quarters at night and kill them in their sleep? Why did nobody sense channeling from the places where the women were killed?

Sleete inspected the door and lock with a careful eye. When Egwene had told Gawyn he could visit the scenes of the murders if he wished, he'd asked if he could bring Sleete with him. In Gawyn's previous interactions with the Warder, Sleete had proven himself to be not only meticulous, but discreet.

Gawyn continued looking. Egwene was nervous about something, he was certain. She wasn't being completely forthcoming about these murders. He found no slits in the carpet or tiles, no cuts in the furniture of the cramped room.

Egwene claimed the murderers were coming in by gateway, but he'd found no evidence of that. True, he didn't know much about gateways yet, and people could reportedly make them hang above the ground so they didn't cut anything. But why would the Black Ajah care about that? Besides, this room was so tiny, it seemed to him it would have been very hard to get in without leaving some trace.

"Gawyn, come here," Sleete said. The shorter man was still kneeling beside the doorway.

Gawyn joined him. Sleete threw the deadbolt a few times in its lock. "This door might have been forced," he said softly. "See the scrape here on the deadbolt? You can pop open this kind of lock by sliding a thin pick in and pushing it on the deadbolt, then putting pressure on the handle. It can be done very quietly."

"Why would the Black Ajah need to force a door?" Gawyn asked.

"Maybe they Traveled into the hallway, then walked until they saw light under a doorway," Sleete said.

"Why not then make a gateway to the other side?"

"Channeling could have alerted the woman inside," Sleete said.

"That's true," Gawyn said. He looked toward the bloody

patch. The desk was set so that the occupant's back would be to the doorway. That arrangement made Gawyn's shoulder blades itch. Who would put a desk like that? An Aes Sedai who thought she was completely safe, and who wanted to be sitting away from the distractions outside. Aes Sedai, for all of their cunning, sometimes seemed to have remarkably underdeveloped senses of self-preservation.

Or maybe they just didn't think like soldiers. Their Warders dealt with that sort of thought. "Did she have a Warder?"

"No," Sleete said. "I've met her before. She didn't have one." He hesitated. "None of the sisters murdered had Warders."

Gawyn gave Sleete a raised eyebrow.

"Makes sense," Sleete said. "Whoever is doing the killing didn't want to alert Warders."

"But why kill with a knife?" Gawyn said. All four had been killed that way. "The Black Ajah doesn't have to obey the Three Oaths. They could have used the Power to kill. Much more direct, much easier."

"But that would also risk alerting the victim or those around," Sleete noted.

Another good point. But still, something about these killings didn't seem to add up.

Or maybe he was just stretching at nothing, struggling to find *something* he could do to help. A part of him thought that if he could aid Egwene with this, maybe she would soften toward him. Perhaps forgive him for rescuing her from the Tower during the Seanchan attack.

Chubain entered a moment later. "I trust Your Lordship has had sufficient time," he said stiffly. "The staff is here to clean."

Insufferable man! Gawyn thought. *Does he have to be so dismissive toward me? I should—*

No. Gawyn forced himself to keep his temper. Once, that hadn't been nearly so hard.

Why *was* Chubain so hostile toward him? Gawyn found himself wondering how his mother would have handled such a man as this. Gawyn didn't often think of her, as doing so brought his mind back to al'Thor. *That* murderer had been allowed to walk away from the White Tower itself! Egwene had held him in her hand, and had released him.

True, al'Thor was the Dragon Reborn. But in his heart, Gawyn wanted to meet al'Thor with sword in hand and ram steel through him, Dragon Reborn or not.

Al'Thor would rip you apart with the One Power, he told himself. *You're being foolish, Gawyn Trakand.* His hatred of al'Thor continued to smolder anyway.

One of Chubain's guards came up, speaking, pointing at the door. Chubain looked annoyed they hadn't found the forced lock. The Tower Guard was not a policing force— the sisters had no need of that, and were more effective at this kind of investigation anyway. But Gawyn could tell that Chubain wished he could stop the murders. Protecting the Tower, and its occupants, was part of his duty.

So he and Gawyn worked for the same cause. But Chubain acted as if this were a personal contest between them. *Though his side did, essentially, meet defeat by Bryne's side in the Tower division,* Gawyn thought. *And as far as he knows, I'm one of Bryne's favored men.*

Gawyn wasn't a Warder, yet he was a friend of the Amyrlin. He dined with Bryne. How would that look to Chubain, particularly now that Gawyn had been given power to look in on the murders?

Light! Gawyn thought as Chubain shot him a hostile glace. *He thinks I'm trying to take his position. He thinks I want to be High Captain of the Tower Guard!*

The concept was laughable. Gawyn could have been First Prince of the Sword—*should* have been First Prince of the Sword—leader of Andor's armies and protector of the Queen. He was son to Morgase Trakand, one of the most influential and powerful rulers Andor had ever known. He had no desire for this man's position.

That wouldn't be how it looked to Chubain. Disgraced by the destructive Seanchan attack, he must feel that his position was in danger.

"Captain," Gawyn said, "may I speak with you in private?"

Chubain looked at Gawyn suspiciously, then nodded toward the hallway. The two of them retreated. Nervous Tower servants waited outside, ready to clean the blood away.

Chubain folded his arms and inspected Gawyn. "What is it you wish of me, my Lord?"

He often emphasized the rank. *Calm,* Gawyn thought. He still felt the shame of how he'd bullied his way into Bryne's camp. He was better than that. Living with the Younglings, enduring the confusion and then the shame of the events surrounding the Tower's breaking, had changed him. He couldn't continue down that path.

"Captain," Gawyn said, "I appreciate you letting me inspect the room."

"I didn't have much choice."

"I realize that. But you have my thanks nonetheless. It's important to me that the Amyrlin see me helping. If I find something the sisters miss, it could mean a great deal for me."

"Yes," Chubain said, eyes narrowing. "I suspect it could."

"Maybe she'll finally have me as her Warder."

Chubain blinked. "Her . . . Warder?"

"Yes. Once, it seemed certain that she would take me, but now . . . well, if I can help you with this investigation, perhaps it will cool her anger at me." He raised a hand, gripping Chubain's shoulder. "I will remember your aid. You call me Lord, but my title is all but meaningless to me now. All I want is to be Egwene's Warder, to protect her."

Chubain wrinkled his brow. Then he nodded and seemed to relax. "I heard you talking. You're looking for marks of gateways. Why?"

"I don't think this is the work of the Black Ajah," Gawyn said. "I think it might be a Gray Man, or some other kind of assassin. A Darkfriend among the Tower staff, perhaps? I mean, look at how the women are killed. Knives."

Chubain nodded. "There were some signs of a struggle, too. The sisters doing the investigation mentioned that. The books swept from the table. They thought it was done by the woman flailing as she died."

"Curious," Gawyn said. "If I were a Black sister, I'd use the One Power, regardless of the fact that others might sense it. Women channel all the time in the Tower; this wouldn't be suspicious. I'd immobilize my victim with weaves, kill her with the Power, then escape before anyone thought oddly of it. No struggle."

"Perhaps," Chubain said. "But the Amyrlin seems confident that this is the work of Black sisters."

"I'll talk to her and see why," Gawyn said. "For now,

perhaps you should suggest to those doing the investigation that it would be wise to interview the Tower servants? Give this reasoning?"

"Yes . . . I think I might do that." The man nodded, seeming less threatened.

The two stepped aside, Chubain waving the servants to enter for their cleaning. Sleete came out, looking thoughtful. He held something up, pinched between his fingers. "Black silk," he said. "There's no way of knowing if it came from the attacker."

Chubain took the fibers. "Odd."

"A Black sister wouldn't seem likely to proclaim herself by wearing black," Gawyn said. "A more ordinary assassin, though, might need the dark colors to hide."

Chubain wrapped the fibers in a handkerchief and pocketed them. "I'll take these to Seaine Sedai." He looked impressed.

Gawyn nodded to Sleete, and the two of them retreated.

"The White Tower is abuzz these days with returning sisters and new Warders," Sleete said softly. "How would anyone—no matter how stealthy—travel the upper levels wearing black without drawing attention?"

"Gray Men are supposed to be able to avoid notice," Gawyn said. "I think this is more proof. I mean, it seems odd that nobody has actually *seen* these Black sisters. We're making a lot of assumptions."

Sleete nodded, eyeing a trio of novices who had gathered to gawk at the guards. They saw Sleete looking and chittered to one another before scampering away.

"Egwene knows more than she's saying," Gawyn said. "I'll talk to her."

"Assuming she'll see you," Sleete said.

Gawyn grunted irritably. They walked down a series of ramps to the level of the Amyrlin's study. Sleete remained with him—his Aes Sedai, a Green named Hattori, rarely had duties for him. She still had her eyes on Gawyn for a Warder; Egwene was being so infuriating, Gawyn had half a mind to let Hattori bond him.

No. No, not really. He loved Egwene, though he was frustrated with her. It had not been easy to decide to give up Andor—not to mention the Younglings—for her. Yet she still refused to bond him.

He reached her study, and approached Silviana. The woman sat at her neat, orderly Keeper's desk in the antechamber before Egwene's study. The woman inspected Gawyn, her eyes unreadable behind her Aes Sedai mask. He suspected that she didn't like him.

"The Amyrlin is composing a letter of some import," Silviana said. "You may wait."

Gawyn opened his mouth.

"She asked not to be interrupted," Silviana said, turning back to the paper she had been reading. "You may wait."

Gawyn sighed, but nodded. As he did so, Sleete caught his eye and gestured that he was going. Why had he accompanied Gawyn down here in the first place? He was an odd man. Gawyn waved farewell, and Sleete vanished into the hallway.

The antechamber was a grand room with a deep red rug and wood trim on the stone walls. He knew from experience that none of the chairs were comfortable, but there was a single window. Gawyn stepped up to it for some air and rested his arm on the recessed stone, staring out over the White Tower grounds. This high up, the air felt crisper, newer.

Below, he could see the new Warder practice grounds. The old ones were where Elaida had begun building her palace. Nobody was sure what Egwene would end up doing with the construction.

The practice grounds were busy, a bustle of figures sparring, running, fencing. With the influx of refugees, soldiers and sell-swords, there were many who presumed themselves Warder material. Egwene had opened the grounds to any who wanted to train and try to prove themselves, as she intended to push for as many women as were ready to be raised over the next few weeks.

Gawyn had spent a few days training, but the ghosts of men he had killed seemed more present down there. The grounds were a part of his past life, a time before everything had gone wrong. Other Younglings had easily—and happily—returned to that life. Already Jisao, Rajar, Durrent and most of his other officers had been chosen as Warders. Before long, nothing would remain of his band. Except for Gawyn himself.

The inner door clicked, followed by hushed voices.

Gawyn turned to find Egwene, dressed in green and yellow, walking over to speak with Silviana. The Keeper glanced at him, and he thought he caught a trace of a frown on her face.

Egwene saw him. She kept her face Aes Sedai serene—she'd grown good at that so quickly—and he found himself feeling awkward.

"There was another death this morning," he said quietly, walking up to her.

"Technically," Egwene said, "it was last night."

"I need to talk to you," Gawyn blurted.

Egwene and Silviana shared a look. "Very well," Egwene said, gliding back into her study.

Gawyn followed, not looking at the Keeper. The Amyrlin's study was one of the grandest rooms in the Tower. The walls were paneled with a pale striped wood, carved to show fanciful scenes, marvelously detailed. The hearth was marble, the floor made of deep red stone cut into diamond blocks. Egwene's large, carved desk was set with two lamps. They were in the shape of two women raising their hands to the air, flames burning between each set of palms.

One wall had bookcases filled with books arranged—it seemed—by color and size rather than by subject. They were ornamental, brought in to trim the Amyrlin's study until Egwene could make her own selections.

"What is it you find so necessary to discuss?" Egwene said, sitting down at her desk.

"The murders," Gawyn said.

"What about them?"

Gawyn shut the door. "Burn me, Egwene. Do you have to show me the Amyrlin every time we speak? Once in a while, can't I see *Egwene*?"

"I show you the Amyrlin," Egwene said, "because you refuse to accept her. Once you do so, perhaps we can move beyond that."

"Light! You've learned to talk like one of them."

"That's because I *am* one of them," she said. "Your choice of words betrays you. The Amyrlin cannot be served by those who refuse to see her authority."

"I accept you," Gawyn said. "I *do*, Egwene. But isn't it important to have people who know you for yourself and not the title?"

"So long as they know that there is a place for obedience."
Her face softened. "You aren't ready yet, Gawyn. I'm sorry."

He set his jaw. *Don't overreact,* he told himself. "Very
well. Then, about the assassinations. We've realized that
none of the women killed had Warders."

"Yes, I was given a report on that," Egwene said.

"Regardless," he said, "it brings my thoughts to a larger
issue. We don't have enough Warders."

Egwene frowned.

"We're preparing for the Last Battle, Egwene," Gawyn
said. "And yet there are sisters without Warders. A *lot* of
sisters. Some had one, but never took another after he died.
Others never wanted one in the first place. I don't think you
can afford this."

"What would you have me do?" she said, folding her
arms. "*Command* the women to take Warders?"

"Yes."

She laughed. "Gawyn, the Amyrlin doesn't have that
kind of power."

"Then get the Hall to do it."

"You don't know what you're saying. The choosing and
keeping of a Warder is a very personal and intimate decision. No woman should be forced to it."

"Well," Gawyn said, refusing to be intimidated, "the
choice to go to war is very 'personal' and 'intimate' as
well—yet all across the land, men are called into it. Sometimes, feelings aren't as important as survival.

"Warders keep sisters alive, and every Aes Sedai is going
to be of vital importance soon. There will be legions upon
legions of Trollocs. Every sister on the field will be more
valuable than a hundred soldiers, and every sister Healing
will be able to save dozens of lives. The Aes Sedai are as-
sets that belong to humanity. You *cannot* afford to let them
go about unprotected."

Egwene drew back, perhaps at the fervor of his words.
Then, unexpectedly, she nodded. "Perhaps there is . . .
wisdom in those words, Gawyn."

"Bring it before the Hall," Gawyn said. "At its core,
Egwene, a sister *not* bonding a Warder is an act of selfishness. That bond makes a man a better soldier, and we'll
need every edge we can find. This will also help prevent the
murders."

"I will see what can be done," Egwene said.

"Could you let me see the reports the sisters are giving?" Gawyn said. "About the murders, I mean?"

"Gawyn," she said, "I've allowed you to be a part of the investigation because I thought it might be good to have a different set of eyes looking things over. Giving you their reports would just influence you to draw the same conclusions as they do."

"At least tell me this," he said. "Have the sisters raised the worry that this might not be the work of the Black Ajah? That the assassin might be a Gray Man or a Dark-friend?"

"No, they have not," Egwene said, "because we *know* that the assassin is not one of those two."

"But the door last night, it was forced. And the women are killed with knives, not the One Power. There are no signs of gateways or—"

"The killer has access to the One Power," Egwene said, speaking very carefully. "And perhaps they are not using gateways."

Gawyn narrowed his eyes. Those sounded like the words of a woman stepping around her oath not to lie. "You're keeping secrets," he said. "Not just from me. From the entire Tower."

"Secrets are needed sometimes, Gawyn."

"Can't you trust me with them?" He hesitated. "I'm worried that the assassin will come for you, Egwene. You don't have a Warder."

"Undoubtedly she *will* come for me, eventually." She toyed with something on her desk. It looked like a worn leather strap, the type used to punish a criminal. Odd.

She? "Please, Egwene," he said. "What's going on?"

She studied him, then she sighed. "Very well. I've told this to the women doing the investigation. Perhaps I should tell you too. One of the Forsaken is in the White Tower."

He lowered his hand to his sword. "What? Where! You have her captive?"

"No," Egwene said. "She's the assassin."

"You know this?"

"I know Mesaana is here; I've dreamed that it is true. She hides among us. Now, four Aes Sedai, dead? It's her, Gawyn. It's the only thing that makes sense."

He bit off questions. He knew very little of Dreaming, but knew she had the Talent. It was said to be like Foretelling.

"I haven't told the entire Tower," Egwene continued. "I worry that if they knew one of the sisters around them is secretly one of the Forsaken, it would divide us all again, as under Elaida. We'd all be suspicious of one another.

"It's bad enough now, with them thinking Black sisters are Traveling in to commit murders, but at least that doesn't make them suspicious of one another. And maybe Mesaana will think that I'm not aware it is her. But there, that's the secret you begged to know. It's not a Black sister we hunt, but one of the Forsaken."

It was daunting to consider—but no more so than the Dragon Reborn walking the land. Light, a Forsaken in the Tower seemed more plausible than Egwene being the Amyrlin Seat! "We'll deal with it," he said, sounding far more confident than he felt.

"I have sisters searching the histories of everyone in the Tower," Egwene said. "And others are watching for suspicious words or actions. We'll find her. But I don't see how we can make the women any more secure without inciting an even more dangerous panic."

"Warders," Gawyn said firmly.

"I will think on it, Gawyn. For now, there is something I need of you."

"If it is within my power, Egwene." He took a step toward her. "You know that."

"Is that so?" she asked dryly. "Very well. I want you to stop guarding my door at night."

"*What?* Egwene, no!"

She shook her head. "You see? Your first reaction is to challenge me."

"It is the duty of a Warder to offer challenge, in private, where his Aes Sedai is concerned!" Hammar had taught him that.

"You are *not* my Warder, Gawyn."

That brought him up short.

"Besides," Egwene said, "you could do little to stop one of the Forsaken. This battle will be fought by sisters, and I am being very careful with the wards I set. I want my quarters to look inviting. If she tries to attack me, perhaps I can surprise her with an ambush."

"Use yourself as bait?" Gawyn was barely able to get the words out. "Egwene, this is madness!"

"No. It's desperation. Gawyn, women I am responsible for are dying. Murdered in the night, in a time when you yourself said we will need every woman."

For the first time, fatigue showed through her mask, a weariness of tone and a slight slump to her back. She folded her hands in front of her, suddenly seeming *worn*.

"I have sisters researching everything we can find about Mesaana," Egwene continued. "She's not a warrior, Gawyn. She's an administrator, a planner. If I can confront her, I can defeat her. But we must *find* her first. Exposing myself is only one of my plans—and you are right, it is dangerous. But my precautions have been extensive."

"I don't like it at all."

"Your approval is not required." She eyed him. "You will have to trust me."

"I do trust you," he said.

"All I ask is that you show it for once."

Gawyn gritted his teeth. Then he bowed to her and left the study, trying—and failing—to keep the door from shutting too hard when he pulled it closed. Silviana gave him a disapproving look as he passed her.

From there, he headed for the training grounds despite his discomfort with them. He needed a workout with the sword.

Egwene let out a long sigh, sitting back, closing her eyes. Why was it so hard to keep her feelings in check when dealing with Gawyn? She never felt as poor an Aes Sedai as she did when speaking with him.

So many emotions swirled within her, like different kinds of wine spilling and mixing together: rage at his stubbornness, burning desire for his arms, confusion at her own inability to place one of those before the other.

Gawyn had a way of boring through her skin and into her heart. That passion of his was entrancing. She worried that if she bonded him, it would infect her. Was that how it worked? What did it feel like to be bonded, to sense another's emotions?

She wanted that with him, the connection that others

had. And it *was* important that she have people she could rely upon to contradict her, in private. People who knew her as Egwene, rather than the Amyrlin.

But Gawyn was too loose, too untrusting, yet.

She looked over her letter to the new King of Tear, explaining that Rand was threatening to break the seals. Her plan to stop him would depend on her gathering support from people he trusted. She had conflicting reports about Darlin Sisnera. Some said he was one of Rand's greatest supporters, while others claimed he was one of Rand's greatest detractors.

She set the letter aside for the moment, then wrote some thoughts on how to approach the Hall on the Warder issue. Gawyn made an excellent argument, though he went too far and assumed too much. Making a plea for women who had no Warders to choose one, explaining all of the advantages and pointing out how it could save lives and help defeat the Shadow . . . that would be appropriate.

She poured herself some mint tea from the pot on the side of her desk. Oddly, it hadn't been spoiling as often lately, and this cup tasted quite good. She hadn't told Gawyn of the other reason she'd asked him to leave her door at nights. She had trouble sleeping, knowing he was out there, only a few feet away. She worried she'd slip and go to him.

Silviana's strap had never been able to break her will, but Gawyn Trakand . . . he was coming dangerously close to doing so.

Graendal anticipated the messenger's arrival. Even here, in her most secret of hiding places, his arrival was not unexpected. The Chosen could not hide from the Great Lord.

The hiding place was not a palace, a fine lodge or an ancient fortress. It was a cavern on an island nobody cared about, in an area of the Aryth Ocean that nobody ever visited. So far as she knew, there was nothing of note or interest anywhere near.

The accommodations were downright dreadful. Six of her lesser pets cared for the place, which was merely three chambers. She'd covered over the entrance with stone, and the only way in or out was by gateway. Fresh water came from a natural spring, food from stores she'd brought in previously, and air through cracks. It was dank, and it was lowly.

In other words, it was precisely the sort of place where nobody would expect to find her. Everyone knew that Graendal could not *stand* a lack of luxury. That was true. But the best part about being predictable was that it allowed you to do the unexpected.

Unfortunately, none of that applied to the Great Lord. Graendal watched the open gateway before her as she relaxed on a chaise of yellow and blue silk. The messenger was a man with flat features and deeply tanned skin, wearing black and red. He didn't need to speak—his presence *was* the message. One of her pets—a beautiful, black-haired woman with large brown eyes who had once been a Tairen high lady—stared at the gateway. She looked frightened. Graendal felt much the same way.

She closed the wood-bound copy of *Alight in the Snow* in her hands and stood up, wearing a dress of thin black silk with ribbons of streith running down it. She stepped through the gateway, careful to project an air of confidence.

Moridin stood inside his black stone palace. The room had no furniture; only the hearth, with a fire burning. Great Lord! A *fire*, on such a warm day? She maintained her composure, and did not begin to sweat.

He turned toward her, the black flecks of *saa* swimming across his eyes. "You know why I have summoned you." Not a question.

"I do."

"Aran'gar is dead, lost to us—and after the Great Lord transmigrated her soul the last time. One might think you are making a habit of this sort of thing, Graendal."

"I live to serve, Nae'blis," she said. Confidence! She had to seem confident.

He hesitated just briefly. Good. "Surely you do not imply that Aran'gar had turned traitor."

"What?" Graendal said. "No, of course not."

"Then how is what you did a *service*?"

Graendal pasted a look of concerned confusion on her face. "Why, I was following the command I was given. Am I not here to receive an accolade?"

"Far from it," Moridin said dryly. "Your feigned confusion will not work on me, woman."

"It is not feigned," Graendal said, preparing her lie. "While I did not expect the Great Lord to be pleased to lose one of the Chosen, the gain was obviously worth the cost."

"What gain?" Moridin snarled. "You allowed yourself to be caught unaware, and foolishly lost the life of one of the Chosen! We should have been able to rely on you, of all people, to avoid stumbling over al'Thor."

He didn't know that she'd bound Aran'gar and left her to die; he thought this was a mistake. Good. "Caught unaware?" she said, sounding mortified. "I never . . . Moridin, how could you *think* that I'd let him find me by accident!"

"You did this *intentionally*?"

"Of course," Graendal said. "I practically had to lead him by the hand to Natrin's Barrow. Lews Therin never was good at seeing facts directly in front of his nose. Moridin, don't you see? How will Lews Therin react to what he has done? Destroying an entire *fortress*, a miniature city of its own, with hundreds of occupants? Killing innocents to reach his goal? Will that sit easily within him?"

Moridin hesitated. No, he had not considered that. She smiled inwardly. To him, al'Thor's actions would have made perfect sense. They were the most logical, and therefore most sensible, means of accomplishing a goal.

But al'Thor himself . . . his mind was full of daydreams about honor and virtue. This event would *not* sit easily within him, and speaking of him as Lews Therin to Moridin would reinforce that. These actions would tear at al'Thor, rip at his soul, lash his heart raw and bleeding. He would have nightmares, wear his guilt on his shoulders like the yoke of a heavily laden cart.

She could vaguely remember what it had been like, taking those first few steps toward the Shadow. Had she ever felt that foolish pain? Yes, unfortunately. Not all of the Chosen had. Semirhage had been corrupt to the bone from the start. But others of them had taken different paths to the Shadow, including Ishamael.

She could see the memories, so distant, in Moridin's eyes. Once, she'd not been sure who this man was, but now she was. The face was different, but the soul the same. Yes, he knew exactly what al'Thor was feeling.

"You told me to hurt him," Graendal said. "You told me to bring him anguish. This was the best way. Aran'gar helped me, though she did not flee when I suggested. That one always *has* confronted her problems too aggressively. But I'm certain the Great Lord can find other tools. We took a risk, and it was not without cost. But the gain . . . Beyond that, Lews Therin now thinks I am dead. That is a large advantage."

She smiled. Not too much pleasure. Merely a little satisfaction. Moridin scowled, then hesitated, glancing to the side. At nothing. "I am to leave you without punishment, for now," he finally said, though he didn't sound pleased about it.

Had that been a communication directly from the Great Lord? As far as she knew, all Chosen in this Age had to go to him in Shayol Ghul to receive their orders. Or at least suffer a visit from that horrid creature Shaidar Haran. Now the Great Lord appeared to be speaking to the Nae'blis directly. Interesting. And worrisome.

It meant the end was very near. There would not be much time left for posturing. She *would* see herself Nae'blis and rule this world as her own once the Last Battle was done.

"I think," Graendal said, "that I should—"

"You are to stay away from al'Thor," Moridin said. "You are not to be punished, but I don't see reason to praise you either. Yes, al'Thor may be hurt, but you still bungled your plan, costing us a useful tool."

"Of course," Graendal said smoothly, "I will serve as it pleases the Great Lord. I was not going to suggest that I move against al'Thor anyway. He thinks me dead, and so best to let him remain in his ignorance while I work elsewhere, for now."

"Elsewhere?"

Graendal needed a victory, a decisive one. She sifted through the different plans she'd devised, selecting the most likely to succeed. She couldn't move against al'Thor? Very well. She would bring to the Great Lord something he'd long desired.

"Perrin Aybara," Graendal said. She felt exposed, having to reveal her intentions to Moridin. She preferred to keep her plots to herself. However, she doubted she'd be able to escape this meeting without telling him. "I will bring you his head."

Moridin turned toward the fire, clasping his hands behind his back. He watched the flames.

With a shock, she felt sweat trickle down her brow. What? She was able to *avoid* heat and cold. What was wrong? She maintained her focus . . . it just didn't work. Not here. Not near him.

That unsettled her deeply.

"He's important," Graendal said. "The prophecies—"

"I know the prophecies," Moridin said softly. He did not turn. "How would you do it?"

"My spies have located his army," Graendal said. "I have already set some plans in motion regarding him, just in case. I retain the group of Shadowspawn given me to cause chaos, and I have a trap prepared. It will break al'Thor, ruin him, if he loses Aybara."

"It will do more than that," Moridin said softly. "But you will never manage it. His men have gateways. He will escape you."

"I—"

"He *will* escape you," Moridin said softly.

The sweat trickled down her cheek, then to her chin. She wiped it casually, but her brow continued to bead.

"Come," Moridin said, striding from the hearth and toward the hallway outside.

Graendal followed, curious but afraid. Moridin led her to a nearby door, set in the same black stone walls. He pushed it open.

Graendal followed him inside. The narrow room was lined with shelves. And on them were dozens—perhaps hundreds—of objects of Power. *Darkness within!* she thought. *Where did he get so many?*

Moridin walked to the end of the room, where he picked through objects on a shelf. Graendal entered, awed. "Is that a shocklance?" she asked, pointing to a long thin bit of metal. "Three binding rods? A *rema'kar*? Those pieces of a sho—"

"It is unimportant," he said, selecting an item.

"If I could just—"

"You are close to losing favor, Graendal," he said, turning and holding a long, spikelike piece of metal, silvery and topped with a large metal head set with golden inlay. "I have found only two of these. The other is being put to good use. You may use this one."

"A dreamspike?" she said, eyes opening wide. How badly she'd wanted to have one of these! "You found *two*?"

He tapped the top of the dreamspike and it vanished from his hand. "You will know where to find it?"

"Yes," she said, growing hungry. This was an object of *great* Power. Useful in so many different ways.

Moridin stepped forward, seizing her eyes with his own. "Graendal," he said softly, dangerously. "I know the key for this one. It will *not* be used against me, or others of the Chosen. The Great Lord will know if you do. I do not wish your apparent habit to be indulged further, not until Aybara is dead."

"I . . . yes, of course." She felt cold, suddenly. How could she feel cold here? And while *still* sweating?

"Aybara can walk the World of Dreams," Moridin said. "I will lend you another tool, the man with two souls. But he is *mine*, just as that spike is mine. Just as you are mine. Do you understand?"

She nodded. She couldn't help herself. The room seemed to be growing darker. That voice of his . . . it sounded, just faintly, like that of the Great Lord.

"Let me tell you this, however," Moridin said, reaching forward with his right hand, cupping her chin. "If you do succeed, the Great Lord will be pleased. Very pleased. That which has been granted you in sparseness will be heaped upon you in glory."

She licked her dry lips. In front of her, Moridin's expression grew distant.

"Moridin?" she asked hesitantly.

He ignored her, releasing her chin and walking to the end of the room. From a table, he picked up a thick tome wrapped in pale tan skin. He flipped to a certain page and studied it for a moment. Then he waved for her to approach.

She did so, careful. When she read what was on the page, she found herself stunned.

Darkness within! "What is this book?" she finally managed to force out. "Where did these prophecies come from?"

"They have long been known to me," Moridin said softly, still studying the book. "But not to many others, not even the Chosen. The women and men who spoke these were isolated and held alone. The Light must never know of these words. We know of their prophecies, but they will never know all of ours."

"But this . . ." she said, rereading the passage. "This says Aybara will die!"

"There can be many interpretations of any prophecy," Moridin said. "But yes. This Foretelling promises that Aybara will die by our hand. You will bring me the head of this wolf, Graendal. And when you do, anything you ask shall be yours." He slapped the book closed. "But mark me. Fail, and you will lose what you have gained. And much more."

He opened a portal for her with a wave of the hand; her faint ability to touch the True Power—that hadn't been removed from her—allowed her to see twisted weaves stab the air and rend it, ripping a hole in the fabric of the Pattern. The air shimmered there. It would lead back to her hidden cavern, she knew.

She went through without a word. She didn't trust her voice to speak without shaking.

CHAPTER
6

Questioning Intentions

Morgase Trakand, once Queen of Andor, served tea. She moved from person to person in the large pavilion Perrin had taken from Malden. It had sides that could be rolled up and no tent floor.

Large though the tent was, there was barely enough room for all who had wanted to attend the meeting. Perrin and Faile were there, of course, sitting on the ground. Next to them sat golden-eyed Elyas and Tam al'Thor, the simple farmer with the broad shoulders and the calm manners. Was this man really the father of the Dragon Reborn? Of course, Morgase had seen Rand al'Thor once, and the boy hadn't looked much more than a farmer himself.

Beside Tam sat Perrin's dusty secretary, Sebban Balwer. How much did Perrin know of his past? Jur Grady was there also, wearing his black coat with a silver sword pin on the collar. His leathery farmer's face was hollow-eyed and still pale from the sickness he'd suffered recently. Neald—the other Asha'man—was not there. He hadn't yet recovered from his snake-bites.

All three Aes Sedai were there. Seonid and Masuri sat with the Wise Ones, and Annoura sat beside Berelain, occasionally shooting glances at the six Wise Ones. Gallenne sat on Berelain's other side. Across from them sat Alliandre and Arganda.

The officers made Morgase think of Gareth Bryne. She hadn't seen him in a long while, not since she'd exiled him for reasons she still couldn't quite explain. Very little about that time in her life made sense to her now. Had she really been so infatuated with a man that she'd banished Aemlyn and Ellorien?

Anyway, those days were gone. Now Morgase picked her way carefully through the room and saw that people's cups were kept full.

"Your work took longer than I'd expected," Perrin said.

"You gave us a duty to attend to, Perrin Aybara," Nevarin replied. "We accomplished it. It took us as much time as needed to do it correctly. Surely you don't imply that we did otherwise." The sandy-haired Wise One sat directly in front of Seonid and Masuri.

"Give over, Nevarin," Perrin grunted as he unrolled a map before him on the ground; it had been drawn by Balwer using instructions from the Ghealdanin. "I wasn't questioning you. I was asking if there were any problems in the burning."

"The village is gone," Nevarin said. "And every plant we found with a *hint* of Blight has been burned to ash. As well we did. You wetlanders would have much trouble dealing with something as deadly as the Blight."

"I think," Faile said, "that you would be surprised."

Morgase glanced at Faile, who locked eyes with the Wise One. Faile sat like a queen, once again dressed to her station in a fine dress of green and violet, pleated down the sides and divided for riding. Oddly, Faile's sense of leadership seemed to have been *enhanced* by her time spent with the Shaido.

Morgase and Faile had quickly gone back to being mistress and servant. In fact, Morgase's life here was strikingly similar to what it had been in the Shaido camp. True, some things were different; Morgase wasn't likely to be strapped here, for instance. That didn't change the fact that—for a time—she and the other four women had been equals. No longer.

Morgase stopped beside Lord Gallenne and refilled his cup, using the same skills she'd cultivated in attending Sevanna. At times, being a servant seemed to require more stealth than being a scout. She wasn't to be seen, wasn't to distract. Had her own servants acted this way around her?

"Well," Arganda said, "if anyone is wondering where we've gone, the smoke from that fire is an easy indicator."

"We're far too many people to think of hiding," Seonid said. Recently, she and Masuri had begun being allowed to speak without reprimand from the Wise Ones, though the Green did still glance at the Aiel women before speaking. It galled Morgase to see that. Sisters of the Tower, made apprentices to a bunch of wilders? It was said to have been done at Rand al'Thor's order, but how would any man— even the Dragon Reborn—be capable of such a thing?

It discomforted her that the two Aes Sedai no longer seemed to resist their station. A person's situation in life could change her dramatically. Gaebril, then Valda, had taught Morgase that lesson. The Aiel captivity had been merely another step in the process.

Each of these experiences had moved her farther away from the Queen she had been. Now she didn't long for fine things or her throne. She just wanted some stability. That, it seemed, was a commodity more precious than gold.

"It doesn't matter," Perrin said, tapping the map. "So, we're decided? We chase after Gill and the others on foot for now, sending scouts by gateway to find them, if possible. Hopefully, we'll catch them before they reach Lugard. How long to the city would you say, Arganda?"

"Depends on the mud," the wiry soldier said. "There's a reason we call this time of year the swamping. Wise men don't travel during the spring melt."

"Wisdom is for those who have time for it," Perrin muttered, counting off distance on the map with his fingers.

Morgase moved to refill Annoura's cup. Pouring tea was more complicated than she'd ever assumed. She had to know whose cup to take aside and fill, and whose to fill while they were holding it. She had to know precisely how high to fill a cup so that it would not spill, and how to pour the tea without rattling the porcelain or splashing. She knew when to not be seen and when to make a slight production out of filling cups in case she'd missed people, forgotten them or misjudged their needs.

She carefully took Perrin's cup from beside him on the ground. He liked to gesture when he spoke, and could knock the cup from her hand if she was unwary. All in all, there was a remarkable art to serving tea—an entire world that Morgase the Queen had never bothered to notice.

She refilled Perrin's cup and placed it back beside him.

Perrin asked other questions about the map—nearby towns, potential sources of resupply. He had a lot of promise as a leader, even if he was rather inexperienced. A little advice from Morgase—

She cut that thought off. Perrin Aybara was a rebel. The Two Rivers was part of Andor, and he'd named himself lord of it, flying that wolfhead banner. At least the flag of Manetheren had been taken down. Flying that had been nothing short of an open declaration of war.

Morgase no longer bristled every time someone named him a lord, but she also didn't intend to offer him any help. Not until she determined how to move him back beneath the cloak of the Andoran monarchy.

Besides, Morgase grudgingly admitted, *Faile is sharp enough to give any advice I would have.*

Faile was actually a perfect complement to Perrin. Where he was a blunt and leveled lance at charge, she was a subtle cavalry bow. The combination of the two—with Faile's connections to the Saldaean throne—was what really worried Morgase. Yes, he'd taken down the Manetheren banner, but he'd ordered that wolfhead banner taken down before. Often, forbidding something was the best way to ensure that it happened.

Alliandre's cup was half empty. Morgase moved over to refill it; like many highborn ladies, Alliandre always expected her cup to be full. Alliandre glanced at Morgase, and there was a faint glimmer of discomfort in those eyes. Alliandre felt uncertain what their relationship should be. That was curious, as Alliandre had been so haughty during their captivity. The person Morgase had once been, the Queen, wanted to sit Alliandre down and give a lengthy explanation of how to better maintain her grandeur.

She'd have to learn on her own. Morgase was no longer the person she had once been. She wasn't sure what she was, but she *would* learn how to do her duty as a lady's maid. This was becoming a passion for her. A way to prove to herself that she was still strong, still of value.

In a way, it was terrifying that she worried about that.

"Lord Perrin," Alliandre said as Morgase moved away. "Is it true that you're planning on sending my people back to Jehannah after you find Gill and his group?"

Morgase continued past Masuri—the Aes Sedai liked

her cup refilled only when she tapped on it lightly with her fingernail.

"I do," Perrin replied. "We all know it wasn't completely your will to join us in the first place. If we hadn't brought you along, you'd never have been captured by the Shaido. Masema is dead. Time to let you return to governing your nation."

"With all due respect, my Lord," Alliandre said. "Why are you recruiting from among my countrymen if not to gather an army for future use?"

"I'm not trying to recruit," Perrin said. "Just because I don't turn them away doesn't mean I intend to enlarge this army any further."

"My Lord," Alliandre said. "But surely it is wise to keep what you have."

"She has a point, Perrin," Berelain added softly. "One need only look at the sky to know the Last Battle is imminent. Why send her force back? I'm certain that the Lord Dragon will have need of every soldier from every land sworn to him."

"He can send for them when he decides to," Perrin said stubbornly.

"My Lord," Alliandre said, "I did not swear to him. I swore to *you*. If Ghealdan will march for Tarmon Gai'don, it should do so beneath your banner."

Perrin stood up, startling several people. Was he leaving? "Just a moment. I need to call for someone," he said as he walked to the open side of the tent and stepped out. "Wil, come here," he called.

A weave of the One Power kept sound from passing in or out. Morgase could see Masuri's weaves, tied off and warding the tent. Their intricacy seemed to mock her own minuscule talent.

Masuri tapped the side of her cup, and Morgase hastened to refill it. The woman liked to sip tea when nervous.

Perrin came back into the tent, followed by handsome young Wil al'Seen carrying a cloth-wrapped bundle.

"Unfurl it," Perrin said.

The young man did so, looking apprehensive. It bore the wolfhead emblem that was Perrin's sigil.

"I didn't make this banner," Perrin said. "I never wanted it, but—upon advice—I let it fly. Well, the reasons for doing that are past. I'd order the thing taken down, but that never seems to work for long." He looked to Wil. "Wil, I want it passed through camp. I'm giving a direct order. I want each and every copy of this blasted banner *burned*. You understand?"

Wil paled. "But—"

"Do it," Perrin said. "Alliandre, you'll swear to Rand as soon as we find him. You won't ride beneath my banner, because I won't *have* a banner. I'm a blacksmith, and that's the end of it. I've stomached this foolishness for too long."

"Perrin?" Faile asked. She looked surprised. "Is this wise?"

Fool man. He should have at least talked to his wife about this. But men would be men. They liked their secrets and their plans.

"I don't know if it's wise. But it's what I'm doing," he said, sitting down. "Be off, Wil. I want those banners burned by tonight. No holdouts, you understand?"

Wil stiffened, then spun and strode from the tent without giving a reply. The lad looked as if he felt betrayed. Oddly, Morgase found herself feeling a little of the same. It was foolish. This was what she wanted—it was what Perrin should do. And yet, the people were frightened, with good reason. That sky, the things that were happening in the world . . . Well, in a time like this, perhaps a man could be excused for taking command.

"You are a fool, Perrin Aybara," Masuri said. She had a blunt way about her.

"Son," Tam addressed Perrin, "the lads put a lot of stock in that banner."

"Too much," Perrin said.

"Perhaps. But it's good to have something to look to. When you took down the other banner, it was hard on them. This will be worse."

"It needs to be done," Perrin said. "The Two Rivers men have gotten too attached to it, started talking like they're going to stay with me instead of going back to their families where they belong. When we get gateways working again, Tam, you'll be taking them and going." He looked at Berelain. "I suppose I can't be rid of you and your men. You'll go back with me to Rand."

"I wasn't aware," Berelain said stiffly, "that you needed

to 'be rid' of us. You seemed far less reluctant to accept my support when demanding the services of my Winged Guardsmen in rescuing your wife."

Perrin took a deep breath. "I appreciate your help, all of you. We did a good thing in Malden, and not just for Faile and Alliandre. It was a thing that needed doing. But burn me, that's over now. If you want to go on to follow Rand, I'm sure he'll have you. But my Asha'man are exhausted, and the tasks I was given are complete. I've got these hooks inside of me, pulling me back to Rand. Before I can do that, I need to be done with all of you."

"Husband," Faile said, her words clipped. "Might I suggest that we begin with the ones who *want* to be sent away?"

"Yes," Aravine said. The former *gai'shain* sat near the back of the tent, easy to overlook, though she had become an important force in Perrin's camp administration. She acted as something of an unofficial steward for him. "Some of the refugees would be happy to return to their homes."

"I'd rather move everyone, if I can," Perrin said. "Grady?"

The Asha'man shrugged his shoulders. "The gateways I've made for scouts haven't taxed me too much, and I think I could make some larger ones. I'm still a little weak, but I am mostly over the sickness. Neald will need more time, though."

"My Lord." Balwer coughed softly. "I have some figures of curious note. Moving as many people as you now have through gateways will take hours, maybe days. It won't be a quick endeavor, as when we approached Malden."

"That's going to be rough, my Lord," Grady said. "I don't think I could hold one open such a long time. Not if you want me strong enough to be in fighting shape, just in case."

Perrin settled back down, inspecting the map again. Berelain's cup was empty; Morgase hurried over to fill it. "All right, then," Perrin said. "We'll start sending some smaller groups of refugees away, but those who want to leave first."

"Also," Faile said. "Perhaps it is time to send messengers to contact the Lord Dragon; he might be willing to send more Asha'man."

Perrin nodded. "Yes."

"Last we knew," Seonid said, "he was in Cairhien. The largest number of the refugees are from there, so we could begin by sending some of them home, along with scouts to meet with the Lord Dragon."

"He's not there," Perrin said.

"How do you know?" Edarra set down her cup. Morgase crept around the perimeter of the tent and snatched it for refilling. Eldest of the Wise Ones, and perhaps foremost among them—it was hard to tell with Wise Ones—Edarra looked strikingly young for her reported age. Morgase's own tiny ability in the One Power was enough to tell her that this woman was strong. Probably the strongest in the room.

"I . . ." Perrin seemed to flounder. Had he a source of information he wasn't sharing? "Rand has a habit of being where you don't expect him. I doubt he's remained in Cairhien. But Seonid is right—it's the best place to start looking."

"My Lord," Balwer said. "I worry about what we might, ahem, blunder into if we are not careful. Fleets of refugees, returning through gateways unexpectedly? We have been out of touch for some time. Perhaps, in addition to contacting the Dragon, we could send scouts to gather information?"

Perrin nodded. "I could approve that."

Balwer settled back, looking pleased, though that man was strikingly good at hiding his emotions. Why did he want so badly to send someone to Cairhien?

"I'll admit," Grady said, "I'm worried about moving all of these people. Even once Neald is well, it's going to be exhausting to hold gateways open long enough to get them all through."

"Perrin Aybara," Edarra said. "There may be a way to fix this problem."

"How?"

"These apprentices have been speaking of something. A circle, it is called? If we linked together, the Asha'man and some of us, then perhaps we could give them the strength to create larger gateways."

Perrin scratched at his beard. "Grady?"

"I've never linked in a circle before, my Lord. But if we could figure it out . . . well, bigger gateways would move more people through faster. That could help a lot."

"All right," Perrin said, turning back to the Wise One. "What would it cost me for you to try this?"

"You have worked too long with Aes Sedai, Perrin Aybara," Edarra said with a sniff. "Not everything must be done at a *cost*. This will benefit us all. I have been contemplating suggesting it for some time."

Perrin frowned. "How long have you known that this might work?"

"Long enough."

"Burn you, woman, why didn't you bring it to me *earlier*, then?"

"You seem hardly interested in your position as chief, most of the time," Edarra said coldly. "Respect is a thing earned and not demanded, Perrin Aybara."

Morgase held her breath at that insolent comment. Many a lord would snap at someone for that tone. Perrin froze, but then nodded, as if that were the expected answer.

"Your Asha'man were sick when I first thought of this," Edarra continued. "It would not have worked before. This is the appropriate time to raise the question. Therefore, I have done so."

She insults Aes Sedai with one breath, Morgase thought, *then acts just like one with the next.* Still, being a captive in Malden had helped Morgase begin to understand Aiel ways. Everyone claimed the Aiel were incomprehensible, but she gave talk like that little credence. Aiel were people, like any other. They had odd traditions and cultural quirks, but so did everyone else. A queen had to be able to understand all of the people within her realm—and all of her realm's potential enemies.

"Very well," Perrin said. "Grady, don't fatigue yourself too much, but start working with them. See if you can manage forming a circle."

"Yes, my Lord," Grady said. The Asha'man always seemed somewhat distant. "Might be good to involve Neald in this. He gets dizzy when he stands, but he's been itching to do something with the Power. This might be a way for him to get back into practice."

"All right," Perrin said.

"We have not finished talking of the scouts we are sending to Cairhien," Seonid said. "I would like to be with the group."

Perrin scratched his bearded chin. "I suppose. Take your

Warders, two Maidens and Pel Aydaer. Be unobtrusive, if you can."

"Also Camaille Nolaisen will go," Faile said. Of course she would add one *Cha Faile* to the group.

Balwer cleared his throat. "My Lord. We are in dire need of paper and new pen nibs, not to mention some other delicate materials."

"Surely that can wait." Perrin frowned.

"No," Faile said slowly. "No, husband, I think this is a good suggestion. We should send one person to collect supplies. Balwer, would you go and fetch the things yourself?"

"If my Lady wishes it," the secretary said. "I have ached to visit this school the Dragon has opened in Cairhien. They would have the supplies we need."

"I suppose you can go, then," Perrin said. "But nobody else. Light! Any more, and we might as well send the whole burning army through."

Balwer nodded, looking satisfied. That one was obviously spying for Perrin now. Would he tell Aybara who she really was? Had he done so already? Perrin didn't act as if he knew.

She gathered up more cups; the meeting was beginning to break up. Of course Balwer would offer to spy for Aybara; she should have approached the dusty man earlier, to see what the price would be to keep his silence. Mistakes like that could cost a queen her throne.

She froze, hand halfway to a cup. *You're not a queen any longer. You have to stop thinking like one!*

During the first weeks following her silent abdication, she'd hoped to find a way to return to Andor, so she could be a resource for Elayne. However, the more she'd considered it, the more she'd realized that she had to stay away. Everyone in Andor *had* to assume that Morgase was dead. Each queen had to make her own way, and Elayne might seem a puppet to her own mother if Morgase returned. Beyond that, Morgase had made many enemies before leaving. Why had she *done* such things? Her memory of those times was cloudy, but her return would only rip open old wounds.

She continued gathering up cups. Perhaps she should have done the noble thing and killed herself. If enemies of the throne discovered who she was, they could use her against Elayne, the same way that the Whitecloaks would have. But for now, she was not a threat. Besides, she was confident that Elayne would not risk Andor's safety, even to save her mother.

Perrin bade farewell to the attendees and gave some basic instructions for the evening camp. Morgase knelt down, using a rag to wipe dirt from the side of a teacup that had rolled over. Niall had told her that Gaebril was dead, and al'Thor held Caemlyn. That would have prompted Elayne to return, wouldn't it? Was she queen? Had the Houses supported her, or had they acted against her because of what Morgase had done?

The scouting party might bring news that Morgase hungered for. She would have to find a way into any meeting discussing their reports, perhaps by offering to serve the tea. The better she grew at her job as Faile's maid, the closer she'd be able to get to important events.

As the Wise Ones made their way from the tent, Morgase caught sight of someone outside. Tallanvor, dutiful as always. Tall, broad of shoulder, he wore his sword at his waist and a look of pointed concern in his eyes.

He'd followed her practically nonstop since Malden, and while she'd complained of it out of principle, she didn't mind. After two months apart, he wanted to take every opportunity to be together. Looking into those beautiful young eyes of his, she could not entertain the notion of suicide, even for the good of Andor. She felt a fool for that. Hadn't she let her heart lead her into enough trouble already?

Malden had changed her, though. She'd missed Tallanvor dearly. And then he'd come for her, when he shouldn't have risked himself so. He was more devoted to her than to Andor itself. And for some reason, that was exactly what she needed. She began to make her way toward him, balancing eight cups in the crook of her arm while carrying the saucers in her hand.

"Maighdin," Perrin said as she passed out of the tent. She hesitated, turning back. Everyone but Perrin and his wife had withdrawn.

"Come back here, please," Perrin said. "And Tallanvor, you might as well come in. I can see you lurking out there. Honestly. It's not as if anyone was going to swoop down and steal her away while she was inside a tent full of Wise Ones and Aes Sedai!"

Morgase raised an eyebrow. From what she'd seen, Perrin himself had followed Faile around lately nearly as much.

Tallanvor shot her a smile as he entered. He took some of the cups from her arm, then both of them presented themselves before Perrin. Tallanvor bowed formally, which gave Morgase a stab of annoyance. He was still a member of the Queen's Guard—the only loyal member, as far as she knew. He shouldn't be bowing to this rural upstart.

"I was given a suggestion back when you first joined us," Perrin said gruffly. "Well, I think it's about time I took it. Lately, you two are like youths from different villages, mooning over one another in the hour before Sunday ends. It's high time you were married. We could have Alliandre do it, or maybe I could. Do you have some tradition you follow?"

Morgase blinked in surprise. Curse Lini for putting that idea in Perrin's head! Morgase felt a sudden panic, though Tallanvor glanced at her questioningly.

"Go change into something nicer if you want," Perrin said. "Gather any you want to witness and be back here in an hour. Then we'll get this silliness over with."

She felt her face grow hot with anger. Silliness? How dare he! And in such a way! Sending her off like a child, as if her emotion—her love—was merely an inconvenience to him?

He was rolling up his map, but then Faile's hand placed on his arm caused him to look up and notice that his orders had not been followed.

"Well?" Perrin asked.

"No," Morgase said. She kept her gaze on Perrin; she didn't want to see the inevitable disappointment and rejection in Tallanvor's face.

"What?" Perrin asked.

"No, Perrin Aybara," Morgase said. "I will *not* be back here in an hour to be married."

"But—"

"If you want tea served, or your tent cleaned, or something packed, then call for me. If you wish your clothing washed, I will oblige. But I am your servant, Perrin Aybara,

not your subject. I am loyal to the Queen of Andor. You
have no authority to give me this sort of command."

"I—"

"Why, the Queen herself wouldn't demand this! Forcing
two people to marry because you're tired of the way they
look at one another? Like two hounds you intend to breed,
then sell the pups?"

"I didn't mean it that way."

"You said it nonetheless. Besides, how can you be sure of
the young man's intentions? Have you spoken to him, asked
him, interviewed him as a lord should in a matter like this?"

"But Maighdin," Perrin said. "He *does* care for you. You
should have seen the way he acted when you were taken.
Light, woman, but it's obvious!"

"Matters of the heart are never obvious." Pulling herself
up to her full height, she almost felt a queen again. "If I
choose to marry a man, I will make that decision on my
own. For a man who claims he doesn't like being in charge,
you certainly do like giving commands. How can you be
sure that I *want* this young man's affections? Do you know
my heart?"

To the side, Tallanvor stiffened. Then he bowed formally
to Perrin and strode from the tent. He was an emotional
one. Well, he needed to know that she would not be shoved
around. Not anymore. First Gaebril, then Valda, and now
Perrin Aybara? Tallanvor would be ill-served if he were to
receive a woman who married him because she was told to
do so.

Morgase measured Perrin, who was blushing. She softened her tone. "You're young at this yet, so I'll give you
advice. There are some things a lord should be involved in,
but others he should *always* leave untouched. You'll learn
the difference as you practice, but kindly refrain from making demands like this one until you've at least counseled
with your wife."

With that, she curtsied—still carrying the teacups—and
withdrew. She shouldn't have spoken to him so. Well, he
shouldn't have made a command like that! It seemed she
had some spark left in her after all. She hadn't felt that firm
or certain of herself since . . . well, since before Gaebril's
arrival in Caemlyn! Though she would have to find Tallanvor and soothe his pride.

She returned the cups to the nearby washing station, then went through the camp, looking for Tallanvor. Around her, servants and workers were busy at their duties. Many of the former *gai'shain* still acted as if they were among the Shaido, bowing and scraping whenever someone so much as looked at them. Those from Cairhien were the worst; they'd been held longest, and Aiel were *very* good at teaching lessons.

There were, of course, a few real Aiel *gai'shain*. What an odd custom. From what Morgase had been able to determine, some of the *gai'shain* here had been taken by the Shaido, then had been liberated in Malden. They retained the white, and so that meant they were now acting as slaves to their own relatives and friends.

Any people could be understood. But, she admitted, perhaps the Aiel would take longer than others. Take, for instance, that group of Maidens loping through camp. Why did they have to force everyone out of their way? There was no—

Morgase hesitated. Those Maidens were heading straight for Perrin's tent. They looked like they had news.

Her curiosity getting the better of her, Morgase followed. The Maidens left two guards by the front tent flaps, but the ward against eavesdropping had been removed. Morgase rounded the tent, trying to look as if she was doing anything *other* than eavesdropping, feeling a stab of shame for leaving Tallanvor to his pain.

"Whitecloaks, Perrin Aybara," Sulin's stout voice reported from inside. "There is a large force of them on the road directly in front of us."

CHAPTER

7

Lighter than a Feather

The air felt calmer at night, though the thunder still warned Lan that not all was well. In his weeks traveling with Bulen, that storm above seemed to have grown darker.

After riding southward, they continued on to the east; they were somewhere near the border between Kandor and Saldaea, on the Plain of Lances. Towering, weathered hills—steep-sided, like fortresses—rose around them.

Perhaps they'd missed the border. There often was no marker on these back roads, and the mountains cared not which nation tried to claim them.

"Master Andra," Bulen said from behind. Lan had purchased a horse for him to ride, a dusty white mare. He still led his packhorse, Scouter.

Bulen caught up to him. Lan insisted upon being called "Andra." One follower was bad enough. If nobody knew who he was, they couldn't ask to come with him. He had Bulen to thank—inadvertently—for the warning of what Nynaeve had done. For that, he owed the man a debt.

Bulen *did* like to talk, though.

"Master Andra," Bulen continued. "If I may suggest, we could turn south at the Berndt Crossroads, yes? I know a waypoint inn in that direction that serves the *very* best quail. We could turn eastward again on the road to South Mettler. A *much* easier path. My cousin has a farm along that road—cousin on my mother's side, Master Andra—and we could—"

"We continue this way," Lan said.

"But South Mettler is a much better roadway!"

"And therefore much better traveled too, Bulen."

Bulen sighed, but fell silent. The *hadori* looked good around his head, and he had proven surprisingly capable with the sword. As talented a student as Lan had seen in a while.

It was dark—night came early here, because of those mountains. Compared to the areas near the Blight, it also felt chilly. Unfortunately, the land here was fairly well populated. Indeed, about an hour past the crossroads they arrived at an inn, windows still glowing with light.

Bulen looked toward it longingly, but Lan continued on. He had them traveling at night, mostly. The better to keep from being seen.

A trio of men sat in front of the inn, smoking their pipes in the darkness. The pungent smoke wound in the air, past the inn's windows. Lan didn't give them much consideration until—as a group—they broke off their smoking. They unhooked horses from the fence at the side of the inn.

Wonderful, Lan thought. Highwaymen, watching the night road for weary travelers. Well, three men shouldn't prove too dangerous. They rode behind Lan at a trot. They wouldn't attack until they were farther from the inn. Lan reached to loosen his sword in its sheath.

"My Lord," Bulen said urgently, looking over his shoulder. "Two of those men are wearing the *hadori*."

Lan spun around, cloak whipping behind him. The three men approached and did not stop. They split around him and Bulen.

Lan watched them pass. "Andere?" he called. "What do you think you're doing?"

One of the three—a lean, dangerous-looking man—glanced over his shoulder, his long hair held back with the *hadori*. It had been years since Lan had seen Andere. He looked as if he'd given up his Kandori uniform, finally; he was wearing a deep black cloak and hunting leathers underneath.

"Ah, Lan," Andere said, the three men pulling up to stop. "I didn't notice you there."

"I'm sure you didn't," Lan said flatly. "And you, Nazar.

You put your *hadori* away when you were a lad. Now you don one?"

"I may do as I wish," Nazar said. He was getting old—he must be past his seventieth year—but he carried a sword on his saddle. His hair had gone white.

The third man, Rakim, wasn't Malkieri. He had the tilted eyes of a Saldaean, and he shrugged at Lan, looking a little embarrassed.

Lan raised his fingers to his forehead, closing his eyes as the three rode ahead. What foolish game were they playing? *No matter,* Lan thought, opening his eyes.

Bulen started to say something, but Lan quieted him with a glare. He turned southward off the road, cutting down a small, worn trail.

Before long, he heard muffled hoofbeats from behind. Lan spun as he saw the three men riding behind him. Lan pulled Mandarb to a halt, teeth gritted. "I'm *not* raising the Golden Crane!"

"We didn't say you were," Nazar said. The three parted around him again, riding past.

Lan kicked Mandarb forward, riding up to them. "Then stop following me."

"Last I checked, we were ahead of you," Andere said.

"You turned this way after me," Lan accused.

"You don't own the roads, Lan Mandragoran," Andere said. He glanced at Lan, face shadowed in the night. "If you haven't noticed, I'm no longer the boy the Hero of Salmarna berated so long ago. I've become a soldier, and soldiers are needed. So I will ride this way if I please."

"I *command* you to turn and go back," Lan said. "Find a different path eastward."

Rakim laughed, his voice still hoarse after all these years. "You're not my captain any longer, Lan. Why would I obey your orders?" The others chuckled.

"We'd obey a king, of course," Nazar said.

"Yes," Andere said. "If *he* gave us commands, perhaps we would. But I don't see a king here. Unless I'm mistaken."

"There can be no king of a fallen people," Lan said. "No king without a kingdom."

"And yet you ride," Nazar said, flicking his reins. "Ride to your death in a land you *claim* is no kingdom."

"It is my destiny."

The three shrugged, then pulled ahead of him.

"Don't be fools," Lan said, voice soft as he pulled Mandarb to a halt. "This path leads to death."

"Death is lighter than a feather, Lan Mandragoran," Rakim called over his shoulder. "If we ride only to death, then the trail will be easier than I'd thought!"

Lan gritted his teeth, but what was he to do? Beat all three of them senseless and leave them beside the road? He nudged Mandarb forward.

The two had become five.

Galad continued his morning meal, noting that Child Byar had come to speak with him. The meal was simple fare: porridge with a handful of raisins stirred in. A simple meal for every soldier kept them all from envy. Some Lords Captain Commander had dined far better than their men. That would not do for Galad. Not when so many in the world starved.

Child Byar stood inside the flaps of Galad's tent, awaiting recognition. The gaunt, sunken-cheeked man wore his white cloak, a tabard over mail underneath.

Galad eventually set aside his spoon and nodded to Byar. The soldier strode up to the table and waited, still at attention. There were no elaborate furnishings to Galad's tent. His sword—Valda's sword—lay on the plain table behind his wooden bowl, slightly drawn. The herons on the blade peeked out from beneath the scabbard, and the polished steel reflected Byar's form.

"Speak," Galad said.

"I have more news about the army, my Lord Captain Commander," Byar said. "They are near where the captives said they would be, a few days from us."

Galad nodded. "They fly the flag of Ghealdan?"

"Alongside the flag of Mayene." That flame of zeal glinted in Byar's eyes. "And the wolfhead, though reports say they took that down late yesterday. Goldeneyes *is* there. Our scouts are sure of it."

"Did he really kill Bornhald's father?"

"Yes, my Lord Captain Commander. I have a familiarity

with this creature. He and his troops come from a place called the Two Rivers."

"The Two Rivers?" Galad said. "Curious, how often I seem to hear of that place, these days. Is that not where al'Thor is from?"

"So it is said," Byar replied.

Galad rubbed his chin. "They grow good tabac there, Child Byar, but I have not heard of them growing armies."

"It is a dark place, my Lord Captain Commander. Child Bornhald and I spent some time there last year; it is festering with Darkfriends."

Galad sighed. "You sound like a Questioner."

"My Lord Captain Commander," Byar earnestly continued, "my Lord, please believe me. I am *not* simply speculating. This is different."

Galad frowned. Then he gestured toward the other stool beside his table. Byar took it.

"Explain yourself," Galad said. "And tell me everything you know of this Perrin Goldeneyes."

Perrin could remember a time when simple breakfasts of bread and cheese had satisfied him. That was no longer the case. Perhaps it was due to his relationship with the wolves, or maybe his tastes had changed over time. These days he craved meat, especially in the morning. He couldn't always have it, and that was fine. But generally he didn't have to ask.

That was the case this day. He'd risen, washed his face, and found a servant entering with a large chop of ham, steaming and succulent. No beans, no vegetables. No gravy. Just the ham, rubbed with salt and seared over the fire, with a pair of boiled eggs. The serving woman set them on his table, then withdrew.

Perrin wiped his hands, crossing the rug of his tent and taking in the ham's scent. Part of him felt he should turn it away, but he couldn't. Not when it was right there. He sat down, took up fork and knife and dug in.

"I still don't see how you can eat that for *breakfast*," Faile noted, leaving the washing chamber of their tent, wiping her hands on a cloth. Their large tent had several curtained di-

visions to it. She wore one of her unobtrusive gray dresses.
Perfect, because it didn't distract from her beauty. It was
accented by a sturdy black belt—she had sent away all of
her golden belts, no matter how fine. He'd suggested finding
her one that was more to her liking, and she'd looked sick.

"It's food," Perrin said.

"I can see," she said with a snort, looking herself over in
the mirror. "What did you think I assumed it was? A rock?"

"I meant," Perrin said between bites, "that food is food.
Why should I care what I eat for breakfast and what I eat for
a different meal?"

"Because it's strange," she said, clasping a cord holding
a small blue stone. She regarded herself in the mirror, then
turned, the loose sleeves of her Saldaean-cut dress swish-
ing. She paused beside his plate, grimacing. "I'm having
breakfast with Alliandre. Send for me if there is news."

He nodded, swallowing. Why should a person have meat
at midday, but refuse it for breakfast? It didn't make sense.

He'd decided to remain camped beside the Jehannah
Road. What else was he to do, with an army of Whitecloaks directly ahead, between him and Lugard? His scouts
needed time to assess the danger. He'd spent much time
thinking about the strange visions he'd seen, the wolves
chasing sheep toward a beast and Faile walking toward a
cliff. He hadn't been able to make sense of them, but could
they have something to do with the Whitecloaks? Their appearance bothered him more than he wanted to admit, but
he harbored a tiny hope that they would prove insignificant
and not slow him too much.

"Perrin Aybara," a voice called from outside his tent.
"Do you give me leave to enter?"

"Come in, Gaul," he called. "My shade is yours."

The tall Aiel strode in. "Thank you, Perrin Aybara," he
said, glancing at the ham. "Quite a feast. Do you celebrate?"

"Nothing besides breakfast."

"A mighty victory," Gaul said, laughing.

Perrin shook his head. Aiel humor. He'd stopped trying to make sense of it. Gaul settled himself on the ground
and Perrin sighed inwardly before picking up his plate and
moving to sit on the rug across from Gaul. Perrin placed the
meal in his lap and continued to eat.

"You need not sit on the floor because of me," Gaul said.

"I'm not doing it because I *need* to, Gaul."

Gaul nodded.

Perrin cut off another bite. This would be so much easier if he grabbed the whole thing in his fingers and started ripping off chunks. Eating was simpler for wolves. Utensils. What was the point?

Thoughts like that gave him pause. He was *not* a wolf, and didn't want to think like one. Maybe he should start having fruit for a proper breakfast, as Faile said. He frowned, then turned back to his meat.

"We fought Trollocs in the Two Rivers," Byar said, lowering his voice. Galad's porridge cooled, forgotten on the table. "Several dozen men in our camp can confirm it. I killed several of the beasts with my own sword."

"Trollocs in the *Two Rivers*?" Galad said. "That's hundreds of leagues from the Borderlands!"

"They were there nonetheless," Byar said. "Lord Captain Commander Niall must have suspected it. We were sent to the place on his orders. You know that Pedron Niall would not have simply jumped at nothing."

"Yes. I agree. But the Two Rivers?"

"It *is* full of Darkfriends," Byar said. "Bornhald told you of Goldeneyes. In the Two Rivers, this Perrin Aybara was raising the flag of ancient Manetheren and gathering an army from among the farmers. Trained soldiers may scoff at farmers pressed into service, but get enough of them together, and they can be a danger. Some are skilled with the staff or the bow."

"I am aware," Galad said flatly, recalling a particularly embarrassing lesson he'd once been given.

"That man, this Perrin Aybara," Byar continued. "He's Shadowspawn, as plain as day. They call him Goldeneyes because his eyes *are* golden, no shade that any person has ever known. We were certain that Aybara was bringing the Trollocs in, using them to force the people of the Two Rivers to join his army. He eventually ran us out of the place. Now he's here, before us."

A coincidence, or something more?

Byar was obviously thinking along the same lines. "My

Lord Captain Commander, perhaps I should have mentioned this earlier, but the Two Rivers wasn't my first experience with this creature Aybara. He killed two of the Children on a forgotten road in Andor some two years ago. I was traveling with Bornhald's father. We met Aybara in a campsite off a main road. He was running with wolves like a wildman! He killed two men before we could subdue him, then escaped into the night after we had him captured. My Lord, he was to be hanged."

"There are others who can confirm this?" Galad asked.

"Child Oratar can. And Child Bornhald can confirm what we saw in the Two Rivers. Goldeneyes *was* at Falme, too. For what he did there alone he should be brought to justice. It is clear. The Light has delivered him to us."

"You're certain our people are among the Whitecloaks?" Perrin asked.

"I could not see faces," Gaul said, "but Elyas Machera's eyes are very keen. He says he's certain he saw Basel Gill."

Perrin nodded. Elyas' golden eyes would be as good as Perrin's own.

"Sulin and her scouts have similar reports," Gaul said, accepting a cup of ale poured from Perrin's pitcher. "The Whitecloak army has a large number of carts, much like the ones we sent ahead. She discovered this early in the morning, but asked me to pass these words to you once you awoke, as she knows that wetlanders are temperamental when disturbed in the morning."

Gaul obviously had no idea that he might be giving offense. Perrin was a wetlander. Wetlanders were temperamental, at least in the opinion of the Aiel. So Gaul was stating an accepted fact.

Perrin shook his head, trying one of the eggs. Overcooked, but edible. "Did Sulin spot anyone she recognized?"

"No, though she saw some *gai'shain*," Gaul said. "However, Sulin is a Maiden, so perhaps we should send someone to confirm what she said—someone who won't demand the opportunity to wash our smallclothes."

"Trouble with Bain and Chiad?" Perrin asked.

Gaul grimaced. "I swear, those women will drive the

mind from me. What man should be expected to suffer such things? Almost better to have Sightblinder himself as a *gai'shain* than those two."

Perrin chuckled.

"Regardless, the captives look unharmed and healthy. There is more to the report. One of the Maidens saw a flag flying over the camp that looked distinctive, so she copied it down for your secretary, Sebban Balwer. He says that it means the Lord Captain Commander himself rides with this army."

Perrin looked down at the last chunk of ham. That was not good news. He'd never met the Lord Captain Commander, but he *had* met one of the Whitecloak Lords Captain once. That had been the night when Hopper had died, a night that had haunted Perrin for two years.

That had been the night when he had killed for the first time.

"What more do you need?" Byar leaned in close, sunken eyes alight with zeal. "We have witnesses who *saw* this man murder two of our own! Do we let him march by, as if innocent?"

"No," Galad said. "No, by the Light, if what you say is true then we cannot turn our backs on this man. Our duty is to bring justice to the wronged."

Byar smiled, looking eager. "The prisoners revealed that the Queen of Ghealdan has sworn fealty to him."

"That could present a problem."

"Or an opportunity. Perhaps Ghealdan is precisely what the Children need. A new home, a place to rebuild. You speak of Andor, my Lord Captain Commander, but how long will they suffer us? You speak of the Last Battle, but it could be months away. What if we were to free an entire nation from the grip of a terrible Darkfriend? Surely the Queen—or her successor—would feel indebted to us."

"Assuming we can defeat this Aybara."

"We can. Our forces are smaller than his, but many of his soldiers are farmers."

"Farmers you just pointed out can be dangerous," Galad said. "They should not be underestimated."

"Yes, but I know we can defeat them. They can be dangerous, yes, but they will break before the might of the Children. This time, finally, Goldeneyes won't be able to hide behind his little village fortifications or his ragtag allies. No more excuses."

Was this part of being *ta'veren*? Could Perrin not escape that night, years ago? He set his plate aside, feeling sick.

"Are you well, Perrin Aybara?" Gaul said.

"Just thinking." The Whitecloaks would not leave him alone, and the Pattern—burn it!—was going to keep looping them into his path until he dealt with them.

"How large is their army?" Perrin asked.

"There are twenty thousand soldiers among them," Gaul replied. "There are several thousand others who have likely never held a spear."

Servants and camp followers. Gaul kept the amusement from his voice, but Perrin could smell it on him. Among the Aiel, nearly every man—all but blacksmiths—would pick up a spear if they were attacked. The fact that many wetlanders were incapable of defending themselves either befuddled or infuriated the Aiel.

"Their force is large," Gaul continued, "but ours is larger. And they have no *algai'd'siswai* nor Asha'man, nor channelers of any type, if Sebban Balwer's word is not in error. He seems to know much of these Whitecloaks."

"He's right. Whitecloaks hate Aes Sedai and think anyone who can use the One Power is a Darkfriend."

"We move against him, then?" Byar asked.

Galad stood. "We have no choice. The Light has delivered him into our hands. But we need more information. Perhaps I should go to this Aybara and let him know that we hold his allies, and then ask his army to meet with us on the field of battle. I'd rather draw him out to make use of my cavalry."

"What do you want, Perrin Aybara?" Gaul asked.

What did he want? He wished he could answer that.

"Send more scouts," Perrin said. "Find us a better place

to camp. We'll want to offer parley, but there's no way under the Light I'm leaving Gill and the others in the hands of the Whitecloaks. We'll give the Children a chance to return our people. If they don't . . . well, then we'll see."

CHAPTER
8

The Seven-Striped Lass

M at sat on a worn stool, his arms leaning against a dark wooden bar counter. The air smelled good—of ale, smoke, and of the washcloth that had recently wiped the counter. He liked that. There was something calming about a good, rowdy tavern that was also kept clean. Well, clean as was reasonable, anyway. Nobody liked a tavern that was *too* clean. That made a place feel new. Like a coat that had never been worn or a pipe that had never been smoked.

Mat flipped a folded letter between two fingers of his right hand. That letter, on thick paper, was sealed with a glob of blood-red wax. He had been carrying it only a short time, but it was already a source of as much aggravation to him as any woman. Well, maybe not an Aes Sedai, but most any other woman. That was saying a lot.

He stopped spinning the letter and tapped it on the counter. Burn Verin for doing this to him! She held him by his oath like a fish caught on a hook.

"Well, Master Crimson?" asked the tavernkeeper. That was the name he was using these days. Best to be safe. "You want a refill or not?"

The tavernkeeper leaned down before him, crossing her arms. Melli Craeb was a pretty woman, with a round face and auburn hair that curled quite fetchingly. Mat would have given her his best smile—there was not a woman he had met who did not melt for his best smile—but he was a married man now. He could not go breaking hearts; it would not be right.

Though, leaning as she did showed some ample bosom
She was a short woman, but she kept the area behind the
bar raised. Yes, a nice bosom indeed. He figured she would
be good for a bit of kissing, perhaps tucked into one of the
booths at the back of the tavern. Of course, Mat did not
look at women anymore, not like that. He did not think
about her for *him* to kiss. Maybe for Talmanes. He was so
stiff, a good kiss and cuddle would do him good.

"Well?" Melli asked.

"What would you do if you were me, Melli?" His empty
mug sat beside him, a few suds clinging to the rim.

"Order another round," she said immediately. "For the
entire bar. It would be downright charitable of you. People
like a charitable fellow."

"I meant about the letter."

"You promised not to open it?" she said.

"Well, not exactly. I promised that if I opened it, I'd do
exactly what it said inside."

"Gave an oath, did you?"

He nodded.

She snatched it from his fingers, causing him to yelp. He
reached to take it back but she pulled away, turning it over
in her fingers. Mat suppressed an urge to reach for it again
he had played more than a few games of take-away, and had
no urge to look the buffoon. A woman liked nothing more
than to make a man squirm, and if you let her do it, she
would only keep going.

Still, he began to sweat. "Now, Melli . . ."

"I could open it for you," she said, leaning back against
the other side of the bar, looking over the letter. Nearby
a man called for another mug of ale, but she waved him
down. The red-nosed man looked as if he had had enough
anyway. Melli's tavern was popular enough that she had
a half-dozen serving girls taking care of the patrons. One
would get to him eventually. "I could open it," she continued to Mat, "and could tell you what's inside."

Bloody ashes! If she did that, he would *have* to do what
it said. Whatever it bloody said! All he had to do was wait
a few weeks, and he would be free. He could wait that long
Really, he could.

"It wouldn't do," Mat said, sitting up with a jerk as she
reached her thumb between two sides of the letter, as if to

rip it. "I'd still have to do what it said, Melli. Don't you do that, now. Be careful!"

She smiled at him. Her tavern, The Seven-Striped Lass, was one of the best in western Caemlyn. Ale with a robust flavor, games of dice when you wanted them, and not a rat to be seen. They probably did not want to risk running afoul of Melli. Light, but the woman could shame the whiskers off a man's cheeks without much trying.

"You never did tell me who it was from," Melli said, turning the letter over. "She's a lover, isn't she? Got you tied up in her strings?"

She had the second part right enough, but a lover? Verin? It was ridiculous enough to make Mat laugh. Kissing Verin would have been about as much fun as kissing a lion. Of the two, he would have chosen the lion. It would have been much less likely to try to bite him.

"I gave my oath, Melli," Mat said, trying not to show his nervousness. "*Don't* you go opening that, now."

"I didn't give any oath," she said. "Maybe I'll read it, and then not tell you what it says. Just give you hints, now and then, as encouragement."

She eyed him, full lips smiling. Yes, she *was* a pretty one. Not as pretty as Tuon, though, with her beautiful skin and large eyes. But Melli was still pretty, particularly those lips of hers. Being married meant he could not stare at those lips, but he did give her his best smile. It was called for, this time, though it could break her heart. He could not let her open that letter.

"It's the same thing, Melli," Mat said winningly. "If you open that letter and I don't do what it says, my oath is as good as dishwater." He sighed, realizing there was *one* way to get the letter back. "The woman who gave it to me was Aes Sedai, Melli. You don't want to anger an Aes Sedai, do you?"

"Aes Sedai?" Melli suddenly looked eager. "I've always fancied going up to Tar Valon, to see if they'll let me join them." She looked at the letter, as if *more* curious about its contents.

Light! The woman was daft. Mat had taken her for the sensible type. He should have known better. He began to sweat more. Could he reach the letter? She was holding it close. . . .

She set it down on the bar before him. She left one finger on the letter, directly in the middle of the wax seal. "You'll introduce me to this Aes Sedai, when you next meet her."

"If I see her while I'm in Caemlyn," Mat said. "I promise it."

"Can I trust you to keep your word?"

He gave her an exasperated look. "What was this whole bloody conversation about, Melli?"

She laughed, turning and leaving the letter on the bar, going to help the gap-toothed man who was still calling for more ale. Mat snatched the letter, tucking it carefully into his coat pocket. Bloody woman. The only way for him to stay free of Aes Sedai plots was to never open this letter. Well, not exactly free. Mat had plenty of Aes Sedai plotting around him; he had them coming out of his ears. But only a man with sawdust for brains would ask for another.

Mat sighed, turning on his stool. A varied crowd clogged The Seven-Striped Lass. Caemlyn was fuller than a lionfish at a shipwreck these days, practically bursting at the seams. That kept the taverns busy. In the corner, some farmers in workcoats fraying at the collars played at dice. Mat had played a few rounds with them earlier, and had paid for his drink with their coins, but he hated gambling for coppers.

The bluff-faced man in the corner was still drinking—must be fourteen mugs sitting empty beside him now—his companions cheering him onward. A group of nobles sat off from the rest, and he would have asked them for a nice game of dice, but the expressions on their faces could have frightened away bears. They had probably been on the wrong side of the Succession war.

Mat wore a black coat with lace at the cuffs. Only a little lace, and no embroidery. Reluctantly, he had left his wide-brimmed hat back in camp, and he had grown a few days' scrub on his chin. That itched like he had fleas, and he looked a bloody fool. But the scrub made him harder to recognize. With every footpad in the city having a picture of him, it was best to be safe. He wished being *ta'veren* would help him for once, but it was best not to count on that. Being *ta'veren* had not been good for anything he could tell.

He kept his scarf tucked low and his coat buttoned, the high collar up nearly to his chin. He had already died once, he was fairly certain, and was not eager to try again.

A pretty serving girl walked by, slender and wide-hipped, with long dark hair she let hang free. He moved to the side, allowing his empty mug to look lonely and obvious on the counter, and she walked over with a smile to refill it. He grinned at her and tipped a copper. He was a married man, and could not afford to charm her, but he *could* keep an eye out for his friends. Thom might like her. A girl might make him stop moping about so much, at least. Mat watched the girl's face for a time to be certain he would recognize her again.

Mat sipped at his ale, one hand feeling at the letter in his pocket. He did not speculate at what was in it. Do that, and he would be only one step from ripping it open. He was a little like a mouse staring at a trap with moldy cheese in it. He did not want that cheese. It could rot, for all he cared.

The letter would probably instruct him to do something dangerous. And embarrassing. Aes Sedai had a fondness for making men look like fools. Light, he hoped that she had not left instructions for him to help someone in trouble. If that were the case, surely she would have seen to it herself.

He sighed and took another pull on his ale. In the corner, the drinking man finally toppled over. Sixteen mugs. Not bad. Mat set aside his own drink, left a few coins as payment, then nodded farewell to Melli. He collected his winnings on the wager regarding the drinking man from a long-fingered fellow in the corner. Mat had bet on seventeen mugs, which was close enough to win some. Then he was on his way, taking his walking stick from the stand by the door.

The bouncer, Berg, eyed him. Berg had a face ugly enough to make his own mother wince. The shoulderthumper did not like Mat, and from the way Berg looked at Melli, that was probably because he figured Mat was trying to make eyes at his woman. Never mind that Mat had *explained* he was married, and did not do that sort of thing any longer. Some men would be jealous no matter what they were told.

The streets of Caemlyn were busy, even at this late hour. The paving stones were damp from a recent shower, though those clouds had passed by and—remarkably—left the sky open to the air. He moved northward along the street, heading for another tavern he knew, one where men diced for silver and gold. Mat was not about any specific task tonight, just listening for rumors, getting a feel for Caemlyn. A lot had changed since he had been here last.

As he walked, he could not help looking over his shoulder. Those bloody pictures had him unnerved. Many of the people on the street seemed suspicious. A few Murandians passed, looking so drunk that he could have lit their breath on fire. Mat kept his distance. After what had happened to him in Hinderstap, he figured he could not be too careful. Light, he had heard stories of *paving stones* attacking people. If a man could not trust the rocks under his feet, what could he trust?

He eventually reached the tavern he wanted, a cheery place called The Dead Man's Breath. It had two toughs out front, holding cudgels they patted against enormous palms. Lots of extra tavern toughs were being hired these days. Mat would have to watch himself, not win too much. Tavern-keepers did not like a man winning too much, as it could bring a fight. Unless the man spent his winnings on food and drink. Then he could win all he liked, thank you very much.

The inside of this tavern was darker than The Seven-Striped Lass had been. The men here hunched low over drinks or games, and there was not much food being served. Just strong drinks. The wooden bar had nails whose heads jutted out a fingernail or so high and jabbed you in the arms. Mat figured they were working to pull themselves free and run for the door.

The tavernkeeper, Bernherd, was a greasy-haired Tairen with a mouth so small it looked like he had swallowed his lips by mistake. He smelled of radishes, and Mat had never seen him smile, not even when tipped. Most tavernkeepers would smile at the Dark One himself for a tip.

Mat hated gambling and drinking in a place where you had to keep one hand on your coin purse. But he had a mind to win some real money tonight, and there were dice games going and coins clinking, so he felt somewhat at home. The lace on his coat did get glances. Why had he taken to wearing that, anyway? Best have Lopin pull it off his cuffs when he got back to the camp. Well, not all of it. Some of it, maybe.

Mat found a game at the back being played by three men and a woman in breeches. She had short golden hair and nice eyes; Mat noticed those purely for Thom's sake. She had a full bosom, anyway, and lately Mat had a mind for women who were more slender through the chest.

In minutes Mat was dicing with them, and that calmed him a measure. He kept his coin pouch in sight, though, laying it on the floor in front of him. Before long, the pile of coins beside it grew, mostly silvers.

"You hear about what happened over at Farrier's Green?" one of the men asked his fellows as Mat tossed. "It was a terrible thing." The speaker was a tall fellow, with a pinched-up face that looked like it had been closed in a door a few times. He called himself Chaser. Mat figured that was because the women ran away from him after they got a look at that face, and he had to run after them.

"What?" Clare asked. She was the golden-haired woman. Mat gave her a smile. He did not dice against women much, as most claimed to find dicing improper. Never mind that they never complained when a man bought them something nice with what he had won. Anyway, dicing with women was not fair, since one of his smiles could set their hearts fluttering and they would get all weak in the knees. But Mat did not smile at girls that way anymore. Besides, she had not responded to any of his smiles anyway.

"Jowdry," Chaser said as Mat shook his dice. "They found him dead this morning. Throat ripped clean out. Body was drained of blood, like a wineskin full of holes."

Mat was so startled that he threw the dice, but did not watch them roll. "What?" he demanded. "What did you say?"

"Here now," Chaser said, looking toward Mat. "It's just someone we knew. Owed me two crowns, he did."

"Drained of blood," Mat said. "Are you sure? Did you see the body?"

"What?" Chaser said, grimacing. "Bloody ashes, man! What's wrong with you?"

"I—"

"Chaser," Clare said. "Will you look at that?"

The lean man glanced down, as did Mat. The dice he had tossed—all three of them—had landed still and were balanced on their *corners*. Light! He had tossed coins so they fell on their sides before, but he had never done anything like this.

Right there, all of a sudden, the dice started rattling inside his head. He almost jumped clear to the ceiling. *Blood
and bloody ashes!* Those dice in his head never meant anything good. They only stopped when something changed,
something that usually meant bad news for poor Matrim
Cauthon.

"I ain't *never* . . ." Chaser said.

"We'll call that a loss," Mat said, tossing a few coins
down and scooping up the rest of his winnings.

"What do you know about Jowdry?" Clare demanded.
She was reaching for her waist. Mat would have bet gold
against coppers on her having a knife there, the way she
glared at him.

"Nothing," Mat said. *Nothing and too much at the same
time.* "Excuse me."

He hastily crossed the tavern. As he did, he noticed one
of the thick-armed toughs from the door standing and talking to Bernherd the tavernkeeper, pointing at a piece of
paper in his hands. Mat could not see what was on it, but he
could guess: his own face.

He cursed and ducked out onto the street. He took the
first alley he saw, breaking into a run.

The Forsaken hunting him, a picture of his face in the
pocket of every footpad in the city and a corpse killed and
drained of its blood. That could only mean one thing. The
gholam was in Caemlyn. It seemed impossible that it could
have gotten here this quickly. Of course, Mat had seen it
squeeze through a hole not two handspans wide. The thing
did not seem to have a right sense of what was possible and
what was not possible.

Blood and bloody *ashes,* he thought, ducking his head.
He needed to collect Thom and get back to the Band's camp
outside of the city. He hastened down the dark, rain-slicked
street. Paving stones reflected the lit oil lamps ahead.
Elayne kept the Queen's Walk well illuminated at night.

He had sent word to her, but had not gotten a reply. How
was that for gratitude? By his count, he had saved her life
twice. Once should have been enough to reduce her to tears
and kisses, but he had not seen even a peck on the cheek.
Not that he wanted one; not from royalty. Best to avoid
them.

You're married to a bloody high lady of the Seanchan,

he thought. *Daughter of the Empress herself.* There was no avoiding royalty now! Not for him. At least Tuon was pretty. And good at playing stones. And very keen of wit, good for talking to, even if she was flaming frustrating most of the . . .

No. No thinking of Tuon right now.

Anyway, he had received no reply from Elayne. He would need to be more firm. It was not just Aludra and her dragons now. The bloody *gholam* was in the city.

He stepped out onto a large, busy street, hands pushed into the pockets of his coat. In his haste, he had left his walking staff back in The Dead Man's Breath. He grumbled to himself; he was *supposed* to be spending his days relaxing, his nights dicing in fine inns, and his mornings sleeping late while waiting for Verin's thirty-day requirement to run out. Now this.

He had a score to settle with that *gholam*. The innocents it had slaughtered while lurking around Ebou Dar were bad enough, and Mat had not forgotten Nalesean and the five Redarms who had been murdered either. Bloody ashes, it had had enough to answer for already. Then it had taken Tylin.

Mat removed a hand from his pocket, feeling at the fox-head medallion, resting—as always—against his chest. He was tired of running from that monster. A plan started to form in his mind, accompanied by the rattling of dice. He tried to banish the image of the Queen lying in bonds Mat himself had tied, her head ripped free. There would have been so much blood. The *gholam* lived on fresh blood.

Mat shivered, shoving his hand back into his pocket as he approached the city gate. Despite the darkness, he could pick out signs of the battle that had been fought here. An arrowhead embedded into the doorway of a building to his left, a dark patch on the wall of a guardhouse, staining the wood beneath the window. A man had died there, perhaps while firing a crossbow out, and had slumped down over the window's ledge, bleeding his lifeblood down the wood.

That siege was over now, and a new Queen—the *right* Queen—held the throne. For once, there had been a battle and he had *missed* it. Remembering that lightened his mood somewhat. An entire war had been fought over the Lion

Throne, and not one arrow, blade or spear had entered the conflict seeking Matrim Cauthon's heart.

He turned right, along the inside of the city wall. There were a lot of inns here. There were always inns near city gates. Not the nicest ones, but almost always the most profitable ones.

Light spilled from doorways and windows, painting the road golden in patches. Dark forms crowded the alleyways except where the inns had hired men to keep the poor away. Caemlyn was strained. The flood of refugees, the recent fighting, the . . . other matters. Stories abounded of the dead walking, of food spoiling, of whitewashed walls suddenly going grimy.

The inn where Thom had chosen to perform was a steep-roofed, brick-fronted structure with a sign that showed two apples, one eaten down to the core. That made it stark white, the other was stark red—colors of the Andoran flag. The Two Apples was one of the nicer establishments in the area.

Mat could hear the music from outside. He entered and saw Thom sitting atop a small dais on the far side of the common room, playing his flute and wearing his patchwork gleeman's cloak. His eyes were closed as he played, his mustache drooping long and white on either side of the instrument. It was a haunting tune, "The Marriage of Cinny Wade." Mat had learned it as "Always Choose the Right Horse," and still was not used to it being performed as slowly as Thom did.

A small collection of coins was scattered on the floor in front of Thom. The inn allowed him to play for tips. Mat stopped near the doorway and leaned back to listen. Nobody spoke in the common room, though it was stuffed so full Mat could have made half a company of soldiers just with the men inside. Every eye was on Thom.

Mat had been all around the world now, walking a great deal of it on his own two feet. He had nearly lost his skin in a dozen different cities, and had stayed in inns far and near. He had heard gleemen, performers and bards. Thom made the entire lot seem like children with sticks, banging on pots.

The flute was a simple instrument. A lot of nobles would rather hear the harp instead; one man in Ebou Dar had told

Mat the harp was more "elevated." Mat figured he would
have gone slack-jawed and saucer-eyed if he had heard Thom
play. The gleeman made the flute sound like an extension of
his own soul. Soft trills, minor scales and powerfully bold
long holds. Such a lamenting melody. Who was Thom sor-
rowing for?

The crowd watched. Caemlyn was one of the greatest
cities in the world, but still the variety seemed incredible. Crusty Illianers sat beside smooth Domani, crafty
Cairhienin, stout Tairens and a sprinkling of Borderlanders.
Caemlyn was seen as one of the few places where one could
be safe from both the Seanchan and the Dragon. There was
a bit of food, too.

Thom finished the piece and moved on to another without opening his eyes. Mat sighed, hating to break up Thom's
performance. Unfortunately, it was time to be moving on
back to camp. They had to talk about the *gholam*, and Mat
needed to find a way to get through to Elayne. Maybe Thom
would go talk to her for him.

Mat nodded to the innkeeper—a stately, dark-haired
woman named Bromas. She nodded to Mat, hoop earrings
catching the light. She was a little older than his normal
taste—but then, Tylin had been her age. He would keep her
in mind. For one of his men, of course. Maybe Vanin.

Mat reached the stage, then began to scoop up the coins.
He would let Thom finish and—

Mat's hand jerked. His arm was suddenly pinned by the
cuff to the stage, a knife sticking through the cloth. The
thin length of metal quivered. Mat glanced up to find Thom
still playing, though the gleeman had cracked an eye before
throwing the knife.

Thom raised his hand back up and continued playing,
a smile showing on his puckered lips. Mat grumbled and
yanked his cuff free, waiting as Thom finished this tune,
which was not as doleful as the other. When the lanky gleeman lowered the flute, the room burst into applause.

Mat favored the gleeman with a scowl. "Burn you, Thom.
This is one of my favorite coats!"

"Be glad I did not aim for the hand," Thom noted, wiping
down the flute, nodding to the cheering and applause of the
inn's patrons. They called for him to continue, but he shook
a regretful head and replaced his flute in its case.

"I almost wish you would have," Mat said, raising his cuff and sticking a finger through the holes. "Blood would not have shown that much on the black, but the stitching will be obvious. Just because you wear more patches than cloak doesn't mean I want to imitate you."

"And you complain that you're not a lord," Thom said, leaning down to collect his earnings.

"I'm not!" Mat said. "And never mind what Tuon said, burn you. I'm no bloody nobleman."

"Ever heard of a farmer complaining that his coat stitches would show?"

"You don't have to be a lord to want to dress with some sense," Mat grumbled.

Thom laughed, slapping him on the back and hopping down. "I'm sorry, Mat. I moved by instinct, didn't realize it was you until I saw the face attached to the arm. By then, the knife was already out of my fingers."

Mat sighed. "Thom," he said grimly, "an old friend is in town. One who leaves folks dead with their throats ripped clean out."

Thom nodded, looking troubled. "I heard about it from some Guardsmen during my break. And we're stuck here in the city unless you decide . . ."

"I'm *not* opening the letter," Mat said. "Verin could have left instructions for me to crawl all the way to Falme on my hands, and I'd bloody have to do it! I know you hate the delay, but that letter could make a much worse delay."

Thom nodded reluctantly.

"Let's get back to camp," Mat said.

The Band's camp was a league outside of Caemlyn. Thom and Mat had not ridden in—walkers were less conspicuous, and Mat would not bring horses into the city until he found a stable that he trusted. The price of good horses was getting ridiculous. He had hoped to leave that behind once he left Seanchan lands, but Elayne's armies were buying up every good horse they could find, and most of the not-so-good ones, too. Beyond that, he had heard that horses had a way of disappearing these days. Meat was meat, and people were close to starving, even in Caemlyn. It made Mat's skin crawl, but it was the truth.

He and Thom spent the walk back talking about the *gholam*, deciding very little other than to make everyone alert and have Mat start sleeping in a different tent every night.

Mat glanced over his shoulder as the two of them crested a hilltop. Caemlyn was ablaze with the light of torches and lamps. Illumination hung over the city like a fog, grand spires and towers lit by the glow. The old memories inside him remembered this city—remembered assaulting it before Andor was even a nation. Caemlyn had never made for an easy fight. He did not envy the Houses that had tried to seize it from Elayne.

Thom stepped up beside him. "It seems like forever since we left here last, doesn't it, Mat?"

"Burn me, but it does," Mat said. "What ever convinced us to go hunting those fool girls? Next time, they can save themselves."

Thom eyed him. "Aren't we about to do the same thing? When we go to the Tower of Ghenjei?"

"It's different. We can't leave her with them. Those snakes and foxes—"

"I'm not complaining, Mat," Thom said. "I'm just thoughtful."

Thom seemed thoughtful a lot, lately. Moping around, caressing that worn letter from Moiraine. It was only a letter. "Come on," Mat said, turning back along the road. "You were telling me about getting in to see the Queen?"

Thom joined him on the dark roadway. "I'm not surprised she hasn't replied to you, Mat. She's probably got her hands full. Word is that Trollocs have invaded the Borderlands in force, and Andor is still fractured from the Succession. Elayne—"

"Do you have any good news, Thom?" Mat said. "Tell me some, if you do. I've a mind for it."

"I wish that The Queen's Blessing were still open. Gill always had tidbits to share."

"Good news," Mat prodded again.

"All right. Well, the Tower of Ghenjei is right where Domon said. I have word from three other ship's captains. It's past an open plain several hundred miles northwest of Whitebridge."

Mat nodded, rubbing his chin. He felt like he could remember something of the tower. A silvery structure, unnatural, in the distance. A trip on a boat, water lapping at the sides. Bayle Domon's thick Illianer accent . . .

Those images were vague to Mat; his memories of the time were full of more holes than one of Jori Congar's alibis. Bayle Domon had been able to tell them where to find the tower, but Mat wanted confirmation. The way Domon bowed and scraped for Leilwin made Mat itch. Neither showed Mat much affection, for all the fact that he had saved them. Not that he had wanted any affection from Leilwin. Kissing her would be about as fun as kissing a stoneoak's bark.

"You think Domon's description will be enough for someone to make us one of those gateways there?" Mat asked.

"I don't know," Thom said. "Though that's a secondary problem, I should think. Where are we going to find someone to make a gateway? Verin has vanished."

"I'll find a way."

"If you don't, we'll end up spending *weeks* traveling to the place," Thom said. "I don't like—"

"I'll find us a gateway," Mat said firmly. "Maybe Verin will come back and release me from this bloody oath."

"Best that one stays away," Thom said. "I don't trust her. There's something off about that one."

"She's Aes Sedai," Mat said. "There's something off about them all—like dice where the pips don't add up—but for an Aes Sedai, I kind of like Verin. And I'm a good judge of character, you know that."

Thom raised an eyebrow. Mat scowled back.

"Either way," Thom said, "we should probably start sending guards with you when you visit the city."

"Guards won't help against the *gholam*."

"No, but what of the thugs who jumped you on your way back to camp three nights back?"

Mat shivered. "At least those were just good, honest thieves. They only wanted my purse, nice and natural. Not a one had a picture of me in their pockets. And it's not like they were twisted by the Dark One's power to go crazy at sunset or anything."

"Still," Thom said.

Mat made no argument. Burn him, but he probably *should* be bringing soldiers with him. A few Redarms, anyway.

The camp was just ahead. One of Elayne's clerks, a man

named Norry, had granted the Band permission to camp in Caemlyn's proximity. They had to agree to allow no more than a hundred men to go into the city on a given day, and had to camp at least a league from the walls, out of the way of any villages and not on anyone's farmland.

Talking to that clerk meant Elayne knew Mat was here. She had to. But she had sent no greetings, no acknowledgment that she owed Mat her skin.

At a bend in the road, Thom's lantern showed a group of Redarms lounging by the side. Gufrin, sergeant of a squad, stood and saluted. He was a sturdy, broad-shouldered man. Not terribly bright, but keen eyed.

"Lord Mat!" he said.

"Any news, Gufrin?" Mat asked.

The sergeant frowned to himself. "Well," he said. "I think there's something you might want to know." Light! The man spoke more slowly than a drunk Seanchan. "The Aes Sedai came back to camp today. While you was away, my Lord."

"All three of them?" Mat asked.

"Yes, my Lord."

Mat sighed. If there had been any hope of this day turning out to be anything other than sour, that washed it away. He had hoped they would stay inside the city for a few more days.

He and Thom continued, leaving the road and heading down a path through a field of blackwasp nettles and knifegrass. The weeds crunched as they walked, Thom's lantern lighting the brown stalks. On one hand, it was good to be back in Andor again; it almost felt like home, with those stands of leatherleaf trees and sourgum. However, coming back to find it looking so dead was disheartening.

What to do about Elayne? Women were troublesome. Aes Sedai were worse. Queens were the worst of the lot. And she was all bloody three. How was he going to get her to give him her foundries? He had taken Verin's offer in part because he thought it would get him to Andor quicker, and therefore to start work on Aludra's dragons!

Ahead, the Band's camp sat on a small series of hills, entrenched around the largest of them at the center. Mat's force had met up with Estean and the others that had gone ahead to Andor, and the Band was well and truly whole again. Fires burned; there was no trouble finding dead wood for fires these days. Smoke lingered in the air, and Mat heard men chatting and calling. It was not too late yet, and Mat did not enforce a curfew. If he could not relax, at least his men could. It might be the last chance they got before the Last Battle.

Trollocs in the Borderlands, Mat thought. *We need those dragons. Soon.*

Mat returned salutes from a few guard posts and parted with Thom, meaning to go find a bed and sleep on his problems for the night. As he did, he noted a few changes he could make to the camp. The way the hillsides were arranged, a light cavalry charge could come galloping through the corridor between them. Only someone very bold would try such a tactic, but he had done just that during the Battle of Marisin Valley back in old Coremanda. Well, not Mat *himself*, but someone in those old memories.

More and more, he simply accepted those memories as his own. He had not asked for them—no matter what those bloody foxes claimed—but he *had* paid for them with the scar around his neck. They had been useful on more than one occasion.

He finally reached his tent, intending to get fresh smallclothes before finding a different tent for the night, when he heard a woman's voice calling to him. "Matrim Cauthon!"

Bloody ashes. He had almost made it. He turned reluctantly.

Teslyn Baradon was not a pretty woman, though she might have made a passable paperbark tree, with those bony fingers, those narrow shoulders and that gaunt face. She wore a red dress, and over the weeks her eyes had lost most of the nervous skittishness she had shown since spending time as a *damane*. She had a glare so practiced she could have won a staring contest with a post.

"Matrim Cauthon," she said, stepping up to him. "I do be needing to speak with you."

"Well, seems that you're doing so already," Mat said, dropping his hand from his tent flap. He had a slight fondness for Teslyn, against his better judgment, but he was not about to invite her in. No more than he would invite a fox into his henhouse, regardless of how kindly he thought of the fox in question.

"So I do be," she replied. "You've heard the news of the White Tower?"

"News?" Mat said. "No, I've heard no news. Rumors, though . . . I've a brainful of those. Some say the White Tower has been reunified, which is what you're probably talking about. But I've also heard just as many claiming that it is still at war. And that the Amyrlin fought the Last Battle in Rand's place, and that the Aes Sedai have decided to raise an army of soldiers by giving birth to them, and that flying monsters attacked the White Tower. That last one is probably just stories of *raken* drifting up from the south. But I think the one about Aes Sedai raising an army of babies holds some water."

Teslyn regarded him with a flat stare. He did not look away. Good thing Mat's father had always said he was more stubborn than a flaming tree stump.

Remarkably, Teslyn sighed, her face softening. "You be, of course, rightly skeptical. But we cannot ignore the news. Even Edesina, who foolishly sided with the rebels, does wish to return. We do plan to go in the morning. As it is your habit to sleep late, I wanted to come to you tonight in order to give you my thanks."

"Your *what*?"

"My thanks, Master Cauthon," Teslyn said dryly. "This trip did not be easy upon any of us. There have been moments of . . . tension. I do not say that I agree with each decision you made. That do not remove the fact that without you, I would still be in Seanchan hands." She shivered. "I pretend, during my more confident moments, that I would have resisted them and eventually escaped on my own. It do be important to maintain some illusions with yourself, would you not say?"

Mat rubbed his chin. "Maybe, Teslyn. Maybe indeed."

Remarkably, she held out her hand to him. "Remember, should you ever come to the White Tower, you do have women there who are in your debt, Matrim Cauthon. I do not forget."

He took the hand. It felt as bony as it looked, but it was warmer than he had expected. Some Aes Sedai had ice running in their veins, that was for certain. But others were not so bad.

She nodded to him. A *respectful* nod. Almost a bow. Mat

released her hand, feeling as unsettled as if someone had kicked his legs out from underneath him. She turned to walk back toward her own tent.

"You'll be needing horses," he said. "If you wait to leave until I get up in the morning, I'll give you some. And some provisions. Wouldn't do for you to starve before you get to Tar Valon, and from what we've seen lately, the villages you'll pass won't have anything to spare."

"You told Joline—"

"I counted my horses again," Mat said. Those dice were still rattling in his head, burn them. "I did another count of the Band's horses. Turns out, we have some to spare. You may take them."

"I did not come to you tonight to manipulate you into giving me horses," Teslyn said. "I do be sincere."

"So I figured," Mat said, turning lifting up the flap to his tent. "That's why I made the offer." He stepped into the tent.

There, he froze. That scent . . .

Blood.

CHAPTER
9

Blood in the Air

M at ducked immediately. That instinct saved his life as something swung through the air above his head.

Mat rolled to the side, his hand hitting something wet as it touched the floor. "Murder!" he bellowed. "Murder in the camp! Bloody murder!"

Something moved toward him. The tent was completely black, but he could hear it. Mat stumbled, but luck was with him as again something *swished* near him.

Mat hit the ground and rolled, flinging his hand to the side. He had left . . .

There! He came up beside his sleeping pallet, his hand grasping at the long wooden haft there. He threw himself backward to his feet, hauling the *ashandarei* up, then spun and slashed—not at the form moving through the tent toward him, but at the wall.

The fabric cut easily and Mat leaped out, clutching his long-bladed spear in one hand. With his other hand, he reached for the leather strap at his neck, his fingernails ripping at his skin in his haste. He pulled the foxhead medallion off and turned in the brush outside the tent.

A weak light came from a nearby lantern on a post at an intersection of camp pathways. By it, Mat made out the figure sliding out the rip in the tent. A figure he had feared to see. The *gholam* looked like a man, slender with sandy hair and unremarkable features. The only thing distinct about the thing was the scar on its cheek.

It was supposed to look harmless, supposed to be forgettable. If most people saw this thing in a crowd, they would ignore it. Right up to the point where it ripped their throat out.

Mat backed away. His tent was near a hillside, and he backed up to it, pulling the foxhead medallion up and wrapping it tightly by its leather strap to the side of his *ashandarei*'s blade. It was far from a perfect fit, but he had practiced this. The medallion was the only thing he knew that could hurt the *gholam*. He worked swiftly, still yelling for help. Soldiers would be no use against this thing, but the *gholam* had said before that it had been ordered to avoid too much notice. Attention might frighten it away.

It did hesitate, glancing toward the camp. Then it turned back to Mat, stepping forward. Its movements were as fluid as silk rippling in the wind. "You should be proud," it whispered. "The one who now controls me wants you more than anyone else. I am to ignore all others until I have tasted your blood."

In its left hand, the creature carried a long dagger. Its right hand dripped blood. Mat felt a freezing chill. Who had it killed? Who else had been murdered in Matrim Cauthon's stead? The image of Tylin flashed in his mind again. He had not seen her corpse; the scene was left to his imagination. Unfortunately, Mat had a pretty good imagination.

That image in his head, smelling the blood on the air, he did the most foolish thing he could have. He attacked.

Screaming in the open darkness, Mat spun forward, swinging the *ashandarei*. The creature was so fast. It seemed to *flow* out of the way of his weapon.

It rounded him, like a circling wolf, footsteps barely making a sound in the dried weeds. It struck, its form a blur, and only a backward jump by reflex saved Mat. He scrambled through the weeds, swinging the *ashandarei*. It seemed wary of the medallion. Light, without that, Mat would be dead and bleeding on the ground!

It came at him again, like liquid darkness. Mat swung wildly and clipped the *gholam* more by luck than anything else. The medallion made a searing hiss as it touched the beast's hand. The scent of burned flesh rose in the air, and the *gholam* scrambled back.

"You didn't have to kill her, burn you," Mat yelled at it. "You could have left her! You didn't want her; you wanted me!"

The thing merely grinned, its mouth an awful black, teeth twisted. "A bird must fly. A man must breathe. I must kill." It stalked forward, and Mat knew he was in trouble. The cries of alarm were loud now. It had only been a few moments, but a few more, and help would arrive. Only a few more moments . . .

"I've been told to kill them all," the *gholam* said softly. "To bring you out. The man with the mustache, the aged one who interfered last time, the little dark-skinned woman who holds your affection. All of them, unless I take you now."

Burn that *gholam*; how did the thing know about *Tuon*? How? It was impossible!

He was so startled that he barely had time to raise the *ashandarei* as the *gholam* leaped for him. Mat cursed, twisting to the side, but too late. The creature's knife flashed in the air. Then the weapon jerked and ripped sideways from its fingers. Mat started, then felt something wrap around him and jerk *him* backward, out of the reach of the *gholam*'s swipe.

Weaves of Air. Teslyn! She stood in front of his tent, her face a mask of concentration.

"You won't be able to touch it directly with weaves!" Mat screamed as her Air deposited him a short distance from the *gholam*. If she had been able to bloody raise him up high enough, he would have been fine with that! But he had never seen an Aes Sedai lift someone more than a pace or so in the air.

He scrambled to the side, the *gholam* charging after him. Then something large flew between them, causing the *gholam* to dodge fluidly. The object—a chair!—crashed into the hillside beside them. The *gholam* spun as a large bench smashed into it, throwing it backward.

Mat steadied himself, looking at Teslyn, who was reaching into his tent with invisible weaves of Air. *Clever woman,* he thought. Weaves could not touch the *gholam*, but something thrown by them could.

That would not stop it. Mat had seen the creature pluck out a knife that had been rammed into its chest; it had shown the indifference a man would show at plucking a burr from his clothing. But now soldiers were leaping over pathways, carrying pikes or swords and shields. The entire camp was being lit up.

The *gholam* gave Mat a glare, then dashed off toward the darkness outside of camp. Mat spun, then froze as he saw two Redarms set pikes against the oncoming *gholam*. Gorderan and Fergin. Both men who had survived the time in Ebou Dar.

"No!" Mat yelled. "Let it—"

Too late. The *gholam* indifferently slid between the pikes, grabbing each man's throat in a hand, then crushing its fingers together. With a spin, it ripped free their flesh, dropping both men. Then it was off into the darkness.

Burn you! Mat thought, starting to dash after it. *I'll gut you and—*

He froze. Blood in the air. From inside his tent. He had nearly forgotten that.

Olver! Mat scrambled back to the tent. It was dark within, though the scent of blood once again assaulted him. "Light! Teslyn, can you—"

A globe of light appeared behind him.

The light of her globe was enough to illuminate a terrible scene inside. Lopin, Mat's serving man, lay dead, his blood darkening the tent floor in a large black pool. Two other men—Riddem and Will Reeve, Redarms who had been guarding his door—were heaped onto his sleeping pallet. He should have noticed that they were missing from their post. Fool!

Mat felt a stab of sorrow for the dead. Lopin, who had only recently shown that he was recovered from Nalesean's death. Light burn him, he had been a good man! Not even a soldier, just a serving man, content to have someone to take care of. Mat now felt terrible for having complained about him. Without Lopin's help, Mat would not have been able to escape Ebou Dar.

And the four Redarms, two of whom had survived Ebou Dar and the *gholam*'s previous attack.

I should have sent word, Mat thought. *Should have put the entire camp on alert.* Would that have done any good? The *gholam* had proven itself practically unstoppable. Mat had the suspicion that it could cut down the entire Band in getting to him, if it needed to. Only its master's command that it avoid attention prevented it from doing so.

He did not see any sign of Olver, though the boy should have been sleeping on his pallet in the corner. Lopin's blood had pooled nearby, and Olver's blanket was soaking it up from the bottom. Mat took a deep breath and began searching through the shambles, overturning blankets and looking behind travel furniture, worried at what he might find.

More soldiers arrived, cursing. The camp was coming alert: horns of warning blowing, lanterns being lit, armor clanking.

"Olver," Mat said to the soldiers gathering at his doorway. He had searched the entire bloody tent! "Has anyone seen him?"

"I think he was with Noal," said Slone Maddow, a wide-eared Redarm. "They—"

Mat shoved his way out of the tent, then ran through camp toward Noal's tent. He arrived just as the white-haired man was stepping out, looking about in alarm.

"Olver?" Mat asked, reaching the older man.

"He's safe, Mat," Noal said, grimacing. "I'm sorry—I didn't mean to alarm you. We were playing Snakes and Foxes, and the boy fell asleep on my floor. I pulled a blanket over him; he's been staying up so late waiting for you these nights that I figured it was best not to wake him. I should have sent word."

"You're *sorry*?" Mat said, grabbing Noal in an embrace. "You bloody wonderful man. You saved his life!"

An hour later, Mat sat with Thom and Noal inside Thom's small tent. A dozen Redarms guarded the place, and Olver had been sent to sleep in Teslyn's tent. The boy did not know how close he had come to being killed. Hopefully he never would.

Mat wore his medallion again, though he needed to find a new leather strap. The *ashandarei* had cut the other one up pretty bad. He would need to find a better way to tie it on there.

"Thom," Mat said softly, "the creature threatened you, and you too, Noal. It didn't mention Olver, but it *did* mention Tuon."

"How would the thing know about her?" Thom asked, scratching at his head.

"The guards found another corpse outside of the camp. Derry." Derry was a soldier who had gone missing a few days back, and Mat had presumed him to have deserted. It happened sometimes, though desertion was irregular in the Band. "He'd been dead a few days."

"It took him that long ago?" Noal said, frowning. Noal's shoulders were stooped and he had a nose the shape of a large, bent pepper growing right out the middle of his face. He had always looked . . . worn to Mat. His hands were so gnarled, they seemed to be all knuckles.

"It must have interrogated him," Mat said. "Found out people I spent time with, where my tent was."

"Is the thing capable of that?" Thom said. "It seemed more like a hound to me, hunting you out."

"It knew where to find me in Tylin's palace," Mat said. "Even after I was gone, it went to her rooms. So either it asked someone, or it was observing. We'll never know if Derry was tortured, or if he just ran across the *gholam* while it was sneaking about the camp and spying. But the thing is clever."

It wouldn't actually go after Tuon, would it? Threatening his friends was probably just a way to unhinge Mat. After all, the thing had shown tonight that it still had orders to avoid too much attention. That didn't console Mat much. If that monster hurt Tuon . . .

There was only one way to make sure that didn't happen.

"So what do we do?" Noal asked.

"We're going to hunt it," Mat said softly, "and we're going to kill the bloody thing."

Noal and Thom fell silent.

"I won't have this thing chasing us all the way to the Tower of Ghenjei," Mat said.

"But *can* it be killed, Mat?" Thom asked.

"Anything can be killed," Mat said. "Teslyn proved that she could still hurt it using the One Power, if she was clever. We'll have to do something similar."

"What?" Noal asked.

"I don't know yet," Mat said. "I want you two to continue your preparations; get us ready so that we can leave for the Tower of Ghenjei as soon as my oath to Verin will let us. Burn me, I *still* need to talk to Elayne. I want Aludra's dragons started. I'll have to write her another letter. Stronger, this time.

"For now, we're going to make some changes. I'm going to start sleeping in the city. A different inn each night. We'll let the Band know it, so if the *gholam* listens, it will find out. There will be no need for it to attack the men.

"You two will need to move to the city too. Until this is done, until it is dead or I am. The question is what to do about Olver. The thing didn't mention him, but . . ."

He saw understanding in Thom's and Noal's eyes. Mat had left Tylin behind, and she was dead now. He was not going to do the same to Olver.

"We'll have to take the boy with us," Thom said. "Either that or send him away."

"I heard the Aes Sedai talking earlier," Noal said, rubbing his face with a bony finger. "They're planning to leave. Maybe send him with them?"

Mat grimaced. The way Olver leered at women, the Aes Sedai would have him strung up by his toes in a day flat. Mat was surprised it had not happened already. If he ever found out which of the Redarms was teaching the boy to act that way around women . . .

"I doubt we'd be able to get him to go," Mat said. "He'd be out of their sight and back here their first night away."

Thom nodded in agreement.

"We'll have to take him with us," Mat said. "Have him stay at the inns inside the city. Maybe that—"

"Matrim Cauthon!" The shrill call came from outside Thom's tent.

Mat sighed, then nodded to the other two and stood up. He stepped out of the tent to find that Joline and her Warders had bullied their way through the Redarms and had nearly yanked open the tent flaps to come stalking in. His appearance drew her up short.

Several of the Redarms looked abashed at having let her through, but the men could not be blamed. Bloody Aes Sedai would bloody do what they bloody pleased.

The woman herself was everything that Teslyn was not. Slender and pretty, she wore a white dress with a deep neckline. She often smiled, though that smile became thin-lipped when she turned it on Mat, and she had large brown eyes. The type of eyes that could suck a man in and try to drown him.

Pretty as she was, Mat did not think of her as a match for one of his friends. He would never wish Joline upon someone he liked. In fact, he was too gentlemanly to wish her on most of his enemies. Best she stayed with Fen and Blaeric, her Warders, who were madmen in Mat's opinion.

Both were Borderlanders—one Shienaran, the other Saldaean. Fen's tilted eyes were hard. He always seemed to be looking for someone to murder; each conversation with him was an interview to see if you fit the criteria. Blaeric's topknot was growing in, and getting longer, but it was still too short. Mat would have mentioned that it looked remarkably like a badger's tail glued to his head, except that he did not feel like being murdered today. It had already been a bloody awful evening.

Joline folded her arms beneath her breasts. "It appears that your reports of this . . . creature that is chasing you were accurate." She sounded skeptical. He had lost five good men, and she sounded skeptical. Bloody Aes Sedai.

"And?" he asked. "You know something about *gholam*?"

"Not a thing," she said. "Regardless, I need to return to the White Tower. I will be leaving tomorrow." She looked hesitant. "I would like to ask if you would lend me some horses for the trip. Whatever you can spare. I will not be picky."

"Nobody in town would sell you any, eh?" Mat said with a grunt.

Her face became even more serene.

"Well, all right," Mat said. "At least you asked nicely this time, though I can see how hard it was for you. I've promised some to Teslyn already. You can have some too. It will be worth it to have you bloody women out of my hair."

"Thank you," she said, her voice controlled. "However, a word of advice. Considering the company you often keep, you might want to learn to control your language."

"Considering the company I keep all too often," Mat said, "it's bloody amazing I don't swear more. Off with you, Joline. I need to write a letter to Her Royal bloody Majesty Queen Elayne the prim."

Joline sniffed. "Are you going to swear at her too?"

"Of course I am," Mat muttered, turning to go back to Thom's tent. "How else is she going to trust that it's really from me?"

CHAPTER
10

After the Taint

I agree with those counts," Elyas said, walking at Perrin's side. Grady walked on the other side, thoughtful in his black coat. Montem al'San and Azi al'Thone—Perrin's two guards for the day—trailed behind.

It was still early in the morning. Perrin was ostensibly checking on guard posts, but he really just wanted to be walking. They'd moved the camp to an elevated meadow along the Jehannah Road. It had a good water supply and was near enough to the road to control it, but far enough back to be defensible.

On one side of the meadow, an ancient statue lay before a patch of trees. The statue had fallen on its side long ago, and most of it was now buried, but an arm rose from the earth, holding the hilt of a sword. The blade was thrust into the ground.

"I shouldn't have sent Gill and the others ahead," Perrin said. "That let them be snatched up by the first passing force."

"You couldn't have anticipated this," Elyas said. "Nor could you have anticipated being delayed. Where would you have left them? Shaido were coming up behind, and if our battle at Malden *hadn't* gone well, Gill and the others would have been trapped between two groups of enemy Aiel."

Perrin growled to himself. His booted feet stuck a little in the sodden ground. He hated the scent of that trampled, stagnant mud mixed with rotting dead plants. It wasn't nearly as bad as the Blight disease, but it seemed to him the whole land was only a few steps away from that.

They approached a guard post. Two men—Hu Barran and Darl Coplin—stood watch here. There would be additional scouts, of course: Two Rivers men in trees, Maidens patrolling the ground. But Perrin had learned that a few men given posts around the camp lent everyone inside a sense of order.

The guards saluted him, though Darl's salute was sloppy. They gave off an odd mixture of scents—regret, frustration, disappointment. And embarrassment. That last one was faint, but still there. Perrin's supposed dalliance with Berelain was still recent in their minds, and Faile's return seemed to increase their discomfort. In the Two Rivers, one did not easily live down a reputation for infidelity.

Perrin nodded to them, then continued on. He didn't do much formal inspecting. If the men knew he would walk by sometime each day, they'd keep themselves in order. For the most part. Last night, he had needed to prod sleeping Berin Thane awake with his boot, and he was always careful to watch for the scent of strong drink among them. He wouldn't put it past Jori Congar to sneak a nip or two while on guard.

"All right," Perrin said. "The Whitecloaks have our people and our supplies." He grimaced, thinking of the grain purchased in So Habor going to fill Whitecloak bellies. "Could we sneak in and free them?"

"I don't see the need for sneaking," Grady said from behind. "Pardon, my Lord, but you seem to be making this a larger problem than it is."

Perrin looked back at the leathery man. "They're Whitecloaks, Grady. They're always a large problem."

"They won't have anyone who can channel the One Power." Grady shrugged, hands clasped behind his back as he walked. With the black coat, the pin and the increasingly soldierlike attitude, he was looking less and less like a farmer. "Neald is feeling better. He and I could pound those Children down until they give us what we want."

Perrin nodded. He hated the idea of letting the Asha'man loose with impunity. The scent of burned flesh in the air, the earth ripped apart and broken. The scents of Dumai's Wells. However, he couldn't afford another distraction like Malden. If there were no other choice, he'd give the order.

Not yet, though. *There are no coincidences with* ta'veren.

The wolves, the Whitecloaks. Things he had been outrunning for some time were returning to hunt him. He'd pushed the Children out of the Two Rivers. Many of the men who had been with him then now followed him here.

"Perhaps it will come to that," Perrin said to Grady, still walking. "But maybe not. We've got a larger force than they do, and with that blasted wolfhead banner finally taken down, they may not realize who we are. We fly the banner of the Queen of Ghealdan, and they're passing through Alliandre's territory. Likely they saw the supplies in our people's carts and decided to 'protect them.' Some discussion, perhaps a little intimidation, may be enough to persuade them to return our people."

Elyas nodded, and Grady seemed to agree, though Perrin wasn't convinced by his own words. The Whitecloaks had haunted him since his early days out of the Two Rivers. Dealing with them had never been simple.

It felt like the time had come. Time to make an end to his troubles with them, one way or another.

He continued his rounds, arriving at the Aiel section of the camp. He nodded at a pair of Maidens lounging on guard with relaxed alertness. They didn't stand up or salute—which suited him fine—though they did nod. He'd apparently gained great *ji* in their eyes by the way he'd planned, then accomplished, the attack on the Shaido.

The Aiel maintained their own guard posts, and he had no reason to inspect them. But he included them in his rounds anyway. It seemed that if he was going to visit the other sections of camp, he should do it here, too.

Grady stopped suddenly and spun toward the Wise Ones' tents.

"What?" Perrin asked urgently, scanning the camp. He couldn't see anything unusual.

Grady smiled. "I think they've managed it." He started into the Aiel camp, ignoring the glares several Maidens gave him. They might very well have tossed him out, Asha'man or no, if Perrin hadn't been there.

Neald, Perrin thought. *He's been working with the Aes Sedai to figure out circles.* If Grady had seen something in the weaves . . .

Perrin followed, and soon they reached a ring of Wise One tents in the center of the Aiel camp, the area between them dried—perhaps by weaves—and the ground packed down. Neald, Edarra and Masuri sat there. Fager Neald was a young Murandian with a mustache that curled to points. He wore no pins on the collar of his black coat, though he'd likely be promoted as soon as the group returned from their excursion. He'd grown in Power since they'd begun.

He was still pale from the snakebites he'd taken, but looked much better than he had only a few days back. He was smiling, staring at the air in front of him, and he smelled exuberant.

A large gateway split the air. Perrin grunted. It appeared to lead back to a place where they'd camped several weeks ago—an open field of no real note.

"It's working?" Grady said, kneeling down beside Neald.

"It's beautiful, Jur," Neald said softly. His voice bore no hint of the bravado he often displayed. "I can *feel saidar*. It's like I'm more complete now."

"You're channeling it?" Perrin asked.

"No. I don't need to. I can *use* it."

"Use it how?" Grady asked, eager.

"I . . . It's hard to explain. The weaves are *saidin*, but I seem to be able to strengthen them with *saidar*. So long as I can make a gateway on my own, it appears that I can increase the Power—and size—with what the women lend me. Light! It's wonderful. We should have done this *months* ago."

Perrin glanced at the two women, Masuri and Edarra. Neither seemed as exultant as Neald. Masuri looked a little sick, and she smelled of fear. Edarra smelled curious and wary. Grady had mentioned that creating a circle this way seemed to require the men to gain control over the women.

"We'll send the scouting group through to Cairhien soon, then," Perrin said, fingering the blacksmith's puzzle in his pocket. "Grady, arrange with the Aiel about that mission, set up the gateways as they ask."

"Yes, my Lord," Grady said, rubbing his leathery face. "I should probably learn this technique rather than continuing on rounds. Though there's something I'll be wanting to talk to you about first. If you've the time."

"If you wish," Perrin said, stepping away from the group. To the side, several of the other Wise Ones came forward and told Neald it was their turn to try the circle with him.

They didn't act at all as if Neald were in charge, and he was quick to obey. He'd been walking lightly around the Aiel since he'd said something a little too frisky to a Maiden and ended up playing Maiden's Kiss.

"What is this about, Grady?" Perrin asked once they were a little way off.

"Well, Neald and I are both well enough to make gateways, it seems," Grady said. "I was wondering if I might . . ." He seemed hesitant. "Well, if I might have leave to slip over to the Black Tower for an afternoon, to see my family."

That's right, Perrin thought. *He's got a wife and a son.* The Asha'man didn't often talk about them. Actually, he didn't often talk about much.

"I don't know, Grady," Perrin said, glancing up at the darkly clouded sky. "We have Whitecloaks ahead, and there's still no telling for sure if those Shaido will loop around and try to ambush us. I'm loath to be without you until I know we're someplace safe."

"It needn't be for long, my Lord," Grady said earnestly. Perrin sometimes forgot how young the man was, only six or seven years older than himself. Grady seemed so much older in that black coat, with his sun-darkened face.

"We'll find a time," Perrin said. "Soon. I don't want to upset anything until we have word of what's been happening since we left." Information could be potent. Balwer had taught him that.

Grady nodded, looking placated, though Perrin hadn't given him anything definite. Light! Even the Asha'man were starting to smell like people who saw him as their lord. They'd been so aloof when this all began.

"You never worried about this before, Grady," Perrin said. "Has something changed?"

"Everything," Grady said softly. Perrin got a whiff of his scent. Hopeful. "It changed a few weeks back. I know that people don't believe it, but I swear to you that it did happen."

"The taint was cleansed?" Perrin asked.

Grady nodded.

The Asha'man insisted that the male half of the Source had been cleaned, though others were skeptical. Perrin believed them. As impossible as it seemed, Grady didn't smell mad when he spoke of this event. Besides, it seemed the sort of thing Rand might have been about. The colors swirled in front of him. He banished them.

"You said it happened, and I trust you, Grady. But what does this have to do with the Black Tower and your family? You want to go see if other Asha'man agree?"

"Oh, they'll agree," Grady said. "It's . . . well, my Lord, I'm a simple man. Sora, she's always been the thinker. I do what needs doing, and that's that. Well, joining the Black Tower, that was something that needed doing. I knew what was going to happen when I was tested. I knew it was in me. It was in my father, you see. We don't talk about it, but it was there. Reds found him young, right after I was born.

"When I joined the Lord Dragon, I knew what would happen to me. A few more years and I'd be gone. Might as well spend them fighting. The Lord Dragon told me I was a soldier, and a soldier can't leave his duty. So I haven't asked to go back before now. You needed me."

"That's changed?"

"My Lord, the taint is *gone*. I'm not going to go mad. That means . . . well, I always had a reason to fight. But now I've got a reason to *live*, too."

Looking into the man's eyes, Perrin understood. What must it have been like? Knowing that you'd eventually go mad and need to be executed. Likely by your friends, who would call it a mercy.

That was what Perrin had sensed in the Asha'man all along, the reason they held themselves apart, often seeming so somber. Everyone else fought for life. The Asha'man . . . they'd fought to die.

That's how Rand feels, Perrin thought, watching the colors swirl again and his friend appear. He was riding his large black horse through a city with muddy streets, speaking with Nynaeve, who rode beside him.

Perrin shook his head and banished the image. "We'll get you home, Grady," he promised. "You'll have some time with her before the end comes."

Grady nodded, glancing at the sky as a low rumble of thunder came from the north. "I just want to talk to her, you know? And I need to see little Gadren again. I won't recognize the lad."

"I'm sure he's a handsome child, Grady."

Grady laughed. It felt odd, but good, to hear that from the man. "Handsome? Gadren? No, my Lord, he might be big for his age, but he's about as pretty as a stump. Still, I love him something fierce." He shook his head, amused. "But I should be off learning this trick with Neald. Thank you, my Lord."

Perrin smiled, watching him go as a Maiden came hurrying into camp. She reported to the Wise Ones, but spoke loud enough to let Perrin hear. "There is a stranger riding along the road toward camp. He flies a flag of peace, but he wears the clothing of these Children of the Light."

Perrin nodded, gathering his guards. As he hastened toward the front of the camp, Tam appeared and fell in beside him. They arrived just as the Whitecloak approached the first guard posts. The man rode a brilliant white gelding, and he carried a long pole with a white banner. His white clothing—mail with a tabard under the cloak—bore a yellow sunburst on the breast.

Perrin felt a sharp sinking feeling. He recognized this man. Dain Bornhald.

"I come to speak with the criminal Perrin Aybara," Bornhald announced in a loud voice, pulling to a stop.

"I'm here, Bornhald," Perrin called, stepping out.

Bornhald looked at him. "It *is* you. The Light has delivered you to us."

"Unless it has also delivered you an army three or four times the size of the one you have now," Perrin called, "then I doubt very much that it will matter."

"We have in our possession people who claim fealty to you, Aybara."

"Well, you can let them ride on back to our camp, and we'll be on our way."

The young Whitecloak turned his mount to the side, scowling. "We have unfinished business, Darkfriend."

"No need for this to turn nasty, Bornhald," Perrin said. "The way I see it, we can still each go our own way."

"The Children would rather die than leave justice undone," Dain said, then spat to the side. "But I will leave that for the Lord Captain Commander to explain. He wishes to see you for himself. I have been ordered to come and tell you that he is waiting beside the road a short ride ahead. He would like you to meet with him."

"You think I'm going to walk into such an obvious trap?" Perrin asked.

Bornhald shrugged. "Come or do not. My Lord Captain Commander is a man of honor, and swears by oath you will return safely—which is more than I'd have given a Dark-friend. You may bring your Aes Sedai, if you have them, for safety." With that, Bornhald turned his mount and galloped away.

Perrin stood thoughtfully, watching him retreat.

"You're not really thinking of going, are you, son?" Tam asked.

"I'd rather know for certain who I'm facing," Perrin said. "And we did ask for parley. Maybe bargain for our people back. Burn me, Tam. I have to at least *try* before attacking them."

Tam sighed, but nodded.

"He mentioned Aes Sedai," Perrin said, "but not Asha'man. I'll bet he doesn't know much about them. Go have Grady dress like a Two Rivers man and tell him to report to me, along with Gaul and Sulin. Ask Edarra if she'll join us too. But *don't* tell my wife about this. We six will go on ahead and see if the Whitecloaks will really meet with us peace-fully. If something goes wrong, we'll have Grady ready to get us out by gateway."

Tam nodded and hurried away. Perrin waited nervously until Tam returned with Gaul, Sulin and Edarra. Grady came a few minutes later, wearing a brown wool cloak and brown and green clothing borrowed from one of the Two Rivers men. He carried a longbow, but walked like a soldier, with his back straight, his eyes keen as he looked about him. There was a particular air of danger to him that no common villager would bear. Hopefully, it wouldn't spoil the disguise.

The six of them broke away from camp, and blessedly, Faile didn't seem to have heard what was happening. Perrin would bring her if there was a longer parley or discussion, but he intended this trip to be quick, and he needed to be able to move without worrying about her.

They went on foot, and found the Whitecloaks a short distance ahead down the road. There looked to be only about a dozen of them, standing near a small tent that had been set up beside the road. They were upwind, which relaxed Perrin a little. He caught scents of anger and disgust, but it didn't *feel* like a trap to him.

As he and the others neared, someone stepped from the small tent, wearing white. The tall man had fine features and short, dark hair. Most women would probably call him handsome. He smelled . . . better than the other Whitecloaks. They had a wild scent to them, like that of a rabid animal. This leader of theirs smelled calm, and not sickly at all.

Perrin glanced toward his companions.

"I do not like this, Perrin Aybara," Edarra said, looking from side to side. "These Children have a sense of wrongness about them."

"Archers could hit us from those trees," Tam said with a grunt, nodding to a stand in the distance.

"Grady, you're holding the Power?" Perrin asked.

"Of course."

"Be ready, just in case," Perrin said, then stepped forward toward the small group of Whitecloaks. Their leader studied Perrin with hands clasped behind his back. "Golden eyes," the man said. "So it is true."

"You're the Lord Captain Commander?" Perrin asked.

"I am."

"What will it take for you to release the people of mine you're holding?"

"My men tell me they tried such an exchange once," the Whitecloak leader said. "And that you deceived them and betrayed them."

"They had kidnapped innocents," Perrin said. "And demanded my life in return. Well, I took my people back. Don't force me to do the same thing here."

The Whitecloak leader narrowed his eyes. He smelled thoughtful. "I will do what is right, Goldeneyes. The cost is irrelevant. My men tell me you murdered several Children a few years back, and have never known justice for it. That you lead Trollocs to attack villages."

"Your men are not very reliable," Perrin said with a growl. "I want a more formal parley, where we can sit down and discuss. Not something improvised like this."

"I doubt that will be needed," the Whitecloak leader said.

"I am not here to bargain. I merely wanted to see you for myself. You wish your people freed? Meet my army on the field of battle. Do this, and I will release the captives, regardless of the outcome. They are obviously not soldiers. I will let them go."

"And if I refuse?" Perrin asked.

"Then it will not bode . . . well for their health."

Perrin ground his teeth.

"Your force will face ours under the Light," the White-cloak leader said. "Those are our terms."

Perrin glanced to the side. Grady met his eyes, and there was an obvious question in them. He could take the White-cloak leader captive right here, with barely a thought.

Perrin was tempted. But they had come under the White-cloak's oath of safety. He would not break the peace. Instead, he turned, and led his people back toward his camp.

Galad watched Aybara withdraw. Those golden eyes were unsettling. He had discounted Byar's insistence that this man was not merely a Darkfriend, but Shadowspawn. However, looking into those eyes, Galad was no longer certain he could dismiss those claims.

To the side, Bornhald let out a breath. "I can't believe you wanted to do this. What if he *had* brought Aes Sedai? We couldn't have stopped the One Power."

"They would not have harmed me," Galad said. "And besides, if Aybara had the ability to assassinate me here with the One Power, he could have done the same to me in my camp. But if he is as you and Child Byar say, then he worries greatly about his image. He didn't lead Trollocs against the Two Rivers directly. He pretended to defend them." Such a man would act with subtlety. Galad had been safe.

He'd wanted to see Aybara himself, and he was glad he had. Those eyes . . . they were almost a condemnation by themselves. And Aybara had reacted to the mention of the murdered Whitecloaks, stiffening. Beyond that, there was the talk his people gave of him in alliance with the Seanchan and having with him men who could channel.

Yes, this Aybara was a dangerous man. Galad had been worried about committing his forces to fighting here, but the Light would see them through it. Better to defeat this

Aybara now, than to wait and face him at the Last Battle. As quickly as that, he made his decision. The right decision. They would fight.

"Come," Galad said, waving to his men. "Let's get back to camp."

CHAPTER
II

An Unexpected Letter

They can't possibly think I'll sign this," Elayne said, tossing the sheaf of papers onto the floor beside her chair.

"It's unlikely that they do," Dyelin said. Her golden hair was pristine, her firm face controlled, her slim body poised. The woman was perfect! It was *unfair* that she should look so pristine while Elayne felt like a sow, fattened up and ripe for the slaughter.

The hearth in Elayne's sitting room crackled warmly. Wine sat in a pitcher on one of the wall's sideboards, but of course she wasn't allowed any of *that*. If one more person tried to offer her bloody goat's milk . . .

Birgitte lounged near the far wall, golden braid hanging over her right shoulder, contrasting with her white-collared red coat and sky-blue trousers. She'd poured herself a cup of tea, and smiled over it, amused by Elayne's annoyance. Elayne could *feel* the emotion through the bond!

They were the only ones in the room. Elayne had retired to the sitting room after accepting the proposal from Ellorien's messenger, explaining that she would like to "consider" the offer in private. Well, she'd consider it! Consider it trash, for that was all it was!

"This is an insult," she said, sweeping her hand toward the pages.

"Do you intend to keep them imprisoned forever, Elayne?" Dyelin asked, raising an eyebrow. "They can't afford to pay a ransom, not after what they spent funding their Succession bid. That leaves you with a decision."

"They can rot," Elayne said, folding her arms. "They raised armies against me and besieged Caemlyn!"

"Yes," Dyelin said flatly. "I believe I was there."

Elayne cursed softly to herself, then stood up and began to pace. Birgitte eyed her; they both knew that Melfane had suggested that Elayne avoid taxing herself. Elayne met the Warder's eyes stubbornly, then continued her pacing. Burn her, and burn that *bloody* midwife! Walking wasn't taxing.

Ellorien was one of the last vocal holdouts to Elayne's rule, and was the most problematic—save, perhaps, for Jarid Sarand. These months marked the beginning of a long period of testing for Elayne. How would she stand on certain issues? How easily would she be pushed? How much did she take after her mother?

They should know that she wouldn't be easily intimidated. But the unfortunate truth was that she stood atop a precarious perch made of teacups, stacked high. Each of those cups was an Andoran House; some had supported her willingly, others grudgingly. Very few of them were as sturdy as she would have liked.

"The captive nobles are a resource," Elayne said. "They should be viewed as such."

Dyelin nodded. The noblewoman had a way of goading Elayne, forcing her to stretch for the answers they both knew she needed to find. "A resource is meaningless unless eventually expended," Dyelin noted. She held a cup of wine. Blasted woman.

"Yes," Elayne said, "but to sell a resource short would be to establish a reputation for carelessness."

"Unless you sell something just before its value plummets," Dyelin said. "Many a merchant has been called foolish for trading ice peppers at a discount, only to be called wise when prices fall even further."

"And these captives? You see their value falling soon?"

"Their Houses have been compromised," Dyelin said. "The stronger your position becomes, Elayne, the less valuable these political captives grow. You shouldn't squander the advantage, but neither should you lock it away until nobody cares anymore."

"You could execute them," Birgitte said.

They both stared at her.

"What?" Birgitte said. "It's what they deserve, and it would establish a hardfisted reputation."

"It's not right," Elayne said. "They should not be killed for supporting someone else for the throne. There can be no treason where there is no Queen."

"So our soldiers can die, but the nobles bloody walk away?" Birgitte asked. Then she raised a hand before Elayne could protest. "Spare the lecture, Elayne. I understand. I don't agree, but I understand. It's always been this way."

Elayne returned to her pacing. She did stop, however, to stomp on Ellorien's proposal as she passed it. That earned her an eye roll from Birgitte, but it felt good. The "proposal" was a list of empty promises that concluded with a demand that Elayne release the captives for "the good of Andor." Ellorien claimed that since the captives had no funds, the crown should pardon them and release them to help rebuild.

Truth be told, Elayne had been considering doing so. But *now* if she released them, the three would see Ellorien as their savior! Any gratitude that Elayne could have gained would instead be given to her rival. Blood and bloody ashes!

"The Windfinders are beginning to ask after the land you promised them," Dyelin noted.

"Already?"

The older woman nodded. "The request still troubles me. Why do they want a sliver of land like that?"

"They earned it," Elayne said.

"Perhaps. Though this does mean that you're the first Queen in five generations to cede a portion of Andor—no matter how small—to a foreign entity."

Elayne took a deep breath, and oddly found herself calmer. Blasted mood swings! Hadn't Melfane promised those would grow less pronounced as the pregnancy progressed? Yet at times she still felt her emotions bouncing around like a ball in a children's game.

Elayne composed herself and sat. "I cannot allow this. The Houses are all looking for opportunities to shoulder their way into power."

"You would be doing the same in their place, I warrant," Dyelin said.

"Not if I knew that the Last Battle was approaching," Elayne snapped. "We need to do something to direct the nobles toward more important matters. Something to unify them behind me, or at least convince them that I'm not to be toyed with."

"And you have a means of achieving this?" Dyelin asked.

"Yes," Elayne said, glancing eastward. "It's time to seize Cairhien."

Birgitte choked quietly on her tea. Dyelin merely raised an eyebrow. "A bold move."

"Bold?" Birgitte asked, wiping her chin. "It's bloody insane. Elayne, you barely have your fingers on Andor."

"That makes the timing even better," Elayne said. "We have momentum. Besides, if we move for Cairhien now, it will show that I mean to be more than a simpering puff of a queen."

"I doubt anyone expects that of you," Birgitte said. "If they do, they probably took one too many knocks to the head during the fighting."

"She's right, however uncouth the presentation," Dyelin agreed. She glanced at Birgitte, and Elayne could feel a stab of dislike through Birgitte's bond. Light! What would it take to make the two of them get along? "Nobody doubts your strength as a queen, Elayne. That won't stop the others from seizing what power they can; they know they're unlikely to be able to get it later."

"I don't have fifteen years to stabilize my rule, like Mother," Elayne said. "Look, we all know what Rand kept saying about me taking the Sun Throne. A steward rules there now, waiting for me, and after what happened to Colavaere, nobody dares disobey Rand's edicts."

"By taking that throne," Dyelin said, "you risk looking as if you're letting al'Thor hand it to you."

"So?" Elayne said. "I had to take Andor on my own, but there is nothing wrong with me accepting his gift of Cairhien. His Aiel were the ones to liberate it. We'd be doing the Cairhienin a favor by preventing a messy Succession. My claim to the throne is strong, at least as strong as anyone else's, and those loyal to Rand will fall behind me."

"And do you not risk overextending yourself?"

"Possibly," Elayne said, "but I think it's worth the risk. In one step I could become one of the most powerful monarchs since Artur Hawkwing."

Further argument was cut off by a polite knock at the

door. Elayne glanced at Dyelin, and the woman's thoughtful expression meant she was considering what Elayne had said. Well, Elayne *would* strike for the Sun Throne, with or without Dyelin's approval. The woman was becoming increasingly useful to Elayne as an advisor—Light be praised that Dyelin hadn't wanted the throne herself!—but a queen could not let herself fall into the trap of relying on any one person *too* much.

Birgitte answered the door, letting in the storklike Master Norry. He was dressed in red and white, his long face characteristically somber. He carried his leather folder under one arm, and Elayne suppressed a groan. "I thought we were finished for the day."

"I thought so as well, Your Majesty," he said. "But several new matters have arisen. I thought that they might be . . . um . . . interesting to you."

"What do you mean?"

"Well, Your Majesty," Norry said, "you know that I am not . . . particularly fond of certain types of work. But in light of recent additions to my staff, I have seen reason to expand my attentions."

"You're talking about Hark, aren't you?" Birgitte said. "How's the worthless piece of grime doing?"

Norry glanced at her. "He is . . . er . . . grimy, I should say." He looked back at Elayne. "But he is rather adept, once given proper motivation. Please forgive me if I have taken liberties, but after the encounters recently—and the guests to your dungeons they provided—I thought it wise."

"What are you talking about, Master Norry?" Elayne asked.

"Mistress Basaheen, Your Majesty," Norry said. "The first instruction I gave our good Master Hark was to watch the Aes Sedai's place of residence—a certain inn known as The Greeting Hall."

Elayne sat upright, feeling a burst of excitement. Duhara Basaheen had repeatedly attempted to gain audience with Elayne by bullying the various members of the palace staff. They all knew now, however, that she was *not* to be admitted. Aes Sedai or not, she was a representative of Elaida, and Elayne intended to have nothing to do with her.

"You had her watched," Elayne said eagerly. "Please tell

me you discovered something I can use to banish that insufferable woman."

"Then I am under no condemnation?" Master Norry asked carefully, still as dry and unexcited as ever. He was yet inexperienced when it came to spying.

"Light, no," Elayne said. "I should have ordered it done myself. You've saved me from that oversight, Master Norry. If what you've discovered is good enough news, I might just be likely to kiss you."

That prompted a reaction; his eyes widened in horror. It was enough to make Elayne laugh, and Birgitte chuckled as well. Dyelin didn't seem pleased. Well, she could go suck on a goat's foot, for all Elayne cared.

"Er . . . well," Norry said, "that wouldn't be necessary, Your Majesty. I had thought that, if there were Darkfriends pretending to be Aes Sedai in the city"—he, like the others, had learned not to refer to Falion and the others as "Aes Sedai" in Elayne's presence—"we might want to keep good watch on any who purported to be from the White Tower."

Elayne nodded eagerly. My, but Norry could ramble!

"I'm afraid I must disappoint Your Majesty," Norry said, obviously noting Elayne's excitement, "if you are hoping for proof that this woman is a Darkfriend."

"Oh."

"However," Norry said, raising a slender finger. "I have reason to believe that Duhara Sedai may have had a hand in the document you seem to be treating with . . . um . . . unusual reverence." He glanced at the pages Elayne had tossed to the floor. One bore the distinct outline of her shoe.

"Duhara has been meeting with *Ellorien*?" Elayne asked.

"Indeed she has," Master Norry said. "The visits are growing more frequent. They are done with some measure of secrecy as well."

Elayne glanced at Dyelin. "Why does *Duhara* want my rivals freed?"

Dyelin looked troubled. "She couldn't be so foolish as to assume she can raise up a movement against you, particularly using a group of broken, bankrupt lords and ladies."

"Your Majesty?" Norry asked. "If I may offer a comment . . ."

"Of course, Master Norry."

"Perhaps the Aes Sedai is trying to curry favor with the

Lady Ellorien. We don't know for certain they conspired on this proposal; it simply seemed likely, judging from the frequency and timing of the Aes Sedai's visits. But she may not have reason to support your enemies so much as she has reason to be in the good graces of *some* of the city's nobility."

It was possible. Duhara wasn't likely to return to the White Tower, no matter how often Elayne suggested that she do so. To go back would be to present Elaida with empty hands and a hostile Andor. No Aes Sedai would be so easily dissuaded. However, if she could return with the loyalty of some of the Andoran nobility, it would be something.

"When Duhara left her inn to visit Ellorien's home," Elayne said, "how did she dress?" Though Ellorien had briefly spoken of returning to her estates, she hadn't left, perhaps realizing that it wasn't politically useful as of yet. She resided in her mansion in Caemlyn at the moment.

"In a cloak, Your Majesty," Norry said. "With the hood drawn."

"Rich or poor?"

"I . . . I don't know," Norry replied, sounding embarrassed. "I could fetch Master Hark. . . ."

"That won't be needed," Elayne said. "But tell me. Did she go alone?"

"No. I believe she always had a rather large contingent of attendants with her."

Elayne nodded. She was willing to bet that while Duhara wore a cloak and drawn hood, she left her Great Serpent ring on and chose a distinctively rich cloak for the subterfuge, along with taking attendants.

"Master Norry," Elayne said, "I fear that you've been played."

"Your Majesty?"

Dyelin was nodding. "She wanted to be seen visiting Ellorien. She didn't want the visits to be official—that would put her too formally against your throne. But she wanted you to know what she was doing."

"She's blatantly mingling with my enemies," Elayne said. "It's a warning. She threatened me earlier, saying that I would not appreciate being in opposition to her and Elaida."

"Ah," Norry said, deflated. "So my initiative wasn't so keen after all."

"Oh, it was still valuable," Elayne said. "If you hadn't had her watched, we'd have missed this—which would have been embarrassing. If someone is going to go out of her way to insult me, then I at least want to be aware of it. If only so that I know whom to behead later on."

Norry paled.

"Figuratively, Master Norry," she said. As much as she'd like to do it. And Elaida too! She dared send a watchdog to "counsel" Elayne? Elayne shook her head. *Hurry up, Egwene. We need you in the Tower. The world needs you there.*

She sighed, turning back to Norry. "You said there were 'several new matters' that needed my attention?"

"Indeed, Your Majesty," he said, getting out his horrible leather folder. He removed a page from it—one he did not regard with nearly as much reverence as most he collected. Indeed, he pinched this one between two fingers and held it aloft, like a man picking up a dead animal found in the gutter. "You will recall your orders regarding mercenary bands?"

"Yes," she said, grimacing. She was getting thirsty. Gloomily, she eyed the cup of warm goat's milk on the table next to her chair. News of battle brought bands of sell-swords eager to offer their services.

Unfortunately for most of the mercenaries, the siege had been a short one. News traveled fast, but weary and hungry soldiers traveled slowly. Soldier bands continued to arrive at the city in a steady flow, the men in them disappointed to find no need for their weapons.

Elayne had begun by sending them away. Then she'd realized the foolishness in this. Every man would be needed at Tarmon Gai'don, and if Andor could provide an extra five or ten thousand soldiers to the conflict, she wanted to do so.

She didn't have the coin to pay them now, but neither did she want to lose them. So instead, she had ordered Master Norry and Captain Guybon to give all of the mercenary bands the same instructions. They were to allow no more than a certain number of soldiers into Caemlyn at a time, and they were to camp no closer than one league from the city.

This was to leave them with the idea that she'd meet with them eventually and offer them work. She just might do that, now that she had decided to take the Sun Throne. Of course, the last sell-swords she'd hired had gone rotten on her more often than not.

Against her better judgment, she picked up the cup of milk and took a sip. Birgitte nodded in satisfaction, but Elayne grimaced. Better to go thirsty!

"Well," Master Norry said, looking over the page in his fingers, "one of the mercenary captains has taken it upon himself to send you a very . . . familiar letter. I wouldn't have brought it to you, but upon second reading it seems that it is something you should see. The ruffian's claims are outlandish, but I would not like to have been the one to ignore them, should they prove . . . um . . . accurate."

Curious, Elayne reached for the paper. Outlandish claims? She didn't know any mercenary captains. The scrawl on the page was uneven, there were numerous crossed out words, and some of the spelling was . . . creative. Whoever this man was, she—

She blinked in surprise as she reached the bottom of the letter. Then she read it again.

Your Royal Bloody Pain in My Back,

We're bloody waiting here to talk to you, and we're getting ~~angry~~ perturbed. (That means angry.) Thom says that you're a queen now, but I figure that changes nothing, sense you acted like a queen all the time anyway. Don't forget that I ~~carried~~ halled your pretty little backside out of a hole in Tear, but you acted like a queen then, so I guess I don't know why I'm suprised now that you act like one when you really are a queen.

So I'm thinking I should treat you like a bloody Queen and send you a bloody letter and all, speaking with high talk and getting your attention. I even used my ring as a signet, like it was ~~paper~~ proper. So here is my formal salutation. So BLOODY STOP TURNING ME AWAY so we can talk. I need your bellfounders. It's bloody important.

—Mat

p.s. Salutation means greeting.

p.p.s. Don't mind the scratched out words and bad spellings. I was going to rewrite this letter, but Thom is laffing so hard at me that I want to be done.

p.p.s. Don't mind me calling your backside pretty. I hardly ever spent any time looking at it, as I've an awareness that you'd pull my eyes out if you saw me. Besides, I'm married now, so that all doesn't matter.

Elayne couldn't decide whether to be outraged or exuberant. Mat was in Andor, and Thom was alive! They'd escaped Ebou Dar. Had they found Olver? How had they gotten away from the Seanchan?

So many emotions and questions welled up in her. Birgitte stood upright, frowning, feeling the emotions. "Elayne? What is it? Did the man insult you?"

Elayne found herself nodding, tears forming in her eyes.

Birgitte cursed, striding over. Master Norry looked taken aback, as if regretting that he'd brought the letter.

Elayne burst into laughter.

Birgitte froze. "Elayne?"

"I'm all right," Elayne said, wiping the tears from her eyes and forcing herself to take a deep breath. "Oh, Light. I needed that. Here, read it."

Birgitte snatched the letter, and as she read, her face lightened. She chuckled. "*You* have a nice backside? He should be talking. Mat's got as fine a rump as comes on a man."

"Birgitte!" Elayne said.

"Well, it's true," the Warder said, handing back the letter. "I find his face far too pretty, but that doesn't mean I can't judge a good backside when I see one. Light, it will be good to have him back! Finally, someone I can go drinking with who doesn't look at me as their bloody military superior."

"Contain yourself, Birgitte," Elayne said, folding the letter up. Norry looked scandalized by the exchange. Dyelin said nothing. It took a lot to faze that woman, and she'd heard worse from Birgitte.

"You did well, Master Norry," Elayne said. "Thank you for bringing this to my attention."

"You do indeed know these mercenaries, then?" he asked, a hint of surprise sounding in his voice.

"They're not mercenaries. Actually, I'm not certain *what* they are. Friends. And allies, I should hope." Why *had* Mat brought the Band of the Red Hand to Andor? Were they loyal to Rand? Could she make use of them? Mat was a scoundrel, but he had a strangely good eye for tactics and warfare. A soldier under his command would be worth ten of the sell-sword riffraff she'd been forced to hire recently.

"My pardon, Your Majesty, for my mistake," Norry said. "I should have brought this to you sooner. My informants told me that this group was recently in the employ of the Crown of Murandy, so I discounted their leader's insistence that he wasn't a mercenary."

"You did well, Master Norry," Elayne said, still feeling amused and insulted. It was odd how often one moved between those two emotions when Matrim Cauthon was involved. "Light knows I've been busy enough. But please, if someone claims to know me personally, at least bring it to Birgitte's attention."

"Yes, Your Majesty."

"Arrange a meeting with Master Cauthon," she said, idly wishing she had time to write him back a letter as insulting as the one he'd written her. "Tell him he must bring Thom with him. To . . . keep him in line."

"As you wish, Your Majesty," Norry said with a characteristically stiff bow. "If I may withdraw . . ."

She nodded in thanks and he left, pulling the door closed. Elayne held Mat's letter idly between two fingers. Could she use Mat, somehow, to help her with the troubles Ellorien was making? As she'd used the Borderlanders? Or was that too obvious?

"Why did he mention bellfounders, do you think?" Birgitte asked.

"It could be something as simple as needing a new bell to ring the hour for his camp."

"But you don't think it's simple."

"Mat's involved," Elayne said. "He has a way of complicating things, and the way he wrote that line makes it smell like one of his schemes."

"True. And if he merely wanted a bell, he could win himself enough to buy it after an hour dicing."

"Come now," Elayne said. "He's not *that* lucky."

Birgitte snorted into her tea. "You need to pay better attention, Elayne. That man could dice with the Dark One and win."

Elayne shook her head. Soldiers, Birgitte included, could be such a superstitious lot. "Make certain to have a few extra Guardswomen on duty when Mat comes. He can be exuberant, and I wouldn't want him to make a scene."

"Who *is* this man?" Dyelin asked, sounding confused.

"One of the other two *ta'veren* who grew up with Rand al'Thor," Birgitte said, gulping down her tea. She'd given up drinking while Elayne was pregnant. At least someone else had to suffer too.

"Mat is . . . a particularly dynamic individual," Elayne said. "He can be very useful when properly harnessed. When he is not—which is most of the time—he can be an outright disaster. But whatever else can be said about the man, he and his Band know how to fight."

"You're going to use them, aren't you?" Birgitte said, eyeing her appreciatively.

"Of course," Elayne said. "And, from what I remember Mat saying, he has a lot of Cairhienin in the Band. They are native sons. If I arrive with that section of the Band as part of my army, perhaps the transition will be easier."

"So you really do intend to go through with this?" Dyelin asked. "Taking the Sun Throne? Now?"

"The world needs unity," Elayne said, standing. "With Cairhien, I begin knitting us all together. Rand already controls Illian and Tear, and has bonds to the Aiel. We're all connected."

She glanced to the west, where she could feel that knot of emotions that was Rand. The only thing she ever sensed from him these days was a cold anger, buried deeply. Was he in Arad Doman?

Elayne loved him. But she didn't intend to see Andor become merely another part of the Dragon's empire. Besides, if Rand *were* to die at Shayol Ghul, who would rule that empire? It could break up, but she worried that someone—Darlin, perhaps—would be strong enough to hold it together. If so, Andor would stand alone between an aggressive Seanchan empire to the southwest, Rand's successor to the northwest and the southeast and the Borderlanders united together in the north and northeast.

She could not let that happen. The woman in her cringed to think of planning for Rand's death, but the Queen could not be so squeamish. The world was changing.

"I realize it will be difficult to administer two nations," Elayne said. "But I *must* hold Cairhien. For the good of both thrones."

She turned and met Dyelin's eyes, and the older woman nodded slowly. "It seems you are committed."

"I am," Elayne said. "But I feel I'm going to need reliable use of Traveling if I'm going to manage it. Let's set up a meeting for me with Sumeko and Alise. We need to discuss the future of the Kin."

CHAPTER
12

An Empty Ink Bottle

Min sat on a window ledge in the Stone of Tear, enjoying the warmth.

The afternoon breeze was refreshing, laden though it was with humidity and the scents of the city below. The Tairens had been calling the weather "chilly," which made Min smile. How would these folk respond to a good Andoran winter, with snow piled up at the sides of buildings and icicles hanging from the eaves?

All that could be said of the weather lately was that it was less sweltering than usual. The warmth that Min was enjoying, however, had nothing to do with the heat in the air.

Sunlight shone upon the city. In the Stone's courtyards, Defenders in their striped sleeves and breeches kept stopping and looking up toward the open sky. The clouds still lurked on the horizon, but they were broken around the city in an unnatural ring. Perfectly circular.

The warmth that Min felt was not caused by the sunlight.

"How can you just sit there?" Nynaeve demanded.

Min turned her head. The window was wide open, and the walls of the Stone were thick. Min sat on the windowsill with her knees bent, her bare toes touching the wall on the other side. Her boots and stockings lay on the floor beside a stack of books.

Nynaeve paced the room. The Stone of Tear had withstood sieges and storms, wars and desolation, but Min wondered if it had ever survived anything quite like Nynaeve al'Meara in a pique. The dark-haired Aes Sedai had spent the last three days stalking through the corridors like a crackling thunderhead, intimidating Defenders, terrifying servants.

"Three days," Nynaeve said. "Three days he's been gone! The Last Battle looms, and the Dragon Reborn is missing."

"He's not missing," Min said softly. "Rand knows where he is."

"You do as well," Nynaeve said, her voice curt.

"I'm not leading you to him, Nynaeve."

"And why not? Surely you can't—"

"He needs to be alone."

Nynaeve cut off. She walked over to the corner table and poured herself a cup of chilled Tremalking black. Chilled tea. That seemed so odd. Tea was meant to be warming during cold days.

Min turned her eyes northward again, into the distant, cloud-smothered haze. As far as she could determine through the bond, she was looking directly at him. Was he in Andor, perhaps? Or in the Borderlands? She'd been tempted to use the bond to seek him out at first, when he'd felt that awful anguish. Pain deeper than the wounds in his side. Agony, anger and despair. In those moments, Rand had seemed more dangerous than he ever had before. Not even that night—when he'd knelt above her, strangling her with one hand—had he been as frightening.

And then . . .

She smiled. And then had come the warmth. It radiated from the bond like the comfort of a winter hearth. Something wonderful was happening, something she'd been awaiting without knowing it.

"It will be all right, Nynaeve," she said.

"How can you say that?" The woman took a sip of her tea. "He didn't destroy Ebou Dar, but that doesn't mean he's not dangerous. You heard what he nearly did to Tam. His own *father*, Min."

"A man should not be condemned for what he 'nearly' did, Nynaeve. He stopped himself."

"He didn't stop himself at Natrin's Barrow."

"That was necessary."

"You didn't believe that at the time."

Min took a deep breath. Nynaeve had been goading her into arguments lately; she certainly had good reason to be tense. Her husband was riding toward his death. The Dragon

Reborn—a man she saw as her charge, still—was wandering alone, and there was nothing Nynaeve could do. And if there was one thing Nynaeve hated, it was being powerless.

"Nynaeve," Min said. "If this lasts much longer, I'll lead you to him. I promise."

The Aes Sedai narrowed her eyes. "'Much longer'?"

"A few days."

"In a few days he could level Cairhien."

"Do you really think he would do that, Nynaeve?" Min asked softly. "Truly?"

"Do I?" Nynaeve gripped her cup of tea, staring down at its contents. "Once I would have laughed at the idea. I knew Rand al'Thor, and the boy still inside him. The man he's become frightens me. I always told him he needed to grow up. And then . . . and then he did." She shivered visibly.

Min started to reply, but motion drew her attention. Two Maidens—Surial and Lerian—guarded the open doorway to the hallway; they'd turned to watch someone approach. There were always Maidens around Min, these days.

Sarene Nemdahl entered the small room a moment later. Min's quarters in the Stone were not expansive—she rarely used them, instead staying with Rand. Her sitting room had a thick blue-and-white rug and a small cherry desk, but nothing else.

Sarene wore her dark hair in its customary beaded braids framing her near-perfect face. "Cadsuane Sedai," Sarene said, "she has need of you."

"Is that so?" Nynaeve said. "Well, perhaps Cadsuane Sedai can—"

"Alanna is gone," Sarene continued, unruffled. "Vanished right from her chambers. The Defenders, they didn't see her go, and there was no sign of a gateway."

"Oh. Well, let's go then." Nynaeve bustled out of the chamber.

"And I'm telling you that I felt nothing," Corele said. She smiled, tapping the side of her nose. "I don't know how she got out. Unless you think she somehow invented flying—which I daresay wouldn't be outside reason, considering some of what has occurred lately."

Fool woman, Cadsuane thought, leveling a flat stare at

Corele. The woman's flippancy was preferable to the self-importance of some other Aes Sedai, but today Cadsuane hadn't the patience for it.

The Yellow shrugged, still smiling, but said nothing further. Cadsuane placed hands on hips, surveying the small chamber. Room for a trunk to hold clothing, a cot for sleeping and a desk. Cadsuane would have expected an Aes Sedai to demand more, even in Tear. Of course, Alanna didn't often reveal her intimate connection to the Dragon. Most didn't know of it.

Two other Aes Sedai—Rafela Cindal and Bera Harkin—stood at the side of the room. Bera said she'd felt Alanna channeling, but nothing demanding. Certainly not enough to create a gateway.

Burn that woman! Cadsuane had thought Alanna well in hand, despite recent stubbornness. She'd obviously slipped out intentionally. The clothing from the trunk was gone and the writing desk was mostly bare. Only an empty ink bottle remained.

"She said nothing to you?" Cadsuane said.

"No, Cadsuane Sedai," Bera replied. "We haven't spoken more than passing words in weeks. I . . . well, I did often hear weeping in her room."

"What is all the fuss about?" a new voice said. Cadsuane glanced at the doorway as Nynaeve arrived and met Cadsuane's stare. "She's only one person, and so far as I understand, she was free to leave when she wished."

"Phaw," Cadsuane said. "The girl isn't 'only one person.' She's a tool. An important one." She reached over to the desk, holding up a sheet of paper that they'd found in the room. It had been folded with a blood-red seal of wax on one side. "Do you recognize this?"

Nynaeve frowned. "No. Should I?"

Lying or truthful? Cadsuane hated not being able to trust the words of someone who called herself an Aes Sedai. But Nynaeve al'Meara had never held the Oath Rod.

Those eyes looked genuinely confused. Nynaeve *should* be trustworthy; she prided herself on her honesty. Unless that was a front. Unless she was Black.

Careful, she thought. *You'll end up as distrustful as the boy is.* Nynaeve hadn't given Alanna the note, which eliminated her last good theory on its origin.

"So, what is it, Cadsuane Sedai?" Nynaeve demanded. At least she used the honorific; Cadsuane nearly chided the girl for her tone. But, truth be told, she felt as frustrated as Nynaeve did. There were times when such emotions were justified. Facing the end of the world with the Dragon Reborn completely out of control was one of them.

"I'm not sure," Cadsuane said. "The letter was opened in haste—the paper was torn. It was dropped on the floor, and the note inside taken, along with clothing and emergency items."

"But why does it matter?" Nynaeve asked. Behind her, Min slipped into the room, two Maidens taking up positions by the door. Had Min yet figured out the real reason the Aiel trailed her?

"Because, Nynaeve," Min said. "She is a pathway to him."

Nynaeve sniffed. "She's been no more helpful than you, Min."

"As persuasive as you can be, Nynaeve," Cadsuane said dryly, "the Shadow has means to make people more forthcoming."

Nynaeve blushed furiously, then began muttering under her breath. Alanna could point the way to the Dragon Reborn. If agents of the Dark One had taken her, there would be no hiding Rand from them. Their traps had been deadly enough when they'd needed to coax and lure him into them.

"We've been fools," Nynaeve said. "There should have been a hundred Maidens guarding her."

"The Forsaken have known where to find him before," Cadsuane said, though inwardly she agreed. She *should* have seen Alanna better watched. "And he has survived. This is simply one more thing to be aware of." She sighed. "Can someone bring us some tea?"

Bera was actually the one who went to fetch it, though Cadsuane hadn't taken any care to cultivate influence with the woman. Well, a reputation was worth something, it appeared.

Bera returned shortly; Cadsuane had stepped out into the hall to think. She accepted the cup and braced herself for the tea's bitter taste—she'd asked for it partially because she needed a moment to think, and an empty-handed woman often looked nervous.

She raised the cup to her lips. What next? Ask the Defenders at the gate of the Stone? Last night, Alanna—after being prodded—had confirmed that al'Thor was still in the same place. Up north, Andor perhaps. For three days. What was the fool boy—

Cadsuane froze. The tea tasted good.

It was wonderful, as a matter of fact. Perfectly sweetened with honey. Faint bitterness and a relaxing flavor. It had been weeks, perhaps months, since Cadsuane had tasted tea that wasn't spoiled.

Min gasped, turning sharply toward the northern quarter of the city. The two Maidens in the doorway were gone in a heartbeat, dashing down the hallway. Cadsuane's suspicions were confirmed; their careful watch of Min had been less about protecting her and more about watching for signs of . . .

"He's here," Min said softly.

CHAPTER
13

For What Has Been Wrought

Min burst from the Dragonwall Gate on the eastern side of the Stone and dashed across the courtyard. What seemed like an entire clan's worth of Aiel flooded out behind her, breaking around Min like deer breaking around an oak. They weaved between startled Defenders and grooms, moving with grace and speed toward the wall.

It was galling how easily they outpaced her—years ago, she'd prided herself on being able to beat any boy she knew in an honest footrace. Now . . . well, too many months spent picking through books, perhaps.

She still outpaced the Aes Sedai, who were bridled by their need to maintain proper decorum. Min had long ago tossed aside all sense of decorum for her towering sheepherder. And so she ran, thankful for her breeches and boots, making for the gate.

And there he was. She pulled up sharply, looking through an open column of Aiel in *cadin'sor* toward the man himself, standing and speaking with two Defenders who were part of the wall guard. He glanced at her as she grew close; he could feel her coming, as she felt him.

Rand had found an old, long brown cloak somewhere. It had sleeves like a coat, though it fell loose from the shoulders. Underneath it, he had on a shirt and fine black trousers.

Now that he was close, the warmth through the bond seemed overwhelming. Couldn't the others see it? It made her want to raise her arm and shade her eyes, though there was nothing to actually see. It was just the bond. Except . . . the air *did* seem to distort around him. Was that a trick of the sunlight? New viewings spun around his head. She normally ignored those, but she couldn't do so now. An open cavern, gaping like a mouth. Bloodstained rocks. Two dead men on the ground, surrounded by ranks and ranks of Trollocs, a pipe with smoke curling from it.

Rand met her gaze, and—despite the bond—she was amazed at what she saw in him. Those gray gemstone eyes of his were deeper. There were faint wrinkles around them. Had those been there before? Surely he was too young for that.

Those eyes did not look young. Min felt a moment of panic as his eyes held hers. Was this the same man? Had the Rand she loved been stolen away, replaced with an ancient *force* of a man she could never know or understand? Had she lost him after all?

And then he smiled, and the eyes—deep though they had become—were his. That smile was something she'd been waiting a very long time to see again. It was now much more confident than the one he'd shown her during their early days together, yet it was still vulnerable. It let her see a part of him that others were never allowed.

That part was the youth, somehow innocent still. She ran up to him and seized him in an embrace. "You woolheaded fool! *Three days?* What have you been doing for *three days?*"

"Existing, Min," he said, wrapping his arms around her. "I wasn't aware that was such a difficult task."

"It has been for me at times." He fell silent, and she was content to hold him. Yes, this was the same man. Changed—and for the better—but still Rand. She clung to him. She didn't care that people were gathering, more and more of them. Let them watch.

Finally she exhaled, reluctantly pulling back. "Rand, Alanna is gone. She vanished earlier today."

"Yes. I felt her go. Northward somewhere. The Borderlands, perhaps Arafel."

"She could be used against you, to find where you are."

He smiled. Light, but it felt good to see that expression on his face again! "The Shadow does not need her to find me,

Min, nor will it ever again. All its eyes are fixed directly upon me, and will be until I blind them."

"What? But Rand—"

"It's all right, Min. The time when it could silence me quietly—and therefore win—has passed. The confrontation is assured and the scream that begins the avalanche has been sounded."

He seemed afire with life. The thrill of it was intoxicating. He left an arm around her—the arm that ended in a stump—as he turned to regard the Aiel. "I have *toh*." Though the courtyard behind them was in chaos, the Aiel stood quietly.

They were ready for this, Min thought. The Aiel weren't hostile, exactly, but they didn't share the excitement of the Defenders. The Tairens thought Rand had returned to lead them to the Last Battle.

"In the Three-fold Land," Rhuarc said, stepping forward, "there is an animal. The meegerling. It looks much like a rat, but it is far more stupid. If you place it near grain, it will go straight toward it, regardless of the danger. No matter how many times it falls in a trench between itself and the food, it will repeat the same action if you move it back to the start. Aiel children amuse themselves with the game." He studied Rand. "I had not thought you would be a meegerling, Rand al'Thor."

"I promise I will never leave you again," Rand said. "Not of my own choice, and not without informing and—if they consent—bringing Maidens as a guard."

The Aiel did not budge. "This will prevent you from earning more *toh*," Rhuarc said. "It will not change what has gone before. And promises have been made before."

"This is true," Rand said, meeting Rhuarc's eyes. "I will meet my *toh*, then."

Something passed between them, something Min didn't understand, and the Aiel parted, looking more relaxed. Twenty Maidens came forward to act as a guard around Rand. Rhuarc retreated with the others, joining a small group of Wise Ones who watched from the periphery.

"Rand?" Min said.

"It will be all right," he said, though there was a grim cast to his emotions. "This was one of the things I needed to fix. One of many." He took his arm from around her and scanned the courtyard, feeling hesitant, as if he were looking for something. Whatever it was, he didn't see it, so he began to stride toward King Darlin, who had just arrived in a hurry.

King Darlin bowed, hand on the pommel of his narrow side-sword. "My Lord Dragon. Are we to march, finally?"

"Walk with me, Darlin," Rand said in reply as he moved through the courtyard. "There is much to do. Who else is here? Narishma, Flinn. Excellent." He nodded to the two black-coated Asha'man who arrived at a run. "Your Aes Sedai? Ah, there they come. Well, that will be next. Kainea, would you be so kind as to gather me some messengers?"

One of the Maidens—a woman with oddly dark hair for an Aiel—ran off to do as requested. Min frowned, keeping pace with Rand and Darlin as the two Asha'man fell into step behind.

Nynaeve and Merise led the group of Aes Sedai. They stopped when they saw Rand approaching, as if to let *him* be the one who came to meet *them*. They pulled together in a clump, fiddling with their clothing, looking more unsettled than Aes Sedai normally did.

Rand crossed the bustling, open courtyard, walking into the shadow of the Stone's towering fortifications, then stepped up to them.

"Rand al'Thor," Nynaeve said, folding her arms as he walked up to them. "You are—"

"An idiot?" Rand finished, sounding amused. "An arrogant fool? An impulsive, wool-headed boy in need of a sound ear-boxing?"

"Er. Yes."

"All true, Nynaeve," he said. "I see it, now. Perhaps I've finally gained a portion of wisdom. I do think you need some new insults, however. The ones you use are wearing out like last year's lace. Someone send for Cadsuane. I promise not to execute her."

The Aes Sedai seemed shocked by his brusque tone, but Min smiled. His confidence had surged again following the confrontation with the Aiel. It was supremely satisfying to see him disarm Aes Sedai, objections and condemnations dying on their lips. Merise sent a servant to fetch Cadsuane.

"Narishma," Rand said, turning. "I need you to visit that

Borderlander army that came looking for me. I'm assuming it's still in Far Madding. Tell the leaders there that I accept their terms and will come in a few days to meet with them."

"My Lord Dragon?" Narishma said. "Is that prudent, considering the nature of that place?"

"Prudent? Prudence is for those who intend to live long lives, Narishma. Darlin, I need the High Lords and Ladies lined up to receive me. One of these arriving messengers should be sufficient for the task. Also, post word that the White Tower has been reunified, and that Egwene al'Vere is the Amyrlin Seat."

"*What?*" Merise said. Several of the other Aes Sedai gasped.

"Rand," Min said. "I doubt the Amyrlin will be pleased to have you publicizing the division."

"A valid point," Rand said. "Darlin, write a proclamation that Egwene al'Vere has succeeded Elaida a'Roihan as the Amyrlin. That should be enough to inform without revealing too much. Light knows I don't need to do anything *else* to make Egwene angry with me. . . ."

"Else?" Corele asked, paling.

"Yes," Rand said offhandedly. "I've already been to the White Tower to see her."

"And they let you *go*?" Corele asked.

"I didn't allow them other options. Darlin, kindly marshal our forces here. I want them gathered by the evening. Flinn, we'll need gateways. Large ones. A circle might be needed."

"Tarwin's Gap?" Nynaeve said, eager.

Rand glanced at her and hesitated. Min could feel his pain—sharp, spiking, *real*—as he spoke. "Not yet, Nynaeve. I've poured hot oil into the White Tower, and it will be boiling soon. Time. We don't have *time!* I will get help to Lan, I vow it to you, but right now I must prepare to face Egwene."

"Face her?" Nynaeve said, stepping forward. "Rand, what have you done?"

"What needed to be done. Where is Bashere?"

"He was out of the city with his men, my Lord Dragon," Flinn said, "running their horses. Should be back soon."

"Good. He's going with me to Arad Doman. You too, Nynaeve. Min." He looked at her, and those unfathomable eyes seemed to draw her in. "I *need* you, Min."

"You have me. Stupid looby."

"*Callandor*," he said. "It plays a part in this. You have to find out how. I cannot seal the Bore the way I tried last time. I'm missing something, something vital. Find it for me."

"I will, Rand." A cold shiver ran through her. "I promise."

"I trust you." He looked up as a figure in a deep hooded cloak walked out of one of the Stone's many guard posts.

"Cadsuane Melaidhrin," Rand said, "I pardon you for past mistakes and I revoke your exile. Not that it was ever anything more than a minor inconvenience to you."

She sniffed, lowering the hood. "If you believe that wearing a cloak in this heat is a 'minor' inconvenience, boy, then you need a lesson in contrast. I trust you see the error in your deed. It strikes me as unsuitable that I should need 'forgiveness' or a 'pardon' in the first place."

"Well, then," Rand said. "Please accept my pardon alongside my apology. You may say I have been under unusual stress of late."

"Of all people," Cadsuane said sternly, "you cannot afford to let the pressure of life drive you."

"On the contrary. I am who I have become because of that pressure, Cadsuane. Metal cannot be shaped without the blows of the hammer. But that is beside the point. You tried to manipulate me, and you failed horribly. But in that failure, you have shown me something."

"Which is?"

"I thought I was being forged into a sword," Rand said, eyes growing distant. "But I was wrong. I'm not a weapon. I never have been."

"Then what are you?" Min asked, genuinely curious.

He merely smiled. "Cadsuane Sedai, I have a task for you, if you will accept it."

"I expect that will depend on the task," she said, folding her arms.

"I need you to locate someone. Someone who is missing, someone I now suspect may be in the hands of well-meaning allies. You see, I've been informed that the White Tower is holding Mattin Stepaneos."

Cadsuane frowned. "And you want him?"

"Not at all. I haven't decided what to do about him yet, so he can stay Egwene's problem for the time. No, the person

I want is probably somewhere in the Caralain Grass. I'll explain more when we are not in the open."

The High Lords and Ladies were gathering. Rand looked toward them, though once again he scanned the courtyard, as if looking for something. Something that made him feel anxious.

He turned back to the High Lords and Ladies. Min watched them skeptically. Aside from Darlin, she'd never been impressed with them. Rand rested his hand on her shoulder. The gathered nobles looked disheveled, apparently summoned from naps or meals, although they wore an assortment of fine silks and ruffles. They looked oddly out of place in the Stone's courtyard, where everyone else had a purpose.

I shouldn't be so harsh on them, Min thought, folding her arms. But then, she had watched their plotting and pandering frustrate Rand. Besides, she'd never been fond of those who thought themselves more important than everyone else.

"Form a line," Rand said, walking up to them.

The High Lords and Ladies looked at him, confused.

"A *line*," Rand said, voice loud and firm. "Now."

They did so, arranging themselves with haste. Rand began to walk down the row, starting with Darlin, looking each man or woman in the eye. Rand's emotions were . . . curious. Perhaps a touch angry. What was he doing?

The courtyard grew still. Rand continued down the line, looking at each of the nobles in turn, not speaking. Min glanced to the side. Near the end of the line, Weiramon kept glancing at Rand, then looking away. The tall man had thinning gray hair, his beard oiled to a point.

Rand eventually reached him. "Meet my eyes, Weiramon," Rand said softly.

"My Lord Dragon, surely I am not worthy to—"

"*Do it.*"

Weiramon did so with an odd difficulty. He looked as if he was gritting his teeth, his eyes watering.

"So it *is* you," Rand said. Min could feel his disappointment. Rand looked to the side, to where Anaiyella stood last in line. The pretty woman had pulled away from Rand, her head turned. "Both of you."

"My Lord—" Weiramon began.

"I want you to deliver a message for me," Rand said. "To the others of your . . . association. Tell them that they cannot hide among my allies any longer."

Weiramon tried to bluster, but Rand took a step closer. Weiramon's eyes opened wide, and Anaiyella cried out, shading her face.

"Tell them," Rand continued, voice soft but demanding, "that I am no longer blind."

"Why . . ." Anaiyella said. "Why are you letting us go?"

"Because today is a day of reunion," Rand said. "Not a day of death. Go."

The two stumbled away, looking drained. The others in the courtyard watched with surprise and confusion. The Aiel, however, began to beat their spears against their shields. Anaiyella and Weiramon seemed to keep to the shadows of the courtyard as they ducked into the Stone.

"Leeh," Rand said. "Take two others. Watch them."

Three Maidens split from those watching over Rand, darting after the two former nobles. Min stepped up to Rand, taking his arm. "Rand? What was that? What did you see in them?"

"The time for hiding is past, Min. The Shadow made its play for me and lost. It is war, not subterfuge, that turns the day now."

"So they're Darkfriends?" Min asked, frowning.

Rand turned to her, smiling. "They are no longer a threat. I—" He cut off suddenly, looking to the side. Min turned, and grew chill.

Tam al'Thor stood nearby. He had just walked out of a nearby entrance into the Stone, pausing on a low set of steps leading down to the courtyard. Rand's emotions grew apprehensive again, and Min realized what he'd been searching for earlier.

Tam looked at his son, falling still. His hair was gray and his face lined, yet he was solid in a way that few people were.

Rand lifted his hand, and the crowd—Aes Sedai included—parted. Rand passed through them, Min following behind, crossing to the steps up the Stone. Rand climbed a few of those steps, hesitant. The courtyard fell silent; even the gulls stopped calling.

Rand stopped on the steps, and Min could feel his reluctance, his shame, his terror. It seemed so strange. Rand— who had faced Forsaken without a tremor—was afraid of his father.

Rand took the last few steps in two sudden strides and grabbed Tam in an embrace. He stood one step down, which brought them near an equal height. In fact, in that posture, Tam almost seemed a giant, and Rand but a child who was clinging to him.

There, holding to his father, the Dragon Reborn began to weep.

The gathered Aes Sedai, Tairens and Aiel watched solemnly. None shuffled or turned away. Rand squeezed his eyes shut. "I'm sorry, Father," he whispered. Min could barely hear. "I'm so sorry."

"It's all right, son. It's all right."

"I've done so much that is terrible."

"Nobody walks a difficult path without stumbling now and again. It didn't break you when you fell. That's the important part."

Rand nodded. They held each other for a time. Eventually, Rand pulled back, then gestured to Min, standing at the base of the steps.

"Come, Father," Rand said. "There is someone I want to introduce to you."

Tam chuckled. "It's been three days, Rand. I've already met her."

"Yes, but *I* didn't introduce you. I need to." He waved to Min, and she raised an eyebrow, folding her arms. He looked at her pleadingly, so she sighed and climbed up the steps.

"Father," Rand said, resting his hand on Min's back. "This is Min Farshaw. And she's very special to me."

CHAPTER
14

A Vow

E gwene walked up the side of a gentle slope, the gras
green at her feet, the air cool and pleasant. Lazy bu
terflies floated from blossom to blossom, like curi
ous children peeking into cupboards. Egwene made he
shoes vanish so she could feel the blades beneath her feet.

She took a deep breath, smiling, then looked up at th
boiling black clouds. Angry, violent, silent despite flashe
of amethyst lightning. Terrible storm above, quiet, placi
meadow beneath. A dichotomy of the World of Dreams.

Oddly, *Tel'aran'rhiod* felt more unnatural to her now tha
it had during her first few visits using Verin's *ter'angrea*
She'd treated this place like a playground, changing he
clothes on a whim, assuming that she was safe. She hadn'
understood. *Tel'aran'rhiod* was about as safe as a bear tra
painted a pretty color. If the Wise Ones hadn't straightene
her out, she might not have lived to become Amyrlin.

Yes, I think this is it. The rolling green hills, the stand
of trees. It was the first place she'd come, well over a yea
ago. There was something meaningful about standing here
having come so far. And yet it seemed she would have t
cover an equal distance before this was done, and in fa
shorter a time.

When she'd been captive in the Tower, she had reminde
herself—repeatedly—that she could focus on only on
problem at a time. The reunification of the White Towe
had to come first. Now, however, both problems and possi
ble solutions seemed uncountable. They overwhelmed he
drowning her in all of the things she *should* be doing.

Fortunately, during the last few days, several unexpecte

stores of grain had been discovered in the city. In one case a forgotten warehouse, owned by a man who had died over the winter. The others were smaller, a few sacks here and there. Remarkably, none of them had borne any kind of rot.

She had two meetings this evening, dealing with other problems. Her biggest difficulty was going to be the perceptions of the people she met with. Neither group would see her as what she had become.

She closed her eyes, willing herself away. When she opened her eyes, she was standing in a large room, deeply shadowed in the corners, its columns rising like thick towers. The Heart of the Stone of Tear.

Two Wise Ones sat on the floor at the center of the room, amid a forest of columns. Above their light brown skirts and white blouses, their faces were distinctly different. Bair's was wrinkled with age, like leather left to cure in the sun. For all her occasional sternness, smile lines wove from her eyes and mouth.

Amys' face was silky smooth, an effect of being able to channel. Her face was not ageless, but she could have been Aes Sedai for the emotion she showed.

The two had their shawls at their waists, their blouses unlaced. Egwene sat before them but left herself wearing wetlander clothing. Amys raised an eyebrow; was she thinking that Egwene should have changed? Or did she appreciate that Egwene did not imitate something she was not? It was difficult to tell.

"The battle within the White Tower is over," Egwene said.

"The woman Elaida a'Roihan?" Amys asked.

"Taken by the Seanchan," Egwene said. "I have been accepted as Amyrlin by those who followed her. My position is far from secure—at times, I feel balanced atop a stone that sits balanced atop another stone. But the White Tower is again whole."

Amys clicked her tongue softly. She raised her hand and a striped stole—an Amyrlin's stole—appeared in it. "I suppose you should be wearing this, then."

Egwene let out a soft, slow breath. It was remarkable to her, sometimes, how much stock she put in the opinions of these women. She took the stole, putting it around her shoulders.

"Sorilea will dislike this news," Bair said, shaking her head. "She still had a hope that you would leave those fools in the White Tower and return to us."

"Please take care," Egwene said, summoning herself a cup of tea. "I am not only one of those fools, my friend, but I am their leader. Queen of the fools, you might say."

Bair hesitated. "I have *toh*."

"Not for speaking the truth," Egwene assured her. "Many of them are fools, but are we not all fools at some point? You did not abandon me to my failures when you found me walking *Tel'aran'rhiod*. In like manner, I cannot abandon those of the White Tower."

Amys' eyes narrowed. "You have grown much since we last met, Egwene al'Vere."

That sent a thrill through Egwene. "I had much need to grow. My life has been difficult of late."

"When confronted by a collapsed roof," Bair said, "some will begin to haul away the refuse, becoming stronger for the process. Others will go to visit their brother's hold and drink his water."

"Have you seen Rand recently?" Egwene asked.

"The *Car'a'carn* has embraced death," Amys said. "He has given up trying to be as strong as the stones, and has instead achieved the strength of the wind."

Bair nodded. "Almost, we will have to stop calling him a child." She smiled. "Almost."

Egwene gave no hint of her shock. She'd expected them to be displeased with Rand. "I wish you to know the respect I have for you. You have much honor for taking me in as you did. I think that the only reason I see farther than my sisters is because you taught me to walk with my back straight and head high."

"It was a simple thing," Amys said, obviously pleased. "One that any woman would have done."

"There are few pleasures more satisfying than taking a cord someone else has knotted," Bair said, "then teasing it straight again. However, if the cord is not of good material, then no untangling will save it. You gave us fine material, Egwene al'Vere."

"I wish that there were a way," Egwene said, "to train more sisters in the ways of the Wise Ones."

"You could send them to us," Amys said. "Particularly

if they need punishing. We wouldn't coddle them like the White Tower."

Egwene bristled. The beatings she'd taken had been "coddling"? That was a fight she didn't want to join, however. The Aiel would always assume wetlander ways to be soft, and there was no changing that assumption.

"I doubt the sisters would agree to that," Egwene said carefully. "But what might work would be to send young women—those still training—to study with you. That was part of why my training was so effective; I wasn't yet set in the ways of the Aes Sedai."

"Would they agree to this?" Bair asked.

"They might," Egwene said. "If we sent Accepted. Novices would be considered too inexperienced, sisters too dignified. But Accepted . . . perhaps. There would need to be a good reason that seems to benefit the White Tower."

"You should tell them to go," Bair said, "and expect them to obey. Have you not the most honor among them? Should they not listen to your counsel when it is wise?"

"Does the clan always do as a chief demands?" Egwene said.

"Of course not," Amys said. "But wetlanders are always fawning over kings and lords. They seem to like being told what to do. It makes them feel safe."

"Aes Sedai are different," Egwene said.

"The Aes Sedai keep implying that we should all be training in the White Tower," Amys said. Her tone indicated what she thought of *that* idea. "They drone on, as noisy as a blind chippabird that cannot tell if it's day or night. They need to see that we will never do such a thing. Tell them that you're sending women to us to study our ways so we can understand one another. It is only the truth; they needn't know that you also expect them to be strengthened by the experience."

"That might work." Egwene was pleased; the plan was only a few hairs off from what she eventually wanted to accomplish.

"This is a topic to consider in easier days," Bair said. "I sense greater trouble in you than this, Egwene al'Vere."

"There is a greater trouble," she said. "Rand al'Thor. Has he told you what he declared when he visited the White Tower?"

"He said he angered you," Amys said. "I find his actions odd. He visits you after all his talk of the Aes Sedai locking him up and putting him in a box?"

"He was . . . different when he came here," Egwene said.

"He has embraced death," Bair said again, nodding. "He becomes the *Car'a'carn* truly."

"He spoke powerfully," Egwene said, "but his words were those of madness. He said he is going to break the seals on the Dark One's prison."

Amys and Bair both froze.

"You are certain of this?" Bair asked.

"Yes."

"This is disturbing news," Amys said. "We will consult with him on this. Thank you for bringing this to us."

"I will be gathering those who resist him." Egwene relaxed. Until that moment, she hadn't been certain which way the Wise Ones would go. "Perhaps Rand will listen to reason if enough voices are present."

"He is not known for his willingness to listen to reason," Amys said with a sigh, rising. Egwene and Bair did so as well. The Wise Ones' blouses were laced in an instant.

"The time is long past for the White Tower to ignore the Wise Ones," Egwene said, "or for the Wise Ones to avoid the Aes Sedai. We must work together. Hand in hand as sisters."

"So long as it isn't some sun-blinded ridiculous thought about the Wise Ones training in the Tower," Bair said. She smiled to show it was a joke, but succeeded only in baring her teeth.

Egwene smiled. She *did* want the Wise Ones to train in the Tower. There were many methods of channeling that the Aes Sedai did better than the Wise Ones. On the other hand, the Wise Ones were better about working together and—Egwene admitted reluctantly—with leadership.

The two groups could learn much from one another. She *would* find a way to tie them together. Somehow.

She fondly bade farewell to the two Wise Ones, watching as they faded from *Tel'aran'rhiod*. Would that their counsel alone proved enough to turn Rand from his insane plan. But it was unlikely.

Egwene took a breath. In an instant she stood in the Hall of the Tower, her feet planted directly on the Flame of Tar

Valon painted on the floor. Seven spirals of color wound out from her, spinning toward the perimeter of the domed chamber.

Nynaeve was not there. Egwene drew her lips to a line. *That woman!* Egwene could bring the White Tower to its knees, turn a staunch member of the Red Ajah to her side, earn the respect of the toughest Wise Ones. But Light help her if she needed the loyalty of her friends! Rand, Gawyn, Nynaeve—all infuriating in their own ways.

She folded her arms to wait. Perhaps Nynaeve would still come. If not, this wouldn't be the first time she had disappointed Egwene. A massive rose window dominated the far wall behind the Amyrlin Seat itself. The Flame at the center sparkled, as if there were sunlight beyond, though Egwene knew those boiling black clouds covered all the sky of the World of Dreams.

She turned from the window, then froze.

There, set into the glass below the Flame of Tar Valon, was a large segment in the shape of the Dragon's Fang. That wasn't part of the original window. Egwene stepped forward, inspecting the glass.

There is a third constant besides the Creator and the Dark One, Verin's meticulous voice said, a memory from another time. *There is a world that lies within each of these others, inside all of them at the same time. Or perhaps surrounding them. Writers in the Age of Legends called it* Tel'aran'rhiod.

Did this window represent one of those, another world where Dragon and Amyrlin ruled Tar Valon side by side?

"That's an interesting window," a voice said from behind her.

Egwene started, spinning. Nynaeve stood there, wearing a dress of bright yellow trimmed with green across the high bodice and along the skirt. She wore a red dot at the center of her forehead, and had her hair woven into its characteristic braid.

Egwene felt a surge of relief. *Finally!* It had been months since she'd seen Nynaeve. Cursing inside for letting herself be surprised, she smoothed her face and embraced the Source, weaving Spirit. A few inverted wards might help keep her from being startled again. Elayne was supposed to arrive a little later.

"I didn't choose this pattern," Egwene said, looking back at the Rose Window. "This is *Tel'aran'rhiod*'s interpretation."

"But the window itself is real?" Nynaeve asked.

"Unfortunately," Egwene said. "One of the holes the Seanchan left when they attacked."

"They *attacked*?" Nynaeve asked.

"Yes," Egwene said. *Something you would have known if you'd ever responded to my summons!*

Nynaeve folded her arms, and the two of them regarded one another across the room, Flame of Tar Valon centering the floor beneath them. This would have to be handled very carefully; Nynaeve could be as prickly as the worst of thornbushes.

"Well," Nynaeve said, sounding distinctly uncomfortable, "I know you're busy, and Light knows I have enough things to be doing. Tell me the news you think I need to know, and I'll be off."

"Nynaeve," Egwene said, "I didn't bring you here only to give you news."

Nynaeve grasped her braid. She knew she should be rebuked for the way she'd avoided Egwene.

"Actually," Egwene continued, "I wanted to ask your advice."

Nynaeve blinked. "Advice on what?"

"Well," Egwene said, strolling across the Flame, "you're one of the few people I can think of who has been in a situation similar to mine."

"Amyrlin?" Nynaeve asked flatly.

"A leader," Egwene said, passing Nynaeve and nodding for her to walk beside her, "that everyone thinks is too young. Who rose to her position abruptly. Who knows she is the right woman for the job, yet has only grudging acceptance from most of those near her."

"Yes," Nynaeve said, walking with Egwene, eyes growing distant. "You could say I know something of being in that situation."

"How did you deal with it?" Egwene asked. "It seems that everything I do, I need to do myself—because if I don't, they ignore me once I'm out of sight. Many assume that I give orders just to be seen making noise, or they resent my position above them."

"How did I deal with it when I was Wisdom?" Nynaeve asked. "Egwene, I don't know if I *did*. I could barely keep myself from boxing Jon Thane's ears half the days, and don't get me talking about Cenn!"

"But eventually they respected you."

"It was a matter of not letting them forget my station. They *couldn't* be allowed to continue to think of me as a young girl. Establish your authority quickly. Be firm with the women in the Tower, Egwene, because they'll begin by seeing how far they can push you. And once you've let them push you a handspan, it's harder than winter molasses to get back what you've lost."

"All right," Egwene said.

"And *don't* come up with idle work for them to do," Nynaeve said. They passed out of the Hall of the Tower, strolling through the hallways. "Get them used to you giving orders, but make those orders good ones. Make sure they don't bypass you. I'd guess that it might be easy for them to start looking to the Sitters or the Ajah heads instead of you; women in Emond's Field started going to the Women's Circle instead of me.

"If you discover that the Sitters are making decisions that should have come before the entire Hall, you have to make a big fuss about it. Trust me. They'll grouse that you're making too much noise over small things, but they'll think twice about doing something important without your attention."

Egwene nodded. It was good advice, though—of course—it came colored by Nynaeve's view of the world. "I think the biggest problem," Egwene said, "is that I have so few true supporters."

"You have me. And Elayne."

"Do I?" Egwene said, stopping in the hallway and looking at Nynaeve. "Do I really have you, Nynaeve?"

The former Wisdom stopped beside her. "Of course you do. Don't be silly."

"And how will it seem," Egwene asked, "if those who know me best refuse my authority? Might it seem to the others that there is something they do not know? Some weakness that only my friends have seen?"

Nynaeve froze. Suddenly, her honesty melted into suspicion, her eyes narrowing. "This wasn't about asking me for advice at all, was it?"

"Of course it was," Egwene said. "Only a fool would ignore the advice of those who support her. But how did it feel for *you*, those first weeks when you became Wisdom? When all the women you were supposed to be leading looked at you only as the girl they had known?"

"Terrible," Nynaeve said softly.

"And were they wrong to do so?"

"Yes. Because I'd become something more. It wasn't me any longer, it was my station."

Egwene met the older woman's eyes, holding them, and an understanding passed between them.

"Light," Nynaeve said. "You caught me quite soundly, didn't you?"

"I *need* you, Nynaeve," Egwene said. "Not just because you're so strong in the Power, not just because you're a clever, determined woman. Not just because you're refreshingly untainted by Tower politics, and not just because you're one of the few who knew Rand before this all began. But because I need people I can trust implicitly. If you can be one of those."

"You'll have me kneeling on the ground," Nynaeve said. "Kissing your ring."

"And? Would you have done it for another Amyrlin?"

"Not happily."

"But you'd have done it."

"Yes."

"And do you honestly think there is another who would do a better job than I?"

Nynaeve hesitated, then shook her head.

"Then why is it so bitter for you to serve the Amyrlin? Not *me*, Nynaeve, but the station."

Nynaeve's face looked as if she'd drunk something very bitter. "This will . . . not be easy for me."

"I've never known you to avoid a task because it was difficult, Nynaeve."

"The station. All right. I'll try."

"Then you might begin by calling me Mother." Egwene held up a finger to cut off Nynaeve's objection. "To remind yourself, Nynaeve. It needn't be permanent, at least not in private. But you must begin *thinking* of me as Amyrlin."

"All right, all right. You've pricked me with enough thorns. I *already* feel as if I've been drinking windsatter's draught all day." She hesitated, then added, "Mother." She almost seemed to choke on the word.

Egwene smiled encouragingly.

"I won't treat you the way women did me after I was first named Wisdom," Nynaeve promised. "Light! Odd to be able to feel as they did. Well, they were still fools. I'll do better; you'll see it. Mother."

It sounded a little less forced that time. Egwene broadened her smile. There were few ways to motivate Nynaeve better than a competition.

Suddenly, a tinkling bell rang in Egwene's mind. She'd almost forgotten her wards. "I think Elayne has arrived."

"Good," Nynaeve said, sounding relieved. "Let's go to her, then." She began striding back toward the Hall, then froze. She glanced back. "If it pleases you, Mother."

I wonder if she'll ever be able to say that without sounding awkward, Egwene thought. *Well, so long as she's trying.* "An excellent suggestion." She joined Nynaeve. Upon arriving in the Hall, however, they found it empty. Egwene folded her arms, looking around.

"Maybe she went looking for us," Nynaeve said.

"We'd have seen her in the hallway," Egwene said. "Besides . . ."

Elayne popped into the room. She wore a regal white gown, sparkling with diamonds. As soon as she saw Egwene, she smiled broadly, rushing over and taking her hands. "You did it, Egwene! We're whole again!"

Egwene smiled. "Yes, though the Tower is still injured. There is much to do."

"You sound like Nynaeve." Elayne glanced at Nynaeve, smiling.

"Thank you," Nynaeve said dryly. ·

"Oh, don't be so silly." Elayne walked over and gave Nynaeve a friendly hug. "I'm glad you're here. I'd worried that you wouldn't come, and Egwene would have to hunt you down and pull your toes off one at a time."

"The Amyrlin," Nynaeve said, "has much better things to do. Isn't that right, Mother?"

Elayne started, looking amazed. She got a glimmer in her eye, and hid a smile. She assumed that Nynaeve had been given a tongue-lashing. But, of course, Egwene knew that wouldn't have worked with Nynaeve; it would be like trying to yank a burr out of your skin when its spines had gone in the wrong way.

"Elayne," Egwene said. "Where did you go, before we returned?"

"What do you mean?" she said.

"When you first came here, we were gone. Did you go somewhere looking for us?"

Elayne seemed perplexed. "I channeled into my *ter'angreal*, went to sleep, and you were here when I appeared."

"Then who set off the wards?" Nynaeve asked.

Troubled, Egwene reset the wards and then—thinking carefully—she wove an inverted ward against eavesdropping but altered it to allow a little bit of sound through. With another weave, she projected that little bit far out around them.

Someone who drew near would hear them as if whispering. They'd edge closer, but the sound would remain a whisper. Perhaps that would draw them closer, inch by inch, as they strained to hear.

Nynaeve and Elayne watched her make the weaves, Elayne looking awed, though Nynaeve nodded thoughtfully to herself.

"Sit, please," Egwene said, making herself a chair and sitting in it. "We have much to discuss." Elayne made herself a throne, probably unconsciously, and Nynaeve made a seat copying the chairs of the Sitters in the room. Egwene, of course, had moved the Amyrlin Seat.

Nynaeve looked from one throne to another, obviously dissatisfied. Maybe that was why she'd resisted these meetings for so long; Egwene and Elayne had risen so far.

It was time for some honey to take away the bitterness. "Nynaeve," Egwene said. "I'd like it very much if you could return to the Tower and teach more of the sisters in your new method of Healing. Many are learning it, but they could use more instruction. And there are others who are reluctant to abandon the old ways."

"Stubborn goats," Nynaeve said. "Show them cherries and they'll still eat the rotten apples, if they've been doing it long enough. I'm not sure it would be prudent for me to come, though. Er, Mother."

"Why is that?"

"Rand," Nynaeve said. "*Someone* has to keep an eye

on him. Someone other than Cadsuane, at least." Her lips turned down at that woman's name. "He's changed recently."

"Changed?" Elayne said, sounding concerned. "What do you mean?"

"Have you seen him recently?" Egwene asked.

"No," Elayne said immediately. Too quickly. It was undoubtedly the truth—Elayne wouldn't lie to her—but there *were* things she was hiding about Rand. Egwene had suspected it for a time. Could she have bonded him?

"He *has* changed," Nynaeve said. "And it's a very good thing. Mother . . . you don't know how bad he grew. There were times when I was terrified of him. Now . . . that's gone. He's the same person—he even talks the same way as before. Quietly, without anger. Before it was like the quiet of a knife being drawn, and now it's like the quiet of a breeze."

"He's awakened," Elayne said suddenly. "He's warm now."

Egwene frowned. "What does that mean?"

"I . . . Actually, I don't know." Elayne blushed. "It came out. Sorry."

Yes, she'd bonded him. Well, that could be useful. Why didn't she wish to speak of it? Egwene would have to talk to her alone sometime.

Nynaeve was studying Elayne with narrowed eyes. Had she noticed as well? Her eyes flickered toward Elayne's chest, then down at her belly.

"You're pregnant!" Nynaeve accused suddenly, pointing at Elayne.

The Andoran queen blushed. That was right, Nynaeve wouldn't know of the pregnancy, though Egwene had heard from Aviendha.

"*Light!*" Nynaeve said. "I didn't think I'd let Rand out of my sight long enough for that. When did it happen?"

Elayne blushed. "Nobody said that he—"

Nynaeve gave Elayne a flat stare, and the Queen blushed further. Both knew Nynaeve's feelings about propriety in these matters—and, in truth, Egwene agreed. But Elayne's private life was none of her business.

"I'm happy for you, Elayne," Egwene said. "And for Rand. I'm not certain what I think of the timing. You should know that Rand is planning to break the remaining seals

upon the Dark One's prison, and in so doing, risk releasing
him upon the world."

Elayne pursed her lips. "Well, there are only three seals
left, and they're crumbling."

"So what if he is running that risk?" Nynaeve said. "The
Dark One will be freed when the final seal crumbles; best if
it happens when Rand is there to battle him."

"Yes, but the seals? That's foolhardy. Surely Rand can
face the Dark One, and defeat him, and seal him away without taking that risk."

"Maybe you're right," Nynaeve said.

Elayne looked troubled.

This was a more lukewarm reception than Egwene had
expected. She'd thought that the Wise Ones would resist
her, while Nynaeve and Elayne would immediately see the
danger.

Nynaeve has been around him too much, Egwene thought.
She was likely caught up by his *ta'veren* nature. The Pattern
bent around him. Those near him would begin to see things
his way, would work—unconsciously—to see his will done.

That had to be the explanation. Normally, Nynaeve was
so levelheaded about these sorts of things. Or . . . well,
Nynaeve wasn't exactly *levelheaded*, really. But she generally did see the right way things needed to be done, so long
as that right way didn't involve her being wrong.

"I need both of you to return to the Tower," Egwene said.
"Elayne, I know what you're going to say—and yes, I realize that you are Queen, and that Andor's needs must be
met. But so long as you haven't taken the oaths, other Aes
Sedai will think you undeserving."

"She's right, Elayne," Nynaeve said. "You needn't visit for
long—enough time to be raised formally to an Aes Sedai
and be accepted into the Green Ajah. The nobles of Andor
won't know the difference, but other Aes Sedai will."

"True," Elayne said. "But the timing is . . . awkward. I
don't know if I want to risk swearing the oaths while pregnant. It might harm the children."

That gave Nynaeve pause.

"You may have a point," Egwene said. "I will have someone look into whether or not the oaths are dangerous in
pregnancy. But Nynaeve, I want you back here for certain."

"It will leave Rand completely unattended, Mother."

"I'm afraid it is impossible to avoid." Egwene met Nynaeve's eyes. "I won't have you as an Aes Sedai free of the oaths. No, close your mouth—I know you try to hold to the oaths. But so long as you are free of the Oath Rod itself, others will wonder if they could be free as well."

"Yes," Nynaeve said. "I suppose."

"So you will return?"

Nynaeve clenched her jaw, and seemed to be fighting an internal battle. "Yes, Mother," she said. Elayne opened her eyes wider in shock.

"This is important, Nynaeve," Egwene said. "I doubt there is anything you alone could do to stop Rand now. We need to gather allies for a unified front."

"All right," Nynaeve said.

"What worries me is the testing," Egwene said. "The Sitters have begun to argue that—while it was all right to raise you and the others in exile—you should still have to go through the testing, now that the White Tower is reunified. They make very good arguments. Perhaps I can argue that your difficult challenges recently should earn you an exemption. We don't have time to teach you two all of the weaves you'd need."

Elayne nodded. Nynaeve shrugged. "I'll do the testing. If I'm going to come back, then I might as well do this properly."

Egwene blinked in surprise. "Nynaeve, these are *very* complex weaves. I haven't had time to memorize all of them; I swear that many are needlessly ornate simply to be difficult." Egwene had no intention of going through the testing herself, and didn't need to. The law was specific. By being made Amyrlin, she had become Aes Sedai. Things weren't as clear in regards to Nynaeve and the others that Egwene had raised.

Nynaeve shrugged again. "The hundred testing weaves aren't so bad. I could show them to you right here, if you wanted me to."

"When have you had time to learn those?" Elayne exclaimed.

"I haven't spent the last few months mooning about and dreaming of Rand al'Thor."

"Securing the throne of Andor is not 'mooning about'!"

"Nynaeve," Egwene cut in, "if you truly have the weaves

memorized, then being raised properly would help me a great deal. It would look less like I'm favoring my friends."

"The testing is supposed to be dangerous," Elayne said. "Are you *sure* you have the weaves in hand?"

"I'll be fine," Nynaeve said.

"Excellent," Egwene said. "I'll expect you here in the morning."

"So soon!" Nynaeve said, aghast.

"The sooner you can hold that Oath Rod, the sooner I'll be able to stop worrying about you. Elayne, we'll still have to do something about you."

"The pregnancy," Elayne said. "It's interfering with my ability to channel. That's getting better—I could get here, thankfully—but it's still a problem. Explain to the Hall it would be too dangerous for me—and for the babes—to undergo the testing while unable to channel consistently."

"They might suggest you wait," Nynaeve said.

"And let me run around without the oaths?" Elayne said. "Though I *would* like to know if anyone's taken the oaths while pregnant before, just to be sure."

"I'll find what I can," Egwene said. "Until then, I have another task for you."

"I *am* rather busy with ruling Andor, Mother."

"I know," Egwene said. "Unfortunately, there's nobody else I can ask. I need more dream *ter'angreal*."

"I might be able to manage," Elayne said. "Assuming I can start channeling reliably."

"What happened to the dream *ter'angreal* you had?" Nynaeve asked Egwene.

"Stolen," Egwene said. "By Sheriam—who, by the way, was Black Ajah."

The two gasped, and Egwene realized that the revelation of the hundreds of Black sisters was unknown to them. She took a deep breath. "Steel yourselves," she said. "I've got a painful story for you. Before the Seanchan attack, Verin came to—"

At that moment, the bell went off in her head again. Egwene willed herself to move. The room blinked around her, and she was suddenly standing outside in the hallway, where her wards were set.

She came face-to-face with Talva, a thin woman with a

bun of golden hair. She had once been of the Yellow Ajah, but was one of the Black sisters who had fled the Tower.

Weaves of Fire sprang up around Talva, but Egwene had already begun working on a shield. She slammed it between the other woman and the Source, immediately weaving Air to snare her.

A sound came from behind. Egwene didn't think; she moved herself, relying on practiced familiarity with *Tel'aran'rhiod*. She appeared behind a woman who was letting loose a jet of Fire. Alviarin.

Egwene snarled, beginning another shield as Alviarin's wave of Fire hit the unfortunate Talva, causing her to scream as her flesh burned. Alviarin spun, then yelped, vanishing.

Burn her! Egwene thought. Alviarin was at the very top of the list of people she wanted captured. The hallway fell still, Talva's corpse—blackened and smoking—slumping to the ground. She'd never awaken; die here, and one died in the real world.

Egwene shivered; that murderous weave had been meant for her. *I relied too much on channeling,* she thought. *Thought happens more quickly than weaves can be made. I should have* imagined *ropes around Alviarin.*

No, Alviarin would still have been able to jump away from ropes. Egwene hadn't been thinking like a Dreamer. Lately, her mind had been on the Aes Sedai and their problems, and weaves had come naturally to her. But she couldn't let herself forget that in this place, thought was more powerful than the One Power.

Egwene looked up as Nynaeve barreled out of the Hall, Elayne following more cautiously. "I sensed channeling," Nynaeve said. She looked at the burned corpse. "Light!"

"Black sisters," Egwene said, folding her arms. "It seems they're making good use of those dream *ter'angreal*. I'd guess they're under orders to prowl the White Tower at night. Perhaps looking for us, perhaps looking for information to use against us." Egwene and the others had done that very thing during Elaida's reign.

"We shouldn't have met here," Nynaeve said. "Next time, we'll use a different place." She hesitated. "If it suits you, Mother."

"It might," Egwene said. "It might not. We'll never defeat them unless we can find them."

"Walking into traps is hardly the best way to defeat them, Mother," Nynaeve said flatly.

"Depends on your preparation," Egwene said. She frowned. Had she just seen a flutter of black cloth, ducking around a corner? Egwene was there in a moment; Elayne's startled curse sounded down the hallway behind her. My but the woman had a tongue on her.

The place was empty. Eerie, almost too silent. That was normal in *Tel'aran'rhiod*.

Egwene remained full of the One Power, but moved back to the other two. She had cleansed the White Tower, but an infestation remained, hiding at its heart.

I will *find you, Mesaana,* Egwene thought, then waved for the others to join her. They moved to the hillside where she'd been earlier, a place where she could give a more detailed explanation of events they'd missed.

CHAPTER
15

Use a Pebble

Nynaeve hastened through the paved streets of Tear, the Asha'man Naeff at her side. She could still feel that storm to the north, distant but terrible. Unnatural. And it was moving southward.

Lan was up there. "Light protect him," she whispered.

"What was that, Nynaeve Sedai?" Naeff asked.

"Nothing." Nynaeve was getting used to having the black-coated men around. She did *not* feel an uncomfortable chill when she looked at Naeff. That would be silly. *Saidin* had been cleansed, with her own help. No need to be uncomfortable. Even if the Asha'man *did* sometimes stare off into nothing, muttering to themselves. Like Naeff, who was looking into the shadow of a nearby building, hand on his sword.

"Careful, Nynaeve Sedai," he said. "There's another Myrddraal following us."

"You're . . . certain, Naeff?"

The tall, rectangular-faced man nodded. He was talented with weaves—particularly Air, which was unusual for a man—and he was very polite to Aes Sedai, unlike some of the other Asha'man. "Yes, I'm certain," he said. "I don't know why I can see them and others cannot. I must have a Talent for it. They hide in shadows, scouts of some sort, I think. They haven't struck yet; I think they're wary because they know I can see them."

He'd taken to night walks through the Stone of Tear, watching the Myrddraal that only he could see. His madness wasn't getting worse, but old injuries wouldn't go away. He'd always bear this scar. Poor man. At least his madness wasn't as bad as some of the others'.

Nynaeve looked forward, marching down the wide, paved street. Buildings passed on either side, designed in Tear's haphazard way. A large mansion, with two small towers and a bronze, gatelike door sat beside an inn of only modest size. Across from them was a row of homes with wrought iron worked into the doors and windows, but a butcher's shop had been built right in the middle of the line.

Nynaeve and Naeff were heading for the All Summers neighborhood, which was just inside the western wall. It wasn't the richest section of Tear, but it was definitely prosperous. Of course, in Tear, there was really only one division: commoner or noble. Many of the nobles still considered commoners completely different—and wholly inferior—creatures.

They passed some of those commoners. Men in loose breeches tied at the ankles, colorful sashes at the waist. Women in high-necked dresses, pale aprons hanging at the front. Wide straw hats with flat tops were common, or cloth caps that hung to one side. Many people carried clogs on a string over their shoulders to use once they returned to the Maule.

The people passing Nynaeve now wore worried faces, some glancing over their shoulders in fear. A bubble of evil had hit the city in that direction. Light send that not too many were hurt, for she didn't have much time to spare. She had to return to the White Tower. It galled her to have to obey Egwene. But obey she would, and leave as soon as Rand returned. He'd gone somewhere this morning. Insufferable man. At least he'd taken Maidens with him. He'd reportedly said he needed to fetch something.

Nynaeve quickened her step, Naeff at her side, until they were nearly running. A gateway would have been faster, but it wouldn't be safe; she couldn't be certain they wouldn't slice into someone. *We're growing too dependent on those gateways,* she thought. *Our own feet hardly seem good enough anymore.*

They turned a corner into a street where a group of nervous Defenders—wearing black coats and silvery breastplates, black and gold sleeves puffing out at the sides—stood in a line. They parted for her and Naeff, and while they looked relieved that she'd arrived, they still clutched their polearms nervously.

The city beyond them looked faintly ... blander than it should. Washed out. The paving stones were a lighter shade of gray, the walls of the buildings a fainter brown or gray than they should have been.

"You have men inside searching for wounded?" Nynaeve asked.

One of the Defenders shook his head. "We've been keeping people out, er, Lady Aes Sedai. It's not safe."

Most Tairens still weren't accustomed to showing Aes Sedai respect. Until recently, channeling had been outlawed in the city.

"Send your men to search," Nynaeve said firmly. "The Lord Dragon will be upset if your timidity costs lives. Start at the perimeter. Send for me if you find anyone I can help."

The guardsmen moved off. Nynaeve turned to Naeff, and he nodded. She turned and took a step into the affected section of town. When her foot hit the paving stone, the stone turned to dust. Her foot sank through the shattered paving stone and hit packed earth.

She looked down, feeling a chill. She continued forward, and the stones fell to powder as she touched them. She and Naeff made their way to a nearby building, leaving a trail of powdered rock behind.

The building was an inn with nice balconies on the second floor, delicate ironwork patterns on the glass windows, and a darkly stained porch. The door was open, and as she lifted her foot up to step onto the low porch, the boards also turned to powder. She froze, looking down. Naeff stepped up beside her, then knelt down, pinching the dust between his fingers.

"It's soft," he said quietly, "as fine a powder as I've ever touched."

The air smelled unnaturally fresh, contrasting strangely with the silent street. Nynaeve took a deep breath, then went into the inn. She had to push forward, walking with the wooden floor at her knees, the boards disintegrating as she touched them.

The inside was dim. The stand-lamps no longer burned. People sat about the room, frozen in midmotion. Most were nobles with fine clothing, the men wearing beards oiled to a

point. One sat at a nearby tall table with long-legged chairs.
He had a mug of morning ale halfway to his lips. He was
motionless, his mouth open to accept the drink.

Naeff's face was grim, although little seemed to surprise
or unsettle Asha'man. As he took another step forward,
Nynaeve lunged and grabbed his arm. He frowned at her,
and she pointed down. Right in front of him—barely visible
beneath the still-whole floorboards right ahead of them—
the ground fell away. He'd been about to step into the inn's
cellar.

"Light," Naeff said, stepping back. He knelt down, then
tapped the board in front of him. It fell to dust, showering
down into the dark cellar below.

Nynaeve wove Spirit, Air and Water to Delve the man sitting at the chair near her. Normally she would touch someone to Delve them, but she hesitated this time. It would work
without touch, but would not be as effective for Healing.

Her Delving found nothing. No life, no sense that he had
ever *been* alive. His body wasn't even flesh. With a sinking
feeling, she Delved other people in the darkened room. A
serving maid carrying breakfast toward three Andoran merchants. A corpulent innkeeper, who must have had trouble
navigating between the close-set tables. A woman in a rich
dress sitting in the very back of the room, primly reading a
small book.

There was no life in any of them. These weren't corpses;
they were husks. Fingers trembling, Nynaeve reached out
and brushed the shoulder of the man at the high table. He
immediately fell to powder, dust showering downward in
a puff. The chair and floorboards underneath did not dis-
solve.

"There is nobody here to save," Nynaeve said.

"Poor people," Naeff said. "Light shelter their souls."

Nynaeve often had trouble feeling pity for the Tairen
nobles—of all the people she had met, they seemed among
the most arrogant. But nobody deserved this. Besides, a
large number of commoners had been caught in this bubble
as well.

She and Naeff made their way out of the building,
Nynaeve's frustration mounting as she tugged on her braid.
She hated feeling helpless. Like with the poor guard who

had started the fire back at the manor house in Arad Doman, or the people who were struck down by strange diseases. The dusty husks this day. What was the good of learning to Heal if she couldn't help people?

And now she had to leave. Go back to the White Tower. It felt like running away. She turned to Naeff. "Wind," she said.

"Nynaeve Sedai?"

"Give the building a gust of wind, Naeff," she said. "I want to see what happens."

The Asha'man did as she asked, his invisible weaves blowing a jet of air. The entire building burst, shattering into dust that blew away, like the white seeds of a dandelion. Naeff turned to her.

"How wide did they say this bubble was?" she asked.

"About two streets wide in all directions."

"We need more wind," she said, beginning a weave. "Create a gust as large as you can. If there *is* anyone wounded in here, we'll find them this way."

Naeff nodded. The two of them strode forward, creating wind. They shattered buildings, causing them to burst and fall. Naeff was far more skilled at the process than she, but Nynaeve was stronger in the One Power. Together, they swept the crumbling buildings, stones and husks before them in a dust storm.

It was exhausting work, but they kept at it. She hoped— against reason—that she might find someone to help. Buildings fell before her and Naeff, the dust getting caught in swirling air. They pushed the dust in a circle, moving inward. Like a woman sweeping the floor.

They passed people frozen on the streets in midstride. Oxen pulling a cart. Heart-wrenchingly, some children playing in an alley. All fell to dust.

They found nobody alive. Eventually, she and Naeff had dissolved all of the broken part of the city and blown the dust into the center. Nynaeve looked at it, kept swirling in place by a small cyclone Naeff had woven. Curious, Nynaeve channeled a tongue of Fire into the cyclone, and the dust caught alight.

Nynaeve gasped; that dust went up like dried paper thrown into a fire, creating a roaring tempest of flames. She and Naeff backed away, but it was over in a flash. It didn't leave any ash behind.

If we hadn't gathered it, she thought, watching the fire fade away, *someone might have dropped a candle on it. A fire like that . . .*

Naeff stilled his winds. The two of them stood in the center of an open circle of bare earth with periodic holes for cellars. On the edges, buildings had been sliced into, rooms open to the air, some structures having collapsed. It was eerie, to see this hollow area. Like a gouged-out eye socket in an otherwise healthy face.

Several groups of Defenders stood at the perimeter. She nodded to Naeff, and they walked to the largest group. "You didn't find anyone?" she demanded.

"No, Lady Aes Sedai," a man said. "Er . . . well, we did find a few, but they were dead already."

Another man nodded, a barrel-like fellow whose uniform was very tight. "Seems anyone who had even a toe inside of that ring fell dead. Found a few of them missing only a foot or part of their arm. But they were dead anyway." The man shuddered visibly.

Nynaeve closed her eyes. The entire world was falling apart, and she was powerless to Heal it. She felt sick and angry.

"Maybe *they* caused it," Naeff said softly. She opened her eyes to see him nodding toward the shadows of a building nearby. "The Fades. There are three of them there, Nynaeve Sedai, watching us."

"Naeff . . ." she said, frustrated. Telling him the Fades weren't real didn't help. *I have to do something,* she thought. *Help someone.* "Naeff, stand still." She took hold of his arm and Delved him. He looked at her, surprised, but didn't object.

She could see the madness, like a dark network of veins digging into his mind. It seemed to pulse, like a small beating heart. She'd found similar corruption recently in other Asha'man. Her skill with Delving was improving, her weaves more refined, and she could find things once hidden to her. She had no idea how to fix what was wrong, though.

Anything should be Healable, she told herself. *Anything but death itself.* She concentrated, weaving all Five Powers.

and carefully prodded at the madness, remembering what
had happened when she'd removed the Compulsion from
Graendal's unfortunate servant. Naeff was better off with
this madness than he would be if she damaged his mind
further.

Oddly, the darkness *did* seem similar to Compulsion.
Was that what the taint had done? Bent the men who used
the One Power with the Dark One's own Compulsion?

She carefully wove a counterweave opposite the madness, then laid it over Naeff's mind. The weave just faded
away, doing nothing.

She gritted her teeth. That *should* have worked. But, as
seemed so common lately, it had failed.

No, she thought. *No, I can't just sit back.* She Delved
deeper. The darkness had tiny, thornlike projections stuck
into Naeff's mind. She ignored the people gathering around
her, and inspected those thorns. She carefully used weaves
of Spirit to pry one free.

It came out with some resistance, and she quickly Healed
the spot where it had punctured Naeff's flesh. The brain
seemed to pulse, looking more healthy. One by one, she
pried the others free. She was forced to maintain her weaves,
holding the barbs back, lest they plunge down again. She
began to sweat. She was already tired from sweeping the
area clean, and no longer could spare concentration to keep
the heat off her. Tear was so muggy.

She continued working, preparing another counterweave.
Once she had pried up each and every thorn, she released
her new weave. The dark patch undulated and shook, like
something *alive.*

Then it vanished.

Nynaeve stumbled back, drained near to exhaustion.
Naeff blinked, then looked around. He raised a hand to his
head.

Light! she thought. *Did I hurt him? I shouldn't have barreled into that. I could have—*

"They're gone," Naeff said. "The Fades . . . I can't see
them anymore." He blinked. "Why would Fades be hiding
in the shadows anyway? If I could see them, they'd have
killed me, and—" He looked at her, focusing. "What did
you *do?*"

"I . . . I think I just Healed your madness." Well, she'd done something to it. What she'd done hadn't been any standard Healing, and hadn't even used Healing weaves. But it had worked, it seemed.

Naeff smiled deeply, seeming bewildered. He took her hand with both of his, then knelt before her, growing teary-eyed. "For months, I have felt as if I were always being watched. As if I would be murdered the moment I turned my back on the shadows. Now I . . . *Thank you.* I need to go find Nelavaire."

"Off with you, then," Nynaeve said. Naeff left her in a dash, running back toward the Stone to search out his Aes Sedai.

I can't let myself begin to think that nothing I do matters. That's what the Dark One wants. As she watched Naeff hasten away, she noticed that the clouds above were breaking. Rand had returned.

Workers began clearing away the rubble of buildings that had half turned to dust, and Nynaeve ended up speaking soothingly to the worried Tairens who began to cluster around the perimeter. She didn't want there to be a panic; she assured everyone that the danger was past, and then she asked to meet with any families who had lost someone.

She was still doing this—talking softly with a thin, worried woman—when Rand found her. The woman was a commoner, wearing a high-necked dress with three aprons and a straw hat. Her husband had worked in the inn Nynaeve had entered. The woman kept glancing at the hole in the ground that had been the cellar.

After a moment, Nynaeve noticed Rand, watching her and standing with his arms behind his back, hand clasping his stump. Two Maidens guarded him, a pair of women named Somma and Kanara. Nynaeve finished speaking with the Tairen, but the woman's tearful eyes wrenched her heart. How would she react, if she lost Lan?

Light protect him. Please, please protect him, she prayed. She unhooked her coin pouch and sent the woman off with it. Perhaps that would help.

Rand stepped up to Nynaeve. "You care for my people. Thank you."

"I care for any who need it," Nynaeve said.

"As you've always done," Rand said. "Along with caring for some who don't need it."

"Like you?" she said, raising an eyebrow.

"No, I've always needed it. That and more."

Nynaeve hesitated. That wasn't something she'd ever expected *him* to admit. Why hadn't he gotten rid of that old cloak? It was faded and dull.

"This is my fault," Rand said, nodding toward the hole in the city.

"Rand, don't be a fool."

"I don't know if anyone can avoid being a fool at times," he said. "I blame myself because of my delays. We've been putting off the confrontation with him for too long. What happened here today? The buildings turned to dust?"

"Yes," Nynaeve said. "Their substance was removed. Everything crumbled the moment we touched it."

"He would do this to the entire world," Rand said, his voice growing soft. "He stirs. The longer we wait—holding on by our fingernails—the more he destroys what remains. We can delay no longer."

Nynaeve frowned. "But Rand, if you let him free, won't that make it even worse?"

"Perhaps for a short burst," Rand said. "Opening the Bore will not free him immediately, though it will give him more strength. It must be done regardless. Think of our task as climbing a tall stone wall. Unfortunately, we are delaying, running laps before attempting the climb. Each step tires us for the fight to come. We must face him while still strong. That is why I must break the seals."

"I . . ." Nynaeve said. "I think I actually believe you." She was surprised to realize it.

"Do you, Nynaeve?" he asked, sounding oddly relieved. "Do you really?"

"I do."

"Then try to convince Egwene. She will stop me, if she can."

"Rand . . . she has called me back to the Tower. I'll need to go today."

Rand looked saddened. "Well, I suspected that she might do that eventually." He took Nynaeve by the shoulder in an odd gesture. "Don't let them ruin you, Nynaeve. They'll try."

"*Ruin* me?"

"Your passion is part of you," Rand said. "I tried to be like them, though I wouldn't have admitted it. Cold. Always in control. It nearly destroyed me. That is strength to some, but it is *not* the only type of strength. Perhaps you could learn to control yourself a little more, but I like you as you are. It makes you genuine. I would not see you become another 'perfect' Aes Sedai with a painted mask of a face and no care for the feelings and emotions of others."

"To be Aes Sedai is to be calm," Nynaeve replied.

"To be Aes Sedai is to be what you decide it is," Rand said, his stump still held behind his back. "Moiraine cared. You could see it in her, even when she was calm. The best Aes Sedai I've known are the ones who others complain aren't what an Aes Sedai should be."

Nynaeve found herself nodding, then was annoyed at herself. She was taking advice from Rand al'Thor?

There was something different about Rand now. Quiet intensity and careful words. He was a man you could take advice from without feeling he was speaking down to you. Like his father, actually. Not that she'd ever admit that to either one of them.

"Go to Egwene," Rand said, releasing her shoulder. "But when you can, I would like it very much if you returned to me. I will need your counsel again. At the very least, I would like you by my side as I go to Shayol Ghul. I cannot defeat him with *saidin* alone, and if we are going to use *Callandor*, I will need two women I trust in the circle with me. I have not decided upon the other. Aviendha or Elayne, perhaps. But you for certain."

"I will be there, Rand." She felt oddly proud. "Hold still for a moment. I won't hurt you. I promise."

He raised an eyebrow, but did nothing as she Delved him. She was *so* tired, but if she was going to leave him, she needed to take this opportunity to Heal his madness. It seemed, suddenly, the most important thing she could do for him. And for the world.

She Delved, staying away from the wounds at his side, which were pits of darkness that seemed to try to suck in her energy. She kept her attention on his mind. Where was the—

She stiffened. The darkness was enormous, covering the entirety of his mind. Thousands upon thousands of the tiny black thorns pricked into his brain, but beneath them was a brilliant white lacing of *something*. A white radiance, like liquid Power. Light given form and life. She gasped. It coated each of the dark tines, driving into his mind alongside them. What did it mean?

She didn't have any idea how to begin working on this. There were so many barbs. How could he even *think* with that much darkness pressing against his brain? And what had created the whiteness? She'd Healed Rand before, and hadn't noticed it then. Of course, she'd never seen the darkness until recently. Her practice with Delving was likely the reason.

She reluctantly withdrew. "I'm sorry," she said. "I can't Heal you."

"Many have tried on those wounds—you yourself included. They are simply unhealable. I don't think on them much, these days."

"Not the wounds in your side," Nynaeve said. "The madness. I . . ."

"You can Heal *madness*?"

"I think I did so in Naeff."

Rand grinned widely. "You never cease to . . . Nynaeve, do you realize that the most Talented of Healers during the Age of Legends had difficulty with diseases of the mind? Many believed it was not possible to Heal madness with the One Power."

"I'll Heal the others," she said. "Narishma, Flinn at the least, before I go. All of the Asha'man probably have at least a hint of this taint upon their minds. I don't know if I'll be able to get to the Black Tower." *Or if I want to go there.*

"Thank you," Rand said, looking northward. "But no, you shouldn't go to the Black Tower. I will need to send someone there, but it will be handled carefully. Something's happening with them. But I have so much to do . . ."

He shook his head, then looked to her. "That is one pit I cannot cross at the moment. Speak well of me to Egwene. I need her to be an ally."

Nynaeve nodded, then—feeling foolish—gave him a hug before hurrying off to seek out Narishma and Flinn. A hug. For the Dragon Reborn. She was turning as silly as Elayne.

She shook her head, thinking that perhaps some time in the White Tower would help her regain her levelheadedness.

The clouds had returned.

Egwene stood at the very apex of the White Tower, on the flat, circular roof, holding to the waist-high wall. Like a creeping fungus—like insects in a swarm—the clouds had closed up above Tar Valon. The sunlight's visit had been welcome, but brief.

The tea was back to tasting stale again. The grain stores they'd discovered were running out, and the next sacks to come in had been filled with weevils. *The Land is One with the Dragon.*

She breathed in, smelling the new air, looking out over Tar Valon. Her Tar Valon.

Saerin, Yukiri and Seaine—three of the sisters who had been the original hunters for the Black Ajah in the Tower—waited patiently behind her. They were among her most ardent supporters now, and her most useful. Everyone expected Egwene to favor the women who had been among those who split from Elaida, so being seen spending time with Aes Sedai who had stayed in the White Tower was helpful.

"What have you discovered?" Egwene asked.

Saerin shook her head, joining Egwene at the wall. The scar on her cheek and the white at her temples made the olive-skinned and blunt-faced Brown look like an aging general. "Some of the information you requested was uncertain even three thousand years ago, Mother."

"Whatever you can give me will help, daughter," Egwene said. "So long as we do not depend on the facts entirely, incomplete knowledge is better than complete ignorance."

Saerin snorted softly, but obviously recognized the quote from Yasicca Cellaech, an ancient Brown scholar.

"And you two?" Egwene asked Yukiri and Seaine.

"We're looking," Yukiri said. "Seaine has a list of possibilities. Some are actually reasonable."

Egwene raised an eyebrow. Asking a White for theories was always interesting, but not always useful. They had a tendency to ignore what was plausible, focusing on remote possibilities.

"Let us begin there, then," Egwene said. "Seaine?"

"Well," Seaine said, "I will begin by saying that one of the Forsaken undoubtedly has knowledge that we can't guess at. So there may be no way to ascertain how she defeated the Oath Rod. For instance, there might be a way to disable it for a short time, or perhaps there are special words that can be used to evade its effects. The rod is a thing of the Age of Legends, and though we've used it for millennia, we don't really *understand* it. No more than we do most *ter'angreal*."

"Very well," Egwene said.

"But," Seaine said, getting out a sheet of paper, "that taken into account, I have three theories on how one might defeat swearing on the rod. First, it is possible that the woman has another Oath Rod. Others were once said to exist, and it's plausible that one rod could release you from the oaths of another. Mesaana could have been holding one secretly. She could have taken the Three Oaths while holding our rod, then somehow used the other to negate those oaths before swearing that she was not a Darkfriend."

"Tenuous," Egwene said. "How would she have released herself without us knowing? It requires channeling Spirit."

"I considered that," Seaine said.

"Not surprising," Yukiri said.

Seaine eyed her, then continued. "This is the reason Mesaana would have needed a second Oath Rod. She could have channeled Spirit into it, then inverted the weave, leaving her linked to it."

"It seems improbable," Egwene said.

"Improbable?" Saerin replied. "It seems ridiculous. I thought you said some of these were plausible, Yukiri."

"This one *is* the least likely of the three," Seaine said. "The second method would be easier. Mesaana could have sent a look-alike wearing the Mirror of Mists. Some unfortunate sister—or novice, or even some untrained woman who could channel—under heavy Compulsion. This woman could have been forced to take the oaths in Mesaana's place. Then, since this person *wouldn't* be a Darkfriend, she could speak truthfully that she wasn't."

Egwene nodded thoughtfully. "That would have taken a lot of preparation."

"From what I've been able to learn about her," Saerin said, "Mesaana was good at preparation. She excelled at it."

Saerin's task had been to discover whatever she could about Mesaana's true nature. They had all heard the stories—who didn't know the names of each of the Forsaken, and their most terrible deeds, by heart? But Egwene put little faith in stories; she wanted something more hardfast, if she could get it.

"You said there was a third possibility?" Egwene asked.

"Yes," Seaine said. "We know that some weaves play with sound. Variations on vocal weaves are used to enhance a voice to project to a crowd, and in the ward against eavesdropping—indeed, they're used in the various tricks used to listen in on what is being said nearby. Complex uses of the Mirror of Mists can change a person's voice. With some practice, Doesine and I were able to fabricate a variation on a weave that would alter the words we spoke. In effect, we said one thing, but the other person *heard* another thing entirely."

"Dangerous ground to walk, Seaine," Saerin said, her voice gruff. "That is the kind of weave that could be used for ill purposes."

"I couldn't use it to lie," Seaine said. "I tried. The oaths hold—so long as the weave was there, I couldn't speak words that I knew another would hear as lies, even if they were truth when they left my lips. Regardless, it was an easy weave to develop. Tied off and inverted, it hung in front of me and altered my words in a way I'd indicated.

"Theoretically, if Mesaana had this weave in force, she could have taken up the Oath Rod and sworn whatever she wished. 'I vow that I will lie whenever I feel like it' for instance. The Oath Rod would have bound her with that vow, but the weaves would have changed the sounds in the air as they passed her lips. We'd have heard her saying the proper oaths."

Egwene gritted her teeth. She'd assumed that defeating the Oath Rod would be difficult. And yet here was a simple weave capable of the feat. She should have known—never use a boulder when a pebble will do, as her mother had often said.

"With this," Egwene said, "they could have been slipping Darkfriends into the ranks of the Aes Sedai for years."

"Unlikely," Saerin said. "None of the Black sisters we captured knew of this weave. If they had, then they'd have tried to use it when we made them reswear the oaths. I suspect that if Mesaana does know this trick, she has kept it to herself. The usefulness of it would vanish once too many people became aware of it."

"Still," Egwene said. "What do we do? Knowing of the weave, we could probably find a way to check for it—but I doubt that the sisters would be willing to go through the reswearing process again."

"And if it were to catch one of the Forsaken?" Yukiri asked. "It might be worth ruffling a few feathers to catch the fox hiding in the henhouse."

"She wouldn't be caught," Egwene said. "Besides, we don't know if she's using one of these methods. Seaine's logic suggests that it might be possible—without too much trouble—to defeat the Oath Rod. The actual method Mesaana used is less important than the possibility of the act."

Seaine glanced at Yukiri. None of the three had questioned Egwene's knowledge that one of the Forsaken was in the White Tower, but she knew they'd been skeptical. Well, at least they now understood that it might be possible to defeat the Oath Rod.

"I want you to continue your work," Egwene said. "You and the others were effective at capturing several Black sisters and unearthing the ferrets. This is much the same thing." *Merely far, far more dangerous.*

"We'll try, Mother," Yukiri said. "But one sister among hundreds? One of the most crafty and evil creatures ever to have lived? I doubt she will leave many clues. Our investigations into the murders have, so far, yielded very little in the way of results."

"Keep at it anyway," Egwene said. "Saerin, what have you to report?"

"Tales, rumors and whispers, Mother," Saerin said with a grimace. "You likely know the most famous stories regarding Mesaana—how she ran the schools in lands conquered by the Shadow during the War of Power. So far as I can tell, those legends are quite true. Marsim of Manetheren speaks of that in detail in her Annals of the Final Nights, and she's often a reliable source. Alrom gathered quite a full report of living through one of those schools, and fragments of it have survived.

"Mesaana wished to be a researcher, but was rejected.

The details are not clear. She also governed the Aes Sedai who went to the Shadow, leading them in battle at times, if Alrom's report is to be believed. I'm not convinced it is; I think it likely Mesaana's leadership was more figurative."

Egwene nodded slowly. "But what of her personality? Who *is* she?"

Saerin shook her head. "The Forsaken are more monsters in the night than real 'personalities' to most, Mother, and much has been lost or misquoted. From what I can tell, among the Forsaken you could think of her as the realist—the one who, rather than sitting high on a throne, steps in and gets her hands dirty. Elandria Borndat's *Seeing Through the Breaking* insists that, unlike Moghedien and Graendal, Mesaana was willing to take the reins directly.

"She was never known as the most skilled or powerful of the Forsaken, but she was extremely capable. Elandria explains that she did what needed to be done. When others would be scheming, she would be carefully building up defenses and training new recruits." Saerin hesitated. "She . . . well, she sounds much like an Amyrlin, Mother. The Shadow's Amyrlin."

"Light," Yukiri said. "Little wonder she set up here." The Gray seemed very unsettled by that.

"The only other thing I could find of relevance, Mother," Saerin said, "was a curious reference from the Blue scholar Lannis, who indicated that Mesaana was second only to Demandred in sheer anger."

Egwene frowned. "I'd assume that all of the Forsaken are full of hate."

"Not hate," Saerin said. "*Anger*. Lannis thought Mesaana was angry—at herself, at the world, at the other Forsaken—because she *wasn't* one of those at the forefront. That could make her very dangerous."

Egwene nodded slowly. *She's an organizer,* she thought. *An administrator who hates being relegated to that position.*

Was that why she'd stayed in the Tower after the Black sisters had been found? Did she desire to bring some great accomplishment to the Dark One? Verin had said that the Forsaken shared one unifying trait: their selfishness.

She tried to deliver a broken White Tower, Egwene thought. *But that has failed. She was probably part of the attempt to kidnap Rand as well. Another fiasco. And the women sent to destroy the Black Tower?*

Mesaana would need something grand to offset so many failures. Killing Egwene would work. That might send the White Tower back into division.

Gawyn had been mortified when she'd said she might use herself as bait. Dared she do so? She gripped the railing, standing above the Tower, above the city that depended on her, looking out on a world that needed her.

Something had to be done; Mesaana had to be drawn out. If what Saerin said was true, then the woman would be willing to fight directly—she wouldn't hide and poke from the shadows. Egwene's task, then, was to tempt her with an opportunity, one that didn't seem obvious, one she couldn't resist.

"Come," Egwene said, walking toward the ramp back down into the Tower. "I have some preparations to make."

CHAPTER
16

Shanna'har

Faile walked the camp in the waning evening light, making her way toward the quartermaster's tent. Perrin had sent their group of scouts through the gateway to Cairhien; they'd return the next morning.

Perrin was still brooding about the Whitecloaks. Over the last several days, the two armies had exchanged several letters, Perrin trying to maneuver for a second, more formal parley while the Whitecloaks insisted on a battle. Faile had given Perrin choice words about sneaking off to meet with the Whitecloaks without her.

Perrin was stalling as he let Elyas and the Aiel scout the Whitecloaks to try to find a way to sneak their people out, but it was unlikely to be an option. He'd succeeded back in the Two Rivers, but there had been only a handful of captives then. Now there were hundreds.

Perrin was not dealing well with his guilt. Well, Faile would talk with him shortly. She continued through the camp, passing the Mayener section to her left, with banners flying high.

I will have to deal with that one soon as well, Faile thought, looking up at Berelain's banner. The rumors about her and Perrin were problematic. She'd suspected that Berelain might try something in Faile's absence, but taking him into her tent at night seemed particularly forward.

Faile's next steps would have to be taken with extreme care. Her husband, his people, and his allies were all balanced precariously. Faile found herself wishing she could ask her mother for advice.

That shocked her, and she hesitated, stopping on the

worn pathway of trampled yellow grass and mud. *Light,* Faile thought. *Look what has happened to me.*

Two years ago, Faile—then called Zarine—had run from her home in Saldaea to become a Hunter for the Horn. She'd rebelled against her duties as the eldest, and the training her mother had insisted she undergo.

She hadn't run because she'd hated the work; indeed, she'd proven adept at everything required of her. So why had she gone? In part for adventure. But in part—she admitted to herself only now—because of all the assumptions. In Saldaea, you *always* did what was expected of you. Nobody wondered if you would do your duty, particularly if you were a relative of the Queen herself.

And so . . . she'd left. Not because she'd hated what she would become, but because she had hated the fact that it had seemed so inevitable. Now here she was, using all of the things her mother had insisted she learn.

It was nearly enough to make Faile laugh. She could tell a host of things about the camp from a mere glance. They'd need to find some good leather for the cobblers soon. Water wasn't a problem, as it had been raining light sprinkles often over the last few days, but dry wood for campfires was an issue. One group of refugees—a collection of former wetlander *gai'shain* who watched Perrin's Aiel with outright hostility—would need attention. As she walked, she watched to make certain the camp had proper sanitation, and that the soldiers were caring for themselves. Some men would show utmost concern for their horses, then forget to eat anything proper—or at least healthy. Not to mention their habit of spending half the night gossiping by the campfires.

She shook her head and continued walking, entering the supply ring, where food wagons had been unloaded for the horde of cooks and serving maids. The supply ring was almost a village itself, with hundreds of people quickly wearing pathways in the muddy grass. She passed a group of dirty-faced youths digging pits in the ground, then a patch of women chattering and humming as they peeled potatoes, children gathering the rinds and throwing them into the pits. There weren't many of those children, but Perrin's force had gathered a number of families from around the countryside who—starving—had begged to join.

Serving men ran baskets of peeled potatoes to cooking pots, which were slowly being filled with water by young women making trips to the stream. Journeyman cooks prepared coals for roasting and older cooks were mixing spices into sauces that could be poured over other foods, which was really the only way to give flavor to such mass quantities.

Elderly women—the few in the camp—shuffled past with bent backs and light wicker baskets bearing herbs clutched on thin arms, their shawls rippling as they chatted with crackling voices. Soldiers hurried in and out, carrying game. Boys between childhood and manhood gathered sticks for tinder; she passed a small gaggle of these who had grown distracted capturing spiders.

It was a tempest of confusion and order coexisting, like two sides of a coin. Strange how well Faile fit in here. Looking back at herself only a few years before, she was amazed to realize that she saw a spoiled, self-centered child. Leaving the Borderlands to become a Hunter for the Horn? She'd abandoned duties, home and family. What had she been thinking?

She passed some women milling grain, then walked around a fresh batch of wild scallions lying on a blanket beside them, waiting to be made into soup. She was glad she'd left and met Perrin, but that didn't excuse her actions. With a grimace, she remembered forcing Perrin to travel the Ways in the darkness, alone. She didn't even recall what he'd done to set her off, though she'd never admit that to him.

Her mother had once called her spoiled, and she'd been right. Her mother had also insisted that Faile learn to run the estates, and all the while Faile had dreamed of marrying a Hunter for the Horn and spending her life far away from armies and the boring duties of lords.

Light bless you, Mother, Faile thought. What would she, or Perrin, have done without that training? Without her mother's teachings, Faile would have been useless. Administration of the entire camp would have rested on Aravine's shoulders. Capable though the woman was as Perrin's camp steward, she couldn't have managed this all on her own. Nor should she have been expected to.

Faile reached the quartermaster's station, a small pavilion at the very heart of the cooking pits. The breeze brought an amalgamation of scents: fat seared by flames, potatoes boiling, peppered sauces spiced with garlic, the wet, sticky scent of potato peelings being carried to the small herd of hogs they'd managed to bring out of Malden.

The quartermaster, Bavin Rockshaw, was a pale-faced Cairhienin with blond speckled through his graying brown hair, like the fur on a mixed-breed dog. He was spindly through the arms, legs and chest, yet had an almost perfectly round paunch. He had apparently worked at quartermastering as far back as the Aiel War, and was an expert—a master as practiced in overseeing supply operations as a master carpenter was at woodworking.

That, of course, meant that he was an expert at taking bribes. When he saw Faile, he smiled and bowed stiffly enough to be formal, but without ornamentation. "I'm a simple soldier, doing his duty," that bow said.

"Lady Faile!" he exclaimed, waving over some of his serving men. "Here to inspect the ledgers, I assume?"

"Yes, Bavin," she said, though she knew there would be nothing suspicious in them. He was far too careful.

Still, she made a cursory motion of going through the records. One of the men brought her a stool, another a table upon which to place the ledgers, and yet another a cup of tea. She was impressed at how neatly the columns added up. Her mother had explained that often, a quartermaster would make many messy notations, referencing other pages or other ledgers, separating different types of supplies into different books, all to make it more difficult to track what was going on. A leader who was befuddled by the notations would assume that the quartermaster *must* be doing his job.

There was none of that here. Whatever tricks of numbering Bavin was using to obscure his thievery, they were nothing short of magical. And he *was* stealing, or at least being creative in how he doled out his foodstuffs. That was inevitable. Most quartermasters didn't really consider it thievery; he was in charge of his supplies, and that was that.

"How odd it is," Faile said as she leafed through the ledger. "The strange twists of fate."

"My Lady?" Bavin asked.

"Hmm? Oh, it is nothing. Only that Torven Rikshan's camp has received their meals each evening a good hour ahead of the other camps. I'm certain that's just by chance."

Bavin hesitated. "Undoubtedly, my Lady."

She continued to leaf through the ledgers. Torven Rikshan was a Cairhienin lord, and had been placed in charge of one of the twenty camps within the larger mass of refugees. He had an usually large number of nobles in his particular camp. Aravine had brought this to Faile's attention; she wasn't certain what Torven had given to receive supplies for meals more quickly, but it wouldn't do. The other camps might feel that Perrin was favoring one over another.

"Yes," Faile said, laughing lightly. "Merely coincidence. These things happen in a camp so large. Why, just the other day Varkel Tius was complaining to me that he had put in a requisition for canvas to repair torn tents, but hasn't had his canvas for nearly a week now. Yet I know for a fact that Soffi Moraton ripped her tent during the stream crossing but had it repaired by that evening."

Bavin was silent.

Faile made no accusations. Her mother had cautioned that a good quartermaster was too valuable to toss into prison, particularly when the next man was likely to be half as capable and equally corrupt. Faile's duty was not to expose or embarrass Bavin. It was to make him worried enough that he kept himself in check.

"Perhaps you can do something about these irregularities, Bavin," she said, closing the ledger. "I loathe to burden you with silly matters, but the problems must not reach my husband's ears. You know how he is when enraged."

Actually, Perrin was about as likely to hurt a man like Bavin as Faile was to flap her arms and fly away. But the camp didn't see it that way. They heard reports of Perrin's fury in battle, along with her occasional arguments with him—provoked by Faile so that they could have a proper discussion—and assumed he had a terrible temper. That was good, so long as they also thought of him as honorable and kind. Protective of his people, yet filled with rage at those who crossed him.

She rose from the stool, handing the ledgers to one of the men, curly-haired and with ink stains on his fingers and jerkin. She smiled at Bavin, then made her way out of the supply ring. She noted with displeasure that the bunch of wild scallions beside the pathway had spoiled in the moments since she'd seen them last, their stalks melted and runny, as if they'd been rotting in the sun for weeks. These spoilings had begun only recently inside of camp, but by reports, it happened far more frequently out in the countryside.

It was hard to tell the hour with the sky so full of clouds, but it seemed from the darkening horizon that her time to meet with Perrin had come. Faile smiled. Her mother had warned her what would happen to her, had told her what was expected of her, and Faile had worried that she would feel trapped by life.

But what Deira *hadn't* mentioned was how fulfilling it would be. Perrin made the difference. It was no trap at all to be caught with him.

Perrin stood with one foot up on the stump of a felled tree, facing north. The hilltop let him look out over the plains toward the cliffs of Garen's Wall rising like the knuckles of a slumbering giant.

He opened his mind, questing out for wolves. There were some in the distance, almost too faint to feel. Wolves stayed away from large gatherings of men.

The camp spread out behind him, watchfires fluttering at its boundaries. This hillside was far enough away to be secluded, but not so distant as to be solitary. He wasn't certain why Faile had asked him to meet her here at dusk, but she'd smelled excited, so he hadn't pried. Women liked their secrets.

He heard Faile coming up the side of the hill, stepping softly on the wet grass. She was good at being quiet—not nearly as good as Elyas or one of the Aiel, but better than one might think of her. But he could smell her scent, soap with lavender. She used that particular soap only on days she deemed special.

She stepped atop the hillside, beautiful, impressive. She wore a violet vest over a long silk blouse of a lighter shade. Where had she gotten the clothing? He hadn't seen her in this fine outfit before.

"My husband," she said, stepping up to him. He could

faintly hear others near the foot of the hill—probably *Cha Faile*. She'd left them behind. "You look concerned."

"It's my fault that Gill and the others were captured, Faile," he said. "My failures continue to mount. It's a wonder anyone follows me."

"Perrin," she said, laying a hand on his arm. "We've spoken of this. You mustn't say such things."

"Why?"

"Because I've never known you to be a liar," she said with a softly chiding tone.

He looked at her. It was growing dark, though he could still make out details. She'd have a harder time seeing them.

"Why do you continue to fight this?" she asked. "You *are* a good leader, Perrin."

"I wouldn't have given myself up for them," he said.

She frowned. "What does that have to—"

"Back in the Two Rivers," Perrin said, turning away from her, looking north again, "I was ready to do it. When the Whitecloaks had Mat's family and the Luhhans, I'd have given myself up. This time, I wouldn't have. Even when I spoke to their leader, asking his price, I knew I wouldn't give myself up."

"You're becoming a better leader."

"How can you say that? I'm growing callous, Faile. If you knew the things I did to get you back, the things I would have done . . ." He fingered the hammer at his side. *The tooth or the claw, Young Bull, it matters not.* He'd thrown away the axe, but could he blame it for his brutality? It was only a tool. He could use the hammer to do the same terrible things.

"It's not callous," Faile said, "or selfish. You're a lord now, and you can't let it be known that capturing your subjects will undermine your rule. Do you think Queen Morgase would abdicate to tyrants who kidnapped her subjects? No leader could rule that way. Your inability to stop evil men does not make you evil yourself."

"I don't want this mantle, Faile. I never have."

"I know."

"Sometimes I wish I'd never left the Two Rivers. I wish I'd let Rand run off to his destiny, leaving regular folk behind to live their lives."

He caught a scent of annoyance from her.

"But if I'd stayed," he added hastily, "I'd never have met you. So I'm glad I left. I'm just saying I'll be glad when this is all through and finished, and I can go back to someplace simple."

"You think the Two Rivers will ever go back to being the way you remember it?"

He hesitated. She was right—when they'd gone, it had already been showing signs of change. Refugees from across the mountains moving in, the villages swelling. Now, with so many men joining him in war, getting ideas into their heads about having a lord . . .

"I could find someplace else," he said, feeling stubborn. "There are other villages. They won't all change."

"And you'd drag me off to one of these villages, Perrin Aybara?" she said.

"I . . ." What would happen if Faile, his beautiful Faile, were confined to a sleepy village? He always insisted that he was only a blacksmith. But was Faile a blacksmith's wife? "I would never force you to do anything, Faile," he said, cupping her face in his hand. He always felt awkward when touching her satin cheeks with his thick, callused fingers.

"I'd go, if you really wanted me to," she replied. That was odd. He'd normally expect a snap from her at his awkward tongue. "But is it what you want? Is it really?"

"I don't know what I want," he said frankly. No, he didn't want to drag Faile off to a village. "Maybe . . . life as a blacksmith in a city, somewhere?"

"If you wish it," she repeated. "Of course, that would leave the Two Rivers without a lord. They'd have to find someone else."

"No. They don't *need* a lord. That's why I have to stop them treating me like one."

"And you think they'd give up on the idea that quickly?" Faile asked, smelling amused. "After they've seen how everyone else does it? After the way they fawned over that fool Luc? After welcoming in all of those people from Almoth Plain, who are used to lords?"

What *would* the Two Rivers folk do if he stepped down as their lord? In a sinking moment of realization, he knew that Faile was right. *Surely they'd pick someone who'd do a better job of it than me,* he thought. *Maybe Master al'Vere.*

But could Perrin trust that? Men like Master al'Vere

or Tam might turn down the position. Might they end up picking someone like old Cenn Buie? Would they have a choice? If Perrin stepped aside, might some person who figured himself highborn *seize* power?

Don't be a fool, Perrin Aybara, he thought. *Almost anyone would be better than you.*

Still, the thought of someone else taking control—someone else being lord—filled him with intense anxiety. And a surprising amount of sadness.

"Now," Faile said, "stop your brooding. I have grand intentions for this evening." She clapped her hands loudly three times, and movements began below. Soon, servants crested the hillside. Perrin recognized them as people she'd appropriated from among the refugees, a group as loyal to her as *Cha Faile*.

They carried canvas, which they spread on the ground. Then they covered that with a blanket. And what was that he smelled coming up from below? Ham?

"What *is* this, Faile?" he asked.

"At first," she said, "I assumed that you had something special planned for our *shanna'har*. I grew nervous when you didn't mention it, however, and so I asked. It appears that you do not celebrate it in the Two Rivers, odd though that is."

"*Shanna'har*?" Perrin asked, scratching his head.

"In the coming weeks," Faile said, "we will have been married one year. This is our first *shanna'har*, our marriage celebration." She folded her arms, watching as her servants arranged a meal on the blanket. "In Saldaea, we celebrate the *shanna'har* each year in the early summer. It is a festival to mark another year together, another year with neither husband nor wife fallen to the Trollocs. Young couples are told to savor their first *shanna'har*, much as one savors the first taste of a succulent meal. Our marriage will only be new to us once."

The servants laid out a meal, including several glass bowls with candles in them. Faile dismissed the servants with a smile and a wave, and they retreated down the side of the hill. Faile had obviously taken care to make the meal look lavish. The blanket was embroidered, perhaps taken from Shaido spoils. The meal was served on silver plates and platters, ham over a bed of boiled barley and capers across the top. There was even wine.

Faile stepped closer to him. "I realize that there has been much, this year, that is not worth savoring. Malden, the Prophet, that harsh winter. But if these things are the cost for being with you, Perrin, then I would pay them freely a dozen times over.

"If all were well, we would spend this next month giving gifts to one another, affirming our love, celebrating our first summer as husband and wife. I doubt we will have the month of ease that is our right, but at least we should spend and enjoy this evening together."

"I don't know if I can, Faile," he said. "The Whitecloaks, the sky . . . Light! The Last Battle itself is almost here. The *Last Battle*, Faile! How can I feast while my people are being held under threat of execution and while the world itself may die?"

"If the world itself is going to die," Faile said, "is this not the time when a man *must* take time to appreciate what he has? Before it is all taken?"

Perrin hesitated. She laid a hand on his arm, her touch so soft. She hadn't raised her voice. Did she want him to yell? It was so hard to tell when she wanted an argument and when she didn't. Maybe Elyas would have advice for him.

"Please," she said softly. "Try to relax for one evening. For me."

"All right," he said, laying his hand on hers.

She led him to the blanket and they settled down, side by side before the array of silver dishes. Faile lit more candles off of the lit ones the servants had left. The night was chilly—the clouds seemed to draw summer warmth away. "Why do this outside?" Perrin said. "And not in our tent?"

"I asked Tam what you do in the Two Rivers for *shanna'har*," she said. "And as I feared, I learned that you don't celebrate it. That is really quite backward, you realize—we'll need to change the custom, once things settle down. Regardless, Tam said that the closest they had was something he and his wife did. Once a year, they would pack up a full meal—as extravagant as they could afford— and hike to a new place in the woods. They would dine there and spend the day with one another." She snuggled up against him. "Our wedding was done in the Two Rivers fashion, so I wished this day to be after that fashion as well."

He smiled. Despite his earlier objections his tension was easing. The food smelled good, and his stomach growled, prompting Faile to sit up and take his plate and hand it to him.

He dug in. He tried to keep his manners, but the food was excellent, and it had been a long day. He found himself ripping into the ham with ferocity, though he tried to take care not to drip on the fancy blanket.

Faile ate more slowly, the scent of amusement mixing with that of her soap.

"What?" Perrin asked, wiping his mouth. She was lit only by the candles, now that the sun was fully down.

"There's much of the wolf in you, my husband."

He froze, noticing that he'd been licking his fingers. He growled at himself, wiping them instead on a napkin. As much as he liked wolves, he wouldn't invite them to the dinner table with him. "Too much of the wolf in me," he said.

"You are what you are, my husband. And I happen to love what you are, so that is well."

He continued to chew on his cut of the ham. The night was quiet, the servants having retreated far enough away that he couldn't smell or hear them. Likely Faile had left orders that they weren't to be disturbed, and with the trees at the base of the hillside, they wouldn't have to worry about being observed.

"Faile," he said softy, "you need to know what I did while you were captive. I did things I worried would turn me into someone you would no longer want. It wasn't only the deal with the Seanchan. There were people in a city, So Habor, that I can't stop thinking of. People that maybe I should have helped. And there was a Shaido, with his hand—"

"I heard about that. It seems that you did what you had to."

"I'd have gone much farther," Perrin admitted. "Hating myself all the way. You spoke of a lord being strong enough to resist letting himself be manipulated. Well, I'll never be that strong. Not if you're taken."

"We shall have to make certain I don't get taken."

"It could ruin me, Faile," he said softly. "Anything else, I think I could handle. But if you are used against me, nothing will matter. I'd do anything to protect you, Faile. *Anything*."

"Perhaps you should wrap me up in soft cloth, then," she said dryly, "and tuck me away in a locked room." Oddly, her scent was not offended.

"I wouldn't do that," Perrin said. "You know I wouldn't. But this means I have a weakness, a terrible one. The type a leader can't have."

She snorted. "You think other leaders don't have weaknesses, Perrin? Every King or Queen of Saldaea has had their own. Nikiol Dianatkhah was a drunkard, despite being known as one of our greatest kings, and Belairah married and put her husband away four times. Her heart always did lead her to trouble. Jonasim had a son whose gambling ways nearly brought her House to ruin, and Lyonford couldn't keep his temper if challenged. Each and every one was a great monarch. And all had their share of weaknesses."

Perrin continued to chew on his food, thoughtful.

"In the Borderlands," Faile said, "we have a saying. 'A polished sword reflects the truth.' A man can *claim* to be diligent in his duties, but if his sword isn't polished, you know that he's been idle.

"Well, your sword is bright, my husband. These last few weeks, you keep *saying* that you led poorly during my captivity. You'd have me believe that you led the entire camp to ruin and dust! But that's not true at all. You kept them focused; you inspired them, maintained a strong presence, and kept the air of a lord."

"Berelain's behind some of that," he said. "I half think the woman would have bathed me herself if I'd gone another day without."

"I'm certain that wouldn't have been good for the rumors," Faile noted dryly.

"Faile, I—"

"I'll deal with Berelain," Faile said. Her voice sounded dangerous. "That's one duty you needn't distract yourself with."

"But—"

"I'll *deal* with her," Faile said, her voice more firm. It was not wise to challenge her when she smelled that way, not unless he wanted to start a full argument. She softened, taking another bite of barley. "When I said you were like a wolf, my husband, I wasn't talking about the way you eat. I was talking about the way you give your attention. You are driven. Given a problem to solve, no matter how grand, and you will see it done.

"Can't you understand? That's a wonderful trait in a leader. It is exactly what the Two Rivers will need. Assuming, of course, that you have a wife to care for some of the smaller issues." She frowned. "I wish you'd spoken to me about the banner before burning it. It will be difficult to raise it again without looking foolish."

"I don't want to raise it again," Perrin said. "That's why I had them burn it."

"But *why*?"

He took another bite of his ham, pointedly not watching her. She smelled curious, almost desperately so.

I can't lead them, he thought. *Not until I know if I can master the wolf.* How could he explain? Explain that he feared the way it took control when he fought, when he wanted something too badly?

He would not rid himself of the wolves; they had become too much a part of him. But where would he leave his people, where would he leave Faile, if he lost himself to what was inside of him?

He again remembered a dirty creature, once a man, locked in a cage. *There is nothing left in this one that remembers being a man . . .*

"My husband," Faile said, resting a hand on his arm. "Please." She smelled of pain. That twisted his heart about.

"It has to do with those Whitecloaks," Perrin said.

"What? Perrin, I thought I said—"

"It has to do," Perrin said firmly, "with what happened to me the first time I met with them. And what I'd begun to discover in the days before."

Faile frowned.

"I've told you that I killed two Whitecloaks," he said. "Before I met you."

"Yes."

"Settle back," he said. "You need to know the whole story."

And so he told her. Hesitantly at first, but the words soon grew easier. He spoke of Shadar Logoth, and of their group being scattered. Of Egwene letting him take the lead, perhaps the first time he'd been forced to do that.

He'd already told her of his meeting with Elyas. She knew much about Perrin, things that he'd never told anyone else, things he'd never even spoken of with Elyas. She knew about the wolf. She knew that he feared he'd lose himself.

But she didn't know what he felt in battle. She didn't know what it had felt like to kill those Whitecloaks, to taste their blood—either in his own mouth, or through his link with the wolves. She didn't know what it had been like to be consumed by anger, fear and desperation when she'd been taken. These were the things he haltingly explained.

He told her of the frenzy he'd gone into when searching for her in the wolf dream. He spoke of Noam and what he feared would happen to him. And of how it related to how he acted when he fought.

Faile listened, sitting quietly atop the hilltop, arms wrapped around her legs, lit by candlelight. Her scents were subdued. Perhaps he should have held some things back. No woman wanted to know what a beast her husband became when he killed, did she? But now that he was speaking, he wanted to be rid of his secrets. He was tired of them.

Each word spoken made him relax more. It did what the meal—touching though it had been—hadn't been able to. In telling her of his struggles, he felt some of his burden lift.

He finished by speaking of Hopper. He wasn't certain why he'd saved the wolf for last; Hopper was part of much Perrin had told before—the Whitecloaks, the wolf dream. But it felt right to reserve Hopper until the end, so he did.

As he finished, he stared at the flame of one of the candles. Two of them had gone out, leaving others still to flicker. That wasn't dim light to his eyes. He had trouble remembering what the days had been like when his senses had been as weak as an ordinary man's.

Faile leaned against him, wrapping his arm around her. "Thank you," she said.

He let out a deep sigh, leaning back against the stump behind him, feeling her warmth.

"I want to tell you about Malden," she said.

"You don't have to," he said. "Just because I—"

"Hush. I was quiet while you spoke. It's my turn."

"All right."

It should have been worrying for him to hear about Malden. He lay with his back to the stump, sky crackling with energy above, the Pattern itself in danger of unraveling, while his wife spoke of being captured and beaten. Yet it was one of the most oddly relaxing things he'd ever experienced.

The events in that city had been important to her, maybe even good for her. Though he was angered at hearing how Sevanna had trussed Faile up naked and left her overnight. Someday he'd hunt that woman down.

Not today, however. Today he had his wife in his arms, and her strong voice was a comfort. He should have realized she would have planned her own escape. In fact, listening to her careful preparation, he began to feel a fool. She'd been worried that he'd get himself killed trying to rescue her—she didn't say it, but he could infer it. How well she knew him.

Faile left some things out. He didn't mind. Faile would be like a penned and caged animal without her secrets. He got a good hint of what she was hiding, though. It was something to do with that Brotherless who had captured her, something about Faile's plans to trick the man and his friends into helping her escape. Perhaps she'd felt a fondness for him, and didn't wish Perrin to regret killing him. That wasn't necessary. Those Brotherless had been with the Shaido, and they had attacked and killed men under Perrin's protection. No act of kindness would redeem that. They deserved their deaths.

That gave him pause. The Whitecloaks probably said very similar things about him. But the Whitecloaks had attacked first.

She finished. It was very late, now, and Perrin reached over to a bundle that Faile's servants had brought up, pulling out a blanket.

"Well?" Faile asked as he settled back, putting his arm around her again.

"I'm surprised that you didn't give me an earful for barreling in like a wild bull and stomping all over your plans."

That made her smell satisfied. It wasn't the emotion he'd expected, but he'd long ago stopped trying to decipher the ways of women's thought.

"I almost brought the matter up tonight," Faile said, "so that we could have a proper argument and a proper reconciliation."

"Why didn't you?"

"I decided that this night should be done in the Two Rivers way."

"And you think husbands and wives don't argue in the Two Rivers?" he asked, amused.

"Well, perhaps they do. But you, husband, always seem uncomfortable when we yell. I'm very glad you've begun to stand up for yourself, as is proper. But I have asked much from you to adapt to my ways. I thought, tonight, I would try to adapt to yours."

Those were words that he had never expected to hear from Faile. It seemed the most personal thing she could ever have given him. Embarrassingly, he felt tears in his eyes, and he pulled her tight.

"Now," she said, "I'm not a docile sheep, mind you."

"I would *never* think that," he said. "Never."

She smelled satisfied.

"I'm sorry I didn't give much thought to you escaping on your own," Perrin said.

"I forgive you."

He looked down at her, those beautiful dark eyes reflecting the candlelight. "Does this mean we can have the reconciliation without the argument?"

She smiled. "I will allow it, this once. And, of course, the servants have strict orders to ensure our solitude."

He kissed her. It felt so very right, and he knew that the worries he'd had—and the awkwardness that had been between them since Malden—were gone. Whether it had been something real or something he imagined, it had passed.

He had Faile back, truly and completely.

CHAPTER
17

Partings, and a Meeting

The morning after the *gholam* attack, Mat woke from dreams rotten as last month's eggs, feeling stiff and aching. He had spent the night sleeping in a hollow he'd found beneath Aludra's supply wagon. He had chosen the location by random chance, using his dice.

He climbed out from under the wagon, standing and rolling his shoulder, feeling it pop. Bloody ashes. One of the best things about having money was *not* having to sleep in ditches. There were beggars who spent nights better than this.

The wagon smelled of sulphur and powders. He was tempted to peek under the oiled tarp that stretched over the back of it, but there would be no point. Aludra and her powders were incomprehensible. So long as the dragons performed, Mat did not mind not knowing how they worked. Well, he did not mind it much. Not enough to risk irritating her.

She was not there at the wagon, fortunately for Mat. She would complain at him again for not having gotten her a bellfounder. She seemed to think him her own personal messenger boy. An unruly one, who refused to do his job properly. Most women had moments like that.

He walked through camp, brushing bits of straw from his hair. He almost went searching for Lopin to have him draw a bath, until he remembered that Lopin was dead. Bloody ashes! Poor man.

Thinking about poor Lopin put Mat in an even more dour mood as he walked toward where he'd find some breakfast. Juilin found him first. The short Tairen thief-catcher wore his flat-topped conical hat and dark blue coat. "Mat," he said. "Is it true? You've given permission for the Aes Sedai to go back to the Tower?"

"They didn't need my permission," Mat said, wincing. If the women heard it said that way, they would tan his hide and make saddle leather from it. "I'm planning to give them horses, though."

"They have them already," Juilin said, looking in the direction of the picket lines. "Said you gave them permission."

Mat sighed. His stomach growled, but food would have to wait. He walked toward the picket lines; he would need to make sure the Aes Sedai did not make off with his best stock.

"I've been thinking I might go with them," Juilin said, joining Mat. "Take Thera to Tar Valon."

"You're welcome to leave any time," Mat said. "I won't hold you here." Juilin was a good enough fellow. A little stiff at times. Well, very stiff. Juilin could make a White-cloak look relaxed. He was not the type you wanted to take with you dicing; he would spend the night scowling at every-one in the tavern and muttering about the crimes they had certainly committed. But he was reliable, and a good hand to have in a pinch.

"I want to get back to Tear," Juilin said. "But the Sean-chan would be so close, and Thera . . . It worries her. She doesn't much like the idea of Tar Valon either, but we don't have many choices, and the Aes Sedai promised that if I came with them, they'd get me work in Tar Valon."

"So, this is parting, then?" Mat said, stopping and turn-ing to him.

"For now," Juilin said. He hesitated, then held out his hand. Mat took it and shook, and then the thief-catcher was off to gather his things and his woman.

Mat thought for a moment, then changed his mind and headed for the cook tent. Juilin would slow the Aes Sedai, probably, and he wanted to fetch something.

A short time later, he arrived at the picket lines fed and carrying a cloth-wrapped bundle under his arm. The Aes Sedai had, of course, created an inordinately large cara-van out of some of his best horses. Teslyn and Joline also seemed to have decided they could commandeer some pack animals and some soldiers to do the loading. Mat sighed and walked into the mess, checking over the horses.

Joline sat on Moonglow, a mare of Tairen stock that had

belonged to one of the men Mat had lost in the fighting to escape the Seanchan. The more reserved Edesina had mounted Firewisp, and was glancing occasionally at two women who stood to the side. Dark-skinned Bethamin and pale, yellow-haired Seta were former *sul'dam*.

The Seanchan women tried very hard to look aloof as the group gathered. Mat sauntered up to them.

"Highness," Seta said, "it is true? You're going to allow these to roam free of you?"

"Best to be rid of them," Mat said, wincing at her choice of titles for him. Did they have to throw around such words like they were wooden pennies? Anyway, the two Seanchan women had changed a great deal since beginning with the group, but they still seemed to find it odd that Mat did not wish to use the Aes Sedai as weapons. "Do you want to go, or do you want to stay?"

"We will go," Bethamin said firmly. She was determined to learn, it seemed.

"Yes," Seta said, "though I sometimes think it might be better to simply let us die, as opposed to . . . Well, what we are, what we represent, means that we are a danger to the Empire."

Mat nodded. "Tuon is a *sul'dam*," he said.

The two women looked down.

"Go with the Aes Sedai," Mat said. "I'll give you your own horses, so you don't have to rely on them. Learn to channel. That'll be more use than dying. Maybe someday you two can convince Tuon of the truth. Help me find a way to fix this without causing the Empire to collapse."

The two women looked to him, more firm and confident, suddenly. "Yes, Highness," Bethamin said. "It is a good purpose for us to have. Thank you, Highness."

Seta actually got tears in her eyes! Light, what did they think he had just promised them? Mat retreated before they could get any more odd ideas in their heads. Flaming women. Still, he could not help feeling sorry for them. Learning that they could channel, worrying they might be a danger to everyone around them.

That's how Rand felt, Mat thought. *Poor fool.* As always, the colors swirled when he thought of Rand. He tried not to do it too often, and before he could banish those colors, he

caught a glimpse of Rand shaving in a fine, gilded mirror
hanging in a beautiful bathing chamber.

Mat gave some orders to get the *sul'dam* horses, then he
walked over toward the Aes Sedai. Thom had arrived and
he strolled over. "Light, Mat," he said. "You look like you
tangled with a briarstitch patch and came out sore."

Mat raised a hand to his hair, which was probably a real
sight. "I lived through the night, and the Aes Sedai are leaving. I've half a mind to dance a jig at that."

Thom snorted. "Did you know those two were going to
be here?"

"The *sul'dam*? I figured."

"No, *those* two." He pointed.

Mat turned, frowning as he found Leilwin and Bayle
Domon riding up. Their possessions were rolled up on the
backs of their horses. Leilwin—then known as Egeanin—
had once been a Seanchan noblewoman, but Tuon had
stripped her name away. She wore a dress with divided
skirts of muted gray. Her short dark hair had grown out,
and hung over her ears. She climbed from her saddle and
stalked in Mat's direction.

"Burn me," Mat said to Thom, "if I can be rid of her, too,
I'll almost start thinking that life has turned fair on me."

Domon followed her as they approached. He was her
so'jhin. Or . . . could he still be *so'jhin*, now that she had
no title? Well, either way, he was her husband. The Illianer
was thick of girth, and strong. He was not too bad a fellow,
except when he was around Leilwin. Which was always.

"Cauthon," she said, stepping up to him.

"Leilwin," he replied. "You're leaving?"

"Yes."

Mat smiled. He really *was* going to do that dance!

"I always intended to make my way to the White Tower,"
she continued. "I set my mind there on the day I left Ebou
Dar. If the Aes Sedai are leaving, I will go with them. A
ship is always wise to join a convoy, when the right opportunity is presented."

"Too bad to see you go," Mat lied, tipping his hat to her.
Leilwin was as tough as a hundred-year oak stuck with bits
of axe left over from the men foolish enough to try to chop it
down. If her horse threw a shoe on the road to Tar Valon, she

would likely sling the animal over her shoulder and carry it the rest of the way.

But she did not like Mat, for all he had done to save her skin. Maybe it was because he had not let her take charge, or maybe because she had been forced to act like his lover. Well, he had not enjoyed that part either. It had been like holding a sword by the blade and pretending that it did not sting.

Though it *had* been fun to watch her squirm.

"Be well, Matrim Cauthon," Leilwin said. "I don't envy the place you've put yourself in. In some ways, I think the winds that carry you may actually be rougher than the ones which have buffeted me, recently." She nodded to him, then turned to go.

Domon reached over, laying a hand on Mat's arm. "You did do as you said. By my aged grandmother! You gave a bumpy ride of it, but you did do as you said. My thanks."

The two of them moved off. Mat shook his head, waving to Thom and strolling over to the Aes Sedai. "Teslyn," Mat said. "Edesina. Joline. All is well?"

"It is," Joline said.

"Good, good," Mat said. "You have sufficient pack animals?"

"They will do, Master Cauthon," Joline said. Then, covering a wince, she added, "Thank you for giving them to us."

Mat smiled broadly. My, but it was amusing to hear her trying to act respectful! She had obviously expected Elayne to welcome her and the others with open arms, not turn them away from the palace without an audience.

Joline eyed Mat, lush lips pressed together. "I would like to have tamed you, Cauthon," she said. "I've still half a mind to return someday and see the job done properly."

"I'll wait breathlessly for that, then," he said, taking the cloth-wrapped package from under his arm. He handed it up to her.

"What is this?" she asked, not reaching for it.

Mat shook the bundle. "Parting gift," he said. "Where I come from, you never let a traveler depart without giving her something for the road. It would be rude."

Reluctantly, she accepted it and peeked inside. She was obviously surprised to find that it contained a collection of about a dozen powdered sweetbuns. "Thank you," she said, frowning.

"I'm sending soldiers with you," Mat said. "They'll bring my horses back once you arrive in Tar Valon."

Joline opened her mouth as if to complain, but then closed it. What argument could she make?

"That will be acceptable, Cauthon," Teslyn said, moving her black gelding closer.

"I'll give them orders to do as you say," Mat said, turning to her. "So you'll have people to command about and make set up your tents. But there's a condition attached."

Teslyn raised an eyebrow.

"I want you to tell the Amyrlin something," he said. "If it's Egwene, this should be easy. But even if it isn't, you tell her. The White Tower has something of mine, and it's nearly time that I reclaimed it. I don't want to, but what I want never seems to matter a whisker, these days. So I'll be coming, and I don't mean to be bloody turned away." He smiled. "Use that exact language."

Teslyn, to her credit, chuckled softly. "I'll see it done, though I doubt the rumors are true. Elaida would not have given up the Amyrlin Seat."

"You might be surprised." Mat surely had been, when he had discovered women calling Egwene Amyrlin. He did not know what had happened up at the White Tower, but he had a sinking feeling that the Aes Sedai had wrapped poor Egwene up in their schemes so soundly that she would never escape. He had half a mind to ride up there himself and see if he could get her out.

But he had other tasks. Egwene would have to see to herself for now. She was a capable girl; she could probably handle it without him for a while.

Thom stood to his side, looking thoughtful. He did not know for sure that Mat had blown the Horn—at least, Mat had never told him. He tried to forget about the bloody thing. But Thom had probably guessed.

"Well, I suppose you should be going," Mat said. "Where's Setalle?"

"She'll be staying here," Teslyn said. "She said that she wanted to keep you from making too many missteps." She raised an eyebrow, and Joline and Edesina nodded sagaciously. They all assumed that Setalle was a former runaway servant from the White Tower, perhaps having fled as a girl because of a misdeed.

Well, that meant he wouldn't be rid of the entire group. Still, if he had to pick one to stay, it would be Mistress Anan. She would probably be wanting to find a way to meet up with her husband and family, who had fled Ebou Dar by ship.

Juilin walked up, leading Thera. Had that frightened wisp of a woman really been the Panarch of Tarabon? Mat had seen mice that were less timid. Mat's soldiers brought out horses for the two of them. All in all, this expedition was costing him some forty animals and a file of soldiers. But it would be worth it. Besides, he intended to retrieve both men and horses—along with information about what was really happening in Tar Valon.

He nodded to Vanin. The thick-waisted horse thief had not been too pleased when Mat had ordered him to go along to Tar Valon and gather information. Mat had figured he would be ecstatic, considering how he doted on the Aes Sedai. Well, he would be even less happy when he found Juilin was along; Vanin tended to step lightly around the thief-catcher.

Vanin mounted a bay gelding. As far as the Aes Sedai knew, he was a senior Redarm and one of Mat's field scouts, but nobody to be suspicious of. He did not look very threatening, except maybe as a danger to a bowl of boiled potatoes. That might be why he was so good at what he did. Mat did not need any horses stolen, but Vanin's talents could be applied to other tasks.

"Well," Mat said, turning back to the Aes Sedai, "I won't keep you further, then." He stepped back, avoiding looking at Joline—who had a predatory cast to her eyes that reminded him all too much of Tylin. Teslyn waved and, curiously, Edesina nodded to him in respect. Juilin had a wave for him and Thom, and Mat got a nod from Leilwin. The woman chewed rocks for breakfast and nails for supper, but she was fair. Maybe he could talk to Tuon, get her reinstated or something.

Don't be a fool, he thought, giving a wave to Bayle Domon. *First you'll need to convince Tuon not to make you* da'covale. He was half convinced she intended to see him as her servant, husband or not. Thinking about that made him sweat around the collar.

Before long, they were making dust along the road. Thom stepped up beside Mat, watching the riders. "Sweetbuns?"

"Tradition among us Two Rivers folk."

"Never heard of that tradition."

"It's very obscure."

"Ah, I see. And what did you do to those buns?"

"Sprinklewort," Mat said. "It'll turn her mouth blue for a week, maybe two. And she won't share the sweetbuns with anyone, except maybe her Warders. Joline is addicted to the things. She must have eaten seven or eight bags' worth since we got to Caemlyn."

"Nice," Thom said, knuckling his mustache. "Childish, though."

"I'm trying to get back to my basic roots," Mat said. "You know, recapture some of my lost youth."

"You're barely twenty winters old!"

"Sure, but I did a lot of living when I was younger. Come on. Mistress Anan is staying, and that gives me an idea."

"You need a shave, Matrim Cauthon." Mistress Anan folded her arms as she regarded him.

He reached up, touching his face. Lopin had always done that, each morning. The man got as sulky as a dog in the rain when Mat did not let him do such things, though lately Mat had been growing out his beard to avoid notice. It still itched like a week-old scab.

He had found Setalle at the supply tents, overseeing the midday meal. Soldiers from the Band hunkered down, chopping vegetables and stewing beans with the furtive expression of men who had been given firm instructions. Setalle was not needed here; the Band's cooks had always been able to prepare meals without her. But there was nothing a woman liked better than finding men who were relaxing, then giving them orders. Besides, Setalle was a former innkeeper and—remarkably—a former Aes Sedai. Mat often found her supervising things that did not need supervising.

Not for the first time, he wished Tuon were still traveling with him. Setalle had usually taken Tuon's side, but staying with the Daughter of the Nine Moons had often kept her busy. Nothing was more dangerous for the sanity of men than a woman with too much time on her hands.

Setalle still wore clothing of the Ebou Dari style, which Mat found pleasant, considering the plunging neckline.

That kind of outfit worked particularly well on a woman as buxom as Setalle. Not that he noticed. She had golden hoops in her ears, a stately demeanor and gray in her hair. The jeweled wedding knife worn around her neck seemed something of a warning, the way it nestled in her cleavage. Not that Mat noticed that, either.

"I've been growing the beard intentionally," Mat said to her statement. "I want to—"

"Your coat is dirty," she said, nodding to a soldier who brought her some onions he had peeled. He sheepishly poured them into a pot, not looking at Mat. "And your hair a mess. You look like you've been in a brawl, and it's not yet noon."

"I'm fine," Mat said. "I'll clean up later. You didn't go with the Aes Sedai."

"Each step toward Tar Valon would take me farther from where I need to be. I need to send word to my husband. When we parted, I didn't suspect that I'd end up in Andor of all places."

"I'm thinking I might be getting access to someone who can make gateways here soon," Mat said. "And I . . ." He frowned as another group of soldiers approached, carrying a few undersized quail they'd hunted. The soldiers looked ashamed of the terrible catch.

Setalle ordered them to pluck the birds without so much as a glance toward Mat. Light, he needed to get her out of his camp. Things would not be normal here until they were all gone.

"Don't look at me like that, Lord Mat," Setalle said. "Noram went into the city to see what kind of provisions he could find. I've noted that without the cook himself here to prod the men, meals don't get done at any reasonable speed. Not all of us like to take lunch when the sun is setting."

"I didn't say a thing," Mat said, keeping his voice even. He nodded to the side. "Can we talk for a moment?"

Setalle hesitated, then nodded and stepped away from the others with him. "What's going on really?" she said softly. "You look like you slept under a hay pile."

"I slept under a wagon, actually. And my tent's stained with blood. Not really looking forward to going there to change clothing right now."

Her gaze softened. "I understand your loss. But that's no excuse to go around looking like you've been living in an alleyway. You'll need to hire another serving man."

Mat scowled. "I never needed one in the first place. I can take care of myself. Look, I have a favor to ask of you. I want you to watch after Olver for a little while."

"For what purpose?"

"That thing might come back," Mat said. "And it could try to hurt him. Besides, I'm going to be leaving with Thom shortly. I might be back. I *should* be back. But if I don't, I . . . Well, I would rather he not be left alone."

She studied him. "He would not be alone. The men in camp seem to have a great deal of fondness for the child."

"Sure, but I don't like the things they're teaching him. The boy needs better examples than that lot."

She seemed amused by that for some reason. "I've already begun instructing the child in letters. I suppose I can watch after him for a time, if need be."

"Great. Wonderful." Mat let out a relieved sigh. Women were always happy for a chance to educate a boy when he was young; Mat thought they assumed they could educate him out of becoming a man if they tried hard enough. "I'll give you some money. You can go into the city and find an inn."

"I've been into the city," Setalle said. "Every inn in the place seems packed to the walls already."

"I'll find a place for you," Mat promised. "Just keep Olver safe. When the time comes, and I have someone to make gateways, I'll have them send you to Illian so you can find your husband."

"A deal," Setalle said. She hesitated, glancing northward. "The . . . others are gone, then?"

"Yes." Good riddance.

She nodded, looking regretful. Maybe she had not been ordering his men about for lunch because she had been offended at seeing them relax. Maybe she had been looking for something to busy herself at.

"I'm sorry," Mat said. "About whatever happened to you."

"The past is gone," she replied. "And I need to leave it be. I should never have even asked to see the item you wear. These last few weeks have made me forget myself."

Mat nodded, parting with her, then went searching for Olver. And after that, he really *should* get around to changing his coat. And burn him, he was going to shave, too. The men looking for him could bloody kill him if they wanted. A slit throat would be better than this itching.

Elayne strolled through the palace's Sunrise Garden. This smaller garden had always been a favored location of her mother's, set atop the roof of the palace's eastern wing. It was rimmed by an oval of white stonework, with a larger, curved wall at the back.

Elayne had a full view of the city below. In earlier years, she had liked the lower gardens precisely because they were a retreat. It was in those gardens that she had first met Rand. She pressed a hand to her belly. Though she felt enormous, the pregnancy was only just beginning to show. Unfortunately, she'd had to commission an entirely new set of gowns. She would probably have to do so again in the coming months. What a bother.

Elayne continued to walk the roof garden. Pink jumpups and white morningstars bloomed in planters. The blossoms weren't nearly as large as they should have been, and already they were wilting. The gardeners complained that nothing helped. Outside the city, grass and weeds were dying in swaths, and the patchwork quilt of fields and crops looked depressingly brown.

It is *coming,* Elayne thought. She continued on her way, walking a path made of springy grass, manicured and kept short. The gardeners' efforts weren't without some results. The grass here was mostly green, and the air smelled of the roses that wove their way up the sides of the wall. Those had brown spots on them, but they *had* bloomed.

A tinkling stream ran through the middle of the garden, lined in carefully placed river stones. That stream ran only when she visited; water had to be carried up to the cistern.

Elayne paused at another vantage point. A Queen couldn't choose seclusion the way a Daughter-Heir could. Birgitte walked up beside her. She folded her arms across her red-coated chest, eyeing Elayne.

"What?" Elayne asked.

"You're in full view," Birgitte said. "Anyone down there with a bow and a good eye could throw the nation right back into a Succession war."

Elayne rolled her eyes. "I'm safe, Birgitte. Nothing will happen to me."

"Oh, well, I apologize," Birgitte said flatly. "The Forsaken are loose and angry with you, the Black Ajah are undoubtedly furious that you've captured their agents, and you've humiliated various nobles who tried to seize the throne from you. *Obviously* you're in no danger whatsoever. I'll run along and take lunch, then."

"You might as well," Elayne snapped. "Because I *am* safe. Min had a viewing. My babes will be born healthy. Min is never wrong, Birgitte."

"Min said your babies would be strong and healthy," Birgitte said. "Not that *you* would be healthy when they arrived."

"How else would they come?"

"I've seen people knocked in the head so hard that they're never the same, girl," Birgitte said. "Some live for years, but never speak another word and have to be fed broth and live with a bedpan. You could lose an arm or two and still bear healthy children. And what about the people around you? Give you no thought to the danger you could cause them?"

"I feel bad for Vandene and Sareitha," Elayne said. "And for those men who died to rescue me. Don't *dare* imply that I feel no responsibility for them! But a queen must be willing to accept the burden of letting others die in her name. We discussed this, Birgitte. We decided that there was no way I could have known that Chesmal and the others would arrive as they did."

"We *decided*," Birgitte said through clenched teeth, "that there was no use arguing any further. But I want you to keep in mind that any number of things could still go wrong."

"They won't," Elayne said, looking out over the city. "My children will be safe, and that means I will be, too. We have until their birth."

Birgitte let out an exasperated sigh. "Foolish, stubborn. . . ." She trailed off as one of the nearby Guardswomen waved to get her attention. Two of the Kin stepped onto the roof. Elayne had asked them to come meet with her.

Birgitte took up a position beside one of the short cherry trees, her arms folded. The two Kinswomen wore unadorned dresses, Sumeko in yellow, Alise in blue. Alise was the shorter of the two, with gray streaking her brown hair, and she was weaker in the Power, so she hadn't slowed in aging as much as Sumeko.

Both women had grown more firm of step lately. No further Kinswomen had disappeared or been murdered; Careane had been behind the killings all along. A member of the Black, hiding among them. Light, but thinking of it made Elayne's skin *crawl*!

"Your Majesty," Alise said, curtsying. She spoke with a calm, smooth voice and a faint Taraboner accent.

"Your Majesty," Sumeko said as well, mimicking her companion's curtsy. The two were deferential—more so to Elayne than they were to other Aes Sedai these days. Nynaeve had given the Kin in general a backbone in regards to the Aes Sedai and the White Tower, though Alise hadn't ever struck Elayne as needing it.

During the siege, Elayne had started to regard the Kinswomen's attitudes with annoyance. Recently, however, she'd been wondering. They had been *extremely* useful to her. How high would their newfound boldness lead them?

Elayne nodded to each of the Kin in turn, then gestured toward a trio of chairs that had been placed in the shade of the drooping cherry trees. The three seated themselves, the stream winding its contrived way past them to the left. There was mint tea. The other two took a cup each, but were careful to add generous amounts of honey. Tea tasted terrible these days without it.

"How are the Kin?" Elayne asked.

The two women glanced at each other. Blast. Elayne was being too formal with them. They knew something was up.

"We are well, Your Majesty," Alise said. "The fear seems to be leaving most of the women. At least, those who had enough sense to feel it in the first place. I suppose those who didn't were the ones who went off on their own and found themselves dead."

"It is good not to have to spend so much time Healing, either," Sumeko noted. "It was becoming very fatiguing. So many wounded, day after day." She grimaced.

Alise was made of stouter material. She sipped her tea, face mild. Not calm and frozen, like an Aes Sedai. Thoughtful and warm, yet reserved. That was an advantage these women had that the Aes Sedai did not—they could be regarded without as much suspicion, as they were not tied directly to the White Tower. But they didn't have its authority, either.

"You can sense that I have something to ask of you," Elayne said, meeting Alise's eyes.

"We can?" Sumeko asked, sounding surprised. Perhaps Elayne had given her too much credit.

Alise nodded in a matronly way. "You've asked much of us while we've been here, Your Majesty. No more than I felt you had a right to ask. So far."

"I have tried to welcome you in Caemlyn," Elayne said. "As I realize you can never return home, not while the Seanchan rule Ebou Dar."

"That is true," Alise agreed. "But one can hardly call Ebou Dar our home. It was merely a place where we found ourselves. Less a home, more a necessity. Many of us roated in and out of the city anyway, to avoid notice."

"Have you considered where you will stay now?"

"We're going to Tar Valon," Sumeko said quickly. "Nynaeve Sedai said—"

"I'm certain there will be a place for some of you there," Elayne interjected. "Those who wish to become Aes Sedai. Egwene will be eager to give a second chance to any Kin who wish to try again for the shawl. But what of the rest of you?"

"We spoke of this," Alise said carefully, eyes narrowing. "We will become associated with the Tower, a place for Aes Sedai to retire."

"Surely you will not move to Tar Valon, though. What good would the Kin be as a place to retire from Aes Sedai politics if they are so near the White Tower?"

"We had assumed we would remain here," Alise said.

"That was my assumption as well," Elayne said carefully. "But assumptions are weak. I wish to give you promises instead. After all, if you were to remain in Caemlyn, I see no reason to not offer you support directly from the Crown."

"At what cost?" Alise asked. Sumeko was watching with a confused frown.

"Not much of one," Elayne said. "Really, not a cost at all. An occasional favor, as you have done the Crown in the past."

The garden fell still. Faint calls from the city below rose up into the air, and the branches shivered in the wind, dropping a few brown leaves between Elayne and the Kin.

"That sounds dangerous," Alise said, taking a sip of her tea. "Surely you're not suggesting that we set up a *rival* White Tower here, in Caemlyn."

"Nothing of the sort," Elayne said quickly. "I *am* Aes Sedai myself, after all. And Egwene has spoken of letting the Kin continue as they have before, so long as they accept her authority."

"I'm not certain we want to 'continue as we have before,'" Alise said. "The White Tower left us to live our lives in terror that we would be discovered. But all the while they were using us. The more we consider that, the less . . . amused that makes us."

"Speak for yourself, Alise," Sumeko said. "*I* intend to be tested and return to the Tower. I *will* join the Yellow, mark my words."

"Perhaps, but they won't have me," Alise said. "I'm too weak in the Power. I won't accept some halfway measure, forced to scrape and bow every time a sister comes along and wants me to wash her clothing. But I won't stop channeling, either. I *won't* give it up. Egwene Sedai has spoken of letting the Kin continue, but if we do, would we be able to work the One Power openly?"

"I assume you would be able to," Elayne said. "Much of this was Egwene's idea. She certainly wouldn't send Aes Sedai to you to retire if they were to be forbidden to channel. No, the days of women outside the Tower channeling in secret have passed. The Windfinders, the Aiel Wise Ones have proven that times must change."

"Perhaps," Alise said. "But giving our services to the Crown of Andor is a very different matter."

"We would make certain not to compete with the Tower's interests," Elayne said. "And you would accept the Amyrlin's authority. So what is the problem? Aes Sedai provide service to monarchs across the land."

Alise sipped her tea. "Your offer has merit. But it depends on the nature of the favors required by the Crown of Andor."

"I would only ask two things of you," Elayne said. "Traveling and Healing. You need not enter our conflicts, you

need not be part of our politics. Simply agree to Heal my
people who are sick, and to assign a group of women each
day to create gateways when the crown wishes."

"That still sounds an awful lot like your own White
Tower," Alise said. Sumeko was frowning.

"No, no," Elayne said. "The White Tower means authority, politics. You would be something else entirely. Imagine
a place in Caemlyn where any person can come to receive
Healing, free of charge. Imagine a city free of disease. Imagine a world where food can travel instantly to those who
need it."

"And a queen who can send troops wherever she needs,"
Alise said. "Whose soldiers can fight one day, then be free
of wounds the next. A queen who can earn a tidy profit by
charging merchants for access to her gateways." She took a
sip of her tea.

"Yes," Elayne admitted. Though she wasn't certain how
she was going to convince Egwene to let her do that part
of it.

"We will want half," Alise said. "Half of anything you
charge for Traveling or Healing."

"Healing is free," Elayne said firmly. "For anyone who
comes, regardless of station. People are treated in order of
the severity of their ailment, not in order of their rank."

"I could agree to this," Alise said.

Sumeko turned to her, eyes wide. "You cannot speak for
us. You yourself threw in my face the Knitting Circle having dissolved, now that we have left Ebou Dar. Besides, by
the Rule—"

"I speak only for myself, Sumeko," Alise said. "And
those who would join me. The Kin as we knew them are
no more. We were dominated by our need to remain secret,
and that is gone now."

Sumeko grew silent.

"You mean to join the Aes Sedai, my friend," Alise said,
laying a hand on her arm. "But they will not have me, nor
will I have them. I need something else, and others will as
well."

"But to tie yourselves to the Crown of Andor. . . ."

"We tie ourselves to the White Tower," Alise said. "But
live in Caemlyn. Both have their benefits. We aren't strong
enough to stand on our own. Andor is as good a place as

any. It has the favor of the White Tower, and the favor of the Dragon Reborn. Mostly, it is here, and so are we."

"You can reorganize," Elayne said, growing excited. "The Rule can be crafted anew. You can decide to let Kin marry now, if you wish. I think that would be for the best."

"Why?" Alise asked.

"Because it will tie them down," Elayne explained. "That will make them less of a threat to the White Tower. It will help differentiate you. It is something that few women in the White Tower do, and it gives you something to make the Kin more attractive as an option."

Alise nodded, thoughtful; Sumeko seemed to be coming around. Elayne was sorry to admit that she wouldn't miss the woman when she left. Elayne intended to push them to restructure how they chose leaders. It would be much more convenient if she could work with one like Alise, as opposed to whomever happened to be the oldest among them.

"I still worry about the Amyrlin," Alise said. "Aes Sedai do not charge for services. What will she say if we start doing so?"

"I will speak with Egwene," Elayne repeated. "I'm certain I can convince her that the Kin, and Andor, are no threat to her."

Hopefully. There was a chance for something incredible in the Kin, a chance for Andor to have constant and inexpensive access to gateways. That would put her on nearly equal ground with the Seanchan.

She spoke with the women for a time longer, making certain they felt she was giving them due attention. Eventually she dismissed them, but found herself lingering in the garden, standing between two planters holding bluebells, their clusters of tiny, vaselike blossoms drooping and wiggling in the breeze. She tried not to look at the planter beside them, which was empty. The bluebells there had flowered in the color of blood, and had actually *bled* something red when cut. The gardeners had pulled them out.

The Seanchan would come for Andor eventually. By then, Rand's armies would likely be weakened and broken from the fighting, their leader possibly dead. Again, it made her heart twist to consider that, but she couldn't shy away from the truth.

Andor would be a prize to the Seanchan. The mines

and rich lands of her realm would tempt them, as would the proximity to Tar Valon. Beyond that, she suspected that those who claimed to be Artur Hawkwing's successors would never be satisfied until they held all that had once belonged to their ancestor.

Elayne looked out over her nation. *Her* nation. Full of those who trusted in her to protect and defend them. Many who had supported her claim to the throne had had little faith in her. But she was their best option, their only option. She would show them the wisdom of their choice.

Securing the Kin would be one step. Sooner or later, the Seanchan would be able to Travel. All they needed to do was capture one woman who knew the weaves, and soon each and every *damane* with the requisite strength would be able to create the portals. Elayne needed access to them as well.

What she didn't have, however, were channelers to use in battle. She knew she couldn't ask this of the Kin. They'd never agree to it, nor would Egwene. Nor would Elayne herself. Forcing a woman to use the Power as a weapon would make her no better than the Seanchan themselves.

Unfortunately, Elayne knew full well the destruction women using the One Power could cause. She'd been bound in a wagon while Birgitte led the attack on the Black Ajah who had kidnapped her here in Caemlyn, but she'd seen its aftermath. Hundreds dead, hundreds more wounded, dozens burned away. Smoking, twisted corpses.

She needed something. An edge against the Seanchan. Something to balance their channelers in combat. The only thing she could think of was the Black Tower. It was on Andor's soil. She'd told them that she considered them part of her nation, but so far she'd gone no further than sending inspection parties.

What would happen to them if Rand died? Dared she try to claim them? Dared she wait for someone else to?

CHAPTER 18

The Strength of This Place

Perrin ran through the darkness. Trails of watery mist brushed his face and condensed in his beard. His mind was foggy, distant. Where was he going? What was he doing? Why was he running?

He roared and charged, ripping through the veiled darkness and bursting into open air. He took a deep breath and landed on the top of a steep hill covered with short, patchy grass, with a ring of trees at its base. The sky rumbled and churned with clouds, like a boiling pot of tar.

He was in the wolf dream. His body slumbered in the real world, on this hilltop, with Faile. He smiled, breathing deeply. His problems had not diminished. In fact, with the Whitecloak ultimatum, they seemed magnified. But all was well with Faile. That simple fact changed so much. With her at his side, he could do anything.

He leaped down from the hillside and crossed the open area where his army camped. They had been here long enough that signs had appeared in the wolf dream. Tents reflected the waking world, though their flaps were in a different position each time he looked at them. Cook-fire pits in the ground, ruts in the pathways, occasional bits of refuse or discarded tools. These would pop into existence, then vanish.

He moved quickly through the camp, each step taking him ten paces. Once he might have found the lack of people in the camp eerie, but he was accustomed to the wolf dream now. This was natural.

Perrin approached the statue at the side of the camp, then looked up at the age-pocked stone, overgrown with lichen of black, orange and green. The statue must have been posed oddly, if it had fallen in such a way. It almost looked as if it had been created this way—an enormous arm bursting from the loam.

Perrin turned to the southeast, toward where the White-cloak camp would be found. He had to deal with them. He was increasingly certain—confident, even—that he could not continue until he had confronted these shadows from the past.

There was one way to deal with them for certain. A careful trap using the Asha'man and Wise Ones, and Perrin could hit the Children so hard that they shattered. He could maybe even destroy them permanently as a group.

He had the means, the opportunity, and the motivation. No more fear in the land, no more Whitecloak mock trials. He leaped forward, soaring thirty feet and falling lightly to the ground. Then he took off, running southeast along the road.

He found the Whitecloak camp in a forested hollow, thousands of white tents set up in tight rings. The tents of some ten thousand Children, along with another ten thousand mercenaries and other soldiers. Balwer estimated that this was the bulk of the remaining Children, though he had been unclear on how he'd gotten that knowledge. Hopefully the dusty man's hatred of the Whitecloaks wasn't clouding his judgment.

Perrin moved among the tents, looking to see if he could discover anything that Elyas and the Aiel had not. It was unlikely, but he figured it was worth an attempt, while he was here. Besides, he wanted to see the place with his own eyes. He lifted flaps, moved between groupings of tents, inspecting the place and getting a feel for it and its occupants. The camp was arranged in a very orderly manner. The insides were less stable than the tents themselves, but what he saw was also kept orderly.

The Whitecloaks liked things neat, tidy and carefully folded. And they liked to pretend the entire world could be polished up and cleaned the same way, people defined and explained in one or two words.

Perrin shook his head, making his way to the Lord Captain Commander's tent. The organization of the tents led him to it easily, at the center ring. It wasn't much larger than the other tents, and Perrin ducked inside, trying to see if he could find anything of use. It was furnished simply, with a bedroll that was in a different position each time Perrin looked at it, along with a table holding objects that vanished and appeared at random.

Perrin stepped up to it, picking up something that appeared there. A signet ring. He didn't recognize the signet, a winged dagger, but memorized it just before the ring vanished from his fingers, too transient to stay long in the wolf dream. Though he'd met with the Whitecloak leader, and corresponded with the man, he didn't know much about the man's past. Perhaps this would help.

He searched through the tent a while longer, finding nothing of use, then went to the large tent where Gaul had explained that many of the captives were being kept. Here, he saw Master Gill's hat appear for a moment, then vanish.

Satisfied, Perrin walked back out of the tent. As he did so, he found something bothering him. Shouldn't he have tried something like this when Faile was kidnapped? He'd sent numerous scouts to Malden. Light, he'd had to restrain himself from marching off to find Faile on his own! But he'd never tried visiting the place in the wolf dream.

Perhaps it would have been useless. But he hadn't considered the possibility, and that troubled him.

He froze, passing a cart parked beside one of the Whitecloak tents. The back was open, and a grizzled silver wolf lay there, watching him.

"I do let my attention grow too narrow, Hopper," Perrin said. "When I get consumed by a goal, it can make me careless. That can be dangerous. As in battle, when concentrating on the adversary in front of you can expose you to the archer on the side."

Hopper cracked his mouth open, smiling after the way of wolves. He hopped from the cart. Perrin could sense other wolves nearby—the others of the pack he had run with before. Oak Dancer, Sparks and Boundless.

"All right," he said to Hopper. "I'm ready to learn."

Hopper sat down on his haunches, regarding Perrin. *Follow,* the wolf sent.

Then vanished.

Perrin cursed, looking about. Where had the wolf gone?

He moved through the camp, searching, but couldn't sense Hopper anywhere. He reached out with his mind. Nothing.

Young Bull. Suddenly Hopper was behind him. *Follow.* He vanished again.

Perrin growled, then moved about the camp in a flash. When he didn't find the wolf, he shifted to the field of grain where he'd met Hopper last time. The wolf wasn't there. Perrin stood among the blowing grain, frustrated.

Hopper found him a few minutes later. The wolf smelled dissatisfied. *Follow!* he sent.

"I don't know how," Perrin said. "Hopper, I don't know where you're going."

The wolf sat down. He sent an image of a wolf pup, joining others of the pack. The pup watched his elders and did what they did.

"I'm not a wolf, Hopper," Perrin said. "I don't learn the way you do. You must explain to me what you want me to do."

Follow here. The wolf sent an image of, oddly, Emond's Field. Then he vanished.

Perrin followed, appearing on a familiar green. A group of buildings lined it, which felt wrong. Emond's Field should have been a little village, not a town with a stone wall and a road running past the mayor's inn, paved with stones. Much had changed in the short time he had been away.

"Why have we come here?" Perrin asked. Disturbingly, the wolfhead banner still flew on the pole above the green. It could have been a trick of the wolf dream, but he doubted it. He knew all too well how eagerly the people of the Two Rivers flew the standard of "Perrin Goldeneyes."

Men are strange, Hopper sent.

Perrin turned to the old wolf.

Men think strange thoughts, Hopper said. *We do not try to understand them. Why does the stag flee, the sparrow fly, the tree grow? They do. That is all.*

"Very well," Perrin said.

I cannot teach a sparrow to hunt, Hopper continued. *And a sparrow does not teach a wolf to fly.*

"But here, you *can* fly," Perrin said.

Yes. And I was not taught. I know. Hopper's scent was full of emotion and confusion. Wolves all remembered everything that one of their kind knew. Hopper was frustrated because he wanted to teach Perrin, but wasn't accustomed to doing things in the way of people.

"Please," Perrin said. "Try to explain to me what you mean. You always tell me I'm here 'too strongly.' It's dangerous, you say. Why?"

You slumber, Hopper said. *The other you. You cannot stay here too long. You must always remember that you are unnatural here. This is not your den.*

Hopper turned toward the houses around them. *This is your den, the den of your sire. This place. Remember it. It will keep you from being lost. This was how your kind once did it. You understand.*

It wasn't a question, though it was something of a plea. Hopper wasn't certain how to explain further.

"I can try," Perrin thought, interpreting the sending as best he could. But Hopper was wrong. This place wasn't his home. Perrin's home was with Faile. He needed to remember that, somehow, to keep himself from getting drawn into the wolf dream too strongly.

I have seen your she in your mind, Young Bull, Hopper sent, cocking his head. *She is like a hive of bees, with sweet honey and sharp stings.* Hopper's image of Faile was that of a very confusing female wolf. One who would playfully nip at his nose one moment, then growl at him the next, refusing to share her meat.

Perrin smiled.

The memory is part, Hopper sent. *But the other part is you. You must stay as Young Bull.* A wolf's reflection in the water, shimmering and growing indistinct as ripples crossed it.

"I don't understand."

The strength of this place, Hopper sent an image of a wolf carved of stone, *is the strength of you.* The wolf thought for a moment. *Stand. Remain. Be you.*

With that, the wolf stood and backed up, as if preparing to run at Perrin.

Confused, Perrin imagined himself as he was, holding that image in his head as strongly as he could.

Hopper ran and jumped at him, slamming his body into Perrin. He'd done this before, somehow *forcing* Perrin out of the wolf dream.

This time, however, Perrin was set and waiting. Instinctively, Perrin pushed back. The wolf dream wavered around him, but then grew firm again. Hopper rebounded off him, though the heavy wolf should have knocked Perrin to the ground.

Hopper shook his head, as if dazed. *Good,* he sent, pleased. *Good. You learn. Again.*

Perrin steadied himself just in time to get slammed by Hopper a second time. Perrin growled, but held steady.

Here, Hopper sent, giving an image of the field of grain. Hopper vanished, and Perrin followed. As soon as he appeared, the wolf slammed into him, mind and body.

Perrin fell to the ground this time, everything wavering and shimmering. He felt himself being pushed away, forced out of the wolf dream and into his ordinary dreams.

No! he thought, holding to an image of himself kneeling among those fields of grain. He *was* there. He imagined it, solid and real. He smelled the oats, the humid air, alive with the scents of dirt and fallen leaves.

The landscape coalesced. He panted, kneeling on the ground, but he was still in the wolf dream.

Good, Hopper sent. *You learn quickly.*

"There's no other option," Perrin said, climbing to his feet.

The Last Hunt comes, Hopper agreed, sending an image of the Whitecloak camp.

Perrin followed, bracing himself. No attack came. He looked around for the wolf.

Something slammed into his mind. There was no motion, only the mental attack. It wasn't as strong as before, but it was unexpected. Perrin barely managed to fight it off.

Hopper fell from the air, landing gracefully on the ground. *Always be ready,* the wolf sent. *Always, but especially when you move.* An image of a careful wolf, testing the air before moving out into an open pasture.

"I understand."

But do not come too strongly, Hopper chided.

Immediately, Perrin forced himself to remember Faile and the place where he slept. His home. He . . . faded slightly. His skin didn't grow translucent, and the wolf dream stayed the same, but he felt more exposed.

Good, Hopper sent. *Always ready, but never holding on too strong. Like carrying a pup in your jaws.*

"That's not going to be an easy balance," Perrin said.

Hopper gave a slightly confused scent. Of course it was difficult.

Perrin smiled. "What now?"

Running, Hopper sent. *Then more practice.*

The wolf dashed away, zipping in a blur of gray and silver off toward the road. Perrin followed. He sensed determination from Hopper—a scent that was oddly similar to the way Tam smelled when training the refugees to fight. That made Perrin smile.

They ran down the road, and Perrin practiced the balance of not being in the dream too strongly, yet being ready to solidify his sense of *self* at any moment. Occasionally Hopper would attack him, trying to throw him from the wolf dream. They continued until Hopper—suddenly—stopped running.

Perrin took a few extra steps, surging ahead of the wolf, before stopping. There was something *in front* of him. A translucent violet wall that cut directly through the roadway. It extended up into the sky and distantly to both the right and the left.

"Hopper?" Perrin asked. "What is this?"

Wrongness, Hopper sent. *It should not be here.* The wolf smelled angry.

Perrin stepped forward and raised a hand toward the surface, but hesitated. It looked like glass. He'd never seen anything like this in the wolf dream. Might it be like the bubbles of evil? He looked up at the sky.

The wall flashed suddenly and was gone. Perrin blinked, stumbling back. He glanced at Hopper. The wolf sat on his haunches, staring at the place where the wall had been. *Come, Young Bull,* the wolf finally sent, standing. *We will practice in another place.*

He loped away. Perrin looked back down the road. Whatever the wall had been, it had left no visible sign of its existence.

Troubled, Perrin followed after Hopper.

"Burn me, where are those archers!" Rodel Ituralde climbed up to the top of the hillside. "I wanted them formed up on

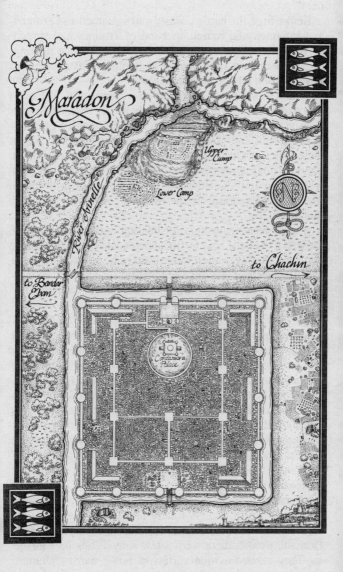

the forward towers an hour ago to relieve the crossbowmen!"

Before him, the battle clanged and screamed and grunted
and thumped and roared. A band of Trollocs had surged
across the river, crossing on ford rafts or a crude floating
bridge fashioned from log rafts. Trollocs *hated* crossing
water. It took a lot to get them over.

Which was why this fortification was so useful. The hillside sloped directly down to the only ford of reasonable size
in leagues. To the north, Trollocs boiled through a pass out
of the Blight and ran right into the River Arinelle. When
they could be forced across, they faced the hillside, which
had been dug with trenches, piled with bulwarks and set
with archer towers at the top. There was no way to reach
the city of Maradon from the Blight except by passing over
this hill.

It was an ideal position for holding back a much larger
force, but even the best fortifications could be overrun, particularly when your men were tired from weeks of fighting.
The Trollocs had crossed and fought their way up the slope
under a hail of arrows, falling into the trenches, having difficulty surmounting the high bulwarks.

The hillside had a flat area at the top, where Ituralde had
his command position, in the upper camp. He called orders
as he looked down on the woven mass of trenches, bulwarks
and towers. The Trollocs were dying to pikemen behind one
of the bulwarks. Ituralde watched until the last Trolloc—an
enormous, ram-faced beast—roared and died with three
pikes in its gut.

It looked as if another surge was coming, the Myrddraal
driving another mass of Trollocs through the pass. Enough
bodies had fallen in the river that it was clogged for the
moment, running red, the carcasses providing a footing for
those running up behind.

"Archers!" Ituralde bellowed. "Where are those bloody—"

A company of archers finally ran past, some of the reserves he'd held back. Most of them had the coppery skin of
Domani, though there were a few stray Taraboners mixed
in. They carried a wide variety of bows: narrow Domani
longbows, serpentine Saldaean shortbows scavenged from
guard posts or villages, even a few tall Two Rivers longbows.

"Lidrin," Ituralde called. The young, hard-eyed officer hurried across the hillside to him. Lidrin's brown uniform was wrinkled and dirty at the knees, not because he was undisciplined, but because there were times when his men needed him more than his laundry did.

"Go with those archers to the towers," Ituralde said. "Those Trollocs are going to try another push. I do *not* want another fist breaking through to the top, hear me? If they seize our position and use it against us, I'm going to have a rotten morning."

Lidrin didn't smile at the comment, as he once might have. He didn't smile much at all anymore; usually only when he got to kill a Trolloc. He saluted, turning to jog after the archers.

Ituralde turned and looked down the back side of the hill. The lower camp was set up there, in the shadow of the steep hillside. This hill had been a natural formation, once, but the Saldaeans had built it up over the years, with one long slope extending toward the river and a steeper one on the opposite side. In the lower camp, his troops could sleep and eat, and their supplies could be protected, all sheltered from enemy arrows by the steep hillside upon which Ituralde now stood.

Both of his camps, upper and lower, were patchwork things. Some of the tents had been purchased from Saldaean villages, some were of Domani make, and dozens had been brought in by gateway from all over the land. A large number of them were enormous Cairhienin things with striped patterns. They kept the rain off his men, and that was enough.

The Saldaeans certainly knew how to build fortifications. If only Ituralde had been able to persuade them to leave their hiding place in the city of Maradon and come help.

"Now," Ituralde said, "where in—"

He cut off as something darkened the sky. He barely had time to curse and duck away as a group of large objects rained down, arcing high to fall on the upper camp, eliciting howls of pain and confusion. Those weren't boulders: they were *corpses*. The hulking bodies of dead Trollocs. The Shadowspawn army had finally set up their trebuchets.

A part of Ituralde was impressed that he'd driven them to it. The siege equipment had undoubtedly been brought to assault Maradon, which was a little to the south. Setting up the trebuchets across the ford to assault Ituralde's lines instead not only would slow the Shadowspawn, but would expose their trebuchets to his counterfire.

He hadn't expected them to hurl carcasses. He cursed as the sky darkened again, more bodies falling, knocking down tents, crushing soldiers.

"Healers!" Ituralde bellowed. "Where are those Asha'man?" He'd pushed the Asha'man hard, since this siege had begun. To the brink of exhaustion. Now he held them back, using them only when Trolloc assaults got too close to the upper camp.

"Sir!" A young messenger with dirt under his fingernails scrambled up from the front lines. His Domani face was ashen, and he was still too young to grow a proper mustache. "Captain Finsas reports the Shadowspawn army moving trebuchets into range. There are sixteen by his count."

"Let Captain Finsas know that his bloody timing could be better," Ituralde growled.

"I'm sorry, my Lord. They rolled them down through the pass before we figured out what was going on. The initial volley hit our watchpost. Lord Finsas himself was wounded."

Ituralde nodded; Rajabi was arriving to take command of the upper camp and organize the wounded. Below, a lot of bodies had hit the lower camp, too. The trebuchets could get the height and range to launch over the hill and fall down on his men in their previously sheltered area. He'd have to pull the lower camp back, farther across the plain toward Maradon, which would delay response times. Bloody ashes.

I never used to swear this much, Ituralde thought. It was that boy, the Dragon Reborn. Rand al'Thor had given Ituralde promises, some spoken, some implied. Promises to protect Arad Doman from the Seanchan. Promises that Ituralde could live, rather than die trapped by the Seanchan. Promises to give him something to do, something important, something vital. Something impossible.

Hold back the Shadow. Fight until help arrived.

The sky darkened again, and Ituralde ducked into the command pavilion, which had a wooden roof as a precaution against siege weapons. He'd feared sprayshot of smaller rocks, not carcasses. The men scattered to help pull the wounded down to the relative safety of the lower camp, and from there across the plain toward Maradon. Rajabi led the effort. The lumbering man had a neck as thick as a ten-year-grown ash and arms nearly as wide. He now hobbled as he walked, his left leg hurt in the fighting and amputated beneath the knee. Asha'man had Healed him as best he could be healed, and he walked on a peg. He'd refused to retire through gateways with the badly injured, and Ituralde hadn't forced him. You didn't throw away a good officer because of one wound.

A young officer winced as a bloated carcass thumped against the top of the pavilion. The officer—Zhell—didn't have the coppery skin of a Domani, though he wore a very Domani mustache and a beauty mark on his cheek in the shape of an arrow.

They could not hold against Trollocs here for much longer, not with the numbers they were fielding. Ituralde would have to fall back, point by point, farther into Saldaea, farther toward Arad Doman. Odd, how he was always retreating toward his homeland. First from the south, now from the northeast.

Arad Doman would be crushed between the Seanchan and the Trollocs. *You'd better keep your word, boy.*

He couldn't retreat into Maradon, unfortunately. The Saldaeans there had made it quite clear they considered Ituralde—and the Dragon Reborn—to be invaders. Bloody fools. At least he had a chance to destroy those siege engines.

Another body hit the top of the command pavilion, but the roof held. From the stink—and, in some cases, splash—of those deceased Trollocs, they'd not chosen the newly dead for this assault. Confident that his officers were seeing to their duties—now was not the time to interfere—Ituralde clasped his hands behind him. Seeing him, soldiers both inside and out of the pavilion stood a little straighter. The best of plans lasted only until the first arrow hit, but a determined, unyielding commander could bring order to chaos by the way he held himself.

Overhead, the storm boiled, clouds of silver and black like a blackened pot hanging above a cook fire, bits of steel shining through at the edges of the crusted soot. It was unnatural. Let his men see that he did not fear it, even when it hailed corpses upon them.

Wounded were carried away, and men in the lower camp began to break it down, preparing to move it farther back. He kept his archers and crossbowmen firing, pikemen ready along the bulwarks. He had a sizable cavalry, but couldn't use them here.

Those trebuchets, if left alone, would wear his men down with boulders and sprayshot—but Ituralde intended to see them burned first, using an Asha'man or a strike force with flaming arrows through a gateway.

If only I could retreat into Maradon. But the Saldaean lord there wouldn't let him in; if Ituralde fell back to the city, he'd get smashed against those walls by the Trollocs.

Bloody, bloody fools. What kind of idiots denied men refuge when an army of Shadowspawn was knocking on their gates?

"I want damage assessments," Ituralde said to Lieutenant Nils. "Prepare the archers for an attack on those siege engines, and bring two of the Asha'man who are on duty. Tell Captain Creedin to watch that Trolloc assault across the ford. They'll redouble their efforts following this barrage, as they'll presume us disordered."

The young man nodded and hastened off as Rajabi limped into the pavilion, rubbing his broad chin. "You guessed right again about those trebuchets. They *did* set them up to attack us."

"I try to always guess right," Ituralde said. "When I don't, we lose."

Rajabi grunted. Overhead, that storm boiled. In the distance, Ituralde could hear Trollocs calling. War drums beating. Men shouting.

"Something's wrong," Ituralde said.

"This whole bloody war is wrong," Rajabi said. "We shouldn't be here; it should be the Saldaeans. Their whole army, not only the few horsemen the Lord Dragon gave us."

"More than that," Ituralde said, scanning the sky. "Why carcasses, Rajabi?"

"To demoralize us."

It was a not-unheard-of tactic. But the first volleys? Why not use stones when they'd do the most damage, and then move to bodies once surprise had been expended? The Trollocs hadn't a mind for tactics, but the Fades . . . they could be crafty. He'd learned that firsthand.

As Ituralde stared at the sky, another massive volley fell, as if spawned by the dark clouds. Light, where had they gotten that many trebuchets? Enough to throw hundreds of dead bodies.

There are sixteen by his count, the boy had said. Not nearly enough. Were some of those carcasses falling too evenly?

It hit him like a burst of frozen rain. Those clever bloody monsters!

"Archers!" Ituralde screamed. "Archers, watch the skies! Those aren't bodies!"

It was too late. As he yelled, the Draghkar unfurled their wings; well over half of the "carcasses" in this volley were living Shadowspawn, hiding among the falling bodies. After the first Draghkar attack on his army a few days back, he'd left archers on permanent rotation watching the skies day and night.

But the archers didn't have orders to fire on falling bodies. Ituralde continued to bellow as he leaped out of the pavilion and whipped his sword from its scabbard. The upper camp became chaos as Draghkar dropped amid the soldiers. A large number of them fell around the command pavilion, their too-large black eyes shining, drawing men toward them with their sweet songs.

Ituralde screamed as loud as he could, filling his ears with the sound of his own voice. One of the beasts came for him, but his yell prevented him from hearing its croon. It looked surprised—as surprised as something so inhuman could look—as he stumbled toward it, pretending to be drawn, then struck an expert thrust through its neck. Dark blood dribbled down across milky white skin as Ituralde yanked his blade free, still screaming.

He saw Rajabi stumble and fall to the ground as one of the Shadowspawn leaped on him. Ituralde couldn't go to him—he was confronted by another of the monsters himself. In a blessed moment, he noticed balls of fire striking down Draghkar in the air—the Asha'man.

But at the same time, in the distance, he heard the war

drums grow louder. As he'd predicted, the churning force of Trollocs would be striking across the ford with as much strength as they ever had. Light, but sometimes he hated being right.

You'd better keep your promise to send me help, boy, Ituralde thought as he fought the second Draghkar, his screaming growing hoarse. *Light, but you'd better!*

Faile strode through Perrin's camp, the air ringing with chattering voices, grunts of exertion and calls of men giving orders. Perrin had sent one last request to the Whitecloaks for parley, and there had been no reply yet.

Faile felt refreshed. She'd spent the entire night nuzzled against Perrin atop their hill. She'd brought plenty of bedding and blankets. In some ways, the grassy hilltop had been more comfortable than their tent.

The scouts had returned from Cairhien this morning; their report would come soon. For now, Faile had bathed and eaten.

It was time to do something about Berelain.

She crossed the trampled grass toward the Mayener section of camp, feeling her anger rise. Berelain had gone too far. Perrin claimed that the rumors came from Berelain's maids, not the woman herself, but Faile saw the truth. The First was a master of manipulating and controlling rumor. That was one of the best ways to rule from a position of relative weakness. The First did so in Mayene, and she did the same here in camp, where Faile was the stronger party as Perrin's wife.

A pair of Winged Guards stood at the entrance to the Mayener section, their breastplates painted crimson, winged helmets shaped like pots and extending down the backs of their necks. They stood up taller as Faile neared, holding lances that were mostly ornamental, pennons flapping with the golden hawk in flight stenciled on their blue lengths.

Faile had to crane to meet their eyes. "Escort me to your lady," she ordered.

The guards nodded, one holding up a gauntleted hand and waving for two other men from inside the camp to take up the watch. "We were told to expect you," the guard told Faile in a deep voice.

Faile raised an eyebrow. "Today?"

"No. The First simply said that should you come, you were to be obeyed."

"Of course I'm to be obeyed. This is my husband's camp."

The guards did not argue with her, though they probably disagreed. Berelain had been sent to accompany Perrin, but he had not been given express command over her or her troops.

Faile followed the men. The ground was, by a miracle, actually starting to dry out. Faile had told Perrin that she wasn't bothered by the rumors, but she *was* frustrated by Berelain's boldness. *That woman*, Faile thought. *How dare she—*

No. No, Faile couldn't continue down that path. A good shouting match would make her feel better, but it would reinforce the rumors. What else would people surmise if they saw her stalk to the First's tent, then scream at her? Faile had to be calm. That would be difficult.

The Mayener camp was arranged with lines of men radiating from a central tent like spokes on a wheel. The Winged Guards didn't have tents—those were with Master Gill—but there was a very orderly arrangement to the groupings. They almost seemed *too* level, the folded blankets, the piles of lances, the horse poles and the periodic firepits. Berelain's central pavilion was lavender and maroon—salvage from Malden. Faile maintained her composure as the two towering guards led her up to the tent. One knocked on the post outside for permission to enter.

Berelain's tranquil voice responded, and the guard pushed back the entrance flap for Faile. As she moved to enter, rustling inside made her step back, and Annoura came out. The Aes Sedai nodded to Faile, the overlapping braids around her face swinging. She seemed displeased; she hadn't regained her mistress's favor yet.

Faile took a deep breath, then stepped into the pavilion. It was cool inside. The floor was covered with a maroon and green rug of a twisting ivy pattern. Though the pavilion looked empty without Berelain's usual travel furniture, she did have a pair of sturdy oak chairs and a light table from Malden.

The First rose. "Lady Faile," she said calmly. Today, she wore the diadem of Mayene. The thin crown had a simple grandeur about it, unornamented save for the golden hawk taking flight as if leaping toward the sunlight streaming in patches through the tent ceiling. Flaps had been removed there to let in the light. The First's dress was gold and green, a very simple belt at her waist, the neckline plunging.

Faile sat in one of the chairs. This conversation was dangerous; it could lead to disaster. But it had to be done.

"I trust you are well?" Berelain said. "The rains of the last few days have not been overly taxing?"

"The rains have been dreadful, Berelain," Faile said. "But I'm not here to talk about them."

Berelain pursed perfect lips. Light, but the woman was beautiful! Faile felt downright dingy by comparison, her nose too large, her bosom too small. Her voice wasn't nearly as melodic as Berelain's. Why had the Creator made people as perfect as Berelain? Was it mockery of the rest of them?

But Perrin didn't love Berelain. He loved Faile. *Remember that.*

"Very well," Berelain said. "I assumed this discussion would come. Let me promise you that the rumors are absolutely false; nothing inappropriate happened between myself and your husband."

"He has told me that already," Faile said, "and I trust his word over yours."

This made Berelain frown. She was a master of political interactions, possessing a skill and subtlety that Faile envied. Despite her youth, Berelain had kept her tiny city-state free from the much larger and powerful Tear. Faile could only guess how much juggling, political double-dealing and sheer cleverness that must have required.

"So why have you come to me?" Berelain asked, sitting down. "If your heart is at ease, then there is no problem."

"We both know that whether or not you slept with my husband is not an issue here," Faile said, and Berelain's eyes widened. "It isn't what happened, but what is *presumed*, that angers me."

"Rumors can be found in any place where people are gathered," Berelain said. "Particularly where men gossip."

"Such strong, persistent rumors are unlikely to have happened without encouragement," Faile said. "Now everyone in the camp—including the refugees sworn to me—assumes that you bedded my husband while I was away. This not only makes me look like a fool, but casts a shadow upon Perrin's honor. He cannot lead if people take him for the type of man who will run to the arms of another woman the moment his wife is away."

"Other rulers have overcome such rumors," Berelain said, "and for many of them, the rumors weren't unfounded. Monarchies survive infidelity."

"Perhaps in Illian or Tear," Faile said, "but Saldaea expects better of its monarchs. As do the people of the Two Rivers. Perrin is *not* like other rulers. The way his men look at him rips him apart inside."

"I think you underestimate him," Berelain said. "He will overcome and he will learn to use rumor for his gain. That will make him stronger as a man and a ruler."

Faile studied the woman. "You don't understand him at all, do you?"

Berelain reacted as if she'd been slapped, pulling back. She obviously didn't like the bluntness of this conversation. That might give Faile some slight advantage.

"I understand men, Lady Faile," Berelain said coldly. "And your husband is no exception. Since you have decided to be candid, I will return in kind. You were clever to take Aybara when you did, welding Saldaea to the Dragon Reborn, but do not think that he will remain yours without contest."

Faile took a deep breath. It was time to make her play. "Perrin's reputation has been severely damaged by what you have done, my Lady First. For my own dishonor, I might have been able to forgive you. But not for his."

"I don't see what can be done."

"I do," Faile said. "And I'm pretty certain one of us is going to have to die."

Berelain remained impassive. "Excuse me?"

"In the Borderlands, if a woman finds that another has been bedding her husband, she is given the option of knife combat." That was true, though the tradition was an old one, rarely observed any longer. "The only way to clear my name is for you and me to fight."

"What would that prove?"

"If nothing else, if you were dead, it would stop anyone

from thinking that you are still sleeping with my husband behind my back."

"Are you actually threatening me in my own tent?"

"This is not a threat," Faile said, remaining firm. Light, she hoped this went the right way. "This is a challenge."

Berelain studied her, eyes calculating. "I will make a public statement. I will publicly chastise my maids for their rumors, and will tell the camp that nothing happened."

"Do you really think that would stop the rumors? You didn't object to them before my return; that is seen as proof. And, of course, now you would be *expected* to act as if nothing happened."

"You can't be serious about this . . . challenge."

"In regards to my husband's honor, Berelain, I am *always* serious." She met the woman's eyes, and saw concern there. Berelain didn't want to fight her. And, of course, Faile didn't want to fight Berelain, and not just because she wasn't certain if she could win or not. Though she *had* always wanted to get revenge on the First for that time when Berelain had taken her knife from her.

"I will make the challenge formally this evening, before the entire camp," Faile said, keeping her voice even. "You will have one day to respond or leave."

"I will not be a party to this foolishness."

"You already are," Faile said, rising. "This is what you set in motion the moment you let those rumors begin."

Faile turned to walk from the tent. She had to work hard to hide her nervousness. Had Berelain seen how her brow prickled with sweat? Faile felt as if she walked on the very edge of a sword. Should word of this challenge get to Perrin, he would be furious. She had to hope that—

"Lady Faile," Berelain said from behind. The First's voice was edged with concern. "Surely we can come to another accommodation. Do not force this."

Faile stopped, heart thumping. She turned back. The First looked genuinely worried. Yes, she believed that Faile was bloodthirsty enough to make this challenge.

"I want you out of Perrin's life, Berelain," Faile said. "I will have that, one way or another."

"You wish me to leave?" Berelain asked. "The tasks the Lord Dragon gave me are finished. I suppose I could take my men and march another direction."

No, Faile didn't want her to go. The disappearance of her troops would be a blow, in the face of that looming White-cloak army. And Perrin would have need of the Winged Guards again, Faile suspected.

"No," Faile said. "Leaving will do nothing for the rumors, Berelain."

"It will do as much as killing me would," the woman said dryly. "If we fight, and you somehow managed to kill me, all that would be said is that you discovered your husband's infidelity and became enraged. I fail to see how that would help your position. It would only *encourage* the rumors."

"You see my problem, then," Faile said, letting her exasperation show through. "There seems to be *no* way to be rid of these rumors."

Berelain studied her. The woman had once promised she would take Perrin. Had all but vowed it. She seemed to have backed off on that, in part, recently. And her eyes showed hints of worry.

She realizes that she let this go too far, Faile thought, understanding. Of course. Berelain hadn't expected Faile to return from Malden. That was why she'd made such a bold move.

Now she realized she'd overextended herself. And she legitimately thought Faile unhinged enough to duel her in public.

"I never wanted this, Berelain," Faile said, walking back into the tent. "And neither did Perrin. Your attentions are an annoyance to us both."

"Your husband did little to dissuade me," Berelain said, arms folded. "During your absence, there were points where he *directly* encouraged me."

"You understand him so little, Berelain." It was amazing how the woman could be so blind while being so clever in other ways.

"So you claim," Berelain said.

"You have two choices right now, Berelain," Faile said, stepping up to her. "You can fight me, and one of us will die. You're right, that wouldn't end the rumors. But it *would* end your chances at Perrin. Either you'd be dead, or you'd be the woman who killed his wife.

"Your other choice," Faile said, meeting Berelain's eyes,

"is to come up with a way to destroy these rumors once and for all. You caused this mess. You will fix it."

And there was her gamble. Faile couldn't think of a way out of the situation, but Berelain was *much* more accomplished in this regard than she was. So Faile came, prepared to manipulate Berelain into thinking she was ready to do something unreasonable. Then let the woman's impressive political acumen attack the situation.

Would it work?

Faile met Berelain's eyes, and allowed herself to feel her anger. Her *outrage* at what had happened. She was being beaten, frozen and humiliated by their common enemy. And during that, Berelain had the *gall* to do something like this?

She held the First's eyes. No, Faile did not have as much political experience as Berelain. But she had something the woman didn't. She loved Perrin. Deeply, truly. She would do *anything* to keep him from being hurt.

The First studied her. "Very well," she said. "So be it. Be proud of yourself, Faile. It is . . . rare that I take myself off a prize I have long desired."

"You haven't said how we could get rid of the rumors."

"There may be a method," Berelain said. "But it will be distasteful."

Faile raised an eyebrow.

"We will need to be seen as friends," Berelain explained. "Fighting, being at odds, this will fuel the rumors. But if we are seen spending time with one another, it will disarm them. That, mixed with a formal renunciation on my part of the rumors, will likely be enough."

Faile sat down in the chair she had been using earlier. Friends? She *detested* this woman.

"It would have to be a believable act," Berelain said, rising and walking over to the serving stand at the corner of the tent. She poured herself some chilled wine. "Only that would work."

"You'll find another man, as well," Faile said. "Someone you can give your attentions to, for a time at least. To prove that you are not interested in Perrin."

Berelain raised the cup. "Yes," she said. "I suspect that would help too. Can you put on such an act, Faile ni Bashere t'Aybara?"

You believed I was ready to kill you over this, didn't you, Faile thought. "I promise it."

Berelain paused, winecup halfway to her lips. Then she smiled, and drank. "We shall see, then," she said, lowering the cup, "what comes of this."

CHAPTER
19

Talk of Dragons

Mat tugged on a sturdy brown coat. The buttons were brass, but other than that, it was free of ornamentation. Made of a thick wool, it had a few holes from arrows that really should have killed him. One of the holes had a bloodstain around it, but that had mostly been washed out. It was a nice coat. He would have paid good coin for a coat like this one, when he lived back in the Two Rivers.

He rubbed his face, looking in the mirror of his new tent. He had shaved off that bloody beard, finally. How did Perrin manage that bloody itching? The man must have sandpaper for skin. Well, Mat would find another way to disguise himself, when needed.

He had nicked himself a few times while shaving. But it was not as if he had forgotten how to take care of himself. He did not need a manservant to do what he could manage on his own. Nodding to himself, he pulled on his hat and grabbed his *ashandarei* from the corner of the tent; the ravens on the blade seemed to perch excitedly in anticipation of battles to come. "Bloody right you do," Mat said, resting the *ashandarei* on his shoulder as he walked out of the tent. He grabbed his pack and slung it over his other shoulder. Starting tonight, he would be spending nights in the city.

He strode through camp, nodding to a group of passing Redarms. He had doubled the watch. He was worried about the *gholam*, but also about the many military camps in the area. Half were mercenaries, half were the retainers of this minor lord or that, coming to pay respects to the Queen—suspiciously arriving *after* the fighting was done.

No doubt each and every one was professing his heart-felt allegiance to Elayne, explaining that his men supported her all along. Their words probably fell a little flat, since Mat had it on good authority from three separate drunks in taverns that Elayne had used Traveling extensively in recruiting her defense. It was easier to feign a delayed arrival when you were responding to a written message.

"Mat! Mat!"

Mat stopped on the pathway outside his tent as Olver came racing up. The boy had taken to wearing a red band around his arm, much as the Redarms did, but he still wore his brown trousers and coat. He was carrying his rolled-up cloth for Snakes and Foxes under one arm and a pack slung over the other.

Setalle stood in the near distance, along with Lussin and Edder, two Redarms that Mat had assigned to watch over her and the boy. They'd be departing for the city soon.

"Mat," Olver said, panting. "You're leaving?"

"I don't have time to play with you now, Olver," Mat said, lowering his *ashandarei* to the crook of his arm. "I have to go meet with a Queen."

"I know," Olver said. "I figured that since we're both going to town, we could ride together and plan. I have some ideas about how to defeat the snakes and the foxes! We're going to show them, Mat. Burn me, but we bloody will!"

"Who taught you that language?"

"Mat," he said. "This is important! We have to plan! We haven't *talked* about what we're going to do."

Silently, Mat cursed himself for discussing the quest to rescue Moiraine where Olver could hear. The boy was not going to take it well when he was left behind.

"I need to think about what I'm going to say to the Queen," Mat said, rubbing his chin. "But I guess you're right, planning is important. Why don't you go tell Noal about your ideas?"

"I already did," Olver said. "And Thom too. And Talmanes."

Talmanes? He was not going with them into the Tower! Light, how much had Olver been spreading the news around?

"Olver," Mat said, squatting down to be on eye level with the boy, "you need to keep quieter. We don't want too many people knowing what we're doing."

"I didn't tell nobody we don't trust, Mat," Olver said. "Don't worry. Most were Redarms."

Great, Mat thought. What would the soldiers think of their commander planning to go off and fight a bunch of creatures from children's stories? Hopefully they would see Olver's comments as the fancies of a young boy.

"Just be careful," Mat said. "I'll come stop by your inn tomorrow, and we can play a game then and talk about it. All right?"

Olver nodded. "All right, Mat. But . . . blood and bloody ashes!" He turned and walked away.

"And stop swearing!" Mat called after him, then shook his head. Bloody soldiers would have Olver corrupted by the time he was twelve.

Mat continued on his way, leaning his spear on his shoulder again. He found Thom and Talmanes mounted at the front of the camp along with a force of fifty Redarms. Thom wore an extravagant wine-red coat and trousers, gold work at the arms, with a shirt bearing white lace at the cuffs and a silken cravat tied at the neck. The buttons were of gleaming gold. His mustaches had been trimmed and neatly combed. The entire outfit was new, including the black cloak, its inner lining of gold.

Mat froze in place. How had the man so perfectly transformed from an old scamp of a gleeman into a royal courtier? Light!

"I see from your reaction that the presentation is effective," Thom said.

"Blood and bloody ashes!" Mat exclaimed. "What happened? Did you take ill from a bad sausage at breakfast?"

Thom whipped his cloak back, revealing that he had his harp out and at his side. He looked like a court-bard! "I figured that if—after all of these years—I was going to make an appearance in Caemlyn, I should look the part."

"No wonder you've been singing for coin every day," Mat said. "The people in those taverns have way too much money."

Talmanes raised an eyebrow—as good as a grin, from that man. At times, he seemed so dour as to make thunderclouds feel cheerful. He also wore a fine outfit, his of deep cobalt and silver. Mat felt at his cuffs. He could have used some lace. If Lopin had been here, he would have set out the proper outfit without Mat even asking. A little lace was good for a man. Made him look presentable.

"Is *that* what you're wearing to visit the Queen, Mat?" Talmanes asked.

"Of course it is." The words left his mouth before he had a chance to think about them. "It's a good coat." He walked over to take Pips' reins.

"Good for sparring in, maybe," Talmanes said.

"Elayne is the Queen of Andor now, Mat," Thom said. "And queens are a particular lot. You should show her respect."

"I *am* showing her bloody respect," Mat said, handing his spear to one of the soldiers, then climbing into the saddle. He took the spear back, then turned Pips so he could regard Thom. "This is a good enough coat for a farmer."

"You're not a farmer anymore, Mat," Talmanes said.

"I am too," Mat said stubbornly.

"But Musenge called you—" Thom began.

"He was mistaken," Mat said. "Just because a man marries someone doesn't mean he suddenly becomes bloody nobility."

Thom and Talmanes exchanged a look.

"Mat," Thom said. "That's actually *exactly* how it works. It's pretty much one of the only ways to become nobility."

"That's the way we do it here, maybe," Mat said. "But Tuon is from Seanchan. Who knows what they do there? We all know how strange they can be. We can't know anything until we talk to her."

Thom frowned. "I'm certain, from things she said, that—"

"We *can't* know anything until we talk to Tuon," Mat repeated, louder this time. "Until then, I'm Mat. None of this Prince of Whatever nonsense."

Thom looked confused, but Talmanes' lips turned ever so slightly up at the side. Burn that man. Mat was inclined to think his solemn nature was all an act. Was he secretly laughing inside?

"Well, Mat," Talmanes said, "you *never* have made any sense, so why should we expect you to now? Onward, then, to meet the Queen of Andor. Certain you don't want to roll in the mud first?"

"I'll be fine," Mat said dryly, pulling his hat down as a soldier tied his pack to the back of his saddle.

He kicked Pips into motion, and the procession began the now-familiar ride to Caemlyn. Mat spent most of the time going over his plan in his head. He had Aludra's papers tucked into a leather folder, and they included her demands. Every bellfounder in Caemlyn, large quantities of bronze and iron, and powders worth thousands of crowns. And she claimed that was the *minimum* of what she needed.

How under the Light was Mat going to get bloody Elayne Trakand to give him all that? He would have to do a lot of smiling. But Elayne had proven resistant to his smiles before, and Queens were not like ordinary folk. Most women, they would smile back or they would scowl at you, so you knew where you stood. Elayne seemed the type to smile at you, then toss you in prison all the same.

For once, it would be nice if his luck could see him off somewhere enjoying a pipe and a game of dice, with a pretty serving girl on his knee and no cares beyond his next throw. Instead, he was married to a Seanchan High Blood and was off to beg the Queen of Andor for her help. How did he get into these situations? Sometimes he thought that the Creator must be like Talmanes. Straight of face, but secretly having a grand time laughing at Mat.

His procession passed numerous camps on the open plains around Caemlyn. All mercenaries were required to stay at least a league away, but the forces of the lords could camp closer. That put Mat in a rough place. There was always tension between sell-swords and loyal armsmen, and with the mercenaries so far from Caemlyn, fights were common. The Band was right in the middle of it.

He did some quick figuring based on the trails of campfire smoke he saw twisting into the air. There were at least ten thousand mercenaries in the area. Did Elayne know what a bubbling kettle she was brewing here? Too much heat, and the whole bloody thing would boil over!

Mat's procession drew attention. He had one of the men flying the banner of the Band of the Red Hand, and his men were developing a reputation. By Mat's count, they were the largest single group—mercenary or lord's force—outside Caemlyn's walls. They were as organized and disciplined as a regular army, and were under the leadership of a personal friend of the Dragon Reborn. His men could not help bragging about that, though Mat would much rather that they had kept quiet.

They passed groups of men waiting by the side of the road, curious to catch a glimpse of "Lord Mat." He kept his eyes forward. If they had expected some fop in a rich coat, then they would be disappointed! Though perhaps he could have chosen a better coat. This one was stiff, and the collar itched.

Of course, more than a few seemed to think Talmanes was "Lord Mat" from the way they pointed, probably because of how he was dressed. Bloody ashes!

This conversation with Elayne was going to be tough. But Mat had a hidden card, one he hoped would be enough to get her to look past the expense of Aludra's proposal. Though he was more afraid she would see what he was doing and want to take part in it. And when a woman wanted to be "part" of something, that meant she wanted to be in charge.

They approached the gate in Caemlyn's white-gray walls, passing the growing outer city. The soldiers waved him on. Mat gave them a tip of the hat, and Thom gave a flourishing wave to the small crowd gathered here. They cheered. Great. Just bloody great.

The march through the New City was uneventful save for *more* crowds watching. Would someone recognize his face from those drawings? Mat wanted to get off the main thoroughfares, but Caemlyn's narrow streets were a twisting mess. A force of fifty horsemen was too large to move through those streets.

They eventually passed through the brilliant white walls of the Inner City, where the roads were wider, the Ogier-built buildings less cramped, and the population thinner. Here, they passed more groups of armed men, including Guardsmen in white and red. Mat could make their camp out ahead, covering the gray paving stones of the courtyard with their tents and horselines.

The Caemlyn palace was like another little city within the city inside the city. It had a low fortified wall, and while its peaks and spires rose into the air, it had more of the look of a war bunker than the Sun Palace did. Odd, how he had never noticed that when he was younger. If Caemlyn fell, this palace could hold on its own. They needed more barracks, though, within that wall. This camping out in the courtyard was ridiculous.

Mat took Talmanes, Thom and a force of ten Redarms as an escort. A tall man in a burnished breastplate, three golden knots on the shoulder of his cloak, waited at the palace entrance. He was a young man, but the way he stood—relaxed, yet poised, hand on the pommel of his sword—indicated he was a practiced soldier. Too bad he had such a pretty face. A life in the military would probably end up wrecking that.

The man nodded to Mat, Thom and Talmanes. "Lord Cauthon?" he asked Mat.

"Just Mat."

The man raised an eyebrow, but said nothing. "My name is Charlz Guybon. I'll lead you to Her Majesty."

She had sent Guybon himself to escort Mat. He was high-ranking, second-in-command of the armies. That was unexpected. Was Elayne afraid of him, or was she was honoring him? Maybe Guybon had wanted to see Mat for himself. She would not honor Mat, not after making him wait so long to get an audience! A fine greeting for an old friend. His suspicions were confirmed when Guybon did not lead them to the Grand Hall, but down to a quiet area of the Palace.

"I've heard much about you, Master Cauthon," Guybon said. He seemed like one of those stiff soldiers. Solid, but maybe a little too solid. Like a bow without enough spring to it.

"From who?" Mat asked. "Elayne?"

"Mostly rumors around the city. People like to talk about you."

They do? Mat thought. "I didn't do half of what they say," he grumbled, "and the other half wasn't my bloody fault."

Guybon laughed. "What of the story of you hanging from a tree for nine days?"

"Didn't happen," Mat said, resisting the urge to tug at the scarf around his neck. Nine days? Where did that come from? He had not even hung for nine bloody minutes! Nine *seconds* had been too long.

"They also say," Guybon continued, "that you never lose at dice or at love, and that your spear never misses its target."

"Wish those second two were true. Burn me, but I wish they were."

"But you *do* always win at dice?"

"Near enough," Mat said, tugging down the brim of his hat. "But don't spread that one, or I'll never find a game."

"They say you slew one of the Forsaken," Guybon noted.

"Not true," Mat said. Where had *that* one come from?

"And the stories of you dueling the King of the Aiel invaders in a battle of honor? Did you really win the Dragon Reborn the loyalty of the Aiel?"

"Bloody ashes," Mat said. "I killed Couladin, but it didn't happen in any kind of duel! I ran into him on the battlefield, and one of us had to die. It wasn't bloody well going to be me."

"Interesting," Guybon said. "I thought that one might be true. At least, it's one of the few that *could* have happened. Unlike. . . ." He trailed off.

"What?" Mat said. They passed an intersection of halls where servants grouped, watching him and the others pass and whispering among themselves.

Guybon looked hesitant. "I'm sure you've heard."

"Doubtful." Burn him! What was next? Had the members of the Band been spreading these rumors? Even they did not know about some of those things!

"Well, there's this rumor that says you stepped into death's domain to challenge him and demand answers to your questions," Guybon said, looking more embarrassed. "And that he gave you that spear you hold and foretold to you your own death."

Mat felt a chill. That one was close enough to the truth to be frightening.

"Silly, I know," Guybon said.

"Sure," Mat said. "Silly." He tried to laugh, but it came out as a cough. Guybon regarded him curiously.

Light, Mat realized, *he thinks I'm dodging the question!* "Only rumors, of course," Mat said quickly. Too quickly, maybe. Blood and bloody ashes!

Guybon nodded, looking thoughtful.

Mat wanted to change the topic, but he did not trust himself to open his bloody mouth. He could see that more and more palace servants had stopped to watch the procession.

He felt like cursing some more at that, but then noticed that many of them seemed focused on Thom.

Thom had been court-bard right here in Caemlyn. He did not talk about it, but Mat knew he had suffered a falling-out with the Queen. Thom had been in virtual exile ever since, coming to Caemlyn only when pressed.

Morgase was dead now, so this was Thom returning from his exile, it seemed. That was probably why he had dressed so finely. Mat looked down at his coat again. *Burn me, I should have worn something nicer.*

Guybon led them to a carved wooden door, bearing the roaring Lion of Andor. He knocked softly, received the call to enter, then gestured Mat toward the door. "The Queen will receive you in her sitting room."

"Thom, you're with me," Mat said. "Talmanes, you watch the soldiers." The nobleman looked crestfallen, but Elayne was undoubtedly going to embarrass Mat, and he did not want Talmanes there to see. "I'll introduce you later," Mat promised. Bloody noblemen. They thought every second thing was an affront to their honor. Mat would have been *happy* to wait outside!

Mat stepped up to the door, taking a deep breath. He had fought in dozens of skirmishes and battles without growing nervous. Now his hands were shaking. Why did he feel as if he were walking directly into an ambush without a scrap of armor on?

Elayne. As Queen. Burn him, but this was going to hurt. He opened the door and strode in.

His eyes found Elayne immediately. She sat beside a hearth, holding a cup of what appeared to be milk. She looked radiant in a gown of deep red and gold. Beautiful, full red lips that Mat would not have minded kissing, if he had not been a married man. Her red-gold hair seemed to shimmer in the hearthlight, and her cheeks were full of color. She seemed to have gained a little weight. Best not to mention that. Or should he? Sometimes women got angry when you mentioned that they looked different, and sometimes they got angry if you did not notice.

She was a pretty thing. Not as pretty as Tuon, of course. Elayne was far too pale, and too tall, and had too much hair. It was distracting. Still, she was pretty. Seemed a waste as a queen. She would have made an excellent serving girl. Ah well. *Somebody* had to be Queen.

Mat glanced at Birgitte, who was the only other one in the room. *She* looked the same. Always did, with that golden braid and high boots, like the hero from the bloody stories. Which was exactly what she was. It was good to see her again; she was one woman he knew who would not snap at him for speaking the truth.

Thom stepped in beside him, and Mat cleared his throat. She would expect him to be formal. Well, he was not going to bow or scrape, and he—

Elayne leaped out of her chair. She ran across the room as Birgitte closed the door. "Thom, I'm so glad that you're all right!" Elayne grabbed him in an embrace.

"Hello, dear one," Thom said fondly. "I hear you've done well for yourself, and for Andor."

Elayne was crying! Mat pulled off his hat, befuddled. Sure, Thom and Elayne had been close, but Elayne was Queen now. Elayne turned toward Mat. "It's good to see you, Mat. Do not think that the Crown has forgotten your service to me. Bringing Thom back to Andor is another debt we owe you."

"Well, um," Mat said. "It really wasn't anything, you know, Elayne. Burn me. You're Queen! How's that feel?"

Elayne laughed, finally releasing Thom. "Such a way with words you have, Mat."

"I'm not going to bow to you or anything," he warned. "Or bother with that 'Your Majesty' nonsense."

"I wouldn't expect it," Elayne said. "Unless we're in public, of course. I mean, I have to keep up appearances for the people."

"I suppose that's true," Mat agreed. It did make sense. He held out a hand to Birgitte, but she chuckled and gave him a hug, slapping him on the back like an old pal meeting for a mug of ale. And, well, perhaps that was what they were. Without the ale.

He could have used some ale.

"Come, sit," Elayne said, gesturing toward the chairs by the fire. "I'm sorry to make you wait so long, Mat."

"It's nothing," he said. "You're busy."

"It's embarrassing," she said. "One of my stewards lumped

you with the mercenary groups. It's so hard to keep track of them all! If you wish, I'll give you leave to camp closer to the city. There's not room inside the walls for the Band, I'm afraid."

"That won't be needed," Mat said, taking one of the seats. "Letting us move closer is kind enough. Thank you." Thom sat, and Birgitte preferred to stand, though she did join them by the hearth, leaning back against the stones.

"You look well, Elayne," Thom said. "Is everything going well with the child?"

"Children," Elayne corrected. "There will be twins. And yes, everything is well. Save for me having to be poked and prodded at nearly every opportunity."

"Wait," Mat said. "*What?*" He glanced again at Elayne's stomach.

Thom rolled his eyes. "Don't you ever *listen* when you're in the city gambling?"

"I listen," Mat muttered. "Usually." He looked accusingly at Elayne. "Does Rand know about this?"

She laughed. "I should hope he isn't too surprised."

"Burn me!" Mat said. "He's the father!"

"The father of my children is a matter of some speculation in the city," Elayne said solemnly. "And the Crown prefers there to *be* speculation, for the time. But enough about me! Thom, you have to tell me everything. How did you escape Ebou Dar?"

"Forget Ebou Dar," Birgitte snapped. "How's Olver? Did you find him?"

"We did," Thom said. "And he is well, though I fear the lad is destined for life as a professional soldier."

"Not a bad life," Birgitte said. "Eh, Mat?"

"There are worse," he said, still trying to get his legs underneath him. How had becoming Queen made Elayne *less* high-and-mighty? Had he missed something? She actually seemed agreeable now!

Well, that was unfair. There were times when she had been agreeable before. They had merely been mixed between times when she had been ordering Mat around. He found himself smiling as Thom related the details of their escape and the capture of Tuon, followed by their travels with Master Luca's menagerie. Drawn from the quiver of a storyteller, the tale sounded a whole lot more impressive than it had been to live. Mat almost thought himself a hero, listening to Thom.

Right before Thom got to the part about Tuon's marriage words, however, Mat coughed and cut in. "And we beat the Seanchan, fled into Murandy, and eventually found an Aes Sedai to get us here through a gateway. By the way, have you seen Verin lately?"

"No," Elayne said. Thom eyed Mat with amusement.

"Blast," Mat said. Well, there went his chance to use her for a gateway to the Tower of Ghenjei. He would worry about that later. He took the leather envelope from his belt, then opened it, taking out Aludra's papers. "Elayne," he said, "I need to talk to you."

"Yes, you mentioned 'bellfounders' in your letter. What trouble have you gotten yourself into, Matrim Cauthon?"

"That's not fair at all," he said, spreading out the sheets. "I'm not the one who gets into trouble. If I—"

"You're *not* going to mention my getting captured in the Stone of Tear again, are you?" she asked with a roll of her eyes.

He stopped. "Of course not. That happened ages ago. I barely remember it."

She laughed, the pretty sound ringing in the room. He felt himself blushing. "Anyway, I'm not in trouble. I just need some resources."

"What kind of resources?" Elayne asked, growing curious as he spread out the papers on the table next to her chair. Birgitte leaned down.

"Well," Mat said, rubbing his chin. "There are three bellfounders in the city; I'll need those. And we're going to need some powders. They're listed on this page. And . . . we'll need a little bit of metal." He winced and handed her one of Aludra's lists.

Elayne read the page, then blinked. "Are you mad?"

"Sometimes I think I might be," he said. "But burn me, I think this will be worth the cost."

"What is it?" Elayne asked as Birgitte looked over one of the sheets, then handed it to Elayne.

"Aludra calls them dragons," Mat said. "Thom says you knew her?"

"Yes, I did," Elayne said.

"Well, these are launching tubes, like the ones for her

fireworks. Only they're made of metal, and they're big. And instead of launching nightflowers, they launch these head-sized chunks of iron."

"Why would you want to launch chunks of iron up into the air?" Elayne said, frown deepening.

"You *don't*," Birgitte said, eyes opening wide. "You launch them at someone else's army."

Mat nodded. "Aludra claims that one of these dragons could launch an iron ball as far as a mile."

"Mother's milk in a cup!" Birgitte said. "You can't be serious."

"She is," Mat said. "And I believe her. You should see what she's created already, and she claims these will be her masterpiece. Look, she shows here the dragons firing on a city wall from a mile away. With fifty dragons and two hundred and fifty soldiers she could knock down a wall like the one around Caemlyn in a few hours."

Elayne looked pale. Did she believe him? Would she be angry at him for wasting her time?

"I know that won't be of much use in the Last Battle," Mat said quickly. "Trollocs don't have walls. But look here. I had her design a spreading shot. Fire it on a line of Trollocs from four hundred paces, and one of these dragons will do the work of fifty bowmen. Burn me, Elayne, but we're going to be at a disadvantage. The Shadow can *always* toss more Trollocs at us than we have soldiers, and the bloody things are twice as hard to kill as a man. We need an advantage. I remember—"

He cut himself off. He had been about to say he remembered the Trolloc Wars, which would not have been a good idea. A man could start some embarrassing rumors that way. "Look," he said. "I know this sounds outrageous, but you have to give it a chance."

She looked up at him, and . . . was she crying again? What had he done?

"Mat, I could kiss you," she declared. "This is exactly what I needed!"

Mat blinked. What?

Birgitte chuckled. "First Norry, now Mat. You'll have to watch yourself, Elayne. Rand will be jealous."

Elayne snorted, looking down at the plans. "The bellfounders aren't going to like this. Most of the craftsmen were looking forward to getting back to daily work, following the siege."

"Oh, I don't know about that, Elayne," Birgitte said. "I've known a craftsman or two in my time. To a person, they complain about royal privilege during war, but as long as the Crown compensates them, they're secretly happy. Steady work is always appreciated. Besides, something like this will make them curious."

"We'll have to keep it secret," Elayne said.

"So you'll do it?" Mat asked, surprised. He had not needed his secret bribe to distract her!

"We'll need proof of one working first, of course," Elayne said. "But if these devices, these dragons, work half as well as Aludra claims . . . well, I'd be a fool not to put every man on them we can!"

"That's right generous of you," Mat said, scratching his head.

Elayne hesitated. "Generous?"

"Building these for the Band."

"For the Band . . . Mat, these will be for Andor!"

"Here now," Mat said. "These are *my* plans."

"And *my* resources!" Elayne said. She sat up straight, suddenly becoming more poised. "Surely you see that the Crown could offer a more stable and useful control for the deployment of these weapons."

To the side, Thom was grinning.

"What are *you* so happy about?" Mat demanded.

"Nothing," Thom said. "You do your mother proud, Elayne."

"Thank you, Thom," she said, favoring him with a smile.

"Whose side are you on?" Mat said.

"Everyone's," Thom said.

"That's not a bloody side," Mat said, then looked back to Elayne. "I put a lot of effort and thought into getting these plans out of Aludra. I've nothing against Andor, but I don't trust anyone with these weapons who isn't me."

"And if the Band were part of Andor?" Elayne asked. She really *did* sound like a queen all of a sudden.

"The Band is beholden to nobody," Mat said.

"That is admirable, Mat," Elayne said, "but it makes you mercenaries. I think that the Band deserves something more, something better. With official backing, you would have access to resources and authority. We could give you a commission in Andor, with your own command structure."

It was actually tempting. Just a little. But it did not matter. He did not think Elayne would be happy to have him in her realm once she knew of his relationship with the Seanchan. He meant to return to Tuon eventually, somehow. If only to work out what she really felt about him.

He had no intention of giving the Seanchan access to these dragons, but he did not fancy giving them to Andor, either. Unfortunately, he had to admit that there was no way he was going to have Andor build them without giving the weapons to the nation, too.

"I don't want a commission for the Band," Mat said. "We're free men, and that's how we like it."

Elayne looked troubled.

"But I'd be willing to split the dragons with you," Mat said. "Some for us, some for you."

"What if," Elayne said, "I built all of the dragons and owned all of them—but promised that only the Band could use them? No other forces would have access to them."

"That would be kind of you," Mat said. "Suspicious, though. No offense."

"It would be better for me if the noble Houses didn't have these, at least not at first. They will spread eventually. Weapons always do. I build them and promise to give them to the Band. No commission, just a contract, hiring you for a long term. You can go at any time. But if you do, you leave the dragons behind."

Mat frowned. "Feels like you're wrapping a chain around my neck, Elayne."

"I'm only suggesting reasonable solutions."

"The day you become reasonable is the day I eat my hat," Mat said. "No offense."

Elayne raised an eyebrow at him. Yes, she had become a queen. Just like that.

"I want the right to keep a few of these dragons," Mat said, "if we leave. One-quarter to us, three-quarters to you. But we'll take your contract, and while we're in your employ, only we use them. As you said."

Her frown deepened. Burn him, but she had grasped the power of those dragons quickly. He could not let her hesitate now. They *needed* the dragons to go into production immediately. And he was not about to let the chance of having them pass the Band by.

Sighing to himself, Mat reached up and undid the strap at the back of his neck, then pulled the familiar foxhead medallion out of his shirt. The second he removed it, he felt more naked than if he had stripped bare. He set it on the table.

Elayne glanced at it, and he could see a flash of desire in her eyes. "What is that for?"

"It's a sweetener," Mat said, leaning forward, elbows on knees. "You get it for one day if you agree to start production on a prototype dragon this evening. I don't care what you do with the medallion—study it, write a bloody book about it, wear it about. But you return it tomorrow. Your word on it."

Birgitte whistled slowly. Elayne had wanted to get her hands on that medallion the moment she discovered he had it. Of course, so had every other bloody Aes Sedai that Mat had met.

"I get the Band in at least a one-year contract," Elayne said, "renewable. We'll pay you whatever you were earning in Murandy."

How did she know about that?

"You can cancel," she continued, "as long as you provide a month's warning—but I keep four dragons out of five. And any men who wish to join the Andoran military must be given the chance."

"I want one out of four," Mat said. "And a new serving man."

"A *what*?" Elayne said.

"A serving man," Mat said. "You know, to take care of my clothing. You'd do a better job of picking than I would."

Elayne looked at his coat, then up at his hair. "That," she said, "I'll give you regardless of how the other negotiations go."

"One out of four?" Mat said.

"I get the medallion for three days."

He shivered. Three days, with the *gholam* in town. She would have him dead. It was already a gamble to give it to her for a day. But he could not think of anything else he could offer. "What do you even think you can do with the thing?" he asked.

"Copy it," Elayne said absently, "if I'm lucky."

"Really?"

"I won't know until I study it."

Mat suddenly had the horrifying image of every Aes Sedai in the world wearing one of those medallions. He shared a look with Thom, who seemed equally surprised to hear this.

But what did that matter? Mat could not channel. Before, he had worried that—if she studied it—Elayne might figure a way to touch him with the One Power when he was wearing it. But if she just wanted to copy it . . . well, he found himself relieved. And intrigued.

"There's been something I've been meaning to mention, Elayne," he said. "The *gholam* is here. In town. It's been killing people."

Elayne remained calm, but he could tell from the way she was even more formal when she spoke that the news worried her. "Then I will be certain to return the medallion to you on time."

He grimaced. "All right," he said. "Three days."

"Very well," she said. "I want the Band to start immediately. I'll be Traveling to Cairhien soon, and I have a feeling they would be a better support force there than the Queen's Guards."

So *that* was what this was about! Elayne was moving on the Sun Throne. Well, that seemed a good use for the men, at least until Mat needed them. Better than letting them sit around getting lazy and picking fights with sell-swords.

"I agree to that," Mat said, "but Elayne, the Band has to be free to fight in the Last Battle, however Rand wants. And Aludra has to supervise the dragons. I have a feeling that she'll insist that she remain with you if the Band breaks off from Andor."

"I have no issues with that," Elayne said, smiling.

"I figured you wouldn't. But, just so we're clear, the Band has control of the dragons until we leave. You can't sell the technology to others."

"Someone will replicate it, Mat," she said.

"Copies won't be as good as Aludra's," Mat said. "I promise you that."

Elayne studied him, blue eyes weighing him, judging

him. "I'd still rather have the Band as a fully commissioned Andoran force."

"Well, I wish I had a hat made all of gold, a tent that could fly and a horse that leaves droppings of diamonds. But we'll both have to settle with what's reasonable, won't we?"

"It wouldn't be unreasonable to—"

"We'd have to do what you said, Elayne," Mat replied. "I won't have it. Some battles aren't worth fighting, and I'm going to decide when my men put themselves at risk. That's that."

"I don't like having men who could leave me at any time."

"You know I won't hold them back merely to spite you," Mat said. "I'll do what's right."

"What you *see* as being right," she corrected.

"Every man should have that option," he replied.

"Few men use it wisely."

"We want it anyway," Mat said. "We demand it."

She glanced—almost imperceptibly—toward the plans and the medallion on the table. "You have it," she said.

"Deal," he said, standing up, spitting in his hand, and holding it out.

She hesitated, stood and spat in her hand, then held it out to him. He smiled and shook it.

"Did you know that I might ask you to take arms against the Two Rivers?" she asked. "Is that why you demanded the right to leave if you want?"

Against the *Two Rivers*? Why under the Light would she want to do that? "You don't need to fight them, Elayne."

"We shall see what Perrin forces me to do," she replied. "But let's not discuss that right now." She glanced at Thom, then reached under her table and pulled out a rolled piece of paper with a ribbon about it. "Please. I want to hear more of what happened during your trip out of Ebou Dar. Will you take dinner with me this evening?"

"We'd be delighted," Thom said, standing. "Wouldn't we, Mat?"

"I suppose," Mat said. "If Talmanes can come. He'll tear my throat out if I don't at least let him meet you, Elayne. Taking dinner with you will have him dancing all the way back to the camp."

Elayne chuckled. "As you wish. I'll have servants show you to some rooms where you can rest until the time arrives." She handed Thom the rolled-up paper. "This will be proclaimed tomorrow, if you will it."

"What is it?" Thom asked, frowning.

"The court of Andor lacks a proper court-bard," she said. "I thought you might be interested."

Thom hesitated. "You honor me, but I can't accept that. There are things I need to do in the next little while, and I can't be tied to the court."

"You needn't be tied to the court," Elayne said. "You'll have freedom to leave and go where you wish. But when you are in Caemlyn, I'd have you be known for who you are."

"I . . ." He took the roll of paper. "I'll consider it, Elayne."

"Excellent." She grimaced. "I'm afraid I have an appointment with my midwife now, but I will see you at dinner. I haven't yet asked what Matrim meant by calling himself a married man in his letter. I expect a full report! No expurgations!" She eyed Mat, smiling slyly. "Expurgation means 'parts cut out,' Mat. In case you weren't bloody aware."

He put his hat on. "I knew that." What had that word been again? Expirations? Light, why had he mentioned his marriage in that letter? He had hoped it would make Elayne curious enough to see him.

Elayne laughed, gesturing them toward the exit. Thom spared a paternal kiss for her cheek before parting—good that it was paternal! Mat had heard some things about those two that he did not want to believe. With Thom old enough to be her grandfather, no less.

Mat pulled open the door, moving to leave.

"And Mat," Elayne added. "If you need to borrow money to buy a new coat, the Crown can lend you some. Considering your station, you really should dress more nicely."

"I'm no bloody nobleman!" he said, turning.

"Not yet," she said. "You don't have Perrin's audacity in naming yourself to a title. I'll see that you get one."

"You wouldn't dare," he said.

"But—"

"See here," he said as Thom joined him in the hallway. "I'm *proud* of who I am. And I like this coat. It's comfortable." He clenched his hands into fists, refusing to scratch at his collar.

"If you say so," Elayne said. "I will see you at dinner. I'll have to bring Dyelin. She's very curious to meet you."

With that, she had Birgitte close the door. Mat stared at it vengefully for a moment, then turned toward Thom. Talmanes and the soldiers waited a short distance down the hallway, out of hearing range. They were being given warm tea by some palace servants.

"That went well," Mat decided, hands on hips. "I worried she wouldn't bite, but I think I reeled her in pretty well." Though the bloody dice were still rolling in his head.

Thom laughed, clapping him on the shoulder.

"What?" Mat demanded.

Thom just chuckled, then glanced down at the scroll in his other hand. "And this was unexpected as well."

"Well, Andor *doesn't* have a court-bard," Mat said.

"Yes," Thom said, looking over the scroll. "But there's a pardon written in here too, for any and all crimes—known and unknown—I may have committed in Andor or Cairhien. I wonder who told her. . . ."

"Told her what?"

"Nothing, Mat. Nothing at all. We have a few hours until dinner with Elayne. What do you say we go buy you a new coat?"

"All right," Mat said. "You think I could get one of those pardons, too, if I asked for it?"

"Do you need one?"

Mat shrugged, walking down the hallway with him. "Can't hurt to be safe. What kind of coat are you going to buy me, anyway?"

"I didn't say *I'd* pay."

"Don't be so stingy," Mat said. "I'll pay for dinner." And bloody ashes, somehow, Mat knew, he would.

CHAPTER
20

A Choice

Y ou must not speak," Rosil said to Nynaeve. The
slender, long-necked woman wore an orange dress
slashed with yellow. "At least, speak only when
spoken to. You know the ceremony?"

Nynaeve nodded, her heart beating treacherously as they
walked into the dungeonlike depths of the White Tower.
Rosil was the new Mistress of Novices, and a member of
the Yellow Ajah by coincidence.

"Excellent, excellent," Rosil said. "Might I suggest you
move the ring to the third finger of your left hand?"

"You may suggest it," Nynaeve said, but did not move the
ring. She *had* been named Aes Sedai. She would not give
in on that point.

Rosil pursed her lips, but said nothing further. The
woman had shown Nynaeve remarkable kindness during
her short time in the White Tower—which had been a relief. Nynaeve had grown to expect that every Yellow sister
would regard her with disdain, or at least indifference. Oh,
they thought she was talented, and many insisted on being
trained by her. But they did not think of her as one of them.
Not yet.

This woman was different, and being a burr in her sandal
was not a good repayment. "It is important to me, Rosil,"
Nynaeve explained, "that I not give any indication of dis-
respect for the Amyrlin. She named me Aes Sedai. To act
as if I were merely Accepted would be to undermine her
words. This test is important—when the Amyrlin raised
me, she never said that I need not be tested. But I *am* Aes
Sedai."

Rosil cocked her head, then nodded. "Yes. I see. You are correct."

Nynaeve stopped in the dim corridor. "I want to thank you, and the others who have welcomed me these last days—Niere and Meramor. I had not assumed I would find acceptance here among you."

"There are some who resist change, dear," Rosil said. "It will ever be so. But your new weaves are impressive. More importantly, they're effective. That earns you a warm welcome from me."

Nynaeve smiled.

"Now," Rosil said, raising a finger. "You *might* be Aes Sedai in the eyes of the Amyrlin and the Tower, but tradition still holds. No speaking for the rest of the ceremony, please."

The lanky woman continued leading the way. Nynaeve followed, biting off a retort. She wouldn't let her nerves rule her.

Deeper into the Tower they wound, and despite her determination to be calm, she found herself increasingly nervous. She *was* Aes Sedai, and she *would* pass this test. She'd mastered the hundred weaves. She didn't need to worry.

Except, some women never returned from the test.

These cellars had a grand beauty to them. The smooth stone floor was leveled carefully. Lamps burned high on the walls; likely, those had required a sister or Accepted to light them with the One Power. Few people came down here, and most of the rooms were used for storage. It seemed a waste to her to put such care in a place rarely visited.

Eventually, they arrived at a pair of doors so large that Rosil had to use the One Power to open them. *It's an indication,* Nynaeve thought, folding her arms. *The vaulted hallways, the enormous door. This is here to show Accepted the importance of what they are about to do.*

The enormous, gatelike doors swung open, and Nynaeve forced herself to master her jitters. The Last Battle was looming. She *would* pass this test. She had important work to be about.

Head raised high, she entered the chamber. It was domed, with stand-lamps around the perimeter. A large *ter'angreal* dominated the center. It was an oval, narrowed at the top and bottom, that sat unsupported.

Many *ter'angreal* looked ordinary. That was not the case here: this oval was *obviously* something worked by the One Power. It was made of metal, but the light changed colors as it reflected off the silvery sides, making the thing seem to glow and shift.

"Attend," Rosil said formally.

There were other Aes Sedai in the room. One from each Ajah, including—unfortunately—the Red. They were all Sitters, an oddity, perhaps because of Nynaeve's notoriety in the Tower. Saerin from the Brown, Yukiri of the Gray, Barasine from the Red. Notably, Romanda from the Yellow was there; she had insisted on taking part. She had been hard with Nynaeve so far.

Egwene herself had come. One more than normal, and the Amyrlin as well. Nynaeve met the Amyrlin's eyes, and Egwene nodded. Unlike the test to be raised to Accepted—which was made entirely by the *ter'angreal*—this test involved the sisters actively working to make Nynaeve prove herself. And Egwene would be among the most harsh. To show that she had been right in raising Nynaeve.

"You come in ignorance, Nynaeve al'Meara," Rosil said. "How will you depart?"

"In knowledge of myself," Nynaeve said.

"For what reason have you been summoned here?"

"To be tried."

"For what reason should you be tried?"

"To show that I am worthy," Nynaeve said.

Several of the women frowned, including Egwene. Those weren't the right words—Nynaeve was supposed to say that she wanted to learn whether or not she was worthy. But she was already Aes Sedai, so by definition she was worthy. She just had to prove it to the others.

Rosil stumbled, but continued. "And . . . for what would you be found worthy?"

"To wear the shawl I have been given," Nynaeve said. She didn't say it to be arrogant. Once again, she simply stated the truth, as she saw it. Egwene had raised her. She wore the shawl already. Why pretend that she didn't?

This test was administered clad in the Light. She began taking off her dress.

"I will instruct you," Rosil said. "You will see this sign upon the ground." She raised her fingers, forming weaves that made a glowing symbol in the air. A six-pointed star, two overlapping triangles.

Saerin embraced the source and wove a weave of Spirit. Nynaeve suppressed the urge to embrace the Source herself.

Only a little longer, she thought. *And then nobody will be able to doubt me.*

Saerin touched her with the weave of Spirit. "Remember what must be remembered," she murmured.

That weave had something to do with memory. What was its purpose? The six-pointed star hovered in Nynaeve's vision.

"When you see that sign, you will go to it immediately," Rosil said. "Go at a steady pace, neither hurrying nor hanging back. Only when you reach it may you embrace the Source. The weaving required must begin immediately, and you may not leave that sign until it is completed."

"Remember what must be remembered," Saerin said again.

"When the weave is complete," Rosil said, "you will see that sign again, marking the way you must go, again at a steady pace, without hesitation."

"Remember what must be remembered."

"One hundred times you will weave, in the order that you have been given and in perfect composure."

"Remember what must be remembered," Saerin said one final time.

Nynaeve felt the weaving of Spirit settle into her. It was rather like Healing. She removed her dress and shift as the other sisters knelt beside the *ter'angreal*, performing complex weaves of all Five Powers. They caused it to glow brightly, the colors on its surface shifting and changing. Rosil cleared her throat, and Nynaeve blushed, handing her the pile of garments, then took off her Great Serpent ring and placed it on top, followed by Lan's ring—which she normally wore around her neck.

Rosil took the clothing. The other sisters were completely absorbed in their work. The *ter'angreal* began glowing a pure white in the center, then started to revolve slowly, moving silently against the stone.

Nynaeve took a deep breath, striding forward. She paused before the *ter'angreal*, stepped through and . . .

. . . and where was she? Nynaeve frowned. This didn't

look like the Two Rivers. She stood in a village made of
huts. Waves lapped against a sandy beach to her left, and
the village ran up a slope toward a rocky shelf to her right.
A distant mountain towered above.

An island of some sort. The air was humid, the breeze
calm. People walked between huts, calling good-naturedly
to one another. A few stopped to stare at her. She looked
down at herself, realizing for the first time that she was naked. She blushed furiously. Who had taken her clothing?
When she found the person responsible she'd switch them
so soundly, they wouldn't be able to sit for weeks!

A robe was hanging from a nearby clothesline. She
forced herself to remain calm as she walked over and pulled
it free. She would find its owner and pay them. She couldn't
very well walk about without a stitch. She threw the robe on
over her head.

The ground shook, suddenly. The gentle waves grew
louder, crashing against the beach. Nynaeve gasped, steadying herself against the clothesline pole. Above, the mountain
began spurting smoke and ashes.

Nynaeve clutched the pole as the rocky shelf nearby began to break apart, boulders tumbling down the incline.
People yelled. She had to do something! As she looked
about, she saw a six-pointed star carved into the ground.
She wanted to run for it, but she knew she needed to walk
carefully.

Keeping calm was difficult. As she walked, her heart
fluttered with terror. She was going to be crushed! She
reached the star pattern just as a large shower of stones
rumbled toward her, smashing huts. Despite her fear,
Nynaeve quickly formed the correct weave—a weave of
Air that formed a wall. She set it in front of herself, and the
stones thudded against the air, forced back.

There were hurt people in the village. She turned from
the star pattern to help, but as she did, she saw the same six-
pointed star woven in reeds and hanging from the door of a
nearby hut. She hesitated.

She *could not* fail. She walked to the hut and passed
through the doorway.

Then she froze. What was she doing in this dark, cold
cavern? And why was she wearing this robe of thick,
scratchy fibers?

She had completed the first of the hundred weaves. She knew this, but nothing else. Frowning to herself, she walked through the cavern. Light shone through cracks in the ceiling, and she saw a greater pool of it ahead. The way out.

She walked from the cavern to find that she was in the Waste. She raised a hand to shade her eyes from the bright sunlight. There wasn't a soul in sight. She walked forward, feet crunching on weeds and scalded by hot stones.

The heat was overwhelming. Soon each step was exhausting. Fortunately, some ruins lay ahead. Shade! She wanted to run for it, but she had to remain calm. She walked up to the stones, and her feet fell on rock shaded by a broken wall. It was so cool, she sighed in relief.

A pattern of bricks lay nearby in the ground, and they made a six-pointed star. Unfortunately, that star was back out in the sunlight. She reluctantly left the shade and walked toward the pattern.

Drums thumped in the distance. Nynaeve spun. Disgusting brown-furred creatures began to climb over a nearby hill, carrying axes that dripped with red blood. The Trollocs looked wrong to her. She'd seen Trollocs before, though she didn't remember where. These were different. A new breed, perhaps? With thicker fur, eyes hidden in the recesses of their faces.

Nynaeve walked faster, but did not break into a run. It was important to keep her calm. That was completely *stupid*. Why would she need to—or want to—keep herself from running when there were Trollocs nearby? If she died because she wasn't willing to hasten her step, it would be her own fault.

Keep composure. Don't move too quickly.

She maintained her steady pace, reaching the six-pointed star as the Trollocs drew close. She began the weave she was required to make and split off a thread of Fire. She sent an enormous spray of heat away from her, burning the nearest of the beasts to cinders.

Jaw set against her fear, she crafted the rest of the required weave. She split her weaves a half-dozen times and finished the complicated thing in mere moments.

She set it in place, then nodded. There. Other Trollocs were coming, and she burned them away with a wave of her hand.

The six-pointed star was carved into the side of an archway of stone. She walked toward it, trying to keep from looking nervously over her shoulder. More Trollocs were coming. More than she could possibly kill.

She reached the archway and stepped through.

Nynaeve finished the forty-seventh weave, which caused the sounds of bells in the air. She was exhausted. She'd had to make this weave while standing on top of an impossibly narrow tower hundreds of feet in the air. Wind buffeted her, threatening to blow her free.

An archway appeared below, in the dark night air. It seemed to grow right out of the pillar's side a dozen feet below her, parallel to the ground, its opening toward the sky. It held the six-pointed star.

Gritting her teeth, she leaped off the spire and fell through the archway.

She landed in a puddle. Her clothing was gone. What had happened to it? She stood up, growling to herself. She was *angry*. She didn't know why, but someone had done . . . something to her.

She was so tired. That was their fault, whoever they were. As she focused on that thought, it became more clear to her. She couldn't remember what they'd done, but they were definitely to blame. She had cuts across both of her arms. Had she been whipped? The cuts hurt something fierce.

Dripping wet, she looked around. She'd completed forty-seven of the hundred weaves. She knew that, but nothing else. Other than the fact that *somebody* very badly wanted her to fail.

She wasn't going to let them win. She rose out of the puddle, determined to be calm, and found some clothing nearby. It was garishly colored, bright pink and yellow with a generous helping of red. It seemed an insult. She put it on anyway.

She walked down a path in the bog, stepping around sinkholes and pools of stagnant water, until she found a six-pointed star drawn in the mud. She began the next weave, which would make a burning blue star shoot into the air.

Something bit at her neck. She slapped her hand at it,

killing a blackfly. Well, no surprise that she'd find those in this dank swamp. She would be glad to—

Another bite on her arm. She slapped at it. The very air started to buzz, flies zipping around her. Nynaeve gritted her teeth, continuing the weave. More and more bites prickled on her arms. She couldn't kill them all. Could she get rid of the flies with a weave? She began a weave of Air to create a breeze around her, but was interrupted as she heard screams.

It was faint over the buzzing of the flies, but it sounded like a child trapped in the bog! Nynaeve took a step toward the sounds and opened her mouth to call, but blackflies swarmed into her mouth, choking her. They got at her eyes, and she had to squeeze them shut.

That buzzing. The screams. The biting. Light, they were in her throat! In her lungs!

Finish the weave. You must *finish the weave.*

She continued, somehow, despite the pain. The sound of the insects was so loud that she could barely hear the whoosh of the fiery star as it blasted into the air. She quickly wove a weave to blow the flies away, and once she did, she looked about. She coughed and trembled. She could feel the flies sticking to the inside of her throat. She didn't see any child in danger. Had it been a trick of her ears?

She did see another six-pointed star, above a door carved into a tree. She walked toward it as the flies buzzed around her again. Calm. She had to be calm! Why? It made no sense! She did it anyway, walking with eyes closed as the flies swarmed her. She reached out, feeling for the door and pulling it open. She stepped through.

She pulled to a stop inside the building, wondering why she was coughing so much. Was she ill? She leaned against the wall, exhausted, angry. Her legs were covered in scrapes, and her arms itched with some kind of insect bites. She groaned, looking down at her garish clothing. What could possibly have possessed her to wear red, yellow and pink together?

She stood up with a sigh and continued down the rickety hallway. The planks that made up the floor rattled as she walked, and the plaster on the walls was broken and crumbling.

She reached a doorway and peeked in. The small

chamber contained four small brass beds; the mattresses had straw peeking from the seams. Each bed bore a young child clutching a ratty blanket. Two of them were coughing, and all four looked pale and sickly.

Nynaeve gasped, hurrying into the room. She knelt beside the first child, a boy of perhaps four years. She checked his eyes, then told him to cough as she listened at his chest. He had the creeping sickness.

"Who is caring for you?" Nynaeve demanded.

"Mistress Mala runs the orphanage," the child said in a weak voice. "We haven't seen her in a long time."

"Please," a young girl said from the next bed. She had bloodshot eyes, her skin so pale it was practically white. "Some water? Could I have some water?" She trembled.

The other two were crying. Pitiful, weak sounds. Light! There wasn't a single window in the room, and Nynaeve saw roaches scuttling under the beds. Who would leave children in such conditions?

"Hush," she said. "I'm here now. I'll care for you."

She'd need to channel to Heal them. Then . . .

No, she thought. *I can't do that. I can't channel until I reach the star.*

She would brew draughts, then. Where was her herb pouch? She looked around the room, searching for a source of water.

She froze; there was another room across the hallway. Had that been there before? A rug on its floor bore the symbol of the six-pointed star. She rose. The children whimpered.

"I'll return," Nynaeve said, stepping toward that room. Each step twisted her heart. She was abandoning them. But no, she was only walking into the next room. Wasn't she?

She reached the rug and began to weave. Just this one quick weaving, then she could help. She found herself crying as she worked.

I've been here before, she thought. *Or a place like it. A situation such as this.*

She found herself more and more angry. How could she channel with those children calling for her? They were dying.

She completed the weave, then watched it blow out jets of air, ruffling her dress. She reached for her braid and held it as a door appeared on the side of the room. A small glass window was set into the top, and it bore the six-pointed star.

She *had* to continue. She heard the weeping children. Tears in her eyes, heart breaking, she walked to the door.

It grew worse. She left people to be drowned, beheaded and buried alive. One of the worst was when she had to form a weave while villagers were consumed by enormous spiders with bright red fur and crystalline eyes. She *hated* spiders.

Sometimes she would appear naked. That stopped bothering her. Though she couldn't remember anything specific but the number of the weave she was on, she understood—somehow—that nudity was *nothing* compared to the terrors she'd seen.

She stumbled through a stone archway, memories of a house on fire fading from her mind. This was the eighty-first weave. She remembered that. That and her fury.

She wore a singed dress of sackcloth. How had she burned it? She stood up straight, holding her head, arms throbbing, back feeling whipped, legs and toes bearing cuts and scratches. She was in the Two Rivers. Except, it *wasn't* the Two Rivers. Not as she remembered it. Some of the buildings smoldered, still burning.

"They're coming again!" a voice yelled. Master al'Vere. Why was he holding a sword? People she knew, people dear to her—Perrin, Master al'Vere, Mistress al'Donel, Aeric Botteger—stood beside a low wall, all holding weapons. Some waved to her.

"Nynaeve!" Perrin called. "Shadowspawn! We need your help!"

Enormous shadows moved on the other side of the wall. Shadowspawn of terrible size—not Trollocs, but something far worse. She could hear roars.

She had to help! She moved toward Perrin, but froze as she saw—across the Green in the other direction—a six-pointed star painted on a hillside.

"Nynaeve!" Perrin sounded desperate. He began striking at something that reached over the wall, tentacles of midnight black. Perrin chopped at them with an axe as one snatched up Aeric and pulled him—screaming—into the darkness.

Nynaeve began to walk toward the star. Calm. Measured.

That was *stupid*. An Aes Sedai had to be calm. She knew that. But an Aes Sedai also needed to be able to act, to do what was needed to help those who needed it. It didn't matter what it cost her personally. These people needed her.

So she started to run.

Even that didn't feel like enough. She ran to get to the star, but still she left people she loved to fight alone. She knew she couldn't channel until she reached the six-pointed star. That made absolutely no sense. Shadowspawn were attacking. She *had to* channel!

She embraced the Source, and something seemed to try to stop her. Something like a shield. She pushed it aside with difficulty and Power flooded her. She began flinging fire at the monster, burning off a tentacle as it grabbed for Perrin.

Nynaeve continued throwing fire until she reached the six-pointed star. There, she wove the eighty-first weave, which created three rings of Fire in the air.

She worked furiously, attacking at the same time. She didn't know the point of creating this weave, but she knew she *had* to finish it. So she increased the strength of the weave, making the burning rings extremely large. Then she began hurling them at the creatures. Massive halos of flame crashed into the dark things, killing them.

There was a six-pointed star on the roof of Master al'Vere's inn. Had it been burned there? Nynaeve ignored it, venting her anger at the things with tentacles.

No. This is important. More important than the Two Rivers. I must go on.

Feeling like an utter coward—but knowing it was the right thing to do—she ran to the inn, passing through the doorway.

Nynaeve lay weeping on the ground beside a broken archway. She was on the last of the hundred weaves.

She could barely move. Her face was streaked with tears. She had hollow memories of fleeing battles, of leaving children to die. Of never being able to do enough.

Her shoulder bled. A wolf's bite. Her legs were flayed, as if she'd walked through a long patch of thorns. All across her body were burns and blisters. She was naked.

She rose to her knees, which were scraped and bleeding. Her braid ended in a smoldering stump about a handspan below her shoulders. She retched to the side, shivering.

So sick, so weak. How could she continue?

No. They will not beat me.

She slowly raised herself to her feet. She was in a small room, harsh sunlight leaking through cracks between the wallboards. A bundle of white cloth lay on the ground. She picked it up, unfolding it. It was a white dress with the colors of the Ajahs banded at the bottom. The clothing of an Accepted in the White Tower.

She dropped it. "I *am* Aes Sedai," she said, stepping over the robe and pushing open the door. Better to go naked than to give in to that lie.

Outside the door, she found another dress, this time yellow. That was more proper. She allowed herself the time to put it on, though she couldn't stop trembling, and her fingers were so tired she could barely make them work. Her blood stained the cloth.

Dress on, she inspected her surroundings. She was on a hillside in the Blight, the ground covered in weeds that bore the distinctive dark marks. Why was there a shack in the Blight, and why had she been inside of it?

She felt so tired. She wanted to go back into the shack and sleep.

No. She would continue. She trudged up the hill. At its top, she looked down on a land covered in broken rubble and pockets of darkness. Lakes, if they could be called that. The liquid looked thick and oily. Dark shapes moved within them. *Malkier,* she thought, stunned that she recognized the place. *The Seven Towers, only rubble now. The Thousand Lakes corrupted. The place of Lan's heritage.*

She stepped forward, but her toe hit something. A stone beneath her feet had been carved with a small symbol. The six-pointed star.

She sighed in relief. It was almost through. She began the final weave.

Below, a man stumbled out from behind a mound of rubble, swinging expertly with his sword. She knew him even at a distance. That strong figure, square face, color-shifting cloak and dangerous way of walking.

"Lan!" she screamed.

He was surrounded by beasts that looked like wolves, but too large. They had dark fur, and their teeth flashed as they lunged toward Lan. Darkhounds, an entire pack.

Nynaeve finished the hundredth weave with a start; she hadn't realized she'd continued it. A shower of colorful specks burst into the air around her. She watched them fall, feeling used. She heard a sound over her shoulder, but when she glanced, there was nothing there. Just the shack.

The six-pointed star hung over a door there, the symbol made of bits of gemstones. That door hadn't been there before. She took a step toward the shack, then looked back.

Lan swung about him with his sword, forcing the Darkhounds away. One bit of saliva from those beasts would kill him.

"Lan," she screamed. "Run!"

He didn't hear her. The six-pointed star. She needed to walk to it!

She blinked, then looked down at her hands. In the direct center of each palm was a tiny scar. Almost unnoticeable. Seeing them sparked a memory in her.

Nynaeve . . . I love you . . .

This was a test. She could remember that now. It was a test to force her to choose between him and the White Tower. She'd made that choice once, but she'd known it wasn't real.

This wasn't real either, was it? She raised a hand to her head, mind cloudy. *That is my husband down there,* she thought. *No. I will not play this game!*

She screamed, weaving Fire and throwing it toward one of the Darkhounds. The creature burst into flames, but the fire didn't seem to hurt it. Nynaeve stepped forward, throwing more fire. Useless! The hounds just kept attacking.

She refused to give in to her exhaustion. She banished it, growing calm, controlled. Ice. They wanted to push her, see what she could do? Well, let it be. She reached out, drawing in an immense amount of the One Power.

Then she wove balefire.

The line of pure light sprang from her fingers, warping the air around it. She hit one of the Darkhounds and seemed to *puncture* it, the light continuing on into the ground. The entire landscape rumbled, and Nynaeve stumbled. Lan fell to the ground. The Darkhounds leaped at him.

NO! Nynaeve thought, righting herself, weaving balefire again. She blasted another hound, then another. More of the monsters leaped from behind rock formations. Where were they all coming from? Nynaeve strode forward, blasting with the forbidden weave.

Each strike made the ground tremble, as if in pain. The balefire shouldn't puncture the ground like that. Something was wrong.

She reached Lan's side. He had broken his leg. "Nynaeve!" he said. "You must go!"

She ignored his words, kneeling down and weaving balefire as another hound rounded the rubble. Their number was increasing, and she was *so* tired. Each time she channeled, she felt it would surely be her last.

But it could not be. Not with Lan in danger. She wove a complex Healing, putting every bit of strength she had left into it, mending his leg. He scrambled up and grabbed his sword, turning to fend off a Darkhound.

They fought together, her with balefire, him with steel. But his swings were lethargic, and it took her a few heartbeats longer each time she made the balefire. The ground was shaking and rumbling, ruins crashing to the ground.

"Lan!" she said. "Be ready to run!"

"What?"

With her last ounce of strength, she wove balefire and aimed it directly downward in front of them. The ground *undulated* in agony, almost like a living thing. The earth split nearby, Darkhounds tumbling in. Nynaeve collapsed, the One Power slipping from her. She was too tired to channel.

Lan grabbed her arm. "We must go!"

She hauled herself to her feet, taking his hand. Together, they ran up the rumbling hillside. Darkhounds howled behind, some of the pack leaping the rift.

Nynaeve ran for all she was worth, clinging to Lan's hand. They crested the hill. The ground was shaking so terribly; she couldn't believe the shack was still standing. She stumbled down the hill toward it, Lan with her.

He tripped, crying out in pain. His hand slipped from her fingers.

She spun. Behind them, a flood of Darkhounds crested the hilltop, snarling, teeth flashing and spittle flying from their mouths. Lan waved for her to go, his eyes wide.

"*No.*" She grabbed him by the arm and, heaving, hauled him down the slope. Together, they tumbled through the doorway, and . . .

. . . and gasping, Nynaeve fell from the *ter'angreal*. She collapsed alone on the cold floor, naked, shaking. In a flood, she remembered it all. Each and every horrible moment of the test. Each betrayal, each frustrating weave. The impotence, the screams of the children, the deaths of people she knew and loved. She wept against the floor, curling up.

Her entire body was afire with pain. Her shoulder, legs, arms and back still bled. She was burned to blisters in swaths across her body, and the greater part of her braid was gone. Her unraveled hair fell across her face as she tried to banish the memories of what she had done.

She heard groans from nearby, and through bleary eyes she saw the Aes Sedai in the circle break off their weaves and slump. She hated them. She hated *each* and *every one* of them.

"Light!" Saerin's voice. "Someone Heal her!"

Everything was growing blurry. Voices grew muddled. Like sounds under water. Peaceful sounds . . .

Something cold washed over her. She gasped, her eyes opening wide at the icy shock of the Healing. Rosil knelt beside her. The woman looked worried.

The pain left Nynaeve's body, but her exhaustion increased tenfold. And the pain inside . . . it remained. Oh, Light. She could hear the children screaming.

"Well," Saerin said from nearby, "seems that she'll live. Now, would someone please tell me what in the name of *creation itself* that was?" She sounded furious. "I've been a part of many a raising, even one where the woman didn't survive. But I have *never*, in all of my days, seen a woman put through what this one just suffered."

"She had to be tested properly," Rubinde said.

"Properly?" Saerin demanded, livid.

Nynaeve didn't have the strength to look at them. She lay, breathing in and out.

"*Properly?*" Saerin repeated. "That wasn't proper. That was downright vengeful, Rubinde! Almost any one of those tests was beyond what I've seen demanded of other women. You should be ashamed. All of you. Light, look what you've done to the girl!"

"It is unimportant," Barasine the Red said in a cold voice. "She failed the test."

"What?" Nynaeve croaked, finally looking up. The *ter'angreal* had fallen dim, and Rosil had fetched a blanket and Nynaeve's clothing. Egwene stood to the side, arms clasped before her. Her face was serene as she listened to the others. She would not have a vote, but the others would, regarding whether Nynaeve had passed the test or not.

"You failed, *child*," Barasine said, regarding Nynaeve with an emotionless stare. "You did not show proper decorum."

Lelaine of the Blue nodded, looking annoyed to be agreeing with a Red. "This was to test your ability to be calm as an Aes Sedai. You did not show that."

The others looked uncomfortable. You weren't supposed to speak of the specifics of a testing. Nynaeve knew that much. She also knew that most of the time, failing and dying were the same thing. Though she wasn't terribly surprised to hear claims that she'd failed, now that she thought about it.

She *had* broken the rules of the test. She'd run in order to save Perrin and others. She'd channeled before she should have. She had trouble summoning regret. Every other emotion was, for the moment, consumed by the hollow loss she felt.

"Barasine does have a point," Seaine said, reluctant. "By the end, you were openly furious, and you ran to reach many of the markers. And then there is the matter of the forbidden weave. Most troubling. I do not say you should fail, but there *are* irregularities."

Nynaeve tried to climb to her feet. Rosil placed a hand on her shoulder to forbid her, but Nynaeve took the arm and used it as support, pulling herself up on unsteady legs. She took the blanket and wrapped it around her shoulders, holding it closed at the front.

She felt so drained. "I did what I had to. Who among you would not run if you saw people in danger? Who among you would forbid herself to channel if she saw Shadowspawn attacking? I acted as an Aes Sedai should."

"This test," Barasine said, "is meant to ensure that a woman is capable of dedicating herself to a greater task. To see that she can ignore the distractions of the moment and seek a higher good."

Nynaeve sniffed. "I completed the weaves I needed to. I maintained my focus. Yes, I broke my calm—but I kept a cool enough head to complete my tasks. One should not demand calmness for the mere sake of calmness, and a prohibition on running when there are people you need to save is foolish.

"My goal in this test was to prove that I deserve to be Aes Sedai. Well, then, I could argue that the lives of the people I saw were more important than gaining that title. If losing my title is what would be required to save someone's life— and if there were no other consequences—I'd do it. Every time. Not saving them wouldn't be serving a higher good; it would just be selfish."

Barasine's eyes opened wide with anger. Nynaeve turned to walk—with some difficulty—to the side of the room, where she could sit on a bench and rest. The women gathered together to speak softly, and Egwene walked—still serene—over to Nynaeve. The Amyrlin sat down beside her. Though she had been allowed to participate in the test, and create some of the experiences that tested Nynaeve, the choice of the raising would be up to the others.

"You've angered them," Egwene said. "And confused them."

"I spoke the truth," Nynaeve grumbled.

"Perhaps," Egwene said. "But I wasn't speaking of your outburst. During the test, you flouted the orders you were given."

"I couldn't flout them. I didn't remember that I'd been given them. I . . . well, actually I could remember what I was supposed to do, but not the reasons." Nynaeve grimaced. "That's why I broke the rules. I thought they were just arbitrary. I couldn't remember why I wasn't supposed to run, so in the face of seeing people die, it seemed silly to walk."

"The rules are supposed to hold strongly, even though you don't remember them," Egwene said. "And you *should not* have been able to channel before reaching the marker. That is in the very nature of the test."

Nynaeve frowned. "Then how—"

"You've spent too much time in *Tel'aran'rhiod*. This

est . . . it seems to function much in the same way as the
World of Dreams. What we create in our minds became
your surroundings." Egwene clicked her tongue, shaking
her head. "I warned them that this might be a danger. Your
practice in the World of Dreams made you innately able to
break the test."

Nynaeve didn't reply to that, feeling sick. What if she *did*
fail? Being cast out of the Tower now, after getting so close?

"I think your infractions might help you, however,"
Egwene said softly.

"What?"

"You're too experienced to have been given this test,"
Egwene explained. "In a way, what happened is proof that
you deserved the shawl when I granted it to you. You performed each of the weaves expertly, with speed and skill.
I particularly liked the way you used 'useless' weaves, on
occasion, to attack the things you saw."

"The fight in the Two Rivers," Nynaeve said. "That one
was you, wasn't it? The others don't know the place well
enough to create it."

"You can sometimes create visions and situations based
on the mind of the woman being tested," Egwene said. "It is
an odd experience, using this *ter'angreal*. One that I am not
certain I understand."

"But the Two Rivers *was* you."

"Yes," Egwene admitted.

"And the last one. With Lan?"

Egwene nodded. "I'm sorry. I thought that if I didn't do
it, nobody would—"

"I am glad that you did," Nynaeve said. "It showed me
something."

"It did?"

Nynaeve nodded, back against the wall, holding the
blanket in place and closing her eyes. "I realized that if I
had to choose between becoming an Aes Sedai and going
with Lan, I'd choose Lan. What people call me doesn't
change anything inside of me. Lan, however . . . he is
more than a title. I can still channel—I can still be me—if
I never become Aes Sedai. But I would never be myself
again if I abandoned him. The world changed when I married him."

She felt . . . freed, somehow, realizing it and saying it.

"Pray the others don't realize that," Egwene said. "I would not be good for them to determine that you woul place anything before the White Tower."

"I wonder if," Nynaeve said, "we sometimes put the Whit Tower—as an institution—before the people we serve. wonder if we let it become a goal in itself, instead of a mean to help us achieve greater goals."

"Devotion is important, Nynaeve. The White Tower pro tects and guides the world."

"And yet, so many of us do it without families," Nynaev said. "Without love, without passion beyond our own par ticular interests. So even while we try to guide the world we separate ourselves from it. We risk arrogance, Egwene We always assume we know best, but risk making ourselve unable to fathom the people we claim to serve."

Egwene seemed troubled. "Don't voice those idea too much, at least not today. They're already frustratee enough with you. But this testing was brutal, Nynaeve I'm sorry. I couldn't be seen favoring you, but perhap I should have put a stop to it. You did what you weren' supposed to, and that drove the others to be increasingl severe. They saw that sick children hurt you, so they pu more and more of them into the test. Many seemed to con sider your victories a personal affront, a contest of wills That drove them to be harsh. Cruel, even."

"I survived," Nynaeve said, eyes closed. "And I learned great deal. About me. And about us."

She wanted to be Aes Sedai, fully and truly embraced She wanted it badly. But in the end, if these people chose t refuse her their approval, she knew she could continue or and do what she needed to do anyway.

Eventually, the Sitters—trailed by Rosil—walked up Nynaeve hauled herself to her feet to be respectful.

"We must discuss the forbidden weave you used," Saerin said, stern.

"It is the only way I know to destroy Darkhounds," Nynaeve said. "It was needed."

"You do not have the right to decide that," Saerin said. "What you did destabilized the ter'angreal. You could have destroyed it, killing yourself and perhaps us. We want you to swear that you will never use that weave again."

"I won't do that," Nynaeve said tiredly.

"And if it means the difference between gaining the shawl or losing it forever?"

"Giving an oath like that would be foolish," Nynaeve said. "I could find myself in a situation where people would die if I didn't use it. Light! I'll be fighting in the Last Battle alongside Rand. What if I were to get to Shayol Ghul and discover that, without balefire, I could not help the Dragon stop the Dark One? Would you have me choose between a foolish oath and the fate of the world?"

"You think you're going to Shayol Ghul?" Rubinde asked, incredulous.

"I'm going to be there," Nynaeve said softly. "It is not a question. Rand has asked it of me, though I would have gone if he hadn't."

They shared a look, seeming troubled.

"If you're going to raise me," Nynaeve said, "then you'll just have to trust my judgment on balefire. If you don't trust me to know when to use a very dangerous weave and when not to, then I'd rather you not raise me."

"I would be careful," Egwene said to the women. "Refusing the shawl to the woman who helped cleanse the taint from *saidin*—the woman who defeated Moghedien herself in battle, the woman married to the King of Malkier—would set a very dangerous precedent."

Saerin looked at the others. Three nods. Yukiri, Seaine and—surprisingly—Romanda. Three shakes of the head. Rubinde, Barasine, Lelaine. That left only Saerin. The deciding vote.

The Brown turned back to her. "Nynaeve al'Meara, I declare that you have passed this test. Narrowly."

To the side, Egwene let out a soft—almost inaudible—sigh of relief. Nynaeve realized she'd been holding her own breath.

"It is done!" Rosil said, clapping her hands together. "Let no one *ever* speak of what has passed here. It is for us to share in silence with she who experienced it. It is done."

The women nodded in agreement, even those who had voted against Nynaeve. Nobody would know that Nynaeve had nearly failed. They had probably confronted her about the balefire directly—rather than seeking formal punishment—because of the tradition of not speaking of what happened in the *ter'angreal*.

Rosil clapped again. "Nynaeve al'Meara, you will spend the night in prayer and contemplation of the burdens you will take up on the morrow, when you don the shawl of an Aes Sedai. It is done." She clapped a third and final time.

"Thank you," Nynaeve said. "But I already have my shawl and—"

She cut off as Egwene gave her a glare. A serene glare, but a glare nonetheless. Perhaps Nynaeve had pushed things far enough tonight already.

"—I will be happy to follow tradition," Nynaeve continued, discarding her objection. "So long as I am allowed to do one very important thing first. Then I will return and fulfill tradition."

Nynaeve needed a gateway to get where she was going. She hadn't specifically told the others she'd be leaving the Tower to see to her task. But she hadn't said she wouldn't, either.

She hustled through the dark camp of tents which sat just outside a partially built wall. The night sky was dim, with those clouds covering it, and fires burned at the perimeter of the camp. Perhaps too many fires. Those here were being extremely cautious. Fortunately, the guards had allowed her into the camp without comment; the Great Serpent ring worked wonders, when applied in the right locations. They'd even told her where to find the woman she sought.

In truth, Nynaeve had been surprised to find these tents outside, rather than inside, the walls of the Black Tower. These women had been sent to bond Asha'man, as Rand had offered. But according to the guards, Egwene's envoy had been made to wait. The Asha'man had said that "others" had the first choice," whatever that meant. Egwene probably knew more; she'd sent messengers back and forth with the women here, particularly to warn them about Black sisters who might be among them. Those they'd known of had vanished before the first messengers arrived.

Nynaeve hadn't the mind to ask more details at the moment. She had another task. She stepped up to the proper tent, feeling so tired from the testing that she felt she would soon tumble to the ground in a flurry of yellow cloth. A few Warders passed through the camp nearby, watching her with calm expressions.

The tent before her was a simple gray thing. It was lit with a faint glow, and shadows moved inside. "Myrelle," Nynaeve said loudly. "I would speak with you." She was surprised at how strong her voice sounded. She didn't feel that she had much strength remaining.

The shadows paused, and then moved again. The tent flaps rustled, and a confused face peered out. Myrelle wore a blue nightgown that was almost translucent, and one of her Warders—a bear of a man with a thick black beard after the Illianer fashion—sat shirtless on the tent floor inside.

"Child?" Myrelle said, sounding surprised. "What are you doing here?" She was an olive-skinned beauty, with long black hair and rounded curves. Nynaeve had to stop herself from reaching for her braid. It was too short now to tug. That was going to take *a lot* of getting used to.

"You have something that belongs to me," Nynaeve said.

"Hmm . . . That depends on opinion, child." Myrelle frowned.

"I was raised today," Nynaeve said. "Formally. I passed the testing. We are equals now, Myrelle." She left the second part unsaid—that Nynaeve was the stronger of the two. Not truly equals, then.

"Return tomorrow," Myrelle said. "I am occupied." She moved to turn back into the tent.

Nynaeve caught the woman's arm. "I have never thanked you," she said, though she had to grit her teeth to get the words out. "I do so now. He lives because of you. I realize that. However, Myrelle, this is *not* a time to push me. Today, I have seen people I love slaughtered, I have been forced to consign children to living torment. I have been burned, scourged and harrowed.

"I swear to you, woman, if you do not pass me Lan's bond *this very moment*, I will step into that tent and teach you the meaning of obedience. Do not press me. In the morning, I swear the Three Oaths. I'm free of them for one more night."

Myrelle froze. Then she sighed and stepped back out of the tent. "So be it." She closed her eyes, weaving Spirit and sending the weaves into Nynaeve.

It felt like an object being shoved physically into her mind. Nynaeve gasped, her surroundings spinning.

Myrelle turned and slipped back into her tent. Nynaeve slid down until she was sitting on the ground. Something was blossoming inside her mind. An awareness. Beautiful, wonderful.

It was him. And he was still alive.

Blessed Light, she thought, eyes closed. *Thank you.*

CHAPTER
21

An Open Gate

W e thought it best," Seonid said, "to let one of us give the full report. I have gathered information from the others for presentation."

Perrin nodded absently. He sat on cushions in the meeting pavilion, Faile at his side. It was crammed full of people again.

"Cairhien is still in a mess, of course," Seonid began. The businesslike Green was a curt woman. Not mean or disagreeable, but even her interactions with her Warders seemed like those of a prosperous farmer with his workers. "The Sun Throne has remained unoccupied for far too long. All know that the Lord Dragon has promised the throne to Elayne Trakand, but she has been struggling to secure her own throne. She has finally done so, by reports."

She looked to Perrin for comment, smelling satisfied. He scratched at his beard. This was important, and he needed to pay attention. But thoughts of his training in the wolf dream kept drawing his mind. "So Elayne is Queen. That must make Rand happy."

"The Lord Dragon's reaction is unknown," Seonid continued, as if checking off another item on a list. The Wise Ones made no comments and asked no questions; they sat on their cushions in a little cluster, like rivets on a hinge. Likely, the Maidens had already told them all of this.

"I am reasonably certain that the Lord Dragon is in Arad Doman," Seonid continued. "Several rumors speak of this—though, of course, there are rumors placing him in many places. But Arad Doman makes sense for him as a tactical conquest, and the unrest there threatens to destabilize the

Borderlands. I'm not certain if it's true that he sent the Aiel there or not."

"He did," Edarra said simply. She offered no further explanation.

"Yes," Seonid said. "Well, many of the rumors say that he is planning to meet the Seanchan in Arad Doman. I suspect he would want the clans there to aid him."

That brought up thoughts of Malden. Perrin imagined *damane* and Wise Ones at war, the One Power ripping through ranks of soldiers, blood, earth and fire spinning in the air. It would be like Dumai's Wells, only worse. He shivered. Anyway, from the visions—and they appeared as Seonid spoke—he knew that Rand was where she said.

Seonid continued, speaking of trade and food resources in Cairhien. Perrin found himself thinking about that strange violet wall he'd seen in the wolf dream. *Idiot,* he told himself sternly. *Keep listening.* Light! He really was a bad ruler. He'd had no trouble running at the front of the wolves when they'd let him hunt. Why couldn't he do the same for his own people?

"Tear is rallying troops," Seonid said. "Rumors say the Lord Dragon commanded King Darlin to gather men for war. There is apparently a king in Tear now, by the way. A curious event. Some say that Darlin will march for Arad Doman, though others say it must be for the Last Battle. Still others insist that al'Thor intends to defeat the Seanchan first. All three options seem plausible, and I can't give more without a trip to Tear myself." She eyed Perrin, smelling hopeful.

"No," Perrin said. "Not yet. Rand isn't in Cairhien, but Andor seems stable. It makes the most sense for me to head there and talk to Elayne. She'll have information for us."

Faile smelled worried.

"Lord Aybara," Seonid said, "do you think the Queen will welcome you? With the flag of Manetheren, and your self-endowed title of Lord . . ."

Perrin scowled. "Both of those fool banners are down now, and Elayne will see things right, once I explain them to her."

"And my soldiers?" Alliandre said. "You will probably want to ask before moving foreign troops onto Andoran soil."

"You *won't* be coming," Perrin said. "I've said it before, Alliandre. You'll be in Jehannah. We'll get you there as soon as we deal with the Whitecloaks."

"Has a decision been made about them, then?" Arganda asked, leaning forward, eager and excited.

"They've demanded a battle," Perrin said. "And they ignore my requests for further parley. I've a mind to give them a fight."

They began talking of that, though it soon became a discussion of what it meant to have a king in Tear. Eventually, Seonid cleared her throat and steered the conversation back to her report.

"The Seanchan are a matter of great discussion in Cairhien," Seonid said. "The invaders seem to be focusing on securing their lands, including Altara. They are still expanding in the west, however, and there are pitched battles on Almoth Plain."

"Expanding toward Arad Doman," Arganda said. "There *is* a battle brewing there."

"Most likely," Seonid said.

"If the Last Battle comes," Annoura said, "then it would be advantageous to have an alliance with the Seanchan." She seemed thoughtful, legs crossed as she sat on her embroidered blue and yellow silk pillow.

"They have chained Wise Ones," Edarra said, her too-young face growing dark. She smelled dangerous. Angry but cold, like the smell before a person planned to kill. "Not just Shaido, who deserve their fate. If there is an alliance with the Seanchan, it will end as soon as the *Car'a'carn*'s work is finished. Already, many of my people speak of a blood feud with these invaders."

"I doubt Rand wants a war between you," Perrin said.

"A year and a day," Edarra said simply. "Wise Ones cannot be taken *gai'shain*, but perhaps the Seanchan ways are different. Regardless, we will give them a year and a day. If they do not release their captives when we demand them after that time, they will know our spears. The *Car'a'carn* cannot demand any more from us."

The pavilion grew still.

"Anyway," Seonid said, clearing her throat. "Once finished with Cairhien, we met up with those who had gone to Andor to check on rumors there."

"Wait," Perrin said. "Andor?"

"The Wise Ones decided to send Maidens there."

"That wasn't the plan," Perrin growled, looking at the Wise Ones.

"You don't control us, Perrin Aybara," Edarra said calmly. "We needed to know if there were still Aiel in the city or not, and if the *Car'a'carn* was there. Your Asha'man complied when we asked them for the gateway."

"The Maidens could have been seen," he grumbled. Well, he *had* told Grady to do the gateways as the Aiel asked him, though he'd been referring to the timing of the departure and the return. He should have been more precise.

"Well, they weren't seen," Seonid sounded exasperated, like one talking with a foolish child. "At least not by anyone they didn't intend to speak with." Light! Was it him, or was she beginning to seem a lot like a Wise One? Was that what Seonid and the others were doing in the Aiel camp? Learning to become *more* stubborn? Light help them all.

"Regardless," Seonid continued, "it was wise of us to visit Caemlyn. Rumor cannot be trusted, particularly not when one of the Forsaken was said to be operating in the area."

"One of the Forsaken?" Gallenne asked. "In Andor?"

Perrin nodded, waving for another cup of warmed tea. "Rand said it was Rahvin, though I was in the Two Rivers when the battle happened." The colors swirled in Perrin's head. "Rahvin was impersonating one of the local noblemen, a man named Gabral or Gabil or some such. He used the Queen—made her fall in love with him, or something—and then killed her."

A serving tray hit the ground with a muted peal.

Porcelain cups shattered, tea spraying into the air. Perrin spun, cursing, and several of the Maidens leaped to their feet, clutching belt knives.

Maighdin stood, looking stunned, arms at her sides. The fallen tray lay on the ground before her.

"Maighdin!" Faile said. "Are you all right?"

The sun-haired serving woman turned to Perrin, looking dazed. "If you please, my Lord, will you repeat what you said?"

"What?" Perrin asked. "Woman, what's wrong?"

"You said one of the Forsaken had taken up residence in

Andor," Maighdin said, voice calm. She gave him as sharp a look as he'd gotten from any Aes Sedai. "Are you certain of what you heard?"

Perrin settled back on his cushion, scratching his chin. "Sure as I can be. It's been some time, now, but I know Rand was convinced. He fought *someone* with the One Power in the Andoran palace."

"His name was Gaebril," Sulin said. "I was there. Lightning struck from an open sky, and there was no doubt it was the One Power. It was one of the Shadow souled."

"There were some in Andor who claimed the *Car'a'carn* spoke of this," Edarra added. "He said that this Gaebril had been using forbidden weaves on wetlanders in the palace, twisting their minds, making them think and do as he wished."

"Maighdin, what's wrong?" Perrin asked. "Light, woman, he's dead now! You needn't fear."

"I must be excused," Maighdin said. She walked from the pavilion, leaving the tray and broken porcelain, bone white, scattered on the ground.

"I will see to her later," Faile said, embarrassed. "She is distraught to find that she'd lived so close to one of the Forsaken. Perhaps she has family in Cairhien."

The others nodded, and other servants moved forward to clean up the mess. Perrin realized he wasn't going to be getting any more tea. *Fool man,* he thought. *You lived most your life without being able to order tea on command. You won't die now that you can't get a refill by waving your hand.*

"Let's move on," he said, settling on his cushions. He could never quite get comfortable on the blasted things.

"My report is finished," Seonid said, pointedly ignoring the servant who was cleaning up porcelain shards in front of her.

"I stand by my earlier decision," Perrin said. "Dealing with the Whitecloaks is important. After that we'll go to Andor, and I'll talk to Elayne. Grady, how are you managing?"

The weathered Asha'man looked up from where he sat in his black coat. "I'm fully recovered from my sickness, my Lord, and Neald almost is as well."

"You still look tired," Perrin said.

"I am," Grady said, "but burn me, I'm better than I was many a day in the field before I went to the Black Tower."

"It's time to start sending some of these refugees where they belong," Perrin said. "With those circles, you can keep a gateway open longer?"

"I'm not right sure. Being in a circle is still tiring. Maybe more so. But I can make much larger gateways with the help of the women, wide enough to drive two wagons through."

"Good. We'll start by sending the ordinary folk home. Each person we see back where they belong will be a stone off my back."

"And if they don't want to go?" Tam asked. "A lot of them have started the training, Perrin. They know what's coming, and they'd rather face it here—with you—than cower in their homes."

Light! Were there no people in this camp who wanted to go back to their families? "Surely there are *some* of them who want to go back."

"Some," Tam said.

"Remember," Faile said, "the weak and the aged were sent away by the Aiel."

Arganda nodded. "I've looked in on these troops. More and more of the *gai'shain* are coming out of their stupor, and when they do, they're hard. Hard as many soldiers I've known."

"Some will want to check on family," Tam said, "but only if you'll let them back. They can see that sky. They know what's coming."

"For now, we'll send back the ones that want to go and remain in their homes," Perrin said. "I can't deal with the others until after I'm done with the Whitecloaks."

"Excellent," Gallenne said eagerly. "You have a plan of attack?"

"Well," Perrin said, "I figure that if they're going to be companionable enough to line up, we'll have at them with my archers and channelers and destroy them."

"I approve of this plan," Gallenne said, "so long as my men can charge to deal with the rabble left at the end."

"Balwer," Perrin said. "Write the Whitecloaks. Tell them we'll fight, and that they should pick a place."

As he said the words, he felt a strange reluctance. It

seemed such a waste to kill so many who could fight against the Shadow. But he didn't see a way around it.

Balwer nodded, smelling fierce. What had the White-cloaks done to Balwer? The dusty secretary was fascinated with them.

The meeting began to break up. Perrin stepped to the tent's open side and watched the separate groups leave, Alliandre and Arganda moving toward their section of the camp. Faile walked beside Berelain; oddly, the two were chatting together. Their scents said they were angry, but their words sounded companionable. What were those two up to?

Only a few wet stains on the ground inside the tent remained of the dropped tray. What was wrong with Maighdin? Erratic behavior like that was disturbing; all too often, it was followed by some manifestation of the Dark One's power.

"My Lord?" a voice asked, preceded by a quiet cough. Perrin turned, realizing that Balwer was waiting behind him. The secretary stood with hands clasped before him, looking like a pile of sticks that children had dressed up in an old shirt and coat.

"Yes?" Perrin asked.

"I happened to overhear several items of, ah, some interest while visiting the scholars of Cairhien."

"You found the supplies, right?"

"Yes, yes. I am quite well stocked. Please, a moment. I do believe you'll be interested in what I overheard."

"Go ahead, then," Perrin said, walking back into the pavilion. The last of the others had left.

Balwer spoke in a soft voice. "First off, my Lord, it appears that the Children of the Light are in league with the Seanchan. It is common knowledge now, and I worry that the force ahead of us was planted to—"

"Balwer," Perrin interrupted, "I know you hate the Whitecloaks, but you've already told me that news a half-dozen times over."

"Yes, but—"

"Nothing more about the Whitecloaks," Perrin said, holding up a hand. "Unless it's *specific* news about this force ahead of us. Do you have any of that?"

"No, my Lord."

"All right, then. Was there anything else you wanted to tell me?"

Balwer showed no signs of annoyance, but Perrin could smell dissatisfaction. Light knew that the Whitecloaks had plenty to answer for, and Perrin didn't blame Balwer for his hatred, but it did grow wearying.

"Well, my Lord," Balwer continued, "I would hazard that the tales of the Dragon Reborn wanting a truce with the Seanchan are more than idle hearsay. Several sources indicate that he has sued their leader for peace."

"But what did he do to his hand?" Perrin asked, dispelling yet another image of Rand from his vision.

"What was that, my Lord?"

"Nothing," Perrin said.

"In addition," Balwer said, reaching into his sleeve, "there are an alarming number of these traveling among cutpurses, slipfingers and footpads in Cairhien." He pulled out a sheet of paper with a sketch of Perrin's face on it. The likeness was alarmingly good. Perrin took the paper, frowning. There were no words on it. Balwer handed him a second one, identical to the first. A third paper followed, this one with a picture of Mat.

"Where did you get these?" Perrin asked.

"As I said, my Lord," Balwer continued, "they are being passed around in certain circles. Apparently there are very large sums of money promised to anyone who can produce your corpse, though I could not determine who would be doing the paying."

"And you discovered these while visiting the scholars at Rand's school?" Perrin asked.

The pinch-faced scribe displayed no emotion.

"Who are you really, Balwer?"

"A secretary. With some measure of skill in finding secrets."

"Some measure? Balwer, I haven't asked after your past. I figure a man deserves to be able to start fresh. But now the Whitecloaks are here, and you have some connection to them. I need to know what it is."

Balwer stood silently for a time. The raised walls of the pavilion rustled.

"My previous employer was a man I respected, my Lord,"

Balwer said. "He was killed by the Children of the Light. Some among them may recognize me."

"You were a spy for this person?" Perrin asked.

Balwer's lips turned down distinctly. He spoke more softly. "I merely have a mind for remembering facts, my Lord."

"Yes, you've got a very good mind for it. Your service is useful to me, Balwer. I'm only trying to tell you that. I'm glad you're here."

The man smelled pleased. "If I may say, my Lord, it is refreshing to work for someone who doesn't see my information as simply a means of betraying or compromising those around him."

"Well, be that as it may, I should probably start paying you better," Perrin said.

That gave Balwer a panicked scent. "That won't be necessary."

"You could demand high wages from any number of lords or merchants!"

"Petty men of no consequence," Balwer said with a twitch of his fingers.

"Yes, but I still think you should be paid more. It's simple sense. If you hire an apprentice blacksmith for your forge and don't pay him well enough, he'll impress your regular customers, then open a new forge across the street the moment he can afford to."

"Ah, but you do not see, my Lord," Balwer said. "Money means nothing to me. The information—that is what is important. Facts and discoveries . . . they are like nuggets of gold. I could give that gold to a common banker to make coins, but I prefer to give it to the master craftsman to make something of beauty.

"Please, my Lord, let me remain a simple secretary. You see, one of the easiest ways to tell if someone is not what he seems is to check his wages." He chuckled. "I've uncovered more than one assassin or spy that way, yes I have. No pay is needed. The opportunity to work with you is its own payment."

Perrin shrugged, but nodded, and Balwer withdrew. Perrin stepped out of the pavilion, stowing the pictures in his pocket. They disturbed him. He'd bet these pictures were in Andor, too, placed by the Forsaken.

For the first time, he found himself wondering if he was going to *need* an army to keep himself safe. It was a disturbing thought.

The wave of bestial Trollocs surged over the top of the hill, overrunning the last of the fortifications. They grunted and howled, thick-fingered hands tearing at the dark Saldaean soil and clutching swords, hooked spears, hammers, clubs and other wicked weapons. Spittle dripped from tusked lips on some, while on others wide, too-human eyes stared out from behind wicked beaks. Their black armor was decorated with spikes.

Ituralde's men stood strong with him at the bottom of the back slope of the hillside. He had ordered the lower camp to disband and retreat as far as they could to the south along the riverbank. Meanwhile, the army had retreated from the fortifications. He hated to surrender the high ground, but getting pushed down that steep hill during an assault would have been deadly. He had room to fall back, so he'd use it, now that the fortifications were lost.

He positioned his forces just at the base of the hill, near where the lower camp had once been. The Domani soldiers wore steel caps and had set their fourteen-foot pikes with butts in the dirt, holding them for more stability, steel points toward the towering wave of Trollocs. A classic defensive position: three ranks of pikemen and shieldmen, pikes slanted toward the top of the slope. When the first rank of pikes killed a Trolloc, they'd fall back and pull their weapons free, letting the second rank step forward to kill. A slow, careful retreat, rank by rank.

A double row of archers behind began loosing arrows, slamming wave after wave up into the Shadowspawn, dropping bodies down the slope. Those rolled, some still screaming, spraying dark blood. A larger number continued down, over their brothers, trying to get at the pikemen.

An eagle-headed Trolloc died on a pike in front of Ituralde. There were chips along the edges of the thing's beak, and its head—set with predatory eyes—sat atop a bull-like neck, the edge of the feathers coated with some kind of dark, oily substance. The monster screeched as it died, voice low and only faintly avian, somehow forming guttural sounds in the Trolloc language.

"Hold!" Ituralde called, turning and trotting his horse down the line of pikemen. "Keep the formation, burn you!"

The Trollocs surged down the hillside, dying on those pikes. It would be a temporary reprieve. There were too many Trollocs, and even a rotating triple pike line would be overwhelmed. This was a delaying tactic. Behind them, the rest of his troops began their retreat. Once the lines had weakened, the Asha'man would assume the burden of defense, buying time for the pikemen to retreat.

If the Asha'man could manage the strength. He'd pushed them hard. Maybe too hard. He didn't know their limits the way he did for ordinary troops. If they were able to break the Trolloc advance, his army would fall back southward. That retreat would take them past the safety of Maradon, but they would not be allowed in. Those inside had rebuffed all Ituralde's attempts at communication. "We do not abet invaders" had been the reply each time. Bloody fools.

Well, the Trollocs would likely form up around Maradon for a sustained siege, giving Ituralde and his men time to fall back to a more defensible position.

"Hold!" Ituralde called again, riding past an area where the Trolloc press was beginning to show results. Atop one of the hilltop fortifications, a pack of wolf-headed Trollocs lurked, wary, while their companions charged down before them. "Archers!" Ituralde said, pointing.

A volley of arrows followed, spraying the wolf-headed Trollocs, or "Minds" as the Dragonsworn in Ituralde's army had started calling them. Trollocs had their own bands and organization, but his men often referred to individuals by the features they displayed. "Horns" for goats, "Beaks" for hawks, "Arms" for bears. Those with the heads of wolves were often among the more intelligent; some Saldaeans claimed to have heard them speaking the human language to bargain with or trick their opponents.

Ituralde knew much about Trollocs now. You needed to know your enemy. Unfortunately, there was huge variety in Trolloc intelligence and personality. And there were many Trollocs who shared physical attributes from various groups. Ituralde swore he'd seen one twisted abomination with the feathers of a hawk but the horns of a goat.

The Trollocs atop the fortification tried to get out of the way of the arrows. A large pack of hulking beasts behind shoved them down the hill with a roar. Trollocs were cowardly things, normally, unless hungry, but if they were whipped into a frenzy, they fought well.

The Fades would follow this initial wave. Once the archers were out of arrows, and Trollocs had softened the men below. Ituralde didn't look forward to that.

Light, Ituralde thought. *I hope we can outrun them.* The Asha'man waited in the distance for his order. He wished he had them closer. But he couldn't risk it. They were too important an asset to lose to a stray arrow.

Hopefully, the front ranks of Trollocs would be severely battered by the pikemen, their carcasses twisted and banked against the pikes—and the Trollocs behind stumbling and falling against their own bloody remnants. Ituralde's remaining Saldaeans would ride as a harrying force at any who got through the Asha'man blasts. Then the pikemen should be able to draw back and follow the rest of the army in retreat. Once past Maradon, they could use gateways to fall back to his next chosen position, a forested pass some ten leagues south.

His men *should* be able to escape. Should. Light, but he hated being forced to command a too-fast retreat like this.

Stay firm, he told himself, continuing to ride and call out the order to hold. It was important that they hear his voice. *That boy is the Dragon Reborn. He'll keep his promises.*

"My Lord!" a voice called. Ituralde's guard split to let a young boy ride up, panting. "My Lord, it's Lieutenant Lidrin!"

"He's fallen?" Ituralde demanded.

"No, my Lord. He's . . ." The boy looked over his shoulder. In the pike line nearby, the soldiers were bulging forward *toward* the Trolloc wave, rather than falling back.

"What in the Light?" Ituralde said, heeling Dawnweave into motion. The white gelding galloped forward, Ituralde's guard and the young messenger joining him in a thunder of hooves.

He could hear Lidrin's yells despite the roar of the battlefield. The young Domani officer was out in front of the pike lines, attacking the Trollocs with sword and shield, bellowing. Lidrin's men had pushed through to defend him, leaving the pikemen confused and disoriented.

"Lidrin, you fool." Ituralde reined his horse to a halt.

"Come!" Lidrin bellowed, raising his sword up before the Trollocs. He laughed loudly, voice half-mad, face splattered with blood. "Come! I will face you all! My sword thirsts!"

"Lidrin!" Ituralde screamed. "Lidrin!"

The man glanced over his shoulder. His eyes were wide with a crazed kind of glee. Ituralde had seen it before, in the eyes of soldiers who fought too long, too hard. "We're going to die, Rodel," Lidrin called. "This way, I get to take them with me! One or two at least! Join me!"

"Lidrin, get back here and—"

The man ignored him, turning back and pressing forward.

"Get his men back here," Ituralde yelled, gesturing. "Close the pike ranks! Quickly. We can't . . ."

The Trollocs surged forward. Lidrin fell in a spray of blood, laughing. His men were too strongly pressed, and they split down the middle. The pikemen reset themselves, but a fist of Trollocs crashed into them. Some Trollocs fell.

Most didn't.

The nearby creatures screeched and howled at seeing the hole in the defenses. They came, scrambling over bodies at the base of the hill, throwing themselves at the pikemen.

Ituralde cursed, then pushed Dawnweave forward. In war, as in farming, you sometimes had to step in and get knee-deep in the muck. He bellowed as he crashed into the Trollocs. His guard rode in around him, closing the gap. The air became a crashing tempest of metal on metal and grunts of pain.

Dawnweave snorted and danced as Ituralde lashed out with his sword. The warhorse disliked being so close to the Shadowspawn, but he was well trained, a gift from one of Bashere's men. He had claimed that a general on the Borderlands needed an animal who had fought Trollocs before. Ituralde blessed that soldier now.

The fighting was brutal. The leading rank of pikemen, and those behind, began buckling. Ituralde briefly heard Ankaer's voice taking command, screaming at the men to get back into line. He sounded frantic. That was bad.

Ituralde swung, doing Heron on the Stump—a horseback sword form—and taking a bull-headed Trolloc across the throat. A spray of fetid brownish blood spurted forth, and the creature fell back against a boar-headed monster. A large red standard—depicting a goat's skull with a fire burning behind it—rose atop the hill. The symbol of the Ghob'hlin Band.

Ituralde turned his horse, dancing out of the way of a wicked axe blow, then urged his mount forward, driving his sword into the Trolloc's side. Around him, Whelborn and Lehynen—two of his best—died as they defended his flank. Light burn the Trollocs!

The entire line was breaking apart. He and his men were too few, but most of his forces had already pulled back. *No, no, no!* Ituralde thought, trying to extricate himself from the battle and take over the command. But if he pulled back, the Trollocs would break through.

He'd have to risk it. He was ready for problems like this.

A trumpet sounded retreat.

Ituralde froze, listening with horror to the haunted sound rolling across the battlefield. The horns weren't supposed to blow unless he, or a member of his guard, gave the order personally! It was too soon, *far* too soon.

Some of the other trumpeters heard the call and took it up, though others did not. They could see that it was far too soon. Unfortunately, that was *worse*. It meant that half of the pikemen began to pull back while the other half held their position.

The lines around Ituralde burst, men scattering as the Trollocs swarmed over them. It was a disaster, as bad a disaster as Ituralde had ever been part of. His fingers felt limp.

If we fall, Shadowspawn destroy Arad Doman.

Ituralde roared, yanking on the reins of his horse and galloping back away from the surging Trollocs. The remaining members of his guard followed.

"Helmke and Cutaris," Ituralde yelled to two of his men, sturdy, long-limbed Domani. "Get to Durhem's cavalry and tell them to attack the center as soon as an opening appears! Kappre, head to Alin's cavalry. Order him to assault the Trollocs on the eastern flank. Sorrentin, go to those Asha'man! I want the Trollocs to go up in flame!"

The horsemen galloped off. Ituralde rode westward, to the place where the pikemen were still holding. He started to rally one of the back ranks and bring it to the bulging section. He almost had it working. But then the Myrddraal came, sliding through the Trolloc ranks like snakes, striking with oily speed, and a flight of Draghkar descended.

Ituralde found himself fighting for his life.

Around him, the battlefield was a terrible mess: ranks destroyed, Trollocs roaming freely for easy kills, Myrddraal trying to whip them into attacking the few remaining pike formations instead.

Fires flew in the air as the Asha'man aimed for the Trollocs, but their fires were smaller, weaker than they had been days ago. Men screamed, weapons clanged, and beasts roared in the smoke beneath a sky of too-black clouds.

Ituralde was breathing hard. His guards had fallen. At least he had seen Staven and Rett die. What of the others? He didn't see them. So many dying. So many. There was sweat in his eyes.

Light, he thought. *At least we gave them a fight. Held out longer than I thought possible.*

There were columns of smoke to the north. Well, one thing had gone well—that Asha'man Tymoth had done his job. The second set of siege equipment was burning. Some of his officers had called it madness to send away one of his Asha'man, but one more channeler wouldn't have mattered in this disaster. And when the Trollocs attacked Maradon, the lack of those catapults would make a big difference.

Dawnweave fell. A Trolloc javelin that had been meant for Ituralde had fallen low. The horse screamed with the weapon lodged in its neck, blood pulsing down its sweat-frothed skin. Ituralde had lost mounts before, and he knew to roll to the side, but was too off-balance this time. He heard his leg snap as he hit.

He gritted his teeth, determined not to die on his back, and forced himself up into a sitting position. He dropped his sword—heron-mark though it was—and lifted up a broken, discarded pike in a fluid motion and rammed it through the chest of an approaching Trolloc. Dark, stinking blood coated the shaft, spurting down onto Ituralde's hands as the Trolloc screamed and died.

There was thunder in the air. That wasn't odd—there was often thunder from those clouds, often eerily disjointed from the bursts of lightning.

Ituralde heaved, pushing the Trolloc to the side by levering the pike. Then a Myrddraal saw him.

Ituralde reached for his sword, gritting his teeth, but knew he had just seen his killer. One of those things could fell a dozen men. Facing it with a broken leg . . .

He tried to stumble to his feet anyway. He failed, falling backward, cursing. He raised his sword, prepared to die as the thing slunk forward, movements like liquid.

A dozen arrows slammed into the Fade.

Ituralde blinked as the creature stumbled. The thunder was getting louder. Ituralde propped himself up, and was amazed to see thousands of unfamiliar horsemen charging in formation through the Trolloc ranks, sweeping the creatures before them.

The Dragon Reborn! He came!

But no. These men flew the Saldaean flag. He looked back. The gates of Maradon were open, and Ituralde's tired survivors were being allowed to limp inside. Fire was flying from the battlements—his Asha'man had been allowed up top to get a vantage on the battlefield.

A force of twenty horsemen broke off and ran down the Myrddraal, trampling it. The last man in the group leaped free of his saddle and hacked at the creature with a hand axe. All across the battlefield, the Trollocs were run down, shot or lanced.

It wouldn't last. More and more Trollocs were rolling through Ituralde's former fortifications and loping down the slope. But the Saldaean relief would be enough, with those gates open, and with the Asha'man blasts wreaking destruction. The remnants of Ituralde's force were fleeing to safety. He was proud to see Barettal and Connel—the last of his guard—stumbling across the field toward him on foot, their mounts no doubt dead, their uniforms bloodied.

He slid his sword into its scabbard and pulled the javelin from Dawnweave's neck. Supporting himself on it, he managed to stand. A rider from the Saldaean force trotted up to him, a man with a lean face, a hooked nose, and a set of bushy black eyebrows. He wore a short, trimmed beard, and he raised a bloodied sword to Ituralde. "You live."

"I do," Ituralde said as his two guards arrived. "You command this force?"

"For now," the man said. "I am Yoeli. Can you ride?"

"Better that than staying here."

Yoeli reached out a hand and pulled Ituralde into his saddle behind him. Ituralde's leg protested with a flare of pain, but there wasn't time to wait for a stretcher.

Two other horsemen took Ituralde's guards onto their horses, and soon they were riding for the city at a gallop.

"Bless you," Ituralde said. "It took you long enough, though."

"I know." Yoeli's voice sounded oddly grim. "I hope you are worth this, invader, for my actions this day will likely cost my life."

"What?"

The man didn't reply. He simply bore Ituralde on thundering hooves into the safety of the city—such as that safety was, considering the city was now besieged by a force of several hundred thousand Shadowspawn.

Morgase walked out of the camp. Nobody stopped her, though some did give her odd looks. She passed the wooded northern rim. The trees were burloak, spaced apart to allow for their great, spreading arms. She moved beneath the boughs, breathing deeply of the humid air.

Gaebril had been one of the Forsaken.

She eventually found a place where a tiny highland stream filled a cleft between two rocks and created a still, clear pool. The tall rocks around it clustered like an ancient, broken throne built for a giant fifteen spans tall.

The trees bore leaves above, though many looked sickly. A thinner patch of clouds blew past, allowing fingers of sunlight to reach down from the overcast sky. That splintered light shone in rays through the clear water, making patches of light on the pool's bottom. Minnows darted between the patches, as if investigating the light.

Morgase rounded the pool, then settled atop a flat boulder. The sounds of the camp could be heard in the distance. Calling, posts being driven into the ground, carts rattling on pathways.

She stared into the pool. Was there anything more

hateful than being made the pawn of another? Of being forced to dance upon their strings like a wooden puppet? In her youth, she'd grown well acquainted with bowing before the whims of others. That had been the only way for her to stabilize her rule.

Taringail had tried to manipulate her. In truth, he'd been successful much of the time. There had been others, too. So many who had pushed her this way or that. She'd spent ten years pandering to whichever faction was the strongest. Ten years slowly building alliances. It had worked. She'd eventually been able to maneuver on her own. When Taringail had died hunting, many had whispered that his passing released her, but those close to her had known that she had already gone a long way toward unseating his authority.

She could remember the very day when she'd cast off the last of those who had presumed to be the real power behind the throne. That was the day that, in her heart, she'd truly become Queen. She'd sworn that she'd never let another manipulate her again.

And then, years later, Gaebril had arrived. After that, Valda, who had been worse. At least with Gaebril, she hadn't realized what was happening. That had numbed the wounds.

Footsteps on fallen twigs announced a visitor. The light from above dimmed, the thinner clouds moving on. The shafts of light faded, and the minnows scattered.

The footsteps stopped beside her stone. "I'm leaving," Tallanvor's voice said. "Aybara has given leave for his Asha'man to make gateways, starting with some of the distant cities. I'm going to Tear. Rumors say there's a king there again. He's gathering an army to fight in the Last Battle. I want to be with it."

Morgase looked up, staring ahead through the trees. It wasn't really a forest. "They say you were as single-minded as Goldeneyes," she said softly. "That you would not rest, that you barely took time to eat, that you spent every moment searching for a way to free me."

Tallanvor said nothing.

"I've never had a man do that for me," she continued. "Taringail saw me as a pawn, Thom as a beauty to be hunted and romanced, and Gareth as a queen to be served. But none of them made me their entire life, their heart.

think Thom and Gareth loved me, but as something to be held and cared for, then released. I didn't think you'd ever let go."

"I won't," Tallanvor said softly.

"You go to Tear. Yet you said you'd never leave."

"My heart stays here," he said. "I know well what it is to love from afar, Morgase. I'd done it for years before this fool's trip began, and I will do it for years yet. My heart is a traitor. Perhaps some Trolloc will do me a favor and rip it free of my chest."

"So bitter," she whispered.

"You have made it amply clear that my attentions are not wanted. A queen and a simple guardsman. Pure foolishness."

"A queen no longer," she said.

"Not in name, Morgase. Just in mind."

A leaf fell from above and struck the pool. With a lobed margin and verdant richness, it should have had a long life yet.

"Do you know the worst part of this?" Tallanvor asked. "It's the hope. The hope I let myself feel. Traveling with you, protecting you, I thought maybe you would see. Maybe you would care. And forget about *him*."

"Him?"

"Gaebril," Tallanvor snapped. "I can see that you still think of him. Even after what he did to you. I leave my heart here, but you left yours in Caemlyn." From the corner of her eye, she could see him turn away. "Whatever it is you saw in him, I don't have it. I'm only a simple, common, *idiot* of a Guardsman who can't say the right words. You fawned over Gaebril, and he all but ignored you. That's how love is. Bloody ashes, I've all but done the same thing with you."

She said nothing.

"Well," he said, "that's why I have to go. You're safe now, and that's all that matters. Light help me, but that's *still* all that I care about!"

He began to walk away, feet crunching twigs.

"Gaebril was one of the Forsaken," she said.

The crunching twigs stopped.

"He was really Rahvin," she continued. "He took over Andor through use of the One Power, forcing people to do as he said."

Tallanvor hissed, twigs crunching as he hastened back to her. "Are you certain?"

"Certain? No. But it *does* make sense. We can't ignore what is happening in the world, Tallanvor. The weather, the way food spoils in a heartbeat, the movements of this Rand al'Thor. He is no false Dragon. The Forsaken must be loose again.

"What would you do, if you were one of them? Raise up an army and conquer? Or simply stroll into a palace and take the Queen as your consort? Twist her mind so that she lets you do as you wish. You'd gain the resources of an entire nation, all with minimal effort. Barely a finger raised . . ."

She raised her head and stared off into the distance. Northward. Toward Andor. "They call it Compulsion. A dark, foul weave that removes the will from your subject. I'm not supposed to know that it exists.

"You say that I think of him. That is true. I think about him and *hate* him. Hate myself for what I let him do. And a part of my heart knows that if he were to appear here and demand something from me, I'd give it. I couldn't help myself. But this thing I feel for him—this thing that blends my desire and my hatred like two locks in a braid—it is not love."

She turned and looked down at Tallanvor. "I know love, Tallanvor, and Gaebril never had it from me. I doubt that a creature like him could comprehend love."

Tallanvor met her eyes. His were dark gray, soft and pure. "Woman, you give me that monster hope again. Be wary of what lies at your feet."

"I need time to think. Would you refrain, for now, from going to Tear?"

He bowed. "Morgase, if you want anything from me—*anything*—all you ever need to do is ask. I thought I made that clear. I'll remove my name from the list."

He withdrew. Morgase watched him, her mind a tempest despite the stillness of the trees and pond before her.

CHAPTER
22

The End of a Legend

A t night, Gawyn couldn't see the White Tower's wounds.

In darkness, one couldn't tell the difference between a beautifully intricate mural and a wall full of mismatched tiles. At night, the most beautiful of Tar Valon's buildings became another dark lump.

And at night, the holes and scars on the White Tower were patched with a bandage of darkness. Of course, on a night as dark as these clouds caused, one also couldn't tell the Tower's color. White or black; at night, it didn't really matter.

Gawyn walked the White Tower grounds, wearing stiff trousers and coat of red and gold. Like a uniform, but of no specific allegiance. He didn't seem to *have* a specific allegiance these days. Almost unconsciously, he found himself walking toward the eastern tower entrance as if to climb up to Egwene's sleeping chambers. He set his jaw, turning the other way.

He should have been sleeping. But after nearly a week of guarding Egwene's door at night, he was—as soldiers liked to say—on a midnight lunch. Perhaps he could have stayed in his rooms to relax, but his quarters in the White Tower's barracks felt confining.

Nearby, two small feral cats stalked through tufts of grass, eyes reflecting the torchlight of a guard post. The cats hunkered low, watching him as if considering—for a brief moment—whether or not he'd be worth attacking. An unseen owl cruised in the air above, the only evidence of its passing a solitary feather that floated down. It was easier to pretend at night. Some men lived their entire lives that way, preferring the curtains of darkness to the open windows of daylight, because they let them see the world all in shadow.

It was summer now, but though the day had been hot, the night was strangely cold. He shivered at a passing breeze. There hadn't been any murders since the death of that unfortunate White. When would the killer strike again? He—or she—could be moving through the hallways at this moment, searching for a solitary Aes Sedai as those cats searched for mice.

Egwene had sent him away from her door, but that didn't mean he couldn't be on watch. What good was it to walk the grounds? He should be indoors, where he had a chance of doing some good. Gawyn made his way to one of the servant entrances.

The low-ceilinged hallway inside was clean and well lit, like the rest of the Tower, though the floor was set with dull gray slate instead of glazed tiles. An open room to his right resounded with laughter and chatting, off-duty guardsmen enjoying time with their comrades. Gawyn gave them barely a glance, but then froze.

He looked back in, recognizing some of the men. "Mazone? Celark? Zang? What are you men about?"

The three looked up with alarm, then chagrin. They were among about a dozen Younglings who were dicing and smoking pipes with the off-duty Tower guardsmen. The Younglings stumbled to their feet and gave salutes, though he was no longer their commander. They didn't seem to realize that.

Celark, foremost among them, hastened over to Gawyn. He was a lean fellow with light brown hair and thick fingers. "My Lord," he said. "Nothing important, my Lord. Just a little harmless fun."

"The Warders don't like this kind of behavior," Gawyn said. "You know that, Celark. If it gets around that you're staying up this late dicing, you'll never convince an Aes Sedai to take you."

Celark grimaced. "Yes, my Lord."

There was something reluctant in that grimace. "What?" Gawyn said. "Out with it, man."

"Well, my Lord," Celark said. "It's that some of us, we aren't so sure that we want to be Warders. Not all of us came here for that, you know. Some were like you, wanting to train with the best. And the rest of us . . . well, things have changed now."

"What things?" Gawyn asked.

"Foolish things, my Lord," the man said, looking down. "You're right, of course. There's early sparring tomorrow. But, well, we've seen war. We're soldiers now. Being a Warder, it's all a man should aspire to. But some of us, we'd rather not see what we have now end. You know?"

Gawyn nodded slowly.

"When I first came to the Tower," Celark said, "I wanted nothing more than to be a Warder. Now I don't know that I want to spend my life protecting one woman, solitary, roving about the countryside."

"You could be Warder to a Brown or White," Gawyn said. "And stay in the Tower."

Celark frowned. "With all respect, my Lord, I think that might be just as bad. Warders . . . they don't live like other men."

"That's for certain," Gawyn said, eyes lifting upward, toward Egwene's distant quarters. He would *not* go seeking that door. He forced his gaze back down to Celark. "There's no shame in choosing a different path."

"The others make it sound like there is."

"The others are wrong," Gawyn said. "Gather those of you who want to remain with the Younglings and report to Captain Chubain tomorrow. I'll speak with him. I'll wager he could use you as a division in the Tower Guard. He lost a lot of men in the Seanchan attack."

Celark relaxed visibly. "You'd do that, my Lord?"

"Of course. It was an honor to lead you men."

"Do you think . . . maybe you could join with us?" The youth's voice was hopeful.

Gawyn shook his head. "I've another path to take. But, the Light willing, I'll end up close enough to keep an eye on you." He nodded toward the room. "Go back to your games. I'll speak to Makzim for you as well." Makzim was the stern, thick-armed Warder currently leading the training sessions.

Celark nodded gratefully, hurrying back to the others. Gawyn continued down the corridor, wishing his choices were as easy as those of his men.

Lost in thought, he'd climbed halfway to Egwene's rooms before he stopped to realize what he was doing. *I need something to distract me.* The hour wasn't too late. Perhaps he could find Bryne and chat.

Gawyn made his way to Bryne's rooms. If Gawyn had a strange position among the Aes Sedai, Bryne's was nearly as odd: Warder to the former Amyrlin, general of Egwene's conquering army, and renowned great captain. Bryne's door was open a crack, emitting a line of light across the blue-tiled corridor. That was his habit when he was in and awake, should one of his officers need him. Many nights Bryne was away, staying at one of his command centers around the island or in a nearby village.

Gawyn knocked softly.

"Come." Bryne's voice was firm and familiar. Gawyn slipped in, then returned the door to its cracked position. Bryne sat at a rickety-looking desk, working on a letter. He glanced at Gawyn. "Just a moment."

Gawyn waited. The walls were papered with maps of Tar Valon, Andor, Cairhien and surrounding regions. Many bore recent notations in red chalk. Bryne was preparing for war. The notations made it clear he felt he'd eventually have to defend Tar Valon itself against Trollocs. Several maps showed villages across the northern part of the countryside, listing their fortifications—if any—and their loyalty to Tar Valon. They'd be used for supply dumps and forward positions. Another map had circles pointing out ancient watchtowers, fortifications and ruins.

There was a methodical inevitability to Bryne's calculations, and a sense of urgency. He wasn't looking to build fortifications, but to use those already in place. He was moving troops into the villages he felt most useful; another map showed progress in active recruitment.

It wasn't until Gawyn stood there—smelling the musty scent of old paper and burning candles—that he felt the reality of the impending war. It was coming soon. The Dragon would break the seals of the Dark One's prison. The place he had told Egwene to meet him, the Field of Merrilor, was marked in bright red on the maps. It was north, on the border of Shienar.

The Dark One. Loose upon the world. Light! It made Gawyn's own problems insignificant.

Bryne finished his letter, sanding the paper, folding it, and reaching for his wax and seal. "It's a little late for calling on people, son."

"I know, but I thought you might be up."

"And so I am." Bryne dribbled wax onto the letter. "What is it you need?"

"Advice," Gawyn said, sitting on a stool.

"Unless it's about the best way to quarter a group of men or how to fortify a hilltop, you'll find my advice lacking. But what is it you want to talk about?"

"Egwene forbade me to protect her."

"I'm certain the Amyrlin had her reasons," Bryne said, calmly sealing the letter.

"Foolish ones," Gawyn said. "She has no Warder, and there is a killer in the Tower." *One of the Forsaken,* he thought.

"Both true," Bryne said. "But what does that have to do with you?"

"She needs my protection."

"Did she *ask* for your protection?"

"No."

"Indeed. As I recall, she didn't ask you to come with her into the Tower either, nor did she ask for you to begin following her about like a hound that has lost his master."

"But she needs me!" Gawyn said.

"Interesting. The last time you thought that, you—with my help—upset weeks' worth of her work to reunite the White Tower. Sometimes, son, our help is not needed. No matter how freely offered, or how urgent that help may seem."

Gawyn folded his arms, unable to lean against the wall, lest he disturb a map showing orchards across the surrounding countryside. One village near Dragonmount was circled four times, for some reason. "So your advice is to let her remain exposed, perhaps to take a knife in the back."

"I haven't given any advice," Bryne said, leafing through some reports on his desk, his firm face lit by flickering candlelight. "I have only made observations, though I think it curious that you conclude that you should leave her alone."

"I . . . Bryne, she doesn't make *sense!*"

The corner of Bryne's mouth raised in a wry smile. He lowered his papers, turning to Gawyn. "I warned you that my advice would be of little use. I'm not sure if there are answers that will suit you. But let me ask this: What is it you want, Gawyn Trakand?"

"Egwene," he said immediately. "I want to be her Warder."

"Well, which is it?"

Gawyn frowned.

"Do you want Egwene, or do you want to be her Warder?"

"To be her Warder, of course. And . . . and, well, to marry her. I love her, Bryne."

"It seems to me that those are two different things. Similar, but separate. But, other than things to do with Egwene, what is it that you want?"

"Nothing," Gawyn said. "She's everything."

"Well, there's your problem."

"How is that a problem? I love her."

"So you said." Bryne regarded Gawyn, one arm on the table, the other resting on his leg. Gawyn resisted the urge to squirm beneath that gaze. "You always were the passionate one, Gawyn. Like your mother and your sister. Impulsive, never calculating like your brother."

"Galad doesn't calculate," Gawyn said. "He just acts."

"No," Bryne said. "Perhaps I spoke wrong—Galad may not be calculating, but he *isn't* impulsive. To be impulsive is to act without careful thought; Galad has given everything a great deal of thought. He's worked out his code of morality that way. He can act quickly and decisively because he's already determined what to do.

"You act with passion. You don't act because of the way you think, but because of the way you feel. In a rush, with a snap of emotion. That gives you strength. You can act when you need to, then sort through the ramifications later. Your instincts are usually good, just like your mother's were. But because of that, you've never had to face what to do when your instincts lead you in the wrong direction."

Gawyn found himself nodding.

"But son," Bryne said, leaning forward. "A man is more than one drive, one goal. No woman wants that in a man. It seems to me that men who spend time making something of themselves—rather than professing their devotion—are the ones who get somewhere. Both with women, and with life itself." Bryne rubbed his chin. "So, if I have advice for you, it's this: Find out who you would be without Egwene, and *then* figure out how to fit her into that. I think that's what a woman—"

"You're an expert on women now?" a new voice asked.

Gawyn turned, surprised, to find Siuan Sanche pushing open the door.

Bryne didn't miss a beat. "You've been there listening long enough, Siuan, to know that's not what the conversation was about."

Siuan snorted, bustling into the room with a pot of tea. "You should be in bed," she said, ignoring Gawyn after a cursory glance.

"Very true," Bryne said casually. "Oddly, the needs of the land don't submit to my whims."

"Maps can be studied in the morning."

"And they can be studied at night. And during the afternoon. Every hour I spend could mean leagues of ground defended if Trollocs break through."

Siuan sighed loudly, handing him a cup, then pouring the tea, which smelled of cloudberry. It was decidedly odd to see Siuan—who, because of her stilling, looked like a woman Gawyn's age—mothering the grizzled General Bryne.

Siuan turned to Gawyn as Bryne accepted his drink. "And you, Gawyn Trakand," she said. "I've been meaning to speak to you. Giving orders to the Amyrlin, telling her what she should do? Honestly. Men seem to think that women are nothing more than their personal messengers, sometimes. You dream up all sorts of ridiculous schemes, then expect us to somehow carry them out."

She eyed him, not looking like she expected any response other than an ashamed lowering of the eyes. Gawyn gave that and then made a hasty exit to avoid further bullying.

He wasn't surprised by anything Bryne had said. The man was nothing if not consistent, and he had repeated the same themes to Gawyn before. Think instead of being impulsive; be deliberate. But he'd spent *weeks* thinking, his ideas chasing one another in circles like flies trapped in a jar. He'd gotten nowhere.

Gawyn walked the hallways, noting Chubain's guards posted at regular intervals. He told himself he *wasn't* climbing to Egwene; he was merely checking on the guards. And yet, he soon found himself in a hallway near the Amyrlin's quarters. Just one hallway over. He'd check on her quickly and . . .

Gawyn froze. *What am I doing?* he thought.

A lot of his nervousness tonight came from not knowing if Egwene was properly guarded or not. He wouldn't be able to sleep until—

No, he told himself forcefully. *This time, I'll do as she asks.* He turned to go.

A sound made him hesitate, glancing over his shoulder. Footfalls and clothing rustling. It was too late for novices, but servants might well be delivering late meals. Bryne and Gawyn weren't the only ones who kept unusual hours in the White Tower.

It came again. So soft, barely audible. Frowning, Gawyn slipped off his boots, then sneaked forward to glance around the corner.

There was nothing. Egwene's door—inlaid with gold in the shape of *Avendesora*—sat closed, the hallway empty. Sighing, Gawyn shook his head, leaning back against the wall to slip his boots back on. He wished Egwene would at least let Chubain set guards at her room. Leaving it unwatched was—

Something moved in the shadow just down from Egwene's doorway. Gawyn froze. There wasn't much of a dark patch there, only a shadow a few inches wide made by an alcove. But as he studied that patch, he had trouble keeping his eyes on it. His gaze slid free, like a dollop of butter on a hot turnip.

It seemed . . . it seemed that the darkness was larger than he had originally thought. Why couldn't he look straight at it?

There was a flash of movement, and something spun in the air. Gawyn threw himself to the side, and steel struck stone. One boot on, he dropped the other as he pulled his sword free. The knife that had been thrown for his heart skidded across the tiled floor.

Gawyn peered round the corner, tense. Someone was fleeing down the hallway. Someone wearing all black, a hood over the head.

Gawyn took off after the person, sword held before him, arms pumping, gait awkward as his unbooted foot hit oppo-

site his booted one. The assassin was extremely fast. Gawyn
bellowed the alarm, his voice echoing through the silent
halls of the Tower; then he cut left. The assassin would have
to turn and come up the hallway here to the right.

Gawyn burst into another hallway, charging on a heading that would cut off the assassin. He skidded around the
corner.

The hallway was empty. Had the assassin doubled back?
Gawyn cursed as he ran forward and reached the original
hallway at the other end. It was empty. A doorway, perhaps? All would be dead ends. If Gawyn waited until help
came . . .

No, Gawyn thought, spinning. *Darkness. Look for darkness.* There was a deep patch of it by a doorframe to his left.
Far too small to hold anyone, but he had that same sense of
disorientation as he looked at it.

A person leaped out, swinging a sword for Gawyn's
head. He whipped his blade into Cutting the Reeds, knocking aside the attack. The assassin was much shorter than
Gawyn, so he should have had a strong advantage in reach.
Yet the assassin moved with a blurring speed, sword darting at Gawyn in a series of thrusts, not using any sword
forms Gawyn recognized.

Gawyn fell into Twisting the Wind, as he was forced to
act as if he were surrounded. He barely kept the attacker at
bay. He could hear yells in the distance—guards responding to his call. He shouted again.

He could sense frustration in the attacker's moves; the assassin had expected to defeat Gawyn quickly. Well, Gawyn
had expected the same, but focusing on this opponent was
very difficult. Gawyn's blows—when he could make them—
hit air when they should have landed on flesh.

Gawyn twisted to the side, raising his blade for Boar
Rushes Down the Mountain. But that gave the assassin an
opening; he flung another knife at Gawyn, forcing him to
the side.

The knife clanged against the wall, and the assassin fled
down the hallway. Gawyn rushed after, but he couldn't keep
up. Soon the assassin was far away, darting to the left. That
direction led to a series of intersections.

Such speed, Gawyn thought, stopping, breathing in and
out in gasps, hands on knees. *It isn't natural.*

Two of Chubain's guards arrived a moment later, swords at the ready. Gawyn pointed. "Assassin. Listening at Egwene's door. Went that way."

One ran where he pointed. The other went to raise the general alarm.

Light! Gawyn thought. *What if I didn't interrupt him listening? What if I interrupted him on his way out?*

Gawyn dashed to Egwene's door, fatigue evaporating. Sword out, he tested the door. It was unlocked!

"Egwene!" he cried, throwing the door open and leaping into the room.

There was a sudden explosion of light and a crashing sound. Gawyn found himself wrapped up in something strong: invisible cords, towing him into the air. His sword fell to the ground, and his mouth filled with an unseen force.

And so it was that he found himself hanging from the ceiling, disarmed, struggling, as the Amyrlin herself walked from her bedroom. She was alert and fully dressed in a crimson dress trimmed with gold.

She did not look pleased.

Mat sat beside the inn's hearth, wishing the fire were a little less warm. He could feel its heat through the layers of his ragged jacket and white shirt, matched by a pair of workman's thick trousers. The boots on his feet had good soles, but the sides were worn. He did not wear his hat, and his scarf was pulled up around the bottom half of his face as he leaned back in the mountain oak chair.

Elayne still had his medallion. He felt naked without it. He had a shortsword sitting by his chair, but that was mostly for show. A walking staff leaned innocently beside it; he would rather use that, or the knives hidden in his coat. But a sword was more visible, and would make the footpads who sauntered through the streets of Low Caemlyn think twice.

"I know why you're asking after him," Chet said. There was a man like Chet in nearly every tavern. Old enough to have seen men like Mat be born, grow up, and die, and willing to talk of all those years if you got enough drink in them. Or often if you didn't.

The stubble on Chet's long face was dappled silver, and he wore a lopsided cap. His patched coat had once been

black, and the red-and-white insignia on his pocket was too
faded to read. It was vaguely military, and one did not usually get scars like the thick, angry one on his cheek and
neck from a bar fight.

"Aye," Chet continued, "many are askin' after the leader
of that Band. Well, this mug of ale is appreciated, so let me
give you some advice. You walk like you know which end
of that sword means business, but you'd be a fool to challenge that one. Prince of Ravens, Lord of Luck. He faced
old death himself and diced for his future, he did. Ain't
never lost a fight."

Mat said nothing. He leaned back in his chair. This was
his fourth tavern this night, and in three of them he had
been able to find rumors about Matrim Cauthon. Barely a
lick of truth to them. Blood and bloody ashes!

Oh, sure, there were tales of other people, too. Most about
Rand, each one making the colors swirl when he heard
them. Tear had fallen to the Seanchan, no Illian, no Rand
had defeated them all and was fighting the Last Battle right
now. No! He visited women in their sleep, getting them
with child. No, that was the Dark One. No, *Mat* was the
Dark One!

Bloody stories. They were supposed to leave Mat alone.
Some he could trace back to the Band—like the story of
a city full of the dead awakening. But many of the people
claimed that the stories had come from their uncle, or cousin,
or nephew.

Mat flicked Chet a copper. The man tipped his hat politely and went to get himself another drink. Mat did not feel
like drinking. He had a suspicion that those pictures of him
were part of why the stories were spreading so quickly. In
the last tavern he had visited, someone had actually pulled
out a copy of the sketch—folded and wrinkled—and shown
it to him. Nobody had recognized him so far, though.

The hearthfire continued to crackle. Low Caemlyn was
growing, and enterprising men had realized that providing
rooms and drinks for the transients could make a healthy
profit. So shanties had started to become taverns, and those
had begun to grow into full inns.

Wood was in high demand, and many of the mercenary
bands had taken to woodcutting. Some worked honestly,
paying the Queen's levy for claims. Others worked less

legally. There had already been hangings for it. Who would have thought? Men hanging for poaching trees? What next? Men hanging for stealing dirt?

Low Caemlyn had changed drastically, roads springing up, buildings being enlarged. A few years, and Low Caemlyn would be a city itself! They'd have to build *another* wall to close it in.

The room smelled of dirt and sweat, but no more so than other taverns. Spills were quickly cleaned up and the serving girls looked eager to have work. One in particular gave him a quiet smile, refilling his mug and showing some ankle. Mat made sure to remember her; she would be good for Talmanes.

Mat lifted up his scarf enough to drink. He felt like a fool wearing the scarf this way. But it was too hot for a hooded cloak, and the beard had been torture. Even with the scarf on his face, he did not stand out too much in Low Caemlyn; he was not the only tough walking around with his face obscured. He explained that he had a bad scar he wanted to cover; others assumed he had a bounty on his head. Both were actually true, unfortunately.

He sat for a time, staring into the dancing flames of the hearth. Chet's warning caused an uncomfortable pit to open in Mat's stomach. The greater his reputation grew, the more likely he would be challenged. There would be great notoriety in killing the Prince of the Ravens. Where had they gotten that name? Blood and bloody ashes!

A figure joined him at the fire. Lanky and bony, Noal looked like a scarecrow who had dusted himself off and decided to go to town. Despite his white hair and leathery face, Noal was as spry as men half his age. When he was handling a weapon, anyway. Other times he seemed as clumsy as a mule in a dining parlor.

"You're quite the notable man," Noal said to Mat, holding out his palms to the fire. "When you stumbled across me in Ebou Dar, I had no idea what illustrious company I'd find myself in. Give this a few more months and you'll be more famous than Jain Farstrider."

Mat hunkered down farther into his chair.

"Men always think it would be grand to be known in every tavern and every city," Noal said softly. "But burn me if it isn't just a headache."

"What do you know of it?"

"Jain complained about it," Noal said softly.

Mat grunted. Thom arrived next. He was dressed as a merchant's servant, wearing a blue outfit that was not too fine, but also not in disrepair. He was claiming to have come to Low Caemlyn to determine whether his master would be well advised to put a shopfront here.

Thom pulled off the disguise with aplomb, waxing his mustaches to points and speaking with a faint Murandian accent. Mat had offered to come up with a backstory for his act, but Thom had coughed and said that he already had one worked out. Flaming liar of a gleeman.

Thom pulled up a chair, seating himself delicately, as if he were a servant who thought highly of himself. "Ah, what a waste of my time this was! My master insists that I associate with such *rabble* as this! And here I find the worst of the lot."

Noal chuckled softly.

"If only," Thom said dramatically, "I had been instead sent to the camp of the majestic, amazing, indestructible, famous Matrim Cauthon! Then I would certainly have—"

"Burn me, Thom," Mat said. "Let a man suffer in peace."

Thom laughed, waving over the serving girl and buying drinks for the three of them. He gave her an extra coin and quietly asked her to keep casual ears from getting too close to the hearth.

"Are you sure you want to meet here?" Noal asked.

"It'll do," Mat said. He did not want to be seen back in camp, lest the *gholam* look there for him.

"All right, then," Noal said. "We know where the tower is, and can get there, assuming Mat procures us a gateway."

"I will," Mat said.

"I haven't been able to find anyone who has gone inside," Noal continued.

"Some say it's haunted," Thom said, taking a slurp from his mug. "Others say it's a relic from the Age of Legends. The sides are said to be of smooth steel, without an opening. I did find a captain's widow's younger son who once heard a story of someone who found great treasures in the tower. He didn't say how the lad had gotten in, though."

"We *know* how to get in," Mat said.

"Olver's story?" Noal asked skeptically.

"It's the best we have," Mat said. "Look, the game and the rhyme are about the Aelfinn and Eelfinn. People knew about them once. Those bloody doorframes are proof of that. So they left the game and the rhyme as warning."

"That game can't be won, Mat," Noal said, rubbing his leathery chin.

"And that's the point of it. You need to cheat."

"But maybe we should try a deal," Thom said, playing with the waxed tip of a mustache. "They did give you answers to your questions."

"Bloody frustrating ones," Mat said. He had not wanted to tell Thom and Noal about his questions—he still had not told them what he had asked.

"But they *did* answer," Thom said. "It sounds like they had some kind of deal with the Aes Sedai. If we knew what it was the Aes Sedai had that the snakes and foxes wanted—the reason they were willing to bargain—then maybe we could trade it to them for Moiraine."

"If she's still alive," Noal said grimly.

"She is," Thom said, staring straight ahead. "Light send it. She *has* to be alive."

"We know what they want." Mat glanced at those flames.

"What?" Noal asked.

"Us," Mat replied. "Look, they can see what's going to happen. They did it to me, they did it to Moiraine, if that letter is any clue. They knew she would leave a letter for you, Thom. They *knew* it. And they still answered her questions."

"Maybe they had to," Thom said.

"Yes, but they don't have to answer straightforwardly," Mat said. "They didn't with me. They answered *knowing* she would come back to them. And they gave me what they did knowing I'd get pulled back, too. They want me. They want us."

"You don't know that for certain, Mat." Thom set his mug of ale on the floor between his feet and got out his pipe. To Mat's right, men cheered a dice game. "They can answer questions, but that doesn't mean they know everything. Could be like Aes Sedai foretellings."

Mat shook his head. The creatures put memories into his head. He figured they were the memories of people who had touched the tower or been into it. The Aelfinn and the

Eelfinn had those memories, and burn him, they probably had his, too. Could they watch him, see through his eyes?

He wished again for his medallion, though it would do no good against them. They were not Aes Sedai; they would not use channeling. "They *do* know things, Thom," Mat said. "They're watching. We won't surprise them."

"Makes them hard to defeat, then," Thom said, lighting a tinder twig with the fire, then using it to light his pipe. "We can't win."

"Unless we break the rules," Mat repeated.

"But they'll know what we're doing," Thom said, "if what you say is true. So we should trade with them."

"And what did Moiraine say, Thom?" Mat said. "In that letter you read every night."

Thom puffed on his pipe, raising an absent hand to his breast pocket, where he kept the letter. "She said to remember what we knew of the game."

"She knows there's no way to win when dealing with them," Mat said. "No trades, Thom, no bargains. We go in fighting and we don't leave until we have her."

Thom hesitated for a moment, then nodded, his pipe beginning to puff.

"Courage to strengthen," Noal said. "Well, we have enough of that, with Mat's luck."

"You don't have to be part of this, you know, Noal," Mat said. "You have no reason to risk yourself on this."

"I'm going," Noal said. "I've seen a lot of places. Most places, actually. But never this one." He hesitated. "It's something I need to do. And that's the end of it."

"Very well," Mat said.

"Fire to blind," Noal said. "What do we have?"

"Lanterns and torches," Mat said, knocking his foot against the sack beside his chair. "And some of those firesticks from Aludra, so we can light them. A few surprises from her, too."

"Fireworks?" Noal asked.

"And a few of those exploding cylinders we used against the Seanchan. She calls them roarsticks."

Thom whistled. "She let you have some?"

"Two. When I presented her with Elayne's agreement, she was ready to let me have almost anything I asked for." Mat grimaced. "She wanted to come along to light them.

Herself! Burn me, but that was a tough argument to end.
But we've got a whole lot of nightflowers." He tapped the
sack beside his chair with the edge of his foot.

"You *brought* them?" Thom asked.

"I wanted to keep them close," Mat said. "And she only
gave them to me today. They're not going to explode by accident, Thom. That doesn't happen very often."

"Well at least move them back from the hearth!" Thom
said. He glanced at his pipe and cursed, then scooted his
chair a few inches from Mat.

"Next," Noal said, "music to dazzle."

"I got us a variety," Thom said. "I'll bring my harp and
flute, but I found us some hand drums and hand cymbals.
They can be strapped to the side of your leg and hit with
one hand. I also bought an extra flute." He eyed Mat. "A
simple one, designed for those with thick, slow fingers."

Mat snorted.

"And finally, iron to bind," Noal said, sliding forward a
pack of his own. It clinked faintly as he untied the top, the
contents reflecting the deep orange hearthlight. "A set of
throwing knives for each of us and two shortswords. Each
of pure iron, no steel. I got us some chains, too, and a band
of iron to clip around the butt of Mat's spear. It might throw
the weight off, though."

"I'll take it," Mat said.

Noal did up his pack again, and the three of them sat
before the hearth for a time. In a way, these things they'd
gathered were an illusion. A way to reassure themselves
that they were doing *something* to prepare.

But Mat remembered those twisted places beyond the
gateways, the angles that were not right, the unnatural landscape. The creatures called snakes and foxes because they
defied standard description.

That place was another world. The preparations he made
with Thom and Noal might help, but they might also be
useless. There was no telling until they stepped into that
tower. It felt like not knowing if you had the right antidote
until after the snake's teeth were already clamped down on
your arm.

Eventually, he bade the other two a good night. Noal
wanted to head back to the Band's camp, which was now
only a ten-minute ride from the city. Thom agreed to go

with him, and they took Mat's pack full of nightflowers—
though both men looked as if they would rather be carrying
a sack full of spiders.

Mat belted his sword on over his coat, took up his staff,
then headed back toward his inn. He did not go directly
there, though, and instead found himself trailing through the
alleys and streets. Shanties and tents had sprung up beside
solid buildings as the city-outside-the-city spread along
the walls, like mold growing on a loaf of bread.

The sky was dark, but the night was still busy, touts calling from within the lit doorways of inns. Mat made sure
the shortsword was visible. There were many who would
think to exploit a lone wanderer at night, particularly outside the city walls, where the arm of the law was a little on
the flabby side.

The air smelled of impending rain, but it often did these
days. He wished it would go on and storm or bloody clear
up. It felt as if the air were holding its breath, waiting for
something. A blow that never fell, a bell that never rang, a
set of dice that never stopped spinning. Just like the ones
that thundered in his head.

He felt at the letter from Verin in his pocket. Would the
dice stop if he opened it? Maybe it was about the *gholam*.
If he did not retrieve his medallion from Elayne soon, the
thing was likely to find him and rip his insides out.

Bloody ashes. He felt like going drinking, forgetting who
he was—and who people *thought* he was—for a while. But
if he got drunk, he was likely to let his face show by accident. Perhaps begin to talk about who he really was. You
never could tell what a man would do when he was drunk,
even if that man was your own self.

He made his way through the city gates and into the New
City. The air began to mist with something that was not
quite rain, as if the sky had listened to his rant and had decided to allow a little sneeze to spray down on him.

Wonderful, he thought, *bloody wonderful.*

The paving stones soon grew wet from the not-rain, and
the streetlamps glowed with balls of vaporous haze. Mat
hunkered down, scarf still covering his face as if he were
a bloody Aielman. Had he not been too hot only a little bit
ago?

He was as eager as Thom to move on and find Moiraine.

She had made a mess of his life, but Mat supposed he owed her for that. Better to live in this mess than to be trapped back in the Two Rivers, living a boring life without realizing how boring it was. Mat was not like Perrin, who had mooned over leaving the Two Rivers before they had even gotten to Baerlon. An image of Perrin flashed in his head, and Mat banished it.

And what of Rand? Mat saw him sitting on a fine chair, staring down at the floor in front of himself in a dark room, a single lamp flickering. He looked worn and exhausted, his eyes wide, his expression grim. Mat shook his head to dispel that image as well. Poor Rand. The man probably thought he was a bloody blackferret or something by now, gnawing on pinecones. But it was likely a blackferret that wanted to live back in the Two Rivers.

No, Mat did not want to go back. There was no Tuon back in the Two Rivers. Light, well, he would have to figure out what to do with Tuon. But he did not want to be rid of her. If she were still with him, he would let her call him Toy without complaining. Well, not much anyway.

Moiraine first. He wished he knew more about the Aelfinn and Eelfinn and their bloody tower. Nobody knew about it, nobody spoke more than legends, nobody had anything useful to say. . . .

. . . nobody but Birgitte. Mat stopped in the street. Birgitte. *She* had been the one to tell Olver how to get into the Tower. How had she known?

Cursing himself for a fool, he turned toward the Inner City. The streets were emptying of the traffic that had burdened them before the almost-rain began. Soon Mat felt he had the whole city to himself; even the cutpurses and beggars withdrew.

For some reason, that put him on edge more than being stared at. It was not natural. Someone should have tried at least to bloody shadow him to see if he was worth picking off. Once again, he longed for his medallion. He had been an idiot to give that away. Better to have cut off his own bloody hand and offered that to Elayne as payment! Was the *gholam* there, in that darkness, somewhere?

There should have been toughs on the street. Cities were full of them. That was practically one of the bloody requirements for a city. A town hall, a few inns and a tavern, and several blunt-faced fellows whose only desire was to pound you into the mud and spend your coin on drink and women.

He passed a courtyard and headed through the Mason's Gate into the Inner City, the white archway almost seeming to glow, rain-slick in the phantom light of the clouded moon. Mat's quarterstaff knocked against the paving stones. The gate guards were huddled and quiet in their cloaks. Like statues, not men at all. The entire place felt like a tomb.

A ways past the gate, he passed an alleyway, and hesitated. He thought he could see a group of shadowy forms inside. Tall buildings rose on either side, grand Ogier masonry. A grunt sounded from inside the alleyway.

"A robbery?" Mat said with relief.

A hulking figure looked back out of the alleyway. Moonlight revealed a fellow with dark eyes and a long cloak. He seemed stunned to find Mat standing there. He pointed with a thick-fingered hand, and three of his companions made for Mat.

Mat relaxed, wiping his brow free of rainwater. So there *were* footpads out this night. What a relief. He had been jumping at nothing!

A thug swung his cudgel at Mat. Mat had worn the shortsword on the right side intentionally; the thug took the bait, assuming that Mat would move to draw the weapon.

Instead, Mat brought up the quarterstaff swiftly, snapping the butt against the man's leg. The footpad stumbled, and Mat swung into the man's head. The drizzle, which was nearly a proper rain by now, sprayed off the cutpurse as he fell, tripping one of his companions.

Mat stepped back and slammed the top of the quarterstaff down on the head of the tripping thug. He went down on top of his companion. The third man looked back toward his leader, who held to the collar of a gangly man Mat could barely make out in the shadows. Mat took the opportunity to leap over the small pile of unconscious thugs, swinging at the third man.

The footpad brought his cudgel up to protect his head, so Mat slammed his quarterstaff into the man's foot. He then swung the quarterstaff, knocking aside the third man's weak parry, and dropped him with a blow to the face.

Mat casually flipped a knife toward the leader of the gang, who was charging forward. The leader gurgled, stumbled in the drizzle, clawing at the knife in his neck. The others Mat would leave unconscious—poor fools, maybe they would take this warning and reform.

Mat stepped to the side as the leader stumbled past, then finally collapsed on top of his three companions. Mat kicked him over, pulled out the knife, then cleaned it. Finally, he glanced at the victim of the robbery.

"Sure am glad to see you," Mat said.

"You . . . you are?" the man asked.

"Sure am," Mat said, standing up straight. "I thought the thieves were not out tonight. A city without cutpurses, well, that's like a field without weeds. And if there were no weeds, what would you need a farmer for? Bloody inhospitable, I tell you."

The rescued man stumbled forward on shaky feet. He seemed confused by what Mat had said, but he scrambled up, taking Mat's hand. "Thank you!" The man had a nasal voice. "Thank you so, so much." In the faint moonlight, Mat could barely make out a wide face with buck teeth atop an awkwardly thin body.

Mat shrugged, setting aside his staff and unwinding his scarf—which was getting sodden—and beginning to wring it free. "I'd stay away from traveling by yourself at night, if I were you, friend."

The man squinted in the darkness. "You!" he said, voice nearly a squeak.

Mat groaned. "Blood and bloody ashes! Can't I go *any-where* without—"

He cut off as the man lunged, a dagger flashing in the faint moonlight. Mat cursed, and snapped his scarf in front of him. The dagger hit the cloth instead of Mat's gut, and Mat quickly twisted his hands, tying the assassin's dagger in lengths of cloth.

The man yelped, and Mat released the scarf and pulled out a pair of knives, one in each hand, releasing them by reflex. They took the assassin in the eyes. One in each eye. Light! Mat had not been aiming for the eyes.

The man collapsed to the wet paving stones.

Mat stood breathing in and out. "Mother's milk in a cup! Mother's *bloody* milk!" He grabbed his quarterstaff, glancing about him, but the gloomy street was empty. "I rescued you. I rescued you, and you try to stab me?"

Mat knelt down beside the corpse. Then, grimly certain what he would find, he fished in the man's pouch. He came out with a couple of coins—gold coins—and a folded-up piece of paper. Moonlight revealed Mat's face on it. He crinkled the paper and shoved it in his pocket.

One in each bloody eye. Better than the man deserved. Mat retied his scarf, grabbed his knives, then walked out onto the street, wishing he had left the assassin to his fate.

Birgitte folded her arms, leaning against a marble pillar and watching as Elayne sat enjoying an evening presentation of "players." Groups like this—acting out stories—had become very popular in Cairhien, and were now trying to achieve the same success in Andor. One of the palace halls, where bards performed, had been adapted to allow the players to act out their stories.

Birgitte shook her head. What was the good of acting out fake stories? Why not go *live* a few stories of your own? Besides, she'd prefer a bard any day. Hopefully this fashion of seeing "players" would die quickly.

This particular story was a retelling of the tragic marriage and death of the Princess Walishen, slain by beasts of the Shadow. Birgitte was familiar with the ballad that the players had adapted to form their story. In fact, they sang parts of it during the performance. It was remarkable how little that song had changed over the years. Some different names, a few different notes, but the same overall.

Much like her own lives. Repeated over and over, but with little variations. Sometimes she was a soldier. Sometimes she was a forest woman, with no formal military training. She'd been a general once or twice, unfortunately. She'd rather leave that particular job for someone else.

She'd been a guard, a noble thief, a lady, a peasant, a killer and a savior. But she had never before been a Warder. The unfamiliarity didn't bother her; in most of her lives, she had no knowledge of what had come before. What she could draw from her previous lives now was a boon, yes, but she had no right to those memories.

That didn't stop her heart from twisting each time one of those memories faded. Light! If she couldn't *be* with Gaidal this time around, couldn't she at least *remember* him? It was as if the Pattern didn't know what to do with her. She'd been forced into this life, shoving other threads aside, taking an unexpected place. The Pattern was trying to weave her in. What would happen when all of the memories faded? Would she remember waking up as an adult with no history? The thought terrified her as no battlefield ever had.

She nodded to one of her Guardswomen, Kaila Bent, who passed by the back row of the makeshift theater and saluted.

"Well?" Birgitte asked, stepping around the corner to speak with Kaila.

"Nothing to report," Kaila said. "All is well." She was a lanky fire-haired woman, and had taken very easily to wearing the trousers and coat of a Guardswoman. "Or, all is as well as it could be while having to suffer through *The Death of Princess Walishen*."

"Stop complaining," Birgitte said, suppressing a wince as the diva—so the players called her—began a particularly shrill aria—so they called a song by yourself. Why did the players need so many new names for things? "You could be out patrolling in the rain."

"I could?" Kaila asked, sounding eager. "Why didn't you say so sooner? Maybe I'll get struck by lightning. That might be preferable."

Birgitte snorted. "Get back to your rounds."

Kaila saluted and left. Birgitte tuned back into the theater, leaning against the pillar. Perhaps she should have brought some wax to stuff in her ears. She glanced over at Elayne. The Queen sat with a calm demeanor, watching the play. At times, Birgitte felt more like a nursemaid than a bodyguard. How did you protect a woman who seemed, at times, so determined to see herself dead?

And yet, Elayne was also so very capable. Like tonight; she'd somehow convinced her most bitter rival to attend this play. That was Ellorien sitting over in the eastern row; the woman's last parting from the palace had been so bitter that Birgitte hadn't expected her to return unless she was in chains. Yet here she was. It whispered of a political maneuver by Elayne that was thirteen steps more subtle than Birgitte had a mind for.

She shook her head. Elayne *was* a queen. Volatility and

all. She'd be good for Andor. Assuming Birgitte could keep that golden-haired head from being lopped off its neck.

After some time suffering through the singing, Kaila approached again. Birgitte stood up straight, curious at the woman's quick pace. "What?" she asked quietly.

"You looked bored," Kaila whispered, "so I thought I'd bring this to you. Disturbance at the Plum Gate." That was the southeastern entrance to the palace grounds. "Someone tried to sneak through."

"Another beggar looking for scraps? Or a spy for one of the lordlings, hoping to listen in?"

"I don't know," Kaila said. "I heard the news thirdhand from Calison as we passed on patrol. He said the Guardsmen have the intruder in custody at the gate."

Birgitte glanced to the side. It looked like another solo was about to begin. "You have command here; hold this post and take reports. I'll go stretch my legs and check on this disturbance."

"Bring me some wax for my ears when you come back, would you?"

Birgitte chuckled, leaving the theater and stepping into a white-and-red palace hallway. Though she had Guardswomen and men with extra bows at the hallways, Birgitte herself carried a sword, for an assassination attempt would most likely turn to close-quarters fighting.

Birgitte trotted down the hallway, glancing out a window when she passed. The sky leaked a strengthening drizzle. Utterly dreary. Gaidal would have liked this weather. He loved the rain. On occasion, she'd joked that drizzle suited his face better, making him less likely to frighten children. Light, but she missed that man.

The most direct route to the Plum Gate took her through the servants' quarters. In many palaces, this would have meant entering a section of the building that was more drab, meant for less important people. But this building had been Ogier built, and they had particular views about such things. The marble stonework here was as grand as it was elsewhere, with tiled mosaics of red and white.

The rooms, while small by royal standards, were each large enough to hold an entire family. Birgitte generally preferred to take her meals in the servants' large, open dining hall. Four separate hearths crackled here in defiance of the

dreary night, and off-duty servants and Guards laughed and
chatted. Some said you could judge a monarch by the way
he treated those who served him. If that were the case, then
the Andoran palace had been designed in a way to encourage the best in its queens.

Birgitte reluctantly passed by the inviting scents of food
and instead pushed her way out into the cold summer storm.
The chill wasn't biting. Just uncomfortable. She pulled up the
hood of her cloak and crossed the slick paving down to the
Plum Gate. The gatehouse was alight with an orange glow,
and the Guardsmen on watch stood outside in wet cloaks,
halberds held to the side.

Birgitte marched up to the gatehouse, water dripping
from the lip of her hood, then pounded on the thick oak
door. It opened, revealing the bald-headed, mustached face
of Renald Macer, sergeant on duty. A stout man, he had
wide hands and a calm temperament. She always thought
he should be in a shop somewhere making shoes, but the
Guard took all types, and dependability was often more important than skill with the sword.

"Captain-General!" he exclaimed. "What are you doing
here?"

"Getting rained on," she snapped.

"Oh, my!" He stepped back, making way for her to enter
the gatehouse. It had a single crowded room. The soldiers
were on storm shift—meaning twice as many men would
work the gate as usual, but they would only have to stand
outside an hour before rotating with the men warming inside the gatehouse.

Three Guardsmen sat at a table, throwing dice into a dicing box while an open-fronted iron stove consumed logs
and warmed tea. Dicing with the four soldiers was a wiry
man with a black scarf wrapped around the bottom of his
face. His clothing was scruffy, his head topped by a mop of
wet brown hair sticking out in all directions. Brown eyes
glanced at Birgitte over the top of the scarf, and the man
sank down a little in his seat.

Birgitte took off her cloak and shook it free of rainwater.
"This is your intruder, I assume?"

"Why, yes," the sergeant said. "How did you hear about
that?"

She eyed the intruder. "He tried to sneak onto the palace grounds, and now you're *dicing* with him?"

The sergeant and the other men looked sheepish. "Well, my Lady—"

"I'm no lady." *Not this time at least.* "I work for a living."

"Er, yes," Macer continued. "Well, he gave up his sword readily, and he doesn't *seem* that dangerous. Just another beggar wanting scraps from the kitchens. Right nice fellow. Thought we'd get him warm before sending him out into that weather again."

"A beggar," she said. "With a sword?"

Sergeant Macer scratched his head. "I guess that *is* kind of odd."

"You could charm the helmet off a general on a battlefield, couldn't you, Mat?" she said.

"Mat?" the man asked in a familiar voice. "I don't know what you mean, my good woman. My name is Garard, a simple beggar who has a quite interesting past, if you care to listen to it—"

She eyed him with a firm gaze.

"Oh, bloody ashes, Birgitte," he complained, taking off the scarf. "I only wanted to get warm for a spell."

"And win the coin off my men."

"A friendly game never hurt a man," Mat said.

"Unless it was against you. Look, why are you *sneaking* into the palace?"

"It took too much bloody work to get in last time," Mat said, sitting back in his chair. "Thought I might pass that up this time."

Sergeant Macer glanced at Birgitte. "You know this man?"

"Unfortunately," she said. "You can release him to my custody, Sergeant. I'll see that Master Cauthon is properly taken care of."

"Master Cauthon?" one of the men said. "You mean the Raven Prince?"

"Oh, for bloody . . ." Mat said, as he stood and picked up his walking staff. "Thanks," he said dryly to Birgitte, throwing on his coat.

She put her cloak back on, then pushed open the door as one of the Guards handed Mat his sword, belt still attached.

Since when had Mat carried a shortsword? Probably a decoy away from the quarterstaff.

The two stepped out into the rain as Mat tied on the belt. "Raven Prince?" she asked.

"I don't want to talk about it."

"Why not?"

"Because I'm getting too bloody famous for my own good, that's why."

"Wait until it tracks you across generations," she said, glancing up at the sky, blinking as a raindrop hit her square in the eye.

"Come on, let's go grab a drink," Mat said, walking toward the gate.

"Wait," she said. "Don't you want to go see Elayne?"

"Elayne?" Mat said. "Blood and ashes, Birgitte, I'm here to talk to *you*. Why do you think I let those Guards catch me? You want a drink or not?"

She hesitated, then shrugged. By putting Kaila on duty in her place, Birgitte had officially gone on break. She knew a fairly decent tavern only two streets from the Palace.

"All right," she said, waving to the Guards and leading Mat onto the rainy street. "But I'll need to have milk or tea instead of ale. We aren't sure if her Warder drinking would be bad for the babies or not." She smiled, thinking of a drunk Elayne trying to talk to her allies after the play. "Though if I make her tipsy, it might be good revenge for some of the things she's done to me."

"I don't know why you let her bond you in the first place," Mat said. The street was nearly empty around them, though the tavern up ahead looked inviting, its yellow light spilling into the street.

"I didn't have a say in the matter," she said. "But I don't regret it. Did you really sneak into the palace to meet with me?"

Mat shrugged. "I have some questions."

"About what?"

He replaced that ridiculous scarf, which she noticed had a rip in the middle. "You know," he said. "*Things*."

Mat was one of the few who knew who she really was. He couldn't mean. . . . "No," she said, turning, "I don't want to talk about it."

"Bloody ashes, Birgitte! I *need* your information. Come on, for an old friend."

"We agreed to keep each other's secrets."

"And I'm not out blabbing yours," Mat said quickly. "But, see, there's this issue."

"What issue?"

"The Tower of Ghenjei."

"That's not an issue," she said. "You stay away from it."

"I can't."

"Of course you can. It's a flaming *building,* Mat. It can't exactly chase you down."

"Very amusing. Look, will you at least hear me out, over a mug? Of, er, milk. I'll buy."

She stopped for a moment. Then she sighed. "Bloody right, you'll buy," she muttered, waving him onward. They entered the inn, known as The Grand Hike, which was crowded beyond usual because of the rain. The innkeeper was a friend of Birgitte's, however, and he had the bouncer toss out a drunkard sleeping in one of the booths to make room for her.

She tossed him a coin in thanks, and he nodded his ugly head to her—he was missing several teeth, one eye, and most of his hair. Best-looking man in the place. Birgitte held up two fingers to order drinks—he knew that she took milk these days—and she waved Mat to the booth.

"I don't rightly think I've ever seen an uglier man than that innkeeper," Mat said as they sat.

"You haven't been alive long enough," she said, leaning back against the wall and putting her booted feet up on the table. There was just room enough for her to do so, sitting on the bench of the booth lengthwise. "If Old Snert were a few years younger, and if someone thought to break his nose in a few places, I might consider him. He's got a fine chest, nice and full of curly hair to get your fingers in."

Mat grinned. "Have I ever mentioned how odd it is to go drinking with a woman who talks about men like that?"

She shrugged. "Ghenjei. Why in the name of Normad's Ears are you wanting to go there?"

"Whose ears?" Mat asked.

"Answer me."

Mat sighed, then absently accepted his mug as the serving girl delivered it. Uncharacteristically, he didn't slap her backside, though he did give her a good leer as she walked away. "The bloody snakes and foxes have a friend of mine," he said, lowering his scarf and taking a pull on his drink.

"Leave him. You can't save him, Mat. If he was foolish enough to go into their realm, he deserves what he got."

"It's a woman," Mat said.

Ah. Birgitte thought. Bloody fool. Heroic, but still a fool.

"I can't leave her," Mat continued. "I owe her. Besides, a good friend of mine is going in whether I want him to or not. I *have* to help."

"Then they'll have all three of you," Birgitte said. "Look, if you go in through the portals, then you're locked into the treaties. They protect you to an extent, but they also restrict you. You'll never get anywhere useful after entering by one of the doorframes."

"And if you go in the other way?" Mat asked. "You told Olver how to open the Tower."

"Because I was telling him a bedtime story! Light, I never thought one of you sap-for-brains would actually *try* to get in!"

"But if we go in that way, can we find her?"

"Maybe," Birgitte said, "but you won't. The treaties won't be in effect, so the Aelfinn and Eelfinn can draw blood. Normally, you only have to worry about tricks with pits or ropes, since they can't. . . ." She trailed off, glancing at him. "How *did* you get hanged, anyway?"

He flushed, looking down into his drink. "They should post a flaming explanation on those doorframes. 'Step through here and they can bloody hang you. And they will. Idiot.'"

Birgitte snorted. They'd talked about the memories he had. She should have put it together. "If you go in the other way, they'll probably try that as well. Shedding blood in their kingdom can have strange effects. They'll try to break your bones with a fall or drug you to sleep. And they *will* win, Mat. It's their world."

"And if we cheat?" Mat asked. "Iron, music, fire."

"That's not cheating. That's being smart. *Everyone* with half a wit who enters through the tower carries those things. But only one out of a thousand makes it back out, Mat."

He hesitated, then fished a small handful of coins out of

his pocket. "What do you think the odds are that if I toss these into the air, they will all come up heads? One in a thousand?"

"Mat . . ."

He tossed them above the table. They came down in a spray, hitting the tabletop. Not a single one of them bounced or rolled from the table onto the floor.

Mat didn't look down at the coins. He met her eyes as they all rolled and vibrated to a stop. She glanced at them. Two dozen coins. Each had landed face up.

"One in a thousand is good odds," he said. "For me."

"Bloody ashes. You're as bad as Elayne! Don't you see? All it takes is one wrong throw. Even you miss once in a while."

"I'll take the chance. Burn me, Birgitte, I know it's stupid, but I'm doing it. How do you know so much about the Tower anyway? You've been into it, haven't you?"

"I have," she admitted.

Mat looked smug. "Well *you* got back out! How'd you manage it?"

She hesitated, then finally took up her mug of milk. "That legend didn't survive, I'm assuming?"

"I don't know it," Mat said.

"I went in to ask them to save the life of my love," she said. "It came after the battle of Lahpoint Hills, where we led the Buchaner rebellion. Gaidal was wounded horribly; a blow to the head that made him unable to think straight. He forgot who I was, some of the time. It tore my heart, so I took him to the Tower to be Healed."

"And how'd you get out?" Mat asked. "How'd you fool them?"

"I didn't," Birgitte said softly.

Mat froze.

"The Eelfinn never Healed him," she continued. "They killed us both. I didn't survive, Mat. That is the end of that particular legend."

He fell silent. "Oh," he finally said. "Well, that's kind of a sad story, then."

"They can't all end in victory. Gaidal and I don't deal well with happy endings anyway. Better for us to burn out in glory." She grimaced, remembering one incarnation when she and he had been forced to grow old together, peacefully.

Most boring life she'd ever known, though at the time—
ignorant of her grander part in the Pattern—she'd been
happy with it.

"Well I'm still going," Mat said.

She sighed. "I can't go with you, Mat. Not and leave
Elayne. She has a death wish the size of your pride, and I
mean to see she survives."

"I don't expect you to go," Mat said quickly. "Burn me,
that's not what I'm asking. And . . ." He frowned. "A death
what the size of my *what*?"

"Never mind," she said, drinking her milk. She had a soft
spot for milk, though she didn't tell people of it. Of course,
she'd be happy when she could drink again; she missed Old
Snert's yeasty drinks. She liked ugly beer as much as she
liked ugly men.

"I came to you because I need help," Mat said.

"What more is there to say? You're taking iron, fire, and
music. Iron will hurt them, ward them, and hold them. Fire
will scare them and kill them. Music will entrance them.
But you'll find that both fire and music grow less and less
effective the longer you use them.

"The tower isn't a place, it's a portal. A kind of gate to the
crossroads between their realms. You'll find both of them
there, Aelfinn snakes and Eelfinn foxes. Assuming they're
working together currently. They have a strange relationship."

"But what do they *want*?" Mat asked. "From us, I mean.
Why do they care?"

"Emotion," Birgitte said. "That's why they built portals
into our world, that's why they entice us in. They feed off
what we feel. They like Aes Sedai in particular, for some
reason. Perhaps those with the One Power taste like a
strong ale."

Mat shivered visibly.

"The inside will be confusing," Birgitte said. "Getting
anywhere specific in there is difficult. Going in through
the tower instead of the doorframes put me in danger, but
I knew that if I could reach that grand hall, I'd be able to
make a deal. You don't get anything free if you go in the
tower, by the way. They'll ask for something, something
dear to you.

"Anyway, I figured out a method to find the grand hall.

Iron dust, left behind me in the intersections where I'd passed so that I knew which ways I'd gone before. They couldn't touch it, you see, and . . . are you sure you've never heard this story?"

Mat shook his head.

"It used to be popular around these parts," she said, frowning. "A hundred years ago or so."

"You sound offended."

"It was a good story," she said.

"If I survive, I'll have Thom compose a bloody ballad about it, Birgitte. Tell me about the dust. Did your plan work?"

She shook her head. "I still got lost. I don't know if they blew away the dust somehow, or if the place is so huge that I never repeated myself. I ended up cornered, my fire going out, my lyre broken, my bowstring snapped, Gaidal unconscious behind me. He could walk some of the days in there, but was too dizzy on others, so I pulled him on the litter I'd brought."

"Some of the *days*?" Mat said. "How long were you in there?"

"I had provisions for two months," Birgitte said, grimacing. "Don't know how long we lasted after those ran out."

"Bloody ashes!" Mat said, then took a long swig of his ale.

"I told you not to go in," Birgitte said. "Assuming you do reach your friend, you'll never get back out. You can wander for weeks in that place and never turn right or left, keep going straight, passing hallway after hallway. All the same. The grand hall could be minutes away, if you knew which direction to take. But you'll keep missing it."

Mat stared into his mug, perhaps wishing he'd ordered something more potent.

"You reconsidering?" she asked.

"No," he said. "But when we get out, Moiraine better bloody appreciate this! *Two months*?" He frowned. "Wait. If you both died in there, how did the story get out?"

She shrugged. "Never did find out. Perhaps one of the Aes Sedai used their questions to ask. Everyone knew I'd gone in. I was called Jethari Moondancer then. You're *sure* you've never heard the story?"

He shook his head again.

She sighed, settling back. Well, not *every* one of the tales about her could live on forever, but she'd thought that one would stand for a few more generations.

She raised her mug to drink the last of her milk. The mug never got there. She froze when she felt a jolt of emotion from Elayne. Anger, fury, *pain*.

Birgitte slammed the mug down on the table, then threw coins down and stood up, cursing.

"What?" Mat said, on his feet in an eyeblink.

"Elayne. In trouble. *Again*. She's hurt."

"Bloody ashes," Mat snapped, grabbing his coat and staff as they ran for the exit.

CHAPTER
23

Foxheads

Elayne turned the strange medallion around in her fingers, tracing the fox's head worked into the front. As with many *ter'angreal*, it was difficult to tell exactly what kind of metal had been used to create it originally. She suspected silver, with the senses of her Talent. However, the medallion was no longer silver. It was something else, something new.

The songmistress of the Lucky Man's Theater Troop continued her song. It was beautiful, pure and high. Elayne sat on a cushioned chair on the right side of the hall, which had been repurposed with a raised area at the front for the players. A pair of Birgitte's Guards stood behind her.

The room was dim, lit only by a line of small flickering lamps set behind blue glass in alcoves on the walls. The blue light was overwhelmed by the burning yellow lanterns set around the front of the platform.

Elayne was barely paying attention. She had often listened to "The Death of Princess Walishen" as a ballad, and didn't really see the point of adding words to it and different players, instead of just having one bard do the entire thing. But it was Ellorien's favorite ballad, and the favorable news out of Cairhien about these players—which nobles there had recently discovered—had many of the nobles in Andor buzzing.

Hence this evening. Ellorien had come at Elayne's invitation; likely she was intrigued. Why had Elayne been so audacious as to invite her? Soon, Elayne would take advantage of having Ellorien here. But not quite yet. Let the

woman enjoy the production first. She'd be expecting a political ambush. She'd wait for Elayne to walk over and sit
in one of the seats near her, or perhaps send a servant with
an offer.

Elayne did neither, instead sitting and regarding the foxhead *ter'angreal*. It was a complex work of art, despite being only a single, solid piece of metal. She could *feel* the
weaves that had been used to create it. Its intricacy was far
beyond the simplicity of the twisted dream rings.

She was doing something wrong in trying to reproduce
the medallion. She carried in her pouch one of her failed
attempts. She'd had copies cast for her, as precise in detail
as her silversmiths could create, though she suspected the
form was not important. The amount of silver seemed to be,
for some reason, but not the shape that silver took.

She'd gotten close. The copy in her pouch didn't work
perfectly. Less powerful weaves slid off anyone holding it,
but very powerful ones could not be deflected for some reason. And, more problematic, it was impossible to channel
while touching the copy.

She could channel while holding the original. Indeed,
she'd been giddy when she'd discovered that holding the
medallion didn't interfere with her weaves at all. Being
pregnant did—that was still a source of frustration to her—
but it *was* possible to hold the foxhead and channel.

But not the copy. She hadn't gotten it quite right. And,
unfortunately, her time was slim. Mat would need his medallion back soon.

She took out the fake and set it on the seat beside her,
then embraced the Source and wove Spirit. Several of the
Kin, a group of whom were watching the production some
seats to the side, glanced up at her as she did so. Most were
too distracted by the song.

Elayne reached over and touched the medallion. Immediately, her weaves unraveled and the Source winked away
from her. Much as if a shield had been placed over her.

She sighed as the song reached its heights. The copy was
so close, yet so frustrating at the same time. She'd never
wear something that prevented her from touching the
Source, not even for the protection it offered.

Still, it was not completely useless. She could give a copy
to Birgitte, perhaps, and a few of the Guardsmen captains.

It wouldn't do for her to create *too* many of these. Not when they could be used so effectively against Aes Sedai.

Could she, perhaps, give one of the copies to Mat? He'd never know, since he couldn't channel himself. . . .

No, she thought, squashing that temptation before it could fly too high. She had promised to return Mat's medallion, and she would. Not some copy that didn't work as well. She tucked both medallions into her dress pocket. Now that she knew she could get Mat to part with his medallion, perhaps she could bully him into giving her more time. Though the presence of the *gholam* did worry her. How to deal with the thing? Perhaps copies of the medallion for all her guards wouldn't be a bad idea after all.

The song finished, the final, high-pitched note dwindling like a candle running out of wick. The end of the play came shortly afterward, men in white masks jumping out of the darkness. A brilliant light flashed, something thrown into one of the lanterns, and when it faded again, Walishen lay dead on the stage, the bell of her red dress splayed around her like spilled blood.

The audience stood to clap. Most of them were Kin, though not a few were attendants of the other High Seats who had been invited. All of those were supporters of hers. Dyelin, of course, and young Conail Northan and the equally young—but twice as proud—Catalyn Haevin.

The final noble here was Sylvase Caeren. What to make of her? Elayne shook her head, slipping the fake foxhead into her pouch and lending a demure clap to the other accolades. The players would be focused only on her. If she didn't give some sign of approval, they'd fret the entire night.

That done, Elayne made her way out to a nearby sitting room, which was furnished with padded, thick-armed chairs for relaxed conversation. There was a bar at the side, manned by a serving man in a crisp red and white uniform. He stood with hands behind his back, waiting respectfully as people ambled in. Ellorien wasn't there, of course—it was basic courtesy for a guest to wait for the host to withdraw first. Though Ellorien and Elayne weren't on the best of terms, it wouldn't do to show poor manners.

Soon after Elayne arrived, Ellorien trailed in. The plump woman was chatting with one of the Kinswomen, pointedly ignoring the High Seats who walked near her. Her conversation sounded forced. She probably could have been expected to avoid the sitting room entirely, but Elayne knew that the woman would want to make certain to express that she had *not* changed her mind about House Trakand.

Elayne smiled, but did not approach the woman, instead turning toward Sylvase as she entered. Of medium build, the blue-eyed girl might have been pretty, save for that expressionless look on her face. Not emotionless, like an Aes Sedai. Completely expressionless. It sometimes seemed like Sylvase was a dressing dummy set up for display. But then, on other occasions, she'd show a hidden depth, a cunning deep down.

"Thank you for the invitation, Your Majesty," Sylvase said evenly, her voice a faintly eerie monotone. "It was most enlightening."

"Enlightening?" Elayne said. "I should hope that it was enjoyable."

Sylvase said nothing. She glanced at Ellorien, and here she finally showed some emotion. An icy kind of dislike, the kind that gave you a shiver. "Why invite *her*, Your Majesty?"

"House Caeren was at odds with Trakand once, too," Elayne said. "Often, those whose loyalty is most difficult to win are the most valuable once it is yours."

"She will not support you, Your Majesty," Sylvase said, her voice still too calm. "Not after what your mother did."

"When my mother took the throne years ago," Elayne said, glancing over at Ellorien, "there were some Houses it was said she'd never win over. And yet she did."

"So? You already have enough support, Your Majesty. You've had your victory."

"One of them."

She left the rest unsaid. There was a debt of honor owed to House Traemane. Courting Ellorien's approval wasn't merely about strengthening the Lion Throne. It was about repairing rifts caused by Elayne's mother while under the influence of Gaebril. It was about recovering her House's reputation, about undoing the wrongs that could be undone.

Sylvase would not understand that. Elayne had learned about the poor girl's childhood; this one would not put much stock in the honor of a High Seat. Sylvase seemed to believe in only two things: power and vengeance. So long as

she supported Elayne and could be guided, she would not
be a liability. But she would never be the strength to House
Trakand that someone like Dyelin was.

"How is my secretary serving your needs, Your Majesty?"
Sylvase asked.

"Well enough, I suppose," Elayne said. So far, he hadn't
produced anything of value, though Elayne hadn't given
him leave to do anything too drastic during his questioning. She was trapped in a conundrum. She'd been hunting
this group of Black Ajah for what seemed like forever. She
finally had them . . . but what did she do with them?

Birgitte had taken the captives alive ostensibly so that
they could be questioned, then tried by the White Tower.
But that meant they had no reason to speak; they knew their
ultimate end would be execution. So Elayne either had to
be willing to bargain with them, or she had to let the questioner take extreme measures.

A queen *had* to be hard enough to allow these things. Or
that was what her teachers and tutors had explained. There
was no question as to the guilt of these women, and they
had already done enough to earn themselves death a dozen
times over. Elayne wasn't certain how far she herself was
willing to descend, however, to pry their secrets free.

Besides, would that actually do any good? Ispan had had
some kind of Compulsion or oaths binding her; these were
likely to have the same. Would they be able to reveal anything useful? If only there were a way to. . . .

She hesitated, missing Sylvase's next comment as a thought
occurred to her. Birgitte wouldn't like it, of course. Birgitte
didn't like *anything*. But Elayne had felt Birgitte move off out
of the Palace somewhere, perhaps doing rounds of the guard
posts outside.

"Excuse me, Sylvase," Elayne said. "I just recalled something that I absolutely *must* do."

"Of course, Your Majesty," the girl said in a flat, almost
inhuman voice.

Elayne moved from her, then quickly greeted—and bade
good evening—to the others. Conail looked bored. He'd
come because it had been expected of him. Dyelin was her
usual pleasant, yet careful, self. Elayne avoided Ellorien.
She greeted everyone else in the room of note. Once finished, she began to walk toward the exit.

"Elayne Trakand," Ellorien called out.

Elayne paused, smiling to herself. She turned, wiping her face of anything other than calculated curiosity. "Yes, Lady Ellorien?"

"Have you invited me here only to ignore me?" the woman demanded from across the room. Other conversations grew quiet.

"Not at all," Elayne said. "I was merely under the impression that you would have a more pleasant time if I did not force you to interact with me. This evening was not intended for political purposes."

Ellorien frowned. "Well what *was* it for, then?"

"To enjoy a good ballad, Lady Ellorien," Elayne said. "And, perhaps, to remind you of days when you often enjoyed entertainment in the company of House Trakand." She smiled and nodded slightly, then left.

Let her think about that, Elayne thought with satisfaction. Ellorien had no doubt heard that Gaebril had been one of the Forsaken. The woman might not believe it, but perhaps she would recall the years of respect she and Morgase had shown one another. Should a few short months be cause to forget years of friendship?

At the bottom of the steps out of the lounge, Elayne found Kaila Bent, one of Birgitte's Guardswoman captains. The lanky fire-haired woman was chatting amiably with a pair of Guardsmen, both of whom seemed quite eager to gain her favor. All three snapped to attention when they noticed Elayne.

"Where did Birgitte go?" Elayne asked.

"She went to investigate a disturbance at the gates, Your Majesty," Kaila said. "I've had word that it was nothing. That mercenary captain who came to visit you earlier tried to sneak onto the palace grounds. Captain Birgitte is questioning him."

Elayne raised an eyebrow. "You mean Matrim Cauthon?"

The woman nodded.

"She's 'questioning' him?"

"That's what I heard, Your Majesty," Kaila replied.

"That means the two of them have gone out for drinks," Elayne said with a sigh. Light, this was a bad time for it.

Or was it a good time? Birgitte couldn't object to Elayne's plan for the Black Ajah if she was out with Mat. Elayne

found herself smiling. "Captain Bent, you are with me."
She left the theater rooms and entered the Palace proper.
The woman followed, waving for the squad of Guards-
women standing in the hallway to follow.

Smiling to herself, Elayne began giving orders. One of the
Guardswomen ran off to deliver them, though she looked
confused at the strange list of commands. Elayne made her
way to her rooms, then sat down, thinking. She would have
to move quickly. Birgitte was in a surly mood; Elayne could
tell that through the bond.

A servant soon arrived, carrying an enveloping black
cloak. Elayne jumped up and slipped it on, then embraced
the Source. It took her three tries! Bloody ashes, but being
pregnant was frustrating sometimes.

She spun weaves of Fire and Air around her, using the
Mirror of Mists to make herself look taller, more imposing.
She fetched her jewelry chest and fished out a small ivory
carving of a seated woman shrouded in her own hair. She
used the *angreal* to pull as much of the One Power into her
as she dared. To anyone watching who could channel, she'd
look imposing indeed.

She glanced back at the Guardswomen. They were confused, obviously, and stood with their hands unconsciously
on their swords. "Your Majesty?" Kaila asked.

"How do I look?" Elayne said, tweaking her weaves to
make her voice deeper.

Kaila's eyes opened wider. "Like a thunderhead given
life, Your Majesty."

"Imposing, then?" Elayne asked, jumping slightly at the
dangerous, almost inhuman sound of her voice. Perfect!

"I'd say so," the lanky Guardswoman said, rubbing her
chin with one hand. "Though the slippers do spoil the effect."

Elayne glanced down, cursing at the pink silk. She wove
some more, making her slippered feet vanish. The weave
would make it appear as if she were floating in the air,
wrapped in a pulsing shroud of darkness, cloak and straps
of black cloth fluttering round her. Her face was hidden
completely in blackness. As an added touch, she created
two faintly glowing pricks of red where the eyes should be.
Like coals radiating with a deep crimson light.

"Light preserve us," one of the Guards whispered.

Elayne nodded to herself, her heart quickening in excitement. She wasn't worried. She'd be safe. Min's viewing promised that. She ran through her plans again. They were solid. But there would be only one way to test them for certain.

Elayne inverted her weaves and tied them off. Then she turned to the Guards. "Turn out the lights," she said to them, "and remain perfectly still. I will return shortly."

"But—" Kaila said.

"That is an order, Guardswoman," Elayne said firmly. "You had best obey it."

The woman hesitated. She likely knew that Birgitte would never let this happen. But Kaila was *not* Birgitte, thankfully. She reluctantly gave the order and the lights in the room were doused.

Elayne reached into her pocket and took out the foxhead medallion, the real one, and held it hidden and tucked in her hand. She took a deep breath, then created a gateway. The ribbon of light was bright in the blackened room, glowing and bathing them in a pale glow, like moonlight. It opened into a room that was similarly dark.

Elayne stepped through and found herself in the Palace dungeons, in one of the cells. A woman knelt on the far side of the cell, beside the sturdy door with a small window at the top, slotted with bars, that let in the only light in the dank cell. There was a small cot to Elayne's right and a bucket for a chamber pot to her left. The tiny room smelled of mold and human waste, and she could clearly hear the scratching of rats nearby. It still seemed too lavish quarters for the woman in front of her.

Elayne had chosen Chesmal with calculation. The woman had seemed to have some authority among the Black, and she was powerful enough that most of the others would bow to her. But she also had seemed more passionate than logical, when Elayne had last encountered her. That would be important.

The tall, handsome woman spun as soon as Elayne entered the cell. Elayne held her breath. Blessedly, the *a'dam* worked. Chesmal threw herself to the straw-covered floor of the cell.

"Great One," the woman hissed. "I had—"

"Silence!" Elayne shouted, her voice booming.

Chesmal cringed, then glanced to the side, as if waiting for the Guards outside to peek in. There would be Kinswomen there to hold Chesmal's shield; Elayne could feel them. Nobody came, despite the sound. The Kin were following Elayne's orders, odd though those orders were.

"You are less than a rat," Elayne said with her disguised voice. "You were sent to see to the Great Lord's glory, but what have you done? Allowed yourself to be captured by these fools, these *children*?"

Chesmal wailed, bowing herself further. "I am dust, Great One. I am nothing! We have failed you. Please, do not destroy me!"

"And why shouldn't I?" Elayne barked. "The work of your particular group has been marked with failure after failure! What have you done that would *possibly* persuade me to allow you to live?"

"We have killed many of these fools who work against the Great Lord!" Chesmal wailed.

Elayne winced, then, steeling herself, created a whip of Air and lashed it across the woman's back. It was no more than Chesmal deserved. "You?" Elayne said. "You had nothing to do with their deaths! Do you think me stupid? Do you think me ignorant!"

"No, Great One," Chesmal wailed, curling up further. "Please!"

"Then give me reason to let you live."

"I have information, Great One," Chesmal said quickly. "One of those we were told to seek, the two men that must be killed at all costs . . . one is here in Caemlyn!"

What's this? Elayne hesitated. "Tell me more."

"He rides with a mercenary group," Chesmal said, sounding relieved to have information that was wanted. "He is the man with the keen eyes who wears the hat and carries the spear marked by ravens!"

Mat? The Darkfriends were hunting *Mat*? He was friends with Rand, true, and *ta'veren*. But what had Mat done to gain the ire of the Forsaken themselves? More disturbing was that Chesmal knew of Mat's presence in the city. He hadn't arrived until *after* the Black sisters had been captured! That meant. . . .

That meant Chesmal and the others were in contact with other Darkfriends. But who? "And how did you discover this? Why was this not reported earlier?"

"I got news this very day, Great One," Chesmal said, sounding more self-assured now. "We are planning an assassination."

"And *how* can you do that while imprisoned?" Elayne demanded.

Chesmal looked up briefly, her square face showing confusion. She said nothing.

I've tipped her off that I don't know as much as I should. Elayne gritted her teeth behind her mask of shadows.

"Great One," Chesmal said. "I have been following my orders carefully. We are almost in a position to begin the invasion, as commanded. Soon, Andor will be awash with the blood of our enemies and the Great Lord shall reign in fire and ash. We will see it done."

What was this? An invasion, of Andor? Impossible! How would it happen? How *could* it happen? And yet, dare she ask the questions? Chesmal seemed to suspect that something was wrong.

"You are not the Chosen who visited me before, are you, Great One?" Chesmal asked.

"Our ways are not to be questioned by one such as you," Elayne growled, punctuating the remark with another switch of Air across the woman's back. "I need to know how much you have been told. So that I can judge the gaps in your understanding. If you are ignorant of. . . . Well, that is to be seen. First, explain to me how much you know of the invasion."

"I know that the deadline nears, Great One," Chesmal said. "If we had longer, perhaps we could plan more extensively. If you could see me freed from these confines, then I could . . ."

She trailed off, glancing to the side.

Deadline. Elayne opened her mouth to demand more, but hesitated. What? She could no longer feel the Kin outside. Had they retreated? And what of Chesmal's shield?

The door rattled, the lock spun, then the door flew open, revealing a group of people on the other side. And they were *not* the group of Guards Elayne had been expecting.

At their head was a man with short black hair, thinning at the sides, and huge mustaches. He wore brown trousers and a black shirt, his coat long, almost an open-fronted robe.

Sylvase's secretary! Behind him were two women. Temaile and Eldrith. Both of the Black Ajah. Both holding to the Source. Light!

Elayne stifled her surprise, meeting their gaze and not giving ground. If she could convince one Black sister that she was of the Forsaken, then perhaps she could convince three. Temaile's eyes opened wide, and she threw herself to her knees, as did the secretary. Eldrith, however, hesitated. Elayne couldn't be certain if it was her stance, her disguise, or her reaction to seeing the three newcomers. Perhaps it was something else entirely. Either way, Eldrith wasn't taken in. The round-faced woman began to channel.

Elayne cursed to herself, forming weaves of her own. She slammed a shield at Eldrith right as she felt one come for her. Fortunately, she was holding Mat's *ter'angreal*. The weave unraveled, and the medallion grew cold in Elayne's hand. Elayne's own weave slid evenly between Eldrith and the Source, cutting her off. The glow of the Power winked out around her.

"What are you doing, you idiot!" Chesmal screeched. "You try to overthrow one of the Chosen? You'll see us all dead!"

"That's not one of the Chosen," Eldrith yelled back. Elayne belatedly thought to weave a gag of Air. "You've been duped! It—"

Elayne got the gag in her mouth, but it was too late. Temaile—who had always looked too delicate to be a Black sister—embraced the Source and looked up. Chesmal's expression turned from horror to anger.

Elayne quickly tied off Eldrith's shield and began weaving another one. A weave of Air hit her. The foxhead medallion grew cold, and—blessing Mat for his timely loan—Elayne placed a shield between Chesmal and the Source.

Temaile gaped at Elayne, obviously stunned to see her weaves fail. Sylvase's secretary wasn't so slow, however. He threw himself forward unexpectedly, ramming Elayne back against the wall with a great deal of force.

Pain laced out from her shoulder, and she felt something

crack. Her shoulder bone? *The babes!* she thought immediately. It was a primal flash of horror and instant terror that
defied all thoughts about Min and viewings. In her surprise,
she let go of the gateway leading back to her room above.
It winked out.

"She has a *ter'angreal* of some kind," Temaile cried.
"Weaves fall off her."

Elayne scrambled, pushing against the secretary and
beginning a weave of Air to thrust him back. As she did,
however, he clawed at her hand, perhaps having noticed
a flash of silvery metal there. The secretary got his long
fingers around the medallion just as Elayne's burst of Air
hit him.

The secretary flew backward, clinging to the medallion.
Elayne growled, still furious. Temaile grinned maliciously,
and weaves of Air sprang up around her. She threw them
forward, but Elayne met them with her own.

The two weaves of Air slammed against one another,
causing the air to churn in the small room. Bits of straw
blew up in a flurry. Elayne's ears protested the sudden pressure. The dark-haired secretary scrambled back from the
battle, clutching the *ter'angreal*. Elayne reached a weave
toward him—but it unraveled.

Elayne yelled in anger, pain throbbing in her shoulder
where she'd hit the wall. The small room was cramped with
so many people in it, and Temaile stood in the doorway, un-
intentionally blocking the secretary from getting away. Or
maybe it was intentional; she probably wanted that medallion. The other two Black sisters hunkered down, air blasting around them, still shielded.

Elayne drew as much through the *angreal* as she dared,
forcing her weave of Air forward, shoving aside the one
Temaile was using to push. The two held for a moment; then
Elayne's burst through, crashing into Temaile and tossing
her out of the cell and against the stone wall outside. Elayne
followed with a shield, though it appeared that Temaile had
been knocked unconscious by the blast.

The secretary bolted for the nearby doorway. Elayne felt
a stab of panic. She did the only thing she could think of.
She picked up Chesmal in a weave of Air and threw her at
the secretary.

Both went down in a heap. A metallic ping sounded in

the air as the foxhead medallion slipped free and hit the ground, rolling through the door.

Elayne took a deep breath, pain flaring across her chest, her arm falling slack. She could no longer hold it up properly. She cradled it in her other arm, angry, clinging to the Source. The sweetness of *saidar* was a comfort. She wove Air and tied up Chesmal, the secretary and Eldrith, who had been trying to crawl toward Elayne unobtrusively.

Calming herself, Elayne pushed past them out of the small cell to check on Temaile in the hallway outside. The woman was still breathing, but was indeed unconscious. Elayne tied her in Air, too, to be certain, then carefully picked up the foxhead medallion. She winced at the pain of her other arm. Yes, she'd broken a bone for certain.

The dark hallway was empty, set with four doorways for cells, lit by only a single stand-lamp. Where were the Guards and Kin? She reluctantly released the weaves that formed her disguise—she wouldn't want any soldiers arriving and mistaking her for one of the Darkfriends. Certainly *someone* had heard some of that racket! In the back of her mind, she could sense concern from Birgitte, who was getting closer. The Warder had undoubtedly felt Elayne's injury.

Almost, Elayne preferred the pain of her shoulder to the lecture she'd get from Birgitte. She winced again, considering that, as she turned and inspected her captives. She'd need to check the other cells.

Of course her babes would be all right. She would be all right. She'd overreacted to the pain; she hadn't *really* been afraid. Still, best to—

"Hello, my Queen," a man's voice whispered in her ear right before a second pain blossomed in her side. She gasped, stumbling forward. A hand reached out and yanked the medallion from her fingers.

Elayne spun, and the room seemed blurry. Something warm ran down her side. She was bleeding! She was so stunned, she felt the Source slip away from her.

Doilin Mellar stood behind her in the hallway, holding a bloodied knife in his right hand, hefting the medallion in his left. His hatchetlike face was broken by a deep smile, almost a leer. Though he wore only rags, he looked as self-assured as a king on his throne.

Elayne hissed and reached for the Source. But nothing happened. She heard chuckling behind her. She hadn't tied off Chesmal's shield! As soon as Elayne released the Source, the weaves would have vanished. Sure enough, Elayne glanced and found weaves cutting her off from the Source.

Chesmal, handsome face flushed, smiled at her. Light! There was blood pooling at Elayne's feet. So much of it.

She stumbled back against the wall of the hallway, Mellar to one side, Chesmal the other.

She *couldn't* die. Min had said . . . *We could be misinterpreting.* Birgitte's voice returned to her. *Any number of things could still go wrong.*

"Heal her," Mellar said.

"What?" Chesmal demanded. Behind her, Eldrith was dusting herself off inside the cell doorway. She'd fallen to the ground when Elayne's weavings of Air dissipated, but her shield was still there. That one Elayne had tied in place.

Think, Elayne told herself, blood dribbling between her fingers. *There has to be a way out. There has to be! Oh, Light! Birgitte, hurry!*

"Heal her," Mellar said again. "The knife wound was to make her drop you."

"Fool," Chesmal said. "If the weaves had been tied off, a wound wouldn't have released us!"

"Then she would have died," Mellar said, shrugging. He eyed Elayne; those handsome eyes of his shone with lust. "And that would have been a pity. For she was promised to *me*, Aes Sedai. I won't have her die here in this dungeon. She doesn't die until *I* have had time to . . . enjoy her." He looked at the Black sister. "Besides, you think those whom we serve would be pleased if they knew you'd let the Queen of Andor die without yielding her secrets?"

Chesmal looked dissatisfied, but she apparently saw the wisdom in his words. Behind them, the secretary slipped out of the cell and—after glancing both ways—slunk down the hallway toward the steps and hurried up them. Chesmal crossed the hallway toward Elayne. Blessedly. Elayne was getting fuzzy-headed. She rested her back against the wall, barely feeling the pain of her broken shoulder, and slid down until she was sitting.

"Idiot girl," Chesmal said. "I saw through your ploy, of course. I was leading you on, knowing that help was coming."

The words were hollow; she was lying for the benefit of the others. The Healing. Elayne needed . . . that . . . Healing. Her mind was growing dull, her vision darkening. She held her hand to her side, terrified for herself, for her children.

Her hand slipped. She felt something through the fabric in the pocket of her dress. The foxhead medallion copy.

Chesmal put her hands on Elayne's head, crafting Healing weaves. Elayne's veins became ice water, her body overwhelmed by a wave of Power. She drew in a deep breath, the agony in her side and shoulder vanishing.

"There," Chesmal said. "Now, quickly, we need to—"

Elayne whipped free the other medallion and held it up. By reflex, Chesmal grabbed it. That made the woman unable to channel. Her weaves vanished, including Elayne's shield.

Chesmal cursed, dropping the medallion. It hit and rolled as Chesmal wove a shield.

Elayne didn't bother with a shield. This time, she wove Fire. Simple, direct, dangerous. The Dark sister's clothing burst into flame before she could finish weaving, and she cried out.

Elayne hauled herself to her feet. The hallway shook and spun—the Healing had taken a lot out of her—but before things stopped spinning, she wove another thread of Fire, lashing it at Mellar. He had risked the life of her children! He had stabbed her! He . . .

The weaves unraveled the moment they touched him. He smiled up at her, stopping something with his foot. The second medallion. "Here now," he said, scooping it up. "Another one? If I shake you, will a third fall free?"

Elayne hissed. Chesmal was still screaming, afire. She fell to the ground, kicking, the hallway growing pungent with the scent of burned flesh. Light! Elayne hadn't meant to kill her. But there wasn't time to spare. She wove Air, snatching up Eldrith again before the woman could escape. Elayne pushed her forward, between herself and Mellar, just in case. He watched with keen eyes, edging forward, holding the two medallions in one hand and his dagger in the other. It still glistened with Elayne's blood.

"We aren't finished, my Queen," he said in a soft voice. "These others were promised power. But my reward was always to be you. I always collect what I am owed." He watched Elayne with care, expecting some trick.

If only she had one! She could barely stand upright. Holding the Source was difficult. She backed away, keeping Eldrith between herself and Mellar. His eyes flicked to the statuesque woman; she stood with arms tied to her sides by Air, floating an inch above the ground. With a jerking motion, he jumped forward and slit Eldrith's throat.

Elayne started, scrambling backward.

"Sorry," Mellar said, and it took Elayne a moment to realize he was addressing Eldrith. "But orders are orders." With that, he ducked, plunging his dagger into Temaile's unconscious body.

He couldn't escape with the medallions! With a surge of strength, Elayne drew in the One Power and wove Earth. She pulled at the ceiling above Mellar as he stood up. Stones shattered, blocks falling downward, causing him to yell and cover his head as he ducked away. Something rang in the air. Metal on stone.

The hallway shook, and dust sprayed in the air. The rain of rocks drove Mellar away, but kept her from chasing. He vanished up the stairwell to the right. Elayne sank down to her knees, feeling drained. But then she saw something glittering among the rubble of the ceiling blocks she'd pulled down. A bit of silvery metal. One of the medallions.

Holding her breath, she grabbed it. Blessedly, the Source didn't leave her. Mellar had escaped with the copy, it seemed, but she still had the original.

She sighed, allowing herself to sit back against the cold stone wall. She wanted to lapse into unconsciousness, but forced herself to tuck away the medallion, then remain awake until Birgitte appeared in the hallway. The Warder panted heavily from having run, her red coat and golden braid wet with rainwater.

Mat stepped down into the hallway after her, wearing a scarf up around his face, his wet brown hair plastered to his head. His eyes darted from side to side, a quarterstaff held at guard.

Birgitte knelt by Elayne's side. "Are you all right?" she asked urgently.

Elayne nodded in exhaustion. "I got myself out of this one." *In a way.* "Did you happen to do the world a favor and kill Mellar on your way in?"

"Mellar?" Birgitte asked, alarmed. "No. Elayne, there's blood on your dress!"

"I'm fine," she said. "Really, I've been Healed."

So Mellar was free. "Quickly," she said. "Search the hallways. The Guards and the Kin who were guarding this place—"

"We found them," Birgitte said. "Stuffed into the bottom of the stairwell. Dead. Elayne, what happened?" To the side, Mat poked at Temaile's corpse, noting the dagger wound in her chest.

Elayne pressed her hands to her abdomen. Her babes would be all right, wouldn't they? "I did something very rash, Birgitte, and I know that you are going to scream at me for it. But would you first please take me to my rooms? I think we should have Melfane look at me. Just in case."

An hour after the failed assassination attempt on Egwene, Gawyn stood alone in a small room that was part of the Amyrlin's chambers. He'd been released from the weaves that had held him, then told to stay put.

Egwene finally strode into the room. "Sit," she said.

He hesitated, but her fierce eyes could have set candles aflame. He sat down on the stool. This small room held several dressers and trunks for clothing. The doorway led out to the larger sitting room where he'd been captured in weaves; a doorway off of that room led to Egwene's bedchamber.

Egwene shut the door, sequestering the two of them from the many guards, Warders and Aes Sedai milling about in the rooms outside. Their conversations made a low hum through the door. Egwene still wore red and gold, and she had golden threads woven into her dark hair. Her cheeks were flushed with anger at him. That made her even more beautiful than usual.

"Egwene, I—"

"Do you realize what you have done?"

"I checked to see if the woman I love was safe, following the discovery of an assassin outside her door."

She folded her arms beneath her breasts. He could almost *feel* the heat of her anger. "Your yelling has drawn half of the White Tower. They saw you captured. The assassin probably knows, now, about my weaves."

"Light, Egwene! You talk as if I did it on purpose. I was only trying to protect you."

"I didn't ask for your protection! I asked for your obedience! Gawyn, don't you see the opportunity we've missed? If you hadn't scared Mesaana away, she'd have walked into my traps!"

"It wasn't one of the Forsaken," Gawyn said. "It was a man."

"You said you couldn't see the face or make out the figure because it was blurred."

"Well, yes," Gawyn said. "But he fought with the sword."

"And a woman couldn't use a sword? The size of the person you saw indicated a woman."

"Maybe, but one of the Forsaken? Light, Egwene, if it had been Mesaana, then she'd have used the Power to burn me to dust!"

"Another reason," Egwene said, "that you should *not* have disobeyed me! Perhaps you're right—perhaps this was one of Mesaana's minions. A Darkfriend or Gray Man. If that were the case, I'd have them captive and be able to learn about Mesaana's plots. And Gawyn, what if you *had* found Mesaana? What could you have done?"

He looked down at the floor.

"I told you that I had taken precautions," she continued. "And still you disobeyed! And now, because of what you've done, the murderer knows that I was anticipating her. She'll be more careful next time. How many lives do you think you just cost us?"

Gawyn kept his hands in his lap, trying to hide the fists that they had formed. He should have felt ashamed, but all he could feel was anger. A rage he couldn't explain—frustration at himself, but mostly at Egwene for turning an honest mistake into a personal affront.

"It seems to me," he said, "that you don't want a Warder at all. Because I'll tell you, Egwene, if you can't stand being looked after, then no man will do."

"Perhaps you are right," she said curtly. Her skirts rustled as she pulled open the door to the hall, went out and then pulled it closed behind her. Not *quite* a slam.

Gawyn stood up and wanted to kick the door. Light, what a mess this had become!

He could hear Egwene through the door, sending the gawkers back to their beds, ordering the Tower Guard to be extra vigilant tonight. That was likely for show. She knew that the assassin wouldn't try again so soon.

Gawyn slipped out of the room and left. She noted his departure, but said nothing to him, instead turning to speak softly with Silviana. The Red had a glare for Gawyn that would have made a boulder wince.

Gawyn passed several guards who—for their parts—seemed respectful of Gawyn. As far as they knew, he'd foiled an attempt on the Amyrlin's life. Gawyn nodded to their salutes. Chubain stood nearby, inspecting the knife that had nearly taken Gawyn in the chest.

Chubain held up the knife to him. "Have you ever seen anything like this?"

Gawyn took the narrow, sleek knife. It was balanced for throwing, with a fine steel blade that looked something like an elongated candle's flame. Set into the center were three bits of blood-colored rock.

"What kind of stone is that?" Gawyn asked, holding the knife up to the light.

"I've never seen it before."

Gawyn turned the knife over a few times. There weren't any inscriptions or carvings. "This came within half a breath of claiming my life."

"You can take it, if you wish," Chubain said. "Maybe you can ask Bryne's men if they've ever seen one like it. We have a second one we found down the hallway."

"It was also intended for my heart," Gawyn said, tucking the knife into his belt. "Thank you. I have a gift for you in return."

Chubain raised an eyebrow.

"You've been complaining of the men you lost," Gawyn said. "Well, I've a group of soldiers I can recommend strongly."

"From Bryne's army?" Chubain asked, lips downturned.

Like many of the Tower Guard, he still regarded Bryne's army as a rival force.

"No," Gawyn said. "Men loyal to the Tower. Some of those who trained to be Warders and who fought with me on Elaida's side. They're feeling displaced now, and they would rather be soldiers than Warders. I'd appreciate it if you'd give them a home. They're solid men and excellent warriors."

Chubain nodded. "Send them to me."

"They'll come to you tomorrow," Gawyn said. "I only ask one thing. Try not to break the group apart. They've been through much together. Their bond gives them strength."

"Shouldn't be difficult," Chubain said. "The Tenth Tower Company was destroyed nearly to a man by those flaming Seanchan. I'll set some veteran officers over your lads and form the new company out of them."

"Thank you," Gawyn said. He nodded toward Egwene's quarters. "Watch over her for me, Chubain. I think she's determined to see herself dead."

"It is ever my duty to defend and uphold the Amyrlin. But where will you be?"

"She made it clear that she wants no Warder," Gawyn said, his mind drifting back to the things Bryne had said to him earlier. What did he want, aside from Egwene? Perhaps it was time to find out. "I think it's past time I went to visit my sister."

Chubain nodded, and Gawyn took his leave. He visited the barracks and gathered his possessions—little more than a change of clothing and a winter cloak—then made his way to the stables and saddled Challenge.

Then he led the horse to the Traveling ground. Egwene maintained a sister on duty there at all times. Tonight's Aes Sedai—a petite, drowsy-eyed Green named Nimri—didn't question him. She made him a gateway to a hillside about an hour's travel from Caemlyn.

And so he left Tar Valon—and Egwene al'Vere—behind.

"What is that?" Lan demanded.

The aged Nazar looked up from his saddlebags, leather *hadori* holding down his powdery white hair. A small stream gurgled near their camp in the middle of a forest of highland pines. Those pines shouldn't have borne half so many brown needles.

Nazar had been tucking something into his saddlebags, and Lan had happened to spot a bit of gold peeking out. "This?" Nazar asked. He pulled the cloth out: a brilliant white flag with a golden crane embroidered in the center. It was a fine work, with beautiful stitching. Lan nearly grabbed it out of Nazar's fingers and ripped it in half.

"Now, I see that expression on your face, Lan Mandragoran," Nazar said. "Well, don't you be getting all self-centered about this. A man has a right to carry his kingdom's flag with him."

"You're a *baker*, Nazar."

"I'm a Borderlander first, son," the man said, tucking the banner away. "This is my heritage."

"Bah!" Lan said, turning away. The others were breaking up camp. He'd grudgingly allowed the three newcomers to join him—they were stubborn as boars, and in the end, he had had to succumb to his oath. He'd promised that he'd accept followers. These men, technically, hadn't asked to ride with him—they'd simply started doing it. That was enough. Besides, if they were going to travel in the same direction, then there was little sense in making two camps.

Lan continued to wipe his face dry from the morning's washing. Bulen was getting bread ready for breakfast. This grove of pines was in eastern Kandor; they were getting close to the border into Arafel. Perhaps he could—

He froze. There were several new tents in their camp. A group of eight men were chatting with Andere. Three of them looked plump around the waist—not warriors, judging by their soft clothing, though they did appear to be Malkieri. The other five were all Shienarans, topknots on their heads, leather bracers on their arms, and horsebows stored in cases on their backs beside long, two-handed swords.

"What is this?" Lan demanded.

"Weilin, Managan and Gorenellin," Andere said, gesturing to the Malkieri. "These others are Qi, Joao, Merekel, Ianor, Kuehn—"

"I didn't ask *who*," Lan said, voice cold. "I asked *what*. What have you done?"

Andere shrugged. "We met them before running into you. We told them to wait along the southern roadway for us. Rakim fetched them last night, while you were sleeping."

"Rakim was supposed to be on watch!" Lan said.

"I watched in his stead," Andere said. "I figured we'd want these fellows."

All three of the plump merchants looked to Lan, then went down on their knees. One was weeping openly. "*Tai'shar Malkier.*"

The five Shienarans saluted Lan. "Dai Shan," one said.

"We have brought what we could to the cause of the Golden Crane," another of the merchants added. "All that we could gather in a little time."

"It is not much," said the third. "But we lend you our swords as well. We may look to have grown soft, but we can fight. We *will* fight."

"I don't need what you brought," Lan said, exasperated. "I—"

"Before you say too much more, old friend," Andere said, laying a hand on Lan's shoulder, "perhaps you should have a look at that." He nodded to the side.

Lan frowned, hearing a rattling sound. He stepped past a patch of trees to look upon the path to the camp. Two dozen wagons were approaching, each piled high with supplies— weapons, sacks of grain, tents. Lan opened his eyes wide. A good dozen warhorses were hitched in a line, and strong oxen pulled the wagons. Teamsters and servants walked alongside them.

"When they said they sold what they could and brought supplies," Andere said, "they meant it."

"We will never be able to move quietly with all of this!" Lan said.

Andere shrugged.

Lan took a deep breath. *Very well.* He would work with it. "Moving quietly appears to be failing anyway. From now on, we will pose as a caravan delivering supplies to Shienar."

"But—"

"You will swear to me," he said, turning toward the men. "Each of you will swear not to reveal who I am or send word to anyone else who might be looking for me. You *will swear it.*"

Nazar looked like he would object, but Lan silenced him with a stern look. One by one, they swore.

The five had become dozens, but it would stop there.

CHAPTER
24

To Make a Stand

B ed rest," Melfane announced, taking her ear from the wooden tube she'd placed against Elayne's chest. The midwife was a short, ample-cheeked woman who today wore her hair tied back by a translucent blue scarf. Her neat dress was of white and matching sky-blue, as if worn in defiance of the perpetually overcast sky.

"What?" Elayne asked.

"One week," Melfane said, wagging a thick finger at Elayne. "You aren't to be on your feet for one week."

Elayne blinked, stunned, her exhaustion fleeing for the moment. Melfane smiled cheerfully as she consigned Elayne to this impossible punishment. Bed rest? For a *week*?

Birgitte stood in the doorway, Mat in the room beyond. He'd stepped out for Melfane's inspection, but otherwise he'd hovered near her almost as protectively as Birgitte. You'd never know they cared for her by the way they spoke, however—the two of them had been sharing curses, each trying to top the other. Elayne had learned a few new ones. Who knew that hundred-legs did those things?

Her babes were safe, so far as Melfane could tell. That was the important part. "Bed rest is, of course, impossible," Elayne said. "I have far too much to do."

"Well, it will have to be done from bed," Melfane replied, her voice pleasant but completely unyielding. "Your body and your child have undergone a great stress. They need time to recover. I will be attending you and making certain you maintain a *strict* diet."

"But—"

"I won't hear any excuses," Melfane interrupted.

"I'm the *Queen*!" Elayne said, exasperated.

"And *I'm* the Queen's midwife," Melfane replied, still calm. "There isn't a soldier or attendant in this palace who won't help me, if I determine that your health—and that of your child—is at risk." She met Elayne's eyes. "Would you like to put my words to the test, Your Majesty?"

Elayne cringed, imagining her own Guards forbidding her to exit her chambers. Or, worse, tying her down. She glanced at Birgitte, but received only a satisfied nod. "It's no more than you deserve," that nod seemed to say.

Elayne sat back in her bed, frustrated. It was a massive four-poster, decorated in red and white. The room was ornate, sparkling with various creations of crystal and ruby. It would make a beautifully gilded prison indeed. Light! This wasn't fair! She did up the front of her gown.

"I see that you're not going to try my word," Melfane said, standing up from the side of the bed. "You show wisdom." She glanced at Birgitte. "I will allow you a meeting with the Captain-General to assess the evening's events. But no more than a half-hour, mind you. I won't have you exerting yourself!"

"But—"

Melfane wagged that finger at her again. "A half-hour, Your Majesty. You are a woman, not a plow beast. You need rest and care." She turned to Birgitte. "Do not upset her unduly."

"I wouldn't dream of it," Birgitte said. Her anger was finally beginning to abate, replaced by amusement. Insufferable woman.

Melfane withdrew to the outer chamber. Birgitte remained where she was, regarding Elayne through narrow eyes. Some displeasure still boiled and churned from the bond. The two regarded one another for a long moment.

"What are we to do with you, Elayne Trakand?" Birgitte finally asked.

"Lock me in my bedroom, it appears," Elayne snapped.

"Not a bad solution."

"And would you keep me here forever?" Elayne asked. "Like Gelfina, from the stories, locked away for a thousand years in the forgotten tower?"

Birgitte sighed. "No. But six months or so would help keep my anxiety levels down."

"We don't have time for that," Elayne replied. "We don't have time for much, these days. Risks must be taken."

"Risks involving the Queen of Andor going alone to face a mob of the Black Ajah? You're like some blood-besotted idiot on the battlefield, charging ahead of his comrades, seeking death without a shield-mate to guard your back!"

Elayne blinked at the anger in the woman.

"Don't you *trust* me, Elayne?" Birgitte asked. "Would you be rid of me, if you could?"

"What? No! Of course I trust you."

"Then *why* won't you let me help you? I'm not supposed to be here, now. I have no purpose other than what circumstance has given me. You made me your Warder, but you won't let me *protect* you! How can I be your bodyguard if you won't tell me when you're putting yourself in danger?"

Elayne felt like pulling the covers up to shield herself from those eyes. How could Birgitte be the one who felt so hurt? Elayne had been the one who'd been wounded! "If it means anything," she said, "I don't intend to do this again."

"No. You'll do something *else* reckless."

"I mean, I intend to be more careful. Maybe you're right, and the viewing isn't a perfect guarantee. It certainly didn't stop me from panicking when I felt a real danger."

"You didn't feel a real danger when the Black Ajah locked you up and tried to cart you away?"

Elayne hesitated. She *should* have been frightened that time, but she hadn't been. Not only because of Min's viewing. The Black Ajah would never have killed her, not under those circumstances. She was too valuable.

Feeling that knife enter her side, pierce her skin, dig toward her womb . . . that had been different. The terror. She could remember the world blackening around her, her heartbeat thudding, growing louder, like the drumbeats at the end of a performance. The ones that came before the silence.

Birgitte regarded Elayne appraisingly. She could feel Elayne's emotions. She was Queen. She could not avoid risks. But . . . perhaps she could rein herself in.

"Well," Birgitte said, "did you at least discover anything?"

"I did," Elayne said. "I—"

At that moment, a scarf-wrapped head appeared in the doorway. Mat had his eyes closed. "You covered up?"

"Yes," Elayne said. "And in a far more fashionable way than you, Matrim Cauthon. That scarf looks ridiculous."

He scowled, opening his eyes and pulling off the scarf, revealing the angular face beneath. "*You* try moving through the city without being recognized," he said. "Every butcher, innkeeper and bloody backroom slipfinger seems to know what I look like these days."

"The Black sisters were planning to have you assassinated," Elayne said.

"What?" Mat asked.

Elayne nodded. "One mentioned you. It sounded like Darkfriends had been searching for you for some time, with the intent of killing you."

Birgitte shrugged. "They're Darkfriends. No doubt they want us *all* dead."

"This was different," Elayne said. "It seemed more . . . intense. I suggest keeping your wits about you the next while."

"That'll be a trick," Birgitte noted. "Seeing as to how he doesn't have any wits in the first place."

Mat rolled his eyes. "Did I miss you explaining what you were doing in the flaming dungeons, sitting in a pool of your own blood, looking for all the world like you'd seen the losing end of a battlefield skirmish?"

"I was interrogating the Black Ajah," Elayne said. "The details are none of your concern. Birgitte, have you a report from the grounds?"

"Nobody saw Mellar leave," the Warder said. "Though we found the secretary's body on the ground floor, still warm. Died from a knife to the back."

Elayne sighed. "Shiaine?"

"Gone," Birgitte said, "along with Marillin Gemalphin and Falion Bhoda."

"The Shadow couldn't leave them in our possession," Elayne said with a sigh. "They know too much. They had to end up either rescued or executed."

"Well," Mat said, shrugging, "you're alive, and three of them are dead. Seems like a reasonably good outcome."

But the ones who escaped have a copy of your medallion, Elayne thought. She didn't speak it, however. She also didn't mention the invasion that Chesmal had spoken of. She would talk of it with Birgitte soon, of course, but first she wanted to consider it herself.

Mat had said the night's events had a "reasonably good outcome." But the more Elayne thought about it, the more dissatisfied she was. An invasion of Andor was coming, but she didn't know when. The Shadow wanted Mat dead, but as Birgitte had pointed out, that was no surprise. In fact, the only *certain* result of the evening's adventures was the sense of fatigue Elayne felt. That and a week confined to her rooms.

"Mat," she said, taking off his medallion. "Here, it's time I gave this back. You should know that it probably saved my life tonight."

He walked over and took it back eagerly, then hesitated. "Were you able to . . ."

"Copy it? Not perfectly. But to an extent."

He put it back on, looking concerned. "Well, that feels good to have back. I've been wanting to ask you something. Now might not be the time."

"Speak of it," Elayne said, tired. "Might as well."

"Well, it's about the *gholam* . . ."

"The city has been emptied of most civilians," Yoeli said as he and Ituralde walked through Maradon's gate. "We're close to the Blight; this is not the first time we've evacuated. My own sister, Sigril, leads the Lastriders, who will watch from the ridge to the southeast and send word if we should fall. She will have sent word to our watchposts around Saldaea, requesting aid. She will light a watchfire to alert us if they come."

The lean-faced man looked at Ituralde, his expression grim. "There will be few troops who could come to our aid. Queen Tenobia took many with her when she rode to find the Dragon Reborn."

Ituralde nodded. He walked without a limp—Antail, one of the Asha'man, was quite skilled with Healing. His men made a hasty camp in the courtyard just inside the city gates. The Trollocs had taken the tents they'd left behind, then lit them on fire at night to illuminate them feasting on the wounded. Ituralde had moved some of his troops into the empty buildings, but he wanted others close to the gate in case of an assault.

The Asha'man and Aes Sedai had worked to Heal Ituralde's men, but only the worst cases could get attention. Ituralde nodded to Antail, who was working with the wounded in a roped-off section of the square. Antail didn't see the nod. He concentrated, sweating, working with a Power Ituralde didn't want to think about.

"Are you certain you want to see them?" Yoeli asked. He held a horseman's long spear on his shoulder, the tip tied with a triangular black and yellow pendant. It was called the Traitor's Banner by the Saldaeans here.

The city bristled with hostility, different groups of Saldaeans regarding one another with grim expressions. Many wore strips of black cloth and yellow cloth twisted about one another and tied to their sword sheaths. They nodded to Yoeli.

Desya gavane cierto cuendar isain carentin, Ituralde thought. A phrase in the Old Tongue. It meant "A resolute heart is worth ten arguments." He could guess what that banner meant. Sometimes a man knew what he must do, though it sounded wrong.

The two of them walked for a time through the streets. Maradon was like most Borderland cities: straight walls, square buildings, narrow streets. The houses looked like fortressed keeps, with small windows and sturdy doors. The streets wound in odd ways, and there were no thatched roofs—only slate shingles, fireproof. The dried blood at several key intersections was difficult to make out against the dark stone, but Ituralde knew what to look for. Yoeli's rescue of his troops had come after fighting among the Saldaeans.

They reached a nondescript building. There would be no way for an outsider to know that this particular dwelling belonged to Vram Torkumen, distant cousin to the Queen, appointed lord of the city in her absence. The soldiers at the door wore yellow and black. They saluted Yoeli.

Inside, Ituralde and Yoeli entered a narrow staircase and climbed three flights of stairs. There were soldiers in nearly every room. On the top floor, four men wearing the Traitor's Banner guarded a large, gold-inlaid door. The hallway was dark: narrow windows, a rug of black, green and red.

"Anything to report, Tarran?" Yoeli asked.

"Not a thing, sir," the man said with a salute. He wore long mustaches and had the bowed legs of a man very comfortable in the saddle.

Yoeli nodded. "Thank you, Tarran. For all you do."

"I stand with you, sir. And will at the end."

"May you keep your eyes northward, but your heart southward, my friend," Yoeli said, taking a deep breath and pushing open the door. Ituralde followed.

Inside the room, a Saldaean man in a rich red robe sat beside a hearth, sipping a cup of wine. A woman in a fine dress did needlework in the chair across from him. Neither looked up.

"Lord Torkumen," Yoeli said. "This is Rodel Ituralde, leader of the Domani army."

The man at the hearth sighed over his cup of wine. "You do not knock, you do not wait for me to address you first, you come during an hour when I have *spoken* of my need for quiet contemplation."

"Really, Vram," the woman said, "you expect *manners* from this man? Now?"

Yoeli quietly rested his hand on the hilt of his sword. The room held a jumble of furniture: a bed on the side of the room that obviously didn't belong there, a few trunks and standing wardrobes.

"So," Vram said, "Rodel Ituralde. You're one of the great captains. I realize it might be insulting to ask, but I must observe formalities. You realize that by bringing troops onto our soil, you have risked a war?"

"I serve the Dragon Reborn," Ituralde said. "Tarmon Gai'don comes, and all previous allegiances, boundaries, and laws are subject to the Dragon's will."

Vram clicked his tongue. "Dragonsworn. I had reports, of course—and those *men* you employ seemed an obvious hint. But it is still so strange to hear. Do you not realize how utterly foolish you sound?"

Ituralde met the man's eyes. He hadn't considered himself Dragonsworn, but there was no use calling a horse a rock and expecting everyone else to agree. "Don't you care about the invading Trollocs?"

"There have been Trollocs before," Vram said. "There have *always* been Trollocs."

"The Queen—" Yoeli said.

"The Queen," Vram interrupted, "will soon return from her expedition to unmask and capture this false Dragon. Once that happens, she will see *you* executed, traitor. You, Rodel Ituralde, will likely be spared because of your station, but I should not like to be your family when they receive the ransom demand. I hope that you have wealth to accompany your reputation. Otherwise, you shall likely spend many of the next years as a general to nothing more than the rats of your cell."

"I see," Ituralde said. "When did you turn to the Shadow?"

Vram's eyes opened wide, and he stood. "You dare name me *Darkfriend*?"

"I've known some Saldaeans in my time," Ituralde said. "I've called some friends; I've fought against others. But never have I known one who would watch men fight Shadowspawn and not offer to help."

"If I had a sword . . ." Vram said.

"May you burn, Vram Torkumen," Ituralde said. "I came here to tell you that, on behalf of the men I lost."

The man seemed shocked as Ituralde turned to go. Yoeli joined him, pulling the door closed.

"You disagree with my accusation?" Ituralde asked, joining the traitor as they returned to the stairs.

"I honestly can't decide if he's a fool or a Darkfriend," Yoeli said. "He'd have to be one or the other to not put together the truth from the winter, those clouds and the rumors that al'Thor has conquered half the world."

"Then you have nothing to fear," Ituralde said. "You won't be executed."

"I killed my countrymen," Yoeli said, "staged a revolt against my Queen's appointed leader, and seized command of the city, though I've not a drop of noble blood."

"That'll change the moment Tenobia returns, I warrant," Ituralde said. "You've earned yourself a title for certain."

Yoeli stopped in the dark stairwell, lit only from above and below. "I see that you do not understand. I have betrayed my oaths and killed friends. I will *demand* execution, as is my right."

Ituralde felt a chill. *Bloody Borderlanders,* he thought. "Swear yourself to the Dragon. He supersedes all oaths. Do not waste your life. Fight beside me at the Last Battle."

"I will not hide behind excuses, Lord Ituralde," the man said, continuing down the steps. "No more than I could watch your men die. Come. Let us see to the housing of those Asha'man. I would like very much to see these 'gateways' you speak of. If we could use them to send messages out and bring supplies in, this could be a very interesting siege indeed."

Ituralde sighed, but followed. They didn't speak of fleeing by way of the gateways. Yoeli wouldn't abandon his city. And, he realized, Ituralde wouldn't abandon Yoeli and his men. Not after what they'd gone through to rescue him.

This was as good a place as any to make a stand. Better than many a situation he'd been in lately, that was for certain.

Perrin entered their tent to find Faile combing her hair. She was beautiful. Each day, he still felt a sense of wonder that she was really back.

She turned to him and smiled in satisfaction. She was using the new silver comb he'd left on her pillow—something he'd traded for from Gaul, who had found it in Malden. If this *shanna'har* was important to her, then Perrin intended to treat it the same way.

"The messengers have returned," Perrin said, closing the flaps to the tent. "The Whitecloaks have chosen a battlefield. Light, Faile. They're going to force me to wipe them out."

"I don't see the trouble with that," she said. "We'll win."

"Probably," Perrin said, sitting down on the pillows beside their sleeping pallet. "But despite the Asha'man doing most of the work at first, we'll have to move in to fight. That means we'll lose people. Good men we need at the Last Battle." He forced himself to relax the fists that he'd clenched. "The Light burn those Whitecloaks for what they've done, and for what they're doing."

"Then it's a welcome opportunity to defeat them."

Perrin grunted a reply, and didn't explain the depth of frustration he felt. He would lose that fight against the Whitecloaks, no matter what happened. Men would die on both sides. Men they *needed*.

The lightning flashed outside, casting shadows on the

canvas ceiling. Faile went over to their trunk, getting out a sleeping shift for herself and setting aside a robe for him. Faile thought a lord should have a robe handy in case he was needed at night. She'd been correct a couple of times so far.

She moved past him, smelling worried, though her expression was pleasant. He had expended all options for a peaceful resolution with the Whitecloaks. It looked like, want it or not, killing would be his lot again very soon.

He stripped to his smallclothes and lay down, then started drifting off before Faile had finished changing.

He entered the wolf dream beneath the great sword impaling the ground. In the distance, he could make out the hill that Gaul had named a "fine watchpoint." The campsite was supplied from behind by a stream.

Perrin turned and sped toward the Whitecloak camp. They sat like a dam in a river, stopping him from continuing onward.

"Hopper?" he called, looking around the Whitecloak camp, still tents standing on an open field. There was no response, so Perrin searched the camp a while longer. Balwer had not recognized the seal Perrin had described. Who led these Whitecloaks?

An hour or so later, Perrin had come to no conclusion about that. However, he was fairly certain which tents they kept their supplies in; those might not be as well guarded as the prisoners, and—with gateways—he might be able to burn their supplies.

Maybe. Their Lord Captain Commander's letters were filled with phrases like: "I am giving your people the benefit of believing they knew not of your nature" and "My patience for your delays wears thin" and "There are only two options. Surrender yourself for proper trial, or bring your army to suffer the Light's judgment."

There was a strange sense of honor to this man, one Perrin had seen hinted at when he'd met the man, but could sense even more through the letters. But who was he? He signed each letter only "Lord Captain Commander of the Children of the Light."

Perrin moved out onto the roadway. Where was Hopper?

Perrin took off at a brisk run. After a few moments, he moved off onto the grass. The earth was so soft, each step seemed to spring his foot back up into the air.

He reached out and thought he sensed something to the south. He ran toward it; he wished to go faster, so he *did*. Trees and hills zipped past.

The wolves were aware of him. It was Oak Dancer's pack, with Boundless, Sparks, Morninglight, and others. Perrin could feel them sending to one another, distant whispers of images and scent. Perrin moved faster, feeling the wind become a roar around him.

The wolves began to move away farther south. *Wait!* he sent. *I must meet with you!*

They returned only amusement. Suddenly, they were heading east, and he pulled to a stop, then turned. He ran as quickly as he knew how, but when he got near, they were suddenly elsewhere. They'd shifted, vanishing from the south and appearing north of him.

Perrin growled, and suddenly he was on all fours. His fur blew, his mouth open as he dashed to the north, drinking in the hissing wind. But the wolves stayed ahead, distant.

He howled. They sent back taunts.

He pushed himself faster, leaping from hilltop to hilltop, bounding over trees, the ground a blur. In moments, the Mountains of Mist sprang up to his left, and he passed along them in a rush.

The wolves turned east. Why couldn't he catch them? He could smell them ahead. Young Bull howled at them, but got no response.

Do not come too strongly, Young Bull.

Young Bull pulled to a halt and the world lurched around him. The main pack continued on to the east, but Hopper sat on his haunches beside a large curving stream. Young Bull had been here before; it was near the den of his sires. He had traveled along the river itself on the back of one of the humans' floating trees. He—

No . . . no . . . remember Faile!

His fur became clothing and he found himself on hands and knees. He glared at Hopper. "Why did you run away?" Perrin demanded.

You wish to learn, Hopper sent. *You grow more skilled. Faster. You stretch your legs and run. This is good.*

Perrin looked back the way he had come, thinking of his speed. He'd bounded from hilltop to hilltop. It had been wonderful. "But I had to become the wolf to do that," Perrin said. "And that threatened to make me here 'too strongly.' What use is training if it makes me do things you've forbidden?"

You are quick to blame, Young Bull. A young wolf howling and yapping outside the den, making a racket. *This is not a thing of wolves.*

Hopper was gone in an eyeblink.

Perrin growled, looking eastward, where he sensed the wolves. He took off after them, going more cautiously. He couldn't afford to let the wolf consume him. He'd end up like Noam, trapped in a cage, his humanity gone. Why would Hopper encourage him to that?

This is not a thing of wolves. Had he meant the accusations, or had he meant what was happening to Perrin?

The others all knew to end the hunt, Young Bull, Hopper sent from a distance. *Only you had to be stopped.*

Perrin froze, pulling to a halt on the bank of the river. The hunt for the white stag. Hopper was there, suddenly, beside the river with him.

"This started when I began to sense the wolves," Perrin sent. "The first time I lost control of myself was with those Whitecloaks."

Hopper lay down, resting his head on his paws. *You often are here too strongly,* the wolf sent. *It is what you do.*

Hopper had told him that, off and on, since he'd known the wolf and the wolf dream. But suddenly, Perrin saw a new meaning to it. It was about coming to the wolf dream, but it was also about Perrin himself.

He'd begun to blame the wolves for what he did, the way he was when fighting, the way he'd become when searching for Faile. But were the wolves the cause of that? Or was it some part of him? Was it possible that that was what caused him to become a wolfbrother in the first place?

"Is it possible," Perrin said, "to run on four legs, but not come here too strongly?"

Of course it is, Hopper sent, laughing after the way of wolves—as if what Perrin had discovered was the most obvious thing in the world. Maybe it was.

Perhaps he wasn't like the wolves because he was a

wolfbrother. Perhaps he was a wolfbrother because he was like the wolves. He didn't need to control them. He needed to control himself.

"The pack," Perrin said. "How do I catch them? Move more quickly?"

That is one way. Another is to be *where you want.*

Perrin frowned. Then he closed his eyes and used the direction the wolves were running to guess where they would be. Something *shifted.*

When he opened his eyes, he was standing on a sandy hillside, tufts of long-bladed grass peeking out of the soil. An enormous mountain with a broken tip—shattered as if it had been slapped by the hand of a giant—rose to his right.

A pack of wolves burst out of the forest. Many of them were laughing. Young Bull, hunting when he should seek the end! Young Bull, seeking the end when he should enjoy the hunt! He smiled, trying to feel good natured about the laughter, though in truth he felt much as he had on the day that his cousin Wil had planted a bucket of wet feathers to drop on Perrin.

Something fluttered in the air. A chicken feather. Wet around the edges. Perrin started, realizing that they were spread around him on the ground. As he blinked, they vanished. The wolves smelled greatly amused, sending images of Young Bull dusted with feathers.

Get lost in dreams here, Young Bull, Hopper sent, *and those dreams become this dream.*

Perrin scratched his beard, fighting down his embarrassment. He'd experienced before the unpredictable nature of the wolf dream. "Hopper," he said, turning to the wolf. "How much could I change about my surroundings, if I wanted?"

If you wanted? Hopper said. *It's not about what you want, Young Bull. It's about what you need. What you know.*

Perrin frowned. Sometimes the wolf's meanings still confused him.

Suddenly, the other wolves in the group turned—as if one—and looked to the southwest. They vanished.

They went here. Hopper sent an image of a distant wooded hollow. The wolf prepared to follow.

"Hopper!" Perrin said, stepping forward. "How did you know? Where they went? Did they tell you?"

No. But I can follow.

"How?" Perrin said.

It is a thing I've always known, Hopper sent. *Like walking. Or jumping.*

"Yes, but *how?*"

The wolf smelled confused. *It is a scent,* he finally replied, though "scent" was much more complex than that. It was a feeling, an impression, and a smell all in one.

"Go somewhere," Perrin said. "Let me try to follow."

Hopper vanished. Perrin walked up to where the wolf had been.

Smell it, Hopper sent distantly. He was near enough to give a sending. By reflex, Perrin reached out. He found dozens of wolves. In fact, he was amazed by how many of them were here, on the slopes of Dragonmount. Perrin had never felt so many gathered in one place before. Why were they here? And did the sky look more stormy in this place than it had in other areas of the wolf dream?

He couldn't sense Hopper; the wolf had closed himself off, somehow, making Perrin unable to place where he was. Perrin settled down. *Smell it,* Hopper had sent. Smell it how? Perrin closed his eyes and let his nose carry the scents of the area to him. Pine cones and sap, quills and leaves, leatherleaf and hemlock.

And . . . something else. Yes, he *could* smell something. A distant, lingering scent that seemed out of place. Many of the scents were the same—the same fecund sense of nature, the same wealth of trees. But those were mixed with the scents of moss and of wet stone. The air was different. Pollen and flowers.

Perrin squeezed his eyes tight, breathing in deeply. Somehow, he built a picture in his mind from those scents. The process was not unlike the way a wolf sending translated into words.

There, he thought. Something *shifted.*

He opened his eyes. He was sitting on a stone outcropping amid pines; he was on the side of Dragonmount, several hours' hike up from where he had been. The stone outcropping was covered in lichen, and it jutted out over the trees spreading below. A patch of violet springbreath grew here, where sunlight could reach the blossoms. It was good to see flowers that weren't wilted or dying, if only in the wolf dream.

Come, Hopper sent. *Follow.*

And he was gone.

Perrin closed his eyes, breathing in. The process was easier this time. Oak and grass, mud and humidity. It seemed each place had its own specific scent.

Perrin *shifted,* then opened his eyes. He crouched in a field near the Jehannah Road. This was where Oak Dancer's pack had gone earlier, and Hopper moved about the meadow, smelling curious. The pack had moved on, but they were still close.

"Can I always do that?" Perrin asked Hopper. "Smell where a wolf went in the dream?"

Anyone can, Hopper said. *If they can smell as a wolf does.* He grinned.

Perrin nodded thoughtfully.

Hopper loped back across the meadow toward him. *We must practice, Young Bull. You are still a cub with short legs and soft fur. We—*

Hopper froze suddenly.

"What?" Perrin asked.

A wolf suddenly howled in pain. Perrin spun. It was Morninglight. The howl cut off, and the wolf's mind winked out, vanishing.

Hopper growled, his scents panicked, angry, and sorrowful.

"What was that?" Perrin demanded.

We are hunted. Go, Young Bull! We must go.

The minds of the other members of the pack leaped away. Perrin growled. When a wolf died in the wolf dream, it was forever. No rebirth, no running with nose to the wind. Only one thing hunted the spirits of the wolves.

Slayer.

Young Bull! Hopper sent. *We must go!*

Perrin continued to growl. Morninglight had sent one last burst of surprise and pain, her last vision of the world. Perrin formed an image from that jumble. Then closed his eyes.

Young Bull! No! He—

Shift. Perrin snapped his eyes open to find himself in a small glade near where—in the real world—his people made camp. A muscular, tanned man with dark hair and blue eyes squatted in the center of the glade, a wolf's corpse at his feet. Slayer was a thick-armed man, and his scent was faintly inhuman, like a man mixed with stone. He wore dark clothing; leather and black wool. As Perrin watched, Slayer began to skin the corpse.

Perrin charged forward. Slayer looked up in surprise. He resembled Lan in an almost eerie fashion, his hard face all angles and sharp lines. Perrin roared, hammer suddenly in his hands.

Slayer vanished in a blink of an eye, and Perrin's hammer passed through empty air. Perrin breathed deeply. The scents were there! Brine, and wood, wet with water. Seagulls and their droppings. Perrin used his newfound skill to hurl himself at that distant location.

Shift.

Perrin appeared on an empty dock in a city he didn't recognize. Slayer stood nearby, inspecting his bow.

Perrin attacked. Slayer brought his head up, eyes widening, his scent growing amazed. He raised the bow to block, but Perrin's swing shattered it.

With a roar, Perrin pulled his weapon back and swung again, this time for Slayer's head. Oddly, Slayer smiled, dark eyes glittering with amusement. He smelled eager, suddenly. Eager to kill. A sword appeared in his raised hand, and he twisted it to block Perrin's blow.

The hammer bounced off too hard, as if it had hit stone. Perrin stumbled, and Slayer reached out, placing a hand against Perrin's shoulder. He shoved.

His strength was *immense.* The shove tossed Perrin backward to the dock, but the wood disappeared as he hit. Perrin passed through empty air and splashed into the water beneath. His bellow became a gurgle; dark liquid surrounded him.

He struggled to swim upward, dropping his hammer, but found that the surface inexplicably became ice. Ropes snaked up from the depths, whipping up around Perrin's arms, yanking him downward. Through the frozen surface above, he could see a shadow moving. Slayer, raising his re-formed bow.

The ice vanished and the water parted. Water streamed

off Perrin, and he found himself staring up at an arrow pointed directly at his heart.

Slayer released.

Perrin willed himself away.

Shift. He gasped, hitting the stone outcropping where he had been with Hopper. Perrin fell to his knees, seawater streaming from his body. He sputtered, wiping his face, heart pounding.

Hopper appeared beside him, panting, his scent angry. *Foolish cub! Stupid cub! Chase down a lion when you're barely weaned?*

Perrin shivered and sat up. Would Slayer follow? Could he? As minutes stretched and nobody appeared, Perrin began to relax. The exchange with Slayer had happened so quickly that it felt like a blur. That strength . . . it was more than any man could have. And the ice, the ropes . . .

"He changed things," Perrin said. "Made the dock vanish beneath me, created ropes to bind me, pushed the water back so that he could get a clear shot at me."

He is a lion. He kills. Dangerous.

"I need to learn. I must face him, Hopper."

You are too young. These things are beyond you.

"Too young?" Perrin said, standing. "Hopper, the Last Hunt is nearly upon us!"

Hopper lay down, head on paws.

"You always tell me that I'm too young," Perrin said. "Or that I don't know what I'm doing. Well, what is the point of teaching me, if not to show me how to fight men like Slayer?"

We will see, Hopper sent. *For tonight, you will go. We are done.*

Perrin sensed a mournful cast to the sending, and also a finality. Tonight, Oak Dancer's pack and Hopper would grieve for Morninglight.

Sighing, Perrin sat with his legs crossed. He concentrated, and managed to imitate the things that Hopper had done in tossing him from the dream.

It faded around him.

He woke on the pallet in his darkened tent, Faile snuggled up beside him.

Perrin lay for a time, staring up at the canvas. The darkness reminded him of the tempestuous sky in the wolf dream. Sleep seemed as far off as Caemlyn. Eventually he rose—carefully extricating himself from Faile—and pulled on his trousers and shirt.

The camp was dark outside, but there was enough light for his eyes. He nodded to Kenly Maerin and Jaim Dawtry, the Two Rivers men who guarded his tent tonight.

"What's the time?" he asked one of them.

"After midnight, Lord Perrin," Jaim said.

Perrin grunted. Distant lightning lit the landscape. He walked off, and the men started to follow. "I'll be fine without guards," he told them. "Watch over my tent—Lady Faile still sleeps."

His tent was near the edge of camp. He liked that; it gave him a little more sense of seclusion, nestled near the hillside at the western side of the camp. Though it was late, he passed Gaul sharpening his spear near a fallen log. The tall Stone Dog stood up and began to follow, and Perrin didn't dismiss him. Gaul felt he hadn't been fulfilling his self-appointed duty of watching after Perrin lately, and had stepped up his efforts. Perrin thought he really just wanted an excuse to stay away from his own tent and the pair of *gai'shain* women who had taken up residence there.

Gaul kept his distance, and Perrin was glad. Was this how all leaders felt? No wonder so many nations ended up at war with one another—their leaders never had any time to think by themselves, and probably attacked to get people to stop pestering them!

A short distance away, he entered a stand of trees with a small pile of logs. Denton—his serving man until they got Lamgwin back—had frowned when Perrin had asked for them. Once a minor lord of Cairhien, Denton had refused to return to his station. He thought of himself as a servant now, and would not let anyone convince him otherwise.

There was an axe. Not the deadly half-moon blade he had once carried to battle, but a sturdy woodsman's axe with a fine steel head and a haft smoothed by the sweaty hands of workers. Perrin rolled up his sleeves, then spat on his hands and picked up the axe. It felt good to hold the worked wood in his hands. He raised it to his shoulder, stood the first log in front of him, then stepped back and swung.

He hit the log straight on, splinters flipping into the dark night air, the log falling into two pieces. He split one of the halves next. Gaul took a seat beside a tree, getting out a spear and continuing to sharpen its head. The rasping of metal against metal accompanied Perrin's *thunk* of axe against wood.

It felt good. Why was it that his mind worked so much better when he was doing something? Loial spoke much of sitting and thinking. Perrin didn't think he himself could figure anything out that way.

He split another log, the axe cutting clear. Was it really true? Could his own nature be to blame for the way he acted, not the wolves? He'd never acted like that back in the Two Rivers.

He split another log. *I always was good at concentrating my attention.* That was part of what had impressed Master Luhhan. Give Perrin a project, and he'd keep working on it until he was done.

He split the halves of that log.

Maybe the changes in him were a result of encountering the outside world. He'd blamed the wolves for many things, and he had placed unnatural demands on Hopper. Wolves weren't stupid or simple, but they did not care about things that humans did. It must have been very hard for Hopper to teach in a way that Perrin would understand.

What did the wolf owe him? Hopper had died during that fateful night, so long ago. The night when Perrin had first killed a man, the night Perrin had first lost control of himself in a battle. Hopper didn't owe Perrin anything, but he had saved Perrin on several occasions—in fact, Perrin realized that Hopper's intervention had helped to keep him from losing himself as a wolf.

He swung at a log, a glancing blow that knocked it to the side. He repositioned and continued, Gaul's quiet sharpening soothing him. He split it.

Perrin grew caught up in what he was doing, maybe too much. That was true.

But at the same time, if a man wanted to get anything done, he had to work on one project until it was complete. Perrin had known men who never seemed to finish anything, and their farms were a mess. He couldn't live like that.

There had to be a balance. Perrin had claimed he had

been pulled into a world filled with problems much larger than he was. He had claimed he was a simple man.

What if he was wrong? What if he was a complex man who had once happened to live a simple life? After all, if he was so simple, why had he fallen in love with such a complicated woman?

The split logs were piling up. Perrin bent down, gathering up quarters, their grain rough against his fingers. Callused fingers; he would never be a lord like those milk-fed creatures from Cairhien. But there were other kinds of lords, men like Faile's own father. Or men like Lan, who seemed more weapon than man.

Perrin stacked the wood. He enjoyed leading the wolves in his dream, but wolves didn't expect you to protect them, or to provide for them, or to make laws for them. They didn't cry to you when their loved ones died beneath your command.

It wasn't the leadership that worried him. It was all the things that came with it.

He could smell Elyas approaching. With his loamy, natural earthen scent he smelled like a wolf. Almost.

"You're up late," Elyas said, stepping up. Perrin heard Gaul rustling, slipping his spear back into its place on his bowcase, then withdrawing with the silence of a sparrow streaking off into the sky. He would stay close, but would not listen in.

Perrin looked up at the dark sky, resting the axe on his shoulder. "Sometimes I feel more awake at night than during the day."

Elyas smiled. Perrin didn't see it, but he could smell the amusement.

"Did you ever try to avoid it, Elyas?" Perrin asked. "Ignore their voices, pretend that nothing about you had changed?"

"I did," Elyas said. He had a soft low voice, one that somehow suggested the earth in motion. Distant rumbles. "I wanted to, but then the Aes Sedai wanted to gentle me. I had to flee."

"Do you miss your old life?"

Elyas shrugged—Perrin could hear the motion, the clothing scraping against itself. "No Warder wants to abandon his duty. Sometimes, other things are more important.

Or . . . well, maybe they are just more *demanding*. I don't regret my choices."

"I can't leave, Elyas. I *won't*."

"I left my life for the wolves. That doesn't mean you have to."

"Noam had to," Perrin said.

"Did he *have* to?" Elyas said.

"It consumed him. He stopped being human."

He caught a scent of worry. Elyas had no answers.

"Do you ever visit wolves in your dreams, Elyas?" Perrin asked. "A place where dead wolves run and live again?"

Elyas turned, eyeing him. "That place is dangerous, Perrin. It's another world, although tied to this one somehow. Legends say the Aes Sedai of old could go there."

"And other people, too," Perrin said, thinking of Slayer.

"Be careful in the dream. I stay away from it." His scent was wary.

"Do you ever have trouble?" Perrin asked. "Separating yourself from the wolf?"

"I used to."

"But not any longer?"

"I found a balance," Elyas said.

"How?"

The older man fell still for a moment. "I wish I knew. It was just something I learned, Perrin. Something you'll have to learn."

Or end up like Noam. Perrin met Elyas' golden eyes, then nodded. "Thank you."

"For the advice?"

"No," Perrin said. "For coming back. For showing me that one of us, at least, can live with the wolves and not lose himself."

"It's nothing," Elyas said. "I had forgotten that it could be nice to be around people for a change. I don't know how long I can stay, though. The Last Hunt is almost here."

Perrin looked up at the sky again. "That it is. Pass the word on to Tam and the others for me. I've made my decision. The Whitecloaks have picked a place to fight. I've decided to go ahead and meet them tomorrow."

"All right," Elyas said. "You don't smell like you want to do it, though."

"It needs to be done," Perrin said. "And that's that." Everyone wanted him to be a lord. Well, this was the sort of thing lords did. Made decisions that nobody wanted to make.

It would still sicken him to give the order. He'd seen a vision of those wolves running sheep toward a beast. It seemed to him that maybe that was what he was doing, running the Whitecloaks toward destruction. They certainly wore the color of sheep's wool.

But what to make of the vision of Faile and the others, approaching a cliff? Elyas moved off, leaving Perrin with the axe still on his shoulder. He felt as if he hadn't been chopping logs, but bodies.

CHAPTER
25

Return to Bandar Eban

Rand and Min did not announce themselves as
they came to Bandar Eban. They stepped through
the gateway into a small alley, guarded by two
Maidens—Lerian and Heidia—along with Naeff, the tall,
square-chinned Asha'man.

The Maidens scouted to the end of the alleyway, peer-
ing suspiciously at the city. Rand stepped forward and laid
a hand on Heidia's shoulder, calming the slender woman,
who seemed anxious at Rand's guard being so few. He wore
his brown cloak.

Overhead, the clouds broke, melting away above the city
in response to Rand's arrival. Min looked upward, feeling
the warmth shine on her face. The alley smelled terrible—of
refuse and waste—but a warm breeze blew through, carrying the stenches away.

"My Lord Dragon," Naeff said. "I don't like this. You
should have greater protection. Let us return and gather—"

"It will be fine, Naeff," Rand said. He turned to Min and
held out his hand.

She took it, joining him. Naeff and the Maidens had orders to follow behind at a distance; they would draw attention.

As Min and Rand stepped out onto one of the Domani
capital's many boardwalks, she raised a hand to her mouth.
It had only been a short time since Rand's departure. How
had the city changed so quickly?

The street was full of sickly, dirty people, crowded
alongside walls, huddled in blankets. There wasn't room to
move on the boardwalks; Min and Rand had to step down

into the mud to continue. People coughed and moaned, and she realized the stenches weren't confined to the alley. The entire *city* seemed to stink. Once, banners had hung from many of these buildings, but they'd been pulled down and ripped apart for blankets or fuel.

Most of the buildings had broken windows, with refugees clogging the doorways and floors inside. As Min and Rand walked, the people around them turned to watch. Some looked delirious. Others looked hungry. And dangerous. Many were Domani, but there seemed to be as many paler-skinned people. Refugees from Almoth Plain or Saldaea, perhaps. Min loosened a knife in her sleeve as they passed a group of young toughs lounging at an alleyway's mouth. Perhaps Naeff had been right. This didn't feel safe.

"I walked through Ebou Dar like this," Rand said softly. Suddenly, she was aware of his pain. A crushing guilt, more hurtful than the wounds in his side. "That was part of what made me change. The people in Ebou Dar were happy and well-fed. They didn't look like these. The Seanchan rule better than I."

"Rand, you aren't responsible for this," Min said. "You weren't here to . . ."

His pain increased, and she realized she'd said the wrong thing. "Yes," he replied softly, "I wasn't here. I *abandoned* this city when I saw that I could not use it as the tool I wished it to be. I forgot, Min. I forgot what this was all about. Tam was so very right. A man must know why he is fighting."

Rand had sent his father—along with one of the Asha'man—to the Two Rivers to prepare and gather them for the Last Battle.

Rand stumbled as he walked, suddenly looking very tired. He sat down on a nearby box. A copper-skinned urchin watched him keenly from a nearby doorway. Across the street, a roadway branched off the main thoroughfare. That one wasn't clogged with people; brutish-looking men with cudgels stood at its mouth.

"They break into gangs," Rand said softly, shoulders bowing. "The rich hire the strong to protect them, to fight away those who come seeking their wealth. But it's not a wealth of gold or jewelry. It's about food, now."

"Rand," she said, going to one knee beside him. "You can't—"

"I know I must go on," Rand said, "but it hurts to know the things that I've done, Min. By turning myself to steel, I pushed out all of these emotions. By allowing myself to care again, to laugh again, I've had to open myself to my failures, too."

"Rand, I see sunlight around you."

He looked up at her, then glanced at the sky.

"Not that sunlight," Min whispered. "A viewing. I see dark clouds, pushed away by the sunlight's warmth. I see you, a brilliant white sword held in your hand, wielded against one of black, held by a faceless darkness. I see trees, growing green again, bearing fruit. I see a field, the crops healthy and full." She hesitated. "I see the Two Rivers, Rand. I see an inn there with the mark of the Dragon's Fang inlaid on its door. No longer a symbol of darkness or hate. A sign of victory and hope."

He looked to her.

Min caught something from the corner of her eye. She turned toward the people sitting on the street, and gaped. Every single one had an image above them. It was remarkable to see so many viewings, all at once, flaring to light above the heads of the sickly, the weak, and the abandoned.

"I see a silver axe above that man's head," she said, pointing to a bearded beggar, who lay against a wall, his chin down against his chest. "He will be a leader in the Last Battle. That woman there—the one sulking in the shadows—she will be trained by the White Tower and become Aes Sedai. I can see the Flame of Tar Valon beside her, and I know what it means. That man over there who looks like a simple street tough? He will save her life. I know he doesn't look like it, but he will fight. All of them will. I can see it!"

She looked at Rand and took his hand. "You will be strong, Rand. You'll do this. You'll lead them. I know it."

"You saw that?" he asked. "In a viewing?"

She shook her head. "I don't need to. I believe in you."

"I almost killed you," he whispered. "When you look at me, you see a murderer. You feel my hand at your throat."

"What? Of course I don't! Rand, meet my eyes. You can sense me through the bond. Do you feel a *sliver* of hesitation or fear from me?"

He searched her eyes with his own, so deep. She didn't back down. She could meet the eyes of this sheepherder.

He sat up straighter. "Oh, Min. What would I do without you?"

She snorted. "You have kings and Aiel chiefs following you. Aes Sedai, Asha'man, and *ta'veren*. I'm certain you'd get along."

"No," Rand said. "You're more vital than them all. You remind me who I am. Besides, you think more clearly than most of those who call themselves my counselors. You could be a queen, if you wished it."

"All I wish for is you, stupid looby."

"Thank you." He hesitated. "Though I could manage without quite so much name calling."

"Life's tough, isn't it?"

He smiled. Then he stood, taking a deep breath. His guilt was still there, but he managed it now, as he managed the pain. Nearby, the refugees perked up. Rand turned toward the bearded wretch Min had indicated earlier; the man sat with his feet in the mud.

"You," the man said to Rand, "you're him. The Dragon Reborn."

"Yes," Rand said. "You were a soldier?"

"I . . ." The man's eyes grew distant. "Another life. I was in the King's Guard, before he was taken, before we were seized by Lady Chadmar, then disbanded." The fatigue seemed to bleed from his eyes as he thought of earlier days.

"Excellent," Rand said. "We need to restore this city, Captain."

"Captain?" the man said. "But I . . ." He cocked his head. Then he stood up and brushed himself off. He suddenly had a faintly military air about him, despite the ripped clothing and the snarled beard. "Well, I suppose you're right. But I don't think it'll be easy. The people are starving."

"I will see to that," Rand said. "I need you to gather your soldiers."

"I don't see many of the other lads here. . . . No, wait. There's Votabek and Redbord." He waved to a pair of the toughs Min had noticed earlier. They hesitated, then walked over.

"Durnham?" one of them asked. "What's this?"

"It's time for the lawlessness in the city to end," Durnham said. "We're going to organize things, clean it up. The Lord Dragon has returned."

One of them spat to the side. He was a burly man with curly black hair, Domani skin, and a thin mustache. "Burn him. He left us. I—" He cut off as he saw Rand.

"I'm sorry," Rand said, meeting the man's eyes. "I failed you. I will not do so again."

The man glanced at his companion, who shrugged. "Lain's never going to pay us. Might as well see what we can do here."

"Naeff," Rand called, waving the Asha'man forward. He and the Maidens stepped up from where they had been watching. "Make a gateway back to the Stone. I want weapons, armor and uniforms."

"I'll do it immediately," Naeff said. "We'll have soldiers bring them—"

"No," Rand said. "Pass the supplies through, into this building here. I'll clear a place for the gateway inside it. But no soldiers are to come." Rand raised his eyes, looking at the street. "Bandar Eban has suffered enough beneath the hands of outsiders. Today, she will not know the hand of a conqueror."

Min stepped back, and watched with wonder. The three soldiers hastened into the building and cleared out the urchins. When Rand saw them, he asked them to be messengers to run errands. They responded. Everyone responded to Rand, when they took time to look at him.

Perhaps another might have thought it some form of Compulsion, but Min saw their faces change, saw hope return as a glimmer in their eyes. They saw something about Rand they could trust. Something, at least, they hoped they could trust.

The three soldiers sent a few of the messenger boys and girls to fetch other former soldiers. Naeff made his gateway. In minutes, the original three soldiers stepped out of the building, wearing silvery breastplates and simple, clean clothing of green. The men had combed their beards and hair and found some water to wash their faces As quickly as that, they stopped looking like beggars and became soldiers. A bit smelly, but soldiers nonetheless.

The woman Min had noted earlier—the one she was certain could learn to channel—came over to speak with Rand. After a bit, she nodded, and soon had gathered women and men to fill buckets from the well. Min frowned at that until they started wiping clean the faces and hands of those who approached.

People began to gather around. Some curious, others hostile, still others merely caught in the flow. The woman and her team began sorting through them and setting them to work. Some to seek out the wounded or sickly, others to take up swords and uniforms. Another woman began interrogating the urchins, discovering where their parents were, if they had any.

Min sat down on the box that Rand had been sitting on. Within the hour, he had a group of soldiers five hundred strong, led by Captain Durnham and his two lieutenants. Many of those five hundred kept glancing down at their clean clothing and silvery breastplates as if amazed.

Rand spoke with many of them, apologizing directly. As he was speaking to one woman, the crowd behind began to shuffle and move. Rand turned to see an aged man approaching, his skin broken by terrible lesions. The crowd kept its distance.

"Naeff," Rand called.

"My Lord?"

"Bring the Aes Sedai through," Rand said. "There are people who require Healing." The woman who had gotten people to fill water buckets led the old man to one side.

"My Lord," Captain Durnham said, marching up. Min blinked. The man had found a razor somewhere and shaved off his beard, revealing a strong chin. He'd left a Domani mustache. Four men followed him as a guard.

"We're going to need more room, my Lord," Durnham said. "That building you chose is overflowing, and more and more are coming, filling the street."

"What do you suggest?" Rand asked.

"The docks," Durnham replied. "They are held by one of the city merchants. I'll wager we can find some near-empty warehouses to use. Those once held food but . . . well, there isn't any left."

"And the merchant who holds the place?" Rand asked.

"My Lord," Captain Durnham said, "nothing you can't deal with."

Rand smiled, then waved for Durnham to lead the way. Rand held his hand out to Min.

"Rand," she said, joining him, "they'll need food."

"Yes," he agreed. He looked southward, toward the nearby docks. "We'll find it there."

"Won't it already have been eaten?"

Rand didn't reply. They joined the newly formed city guard, walking at the head of a force in green and silver. Behind them trailed a growing throng of hopeful refugees.

The enormous docks of Bandar Eban were some of the most impressive in the world. They lay in a half-moon at the base of the city. Min was surprised to see how many ships were there, most of them Sea Folk vessels.

That's right, Min thought. *Rand had them bring food to the city.* But it had spoiled. As Rand had left the city, he'd gotten word that all of the food on those ships had fallen to the Dark One's touch.

Someone had set up blockades at the base of the roadway. Other roads to the docks looked similarly inhibited. Uniformed soldiers peeked out nervously from behind the barricade as Rand's force walked up.

"Stop right there!" a voice called. "We don't—"

Rand lifted his hand, then waved it casually. The barricade—formed of furniture and planks—rumbled, then slid to the side with a grinding of wood. Men cried out from behind, scrambling away.

Rand left the barricade slumped at the side of the road. He stepped forward, and Min could sense peace inside of him. A ragged-looking group of men with cudgels stood in the road, eyes wide. Rand picked one at the front. "Who is it that blocks my people from these docks and seeks to hoard food for himself? I would . . . speak with this person."

"My Lord Dragon?" a surprised voice asked.

Min glanced to the side. A tall, lean man in a red Domani coat hustled toward them from the docks. His shirt had once been fine and ruffled, but was now wrinkled and unkempt. He looked exhausted.

What was his name? Min thought. *Iralin. That's it. Master of the docks.*

"Iralin?" Rand asked. "What is going on here? What have you done?"

"What have *I* done?" the man demanded. "I've been trying to keep everyone from rushing those ships for the spoiled food! Anyone who eats it gets sick and dies. The people won't listen. Several groups tried to storm the docks for the food, so I decided not to let them kill themselves eating it."

The man's voice had never been that angry before. Min remembered him as peaceable.

"Lady Chadmar fled an hour after you left," Iralin continued. "The other members of the Council of Merchants ran within the day. Those burning Sea Folk claim they won't sail away until they've unloaded their wares—or until I give them payment to do something else. So I've been waiting for the city to starve itself, eat that food and die, or go up in another riot of flame and death. *That's* what I've been doing here. What have *you* been doing, Lord Dragon?"

Rand closed his eyes and sighed. He did not apologize to Iralin as he had the others; perhaps he saw that it would not have meant anything.

Min glared at Iralin. "He has weights upon his shoulders, merchant. He cannot watch over each and every—"

"It is all right, Min," Rand said, laying his hand on her arm and opening his eyes. "It is no more than I deserve. Iralin. Before I left the city, you told me that the food on those ships had spoiled. Did you check every barrel and sack?"

"I checked enough," Iralin said, still hostile. "If you open a hundred sacks and you find the same thing in every one, you figure out the pattern. My wife has been trying to figure out a safe method of sifting the rotted grain from the safe grain. If there's any safe grain to be had."

Rand began walking toward the ships. Iralin followed, looking confused, perhaps because Rand hadn't yelled at him. Min joined them. Rand approached a Sea Folk vessel sitting low in the water, moored by ropes. A group of Sea Folk lounged atop it.

"I would speak with your Sailmistress," Rand called.

"I am she," said one of the Sea Folk, a woman with white in her straight black hair and a pattern of tattoos across her right hand. "Milis din Shalada Three Stars."

"I made a deal," Rand called up, "for food to be delivered here."

"That one doesn't want it delivered," Milis said, nodding to Iralin. "He won't let us unload; says that if we do, he'll have his archers loose on us."

"I wouldn't be able to hold the people back," Iralin said. "I've had to spread rumors in town that the Sea Folk are holding the food hostage."

"You see what we suffer for you?" Milis said to Rand. "I begin to wonder about our Bargain with you, Rand al'Thor."

"Do you deny that I am the Coramoor?" Rand asked, meeting her eyes. She seemed to have trouble looking away from him.

"No," Milis said. "No, I guess that I do not. You will want to board the *Whitecap*, I suppose."

"If I may."

"Up with you, then," she said.

Once the gangplank was in place, Rand strode up it, followed by Min with Naeff and the two Maidens. After a moment, Iralin came, too, followed by the captain and some of his soldiers.

Milis led them to the center of the deck, where a hatch and ladder led down to the ship's hold. Rand climbed down first, moving awkwardly, being one-handed. Min followed.

Beneath, light peeked through slots in the deck, illuminating sack upon sack of grain. The air smelled dusty and thick.

"We'll be glad to have this cargo gone," Milis said softly, coming down next. "It's been killing the rats."

"I would think you'd appreciate that," Min said.

"A ship without rats is like an ocean without storms," Milis said. "We complain about both, but my crew mutters every time they find one of the vermin dead."

There were several open sacks of grain nearby, turned on their sides, spilling dark contents across the floor. Iralin had spoken of trying to sift the bad from the good, but Min didn't see any good. Just shriveled, discolored grains.

Rand stared at the open sacks as Iralin came down into the hold. Captain Durnham shuffled down the ladder last with his men.

"Nothing stays good any longer," Iralin said. "It's not just this grain. People brought winter stores from the farms with them. They're all gone. We're going to die, and that's that. We won't *reach* the bloody Last Battle. We—"

"Peace, Iralin," Rand said softly. "It is not so bad as you think." He stepped forward and yanked free the tie on the top of a sack. It fell to the side, and golden barley spilled from it across the floor of the hold, not a single speck of darkness on it. The barley looked as if it had just been harvested, each grain plump and full.

Milis gasped. "What did you do to it?"

"Nothing," Rand said. "You merely opened the wrong sacks. The rest are all good."

"Merely . . ." Iralin said. "We *happened* to open the *exact* number of bad sacks without reaching one of the good ones? That's ridiculous."

"Not ridiculous," Rand said, laying his hand Iralin's shoulder. "Simply implausible. You did well here, Iralin. I'm sorry to have left you in such a predicament. I'm naming you to the Merchant Council."

Iralin gaped.

To the side, Captain Durnham pulled open another sack. "This one's good."

"So's this one," said one of his men.

"Potatoes here," another soldier said from beside a barrel. "Look as good as any I've had. Better than most, actually. Not dried up, like you'd expect from winter leftovers."

"Spread the word," Rand said to the soldiers. "Gather your men to set up distribution in one of the warehouses. I want this grain well guarded; Iralin was wise to worry that the people would rush the docks. Don't give out uncooked grain—that will turn people to hoarding and bartering with it. We'll need cauldrons and fires to cook some of it. Move the rest to stores. Hurry, now."

"Yes, sir!" Captain Durnham said.

"The people I've gathered so far will help," Rand said. "They won't steal the grain; we can trust them. Have them unload the ships and burn the bad grain. There should be thousands of sacks that are still good."

Rand looked to Min. "Come. I need to organize the Aes Sedai for Healing." He hesitated, looking at the stunned Iralin. "Lord Iralin, you are steward of the city for now, and Durnham is your commander. You will soon have sufficient troops to restore order."

"Steward of the city . . ." Iralin said. "Can you *do* that?"

Rand smiled. "Somebody must. Hurry about your work;

there is much to do. I can only remain here long enough for you to make things stable. A day or so."

Rand turned to climb up the ladder.

"A day?" Iralin said, still standing in the hold with Min. "To get things stable? We can't possibly do it in that time. Can we?"

"I think you'll be surprised by him, Lord Iralin," Min said, gripping the ladder and starting to climb. "I am, each day."

CHAPTER
26

Parley

Perrin rode Stepper out of camp, leading a large army. They didn't fly the wolfhead banner. So far as he knew, his order to burn the things had been followed. He was less certain of that decision now.

There was an odd scent in the air. A staleness. Like the inside of a room that had been left locked up for years. Stepper trotted onto the Jehannah Road. Grady and Neald flanked Perrin directly, and they smelled eager.

"Neald, you sure you're ready?" Perrin asked as he turned the army to the southeast.

"I feel as strong as I ever have, my Lord," Neald answered. "Strong enough to kill some Whitecloaks. I've always wanted a chance to do that."

"Only a fool looks for a chance to kill," Perrin said.

"Er, yes, my Lord," Neald said. "Though, maybe I should mention—"

"No need to speak of that," Grady interrupted.

"What?" Perrin asked.

Grady looked embarrassed. "It's nothing, I'm sure."

"Say it, Grady," Perrin said.

The older man took a deep breath. "We tried to make a gateway this morning to send refugees back, and it didn't work. One time earlier, it happened, too. Weaves fell apart and unraveled on us."

Perrin frowned. "Other weaves work fine?"

"They do," Neald said quickly.

"Like I said, my Lord," Grady said. "I'm sure it will work when we try again. Just not enough practice."

It wasn't likely that they'd need Traveling to retreat from this battle—not with only two Asha'man and so large a force. But it was still disconcerting to lose the chance. It had better not happen with other weaves. He was depending on Grady and Neald to confuse and disrupt the initial Whitecloak charge.

Maybe we should turn back, Perrin thought, but squelched the thought immediately. He didn't like having to make this decision. It made him sick to think of fighting, man against man, when their real enemy was the Dark One. But his hand had been forced.

They continued on, his hammer in its strap at his side. Hopper had implied it was no different from the axe. To the wolf, one weapon was like another.

Mayener Winged Guards rode beside him, red-painted breastplates gleaming, looking like graceful hawks ready to swoop. Alliandre's soldiers, straightforward and determined, rode behind, like boulders poised to crush. Two Rivers longbowmen, like sapling oaks, were nimble yet sturdy. Aiel, like adders with razor teeth. Wise Ones, reluctantly drawn along, uncertain thunderheads boiling with unpredictable energy. He didn't know if they would fight for him.

The rest of his army was less impressive. Thousands of men with a range of experience and age—some mercenaries, some refugees from Malden, some women who had seen the Maidens and *Cha Faile* and insisted on being trained alongside the men. Perrin hadn't stopped them. The Last Battle was coming. Who was he to forbid those who wanted to fight?

He *had* considered forbidding Faile to come today, but he'd known how that would turn out. Instead, he placed her at the back, surrounded by Wise Ones and *Cha Faile*, accompanied by Aes Sedai.

Perrin gripped his reins tighter, listening to the marching feet. Few of the refugees had armor. Arganda had called them light infantry. Perrin had another term for them: "innocents with blades." Why did they follow him? Couldn't they see that they would fall first?

They trusted him. Light burn them, they *all* trusted him! He rested his hand on his hammer, smelling the damp air mixed with fear and excitement. The thunder of hooves and footsteps, reminding him of the dark sky. Thunder with no lightning. Lightning with no thunder.

The battlefield was ahead, a broad green grassland lined on the far end by troops in white. That Whitecloak army wore silver breastplates shined to perfection, their tabards and cloaks a pure white. This grassy plain was a good place to have a battle. It would also be a good place to plant crops.

To understand a thing, you must understand its parts and its purpose.

What had been the purpose of his war axe? To kill. That was why it had been made. That was all it had been good for.

But the hammer was different.

Perrin pulled Stepper up sharply. Beside him, the Asha'man stopped, and the entire column of troops started to pull to a halt. Groups bunched up as they slowed; yelled orders replaced the sounds of marching.

The air was still, the sky overhead dreary. He couldn't smell the grass or the distant trees for the dust in the air and the men sweating in their armor. Horses snorted, a number of them nibbling at the grass. Others shuffled, catching the tension of their riders.

"My Lord?" Grady asked. "What is it?"

The Whitecloak army was already in position with a V formation of riders at the front. They waited, lances upright, ready to be lowered to spill blood.

"The axe only kills," Perrin said. "But the hammer can either create or kill. *That* is the difference."

It made sense to him, suddenly. That was why he'd needed to throw the axe away. He could *choose* not to kill. He would not be pushed into this.

He turned to Gaul, who stood with several Maidens a short distance away. "I want the Aes Sedai and Wise Ones up here now." Perrin hesitated. "Order the Aes Sedai, but *ask* the Wise Ones. Order the Two Rivers men up as well."

Gaul nodded and ran to do as asked. Perrin turned back to the Whitecloaks. For all their faults, the Whitecloaks considered themselves honorable. They wouldn't attack until Perrin was in position.

The cluster of Wise Ones and Aes Sedai joined him at the front. Faile, he noticed, rode with them. Well, he *had* told her to stay with them. He held out a hand to her, inviting her next to him. The Two Rivers men came up on the flank of his force.

"Gaul said you were very polite," Edarra noted to Perrin. "That means you want something from us that we will not want to do."

Perrin smiled. "I want you to help me prevent this battle."

"You do not wish to dance the spears?" Edarra asked. "I have heard some of what these men in white have done in the wetlands. I think they wear white to hide what is dark inside of them."

"They're confused," Perrin said. "Well, they're more than confused. They're Light-cursed frustrating. But we shouldn't be fighting them, not with the Last Battle coming. If we squabble among ourselves, we will lose to the Dark One."

Edarra laughed. "I would like to see someone tell that to the Shaido, Perrin Aybara. Or, rather, I would like to have seen someone suggest that to you when they still held your wife!"

"Well, the Shaido needed killing," he said. "But I don't know if these Whitecloaks do. Maybe they only need a good fright. I want you and the Aes Sedai to blast the ground in front of their army."

"You ask something you should not, Aybara," Seonid said sternly. "We will not take part in your battle." The diminutive Green met his eyes, voice crisp and curt.

"You're not taking part in battle," Perrin said. "You're preventing one."

Seonid frowned. "I'm afraid it would be the same, in this case. If we attack the earth, it would be using the One Power as a weapon. We could hurt those men. I'm sorry."

Perrin ground his teeth, but did not force them. The Wise Ones and Asha'man would probably be enough. He turned to the Two Rivers men. "Tam, tell the men to nock arrows and be ready to launch a volley."

Tam nodded, sending a runner with the order. The Two Rivers men lined up. This was beyond the range of most bows, but a good pull on a Two Rivers longbow could manage it.

Perrin nodded to the Wise Ones, then motioned toward the Asha'man. Before anything else could be said, the ground in front of the Whitecloaks erupted. A rumble shook the meadow, dirt exploding into the air. Grady and Neald moved their horses forward.

The Whitecloaks' horses reared and men shouted in terror. A small group of men at the very front didn't seem disturbed by the explosions, and they kept their horses under control. Those would be the leaders. Indeed, Perrin's eyes could make out the Lord Captain Commander himself sitting there.

Dirt sprayed into the air again, falling to pelt the trench beneath. The Wise Ones wore that look of concentration that came with channeling.

"Can one of you enhance my voice?" Perrin asked.

"I can do it," Grady said. "I saw the M'Hael do it once."

"Good," Perrin said, turning to Tam. "Once the channelers stop, tell the men to give me a couple of long volleys. Try and hit that trench."

A few moments later, the explosions ended. The Two Rivers men drew a volley and loosed it. Thick shafts rose in an arc, and soon the rift bristled with arrows. Perrin watched the Whitecloak army. They had broken ranks, standing in disorder.

A clank of armor matched by hoofbeats announced Arganda's arrival. The First Captain of Ghealdan wore his plumed helm, his eyes hard beneath it. "What was the point of that, if I may ask, Lord Aybara?" He smelled hostile. "You just gave away our advantage! An ambush could have killed thousands and broken their initial charge."

"Yes," Perrin said. Faile still rode at his other side. "And they know it. Look at their lines, Arganda. They're worried. The Whitecloaks are realizing what they'd have to go through to charge us. If I was willing to give them this as a warning burst, what was I holding back?"

"But that was the extent of what we can do," Faile said.

"They don't know that." Perrin grinned. "It would be stupid of us to commit everything we have in a warning blast like that."

Arganda held his tongue, though he obviously was thinking that very thing. He was a soldier to the bone. An axe. There was nothing wrong with that, but Perrin had to be the hammer. When he pointed, men like Arganda killed.

"Grady," Perrin said. "My voice, please? I wouldn't mind if our army could hear what I say, too."

"I can manage that," Grady said.

Perrin took a deep breath, then spoke. "I am Perrin Aybara!" his voice boomed across the plain. "I am friend to the Dragon Reborn, and I serve here at his command. I am marching to the Last Battle. Lord Captain Commander, you demanded I meet with you on your terms before, and I came. I ask you to return the honor here, and meet as I request. If you are determined to kill me before I ride against the Shadow, at least do me the service of giving me one last chance to prevent spilling blood this day!"

He nodded to Grady, and the man released his weave. "Do we have a pavilion we could set up for parley?"

"Back at the camp," Faile said.

"I can try a gateway," Neald said, knuckling his mustache—or, at least, the thin bit of fur on his face that he called a mustache, waxed to points.

"Try it."

He concentrated. Nothing happened. The young man blushed furiously. "Doesn't work. Not Traveling *or* Skimming."

"I see," Perrin said. "Well, let's send a rider back. We should be able to have the tent set up here in minutes. I don't know if they'll agree to meet, but I want to get ready, in case they do. Bring Berelain and Alliandre back as well, and perhaps someone with drinks and the chairs and table from my tent."

The proper orders were given, and a Two Rivers man—Robb Solter—rode off, Maidens trailing after him. The Whitecloaks seemed to be considering his proposition. Good.

Arganda and most of the others spread out to pass the word about what was happening, though they couldn't possibly have missed Perrin's announcement. Everyone seemed to be doing what they should, so Perrin sat back in his saddle to wait.

Faile sidled her horse up to him. She smelled intrigued.

"What?" Perrin asked.

"Something's changed about you. I'm trying to figure out what."

"I'm stalling," Perrin said. "I haven't made any decisions yet. But I don't want to kill these men. Not yet. Not unless I have to."

"They're not going to give any ground, husband," Faile said. "They've already judged you."

"We'll see," he said. He looked up at the sky, thinking of the strange scent and the fact that the Asha'man gateways weren't working. Slayer was prowling this area in the wolf dream and there was that wall of glass. Something felt very wrong on the wind, and his senses itched at him. Be wary. Be prepared.

The hammer could kill or create. He didn't know which situation this was yet. He didn't intend to strike until he did.

Galad sat on the grassy plain that should have been a field of battle, looking at the trench torn in the ground, bristling with hundreds of arrows.

He was prepared for Aes Sedai. An Aes Sedai could not hurt someone unless she or her Warder was in danger, and Galad had given very specific orders to his people *not* to engage—or even go near—Aes Sedai. If the Children saw Aes Sedai, they were to stop and nod their heads, turning their weapons away. If his men showed plainly that they would not harm Aes Sedai, then the sisters should be useless in battle.

Many of the Children did not believe this. They called the stories of the Three Oaths deliberate fabrications. They hadn't lived in the White Tower. Galad didn't like most Aes Sedai, and he certainly didn't trust them, but he knew that the oaths *did* hold.

Galad's men moved back into line, muttering. He raised his looking glass, inspecting Aybara's front line. Men in black coats. Several Aiel women, including one of those who had come with Aybara to their first meetings. A channeler, no doubt. He imagined the ground exploding beneath his charging forces, knocking the cavalry into the air, others falling into the trench while the later lines stalled in confusion, prey to those impressive longbows.

Bornhald rode up to Galad, his face angry. "We aren't really going to parley, are we?"

Galad lowered his looking glass. "Yes. I think we are."

"But we already met with him!" Bornhald said. "You said you wanted to see those eyes, as proof he was Shadowspawn, and you saw them. What more do you need?"

Byar nudged his mount closer. He often acted as a guard to Galad, these days. "He can't be trusted, my Lord Captain Commander."

Galad nodded at the trench. "He could have destroyed us with that attack."

"I agree with Byar," Bornhald said. "He wants to draw you out, then kill you to demoralize us."

Galad nodded slowly. "That's possible." He turned to Lord Captain Harnesh, who rode nearby. "If I die, I want you to take command and charge. Attack without mercy; repeal my order to avoid Aes Sedai. Kill anyone who seems to be channeling. Make it a priority. It's possible that we do not understand what is happening here."

"But you're still going?" Bornhald asked.

"Yes," Galad said. He had let Bornhald and Byar goad him into battle, but now he wondered if he'd been too hasty. He *had* seen those eyes, and had heard the testimonies of both his Children and some of those who had ridden with Aybara. It had seemed clear that attacking was the thing to do.

But Aybara was right. He had come to meet with Galad when asked. Perhaps there was a way to prevent bloodshed. Galad did not believe it, but if there was even a chance, then delaying was the right thing. It was as simple as that.

Bornhald did not seem pleased. His anger at the man who had killed his father was understandable, but it could not be allowed to guide the Children. "You may come with me," Galad said, nudging his horse forward. "That goes for you as well, Child Byar. The Lords Captain should remain behind, scattered through the men, lest Aybara leave us without leaders."

Harnesh saluted. Bornhald reluctantly fell into place beside Galad, as did Byar, whose eyes burned with a wild zeal that matched Bornhald's anger. Both had experienced defeat and indignity at the hands of this Perrin Aybara. Galad also took fifty Children as guards, riding in formation behind him.

A pavilion was set up by the time they arrived. Flat-topped and simple, it had four poles stretching the brownish-gray canvas. There was a small square table under it, accompanied by two chairs.

Aybara sat on one side of the table. He stood up as Galad approached; today, the large man wore a green coat and brown trousers—both well crafted but plain—and had that hammer slung at his waist. The clothes had an earthy sensibility to them. No, this was not a man of palaces, but a man of fields and forests. A woodsman who had risen to be a lord.

A pair of Two Rivers men stood at the back of the pavilion, holding powerful Two Rivers longbows. They were said to be independent farmers and herdsmen of old, sturdy stock. And they had chosen this Perrin Aybara to lead them.

Galad walked toward the pavilion. Byar and Bornhald joined him, though the other fifty remained mounted outside.

Unlike their last meeting, there were Aes Sedai here, three whom he could spot. A short Cairhienin woman; a slim, pleasant-looking woman in a simple dress; a stocky woman whose numerous braids meant she was likely from Tarabon. They stood with the group of Aiel women in shawls, guarded by a handful of Maidens of the Spear. Well, those Aiel did give credence to the claim that Aybara had been sent by the Dragon Reborn.

Galad rested his hand casually on the pommel of his sword, looking over the pavilion's other occupants.

And then he froze. A strikingly beautiful woman stood behind Aybara's chair. No, not beautiful, *gorgeous*. Lustrous black hair streamed down past her neck; it seemed to shine. She wore a red gown, thin enough to accentuate her form and deeply cut enough to expose swelling bosom.

And those eyes. So dark, with long beautiful lashes. He seemed . . . pulled toward them. Why hadn't this woman come last time?

"You appear surprised," Aybara said as he sat back down. He had a gruff voice. "The Lady First is here at the Lord Dragon's command, as I am. Didn't you notice the flag of Mayene above my forces?"

"I . . ." Galad snapped his mouth closed, executing a bow to the woman. Berelain sur Paendrag Paeron? She was said to be a marvelous beauty, but those tales did her little justice. Galad tore his eyes from her and forced himself to take the seat opposite Aybara. He had to concentrate on his foe.

Those golden eyes were as unsettling as he remembered. So strange to look into. Yes, this man couldn't be anything *other* than Shadowspawn. Why would so many follow such a creature? Why would *she* follow such a creature?

"Thank you for coming," Aybara said. "Our last meeting was hasty. We'll do it proper, this time. You should be made aware that this woman beside me is Alliandre Maritha Kigarin, Queen of Ghealdan, Blessed of the Light, Defender of Garen's Wall." So, that stately, dark-haired woman was the current Queen of Ghealdan. Of course, with the unrest here lately, there were probably a half-dozen people trying to claim the throne. She was pretty, but completely overshadowed by Berelain.

Perrin nodded toward a third woman. "This is Faile ni Bashere t'Aybara, my wife and cousin to the Queen of Saldaea." Aybara's wife regarded Galad with suspicion. Yes, she was obviously Saldaean, by that nose. Bornhald and Byar hadn't known of her royal connections.

Two monarchs in the tent, and both behind Aybara. Galad rose from his seat and gave a bow to Alliandre to match the one he'd given Berelain. "Your Majesty."

"You're very polite, Lord Captain Commander," Berelain said. "And those were elegant bows. Tell me, where did you receive such training?"

Her voice was like music. "In the court of Andor, my Lady. I am Galad Damodred, stepson of the departed Queen Morgase and half-brother of Elayne Trakand, the rightful Queen."

"Ah," Perrin said. "About time I put a name to you. Wish you'd said that last time."

Berelain stared into his eyes, and she smiled, looking as if she wanted to step forward. She caught herself, however. "Galad Damodred. Yes, I *thought* I recognized something in your face. How is your sister?"

"I hope she is well," Galad said. "I have not seen her in some time."

"Elayne's fine," Perrin said gruffly. "Last I heard—which was only a few days back—she'd secured her claim to the throne. I wouldn't be surprised if she's looking to marry Rand by now. If she can pull him away from whatever realm he's conquering."

Behind Galad, Byar hissed softly. Had Aybara intended insult by indicating a relationship between Elayne and the Dragon Reborn? Unfortunately, Galad knew his sister all too well. She was impulsive, and she *had* shown an unseemly fascination with young al'Thor.

"My sister may do as she wishes," Galad said, surprised at how easily he contained his annoyance at both her and the Dragon Reborn. "We are here to discuss you, Perrin Aybara, and your army."

Aybara leaned forward, laying two hands on the table. "We both know this isn't about my army."

"What is it about, then?" Galad asked.

Aybara met his gaze with those unnatural eyes of his. "It's about a pair of Children of the Light I killed two years back. Now every time I turn around, it seems that there is a group of you snapping at my heels."

It wasn't often that a murderer was so open about what he had done. Galad heard the rasp of a sword being drawn behind him, and raised a hand. "Child Bornhald! You *will* control yourself!"

"*Two* Children of the Light, Shadowspawn?" Bornhald spat. "And what of my father?"

"I had nothing to do with his death, Bornhald," Aybara said. "Geofram was killed by the Seanchan, unfortunately. For a Whitecloak, he seemed like a reasonable man, though he was planning to hang me."

"He was to hang you for the murders you just confessed to," Galad said calmly, shooting a glance at Bornhald. The man snapped his sword back in its sheath, but his face was red.

"They weren't murders," Aybara said. "They attacked me. I fought back."

"That is not what I have heard," Galad said. What game was this man playing? "I have sworn testimony that you were hiding underneath a cleft in the rock. When the men asked you to come out, you jumped out screaming and attacked them without provocation."

"Oh, there was provocation," Aybara said. "Your Whitecloaks killed a friend of mine."

"The woman who was with you?" Galad asked. "From what I hear, she escaped safely." He'd been shocked when Bornhald had mentioned *that* name. Egwene al'Vere. Another woman who seemed to prefer dangerous company.

"Not her," Perrin said. "A friend named Hopper. And after him, a companion of his. They were wolves."

The man was condemning himself further! "You make friends of wolves, known to be creatures of the Shadow?"

"Wolves aren't of the Shadow," Aybara said. "They hate Shadowspawn as much as any man I've known."

"And how do you know this?"

Aybara said nothing further. There was more there. Byar said this man seemed able to command wolves, run with them, like a wolf himself. That testimony was part of what had persuaded Galad that battle was the only recourse. It seemed that Byar's words had not been exaggeration.

But there was no need, yet, to dwell on that. Aybara had admitted to murder. "I don't accept the killing of wolves as something to exonerate you," Galad said. "Many hunters slay wolves who attack their flocks or threaten their lives. The Children did nothing wrong. Your attack on them, therefore, was unprovoked murder."

"There was far more to it than that," Aybara said. "But I doubt I'll convince you of that."

"I cannot be convinced of something that isn't true," Galad said.

"And you won't leave me alone, either," Aybara said.

"We are at an impasse, then," Galad said. "You have confessed to crimes that I, as a servant of justice, *must* see righted. I cannot walk away. You see why I felt further parley was useless?"

"What if I were willing to stand trial?" Perrin asked.

Aybara's bold-nosed wife rested a hand on his shoulder. He reached up and laid his hand on it, but did not turn away from Galad.

"If you will come and accept punishment from us for what you've done . . ." Galad said. It would mean execution. Surely the creature wouldn't give himself up.

At the back of the pavilion, a group of servants had arrived and were preparing tea. Tea. At a war parley. Obviously Aybara had little experience with this kind of thing.

"Not punishment," Aybara said sharply. "A trial. If I am proven innocent, I go free and you—the Lord Captain Commander—instruct your men to stop hounding me. Especially Bornhald and that one behind you who growls like a pup seeing his first leopard."

"And if you are proven guilty?"

"That depends."

"Don't listen to him, my Lord Captain Commander!"

Byar said. "He promised to give himself to us once before, then betrayed his word!"

"I did not!" Aybara said. "*You* did not fulfill your part of the bargain!"

"I—"

Galad slapped the table. "This is useless. There will be no trial."

"Why not?" Aybara demanded. "You talk of justice, but won't offer me a trial?"

"And who would judge it?" Galad asked. "Would you trust me to do so?"

"Of course not," Perrin said. "But Alliandre can. She's a queen."

"And your companion," Galad said. "I mean her no insult, but I fear she would acquit you without hearing evidence. Even the Lady First would not be adequate—though I would, of course, trust her word, I fear that my men would not."

Light, but that woman was beautiful! He glanced at her for a moment, and found her blushing as she regarded him. It was faint, but he was sure he saw it. He found himself blushing as well.

"The Aes Sedai, then," Aybara said.

Galad tore his eyes away from Berelain and looked at Aybara, giving him a flat stare. "If you think that a judgment by one from the White Tower would satisfy my men, you know little of the Children of the Light, Perrin Aybara."

Aybara's eyes grew hard. Yes, he knew that. It was too bad. A trial would have been a tidy end to this. A serving woman approached the table with two cups of tea, but there was no need. This second parley was over.

"You're right, then," Aybara said, looking frustrated. "This meeting was pointless."

"No," Galad said, stealing another glance at Berelain. "Not pointless for me." He knew more of Aybara's strength; that would help him in battle. Beyond that, it had been right to delay fighting for a short time to make certain it was needed. There was still plenty of light in the day for the fighting to proceed.

But . . . what of that woman . . . the Lady First? He forced himself to look away. It was difficult.

Galad stood, and bowed to Alliandre, then to Berelain. He moved to leave.

Then he heard a gasp. Oddly, it came from the serving woman who had brought the tea. Galad glanced at her.

It was Morgase.

Galad froze, completely still. He'd been trained by swordmaster after swordmaster never to let his surprise overwhelm him, but at that moment, their careful training was for naught. That *was* his stepmother. That red-gold hair he had tugged as a child. That face, so beautiful and strong. Those eyes. Those were her eyes.

A ghost? He had heard the stories. Manifestations of the Dark One's evil returning the dead to life. But nobody else in the pavilion seemed uneasy, and this woman was too real. Hesitantly, Galad reached out and touched the apparition on the cheek. The skin was warm.

"Galad?" she said. "What are you doing here? How—"

She cut off as he seized her in an embrace, causing those around him on both sides to jump in surprise. She jumped, too. She lived! How?

I killed Valda, Galad thought immediately. *Killed him for the death of my mother. Who is not dead. I have done evil.*

No. Valda had deserved to die for the assault on Morgase. Or was that part true? He had spoken to Children sure that it was, but they'd also been sure she was dead.

He would sort that out later. Right now, he needed to stop embarrassing himself in front of his men. He released his stepmother, but she kept hold of his arm. She looked dazed. He had rarely seen her that way.

Perrin Aybara had stood up and was watching them with a frown. "You know Maighdin?"

"Maighdin?" Galad asked. She wore a simple dress and no jewelry. Was she trying to hide as a servant? "Aybara, this is Morgase Trakand, Defender of the Realm, Protector of the People, High Seat of House Trakand. She is your *queen*!"

That brought a stillness to the pavilion. Aybara scratched at his beard thoughtfully. His wife watched Morgase with eyes wide, either shocked or angry.

"Maighdin," Aybara said, "is this true?"

She lifted her chin, staring Aybara in the eyes. How could they not see the Queen in her?

"I *am* Morgase Trakand," she said. "But I have renounced my throne in favor of Elayne. Before the Light, I will never again claim the crown."

Galad nodded. Yes. She must have feared that Aybara would use her against Andor. "I'm taking you back to my camp, Mother," Galad said, still watching Aybara. "Then we can discuss the way you were treated by this man."

She turned level eyes on Galad. "An order, Galad? Have I no say in the matter?"

He frowned, leaning in and speaking in a whisper. "Does he have others captive? What leverage does he have over you?"

She shook her head and replied softly, "This man is not what you think he is, Galad. He's rough-cut, and I certainly don't like what he's doing to Andor, but he is no friend of the Shadow. I have more to fear from your . . . associates than from Perrin Aybara."

Yes, she did have reason to distrust the Children. Good reason. "Will you come with me, my Lady? I promise you that you may leave and return to Aybara's camp at any time. Whatever you suffered from the Children in the past, you *will* be safe now. I vow this."

Morgase gave him a nod.

"Damodred," Aybara said, "wait a moment."

Galad turned, laying his hand on his sword pommel again. Not as a threat, but a reminder. Many of those in the pavilion had begun to whisper. "Yes?" Galad asked.

"You wanted a judge," Aybara said. "Would you accept your mother in that position?"

Galad didn't hesitate. Of course; she'd been a queen since her eighteenth nameday, and he had seen her sit in judgment. She was fair. Harsh, but fair.

But would the other Children accept her? She'd been trained by the Aes Sedai. They'd see her as one of them. A problem. But if it gave a way out of this, perhaps he could make them see the truth.

"I would," Galad said. "And if I vouched for her, my men would as well."

"Well," Aybara said, "I'd accept her, too."

Both men turned to Morgase. She stood in her simple yellow dress, looking more a queen by the moment. "Perrin," she said, "if I sit in judgment, I will not temper my decisions. You took me in when we needed shelter, and for that I am appreciative. But if I decide that you have committed murder, I will not hold back my decision."

"That will do," Aybara said. He seemed sincere.

"My Lord Captain Commander," Byar said softly in Galad's ear, sounding fervent. "I fear this would be a farce! He's not said he would submit to punishment."

"No, I have not," Aybara said. How had he heard those whispers? "It would be meaningless. You think me a Darkfriend and a murderer. You wouldn't accept my word on taking punishment, not unless I was in your custody. Which I won't allow."

"See?" Byar said, more loudly. "What is the point?"

Galad met Aybara's golden eyes again. "It will give us a trial," he said, growing more certain. "And legal justification. I'm beginning to see, Child Byar. We *must* prove our claims, otherwise we are no better than Asunawa."

"But the trial will not be fair!"

Galad turned to the tall soldier. "Are you questioning my mother's impartiality?"

The gaunt man froze, then shook his head. "No, my Lord Captain Commander."

Galad turned back to Aybara. "I ask Queen Alliandre to grant that this trial be legally binding in her realm."

"If Lord Aybara requests it, I will." She sounded uncomfortable.

"I do request it, Alliandre," Perrin said. "But only if Damodred agrees to release all of my people that he's holding. Keep the supplies, but let the people go, as you promised me you would before."

"Very well," Galad said. "It will happen once the trial begins. I promise it. When will we meet?"

"Give me a few days to prepare."

"In three days, then," Galad said. "We hold the trial here, in this pavilion, in this place."

"Bring your witnesses," Aybara said. "I'll be here."

CHAPTER
27

A Call to Stand

I *am not opposed to questioning the Lord Dragon,* Egwene read from the letter as she sat in her study. *Indeed, the more absolute a man's power becomes, the more necessary questioning becomes. However, know that I am not a man who gives his loyalty easily, and I have given my loyalty to him. Not because of the throne he provided me, but because of what he has done for Tear.*

Yes, he grows more erratic by the day. What else are we to expect from the Dragon Reborn? He will break the world. We knew this when we gave him our allegiance, much as a sailor must sometimes give his loyalty to the captain who steers his ship straight for the strand. When an unnavigable tempest rises behind, the strand is the only option.

Still, your words bring me concern. The destruction of the seals is not something we should undertake without careful discussion. The Lord Dragon charged me with raising him an army, and I have done so. If you provide the gateways you have promised, I will bring some troops to this meeting place, along with the loyal High Lords and Ladies. Be warned, however, that the Seanchan presence to my west continues to weigh heavily upon my mind. The bulk of my armies must remain behind.

High Lord Darlin Sisnera,
King of Tear
beneath the rule
of the Dragon Reborn
Rand al'Thor

Egwene tapped the sheet with one finger. She was impressed—Darlin had committed his words to paper, rather than sending a messenger with them memorized. If a messenger fell into the wrong hands, his words could always be denied. Convicting a man of treason based on the testimony of one messenger was difficult.

Words on paper, however . . . Bold. By writing them, Darlin said, "I do not care if the Lord Dragon discovers what I have written. I stand by it."

But leaving behind the bulk of his army? That would not do. Egwene inked her pen.

King Darlin. Your concern for your kingdom is well measured, as is your loyalty to the man you follow.

I know that the Seanchan are a danger to Tear, but let us not forget that the Dark One, not the Seanchan, is our primary concern during these worst of days. Perhaps it is easy to think yourself safe from the Trollocs when so distant from the battle lines, but how will you feel once the cushions of Andor and Cairhien have fallen? You are separated from the Seanchan by hundreds of miles.

Egwene paused. Tar Valon had been separated from the Seanchan by hundreds of miles, and had nearly been destroyed. He was right to be afraid, and he *was* a good king for considering it. But she needed his army at the Field of Merrilor. Perhaps she could offer a way for him to both be safe and help with Rand.

Illian holds for now, she wrote. *And gives you a buffer between the Seanchan and yourself. I will provide you with gateways and a promise. If the Seanchan move against Tear, I will give you gateways so you can return immediately and defend your nation.*

She hesitated. Chances were good that the Seanchan had Traveling now. Nobody was safe from them, no matter how far or close they might be. If they decided to strike for Tear, even giving Darlin gateways back might not be enough to help.

She felt a shiver, remembering her own time with the Seanchan, captive as a *damane*. She loathed them with a hatred that sometimes worried her. But Darlin's support was *essential* to her plans. She gritted her teeth and continued writing.

The Dragon Reborn must see our full forces marshaled to oppose his brash intentions. If he sees this as halfhearted, we will never dissuade him from his course. Please come with all of your troops.

She sanded the letter, then folded and sealed it. Darlin and Elayne were monarchs of two of the most powerful kingdoms. Both were very important to her plans.

Next she would respond to a letter from Gregorin den Lushenos of Illian. She hadn't yet told him directly that she had Mattin Stepaneos at the White Tower, but had hinted at it. She'd also spoken to Mattin himself, letting him know he was free to leave, if he wished. She would *not* be in the habit of holding monarchs against their will.

Unfortunately, Mattin was now afraid for his life, should he return. He'd been gone too long, and he viewed Illian as being in the Dragon Reborn's pocket. Which it probably was. What a mess.

One problem at a time. Gregorin, the steward in Illian, was very hesitant to support her cause—he seemed more intimidated by Rand than Darlin was, and the Seanchan were not a distant concern for him. They were practically pounding on his city gates.

She wrote Gregorin a firm letter, giving a promise like the one she'd given Darlin. Perhaps she could arrange to keep Mattin away—something both men might want, though she wouldn't let Gregorin know that—in exchange for him bringing his armies northward.

Obliquely, she realized what she was doing. She was using Rand's proclamation as a beacon by which to gather and tie the monarchs to the White Tower. They would come to support her arguments against breaking the seals. But in the end, they would serve humankind in the Last Battle.

A knock came at her door. She looked up as Silviana peeked in. The woman held up a letter. It was curled tightly from having been carried in by pigeon.

"Your expression is grim," Egwene noted.

"The invasion has begun," she said. "Watchtowers across the Blightborder go silent, one at a time. Waves of Trollocs advance beneath clouds that boil black. Kandor, Arafel and Saldaea are at war."

"Do they hold?" Egwene asked with a spike of fear.

"Yes," Silviana said. "But news is uncertain and piecemeal. This letter—which is from an eyes-and-ears I trust—claims that an assault this massive has not been seen since the Trolloc Wars."

Egwene took a deep breath. "What of Tarwin's Gap?"

"I don't know."

"Find out. Call Siuan in here. She might have more. The Blue network is the most extensive." Siuan wouldn't know everything, of course, but she would have her fingers in it.

Silviana nodded curtly. She didn't say the obvious—that the Blue network was the Blue Ajah's, not to be preempted by the Amyrlin. Well, the Last Battle was at hand. Some concessions had to be made.

Silviana closed the door softly, and Egwene picked up her pen to finish her screed to Gregorin. She was interrupted by another knock, this one much more hasty. Silviana threw open the door a second later.

"Mother," she said. "They're meeting. As you said they would!"

Egwene felt a stab of annoyance. She calmly put down her pen and stood. "Let us be to it, then."

She walked from her study, pace hurried. In the Keeper's antechamber, she passed a pair of Accepted—Nicola, who had just been raised, and Nissa. She'd like them both raised to the shawl before the Last Battle. They were young, but powerful, and every sister would be needed—even one who, like Nicola, had proved to have terrible judgment in the past.

These two had brought the news about the Hall; the novices and Accepted were among the most loyal to Egwene, but were often ignored by the sisters. For now, they remained behind as Egwene and Silviana hurried toward the Hall.

"I can't believe they would try this," Silviana said softly as they walked.

"It's not what you think," Egwene guessed. "They won't try to depose me. The division is too fresh in their minds."

"Then why meet without you?"

"There are ways to move against an Amyrlin without deposing her."

She'd been expecting this for some time, but that didn't

make it any less frustrating. Aes Sedai would, unfortunately, be Aes Sedai. It had only been a matter of time before someone decided to try wrenching power from her.

They reached the Hall. Egwene pushed open the doors and stepped in. Her appearance was met with cool Aes Sedai gazes. The seats weren't all filled, but two-thirds of them were. She was surprised to see three Red Sitters. What of Pevara and Javindhra? It appeared that their extended absence during this time had prompted the Red to action. They had been replaced by Raechin and Viria Connoral. The sisters were the only siblings in the White Tower, now that Vandene and Adeleas were dead; an odd choice, but not unexpected.

Both Romanda and Lelaine were in attendance. They met Egwene's gaze evenly. How strange to see them here with so many sisters who they had been at odds with. A common foe—Egwene—could heal any number of rifts. She should have been pleased at that, perhaps.

Lelaine was the only Blue, and there was also only one Brown: Takima, who looked sick. The ivory-skinned Brown wouldn't meet Egwene's gaze. There were two Whites, two Yellows—including Romanda—two Grays, and all three Greens. Egwene gritted her teeth when she saw that. That was the Ajah she would have joined, but it gave her the most grief!

Egwene did not chastise them for meeting without her; she simply strode down between them, Silviana announcing her. Egwene turned and sat down on the Amyrlin Seat, her back to the huge rose window.

There, she sat quietly.

"Well?" Romanda finally asked. Her gray hair up in a bun, she looked like a mother wolf sitting atop the ledge out front of her den. "Are you going to say anything, Mother?"

"You did not inform me of this meeting," Egwene said, "so I assume you do not want my words. I have come merely to watch."

That seemed to make them more uncomfortable. Silviana walked to her side, brandishing one of her best expressions of displeasure.

"All right, then," Rubinde said. "I believe we were going to hear from Saroiya next."

The blocky White was one of the Sitters who had left th[e] Tower when Elaida was raised, but she had made her shar[e] of trouble in Salidar. Egwene was not surprised to see he[r] here. The woman stood, pointedly not looking at Egwen[e]. "I will add my testimony. During the days of . . . uncer[-] tainty within the Tower"—that would mean the division [a] few sisters liked to speak of it outright—"the Amyrlin di[d] exactly as Romanda indicated. We were taken by surpris[e] when she called for a declaration of war.

"Within the law, there are provisions that give the Amy[r-] lin almost total power when official war is declared. B[y] being goaded into making war with Elaida, we gave th[e] Amyrlin the means to subject the Hall to her will." Sh[e] looked around the room, but did not turn to Egwene. "It i[s] my opinion that she will try something similar again. Tha[t] must be prevented. The Hall is meant to be a balance upo[n] the Amyrlin's power."

She sat down.

Hearing the words actually relieved Egwene. One coul[d] never be certain what kinds of scheming were happening i[n] the White Tower. This meeting meant her plans were pro[-] ceeding as hoped, and that her enemies—or, well, her re[-] luctant allies—hadn't seen what she was *really* doing. The[y] were busy reacting to things she'd done months ago.

That didn't mean they weren't dangerous. But when [a] person anticipated danger, it could be handled.

"What can we do?" Magla asked. She glanced at Egwen[e]. "To be prudent, I mean. To make certain the Hall of th[e] Tower is in no way limited."

"We cannot declare war," Lelaine said firmly.

"And yet, to avoid it?" Varilin said. "War is declare[d] between halves of the White Tower, but not against th[e] Shadow?"

"War," Takima said hesitantly, "is *already* declare[d] against the Shadow. Need there be an official proclamation[?] Is not our existence enough? Indeed, do not the oaths mak[e] our position clear?"

"But we must make some kind of declaration," Romand[a] said. She was eldest among them, and would be the on[e] running the meeting. "Something to make the position c[of] the Hall known, to dissuade the Amyrlin from an impru[-] dent call for war."

Romanda didn't seem embarrassed at all by what they had done here. She looked directly at Egwene. No, she and Lelaine would not quickly forgive Egwene for choosing a Red as her Keeper.

"But how would we send such a message?" Andaya asked. "I mean, what are we to do? Make a pronouncement from the Hall that there won't be a declaration of war? Would that not sound ridiculous?"

The women fell silent. Egwene found herself nodding, though not specifically to what was being said. She had been raised through unconventional circumstances. Left alone, the Hall would try to establish its power as greater than hers. This day could easily have meant a step toward that. The Amyrlin Seat's strength had not been constant through the centuries—one could rule almost totally while another was controlled by the Sitters.

"I believe the Hall acts in wisdom," Egwene said, speaking very carefully.

The Sitters turned to her. Some looked relieved. Those who were more familiar with her, however, looked suspicious. Well, that was good. Better they regard her as a threat than as a child to be bullied. She hoped they would eventually respect her as their leader, but there was only so much she could do with the time given.

"The war between factions within the Tower was a different type of battle," Egwene continued. "It was deeply and individually my battle, as Amyrlin, for that division was initially *about* the Amyrlin Seat.

"But the war against the Shadow is more vast than any one person. It is greater than you or I, greater than the White Tower. It is the war of all life and creation, from the most destitute of beggars to the most powerful of queens."

The Sitters considered that in silence.

Romanda spoke first. "And so you would not oppose the Hall taking over prosecution of the war, managing General Bryne's armies and the Tower Guard?"

"That depends," Egwene said, "upon how the provision was worded."

There was movement in the hallway outside, and Saerin bustled into the Hall, accompanied by Janya Frende. They shot Takima withering glances, and she shrank down like a threatened bird. Saerin and Egwene's other supporters would

have been informed of this meeting just after Egwene herself was.

Romanda cleared her throat. "Perhaps we should see if
there is anything in the Law of War that can help."

"I'm certain you have studied it quite thoroughly now,
Romanda," Egwene said. "What is it you propose?"

"There is a provision for the Hall taking up prosecution
of a war," Romanda said.

"That requires the Amyrlin's assent," Egwene said idly.
If that was Romanda's game, then how had she intended to
get Egwene's approval after meeting without her? Perhaps
she'd had a different plan.

"Yes, it would require the Amyrlin's agreement," said
Raechin. She was a tall, dark-haired woman, and liked to
wear her hair in a coil of braids atop her head. "But you said
that you thought us wise to take this measure."

"Well," Egwene said, trying to sound as if she were being
pressed into a corner, "agreeing with the Hall is quite different from allowing a provision to ban me from the day-to-day
workings of the army. What is the Amyrlin Seat to do, if not
see to the war?"

"By reports, you've been dedicating yourself to wran-
gling kings and queens," Lelaine said. "That seems a fine
task for the Amyrlin."

"Then you'll stand for such a provision?" Egwene said.
"The Hall sees to the army, while I am given authority for
dealing with the monarchs of the world?"

"I . . ." Lelaine said. "Yes, I'd stand for that."

"I suppose I could agree," Egwene said.

"Shall we put it to a vote?" Romanda said quickly, as if
pouncing on the moment.

"Very well," Egwene said. "Who will stand for this motion?"

Rubinde rose to her feet, and was joined by Faiselle and
Farnah, the other Greens. Raechin and her sister stood
quickly, though Barasine was watching Egwene with eyes
narrowed. Magla stood next, and Romanda reluctantly
joined her. Ferane rose slowly. Lelaine was next. She and
Romanda shot daggered glances at one another.

That was nine. Egwene's heart beat quickly as she
glanced at Takima. The woman seemed very disturbed, as

if trying to sort through Egwene's plan. The same went for Saroiya. The calculating White studied Egwene, tugging her ear. Suddenly, her eyes went wide, and she opened her mouth to speak.

At that moment, Doesine and Yukiri arrived, striding into the room. Saerin stood immediately. Slim Doesine glanced at the women around her. "What motion are we standing for?"

"An important one," Saerin said.

"Well, I suppose I'll stand for it, then."

"As will I," Yukiri said.

"The lesser consensus is given, it seems," Saerin said. "The Hall is given authority over the White Tower's army, while the Amyrlin is given authority and responsibility for dealing with the world's monarchs."

"No!" Saroiya said, climbing to her feet. "Don't you see? *He* is a king! He holds the Laurel Crown. You've just given the Amyrlin sole responsibility for dealing with the Dragon Reborn!"

There was silence in the Hall.

"Well," Romanda said, "surely she . . ." She trailed off as she turned, seeing Egwene's serene face.

"I suppose someone should ask for the greater consensus," Saerin said dryly. "But you've managed to hang yourselves quite efficiently with the lesser rope already."

Egwene stood. "I meant what I said about the Hall's choices being wise, and nobody has hanged herself. It *is* wise of the Hall to put me in charge of dealing with the Dragon Reborn—he will need a firm, familiar hand. You are also wise to see that the details of managing the army were demanding too much of my attention. You will want to choose someone among you to go through and approve all of General Bryne's supply requests and recruitment schemes. I assure you, there are a multitude of them.

"I am pleased that you have seen the need to aid the Amyrlin, though I am deeply *displeased* at the secretive nature of this meeting. Do not try to deny that it was done in secret, Romanda. I see you preparing to object. If you wish to speak, know that I will pin you by the Three Oaths into answering directly."

The Yellow bit off her comment.

"How can you not have learned the foolishness of acts like this?" Egwene said. "Is your memory so short?" She looked at the women in turn, and was satisfied by the number who winced.

"It is time," Egwene said, "for a change to be made. I propose that there be no further meetings of this nature. I propose that it be written into Tower law that if any Sitter leaves the White Tower, her Ajah must appoint a surrogate to vote for her while absent. I propose that it be written into Tower law that no meeting of the Hall can be convened unless every Sitter or her surrogate either is present, or has sent word *directly* that she cannot attend. I propose that the Amyrlin *must* be informed—and given a reasonable amount of time to attend if she wishes—of every meeting of the Hall, save when she cannot be found or is indisposed in some way."

"Bold changes, Mother," Saerin said. "You propose altering traditions that have been established for centuries."

"Traditions that hitherto have been used only for treachery, backbiting and division," Egwene said. "It is time for this hole to be closed, Saerin. The last time it was used effectively, the Black Ajah manipulated us into casting down an Amyrlin, raising a fool in her place, and dividing the Tower. Are you aware that Kandor, Saldaea and Arafel are swarming with Shadowspawn?"

Several of the sisters gasped. Others nodded, including Lelaine. So the Blue network was still reliable. Good.

"The Last Battle is here," Egwene said. "I will *not* withdraw my proposal. Either you will stand now, or you will be known—through all time—as one of those who refused. At the dusk of an Age, can you not stand for openness and Light? Will you not—for all of our sakes—make it impossible for a meeting of the Hall to be called without your presence? To leave any out means the possibility that *you* will be left out."

The women were silent. One by one, those who were standing sat back down to prepare for the new vote.

"Who will stand for this motion?" Egwene asked.

They stood. Blessedly, they stood—one at a time, slowly, reluctantly. But they did it. Every one of them.

Egwene let out a deep breath. They might squabble and

scheme, but they knew right when they saw it. They shared the same goals. If they disagreed, it was because they had different views on how to reach those goals. Sometimes it was hard to remember that.

Looking shaken by what they'd done, the Sitters allowed the meeting to break up. Outside, sisters had begun to gather, surprised to find the Hall meeting. Egwene nodded to Saerin and the others of her supporters and walked from the room, Silviana at her side.

"That was a victory," the Keeper said once they were alone. She sounded satisfied. "But you did still give up control of our armies."

"I had to," Egwene said. "They could have pulled command away from me at any time; this way, I got something in return."

"Authority over the Dragon Reborn?"

"Yes," Egwene said, "but I was referring more to closing that loophole in Tower law. So long as it was possible for the Hall to meet in relative secret, my authority—the authority of any Amyrlin—could be circumvented. Now, if they want to maneuver, they'll have to do it in front of my face."

Silviana gave a rare smile. "I suspect that since something like today is a result of such maneuvering, Mother, they will be more hesitant in the future."

"That's the idea," Egwene said. "Though I doubt Aes Sedai will ever stop trying to maneuver. They simply cannot be allowed to dice with the Last Battle or the Dragon Reborn."

Back at Egwene's study, Nicola and Nissa still waited. "You did well," Egwene told them. "*Very* well. In fact, I'm of a mind to give you more responsibility. Go to the Traveling ground, and go to Caemlyn—the Queen there will be expecting you. Return with the items she gives you."

"Yes, Mother," Nicola said, grinning. "What will she give us?"

"*Ter'angreal*," Egwene said. "Used for visiting the World of Dreams. I'm going to begin training you, and some others, in their use. Do *not* use them without my express permission, however. I will send some soldiers with you." That should be enough to keep the two in line.

The two Accepted curtsied and trotted away, excited.

Silviana looked at Egwene. "You didn't swear them to silence. They are Accepted, and they *will* brag about being
trained with the *ter'angreal*."

"I'm depending on it," Egwene said, walking to the study
door.

Silviana raised an eyebrow.

"I don't intend to let the girls come to harm," Egwene
said. "In fact, they'll be doing a lot less in *Tel'aran'rhiod*
than they probably suspect from what I just said. Rosil has
been lenient with me so far, but she'll never let me put Accepted in danger. This is just to start the proper rumors."

"What rumors?"

"Gawyn scared off the assassin," Egwene said. "There
hasn't been a murder in days, and I suppose we should
bless him for that. But the killer is still hiding, and I've
glimpsed Black sisters watching me in *Tel'aran'rhiod*. If I
can't catch them here, then I will catch them there. But first
I need a way to trick them into thinking they know where
to find us."

"So long as you intend them to find you, and not those
girls," Silviana said, voice calm—but iron. She had been
the Mistress of Novices.

Egwene found herself grimacing, thinking of the things
that had been expected of her as an Accepted. Yes, Silviana
was right. She would have to take care not to subject Nicola
and Nissa to similar dangers. *She* had survived, and was
stronger for it, but Accepted should not be put through such
trials unless there was no other choice.

"I will take care," Egwene said. "I simply need them to
spread the rumor that I have a very important meeting coming up. If I lay the groundwork properly, our phantom won't
be able to resist coming to listen in."

"Bold."

"Essential," Egwene said. She hesitated, hand on her
door. "Speaking of Gawyn, have you found out where in the
city he's run off to?"

"Actually, Mother, I had a note on this earlier today. It
appears that . . . well, he *isn't* in the city. One of the sisters
delivering your messages to the Queen of Andor returned
with news of seeing him there."

Egwene groaned, closing her eyes. *That man will be the*

death of me. "Tell him to return. Infuriating though he is, I'm going to need him in the coming days."

"Yes, Mother," Silviana said, taking out a sheet of paper.

Egwene entered her study to continue her letters. Time was short. Time was so very, very short.

CHAPTER
28

Oddities

W hat are you planning, husband?" Faile asked.
They were back in their tent, following the
parley with the Whitecloaks. Perrin's actions
had surprised her—which was invigorating, yet also disturbing.

He took off his coat. "I smell a strangeness on the wind,
Faile. Something I've never smelled before." He hesitated,
glancing at her. "There are no wolves."

"No wolves?"

"I can't sense any nearby," Perrin said, eyes distant. "There
were some before. Now they're gone."

"You said that they don't like being close to people."

He pulled off his shirt, exposing a muscled chest covered
in curling brown hair. "There were too few birds today, too
few creatures in the underbrush. Light burn that sky. Is that
causing this, or is it something else?" He sighed, sitting
down on their sleeping pallet.

"You're going to go . . . there?" Faile asked.

"Something's wrong," he repeated. "I need to learn what
I can before the trial. There might be answers in the wolf
dream."

The trial. "Perrin, I don't like this idea."

"You're angry about Maighdin."

"Of *course* I'm angry about Maighdin," she said. They'd
been through Malden together, and she hadn't told Faile
that she was the *Queen of bloody Andor*? It made Faile look
like a fool—like a small-town braggart, extolling her skill
with the sword in front of a passing blademaster.

"She didn't know if she could trust us," Perrin said. "She

was fleeing one of the Forsaken, it seems. I'd have hidden myself, too."

Faile glared at him.

"Don't look at me like that," he said. "She didn't do it to make you look bad, Faile. She had her reasons. Let it go."

That made her feel a little better; it was so nice that he would stand up for himself now. "Well, it makes me wonder who Lini will turn out to be. Some Seanchan queen? Master Gill, the King of Arad Doman in hiding?"

Perrin smiled. "I suspect they're her attendants. Gill is who he says he is, at least. Balwer is probably having a fit for not having figured this out."

"I bet he did figure it out," Faile said, kneeling beside him. "Perrin, I meant what I said about this trial. I'm worried."

"I won't let myself be taken," he said. "I only said I'd sit through a trial and give them a chance to present evidence."

"Then what's the point?" Faile said.

"It gives me more time to think," he said, "and it might stop me from having to kill them. Their captain, Damodred—something about him smells better than many of the rest. Not rabid with anger or hate. This will get our people back and let me plead my side. It feels good for a man to be able to have his say. Maybe that's what I've needed, all this time."

"Well, all right," Faile said. "But in the future, please consider *warning me* of your plans."

"I will," he said, yawning and lying back. "In truth, it didn't occur to me until the last moment."

Faile kept her tongue with some difficulty. At least something good had come from that parley. She'd watched Berelain when she'd met Damodred, and she'd rarely seen a woman's eyes light up so brightly. Faile might be able to make use of that.

She looked down. Perrin was already snoring softly.

Perrin found himself sitting with his back against something hard and smooth. The too-dark, almost *evil* sky of the wolf dream boiled above the forest, which was a mixture of fir, oak and leatherleaf.

He stood up, then turned and looked at what he had been

leaning against. A massive steel tower stretched toward the turbulent sky. Too straight, with walls that looked like a single piece of seamless metal, the tower exuded a completely *unnatural* feel.

I told you this place was evil, Hopper sent, suddenly sitting next to Perrin. *Foolish cub.*

"I didn't come here by choice," Perrin protested. "I woke here."

Your mind is focused on it, Hopper said. *Or the mind of one to whom you are connected.*

"Mat," Perrin said, without understanding how he knew. The colors didn't appear. They never did in the wolf dream.

As foolish a cub as yourself?

"Maybe more foolish."

Hopper smelled incredulous, as if unwilling to believe that was possible. *Come,* the wolf sent. *It has returned.*

"What has—"

Hopper vanished. Perrin followed with a frown. He now could easily catch the scent of where Hopper had gone. They appeared on the Jehannah Road, and that strange violet glass wall was there again, slicing the roadway in half, extending high in the air and into the distance in either direction. Perrin walked up to a tree. Its bare branches seemed trapped in the glass, immobile.

Hopper paced nearby. *We have seen this thing before,* he sent. *Long, long ago. So many lives ago.*

"What is it?"

A thing of men.

Hopper's sending included confused images. Flying, glowing discs. Impossibly tall structures of steel. Things from the Age of Legends? Hopper didn't understand their use any more than he understood the use of a horse cart or a candle.

Perrin looked down the roadway. He didn't recognize this section of Ghealdan; it must be farther toward Lugard. The wall had appeared in a different place than it had last time.

A thought occurring to him, Perrin moved down the roadway in a few jumping bursts. A hundred paces away, he looked back and confirmed his suspicions. That glass didn't make a wall, but an enormous *dome*. Translucent, with a violet tint, it seemed to extend for leagues.

Hopper moved at a blur, coming to stand beside him. *We must go.*

"He's in there, isn't he?" Perrin asked. He reached out. Oak Dancer, Sparks and Boundless were near. Ahead, inside the dome. They responded with quick, frantic sendings, at hunt and being hunted.

"Why don't they flee?" Perrin asked.

Hopper sent confusion.

"I'm going to them," Perrin said, willing himself forward.

Nothing happened.

Perrin felt a stab of panic in his gut. What was wrong? He tried again, this time trying to send himself to the base of the dome.

It worked. He arrived in an eyeblink, that glasslike surface rising in a cliff face before him. *It's this dome,* he thought. *It's blocking me.* Suddenly, he understood the trapped feeling the wolves had sent. They couldn't get away.

Was that the purpose of this dome, then? To trap wolves so that Slayer could kill them? Perrin growled, stepping up to the surface of the dome. He couldn't pass in by imagining himself there, but perhaps he could get through by more mundane means. He raised a hand, then hesitated. He didn't know what touching the surface would do.

The wolves sent images of a man in black and leather, with a harsh, lined face and a smile curling on his lips as he launched arrows. He smelled wrong, so wrong. He also smelled of dead wolves.

Perrin couldn't leave them in there. No more than he could leave Master Gill and the others to the Whitecloaks. Furious at Slayer, he touched the surface of the dome.

His muscles suddenly lost strength. They felt like water, his legs unable to hold him up. He fell to the ground, hard. His foot was still touching the dome—passing through it. The dome appeared to have no substance.

His lungs no longer worked; inflating his chest was too difficult. Panicked, he imagined himself elsewhere, but it didn't work. He was trapped, as surely as the wolves!

A gray-silver blur appeared next to him. Jaws grabbed his shoulder. As Hopper pulled him free of the violet dome, Perrin immediately felt his strength return. He gasped for breath.

Foolish cub, Hopper sent.

"You'd leave them?" Perrin said, voice ragged.

Not foolish to dig in the hole. Foolish for not waiting for me in case hornets came out. Hopper turned toward the dome. *Help me if I fall.* He padded forward, then touched his nose to the dome. Hopper stumbled, but righted himself and continued on slowly. On the other side, he collapsed, but his chest continued to move.

"How did you do it?" Perrin asked, rising.

I am me. Hopper as he saw himself—which was identical to who he was. Also scents of strength and stability.

The trick, it seemed, was to be in complete control of who you were. Like many things in the wolf dream, the strength of one's mental image was more powerful than the substance of the world itself.

Come, Hopper sent. *Be strong, pass through.*

"I have a better idea," Perrin said, standing up. He charged forward at full speed. He hit the violet dome and immediately went limp, but his momentum carried him to the other side, where he rolled to a stop. He groaned, shoulder hurt, arm scraped.

Foolish cub, Hopper sent. *You must learn.*

"Now isn't the time," Perrin said, climbing to his feet. "We have to help the others."

Arrows in the wind, thick, black, deadly. The hunter's laughter. The scent of a man who was stale. The killer was *here.* Hopper and Perrin ran down the road, and Perrin found that he could increase his speed within the dome. Tentatively, he tried jumping forward with a thought, and it worked. But when he tried to send himself outside, nothing happened.

So the dome was a barrier. Within it, he could move freely, but he could not move to a place outside it by imagining himself elsewhere. He had to pass the dome's wall physically if he wanted out.

Oak Dancer, Boundless and Sparks were ahead. And Slayer, too. Perrin growled—frantic sendings flooded him. Dark woods. Slayer. He seemed so tall to the wolves, a dark monster with a face chiseled as if from rock.

Blood on the grass. Pain, anger, terror, confusion. Sparks was wounded. The other two jumped back and forth, taunting and distracting Slayer while Sparks crawled toward the border of the dome.

Care, Young Bull, Hopper sent. *This man hunts well. He moves almost like a wolf, though he is something wrong.*

"I'll distract him. You get Sparks."

You have arms. You carry. There was more to the sending than that, of course: Hopper's age and experience, Perrin still a pup.

Perrin gritted his teeth, but didn't argue. Hopper *was* more experienced than he was. They parted, Perrin reaching out for Sparks, finding where he was—hidden within a patch of trees—and taking himself directly there.

The dark brown wolf had an arrow in his thigh, and he was whimpering softly, trailing blood as he crawled. Perrin knelt quickly and pulled the arrow out. The wolf continued to whimper, smelling frightened. Perrin held the arrow up. It *smelled* evil. Disgusted, he tossed it aside and picked up the wolf.

Something crackled nearby, and Perrin spun. Boundless leaped between two trees, smelling anxious. The other two wolves were leading Slayer away.

Perrin turned and ran toward the dome's nearest edge, carrying Sparks. He couldn't leap directly to the edge of the dome because he didn't know where it was.

He burst from the trees, heart thumping. The wolf in his arms seemed to grow stronger as they left the arrow behind. Perrin ran more quickly, using a speed that felt reckless, moving hundreds of paces with blurring speed. The dome wall approached, and he pulled to a stop.

Slayer was suddenly there, standing before him, bow drawn. He wore a black cloak that billowed around him; he was no longer smiling, and his eyes were thunderous.

He released. Perrin *shifted* and never saw where the arrow landed. He appeared in the place where he'd first entered the dome; he should have gone there first. He hurled himself through the violet dome, collapsing on the other side, sending Sparks tumbling.

The wolf yelped. Perrin hit hard.

Young Bull! Sparks sent an image of Slayer, dark like a thunderhead, standing right inside the barrier with bow drawn.

Perrin didn't look. He *shifted*, sending himself to the slopes of Dragonmount. Once there, he leaped to his feet, anxious, hammer appearing in his hand. Groups of nearby wolves sent greeting. Perrin ignored them for the moment.

Slayer did not follow. After a few tense moments, Hopper appeared. "Did the others get away?" Perrin asked.

They are free, he sent. *Whisperer is dead.* The sending showed the wolf—from the viewpoint of the others in the pack—being killed moments after the dome appeared. Sparks had taken an arrow as he nuzzled at her side in panic.

Perrin growled. He nearly jumped away to confront Slayer again, but a caution from Hopper stopped him. *Too soon! You must learn!*

"It's not only him," Perrin said. "I need to look at the area around my camp and that of the Whitecloaks. Something smells wrong there in the waking world. I need to see if something is odd there."

Odd? Hopper sent the image of the dome.

"It is probably related." The two oddities seemed likely to be more than mere coincidence.

Search another time. Slayer is too strong for you.

Perrin took a deep breath. "I have to face him eventually, Hopper."

Not now.

"No," Perrin agreed. "Not now. Now we practice." He turned to the wolf. "As we will do every night until I am ready."

Rodel Ituralde rolled over in his cot, neck slick with sweat. Had Saldaea always been this hot and muggy? He wished for home, the cool ocean breezes of Bandar Eban.

Things felt *wrong*. Why hadn't the Shadowspawn attacked? A hundred possibilities rattled in his mind. Were they waiting for new siege engines? Were they scouting out forests in order to build them? Or were their commanders content with a siege? The entire city was surrounded, but there *had* to be enough Trollocs out there to overwhelm it now.

They had taken to beating drums. All hours. Thump, thump, thump. Steady, like the heartbeat of an enormous animal, the Great Serpent itself, coiling around the city.

Dawn was beginning to shine outside. He hadn't turned in until well after midnight. Durhem—who commanded the morning watch—had ordered that Ituralde not be disturbed until noon. His tent was in a shadowed alcove of the courtyard. He had wanted to be close to the wall, and had refused a bed. That had been foolish. Though a cot had been fine for him in previous years, he wasn't as young as he'd once been. Tomorrow, he'd move.

Now, he told himself, *sleep.*

It wasn't that easy. The accusation that he was Dragonsworn left him unsettled. In Arad Doman, he'd been fighting for his king, someone he'd believed in. Now he was fighting in a foreign land for a man he'd met only once. All because of a gut feeling.

Light, but it was hot. Sweat ran down his cheeks, making his neck itch. It shouldn't be this hot so early in the morning. It wasn't natural. Those burning drums, still pounding.

He sighed, climbing off his sweat-dampened cot. His leg ached. It had for days now.

You're an old man, Rodel, he thought, stripping off his sweaty smallclothes and getting out some freshly washed ones. He stuffed his trousers into knee-high riding boots. A simple white shirt with black buttons went on next, and then his gray coat, buttoning straight up to the collar.

He was strapping on his sword when he heard hurried footsteps outside, followed by whispers. That conversation grew heated, and he stepped outside just as someone said, "Lord Ituralde will wish to know!"

"Know what?" Ituralde asked. A messenger boy was arguing with his guards. All three turned toward him sheepishly.

"I'm sorry, my Lord," Connel said. "We were instructed to let you sleep."

"A man who can sleep in this heat must be half-lizard, Connel," Ituralde said. "Lad, what's the word?"

"Captain Yoeli is on the wall, sir," the youth said. Ituralde recognized the young man—he'd been with him from near the beginning of this campaign. "He said you should come."

Ituralde nodded. He laid a hand on Connel's arm. "Thank you for watching me, old friend, but these bones aren't so frail as you think."

Connel nodded, blushing. The guard fell into place behind as Ituralde crossed the courtyard. The sun had risen. Many of his troops were up. Too many. He wasn't the only one having difficulty sleeping.

Atop the wall, he was greeted by a disheartening sight. On the dying land, thousand upon thousands of Trollocs camped, burning fires. Ituralde didn't like to think about where the wood for those fires came from. Hopefully all of the nearby homesteaders and villagers had heeded the call to evacuate.

Yoeli stood gripping the crenelated stone of the wall, next to a man in a black coat. Deepe Bhadar was senior among the Asha'man whom al'Thor had given him, one of only three who wore both the Dragon and the sword pins on his collar. The Andoran man had a flat face and black hair that he wore long. Ituralde had sometimes heard some of the black-coated men mumbling to themselves, but not Deepe. He seemed fully in control.

Yoeli kept glancing at the Asha'man; Ituralde didn't feel comfortable with men who could channel either. But they were an excellent tool, and they hadn't failed him. He preferred to let experience, instead of rumor, rule him.

"Lord Ituralde," Deepe said. The Asha'man never saluted Ituralde, just al'Thor.

"What is it?" Ituralde asked, scanning the hordes of Trollocs. They didn't seem to have changed since he'd bedded down.

"Your man claims to be able to *feel* something," Yoeli said. "Out there."

"They have channelers, Lord Ituralde," Deepe said. "I suspect at least six, perhaps more. Men, since I can feel the Power they're wielding, doing something powerful. If I squint at the far camps, I think I can sometimes see weaves, but it may be my imagination."

Ituralde cursed. "That's what they've been waiting for."

"What?" Yoeli asked.

"With Asha'man of their own—"

"They are *not* Asha'man," Deepe said fervently.

"All right, then. With *channelers* of their own, they can tear this wall down easily as knocking over a pile of blocks, Yoeli. That sea of Trollocs will surge in and fill your streets."

"Not so long as I stand," Deepe said.

"I like determination in a soldier, Deepe," Ituralde said, but you *look* as exhausted as I feel."

Deepe shot him a glare. His eyes were red from lack of sleep, and he clenched his teeth, the muscles in his neck and face tense. He met Ituralde's eyes, then took a long, forced breath.

"You are correct," Deepe said. "But neither of us can do anything about that." He raised his hand, doing something that Ituralde couldn't see. A flash of red light appeared over his hand—the signal he used to draw the others to him. "Prepare your men, General, Captain. It will not be long. They cannot continue to hold that kind of Power without . . . consequences."

Yoeli nodded, then hurried away. Ituralde took Deepe's arm, drawing his attention.

"You Asha'man are too important a resource to lose," Ituralde said. "The Dragon sent us here to help, not to die. If this city falls, I want you to take the others and whatever wounded you can and get out. Do you understand, soldier?"

"Many of my men will not like this."

"But you know it is for the best," Ituralde said. "Don't you?"

Deepe hesitated. "Yes. You are correct, as you so often are. I will get them out." He spoke in a lower voice. "This is hopeless resistance, my Lord. Whatever is happening out there, it will be deadly. It galls me to suggest it . . . but what you have said about my Asha'man applies to your soldiers as well. Let us flee." He said the word "flee" with bitterness.

"The Saldaeans wouldn't leave with us."

"I know."

Ituralde considered it. Finally, he shook his head. "Every day we delay up here keeps these monsters away from my homeland a day longer. No, I cannot go, Deepe. This is still the best place to fight. You've seen how fortified those buildings are; we can hold inside for a few days, split apart, keep the army busy."

"Then my Asha'man could stay and help."

"You have your orders, son. You follow them. Understand?"

Deepe snapped his jaw shut, then nodded curtly. "I will take—"

Ituralde didn't hear the rest. An explosion hit.

He didn't feel it arrive. He was standing with Deepe one moment, then found himself on the floor of the wall walk, the world strangely silent around him. His head screamed with pain and he coughed, raising a trembling hand to find his face bleeding. There was something in his right eye; it seared with pain when he blinked. Why was everything so quiet?

He rolled over, coughing again, right eye squeezed shut, the other watering. The wall ended a few inches away from him.

He gasped. An enormous chunk of the northern wall was simply *gone*. He groaned, looking back in the other direction. Deepe had been standing beside him . . .

He found the Asha'man lying on the wall walk nearby, head bleeding. His right leg ended in a ragged rip of flesh and broken bone above where the knee should have been. Ituralde cursed and stumbled forward, dropping to his knees beside the man. Blood was pooling beneath Deepe, but he was still twitching. Alive.

I need to sound the alarm . . .

Alarm? That explosion would have been alarm enough. Inside the wall, buildings were demolished, crushed by stones flying in a spray away from the hole. Outside, Trollocs were loping forward, carrying rafts to cross the moat.

Ituralde pulled the Asha'man's belt off and used it to bind his thigh. It was all he could think to do. His head was still throbbing from the explosion.

The city is lost . . . Light! It's lost, just like that.

Hands were helping him up. Dazedly he glanced about. Connel; he'd survived the blast, though his coat was torn to shreds. He pulled Ituralde away while a pair of soldiers took Deepe.

The next minutes were a blur. Ituralde stumbled down the stairs from the wall, nearly pitching headfirst fifteen feet onto the cobbles. Only Connel's hands kept him from falling. And then . . . a tent? A large open-sided tent? Ituralde blinked. A battlefield should not be so quiet.

Waves of heat washed over him. He screamed. Sound assaulted his ears and mind. Screams, rock breaking, trumpets sounding, drums throbbing. Men dying. It all hit him at once, as if plugs had been yanked from his ears.

He shook himself, gasping. He was in the sick tent. Antail—the quiet, thin-haired Asha'man—stood above him. Light, but Ituralde felt exhausted! Too little sleep mixed with the strain of being Healed. As the sounds of battle consumed him, he found his eyelids treacherously heavy.

"Lord Ituralde," Antail said, "I have a weave that will not make you well, but it will make you think you are well. It could be harmful to you. Do you want me to proceed?"

"I . . ." Ituralde said. The word came out as a mumble. "It . . ."

"Blood and bloody ashes," Antail muttered. He reached forward. Another wave of Power washed through Ituralde. It was like a broom sweeping through him, pushing away all of the fatigue and confusion, restoring his senses and making him feel as if he'd had a perfect night's rest. His right eye didn't hurt anymore.

There was something lingering, deep down, an exhaustion in his bones. He could ignore that. He sat up, breathed in and out, then looked to Antail. "Now *that* is a useful weave, son. You should have told me you could do this!"

"It's dangerous," Antail repeated. "More dangerous than the women's version, I'm told. In some ways more effective. You're trading alertness now for a more profound exhaustion later on."

"Later on, we won't be in the middle of a city that is falling to the Trollocs. Light willing, at least. Deepe?"

"I saw to him first," Antail said, gesturing to the Asha'man lying on a nearby cot, his clothing singed and his face bloodied. His right leg ended in a healed stump, and he appeared to be breathing, though unconscious.

"Connel!" Ituralde said.

"My Lord," the soldier said, stepping up. He'd found a squad of soldiers to act as a personal guard.

"Let's investigate this mess," Ituralde said. He ran out of the sick tent, toward Cordamora Palace. The city was in chaos, groups of Saldaeans and Domani rushing this way and that. Connel, showing foresight, sent a messenger to find Yoeli.

The palace stood nearby, just before the front gate. Its wall had been damaged in the blast, but the building still looked hale. Ituralde had been using it as a command post. Men would expect to find him here. They ran inside, Connel carrying Ituralde's sword—the belt had been cut free at some point. They climbed to the third floor, then ran out onto a balcony that surveyed the area broken by the blast.

As he'd originally feared, the city was lost. The swath of broken wall was being defended by a hastily assembled jumble of defenders. A mounting tide of Trollocs were throwing down rafts on the moat, some beginning to surge forward, followed by Fades. Men ran through the streets, disoriented.

If he'd had more time to prepare, he could have held, as he'd told Deepe. Not now. *Light, but this defense has been one disaster after another.*

"Gather the Asha'man," Ituralde ordered. "And any of my officers you can find. We will organize the men into a retreat through gateways."

"Yes, my Lord," Connel said.

"Ituralde, no!" Yoeli burst out onto the balcony, uniform dirtied and ripped.

"You survived," Ituralde said, relieved. "Excellent. Man, your city is lost. I'm sorry. Bring your men with us and we can—"

"Look!" Yoeli said, pulling Ituralde to the side of the balcony, pointing to the east. A thick column of smoke rose in the distance. A village the Trollocs had burned?

"The watchfire," Yoeli continued. "My sister has seen aid coming! We *must* stand until they arrive."

Ituralde hesitated. "Yoeli," he said softly, "if a force has come, it can't be large enough to stop this horde of Trollocs. And that's assuming it's not a ruse. The Shadowspawn have proven clever in the past."

"Give us a few hours," Yoeli said. "Hold the city with me and send scouts through those gateways of yours to see if a force really is coming."

"A few hours?" Ituralde said. "With a hole in your wall? We're overwhelmed, Yoeli."

"Please," Yoeli pled. "Are you not one of those they name Great Captain? Show me what that title means, Lord Rodel Ituralde."

Ituralde turned, back at the broken wall. Behind him, in the palace's top room, he could hear his officers gathering. The line at the wall was fragmenting. It wouldn't be long now.

Show me what that means.

Perhaps . . .

"Tymoth, are you here?" Ituralde bellowed.

A red-haired man in a black coat stepped onto the balcony. He'd be in command of the Asha'man now that Deepe had fallen. "Here, Lord Ituralde."

"Gather your men," Ituralde said urgently. "Take command of that gap and have the soldiers there retreat. I want the Asha'man to hold the breach. I need a half-hour. I want all of your energy—everything you've got—to hit those Trollocs. You hear me? *Everything* you've got. If you can channel enough to light a candle when this is done, I'll have your hides."

"Sir," the Asha'man said. "Our retreat?"

"Leave Antail in the Healing tent," Ituralde said. "He can make a large enough gateway for the Asha'man to run. But everyone else, *hold that breach*!"

Tymoth dashed away. "Yoeli," Ituralde said, "your job is to gather your forces and stop them from running through the city like . . ." He paused. He'd been about to say, "like it's Tarmon bloody Gai'don." *Burn me!* ". . . like there is nobody in command. If we are going to hold, we will need to be *organized* and *disciplined*. I need four cavalry companies formed up in the courtyard in ten minutes. Give the orders."

"Yes, my Lord," Yoeli said, snapping to it.

"Oh," Ituralde said, turning. "I'm going to need a couple of cartloads of firewood, as many barrels of oil as you can come up with, and all of the wounded in either army who can still run but who have face or arm wounds. Also, get me anyone in the city who's ever held a bow. Go!"

Nearly an hour later, Ituralde stood, hands clasped behind his back, waiting. He'd moved in from the balcony to look out a window, as to not expose himself. But he still had a good view of the fighting.

Outside the palace, the Asha'man line was finally weakening. They'd given him the better part of an hour, blasting back wave after wave of Trollocs in an awesome display of Power. Blessedly, the enemy channelers had not appeared. After that show of power, hopefully they were drained and exhausted.

It felt like dusk, with those oppressive clouds overhead and the masses of figures darkening the hillsides beyond the city. The Trollocs, fortunately, didn't bring ladders or siege towers. Only wave after wave at that breach, whipped into attack by the Myrddraal.

Already, some of the black-coated men were limping away from the breach, looking exhausted. The last few threw a final blast of Fire and erupting Earth, then followed their companions. They left the gap completely open and undefended, as ordered.

Come on, Ituralde thought as the smoke cleared.

The Trollocs peered through the smoke, climbing over the carcasses of those the Asha'man had killed. The Shadowspawn loped on hooves or thick paws. Some sniffed the air.

The streets inside the gap were filled with carefully placed men who were bloodied and wounded. They began to scream as the Trollocs entered, running as commanded. Likely none of their fear was feigned. The scene looked more terrible now that many of the nearby buildings were smoldering, as if from the blast, roofs on fire, smoke pouring from windows. The Trollocs wouldn't know that the slate roofs had been designed *not* to burn, and laws kept buildings from containing too much wood.

Ituralde held his breath. The Trollocs broke, running into the city, howling and roaring, groups breaking apart as they saw the opportunity to pillage and slaughter.

The door behind Ituralde slammed open, and Yoeli hastened in. "The last ranks are placed. Is it working?"

Ituralde didn't answer; the proof was below. The Trollocs assumed their battle won—the blasting Power of the Asha'man had the air of one final stand, and the city appeared to be in chaos. The Trollocs all ran down the streets with obvious glee. Even the Myrddraal who entered appeared at ease.

The Trollocs avoided the burning buildings and the palace, which was walled. They moved deeper into the city, pursuing the fleeing soldiers down a wide avenue on the eastern side of the city. Carefully piled rubble encouraged the bulk of them down this avenue.

"Do you have aspirations of being a general, Captain Yoeli?" Ituralde asked softly.

"My aspirations are not important," Yoeli said. "But a man would be a fool not to hope to learn."

"Then pay attention to this lesson, son." Below, shutters on windows were flung open on buildings along the avenue the Trollocs had taken. Bowmen surged out onto balconies. "If you ever have so much as an *impression* that you're doing what your enemy expects you to do, then do something else."

The arrows fell, and Trollocs died. Large crossbows that shot quarrels almost the size of spears targeted the Fades, and many could be seen lurching across the pavement, not knowing that they were already dead, as scores of Trollocs linked to them fell. Confused, enraged, the still-living creatures began to bellow and pound in the doors of the buildings filled with archers. But as they did so, the thunder began. Hoofbeats. Yoeli's best cavalry charged down the streets, lances forward. They trampled the Trollocs, slaughtering them.

The city became an enormous ambush. A man couldn't ask for better vantages than those buildings, and the streets were wide enough to allow a charge by those who knew the layout. The Trollocs went from bellowing in joy to screaming in pain, and scrambled over one another in their haste to get away. They entered the courtyard by the broken wall.

The Saldaean horsemen followed, their hooves and flanks wet with the noxious blood of the fallen. Men appeared at windows of "burning" buildings—the fires carefully created in sectioned-off rooms—and began loosing arrows down into the large courtyard. Others tossed new lances to the horsemen, who, reequipped, lined up and rode into the Trollocs. The arrows stopped falling, and the cavalry made a sweeping charge across the courtyard.

Hundreds of Trollocs died. Perhaps thousands. Those that didn't die scrambled out of the gap. Most of the Myrddraal fled. Those that did not were targets for the archers. Killing one of them could kill dozens of Trollocs linked to them. The Fades went down—many sprouting dozens of arrows.

"I'll give the order to unite and hold the breach again," Yoeli said eagerly.

"No." Ituralde said.

"But—"

"Fighting at the breach will gain us nothing," Ituralde

said. "Give the orders for the men to move to different buildings, and have the archers take different positions. Are there warehouses or other large buildings that can hide the horsemen? Move them there, quickly. And then we wait."

"They won't be caught again."

"No," Ituralde said. "But they'll be slow and cautious. If we fight them head on, we lose. If we hold, buy time, we win. That's the only way out of this, Yoeli. To survive until help comes. If it's coming."

Yoeli nodded.

"Our next trap won't kill as many," Ituralde said, "but Trollocs are cowards at heart. The knowledge that any roadway could suddenly turn into a death trap will make them hesitate, and will earn us more time than would losing half of our men holding that wall."

"All right," Yoeli said. He hesitated. "But . . . doesn't this mean that they're anticipating us? This phase of the plan will work only because they expect our ambushes."

"I suppose that's true."

"So shouldn't we do something different? You said that if we've got a hint that the enemy knows what we're going to do, we should change plans."

"You're thinking about it too much, son. Go do as I commanded."

"Er, yes, my Lord." He hurried away.

This, Ituralde thought, *is why I should never teach tactics.* It was hard to explain to students that there was a rule that trumped all of the others: Always trust your instincts. The Trollocs would be afraid. He could use that. He'd use anything they gave him.

He didn't like to think too long about that rule, lest he dwell on the fact that he'd violated it already. Because his every instinct screamed that he should have abandoned this city hours ago.

CHAPTER
29

A Terrible Feeling

W hat is Perrin plotting, do you think?" Berelain asked as she strolled beside Faile and Alliandre. Faile didn't answer. The late afternoon was softly lit by a distant sun shrouded in clouds. Soon it would make the horizon burn as it sank down for the night. In two days, Perrin would go on trial. He'd delayed specifically, she knew, to gain more time for the Asha'man to work out the strange problem with gateways.

Their army was growing, still more people flooding to them. Scout reports indicated that the Whitecloak force was growing as well. More slowly, but still growing. In days like these, an army was a symbol of strength and—at the very least—food.

A stand of fingeroot trees glutted themselves on the water of the stream near Perrin's war camp. Such strange plants they were, with those roots that dipped into the water. Trunks like flowing glass that had pooled while hardening. There was nothing like them up in Saldaea. It seemed that two wrong steps here could lead you into a swamp.

"No answer for me?" Berelain asked. She seemed distracted these days. "I've been thinking. Perhaps it would be good to send an envoy to the Whitecloak army. Do you think Perrin would allow me to go and speak with them? Perhaps I could make a personal appeal on his behalf."

She *kept* bringing up that topic. "No," Faile said. "You know his mind is made up on this trial, Berelain."

The First pursed her lips, but did not press further. The three continued their walk, accompanied by ten Maidens.

Once, Faile might have complained about the attention. That was before she'd been taken so unexpectedly, and so easily.

In the distance, she saw a small group of refugees leaving the camp, walking away to the southeast, cross-country. Before things had gone wrong with the gateways, about ten thousand had been sent to rural areas in Cairhien. All had instructions to remain quiet. Perrin didn't want his location known yet. Women would be still, but of course the men would gossip; they always did.

Few knew that gateways failed; Perrin had told the people that he needed the Asha'man strong, in case there was fighting with the Whitecloaks. It was true enough. Still, some refugees had asked to leave, going on foot. To these, Faile gave bits of gold or a jewel from Sevanna's store and wished them the best. She was surprised at how many wanted to return to homes that were in Seanchan-controlled lands.

Despite the departures, the size of Perrin's force was swelling day by day. Faile and the others passed a large group practicing with swords. The refugees who had decided to train were now some twenty-five thousand strong. They practiced late into the day, and Faile could still hear barked orders from Tam.

"Well." Berelain continued her musings. "What *will* Perrin do? Why set up this trial? He wants something from those Whitecloaks." She stepped around a gnarled fingeroot. The First, like so many others, read much more into Perrin's actions than there was to find. He'd be amused if he knew the plots they ascribed to him.

And she claims to understand men, Faile thought. Perrin was by no means stupid, nor was he the simple man he sometimes claimed to be. He planned, he thought, and he was careful. But he was also direct. Deliberate. When he said something, he meant it.

"I agree with Berelain," Alliandre said. "We should just leave, march away. Or attack those Whitecloaks."

Faile shook her head. "It bothers Perrin when people think he did something wrong. As long as the Whitecloaks continue to insist he is a murderer, his name will not be clear." He was being bullheaded and foolish, but there *was* a nobility about it.

So long as it didn't get him killed. However, she loved him for that very sense of honor. Changing him would be ill-advised, so she had to make certain others didn't take advantage of him.

As she always did when they discussed the Whitecloaks, Berelain got a strange look in her eyes, and she glanced—perhaps unconsciously—in the direction their army camped. Light. She wasn't going to ask *again* if she could go speak to them? She had come up with a dozen different reasons why she wanted to.

Faile noticed a large group of soldiers trying to look inconspicuous as they rounded the inside of the camp, keeping pace with Faile and their guards on their promenade. Perrin wanted her well protected.

"This young Lord Captain Commander," Alliandre said idly. "He looks quite striking in that white uniform, wouldn't you say? If you can get past that sunburst on his cloak. Such a beautiful man."

"Oh?" Berelain said. Surprisingly, warm color rose in her cheeks.

"I'd always heard that Morgase's stepson was a handsome man," Alliandre continued. "But I hadn't anticipated him being so . . . pristine."

"Like a statue carved from marble," Berelain whispered, "a relic from the Age of Legends. A perfect thing left behind. For us to worship."

"He's passable," Faile said with a sniff. "I prefer a bearded face, myself."

It wasn't a lie—she loved a bearded face, and Perrin *was* handsome. He had a burly power to him that was *quite* appealing. But this Galad Damodred was . . . well, it wasn't fair to compare him to Perrin. That would be like comparing a stained glass window to a cabinet made by a master carpenter. Both were excellent examples of their craft, and it was hard to weigh them against one another. But the window certainly did shine.

Berelain's expression seemed distant. She was definitely taken with Damodred. Such a short time for it to have happened. Faile told Berelain that finding another man for her attentions would help with the rumors, but the Whitecloak commander? Had the woman lost all sense?

"So what do we do?" Alliandre asked as they rounded

the south side of the camp, halfway to the point from which they'd started.

"About the Whitecloaks?" Faile asked.

"About Maighdin," Alliandre said. "Morgase."

"I can't help feeling that she took advantage of my kindness," Faile said. "After all we went through together, she didn't tell me who she was?"

"You seem to be determined to give her very little credit," Berelain said.

Faile didn't reply. She'd been thinking about what Perrin said, and he was probably right. Faile should not be so angry with her. If Morgase really had been fleeing one of the Forsaken, it was a miracle that she was still alive. Besides, she herself had lied about who she was, when first meeting Perrin.

In truth, her anger was because Morgase was going to judge Perrin. She *presumed* to judge Perrin. Maighdin the lady's maid might be grateful, but Morgase the Queen would see Perrin as a rival. Would Morgase *really* treat this judgment fairly, or would she take the chance to discredit a man who had raised himself up as a lord?

"I feel as you do, my Lady," Alliandre said softly.

"And how is that?"

"Deceived," Alliandre said. "Maighdin was our friend. I thought I knew her."

"You would have acted exactly as she did in that situation," Berelain said. "Why give away information if you don't have to?"

"Because we were friends," Alliandre said. "After what we went through together, it turns out that she's *Morgase Trakand*. Not just a queen—*the Queen*. The woman's a legend. And she was here, with us, serving us tea. Poorly."

"You have to admit," Faile said thoughtfully, "she did get better with the tea."

Faile reached to her throat, touching the cord that bore Rolan's stone. She didn't wear it every day, but she did so often enough. Had Morgase been false that entire time they'd been with the Shaido? Or had she, in a way, been more true? With no titles to live up to, she hadn't been forced to be the "legendary" Morgase Trakand. Under circumstances like that, wouldn't a person's true nature be more likely to show through?

Faile gripped the cord. Morgase would not turn this trial against Perrin out of spite. But she *would* offer judgment in honesty. Which meant Faile needed to be prepared, and have ready—

Screams sounded nearby.

Faile reacted immediately, spinning toward the woods. She instinctively anticipated Aiel leaping from the bushes to kill and capture, and she felt a moment of sheer panic.

But the screams were coming from *inside* camp. She cursed, turning about, but felt something tug at her belt. She looked down with a start to see her belt knife pull itself from its sheath and flip into the air.

"A bubble of evil!" Berelain said, stumbling to the side.

Faile ducked, throwing herself to the ground as her knife flipped through the air toward her head. It narrowly missed. As Faile came up in a crouch, she saw with a start that Berelain was facing down a dagger, one that looked—from the damage to Berelain's shirt—to have ripped its way free of a hidden sheath inside her sleeve.

Beyond Berelain, the camp was in a tumult. The nearby practicing refugees were scattering, swords and spears flipping through the air of their own volition. It looked as if *every weapon* in the camp had suddenly sprung to life, rising up to attack its master.

Motion. Faile dodged to the side as her knife came back for her, but a white-haired figure in brown snatched the weapon from the air, holding it in a tight grip. Sulin rolled, clinging to it, her teeth gritted as she wrenched it from the air and slammed it down onto a stone, breaking the blade from the hilt.

It stopped moving. Sulin's spears, however, pulled from their place on her back and spun in the sky, tips pointing toward her.

"Run!" the Maiden said, turning and trying to face all three spears at once.

"Where?" Faile demanded, picking up a stone from the ground. "The weapons are everywhere." Berelain was struggling with her dagger. She'd grabbed it, but it was fighting her, wrenching her arms from side to side. Alliandre was surrounded by *three* knives. Light! Faile suddenly felt lucky for having worn only one today.

Several of the Maidens charged in to help Alliandre,

throwing stones at the knives, dodging spears that lunged for them. Berelain was alone.

Gritting her teeth—feeling half a fool for helping the woman she hated—Faile jumped in and placed her hands over Berelain's, lending her strength to that of the First. Together, they wrenched the dagger to the side, toward the ground, where they could drive its point into the earth. When they did, remarkably, it stopped moving.

Faile released it hesitantly, then looked up at the disheveled Berelain. The woman pressed her right hand to her other palm, stanching the blood from a cut she'd taken. She nodded at Faile. "Thank you."

"What stopped it?" Faile asked, heart thumping. Shouts sounded from around the camp. Cursing. Clangs from weapons.

"The dirt?" Berelain asked, kneeling.

Faile dug her fingers into the loam. She turned, noticing with alarm that one of the Maidens was down, though others had felled several of the flying spears. Faile tossed her handful of soil at one that was still whipping about.

When the dirt touched the spear, the weapon dropped. Sulin saw it, eyes widening behind her veiled face. She dropped the stones she'd been wielding and took up a handful of soil, spraying it over her head as a spear drove for her heart.

The dirt stopped it, and it fell to the ground. Nearby, the soldiers who had been following along to guard Faile and the others were having a worse time of things. They had backed into a circle, using their shields to block incoming weapons, hunkered down with worried expressions.

"Quickly!" Faile said to the Maidens, digging both hands into the soil. "Spread the word! Let the others know how to stop the weapons!" She threw soil at the daggers beside Alliandre, dropping two with one throw, then began running for the nearby soldiers.

"There is no need for you to apologize, Galad," Morgase said softly. "You couldn't have known what was happening in the Fortress of the Light. You were leagues and leagues away."

They sat in his tent, chairs facing each other, late-afternoon light shining on the walls. Galad sat with hands clasped before him as he leaned forward. So thoughtful. She remembered her first impressions of him, long ago when she'd married his father. The young child had simply been part of the deal, and while Morgase had adopted him, she had always worried that he felt less loved than his siblings.

Galad had always been so solemn. Quick to point out when someone did something wrong. But unlike other children—Elayne especially—he had not used his knowledge as a weapon. She should have seen. She should have realized he'd be attracted to the Whitecloaks for their vision of a world that was black and white. Could she have prepared him better? Shown him that the world was not black and white—it wasn't even gray. It was full of colors that sometimes didn't fit into any spectrum of morality.

He looked up, hands still clasped, eyes troubled. "I accused Valda wrongly. When I went to him, I said I was demanding Trial Beneath the Light because he had abused you and killed you. Half was wrong. I have done something where I was in error, at least in part. Regardless of that fact, I'm pleased that I killed him."

Her breath caught in her throat. Valda had reputedly been one of the greatest swordsmen alive. And Galad had bested him in a duel? This youth? But he was a youth no longer. Galad had made his choices, and she had a difficult time judging him for them. In some ways, they seemed more admirable than her own choices.

"You did well," she said. "Valda was a snake. I am certain he was behind Niall's death. Galad, you did the world a service."

He nodded. "For what he did to you, he deserved death. But I shall need to release a statement anyway." He rose, clasping his hands behind his back as he walked, his white clothing seeming to glow in the light. "I will explain that my accusation of murder was false, but that Valda still deserved death for his other offenses. Dire offenses." He stopped for a moment. "I wish I had known."

"There was nothing you could have done, son," she said. "My captivity was my own fault. For trusting my enemies."

Galad waved a hand. "There was no resisting Gaebril, if what you have heard is true. As for your captivity, you did *not* trust your enemies. You were betrayed, like all of us, by

Valda. The Children are never the enemies of a person who walks in the Light."

"And Perrin Aybara?" she asked.

"Shadowspawn."

"No, son. I don't like some of the things he is doing, but I promise you, he is a good man."

"Then the trial will prove that," Galad said.

"Good men can make mistakes. If you proceed with this, it could end in a way that none of us wish."

Galad froze, frowning. "Mother, are you implying that he should be allowed to escape his crime?"

"Come," she said, gesturing. "Sit back down. You're dizzying me with that pacing about."

Perhaps he'd risen to the position of Lord Captain Commander only recently, but he already seemed to bristle at taking an order. He did sit, however.

Oddly, she felt like a queen again. Galad hadn't seen her during the hard months. He thought of her as the old Morgase, so around him, she actually *felt* like the old Morgase. Almost.

Niall had held her as a prisoner, but had respected her and she had begun to think that she might be able to respect him as well. What had happened to the board where she and Niall had played stones so often? She hated to think of it broken in the Seanchan assault.

Would Galad become a Lord Captain Commander like Niall, or perhaps someone better? The Queen in her, the Queen reawakened, wanted to find a way to bring his light out and stifle the shadow.

"Galad," she said. "What are you going to do?"

"About the trial?"

"No. With this army of yours."

"We will fight at the Last Battle."

"Admirable," she said. "But do you know what that means?"

"It means fighting alongside the Dragon Reborn."

"And the Aes Sedai."

"We can serve alongside the witches for a time, if it is in the name of the greater good."

She closed her eyes, breathing out. "Galad, listen to yourself. You name them witches? You went to train with them perhaps to become a Warder!"

"Yes."

She opened her eyes. He seemed so earnest. But even the most deadly and violent of hounds could be earnest. "Do you know what they did to Elayne, Mother?" he asked.

"You mean losing her?" Morgase still harbored anger over that.

"They sent her out on missions," he said, voice laced with disgust. "They refused to let me see her, probably because she was out being put into danger. I met her later, outside the Tower."

"Where was she?" Morgase asked, eager.

"Here in the south. My men name the Aes Sedai witches. Sometimes, I wonder how far off from the truth that is."

"Galad . . ."

"Not all women who wield the One Power are evil inherently," he said. "That is a mistaken tradition of the Children. *The Way of the Light* doesn't make that claim; it just says that the temptation to use the One Power can corrupt. I believe that the women who now run the White Tower have let their schemes and selfish plots blind them."

She nodded, not wishing to argue the point. Thank the Light Elaida wasn't here to hear that logic!

"Either way," he said. "We will fight alongside them, and the Dragon Reborn, and this Perrin Aybara if need be. The struggle against the Shadow outweighs all other concerns."

"Then let us join that struggle," she said. "Galad, forget this trial! Aybara intends to disband some of his army and give the rest to al'Thor."

He met her eyes, then nodded. "Yes. I can see now that the Pattern has led you to me. We will travel with you. *After* the trial has finished."

She sighed.

"I don't do this by choice," Galad said, rising again. "Aybara himself suggested that he be tried. The man's conscience weighs against him, and to deny him this opportunity would be wrong. Let him prove his innocence to us, and to himself. Then we can continue." He hesitated, reaching out and touching the white-scabbarded sword on his dressing table. "And if we continue without him, then he will rest in the Light, having paid for his crimes."

"Galad," she said, "you know Lini was among the people you took from Perrin's camp."

"She should have spoken up, revealed herself to me. I would have set her free."

"And yet she did not. I have heard you all but threatened to execute the prisoners if Perrin didn't come to battle. Would you have actually done this?"

"Their blood would have been on his head."

"Lini's blood, Galad?"

"I . . . I would have seen her among them and removed her from danger."

"So you would have killed the others," Morgase said. "People who did no wrong, who were guilty of nothing more than being beguiled by Aybara?"

"The executions would never have occurred. It was merely a threat."

"A lie."

"Bah! What is the point of this, Mother?"

"To make you think, son," Morgase said. "In ways that I should have encouraged before, rather than leaving you to your simple illusions. Life is not so easy as the toss of a coin, one side or the other. Have I ever told you of the trial of Tham Felmley?"

Galad shook his head, looking irritated.

"Listen to me. He was a brickmason in Caemlyn, a reputable one. He was accused of murdering his brother in the early days of my reign. He had enough repute, and the case was important enough, that I judged it myself. He hanged at the end of it."

"A fitting end for a murderer."

"Yes," Morgase said. "Unfortunately, the murderer went free. One of his workers had actually done the deed. It didn't come out until two years later, when the man was taken for another murder. He laughed at us then, as we hanged him. Felmley had been innocent all along. The real man, the murderer, was one of those to condemn him during the original trial."

Galad fell silent.

"It's the only time," Morgase said, "where I know for certain that I hanged someone by mistake. So you tell me, Galad. Should I hang for *my* mistake in condemning an innocent man?"

"You did your best, Mother."

"And a man is still dead who did not deserve it."

Galad looked troubled.

"The Children like to speak of the Light protecting them," Morgase said, "of guiding their judgment and leading people to justice. That isn't how it works, Galad. Valda, claiming the blessing of the Light, could do terrible things. And I, hoping for the Light's aid, have killed unjustly.

"I'm not saying that Aybara is innocent. I haven't heard enough either way. But I want you to understand. Sometimes a good man *can* do wrong. At times, it is appropriate to punish him. At other times, punishment serves nobody, and the best thing to do is to let him continue and learn. As I continued and learned, after making such a poor judgment."

Galad frowned. That was good. Finally, he shook his head, his face clearing. "We shall see what the trial brings. It—"

There was a knock on the post outside. Galad turned, his frown deepening. "Yes?"

"My Lord Captain Commander," a Whitecloak said, lifting the flap and stepping into the tent. He was a lean man with sunken eyes that had dark patches beneath them. "We've just had word from the creature Aybara's camp. They're asking to push back the day of the trial."

Galad stood. "For what purpose?" he demanded.

"A disturbance in their camp, they claim," the Whitecloak said. "Something about wounded needing tending. My Lord Captain Commander . . . it is obviously a ploy. A trick of some sort. We should attack them, or at the very least, deny this pointless extension."

Galad hesitated. He looked at Morgase.

"It is no ploy, son," she said. "I can promise you that. If Aybara says he needs more time, he's being honest with you."

"Bah," Galad said, waving the messenger away. "I shall consider it. Alongside the things you have said, Mother. Perhaps some extra time to consider would be . . . welcomed."

"The channelers say they are working as hard as they can," Gaul explained, walking beside Perrin through camp as they checked the various sections. "But they say it could take days to see to everyone."

The sun was sinking toward the horizon, but it would probably be a long night for many of them, tending the wounded.
Thousands had been wounded, though most wounds—
fortunately—were not bad. They'd lost some people. Too
many, maybe as many as had fallen to the snake bites.

Perrin grunted. Gaul himself had his arm in a sling; he'd
fended off his spears, only to have one of his arrows nearly
kill him. He'd blocked it with his forearm. When Perrin had
asked, he'd laughed and said that it had been years since
he'd shot himself with his own arrow. Aiel humor.

"Have we heard back from the Whitecloaks?" Perrin
asked, turning to Aravine, who walked on his other side.

"Yes," she said. "But nothing specific. Their commander
said he'd 'think' about giving us more time."

"Well, he's not the one who will decide," Perrin said, going into the Mayener section of camp to check on Berelain's
people. "I'm not going to risk a battle with a quarter of my
men wounded and my Asha'man dead tired from Healing.
We go to this trial when I say so, and if Damodred dis-
agrees, he can just go ahead and attack us."

Gaul grunted his agreement. He wore his spears, but
Perrin noticed they were strapped more tightly in place
than usual. Aravine carried a lantern, though they hadn't
needed to light it yet. She was anticipating a late night as
well.

"Let me know when Tam and Elyas get back," Perrin
said to Gaul. Perrin had sent each one separately to visit
nearby villages and make certain the people there—the
ones who hadn't joined a passing army—hadn't suffered
from the bubble of evil.

Berelain had composed herself, her hand bandaged. She
gave the report to him herself, from her tent, saying how
many of her soldiers had been wounded, giving the names
of the men they'd lost. Only six from her camp.

Perrin yawned as he left the tent, sending Aravine to
check on the Aes Sedai. Gaul had run off to help with
carrying some of the wounded, and Perrin found himself
alone as he walked down the path toward Alliandre's section of camp.

His hammer hadn't tried to kill him. So far as he knew,
it was the only weapon on anyone's person that hadn't responded to the bubble of evil. What did it mean?

He shook his head, then hesitated, pausing in thought as he heard someone jogging along the path toward him. He caught Tam's scent, and turned to meet the sturdy man as he arrived.

"Perrin, son," Tam said, out of breath from running. "Something unusual just happened."

"The bubble of evil hit the village?" Perrin asked, alarmed. "Were people hurt?"

"Oh, no," Tam said. "Not that. The village was fine. They didn't even notice anything was wrong. This is something else." Tam smelled odd. Thoughtful, worried.

Perrin frowned. "What? What's happening?"

"I . . . well, I have to go, son," Tam said. "Leave the camp. I don't know when I'll be back."

"Is this—"

"It has nothing to do with the Whitecloaks," Tam said. "I've been told I can't say much. But it's about Rand."

The colors swirled. Rand walked the hallways of the Stone of Tear. His expression was dark. Dangerous.

"Perrin," Tam said, "I think this is something I need to do. It involves Aes Sedai, and I *have* to leave you now. I can't say anything else. They made me swear it."

Perrin looked into Tam's eyes and saw the sincerity there. He nodded. "All right, then. You need any help? Someone to go with you, wherever you're going?"

"I'll be all right," Tam said. He smelled embarrassed. What was going on? "I'll try to get you some help, son." He laid a hand on Perrin's shoulder. "You've done well here. I'm proud of you, and your father would be too. Keep it up. I'll see you at the Last Battle, if not before."

Perrin nodded. Tam hurried off toward his tent, perhaps to pack.

It was hard to look regal while being carried atop the Caemlyn city wall on a litter, but Elayne did her best. Sometimes getting what you wanted was more important than looking regal.

Bed rest! For a queen! Well, in order to keep Melfane from hovering over her, she'd given an oath that she would stay off her feet. But she'd said nothing about staying in her bedroom.

Four Guardsmen carried the litter high on their shoulders. Elayne sat safely between armrests, wearing a crimson gown, hair carefully brushed, the Rose Crown of Andor atop her head.

The day was muggy, the weather turning warm, the sky still dark with clouds. She spared a moment to feel guilty for making the poor men, in dress uniform, carry her through this early-summer heat. But these men would ride to battle in her name; they could stand a little warm weather. How often did Guardsmen get the honor of carrying their queen, anyway?

Birgitte strode alongside the bed, and the bond indicated that she was amused. Elayne had feared she'd try to stop this excursion, but instead she had *laughed*! Birgitte must have determined that this day's activities—though bound to upset Melfane—were no real risk to Elayne or her babes. To the Warder, that meant this was an opportunity to see Elayne get paraded through town looking foolish.

Elayne winced. What would the people say? The Queen, riding a litter, being marched to the outer wall? Well, Elayne wasn't about to let rumors keep her from seeing the test firsthand, and she wasn't about to be bullied by a tyrannical midwife.

She had quite a view from the wall. The fields leading to Aringill lay open to her left; the city bustled to her right. Those fields were too brown. Reports from around the realm were dire. Nine fields in ten had failed.

Elayne's porters carried her up to one of the wall's tower turrets, then hit a snag as they realized the poles on the litter were too long to make the turns on the stairs inside the tower; the demonstration was supposed to happen atop it. Luckily, there were alternative short handholds for just such situations. They removed the poles, switched to the handholds, and proceeded.

While they carried her up, she distracted herself by thinking about Cairhien. The noble Houses there all *claimed* to be eagerly awaiting her arrival to take the throne, and yet none offered more than the most flaccid support. *Daes Dae'mar* was fully in effect, and the posturing for Elayne's ascent—or her failure to ascend—had begun the moment Rand had mentioned that he intended the nation to be hers.

In Cairhien, a hundred different political winds always

blew in a hundred different directions. She didn't have time to learn all of the different factions before she took the throne. Besides, if she was seen as playing the game, she could be seen as someone to defeat. She had to find a way to seize the Sun Throne *without* mixing too much in the local House politics.

Elayne's litter creaked up and crested the lip of the tower's turret. Atop the tower, Aludra stood with one of her prototype dragons. The bronze tube was quite long and set in a framework of wood. It was just a dummy, for display. A second, working dragon had been set up atop the next tower down the wall. It was far enough away that Elayne wouldn't be in danger if something went wrong.

The slender Taraboner woman seemed to take no thought for the fact that she was delivering a potentially world-changing weapon to the queen of a foreign country; all Aludra seemed to want was a way to get back at the Seanchan, or so Mat had explained. Elayne had spent some time with the woman while traveling with Luca's menagerie, but still wasn't certain how trustworthy she was. She'd have Master Norry keep an eye on her.

Assuming, of course, that the dragons worked. Elayne spared another glance for the people down below. Only then did she realize how high up she really was. Light!

I'm safe, she reminded herself. *Min's viewing.* Not that she said anything like that to Birgitte, not any longer. And she *did* intend to stop taking so many risks. This wasn't a risk. Not really.

She turned away before she grew dizzy and inspected the dragon more closely. It was shaped like a large bronze bell, though longer and narrower. Like an enormous vase turned on its side. Elayne had received more than one missive from the city's irate bellfounders. Aludra insisted that her orders be carried out *exactly* and had forced the men to recast the tube three times.

Late the previous night, a loud crack had sounded across the city. As if a stone wall had fallen somewhere or a bolt of lightning had struck. This morning Elayne had received a note from Aludra.

First test a success, it had read. *Meet me today on city wall for demonstration.*

"Your Majesty," Aludra said. "You are . . . well, yes?"

"I will be fine, Aludra," Elayne said, trying to maintain her dignity. "The dragon is ready?"

"It is," Aludra said. She wore a long brown dress, her black wavy hair loose, coming down to her waist. Why no braids today? Aludra didn't seem to care for jewelry, and Elayne had never seen her wear any. A group of five men from Mat's Band of the Red Hand stood with her, one carrying what appeared to be a chimney brush of some sort. Another had a metal sphere in his hands, and another carried a small wooden cask.

Elayne could see a similar group on the next tower over. Someone there raised a hat into the air and waved at her. Mat wanted to watch from the tower with the working dragon, it seemed. Foolhardy man. What if the thing exploded like a nightflower?

"The demonstration, then," Aludra said, "we shall begin. These men here will show you what is being done on the other tower." She hesitated as she regarded Elayne. "Her Majesty, I think we should prop her up, so that she can see the display."

A few minutes later, they'd located some small boxes to place beneath the litter and elevate Elayne so that she could see over the tower's crenelations. It appeared that something had been constructed on a distant hillside, though it was too far for Elayne to make out. Aludra pulled out several looking glasses and handed one each to Elayne and Birgitte.

Elayne raised her glass to her eye. Dressing dummies. Aludra had set up some fifty of them in ranks on the far hill. Light! Where had she gotten so many? Likely, Elayne would be getting some wordy missives from gownmakers across the city.

Mat had promised this would be worth practically any cost. Of course, that was Mat. He wasn't exactly the most reliable person around.

He's not the one who lost an invaluable ter'angreal *to the Shadow,* she reminded herself. She grimaced. In her pouch, she carried another replica of the foxhead. It was one of three she'd created so far. If she was going to be confined to her bed, then she might as well make use of her time. It would be a lot less frustrating if she could channel consistently.

All three of the replica foxhead medallions worked as the

first replica had. She couldn't channel while wearing one, and a powerful weave could overwhelm them. She really needed that original back for further study.

"You can see, Your Majesty," Aludra said in a stiff voice, as if unaccustomed to giving a demonstration, "that we've tried to re-create the conditions under which you might make use of the dragons, yes?"

Except instead of fifty dressing dummies, we'll have a hundred thousand Trollocs, Elayne thought.

"The next tower, you should look at it," Aludra said, gesturing.

Elayne turned the glass to look at the next tower down the wall. She could see five members of the Band there, dressed in uniforms, waiting with another dragon. Mat was looking in the thing, right down the tube.

"These have trained somewhat on the dragons," Aludra continued. "But they do not have the efficiency I would like. They will do for now, yes?"

Elayne lowered her glass as the men pulled the dummy tube back—it was on a set of wheels—and rotated it up a bit toward the sky. One poured some black powder in from his cask, then another stuffed in a wad of something. This was followed by the man with the long pole ramming it down the tube. That wasn't a chimney brush he held, but some kind of tool used for packing.

"That looks like the powder inside a nightflower," Birgitte said. She felt wary.

Aludra shot the Warder a glance. "And how do you know what is inside a nightflower, Maerion? You do realize how dangerous it is to open one of those, yes?"

Birgitte shrugged.

Aludra frowned, but got no response, so took a deep breath and calmed herself. "The device, it is perfectly safe. We set up the other dragon to do the firing, so there would be no danger, yes? But there would not be danger anyway. The casting is good and my calculations, they are perfect."

"Elayne," Birgitte said, "I still think we'd be better off watching from the wall down below. Even if this one beside us isn't going to be lit."

"After all I went through to get up here?" Elayne asked. "No thank you. Aludra, you may proceed."

She ignored Birgitte's annoyance. Did Aludra really

think she could hit one of those dressing dummies with her iron sphere? That was a long way to go, and the sphere was so small, barely wider than a man's outstretched palm. Had Elayne invested all of this effort to get something that would work more poorly than a catapult? This dragon sounded as if it could throw its sphere farther, but the boulders tossed by a catapult were many times larger.

The men finished. The remaining man touched a small torch to a fuse sticking out of the sphere and rolled it into the tube; then they turned the tube to face directly outward.

"You see?" Aludra said, patting the dragon. "Three men is best. Four for safety, in case one falls. One could do the work if he had to, but it would be slow."

The men stepped back as Aludra got out a red flag. She held it up in the air, signaling the other team on the next tower down the wall. Elayne focused on them with the glass. One carried a small torch. Mat watched with a curious expression.

Aludra lowered her flag. The soldier touched his burning torch to the side of the dragon.

The explosive sound that followed was so powerful that it made Elayne jump. The boom was as sharp as a thunderclap, and she heard in the distance what sounded like an echo of the explosion. She raised a hand to her breast, and remembered to draw breath.

A pocket on the hillside exploded in a massive spray of dust and earth. The ground seemed to tremble! It was as if an Aes Sedai had torn up the earth with a weave, but the One Power hadn't been used at all.

Aludra seemed disappointed. Elayne raised her looking glass to her eye. The blast had missed the dressing dummies by a good twenty paces, but had ripped a hole in the ground five paces wide. Did the ball explode like a nightflower to cause that? This device wasn't merely an improved catapult or trebuchet; it was something else. Something capable of smashing an iron sphere into the ground with such force that it blew open a hole, then perhaps exploded on its own.

Why, she could line an entire wall with these dragons! With all of them firing together. . . .

Aludra raised her flag again; Elayne watched with her glass as the men on the next tower over cleaned, then reloaded, the tube. Mat was holding his ears and scowling, which gave Elayne a smile. He really *should* have watched from her tower. The reloading process took a very short time, perhaps three minutes. And Aludra said she intended to see it happen more quickly?

Aludra wrote a set of orders and sent it by messenger to the men. They changed the dragon's position slightly. She waved her flag; Elayne steeled herself for another explosion, but still jumped when it came.

This time, the blast was dead-on, hitting in the very center of the rank of dressing dummies. Their tattered remnants spun through the air. The blow destroyed five or six, and knocked down a good dozen of them.

With the ability to fire every two minutes, hit so far away, and deal such destruction, these weapons would be *deadly*. As deadly as *damane*, perhaps. Birgitte was still looking through her looking glass, and while her face was impassive, Elayne could feel the woman's amazement.

"The weapon, you find it pleasing?" Aludra asked.

"I find it pleasing, Aludra," Elayne said, smiling. "I find it pleasing indeed. The resources of the entire city are yours, the resources of all Andor. There are several more bellfounders in Andor." She glanced at the Illuminator. "But you *must* keep the plans and designs a secret. I will send Guards with you. We can't afford to let any of the bellfounders consider the value of leaving home and selling information to our enemies."

"So long as they don't reach the Seanchan," Aludra said, "I care not."

"Well, *I* do," Elayne said. "And I'm the one who will see these things used properly. I'll need an oath out of you, Aludra."

The woman sighed, but gave it. Elayne had no intention of turning them against anyone other than Trollocs and Seanchan. But she would feel much more secure about her nation knowing that she had these at her disposal.

She smiled as she considered it, and found it difficult to contain her excitement. Birgitte finally lowered her glass. She felt . . . solemn.

"What?" Elayne asked as the Guards took turns with her glass, inspecting the devastation. She felt some odd indigestion. Had she eaten something bad for lunch?

"The world just changed, Elayne," Birgitte said, shaking her head, long braid swinging slightly. "It just changed in a very large way. I have a terrible feeling that it's only the beginning."

CHAPTER
30

Men Dream Here

These Whitecloaks are a tight-lipped group, my Lady," Lacile said with a smug smile, "but they're still men. Men who haven't seen a woman in a while, I think. That always makes them lose what few brains they have."

Faile walked the horselines, the sky dark, lantern held before her. Perrin was asleep; he'd retired early these last few days, seeking the wolf dream. The Whitecloaks had reluctantly agreed to delay the trial, but Perrin still should have been preparing his words to speak there. He grumbled that he already knew what he was going to say. Knowing him, he'd just tell Morgase what had happened, straightforward as usual.

Lacile and Selande walked on either side of Faile. Other members of *Cha Faile* walked behind, keeping careful watch for anyone close enough to be within earshot.

"I think the Whitecloaks knew we were there to spy," Selande said. The short, pale woman walked with hand on her sword. The stance didn't seem as awkward as it once had; Selande had taken her sword training seriously.

"No, I doubt they guessed," Lacile replied. She still wore a simple tan blouse and darker brown skirt. Selande had changed back to breeches and sword immediately upon returning—she still bore a cut on her arm from where that sword had tried to kill her—but Lacile seemed to be savoring her time in the skirt.

"They barely said anything of use," Selande said.

"Yes," Lacile replied, "but I think they're merely in that habit. Our excuse of checking on Maighdin and the others was a reasonable one, my Lady. We were able to deliver your note, then do a little chatting with the men. I teased out enough to be of some use."

Faile raised an eyebrow, though Lacile fell quiet as they passed a groom working late, brushing down one of the horses.

"The Whitecloaks respect Galad," Lacile said once out of the groom's earshot. "Though some grumble about the things he's been telling them."

"What things?" Faile asked.

"He wants them to ally with the Aes Sedai for the Last Battle," Lacile explained.

"Anyone could have told you they would dislike that idea," Selande said. "They're Whitecloaks!"

"Yes," Faile said, "but it means that this Galad is more reasonable than his men. A useful tip, Lacile."

The young woman swelled, brushing her short hair back in a modest gesture, throwing back the red ribbons she had tied there. She'd taken to wearing twice as many now, since her Shaido captivity.

Up ahead, a lanky figure stepped between two of the horses. He had a thick mustache, Taraboner style, and though he was young, he had the air of one who had seen much in his life. Dannil Lewin, the man in charge of the Two Rivers men now that Tam had mysteriously decided to depart. Light send that Tam was safe, wherever he'd gone.

"Why, Dannil," Faile said, "what an odd coincidence to see you here."

"Coincidence?" he asked, scratching at his head. He held his bow in one hand, staff-like, though he kept glancing at it, wary. A lot of people did that with their weapons now. "You asked me to come here."

"It must be a coincidence nonetheless," Faile said, "in case anyone asks. Particularly if that somebody is my husband."

"I don't like keeping things from Lord Perrin," Dannil said, falling into step with her.

"And you'd prefer to risk letting him be beheaded by a group of rabid Whitecloaks?"

"No. None of the men do."

"You've done what I asked, then?"

Dannil nodded. "I spoke to Grady and Neald. Lord Perrin has already ordered them to stay nearby, but we talked. Grady said he'd have weaves of Air ready, and will grab Lord Perrin and get out if things get ugly, Neald covering the retreat. I've talked to the men from the Two Rivers. A group of archers in the trees will be ready to provide a distraction."

Faile nodded. Neither Asha'man had been wounded in this bubble of evil, fortunately. Each had been carrying a knife, but reports said they'd looked at the floating weapons, then nonchalantly waved hands and blasted them from the air. When messengers with news of Faile's earth-throwing trick had reached the section of camp the Asha'man had been in, they'd found this area in much less chaos, Grady and Neald striding through camp and felling weapons wherever they saw them.

Part of the reason for the delay before the trial was to take care of Healing. But another large reason was because Perrin wanted to give time to the camp's smiths and craftsmen to make replacement weapons for those who had lost theirs, just in case the trial turned to a battle. And Faile was increasingly certain that it would.

"Lord Perrin won't like being pulled away from fighting," Dannil said. "Not one bit."

"That tent could turn into a death trap," Faile said. "Perrin can lead the battle if he wants, but from a safer position. You will get him out."

Dannil sighed, but nodded. "Yes, my Lady."

Perrin was learning not to fear Young Bull.

Step by step, he learned balance. The wolf when the wolf was needed; the man when the man was needed. He let himself be drawn into the hunt, but kept Faile—his home—in his mind. He walked the edge of the sword, but each step made him more confident.

Today, he hunted Hopper, wily and experienced prey. But Young Bull was quick to learn, and having the mind of a man gave him advantages. He could think like something, or someone, that he was not.

Was this how Noam had begun? Where would this path of understanding lead? There was a secret to this, a secret Young Bull had to find for himself.

He could not fail. He *had* to learn. It seemed that—
somehow—the more confident he became in the wolf
dream, the more comfortable he became with himself in
the waking world.

Young Bull charged through an unfamiliar forest. No, a
jungle, with hanging vines and wide-fronded ferns. The underbrush was so thick that a rat would have trouble squeezing through. But Young Bull *demanded* that the world
open before him. Vines pulled back. Shrubs bent. Ferns
retracted, like mothers pulling their children out of the way
of a galloping horse.

He caught glimpses of Hopper bounding ahead. His prey
vanished. Young Bull didn't break pace, charging through
that spot and catching the scent of Hopper's destination.
Young Bull *shifted* onto an open plain with no trees and an
unfamiliar scrub patching the ground. His prey was a series of streaking blurs in the distance. Young Bull followed,
each bound carrying him hundreds of paces.

Within seconds, they approached an enormous plateau.
His prey ran directly *up* the side of the stone shelf. Young
Bull followed, ignoring what was "right." He ran with the
ground far below at his back, nose toward that boiling sea
of black clouds. He leaped over clefts in the rock, ricocheting
between two sides of a rift, cresting the top of the plateau.

Hopper attacked. Young Bull was ready. He rolled, coming up on all fours as his prey leaped over his head, passed
over the cliff's edge, but then vanished in a flash and was
back standing on the lip of the cliff.

Young Bull became Perrin holding a hammer made of
soft wood. Such things were possible in the wolf dream; if
the hammer hit, it would not harm.

Perrin swung, the air cracking with the sudden speed of
his motion. But Hopper was equally fast, dodging out of the
way. He rolled, then leaped at Perrin's back, fangs glistening. Perrin growled and *shifted* so that he was standing a
few feet from where he had been. Hopper's jaws snapped
open air, and Perrin swung his hammer again.

Hopper was suddenly shrouded in a deep mist. Perrin's
hammer slammed down through it, hitting the ground. It
bounced off. He cursed, spinning. In the fog, he couldn't
see, couldn't catch Hopper's scent.

A shadow moved in the mist and Perrin lunged, but it was only a pattern in the air. He spun and found shadows moving all around him. The shapes of wolves, men, and other creatures he couldn't see.

Make the world yours, Young Bull, Hopper sent.

Perrin focused, thinking of dry air. Of the musty scent of dust. That was what the air should be like, in an arid landscape like this.

No. It wasn't what the air *should* be like. It was how the air *was*! His mind, his will, his feelings slammed against something else. He pushed through.

The mists vanished, evaporating in the heat. Hopper sat on his haunches a short distance away. *Good,* the wolf sent. *You learn.* He glanced sideways, looking toward the north, seeming distracted by something. Then he was gone.

Perrin caught his scent and followed to the Jehannah Road. Hopper dashed along outside the strange violet dome. They jumped back to this place frequently to see if the dome ever vanished. So far, it had not.

Perrin continued the chase. Was the dome meant to trap wolves inside? But if that was the case, why had Slayer not sprung his trap at Dragonmount, where so many wolves had for some reason gathered?

Perhaps the dome had another purpose. Perrin memorized a few notable rock formations along the perimeter of the dome, then followed Hopper to a low shelf of rock. The wolf leaped from it, vanishing in midair, and Perrin followed.

He caught the scent of Hopper's destination in midjump, then took himself there, still in motion. He appeared about two feet above a shimmering blue expanse. Stunned, he fell and splashed into the water.

He swam frantically, dropping his hammer. Hopper stood on top of the water, bearing a wolfish expression of disapproval. *Not good,* the wolf added. *You still need to learn.*

Perrin sputtered.

The sea grew tempestuous, but Hopper sat placidly upon the rolling waves. Again he glanced northward, but then turned back to Perrin. *Water troubles you, Young Bull.*

"I was just surprised," Perrin said, swimming hard.

Why?

"Because I didn't expect this!"

Why expect? Hopper sent. *When you follow another, you could end up anywhere.*

"I know." Perrin spat out a mouthful of water. He gritted his teeth, then imagined himself standing on the water like Hopper. Blessedly, he rose out of the sea to stand atop its surface. It was a strange sensation, the sea undulating beneath him.

You will not defeat Slayer like this, Hopper sent.

"Then I will keep learning," Perrin said.

There is little time.

"I will learn more quickly."

Can you?

"We have no other choice."

You could choose not to fight him.

Perrin shook his head. "Do we run from our prey? If we do, they'll hunt us instead. I will face him, and I need to be prepared."

There is a way. The wolf smelled of worry.

"I'll do what I have to."

Follow. Hopper vanished, and Perrin caught an unexpected scent: refuse and mud, burning wood and coal. People.

Perrin *shifted* and found himself atop a building in Caemlyn. He had visited this city only twice, and briefly, and seeing the beautiful Inner City before him—ancient buildings, domes and spires rising atop the hill like majestic pines atop a crowned mountain—gave him pause. He was near the old wall, beyond which spread the New City.

Hopper sat at his side, looking over the beautiful city. Much of the city itself was said to be Ogier-built, and Perrin could believe it, with that marvelous beauty. Tar Valon was said to be more grand than Caemlyn. Perrin had trouble believing that was possible.

"Why are we here?" Perrin asked.

Men dream here, Hopper replied.

In the real world, they did. Here, the place was empty. It was light enough to be day, despite that storm overhead, and Perrin felt there should be people crowding the streets. Women, going to and from market. Nobles atop horses. Wagons bearing barrels of ale and sacks of grain. Children scampering, slipfingers searching for marks, workers replacing paving stones, enterprising hawkers offering meat pies to them all.

Instead, there were hints. Shadows. A fallen handkerchief on the street. Doors that were open one moment, then closed the next. A thrown horseshoe sticking from the mud of an alleyway. It was as if all of the people had been whisked away, snatched by Fades or some monster from a gleeman's dark tale.

A woman appeared momentarily below. She wore a beautiful green and gold dress. She stared at the street, eyes glazed over, then was gone. People did occasionally appear in the wolf dream. Perrin figured it must happen to them when they were asleep, part of their natural dreams.

This place, Hopper said, *is not only a place of wolves. It is a place of all.*

"Of all?" Perrin asked, sitting down on the rooftiles.

All souls know this place, Hopper said. *They come here when they reach for it.*

"When they're dreaming."

Yes, Hopper said, lying down beside him. *The fear-dreams of men are strong. So very strong. Sometimes, those terrible dreams come here.* That sending was an enormous wolf, the size of a building, knocking aside much smaller wolves who tried to snap at him. There was a scent of terror and death about the wolf. Like . . . a nightmare.

Perrin nodded slowly.

Many wolves have been caught in the pains of these fear-dreams. They appear more commonly where men might walk, though the dream lives without those who created it.

Hopper looked at Perrin. *Hunting in the fear-dreams will teach you strength. But you might die. It is very dangerous.*

"I don't have time to be safe anymore," Perrin said. "Let's do it."

Hopper didn't ask if he was certain. He jumped down to the street, and Perrin followed, landing softly. Hopper began to lope forward, so Perrin broke into a jog.

"How do we find them?" Perrin asked.

Smell fear, Hopper sent. *Terror.*

Perrin closed his eyes, breathing in deeply. Just as doors flashed open and closed, in the wolf dream he could sometimes smell things there for a moment, then gone. Musty winter potatoes. The dung of a passing horse. A pie, baking.

When he opened his eyes, he saw none of these things. They weren't really there, but they *almost* were. They *could* have been.

There, Hopper said, vanishing. Perrin followed, appearing beside the wolf outside of a narrow alleyway. Inside, it looked too dark to be natural.

Go in, Hopper said. *You will not last long your first time. I will come for you. Remember it is* not. *Remember it is* false.

Feeling worried, but determined, Perrin stepped into the alleyway. The walls to either side were black, as if they'd been painted. Only . . . these walls were too dark to be painted. Was that a tuft of grass beneath his foot? The sky above had stopped boiling, and he thought he could see stars peeking down. A pale moon, far too large, appeared in the sky, shrouded in clouds. It gave a cold glow, like ice.

He wasn't in the city anymore. He turned about, alarmed, to find himself in a forest. The trees had thick trunks and were of no species he could recognize. Their branches were naked. The bark was a faint gray, lit by the phantom light above, and looked like bone.

He needed to get back to the city! Out of this terrible place. He turned around.

Something flashed in the night, and he spun. "Who's there!" he shouted.

A woman burst from the darkness, running in a mad scramble. She wore a loose white robe, little more than a shift, and she had long dark hair streaming behind her. She saw him and froze, then turned and made as if to run in a different direction.

Perrin cut her off, snatching her hand, pulling her back. She struggled, feet marring the loamy dark ground beneath as she tried to pull away. She was gasping. In and out. In and out. She smelled frantic.

"I need to know the way out!" Perrin said. "We have to return to the city."

She met his eyes. "He's coming," she hissed. Her hand slipped from his and she ran, vanishing into the night, the darkness enfolding her like a shroud. Perrin took a step forward, hand outstretched.

He heard something behind him. He turned slowly to find something enormous. A looming shadow that sucked in the moonlight. The thing seemed to draw breath away, absorbing his very life and will.

The thing reared up taller. It was taller than the trees, a hulking monster with arms as thick as barrels, its face and body lost in shadow. It opened deep red eyes, like two huge coals flaring to life.

I need to fight it! Perrin thought, hammer appearing in his hand. He took a step forward, then thought better of it. Light! That thing was *enormous*. He couldn't fight it, not out in the open like this. He needed cover.

He turned and ran through the hostile woods. The thing followed. He could hear it snapping branches, its footsteps making the earth shake. Ahead of him, he saw the woman, her thin white gown slowing her as it caught on a branch. She pulled free and continued to run.

The creature loomed. It would catch him, consume him, destroy him! He yelled for the woman, reaching out toward her. She glanced over her shoulder at him, and tripped.

Perrin cursed. He scrambled to her side, to help her up. But the thing was so close!

It was a fight, then. His heart was thumping as quickly as a woodlark pecking a tree. Hands sweaty, he turned, gripping his hammer to face the terrible thing behind. He placed himself between it and the woman.

It reared up, growing larger, those red eyes blazing with fire. Light! He couldn't fight that, could he? He needed an edge of some kind. "What is that thing?" he desperately asked of the woman. "Why does it chase us?"

"It's *him*," she hissed. "The Dragon Reborn."

Perrin froze. The Dragon Reborn. But . . . but that was Rand. *It's a nightmare,* he reminded himself. *None of this is real. I can't let myself be caught up in it!*

The ground trembled, as if moaning. He could feel the heat of the monster's eyes. A scrambling sound came from behind as the woman ran, leaving him.

Perrin stood up, legs shaking, every instinct crying for him to run. But no. He couldn't fight it, either. He could *not* accept this as real.

A wolf howled, then leaped into the clearing. Hopper seemed to push back the darkness. The creature bent down toward Perrin, reaching a massive hand as if to crush him.

This was an alley.

Inside of Caemlyn.

It wasn't real.

It was not.

The darkness around them faded. The enormous dark shadow creature warped in the air, like a piece of cloth being stretched. The moon vanished. A small pocket of ground—the dirty, trampled earth of an alley—appeared at their feet.

Then, with a snap, the dream was gone. Perrin stood in the alley again, Hopper at his side, no sign of the forest or the terrible creature that someone had viewed as the Dragon Reborn.

Perrin exhaled slowly. Sweat dripped from his brow. He reached up to wipe it away, then willed the sweat away instead.

Hopper vanished, and Perrin followed, finding himself on the same rooftop as before. He sat down. Merely thinking of that shadow made him shiver. "It felt so real," he said. "A piece of me knew it was a nightmare. I couldn't help but try to fight, or try to run. When I did either, it grew stronger, didn't it? Because I accepted it was real?"

Yes. You must not believe what you see.

Perrin nodded. "There was a woman in there. Part of the dream? She wasn't real either?"

Yes.

"Maybe she was the one who dreamed it," Perrin said. "The one having the original nightmare, caught up in it and trapped here in the World of Dreams."

Men who dream do not stay here long, Hopper sent. To him, that was the end of the discussion. *You were strong, Young Bull. You did well.* He smelled proud.

"It helped when she called the thing the Dragon Reborn. That *showed* it wasn't real. Helped me believe it wasn't."

You did well, foolish cub, Hopper repeated. *Perhaps you can learn.*

"Only if I keep practicing. We need to do that again. Can you find another?"

Yes, Hopper sent. *There are always nightmares when your kind is near. Always.* The wolf turned northward again, however. Perrin had thought that the thing that had been distracting him earlier was the dreams, but it didn't seem to have been the case.

"What is up there?" Perrin asked. "What is it you keep looking toward?"

It comes, Hopper sent.

"What?"

The Last Hunt. It begins. Or it does not.

Perrin frowned, standing. "You mean . . . right now?"

The decision will be made. Soon.

"What decision?" Hopper's sendings were confusing, and he couldn't decipher them. Light and darkness, a void and fire, a coldness and a terrible, terrible heat. Mixed with wolves howling, calling, lending strength.

Come. Hopper stood, looking to the northeast.

Hopper vanished. Perrin *shifted* after him, appearing low down on the slopes of the Dragonmount, beside an outcropping of stone.

"Light," Perrin said softly, looking up in awe. The storm that had been brewing for months had come to a head. A massive black thunderhead dominated the sky, covering the top of the mountain. It spun slowly in the air, an enormous vortex of blackness, emitting bolts of lightning that connected to the clouds above. In other parts of the wolf dream the clouds were tempestuous, yet distant. This felt immediate.

This was . . . the focus of something. Perrin could feel it. Often, the wolf dream reflected things in the real world in strange or unexpected ways.

Hopper stood on the outcropping. Perrin could feel wolves all across the slopes of Dragonmount. In even greater numbers than he'd felt here recently.

They wait, Hopper said. *The Last Hunt comes.*

As Perrin reached out, he found that other packs were coming, still distant but moving toward Dragonmount. Perrin looked upward at the monstrous peak. The tomb of the Dragon, Lews Therin. It was a monument to his madness, to both his failure and his success. His pride and his self-sacrifice.

"The wolves," Perrin said. "They gather for the Last Hunt?"

Yes. If it occurs.

Perrin turned back to Hopper. "You said that it would. 'The Last Hunt comes,' you said."

A choice must be made, Young Bull. One path leads to the Last Hunt.

"And the other?" Perrin asked.

Hopper didn't respond immediately. He turned toward Dragonmount. *The other path does not lead to the Last Hunt.*

"Yes, but what *does* it lead to?"

To nothing.

Perrin opened his mouth to press further, but then the weight of Hopper's sending hit him. "Nothing" to the wolf meant a vacant den, all of the pups taken by trappers. A night sky empty of stars. The moon fading. The smell of old blood, dry, stale and flaked away.

Perrin closed his mouth. The sky continued to churn with that black storm. He smelled it on the wind, the smell of broken trees and dirt, of flooded fields and lightning fires. As so often, particularly recently, those scents seemed to contrast with the world around him. One of his senses told him he was in the very center of a catastrophe while the others saw nothing amiss.

"This choice. Why don't we just make it?"

It is not our choice, Young Bull.

Perrin felt drawn to the clouds above. Despite himself, he began to walk up the slope. Hopper loped up beside him. *It is dangerous above, Young Bull.*

"I know," Perrin said. But he couldn't stop. Instead, he increased his speed, each step launching him just a little farther. Hopper ran beside him, passing trees, rocks, groups of watching wolves. Upward Perrin and Hopper went, climbing until the trees dwindled and the ground grew cold with frost and ice.

Eventually, they approached the cloud itself. It seemed a dark fog, shaking with currents as it spun. Perrin hesitated at the perimeter, then stepped inside. It was like stepping into the nightmare. The wind was suddenly violent, the air buzzing with energy. Leaves and dirt and grit blew in the tempest, and he had to raise a hand against it.

No, he thought.

A small bubble of calm air opened around him. The tempest continued to blow just inches from his face, and he had to strain to keep from being claimed by it again. This storm wasn't a nightmare or a dream; it was something more vast, something more *real*. This time, Perrin was the one creating something abnormal with the bubble of safety.

He pressed forward, soon leaving tracks in snow. Hopper strode against the wind, lessening its effect on him as well. He was stronger at it than Perrin was—Perrin barely managed to keep his own bubble up. He feared that without it, he would be sucked into the storm and tossed into the air. He saw large branches rip past in the air, and even some smaller trees.

Hopper slowed, then sat down in the snow. He looked upward, toward the peak. *I cannot stay,* the wolf sent. *This is not my place.*

"I understand," Perrin said.

The wolf vanished, but Perrin continued. He couldn't explain what drew him, but he knew that he needed to witness. Someone did. He walked for what seemed like hours, focused completely on only two things: keeping the winds off him and putting one foot in front of the other.

The storm grew increasingly violent. It was so bad here that he couldn't keep all of the storm off, just the worst of it. He passed the ridged lip where the mountaintop was broken, picking his way alongside it, hunkered against the gusts, a steep fall on either side. Wind began to whip at his clothing, and he had to squint his eyes against the dust and snow in the air.

But he continued on. Striving for the peak, which rose ahead, rising above the blasted-out side of the mountain. He knew that atop that point, he would find what he searched for. This horrible maelstrom was the wolf dream's reaction to something great, something terrible. In this place, sometimes things were more real than in the waking world. The dream reflected a tempest because something very important was happening. He worried that it was something terrible.

Perrin pressed forward, shoving his way through the snows, crawling up rock faces, his fingers leaving skin sticking to the frigid stones. But he had trained well these last few weeks. He leapt chasms he shouldn't have been able to leap and climbed rocks that should have been too high for him.

A figure stood at the very top of the jagged, broken tip of the mountain. Perrin kept pressing onward. Someone needed to watch. Someone needed to be there when it happened.

Finally, Perrin heaved atop one last stone and found himself within a dozen feet of the top. He could make out the figure now. The man stood at the very heart of the vortex of winds, staring eastward, motionless. He was faint and translucent, a reflection of the real world. Like a shadow. Perrin had never seen anything like it.

It was Rand, of course. Perrin had known that it would be. Perrin held to the stone with one ragged hand and pulled his cloak close with the other—he'd created the cloak several cliff faces ago. He blinked through reddened eyes, gazing upward. He had to focus most of his concentration on pushing back some of the winds to keep himself from being flung out into the tempest.

Lightning flashed suddenly, thunder sounding for the first time since he'd begun climbing. That lightning began to arc in a dome around the top of the mountain. It threw light across Rand's face. That hard, impassive face, like stone itself. Where had its curves gone? When had Rand gained so many lines and angles? And those eyes, they seemed made of marble!

Rand wore a coat of black and red. Fine and ornamented, with a sword at his waist. The winds didn't affect Rand's clothes. Those fell unnaturally still, as if he really were just a statue. Carved from stone. The only thing that moved was his dark red hair, blowing in the wind, thrown and spun.

Perrin clung to the rocks for his life, cold wind biting into his cheeks, his fingers and feet so numb he could barely feel them. His beard bristled with dusty ice and snow. Something black began to spin around Rand. It wasn't part of the storm; it seemed like night itself leaking from him. Tendrils of it grew from Rand's own skin, like tiny hands curling back and wrapping around him. It seemed evil itself given life.

"Rand!" Perrin bellowed. "Fight it! Rand!"

His voice was lost in the wind, and he doubted that Rand could have heard him anyway. The darkness continued to seep out, like a liquid tar coming through Rand's pores, creating a miasma of pitch around the Dragon Reborn. Within moments, Perrin could barely see Rand through the blackness. It enclosed him, cutting him off, banishing him. The Dragon Reborn was gone. Only evil remained.

"Rand, please . . ." Perrin whispered.

And then—from the midst of the blackness, from the center of the uproar and the tempest—a tiny sliver of light split through the evil. Like a candle's glow on a very dark night. The light shone upward, toward the distant sky, like a beacon. So frail.

The tempest buffeted it. The winds stormed, howled, and screamed. The lightning beat against the top of the rocky peak, blasting free chunks of rock, scoring the ground. The blackness undulated and pulsed.

But still the light shone.

A web of cracks appeared down the side of the shell of evil blackness, light shining from within. Another fracture joined it, and another. Something strong was inside, something glowing, something *brilliant*.

The shell exploded outward, vaporizing and releasing a column of light so bright, so incredible that it seemed to sear the eyes from Perrin's head. But he looked on anyway, not raising arm to shade or block the resplendent image before him. Rand stood within that light, mouth open as if bellowing toward the skies above. The sun-yellowed column shot into the air, and the storm seemed to *shudder*, the entire sky itself undulating.

The tempest vanished.

That column of fiery light became a column of sunlight streaming down, illuminating the peak of Dragonmount. Perrin pulled his fingers free from the rock, gazing on with wonder at Rand standing within the light. It seemed so long, so very long, since Perrin had seen a ray of pure sunlight.

The wolves began to howl. It was a howl of triumph, of glory and of victory. Perrin raised his head and howled as well, becoming Young Bull for a moment. He could feel the pool of sunlight growing, and it washed over him, its warmth banishing the frozen chill. He barely noticed when Rand's image vanished, for he left that sunlight behind.

Wolves appeared around Perrin, flashing into existence midleap. They continued to bay, jumping at one another, exulting and dancing in the sunlight as it washed over them. They yipped and barked, tossing up patches of snow as they bounded. Hopper was among them, and he leaped into the air, soaring over to Perrin.

The Last Hunt begins, Young Bull! Hopper screamed. *We live. We live!*

Perrin turned back to the place where Rand had stood. If that darkness had taken Rand . . .

But it hadn't. He smiled broadly. "The Last Hunt has come!" he screamed to the wolves. "Let it begin!"

They howled their agreement, as loud as the storm had been just moments before.

CHAPTER
31

Into the Void

Mat dumped the rest of the wine into his mouth, savoring the sweet, cool taste. He brought the cup down and tossed a handful of dice. They tumbled to the wooden floor of the tavern, clacking against one another.

The air was thick. Thick with sounds, thick with curses, thick with scents. Smoke, pungent liquors, a steak that had been peppered so much that you could hardly taste the meat. That was probably for the best. Even in Caemlyn, meat spoiled unpredictably.

The pungent men around Mat watched his dice fall: one of the men stank of garlic, another of sweat, a third of a tannery. Their hair was stringy, their fingers were grimy, but their coin was good. The game was called Koronko's Spit, and hailed from Shienar.

Mat did not know the rules.

"Five ones," said the man who stank of garlic. His name was Rittle. He seemed unsettled. "That's a loss."

"No it's not," Mat said softly. Never mind that he did not know the rules. He knew he had won; he could feel it. His luck was with him.

Good thing, too. He needed it tonight.

The man that smelled of a tannery reached for his belt, where he carried a wicked knife. His name was Saddler, and he had a chin that could have been used to sharpen swords. "I thought you said you didn't know this game, friend."

"I don't," Mat said. "Friend. But that's a win. Do we need to ask around the room to see if anyone else can confirm it?"

The three men looked at each other, expressions dark. Mat stood up. The inn had walls dark from years of men smoking pipes inside it, and the windows—though of fine glass—had grown opaque with dirt and smoke. It was a tradition that they never be cleaned. The weathered sign out front had a wagon wheel painted on it, and the official name was The Dusty Wheel. Everyone called it The Rumor Wheel instead; it was the best place in Caemlyn to listen to rumors. Most of them were untrue, but that was half the fun.

Most everyone in the place was drinking ale, but Mat had taken a fancy to good red wine lately. "Want some more, Master Crimson?" Kati, the serving woman, asked. She was a raven-haired beauty with a smile so wide it reached halfway to Cairhien. She had been flirting with him all night. Never mind that he had *told* her he was married. He had not even smiled at her. Well, not much. And hardly his best smile. Some women could not see the truth of things, even if it was written on their own foreheads, that was a fact.

He waved her away. Only one cup tonight, for courage. Burn him, but he needed a little of that. With resignation, he took the scarf off his neck and dropped it to the side. He untucked the foxhead medallion—Light, but it felt good to be wearing that again!—and hung it out front of his clothing. He wore the new red and silver coat that Thom had bought him.

Mat took his *ashandarei* from beside the wall and pulled off the cloth cover, revealing the blade. He set it over his shoulder. "Hey," he said in a loud voice. "Anyone in the bloody place know the rules for Koronko's Spit?"

The three men he had been dicing regarded the weapon; the third of them, Snelle, stood up, hooking his thumbs into the top of his trousers, pushing back his coat and showing the shortsword buckled at his waist.

Most people ignored Mat at first. Conversations rang, stories about the Borderlander army that had passed, about the Queen's pregnancy, about the Dragon Reborn, about mysterious deaths or not so mysterious ones. Everyone had a rumor to share. Some of the inn's occupants wore little better than rags, but some wore the finest of clothing. Nobles, commoners and everything in between came to The Rumor Wheel.

A few men by the bar glanced at Mat because of the outburst. One hesitated, blinking. Mat reached down and took his wide-brimmed black hat off the table beside him, holding it by the crown, then set it on his head. The man nudged his companions. The sweaty, balding man Mat had been dicing with raised fingers to his chin, rubbing it in thought, as if trying to remember something.

Snelle smiled at Mat. "Looks like nobody answered you, *friend*. Guess you'll have to trust us. You shouldn't have thrown if you didn't ask the rules. Now, are you going to pay, or—"

Rittle's eyes opened wide, and he stood hastily and took his friend's arm. He leaned in, whispering something. Snelle looked down at Mat's medallion. He looked up and met Mat's eyes.

Mat nodded.

"Excuse us," Rittle said, stumbling away. The other two joined him. They left their dice and coins on the ground.

Mat casually knelt down, scooping up the coins and dumping them in his pouch. He left the dice. They were loaded, meant to almost always throw threes. He had been able to judge that from a few quick throws before laying down coins.

Whispers moved through the inn's common room like a swarm of ants covering a corpse. Chairs scooted back. Conversations changed tempo, some silencing, others becoming urgent. Mat stood up to go. People hastened out of his way.

Mat left a golden crown on the edge of the bar, then tipped his hat to Hatch, the innkeeper. The man stood behind the bar wiping a glass, his wife next to him. She was a pretty one, but Hatch kept a special cudgel for thumping men who looked too long. Mat gave her only a short look, then.

Mat pulled off his black scarf, leaving it on the floor. It had a hole in it now anyway. He stepped out into the night, and the moment he did, the dice stopped thundering in his head.

It was time to get to work.

He walked out onto the street. He had spent all evening with his face uncovered. He was certain he had been recognized a few times, mostly by men who had slipped out into the night without saying anything. As he walked down off the inn's front porch, people gathered at the windows and doorway.

Mat tried not to feel like all of those eyes were knives sticking into his back. Light, he felt like he was dangling from another noose. He reached up and felt at the scar on his neck. It had been a long while since he had gone about with his neck uncovered. Even with Tylin, he had normally left the scarf on.

Tonight, though, he danced with Jak o' the Shadows. He tied his medallion to the *ashandarei*. He affixed it so that the medallion rested against the flat of the blade, and one edge hung out over the tip. It would be hard to use—he would have to hit with the flat of the blade in most cases to touch the medallion to flesh—but it gave him much better reach than swinging the medallion by hand.

Medallion in place, he picked a direction and began walking. He was in the New City, a place heaped with man-made buildings, a contrast to the fine Ogier work elsewhere in Caemlyn. These buildings were well built, but were narrow and thin, up close next to one another.

The first group tried to kill him before he was one street away from The Rumor Wheel. There were four of them. As they charged him, a group of shadows leaped from a nearby alleyway, Tálmanes at their head. Mat spun on the killers, who pulled up short as his soldiers joined him. The street toughs fled in a scramble and Mat nodded to Talmanes.

The men of the Band faded back into the darkness, and Mat continued on his way. He walked slowly, carrying his *ashandarei* on his shoulder. His men had been told to keep their distance unless he was attacked.

He ended up needing them three more times through the hour, each time scaring away a larger group of thugs. The last time, the Band and he actually clashed with the assassins. The thugs were no match for trained soldiers, even on the darkened streets that were their home. The exchange left five of the thugs dead, but only one of his men wounded. Mat sent Harvell away with a guard of two.

It grew later and later. Mat began to worry that he would have to repeat this act the next night, but then he noticed someone standing in the street ahead. The paving stones

were wet from a misting earlier in the night, and they reflected the diffused light of a hidden slivered moon.

Mat stopped, lowering his weapon to his side. He
could not make out details about the figure, but the way it
stood . . .

"You think to ambush me?" the *gholam* asked, sounding
amused. "With your men who squish and rip, who die so
easily, almost at a touch?"

"I'm tired of being chased," Mat said loudly.

"So you deliver yourself to me? What a kind gift."

"Sure," Mat said, lowering his *ashandarei*, foxhead on
the back gleaming faintly. "Just mind the sharp edges."

The thing slid forward, and Mat's men lit lanterns. The
men of the Band set the lanterns on the ground, then backed
away, a few of them dashing off to deliver messages. They
had strict orders not to interfere. Tonight would probably
strain their oaths to him on that.

Mat planted himself and waited for the *gholam*. Only a
hero charged a beast like that, and he was no bloody hero.
Though his men would be trying to clear away anyone on
the streets, trying to keep the area empty so nobody would
scare the *gholam* away. That was not heroism. It might have
been stupidity, though.

The *gholam*'s fluid movements threw lanternlight shadows across the road. Mat met it with a sweep of his *ashandarei*, but the beast danced to the side, easily evading him.
Bloody ashes, but the thing was fast! It reached out, swiping
at the front of the *ashandarei* with the knife it held.

Mat yanked the *ashandarei* back, not letting the monster
cut the medallion free. It danced around Mat, and he spun,
staying inside the ring of lanterns. He had chosen a relatively wide street, remembering with a shiver that day in the
alleyway of Ebou Dar where the *gholam* had nearly taken
him in close quarters.

The beast slid forward again, and Mat feinted, drawing
it in. He almost miscalculated, but twisted the *ashandarei*
in time to slap the *gholam* with the flat of the weapon. The
medallion let out a hiss as it touched the *gholam*'s arm.

The *gholam* cursed and backed away. Wavering lanternlight illuminated its features, leaving pockets of darkness
and pockets of light. It was smiling again, despite the wisp
of smoke rising from its arm. Before, Mat had thought this

creature's face unremarkable, but in the uneven light—and with that smile—it took on a terrifying cast. More angular, reflected lanternlight making its eyes glow like tiny yellow flames consumed by the darkness of its sockets.

Nondescript by day, a horror by night. This thing had slaughtered Tylin while she lay helpless. Mat gritted his teeth. Then he attacked.

It was a bloody stupid thing to do. The *gholam* was faster than he was, and Mat had no idea if the foxhead could kill it or not. He attacked anyway. He attacked for Tylin, for the men he'd lost to this horror. He attacked because he had no other option. When you really wanted to see what a man was worth, you backed him into a corner and made him fight for his life.

Mat was in the corner now. Bloodied and harried. He knew this thing would eventually find him—or, worse, find Tuon or Olver. It was the kind of situation where a sensible man would have run. But he was a bloody fool instead. Staying in the city because of an oath to an Aes Sedai? Well, if he died, he would go out with weapon in hand.

Mat became a swirling cyclone of steel and wood, yelling as he attacked. The *gholam*, seeming shocked, actually backed away. Mat slammed his *ashandarei* into its hand, burning the flesh, then spun and knocked the dagger from its fingers. The creature leaped away, but Mat lunged forward, ramming the butt of his spear between the thing's legs.

It went down. Its motions were fluid, and it caught itself, but it *did* go down. As it threw itself to its feet, Mat slashed the *ashandarei*'s blade at its heel. He neatly severed the *gholam*'s tendon, and if the thing had been human, it would have collapsed. Instead, it landed without even a wince of pain, and no blood seeped free of the cut.

It spun and lunged at Mat with clawed fingers. He was forced to stumble back, swinging the *ashandarei* to ward it away. The creature grinned at him.

Then, oddly, it turned and ran.

Mat cursed. Had something scared it away? But no, it was not fleeing. It was going for his men!

"Retreat!" Mat called at them. "Back! Burn you, you bloody monster. I'm here! Fight me!"

The members of the Band scattered at his orders, though

Talmanes hung back, wearing a grim expression. The *gholam* laughed, but did not chase down the soldiers. Instead, the thing kicked over the first lantern, causing it to wink out. It ran around the circle, kicking at each one, plunging the street into darkness.

Bloody ashes! Mat chased after the creature. If it managed to get all of those lights out, with that cloud cover, Mat would be left fighting it unable to see!

Talmanes—blatantly ignoring his own safety—leaped forward and snatched his lantern up to protect it. He fled down the street, and Mat cursed as the *gholam* chased after.

Mat dashed behind them. Talmanes had a good lead, but the *gholam* was so quick. It nearly got to him, and Talmanes jerked to the side, backing up the steps of a nearby building. The monster lunged for him, and Talmanes stumbled backward as Mat ran toward them for all he was worth.

The lantern fell from Talmanes' fingers and splashed oil across the front of the building. The dry wood came alight, tongues of flame rippling across the lamp oil, illuminating the *gholam*. It leaped for Talmanes.

Mat threw his *ashandarei*.

The broad-bladed spear was not meant for throwing, but he did not have a knife handy. He aimed for the *gholam*'s head. One would have never known that, for he missed pitifully. Fortunately, the weapon dipped down and passed between the *gholam*'s legs.

The monster tripped, thudding heavily to the paving stones. Talmanes scrambled back up the steps of the now-blazing building.

Bless this luck of mine, Mat thought.

The *gholam* stood up and made a motion to follow Talmanes, but then looked down at what had tripped it. The creature looked at Mat with a wicked grin, half its face cast in the light of the burning building. The creature picked up Mat's *ashandarei*—foxhead medallion still tied to the front—then whipped its hand to the side, tossing the weapon away. The *ashandarei* crashed through a window and passed into the burning building.

Lamps sparked on inside, as if those living there were only now noticing the fight happening in their proximity. Talmanes gave Mat a look, and they met eyes. The Cairhienin man threw himself against the door into the burning building and broke in. The *gholam* spun on Mat, backlit by the growing flames. They blazed quickly, and Mat's heart thumped with alarm as the creature came for him, unnaturally fast.

Mat reached into his coat pockets with sweaty fingers. Right before the *gholam* reached him—hands going for Mat's neck—Mat pulled something out with each hand, slamming them forward into the *gholam*'s palms. Hissing rang in the air, like meat being placed on a grill, and the *gholam* screeched in pain. It stumbled, wide-eyed, as it looked at Mat.

Who held a foxhead medallion in each hand.

He whipped them out, each held on a long, thick chain, spinning. The medallions caught firelight, seeming to glow as Mat whipped them at the *gholam*, striking it on the arm.

The creature howled, backing up another step. "How?" it demanded. "How!"

"Don't rightly know myself." Elayne had said her copies weren't perfect, but it seemed they did the job well enough. So long as they hurt the *gholam*, he didn't care about their other abilities. Mat grinned, spinning the second medallion forward. "Guess I just got lucky."

The *gholam* glared at him, then stumbled up the steps toward the burning building. It dashed inside, perhaps deciding to flee. Mat was not about to let it escape, not this time. He charged it up the steps and ducked through the flaming doorway, reaching out a hand as Talmanes tossed his *ashandarei* to him from a side hallway.

Mat caught the weapon, leaving the medallions wrapped around his forearms. The *gholam* spun on him; the hallway was already burning, the heat from the sides and above oppressive. Smoke lined the ceiling. Talmanes coughed, a kerchief held to his face.

The *gholam* turned on Mat, snarling and attacking. Mat met the beast in the middle of the wide hallway, bringing up his *ashandarei* to block the *gholam*'s clawlike hands. The butt of Mat's *ashandarei* had been singed from sitting in the fire, and the wood smoldered at the end. It left a trail of smoke in the air.

He attacked for all he was worth, spinning the *ashandarei*, the back end leaving a whirl of smoke around him. The *gholam* tried to strike at him, but Mat dropped the *ashandarei* with one hand and flung one of the medallions like a knife, hitting the creature in the face. It howled and stumbled back, face burned and smoking. Mat stepped forward, slamming the end of the *ashandarei* against the medallion as it hit the floor, flipping it back up and hitting the creature again.

He pushed forward, slashing with the *ashandarei*, and several of the creature's fingers flew free. Sure, it did not bleed and did not seem to feel pain from ordinary wounds, but *that* would slow it a bit.

The *gholam* recovered, hissing, eyes wide with anger. Its smile was gone now. It leaped forward in a blur, but Mat spun and sliced down the creature's tan shirt, exposing its chest. Then he whipped the second medallion to the side, hitting the *gholam* as it clawed at his arm, slicing his skin and spraying blood across the wall.

Mat grunted. The *gholam* howled and stumbled back, farther down the burning hallway. Mat was sweating from the heat, from the exertion. Mat could not fight this creature. Not for long. That did not matter. He pushed forward, letting his *ashandarei* become a blur. He slapped the flat of it—with the medallion—against the *gholam*. When the beast recovered, he flung the second medallion at its face, making it duck. But then he kicked the third one up to hit it on the neck.

He left lines of smoke in the air as he spun the *ashandarei*, grabbing it in two hands again. The end of his weapon glowed and smoldered. He found himself yelling in the Old Tongue.

"*Al dival, al kiserai, al mashi!*" For light, glory, and love!

The *gholam* stepped back, snarling at the barrage. It looked over its shoulder, seeming to notice something behind, but Mat's attack drew its attention back.

"*Tai'daishar!*" True Blood of Battle!

Mat forced the creature toward an open doorway at the back of the hallway. The room beyond was entirely dark. No light of the fires reflected off walls there.

"*Carai manshimaya Tylin. Carai an manshimaya Nalesean. Carai an manshimaya ayend'an!*" Honor of my blade for Tylin. Honor of my blade for Nalesean. Honor of my blade for the fallen.

The call of vengeance.

The *gholam* backed into the darkened room, stepping onto a bone white floor, eyes flickering down.

Taking a deep breath, Mat leaped through the doorway with a final burst of strength and slammed the smoldering butt of his *ashandarei* into the side of the creature's head. A spray of sparks and ash exploded around its face. The creature cursed and stumbled to the right.

And there, it nearly stepped off the edge of a platform hanging above an expansive void. The *gholam* hissed in anger, hanging with one leg over the void, flailing to keep its balance.

From this side, the doorway into the room was ringed by a glowing white light—the edges of a gateway made for Skimming. "I don't know if you can die," Mat said softly. "I hope to the Light that you can't." He raised a boot and slammed it into the thing's back, throwing it off the platform into the darkness. It fell, twisting in the air, looking up at him with horror.

"I hope you can't die," Mat said, "because I'm going to enjoy the thought of you falling through that blackness forever, you misbegotten son of a goat's droppings." Mat spit over the side, sending a bit of bloody spittle down, plummeting after the *gholam*. Both disappeared into the blackness below.

Sumeko walked up beside him. The stout Kinswoman had long dark hair and the air of a woman who did not like being ordered about. Nearly every woman had that same air. She'd been standing just inside the gateway, to the side where she would be unseen from the hallway. She had to be there to maintain the white platform, which was in the shape of a large book. She raised an eyebrow at him.

"Thanks for the gateway," Mat said, shouldering his *ashandarei*, the butt still trailing a thin line of smoke. She'd made the gateway from inside the palace, using it to travel to this point and open the gateway in the hallway. They'd hoped that would keep the *gholam* from feeling her channel, as she'd made the weaves in the palace.

Sumeko sniffed. Together, the two walked out through the gateway and into the building. Several of the Band were hurriedly putting out the fire. Talmanes rushed up to Mat as he gateway vanished, accompanied by another of the Kins-women, Julanya.

"You sure that darkness goes on forever?" Mat asked. Julanya was a plump, pretty woman who would have fit nicely on Mat's knee. The white in her hair did not detract from her prettiness at all.

"Near as we can tell, it does," Sumeko said. "This was quite nearly bungled, Matrim Cauthon. The thing didn't seem surprised by the gateway. I think it sensed it anyway."

"Still managed to fight it off the platform," Mat said.

"Barely. You should have let us deal with the beast."

"Wouldn't have worked," Mat said, taking a wetted ker-chief from Talmanes. Sumeko glanced at his arm, but Mat didn't ask for Healing. That cut would heal right nicely. Might even have a good scar. Scars impressed most women, so long as they were not on the face. What did Tuon think of them?

Sumeko sniffed. "The pride of men. Do not forget that we lost some of our own to that thing."

"And I'm glad I could help you get revenge," Mat said. He smiled at her, though she was right; it *had* nearly been bun-gled. He was certain the *gholam* had felt the Kinswoman beyond that doorway as they approached. Fortunately, though, the thing hadn't seemed to consider a woman who could channel to be a threat.

Talmanes handed Mat back the two fallen medallions. He tucked them away and untied the one on his *ashandarei*, slipping it back onto his neck. The Kin watched those me-dallions with a predatory hunger. Well, they could do that all they wanted. He intended one for Olver and the other for Tuon, once he could find her.

Captain Guybon, Birgitte's second-in-command, walked into the building. "The beast is dead?"

"No," Mat said, "but close enough for a Crown contract."

"Crown contract?" Guybon asked, frowning. "You asked the Queen's aid on this endeavor. This wasn't done on her contract."

"Actually," Talmanes said, clearing his throat, "we just rid the city of a murderer who has taken, at last count, nearly a dozen of her citizens. We're entitled to combat pay, I surmise." He said it with a completely straight face. Bless the man.

"Bloody right," Mat said. Stopping the *gholam and* getting paid for it. That sounded like a sunny day for a change. He tossed his kerchief to Guybon and walked away, leaving behind the Kinswomen who folded their arms and watched with displeasure. Why was it a woman could look angry with a man even when he had done exactly what he had said he would, risking his neck even?

"Sorry about the fire, Mat," Talmanes said. "Didn't mean to drop the lantern like that. I know I was just supposed to lead him into the building."

"Worked out fine," Mat said, inspecting the butt of his *ashandarei.* The damage was minor.

They had not known where—or if—the *gholam* would attack him, but Guybon had done his job well, getting everyone out of the nearby buildings, then picking a hallway that the Kinswoman would make the gateway into. He'd sent a member of the Band to tell Talmanes where to go.

Well, Elayne and Birgitte's idea with the gateway had worked out, even if it hadn't been the way they'd planned. It was still better than what Mat had been able to come up with; his only idea had been to try to stuff one of those medallions down the *gholam*'s throat.

"Let's collect Setalle and Olver from their inn," Mat said, "and get back to camp. Excitement's over for now. About bloody time."

CHAPTER

32

A Storm of Light

The city of Maradon burned. Violent, twisting columns of smoke rose from dozens of buildings. The careful city planning kept the fires from spreading too quickly, but did not stop them entirely. Human beings and tinder. They went together.

Ituralde crouched inside a broken building, rubble to his left, a small band of Saldaeans to his right. He'd abandoned the palace early on; it had been swarmed with Shadowspawn. He'd left it packed with all the oil they'd been able to find, then had the Asha'man set it aflame, killing hundreds of Trollocs and Fades trapped inside.

He glanced out the window of his current hiding place. He could have sworn he'd seen a patch of bare sky out the window, but the ash and smoky haze in the air made it difficult to tell. A building nearby burned so intensely that he could feel the heat through the stone.

He used the smoke and the fire. Almost everything on a battlefield could be an advantage. In this case, once Yoeli had accepted that the city was lost, they'd stopped defending it. Now they used the city as a killing ground.

The streets created a maze that Ituralde—with the help of the Saldaeans—knew and his enemies did not. Every rooftop was a ridge to give high ground, every alley a secret escape route, every open square a potential trap.

The Trollocs and their commanders had made a mistake. They assumed that Ituralde cared about protecting the city. They mistook him. All he cared about now was doing as much damage to them as possible. So, he used their assumptions against them. Yes, their army was large. But any man who had ever tried to kill rats knew that the size of his hammer didn't matter so long as the rats knew how to hide.

A hesitant group of the creatures shuffled down the blackened street outside Ituralde's building. The Trollocs snapped and hooted warily at one another. Some sniffed at the air, but the smoke ruined their sense of smell. They completely missed Ituralde and his small band, just inside the building.

Hoofbeats rang on the other end of the street. The Trollocs began to shout, and a group hurried to the front, setting wickedly barbed spears down with the butts against the cobbles. Charging that would be death for cavalry. The Trollocs were learning to be more careful.

But they weren't learning well enough. The cavalry came into view, revealing one man leading a group of wounded and exhausted horses. A distraction.

"Now," Ituralde said. The archers around him sprang up and began shooting out the windows at the Trollocs. Many died; others spun and charged.

And from a side street a cavalry charge—the horses' hooves covered with rags to dampen sound—galloped out, their approach covered by the louder hooves of the diversionary horses. The Saldaeans ripped through the Trollocs, trampling and killing.

The archers whooped and took out swords and axes to finish off the wounded Trollocs. No Fade with this group, bless the Light. Ituralde stood up, a wet handkerchief to his face against the smoke. His weariness—once buried deep—was slowly resurfacing. He was worried that when it hit him, he'd drop unconscious. Bad for morale, that.

No, he thought, *hiding in the smoke while your home burns, knowing that the Trollocs are slowly penning you in . . .* that's *bad for morale.*

His men finished off the fist of Trollocs, then hastened to another pre-decided building that they could hide in. Ituralde had about thirty archers and a company of cavalry, which he moved among five independent bands of irregular fighters similar to this one. He waved his men back into hiding while his scouts brought him information. Even with the scouts, it was difficult to get a good read on the large city. He had vague ideas of where the strongest resistance was, and sent what orders he could, but the battle was spread over too large an area for him to be able to coordinate the fighting effectively. He hoped Yoeli was well.

The Asha'man were gone, escaping at his order through the tiny gateway—only large enough to crawl through—that Antail had made. Since they'd gone—it was hours ago now—there had been no sign of whatever "rescuers" were supposedly coming. Before the Asha'man left, he'd sent a scout through a gateway to that ridge where the Lastriders had been said to watch. All that the scout found was an empty camp, the fire burning unattended.

Ituralde joined his men inside the new hiding place, leaving his handkerchief—now stained with soot—on the doorknob to give the scouts a clue to his location. Once inside, he froze, hearing something outside.

"Hush," he said to the men. They stilled their clinking armor.

Footfalls. Many of them. That was a Trolloc band for certain; his men had orders to move silently. He nodded to his soldiers, holding up six fingers. Plan number six. They'd hide, waiting, hoping the creatures would pass them by. If they didn't—if they delayed, or started searching the nearby buildings—his team would burst out and broadside them.

It was the riskiest of the plans. His men were exhausted and the cavalry had been sent to another of his groups of defenders. But better to attack than be discovered or surrounded.

Ituralde sidled up to the window, waiting, listening, breathing shallowly. Light, but he was tired. The group marched around the corner outside, footfalls in unison. That was odd. The Trollocs raiding the city were hunting in packs, not marching in formation.

"My Lord," one of his men whispered. "There aren't any hooves."

Ituralde froze. The man was right. His tiredness was making him stupid. *That's an army of hundreds,* he thought. He got to his feet, coughing despite himself, and pushed open the door. He stepped outside.

A gust of wind blew down the street as Ituralde's men piled out behind him. The wind cleared the smoke for a moment, revealing a large troop of infantry kitted out in silvery armor and carrying pikes. They seemed ghosts for a moment—glowing in a phantom golden light from above, a sun he had not seen in months.

The newcomers began to call as they saw him and his men, and two of their officers charged up to him. They were Saldaean. "Where is your commander?" one asked. "The man Rodel Ituralde?"

"I . . ." Ituralde found himself coughing. "I am he. Who are you?"

"Bless the Light," one of the men said, turning back to the others. "Pass the word to Lord Bashere! We've found him!"

Ituralde blinked. He looked back at his filthy men, faces blackened with soot. More than a few had an arm in a sling. He'd started with two hundred. Now there were fifty. They should be celebrating, but most of them sat down on the ground, closing their eyes.

Ituralde found himself laughing. "Now? The Dragon sends help *now*?" He stumbled, then sat down, staring up at the burning sky. He was laughing, and he could not stop. Soon tears began streaking down his cheeks.

Yes, there was sunlight up there.

Ituralde had regained some composure by the time the troops led him into a well-defended sector of the city. The smoke here was much less thick. Supposedly, al'Thor's troops—led by Davram Bashere—had reclaimed most of Maradon. What was left of it. They'd been putting out the fires.

It was so odd to see troops with shiny armor, neat uniforms, clean faces. They'd swept in with large numbers of Asha'man and Aes Sedai, and an army that—for now—had been enough to drive the Shadowspawn back to the hillside fortifications above the river. Al'Thor's men led him to a tall building inside the city. With the palace burned out, mostly destroyed, it looked like they'd picked this building as a command center.

Ituralde had been fighting a draining war for weeks now. Al'Thor's troops seemed almost *too* clean. His men had been dying while these men washed and slept and dined on hot food?

Stop it, he told himself, entering the building. It was

far too easy to blame others when a battle went wrong. It wasn't the fault of these men that their lives had been easier than his recently.

He labored up the stairs, wishing they'd let him be. A good night's sleep, a wash, and *then* he could meet with Bashere. But no, that wouldn't do. The battle wasn't over, and al'Thor's men would need information. It was just that his mind was failing him, working very slowly.

He reached the top floor and followed Bashere's soldiers into a room to the right. Bashere stood there, wearing a burnished breastplate without the matching helmet, hands clasped behind his back as he looked out the window. He wore one of those overly large Saldaean mustaches and a pair of olive trousers stuffed into knee-high boots.

Bashere turned and started. "Light! You look like death itself, man!" He turned to the soldiers. "He should be in the Healer's tent! Someone fetch an Asha'man!"

"I'm all right," Ituralde said, forcing sternness into his voice. "I look worse than I feel, I'd warrant."

The soldiers hesitated, looking to Bashere. "Well," the man said, "at least get him a chair and something to wipe his face with. You poor fellow; we should have been here days ago."

Outside, Ituralde could hear the sounds of distant battle. Bashere had chosen a tall building, one from which he could survey the fighting. The soldiers brought a chair, and—for all his wish to show a strong face to a fellow general— Ituralde sat with a sigh.

He looked down, and was amazed to see how dirty his hands were, as though he'd been cleaning a hearth. No doubt his face was soot-covered, streaked with sweat, and there was likely still dried blood on it. His clothing was ragged from the blast that had destroyed the wall, not to mention a hastily bandaged cut on his arm.

"Your defense of this city was nothing short of stunning, Lord Ituralde," Bashere said. There was a formality to his tone—Saldaea and Arad Doman were not enemies, but two strong nations could not share a border without periods of animosity. "The number of Trollocs dead compared to the number of men you had . . . and with a gap that large in the wall . . . Let me say that I'm impressed." Bashere's tone implied that such praise was not easily given.

"What of Yoeli?" Ituralde asked.

Bashere's expression grew grim. "My men found a small band defending his corpse. He died bravely, though I was surprised to find him in command and Torkumen—a distant cousin of mine, the presumed leader of the city— locked in his rooms, and abandoned, where the Trollocs could have gotten him."

"Yoeli was a good man," Ituralde said stiffly. "Among the bravest I've had the honor of knowing. He saved my life, brought my men into the city *against* Torkumen's orders. It's a burning shame to lose him. A burning shame. Without Yoeli, Maradon wouldn't stand right now."

"It hardly stands anyway," Bashere said somberly.

Ituralde hesitated. *He's uncle to the Queen—this city is probably his home.*

The two looked at one another, like old wolves, leaders of rival packs. Stepping softly. "I'm sorry for your loss," Ituralde said.

"The city stands as well as it does," Bashere said, "because of you. I'm not angry, man. I'm saddened, but not angry. And I'll take your word on Yoeli. To be frank, I've never liked Torkumen. For now, I've left him in the room where we found him—still alive, thankfully—though I'll hear thunder from the Queen for what's been done to him. She's always been fond of him. Bah! She normally has better judgment."

Bashere nodded to the side when he spoke of Torkumen, and—with a start—Ituralde realized that he recognized this building. This was Torkumen's home, where Yoeli had brought Ituralde on his first day in the city. It made sense to choose this building as a command post—it was close enough to the northern wall to have a good view of the outside, but far enough away from the blast to have survived, unlike the Council Hall.

Well, it would have served Torkumen right if the Trollocs had gotten him. Ituralde sat back, closing his eyes, as Bashere consulted with his officers. Bashere was capable, that much was obvious. Very quickly he'd swept the city clean; once the Trollocs had realized that there was a larger force to fight, they'd abandoned the city. Ituralde could feel pride that, in part, his tenacity was what had made them so quick to run.

Ituralde continued to listen. Most of Bashere's troops

had come into the city through gateways, after sending in one scout to find safe places to make them. Fighting in the streets wouldn't work for him as it had Ituralde; the hit-and-hide tactic had been devoted to doing as much damage as possible before getting killed. It was a losing tactic.

The Trollocs had pulled back into the fortifications, but they wouldn't stay there for long. As he sat with closed eyes, struggling to stay awake, Ituralde heard Bashere and his captains come to the same dire conclusion Ituralde had. Maradon was lost. The Shadowspawn would wait for night, then swarm in again.

After all this, they'd just flee? After Yoeli had died holding the city? After Rajabi had been killed by a Draghkar? After Ankaer and Rossin had fallen during the skirmishes inside the walls? After all the bloodshed, they finally saw help arrive, only to have it prove insufficient?

"Perhaps we could push them off that hilltop," one of Bashere's men said. "Clean out the fortifications."

He didn't sound very optimistic.

"Son," Ituralde said, forcing his eyes open, "I held that hill for weeks against a superior force. Your people built it up well, and the problem with well-built fortifications is that your enemy can turn them against you. You'll lose men attacking there. A lot of them."

The room fell silent.

"We leave, then," Bashere said. "Naeff, we'll need gateways."

"Yes, Lord Bashere." Square-faced and lean of build, the man wore the black coat and the Dragon pin of an Asha'man.

"Malain, gather the cavalry and organize them outside; make it look as if we're going to try an assault against their fortifications. That'll keep them eager and waiting. We'll evacuate the wounded, then we'll have the cavalry charge in the other direction into—"

"By the Light and my hope for rebirth!" a voice suddenly exclaimed. Everyone in the room turned in shock; that wasn't the sort of oath you heard every day.

A young soldier stood by the window, looking out with a looking glass. Bashere cursed, and hurried to the window, the others crowding around, several taking out looking glasses.

What now? Ituralde thought, standing despite his fatigue and hurrying over. *What could they possibly have come up with? More Draghkar? Darkhounds?*

He peered out the window, and someone handed him a looking glass. He raised it, and as he'd guessed, the building was on enough of a rise to look out over the city wall and onto the killing field outside and beyond. The tower positions on the crest of the hill were clustered with ravens. Through the glass, he could see Trollocs clogging the heights, holding the upper camp, the towers, and the bulwarks there.

Beyond the hill, surging down through the pass, was an awesome force of Trollocs, many times the number that had assaulted Maradon. The wave of monsters seemed to continue on forever.

"We need to go," Bashere said, lowering his looking glass. "Immediately."

"Light!" Ituralde whispered. "If that force gets past us, there won't be anything in Saldaea, Andor, or Arad Doman that can stop it. Please tell me the Lord Dragon made peace with the Seanchan, as he promised?"

"In that," a quiet voice said from behind, "as in so many other things, I have failed."

Ituralde spun, lowering his looking glass. A tall man with reddish hair stepped into the room—a man whom Ituralde felt he had never met before, despite the familiar features.

Rand al'Thor had changed.

The Dragon Reborn had that same self-confidence, that same straight back, that same attitude expecting obedience. And yet, at the same time, everything seemed different. The way he stood, no longer faintly suspicious. The way he studied Ituralde with concern.

Those eyes, cold and emotionless, had once convinced Ituralde to follow this man. Those eyes had changed, too. Ituralde had not noted wisdom in them before.

Don't be a thickheaded fool, Ituralde thought, *you can't tell if a man is wise by looking at his eyes.*

And yet he could.

"Rodel Ituralde," al'Thor said, stepping forward and laying a hand on Ituralde's arm. "I left you and your men stranded and overwhelmed. Please forgive me."

"I made this choice myself," Ituralde said. Oddly, he felt less tired than he had just moments ago.

"I have inspected your men," al'Thor said. "There are so few left, and they are broken and battered. How did you hold this city? What you have done is a miracle."

"I do what needs to be done."

"You must have lost many friends."

"I . . . Yes." What other answer was there? To dismiss it as nothing would be to dishonor them. "Wakeda fell today. Rajabi . . . well, a Draghkar got him. Ankaer. He lasted until this afternoon. Never did find out why that trumpeter sounded early. Rossin was looking into it. He's dead, too."

"We need to get out of the city," Bashere said, his voice urgent. "I'm sorry, man. Maradon is lost."

"No," al'Thor said softly. "The Shadow will not have this city. Not after what these men did to hold it. I *will not* allow it."

"An honorable sentiment," Bashere said, "but we don't . . ." He trailed off as al'Thor looked at him.

Those eyes. So *intense*. They seemed almost alight. "They will not take this city, Bashere," al'Thor said, an edge of anger entering his quiet voice. He waved to the side, and a gateway split the air. The sounds of drums and Trollocs yelling grew closer, suddenly. "I'm tired of letting him hurt my people. Pull your soldiers back."

With that, al'Thor stepped through the gateway. A pair of Aiel Maidens hurried into the room, and he left the gateway open long enough for them to leap through behind him. Then he let it vanish.

Bashere looked stunned, mouth half-open. "Curse that man!" he finally said, turning to the window again. "I thought he wasn't going to do this sort of thing any longer!"

Ituralde joined Bashere, raising his looking glass, looking out through the enormous gap in the wall. Outside, al'Thor was crossing the trampled ground, wearing his brown cloak and followed by the two Maidens.

Ituralde thought he could hear the sounds of the howling Trollocs. Their drums beat. They saw three people alone.

The Trollocs surged forward, charging across the ground. Hundreds. Thousands. Ituralde gasped. Bashere uttered a quiet prayer.

Al'Thor raised one hand, then thrust it—palm forward—toward the tide of Shadowspawn.

And they started to die.

It began with waves of fire, much like the ones Asha'man used. Only these were far larger. The flames burned terrible swaths of death through the Trollocs. They followed the course of the land, seeping up the hill and down into the trenches, filling them with white-hot fire, searing and destroying.

Clouds of Draghkar spun in the sky, diving for al'Thor. The air above him turned blue, and shards of ice exploded outward, spraying the air like arrows from the bows of an entire banner of archers. The beasts shrieked their inhuman agony, carcasses tumbling to the ground.

Light and Power exploded from the Dragon Reborn. He was like an entire army of channelers. Thousands of Shadowspawn died. Deathgates sprang up, striking across the ground, killing hundreds.

The Asha'man Naeff—standing beside Bashere—gasped. "I've never seen so many weaves at once," he whispered. "I can't track them all. He's a storm. A storm of Light and streams of Power!"

Clouds began to form and swirl above the city. The wind picked up, howling, and lightning struck from above. Blasts of thunder overpowered the sounds of drums as Trollocs tried in vain to get to al'Thor, climbing over the burning carcasses of their brethren. The swirling white clouds crashed into the black, boiling tempest, intermingling. Wind spun around al'Thor, whipping at his cloak.

The man himself seemed to be glowing. Was it the reflection of the swaths of fire, or perhaps the lightning blasts? Al'Thor seemed brighter than them all, his hand upraised against the Shadowspawn. His Maidens hunched near the ground on either side of him, eyes forward, shoulders set against the great wind.

Clouds spinning about one another made funnels into the masses of Trollocs, sweeping across the top of the hill, taking up the creatures into the air. Great waterspouts rose behind, made of flesh and fire. The beasts rained down, falling upon the others. Ituralde watched with awe, the hair on his arms and head rising. There was an *energy* to the very air itself.

A scream came from nearby. Within the building, in one of the nearby rooms. Ituralde did not turn away from the window. He *had* to watch this beautiful, terrible moment of destruction and Power.

Waves of Trollocs broke, the drums faltering. Entire legions of them turned and fled, stumbling up the hillside and over one another, fleeing back toward the Blight. Some remained firm—too angry, too intimidated by those driving them, or too stupid to flee. The tempest of destruction seemed to come to a peak, flashes of light blasting down in time with howling wind, thrumming waves of burning flame, tinkling shards of ice.

It was a masterwork. A terrible, destructive, wonderful masterwork. Al'Thor lifted his hand toward the sky. The winds grew faster, the lightning strikes larger, the fires hotter. Trollocs screamed, moaned, howled. Ituralde found himself trembling.

Al'Thor closed his hand into a fist, and it all ended.

The last of the wind-seized Trollocs dropped from the sky like leaves abandoned by a passing breeze. Everything fell silent. The flames died, the black and white clouds cleared and opened to a blue sky.

Al'Thor lowered his hand. The field before him was piled with carcasses atop carcasses. Tens of thousands of dead Trollocs smoldering. Directly before al'Thor, a pile a hundred paces wide formed a ridge five feet tall, a mound of dead that had nearly reached him.

How long had it taken? Ituralde found that he could not gauge the time, though looking at the sun, at least an hour had passed. Perhaps more. It had seemed like seconds.

Al'Thor turned to walk away. The Maidens rose on shaky feet, stumbling after him.

"What was that scream?" Naeff asked. "The one nearby, in the building. Did you hear it?"

Ituralde frowned. What *had* that been? He crossed the room, the others—including several of Bashere's officers—following. Many others stayed in the room, however, staring out at the field that had been cleansed by ice and by fire. It was odd, but Ituralde hadn't been able to spot a single fallen tower atop the hill. It was as if al'Thor's attacks had somehow affected only the Shadowspawn. Could a man really be that precise?

The hallway outside was empty, but Ituralde had a suspicion now of where the scream had come from. He walked to Lord Torkumen's door; Bashere unlocked it, and they went inside.

It seemed empty. Ituralde felt a spike of fear. Had the man escaped? He pulled out his sword.

No. A figure was huddled in the corner beside the bed, fine clothing wrinkled, doublet stained with blood. Ituralde lowered his sword. Lord Torkumen's eyes were gone. He appeared to have put them out with a writing quill; the bloodied implement lay on the ground beside him.

The window was broken. Bashere glanced out of it. "Lady Torkumen is down there."

"She jumped," Torkumen whispered, clawing at his eye sockets, fingers covered with blood. He sounded dazed. "That light . . . That terrible *light*."

Ituralde glanced at Bashere.

"I cannot watch it," Torkumen muttered. "I cannot! Great Lord, where is your protection? Where are your armies to rend, your swords to strike? That Light eats at my mind, like rats feasting on a corpse. It burns at my thoughts. It killed me. That light killed me."

"He's gone mad," Bashere said grimly, kneeling down beside the man. "Better than he deserved, judging by those ramblings. Light! My own cousin a Darkfriend. And in control of the city!"

"What is he talking about?" one of Bashere's men said. "A light? Surely he couldn't have seen the battle. None of these windows face the right way."

"I'm not sure he was talking about the battle, Vogeler," Bashere said. "Come on. I suspect the Lord Dragon is going to be tired. I want to see that he's cared for."

This is it, Min thought, tapping the page. She sat on her windowsill in the Stone of Tear, enjoying the breeze. Trying not to think of Rand. He wasn't hurt, but his emotions were so strong. Anger. She'd hoped he wouldn't be so angry ever again.

She shook off the worrying; she had work to do. Was she following the wrong thread? Was she interpreting in the wrong way? She read the line again. *Light is held before the maw of the infinite void, and all that he is can be seized.*

Her speculation cut off as she saw a light appear from the room across the hall. She dropped her book and leaped down to the floor. Rand was suddenly close. She could feel it through the bond.

Two Maidens guarded the room across the hall, mostly to prevent people from wandering in and getting hurt by gateways. The one that had opened now led to a place that smelled of smoke. Rand stumbled through. Min ran to him. He looked exhausted, eyes red, face wan. He leaned against her with a sigh, letting her help him to a chair.

"What happened?" Min demanded of Evasni, the Maiden who came through next. She was a lanky woman with dark red hair, cut short with a tail in the back like that of most Maidens.

"The *Car'a'carn* is well," the woman said. "Though he is like a youth who ran one more lap around the camp than everyone else, only to prove that he could."

"He gained much *ji* today," Ifeyina—the other Maiden—said, almost in argument. Her voice was solemn.

Rand sighed, settling back in the chair. Bashere followed out of the gateway, boots hitting stone. Min heard calls from down below—a group of wounded soldiers being brought through a larger gateway. The Stone's courtyards were alive with activity, Aes Sedai Healers running to care for the bloodied, sooty men.

After Bashere came a lean Domani man in his middle years. Rodel Ituralde. He looked much the worse for wear, with dried blood on his filthy face, his clothing ripped, and wearing a clumsy bandage on his arm. Rand had no visible wounds. His clothing was clean, though he insisted on still wearing that aged brown cloak. But Light, he looked tired.

"Rand," Min said, kneeling down. "Rand, are you all right?"

"I grew angry," Rand said softly. "I had thought myself beyond that."

She felt a chill.

"It was not a terrible anger, like before," Rand said. "It was not the anger of destruction, though I did destroy. In Maradon, I saw what had been done to men who followed

me. I saw Light in them, Min. Defying the Dark One no
matter the length of his shadow. We will live, that defiance
said. We will love and we will hope.

"And I saw him trying so hard to destroy that. He knows
that if he could break them, it would mean something.
Something much more than Maradon. Breaking the spirit
of men . . . he *thirsts* for that. He struck far harder than
he otherwise would have because he wanted to break my
spirit." His voice grew softer and he opened his eyes, looking down at her. "And so I stood against him."

"What you did was amazing," Bashere said, standing beside Min with his arms folded. "But did you let him drive
you to it?"

Rand shook his head. "I have a right to my anger, Bashere.
Don't you see? Before, I tried to hold it all hidden within.
That was wrong. I *must* feel. I must hurt for the pains, the
deaths, the losses of these people. I have to cling to these
things so I know why I am fighting. There are times when
I need the void, but that does not make my anger any less a
part of me."

He seemed to be growing more confident with each
word, and Min nodded.

"Well, you saved the city," Bashere said.

"Not soon enough," Rand said. Min could feel his sorrow. "And my actions today may still have been a mistake."

Min frowned. "Why?"

"It came too close to a confrontation between us," Rand
said. "That *must* happen at Shayol Ghul, and at the right
time. I cannot afford to let him provoke me. Bashere is
right. Nor can I afford to let the men assume that I will
always be able to step in and save them."

"Perhaps," Bashere said. "But what you did today . . ."

Rand shook his head. "I am not to fight this war, Bashere.
Today's battle exhausted me beyond what I should have allowed. If my enemies were to come upon me now, I'd be
finished. Besides, I can only fight in one place at a time.
What is coming will be grander than that, grander and
more terrible than any one man could hope to hold back.
I will organize you, but I must leave you. The war will be
yours."

He fell silent, and Flinn stepped through the gateway, letting it slide closed.

"I must rest now," Rand said softly. "Tomorrow I meet with your niece and the other Borderlanders, Bashere. I now not what they will require of me, but they *must* return o their posts. If Saldaea was in such a state with one of the great captains leading the defense, I can only guess what he other Borderland nations are suffering."

Min helped him to his feet. "Rand," she said softly. "Cadsuane returned, and she had someone with her."

He hesitated. "Take me to her."

Min winced. "I shouldn't have mentioned it. You should est."

"I will," he said. "Don't worry."

She could still sense his exhaustion. But she didn't argue. They walked from the room. "Rodel Ituralde," Rand said, ausing by the doorway. "You will wish to accompany me. cannot repay you for the honor you have shown, but I do ave something I can give."

The grizzled Domani nodded, following. Min helped Rand down the corridor, worrying about him. Did he *have* o push himself this hard?

Unfortunately, he does. Rand al'Thor was the Dragon Reborn. He'd be bled dry, ground down, used up before this vas through. It was almost enough to make a woman stop rying.

"Rand . . ." she said, Ituralde and several Maidens trailing them. Fortunately, Cadsuane's room wasn't far.

"I will be all right," he said. "I promise. Have you news f your studies?" He was trying to distract her.

Unfortunately, that question just sent her to another vorry. "Have you ever wondered why *Callandor* is so often alled a 'fearful blade' or 'the blade of ruin' in the prophecies?"

"It's such a powerful *sa'angreal*," he said. "Maybe it's ecause of the destruction it can cause?"

"Maybe," she said.

"You think it's something else."

"There's a phrase," Min said, "in the Jendai Prophecy. I vish we knew more of them. Anyway, it says 'and the Blade vill bind him by twain.'"

"Two women," Rand said. "I need to be in a circle with vo women to control it."

She grimaced.

"What?" Rand said. "You might as well be out with it Min. I need to know."

"There's another phrase, from *The Karaethon Cycle* Anyway, I think that *Callandor* might be flawed beyon that. I think it might . . . Rand, I think it might make yo weak, open you to attack, if you use it."

"Perhaps that's how I'll be killed, then."

"You *aren't* going to be killed," Min said.

"I—"

"You'll live through this, sheepherder," she insisted. "I'n going to see that you do."

He smiled at her. He looked so tired. "I almost believ that you'll do it, Min. Perhaps I'm not the one the Patter bends around, but you." He turned, then knocked on a doo in the hallway.

It cracked, Merise peeking out. She looked Rand up an down. "You seem as if you can barely stand on your ow feet, al'Thor."

"True indeed," he replied. "Is Cadsuane Sedai here?"

"She has done as you asked," Merise replied. "And, might say, she's been *very* accommodating, considerin how you—"

"Let him in, Merise," Cadsuane's voice said from inside

Merise hesitated, then gave Rand a glare as she pulle the door open all the way. Cadsuane sat in a chair, speakin with an older man whose long, gray hair fell loose to hi shoulders. He had a large beak of a nose and regal clothing

Rand stepped to the side. Behind them, someone gasped Rodel Ituralde stepped up to the doorway, seeming stunned and the man in the room turned. He had kindly eyes an coppery skin.

"My liege," Ituralde cried, hastening forward, then goin down on one knee. "You live!"

Min felt an overwhelming sense of happiness from Rand Ituralde, it appeared, was weeping. Rand stepped back "Come, let's go to my rooms and rest."

"The King of Arad Doman. Where did she find him? Min said. "How did you know?"

"A friend left me a secret," Rand said. "The White Towe collected Mattin Stepaneos to 'protect' him. Well, it wasn' too much of a leap to wonder if they might have don that with other monarchs. And if they sent sisters to Ara

Doman to seize him months ago, before any of them knew of gateways, they could have gotten trapped in the snows on their return trip." He seemed so relieved. "Graendal never had him. I didn't kill him, Min. One innocent I assumed that I'd killed still lives. That's something. A small something. But it helps."

She helped him walk the rest of the way to their rooms, content—for the moment—to share in his warm sense of joy and relief.

CHAPTER
33

A Good Soup

Siuan's soup was surprisingly good.

She took another sip, raising an eyebrow. It was simple—broth and vegetables, bits of chicken—but when most food tasted stale at best, this seemed a wonder. She tried the biscuit. No weevils? Delightful!

Nynaeve had just fallen silent, her own bowl steaming in front of her. Newly raised, she'd taken the oaths earlier in the day. They were in the Amyrlin's study, shutters open and spilling in golden light, new rugs of green and gold on the floor.

Silently, Siuan chided herself for getting distracted by the soup. Nynaeve's report demanded consideration. She'd spoken of her time with Rand al'Thor, and specifically of events such as the cleansing. Of course, Siuan had heard the reports that *saidin* had been cleansed; an Asha'man had visited the camp during the division. She had remained skeptical, but there was little denying it now.

"Well," the Amyrlin said, "I am very glad for this longer explanation, Nynaeve. Though *saidin* being cleansed does make it less unsettling to consider Asha'man and Aes Sedai bonding one another. I wish Rand had been willing to speak to me of that during our meeting." She said it evenly, though Siuan knew she looked on men bonding women with as much pleasure as a captain looked on a fire in his hold.

"I suppose," Nynaeve said, lips turning down. "If it matters, Rand didn't approve the men bonding women."

"It doesn't matter if he did or not," Egwene said. "The Asha'man are his responsibility."

"As the Aes Sedai who chained him and beat him are yours, Mother?" Nynaeve asked.

"Inherited from Elaida, perhaps," Egwene said, eyes narrowing just slightly.

She was right to bring Nynaeve back, Siuan thought, taking a sip of soup. *She takes his side far too often for comfort.*

Nynaeve sighed, taking her spoon to begin her soup. "I didn't mean that as a challenge, Mother. I just want to show how he thinks. Light! I didn't approve of much of what he did, particularly lately. But I can see how he got there."

"He *has* changed, though," Siuan said thoughtfully. "You said so yourself."

"Yes," Nynaeve said. "The Aiel say he's embraced death."

"I've heard that from them, too," Egwene said. "But I looked into his eyes, and something else has changed, something inexplicable. The man I saw . . ."

"He didn't seem like one to destroy Natrin's Barrow?" Siuan shivered as she thought of that.

"The man I saw wouldn't need to destroy such a place," Egwene said. "Those inside would just follow him. Bend to his wishes. Because he *was.*"

The three fell silent.

Egwene shook her head and took a sip of her soup. She paused, then smiled. "Well, I see the soup is good. Perhaps things aren't as bad as I thought."

"The ingredients came from Caemlyn," Nynaeve noted. "I overheard the serving girls talking."

"Oh."

More silence.

"Mother," Siuan said, speaking carefully. "The women are still worried about the deaths in the Tower."

"I agree, Mother," Nynaeve said. "Sisters stare at one another with distrust. It worries me."

"You both should have seen it before," Egwene said. "During Elaida's reign."

"If it was worse than this," Nynaeve said, "I'm glad that I didn't." She glanced down at her Great Serpent ring. She did that a lot, recently. As a fisher with a new boat often glanced toward the docks and smiled. For all her complaints that she *was* Aes Sedai, and for all the fact that she'd been wearing that ring for a long time now, she was obviously satisfied to have passed the testing and taken the oaths.

"It was terrible," Egwene said. "And I don't intend to let it go back to that. Siuan, the plan must be put into motion."

Siuan grimaced. "I've been teaching the others. But I don't think this is a good idea, Mother. They're barely trained."

"What's this?" Nynaeve asked.

"Aes Sedai," Egwene said. "Carefully chosen and given dream *ter'angreal*. Siuan is showing them how *Tel'aran'rhiod* works."

"Mother, that place is dangerous."

Egwene took another sip of soup. "I believe I know that better than most. But it *is* necessary; we must lure the killers into a confrontation. I'll arrange for a 'secret' meeting among my most loyal Aes Sedai, in the World of Dreams, and perhaps lay clues that other people of importance will be attending. Siuan, you've contacted the Windfinders?"

"Yes," Siuan said. "Though they want to know what you'll give them to agree to meet with you."

"The loan of the dream *ter'angreal* will be enough," Egwene said dryly. "Not everything has to be a bargain."

"To them, it often does," Nynaeve said. "But that's beside the point. You're bringing *Windfinders* to this meeting to lure Mesaana?"

"Not exactly," Egwene said. "I'll see the Windfinders at the same time, in a different place. And some Wise Ones as well. Enough to hint to Mesaana—assuming she's got spies watching the other groups of women who can channel— that she *really* wants to spy on us in *Tel'aran'rhiod* that day.

"You and Siuan will hold a meeting in the Hall of the Tower, but it will be a decoy to draw Mesaana or her minions out of hiding. With wards—and some sisters watching from hidden places—we'll be able to trap them. Siuan will send for me as soon as the trap is sprung."

Nynaeve frowned. "It's a good plan, save for one thing. I don't like you being in danger, Mother. Let me lead this fight. I can manage it."

Egwene studied Nynaeve, and Siuan saw some of the real Egwene. Thoughtful. Bold, but calculating. She also saw Egwene's fatigue, the weight of responsibility. Siuan knew that feeling well.

"I'll admit you have a valid concern," Egwene said. "Ever since I let myself get captured by Elaida's cronies outside of Tar Valon, I've wondered if I become too directly involved, too directly in danger."

"Exactly," Nynaeve said.

"However," Egwene said, "the simple fact remains that I am the one among us who is most expert at *Tel'aran'rhiod*. You two are skilled, true, but I have more experience. In this case, I am not just the leader of the Aes Sedai, I am a tool that the White Tower must use." She hesitated. "I dreamed this, Nynaeve. If we do not defeat Mesaana here, all could be lost. All *will* be lost. It is not a time to hold back any of our tools, no matter how valuable."

Nynaeve reached for her braid, but it now came only to her shoulders. She gritted her teeth at that. "You might have a point. But I don't like it."

"The Aiel dreamwalkers," Siuan said. "Mother, you said you'll be meeting with them. Might they be willing to help? I'd feel much better about having you fight if I knew they were around to keep an eye on you."

"Yes," Egwene said. "A good suggestion. I will contact them before we meet and make the request, just in case."

"Mother," Nynaeve said. "Perhaps Rand—"

"This is a matter of the Tower, Nynaeve," Egwene said. "We will manage it."

"Very well."

"Now," Egwene continued, "we need to figure out how to spread the right rumors so that Mesaana won't be able to resist coming to listen . . ."

Perrin hit the nightmare running. The air bent around him, and the city houses—this time of the Cairhienin flat-topped variety—disappeared. The road became soft beneath his feet, like mud, then turned to liquid.

He splashed in the ocean. *Water again?* he thought with annoyance.

Deep red lightning crashed in the sky, throwing waves of bloody light across the sea. Each burst revealed shadowed creatures lurking beneath the waves. Massive things, evil and sinuous in the spasming red lightning.

People clung to the wreckage of what had once been a ship, screaming in terror and crying out for loved ones. Men on broken boards, women trying to hold their babies above the water as towering waves broke over them, dead bodies bobbing like sacks of grain.

The things beneath the waves struck, snatching people from the surface and dragging them into the depths with splashes of fins and sparkling, razor-sharp teeth. The water was soon bubbling red that didn't come from the lightning.

Whoever had dreamed *this* particular nightmare had a singularly twisted imagination.

Perrin refused to let himself be drawn in. He squelched his fear, and did not swim for one of those planks. *It isn't real. It isn't real. It isn't real.*

Despite his understanding, part of him knew that he was going to die in these waters. These terrible, bloody waters. The moans of the others assaulted him, and he yearned to try to help them. They weren't real, he knew. Just figments. But it was hard.

Perrin began to rise from the water, the waves turning back into ground. But then he cried out as something brushed his leg. Lightning crashed, breaking the air. A woman beside him slipped beneath the waves, tugged by unseen jaws. Panicked, Perrin was suddenly back in the water, there in a heartbeat, floating in a completely different place, one arm slung over a piece of wreckage.

This happened sometimes. If he wavered for a moment—if he let himself see the nightmare as real—it would pull him in and actually move him, fitting him into its terrible mosaic. Something moved in the water nearby, and he splashed away with a start. One of the surging waves raised him into the air.

It isn't real. It isn't real. It isn't real.

The waters were so cold. Something touched his leg again, and he screamed, then choked off as he gulped in a mouthful of salty water.

IT ISN'T REAL!

He was in Cairhien, leagues from the ocean. This was a street. Hard stones beneath. The smell of baked bread coming from a nearby bakery. The street lined with small, thin-trunked ash trees.

With a bellowing scream, he clung to this knowledge as the people around him held to their flotsam. Perrin knotted his hands into fists, focusing on reality.

There *were* cobblestones under his feet. Not waves. Not water. Not teeth and fins. Slowly, he rose from the ocean again. He stepped out of it and set his foot on the surface, feeling solid stone beneath his boot. The other foot followed. He found himself on a small, floating circle of stones.

Something enormous surged from the waters to his left, a massive beast part fish and part monster, with a maw so wide that a man could walk into it standing upright. The teeth were as large as Perrin's hand, and they glittered, dripping blood.

It was *not* real.

The creature exploded into mist. The spray hit Perrin, then dried immediately. Around him, the nightmare bent, a bubble of reality pressing out from him. Dark air, cold waves, screaming people ran together like wet paint.

There was no lightning—he did *not* see it light his eyelids. There was no thunder. He could *not* hear it crashing. There were no waves, not in the middle of landlocked Cairhien.

Perrin snapped his eyes open, and the entire nightmare broke apart, vanishing like a film of frost exposed to the spring sunlight. The buildings reappeared, the street returned, the waves retreated. The sky returned to the boiling black tempest. Lightning that was bright and white flashed in its depths, but there was no thunder.

Hopper sat on the street a short distance away. Perrin walked over to the wolf. He could have jumped there immediately, of course, but he didn't like the idea of doing everything easily. That would bite at him when he returned to the real world.

You grow strong, Young Bull, Hopper sent approvingly.

"I still take too long," Perrin said, glancing over his shoulder. "Every time I enter, it takes me a few minutes to regain control. I need to be faster. In a battle with Slayer, a few minutes might as well be an eternity."

He will not be so strong as these.

"He'll still be strong enough," Perrin said. "He's had years to learn to control the wolf dream. I only just started."

Hopper laughed. *Young Bull, you started the first time you came here.*

"Yes, but I just started training a few weeks back."

Hopper continued laughing. He was right, in a way. Perrin *had* spent two years preparing, visiting the wolf dream at night. But he still needed to learn as much as he could. In a way, he was glad for the delay before the trial.

But he could not delay too long. The Last Hunt was upon them. Many of the wolves were running to the north; Perrin could feel them passing. Running for the Blight, for the Borderlands. They were moving both in the real world and in the wolf dream, but those here did not *shift* there directly. They ran, as packs.

He could tell that Hopper longed to join them. However, he remained behind, as did some others.

"Come on," Perrin said. "Let's find another nightmare."

The Rose March was in bloom.

That was incredible. Few other plants had bloomed in this terrible summer, and those that did had wilted. But the Rose March was blooming, and fiercely, hundreds of red explosions twisting around the garden framework. Voracious insects buzzed from flower to flower, as if every bee in the city had come here to feed.

Gawyn kept his distance from the insects, but the scent of roses was so pervasive that he felt bathed in it. Once he finished his walk, his clothing would probably smell of the perfume for hours.

Elayne was speaking with several advisors near one of the benches beside a small, lily-covered pond. She was showing her pregnancy, and seemed radiant. Her golden hair reflected the sunlight like the surface of a mirror; atop that hair, the Rose Crown of Andor looked almost plain by comparison.

She often had much to do these days. He'd heard hushed reports of the weapons she was building, the ones she thought might be as powerful as captive *damane*. The bellfounders in Caemlyn had been working straight through the nights, from what he'd heard. Caemlyn was preparing for war, the city abuzz with activity. She didn't often have time for him, though he was glad for what she could spare.

She smiled at him as he approached, then waved off her attendants for the moment. She walked to him and gave him a fond kiss on the cheek. "You look thoughtful."

"A common malady of mine lately," he said. "You look distracted."

"A common malady of *mine* lately," she said. "There is always too much to do and never enough of me to do it.

"If you need to—"

"No," she said, taking his arm. "I need to speak to you. And I've been told that a walk around the gardens once a day will be good for my constitution."

Gawyn smiled, breathing in the scents of roses and mud around the pond. The scents of life. He glanced up at the sky as they walked. "I can't believe how much sunlight we've been seeing here. I'd nearly convinced myself that the perpetual gloom was something unnatural."

"Oh, it probably is," she said nonchalantly. "A week back the cloud cover in Andor broke around Caemlyn, but nowhere else."

"But . . . how?"

She smiled. "Rand. Something he did. He was atop Dragonmount, I think. And then . . ."

Suddenly, the day seemed darker. "Al'Thor again," Gawyn spat. "He follows me even here."

"Even here?" she said with amusement. "I believe these gardens are where we first met him."

Gawyn didn't reply to that. He glanced northward, checking the sky in that direction. Ominous dark clouds hung out there. "He's the father, isn't he?"

"If he were," Elayne said without missing a beat, "then it would be prudent to hide that fact, wouldn't it? The children of the Dragon Reborn will be targets."

Gawyn felt sick. He'd suspected it the moment he'd discovered the pregnancy. "Burn me," he said. "Elayne, how could you? After what he did to our mother!"

"He did nothing to her," Elayne said. "I can produce witness after witness that will confirm it, Gawyn. Mother vanished *before* Rand liberated Caemlyn." There was a fond look in her eyes as she spoke of him. "Something is happening to him. I can feel it, feel him changing. Cleansing. He drives back the clouds and makes the roses bloom."

Gawyn raised an eyebrow. She thought the roses bloomed

because of *al'Thor*? Well, love could make a person think strange things, and when the man she spoke of was the Dragon Reborn, perhaps some irrationality was to be expected.

They approached the pond's small dock. He could remember swimming there as a child, then getting an earful for it. Not from his mother, from Galad, though Gawyn's mother had given him a stern, disappointed look. He'd never told anyone that he'd been swimming only because Elayne had pushed him in.

"You're never going to forget that, are you?" Elayne asked.

"What?" he asked.

"You were thinking of the time you slipped into the pond during Mother's meeting with House Farah."

"Slipped? You *pushed* me!"

"I did nothing of the sort," Elayne said primly. "You were showing off, balancing on the posts."

"And you shook the dock."

"I stepped onto it," Elayne said. "Forcefully. I'm a vigorous person. I have a forceful stride."

"A forceful— That's a downright lie!"

"No, I'm merely stating the truth creatively. I'm Aes Sedai now. It's a talent of ours. Now, are you going to row me on the pond, or not?"

"I . . . Row you? When did that come up?"

"Just now. Weren't you listening?"

Gawyn shook a bemused head. "Fine." Behind them, several Guardswomen took up posts. They were always near, often led by the tall woman who fancied herself an image of Birgitte from the stories. And maybe she did look like Birgitte at that—she went by the name, anyway, and was serving as Captain-General.

The Guards were joined by a growing group of attendants and messengers. The Last Battle approached, and Andor prepared—and, unfortunately, many of those preparations required Elayne's direct attention. Though Gawyn had heard a curious story of Elayne having been carried up on the city wall in her bed a week or so back. So far, he hadn't been able to pin her down on whether that was true or not.

He waved to Birgitte, who gave him a scowl as he led Elayne to the pond's small rowboat. "I promise not to dump her in," Gawyn called. Then, under his breath, "Though I might row 'forcefully' and upend us."

"Oh, hush," Elayne said, settling down. "Pondwater wouldn't be good for the babies."

"Speaking of which," Gawyn said, pushing the boat off with his toe, then stepping into it. The vessel shook precariously until he sat down. "Aren't you supposed to be walking for your 'constitution'?"

"I'll tell Melfane I needed to take the opportunity to re-form my miscreant brother. You can get away with all kinds of things if you're giving someone a proper scolding."

"And is that what I'm getting? A scolding?"

"Not necessarily." Her voice was somber. Gawyn shipped the oars and slipped them into the water. The pond wasn't large, barely big enough to justify a boat, but there was a serenity about being upon the water, amid the pond-runners and the butterflies.

"Gawyn," Elayne said, "why have you come to Caemlyn?"

"It's my home," he said. "Why shouldn't I come here?"

"I worried about you during the siege. I could have used you in the fighting. But you stayed away."

"I explained that, Elayne! I was embroiled in White Tower politics, not to mention the winter snows. It burns me that I couldn't help, but those women had their fingers on me."

"I'm one of 'those women' myself, you know." She held up her hand, Great Serpent ring encircling her finger.

"You're different," Gawyn said. "Anyway, you're right. I *should* have been here. I don't know what other apologies you expect me to make, though."

"I don't expect any apologies," Elayne said. "Oh, Gawyn, I wasn't chastising you. While I certainly could have used you, we managed. I also worried about you getting caught between defending the Tower and protecting Egwene. It seems that worked out as well. So, I ask. Why have you come here now? Doesn't Egwene need you?"

"Apparently not," Gawyn said, backing the boat. A massive draping willow grew from the side of the pond here, hanging down branches like braids to dangle above the water. He raised his oars outside those branches and the boat stilled.

"Well," Elayne said. "I won't presume to pry into that—at least, not at the moment. You are always welcome here, Gawyn. I'd make you Captain-General if you asked, but I don't think you want it."

"What makes you say that?"

"Well, you've spent the majority of your time here moping around these gardens."

"I have *not* been moping. I've been pondering."

"Ah, yes. I see *you've* learned to speak the truth creatively, too."

He snorted softly.

"Gawyn, you haven't been spending time with any of your friends or acquaintances from the palace. You haven't been stepping into the role of a prince or Captain-General. Instead you merely . . . ponder."

Gawyn looked out across the pond. "I don't spend time with the others because they all want to know why I wasn't here for the siege. They keep asking when I'm going to take my station here and lead your armies."

"It's all right, Gawyn. You don't have to be Captain-General, and I can survive with my First Prince of the Sword absent, if I must. Though I'll admit, Birgitte is rather upset with you for not becoming Captain-General."

"Is *that* the reason for the glares?"

"Yes. But she will manage; she's actually good at the job. And if there's anyone I'd want you protecting, it would be Egwene. She deserves you."

"And what if I've decided I don't want her?"

Elayne reached forward, resting her hand on his arm. Her face—framed in golden hair, topped by that matching crown—looked concerned. "Oh, Gawyn. What has happened to you?"

He shook his head. "Bryne thinks I was too accustomed to succeeding, and didn't know how to react when things started to upend on me."

"And what do you think?"

"I think it's been good for me to be here," Gawyn said, taking a deep breath. Some women were walking along the path around the pond, led by a woman with bright red hair that was streaked with white. Dimana was some kind of failed student of the White Tower. Gawyn wasn't quite certain about the nature of the Kin and their relationship with Elayne.

"Being here," he said, "reminded me of my life before. It's been particularly liberating to be free of Aes Sedai. For a time, I was *sure* that I needed to be with Egwene. When I left the Younglings to ride to her, it felt like the best choice I'd ever made. And yet, she seems to have moved beyond needing me. She's so concerned with being strong, with being the Amyrlin, that she doesn't have room for anyone who won't bow to her every whim."

"I doubt that it's as bad as you say, Gawyn. Egwene . . . well, she *has* to put forward a strong front. Because of her youth, and the way she was raised. But she's not arrogant. No more so than is necessary."

Elayne dipped her fingers in the water, startling a goldenback fish. "I've felt the way she must be feeling. You say she wants someone to bow and scrape for her, but what I'd bet she really wants—what she really *needs*—is someone she can trust completely. Someone she can give tasks, then not worry about how they will be handled. She has enormous resources. Wealth, troops, fortifications, servants. But there's only *one* of her, and so if everything requires her attention directly, she might as well have no resources at all."

"I . . ."

"You say you love her," Elayne said. "You've told me you're devoted to her, that you'd die for her. Well, Egwene has armies full of those kinds of people, as do I. What is truly unique is someone who does what I tell them. Better, someone who does what they know I'd tell them, if I had the chance."

"I'm not sure I can be that man," Gawyn said.

"Why not? Of all the men ready to support a woman of Power, I'd have thought it would be you."

"It's different with Egwene. I can't explain why."

"Well, if you wish to marry an Amyrlin, then you must make this choice."

She was right. It frustrated him, but she was right. "Enough about that," he said. "I notice the topic moved away from al'Thor."

"Because there was no more to say about him."

"You have to stay away from him, Elayne. He's danger-ous."

Elayne waved her hand. "*Saidin* is cleansed."

"Of course *he* would say that."

"You hate him," Elayne said. "I can hear it in your voice. This isn't about Mother, is it?"

He hesitated. She'd grown so good at twisting a con-versation. Was that the queen in her, or the Aes Sedai? He nearly turned the boat back toward the dock. But this was Elayne. Light, but it felt good to talk to someone who really understood him.

"Why do I hate al'Thor?" Gawyn said. "Well, there's Mother. But it's not just her. I hate what he's become."

"The Dragon Reborn?"

"A tyrant."

"You don't know that, Gawyn."

"He's a sheepherder. What right does he have to cast down thrones, to change the world as he does?"

"Particularly while you huddled in a village?" He'd told her most of what had happened to him in the last few months. "While he conquered nations, you were being forced to kill your friends, then were sent to your death by your Amyrlin."

"Exactly."

"So it's jealousy," Elayne said softly.

"No. Nonsense. I . . ."

"What would you do, Gawyn?" Elayne asked. "Would you duel him?"

"Maybe."

"And what would happen if you won and ran him through as you've said you wanted to do? Would you doom us all to satisfy your momentary passion?"

He had no reply to that.

"That's not just jealousy, Gawyn," Elayne said, taking the oars from him. "It's selfishness. We can't afford to be shortsighted right now." She began to row them back de-spite his protest.

"This," he said, "coming from the woman who person-ally raided the Black Ajah?"

Elayne blushed. He could tell that she wished he'd never

found out about that event. "It was needed. And besides, I did say 'we.' You and I, we have this trouble. Birgitte keeps telling me I need to learn to be more temperate. Well, you'll need to learn the same thing, for Egwene's sake. And she does need you, Gawyn. She may not realize it; she may be convinced she needs to hold up the world herself. She's wrong."

The boat thumped against the dock. Elayne unshipped the oars and held out a hand. Gawyn climbed out, then helped her up onto the dock. She gripped his hand fondly. "You'll sort it out," she said. "I'm releasing you from any responsibility to be my Captain-General. For now, I won't appoint another First Prince of the Sword, but you can hold that title with duties in abeyance. So long as you show up for the occasional state function, you needn't worry about anything else that might be required of you. I will publish it immediately, citing a need for you to be doing other work at the advent of the Last Battle."

"I . . . Thank you," he said, though he wasn't certain he felt it. It sounded too much like Egwene's insistence that he didn't need to guard her door.

Elayne squeezed his hand again, then turned and walked up to the attendants. Gawyn watched her speak to them in a calm tone. She seemed to grow more regal by the day; it was like watching a flower blossom. He wished he'd been in Caemlyn to view the process from the start.

He found himself smiling as he turned to continue his way along the Rose March. His regrets had trouble taking hold before a healthy dose of Elayne's characteristic optimism. Only she could call a man jealous and make him feel good about it.

He passed through waves of perfume, feeling the sun on his neck. He walked where he and Galad had played as children, and he thought of his mother walking these gardens with Bryne. He remembered her careful instruction when he misstepped, then her smiles when he acted as a prince should. Those smiles had seemed like the sun rising.

This place *was* her. She lived on, in Caemlyn, in Elayne—who looked more and more like her by the hour—in the safety and strength of Andor's people. He stopped beside the pond, the very spot where Galad had saved him from drowning as a child.

Perhaps Elayne was right. Perhaps al'Thor hadn't had anything to do with Morgase's death. If he had, Gawyn would never prove it. But that didn't matter. Rand al'Thor was already condemned to die at the Last Battle. So why keep hating the man?

"She is right," Gawyn whispered, watching the hawkflies dance over the surface of the water. "We're done, al'Thor. From now on, I care nothing for you."

It felt like an enormous weight lifting from his shoulders. Gawyn let out a long, relaxed sigh. Only now that Elayne had released him did he realize how much guilt he'd felt over his absence from Andor. That was gone now, too.

Time to focus on Egwene. He reached into his pocket, slipping out the assassin's knife, and held it up in the sunlight, inspecting those red stones. He *did* have a duty to protect Egwene. Supposing she railed against him, hated him, and exiled him; wouldn't it be worth the punishments if he managed to preserve her life?

"By my mother's grave," a voice said sharply from behind. "Where did you get *that*?"

Gawyn spun. The women he'd noticed earlier were standing behind him on the path. Dimana led them, her hair streaked with white, her face wrinkled around the eyes. Wasn't working with the Power supposed to stop those signs of aging?

There were two people with her. One was a plump young woman with black hair, the other a stout woman in her middle years. The second was the one who had spoken; she had wide, innocent-looking eyes. And she seemed horrified.

"What is that, Marille?" Dimana asked.

"That knife," Marille said, pointing at Gawyn's hand. "Marille has seen one like it before!"

"*I* have seen it before," Dimana corrected. "You are a person and not a thing."

"Yes, Dimana. Much apologies, Dimana. Marille . . . I will not make the mistake again, Dimana."

Gawyn raised an eyebrow. What was wrong with this person?

"Forgive her, my Lord," Dimana said. "Marille spent a long time as a *damane*, and is having difficulty adjusting."

"You're Seanchan?" Gawyn said. *Of course. I should have noticed the accent.*

Marille nodded vigorously. A former *damane*. Gawyn felt a chill. This woman had been trained to kill with the Power. The third woman remained silent, watching with curious eyes. She didn't look nearly as subservient.

"We should be moving on," Dimana said. "It isn't good for her to see things that remind her of Seanchan. Come, Marille. That is merely a token Lord Trakand won in battle, I suspect."

"No, wait," Gawyn said, holding up a hand. "You recognize this blade?"

Marille looked to Dimana, as if requesting permission to answer. The Kinswoman nodded sufferingly.

"It is a Bloodknife, my Lord," Marille said. "You did not win it in battle, because men do not defeat Bloodknives. They are unstoppable. They only fall when their own blood turns against them."

Gawyn frowned. What nonsense was this? "So this is a Seanchan weapon?"

"Yes, my Lord," Marille said. "Carried by the Bloodknives."

"I thought you said this *was* a Bloodknife."

"It is, but that is also who carries them. Shrouded in the night, sent by the Empress's will—may she live forever—to strike down her foes and die in her name and glory." Marille lowered her eyes farther. "Marille speaks too much. She is sorry."

"*I* am sorry," Dimana said, a hint of exasperation in her tone.

"I am sorry," Marille repeated.

"So these . . . Bloodknives," Gawyn said. "They're *Seanchan* assassins?" He felt a deep chill. Could they have left behind suicide troops to kill Aes Sedai? Yes. It made sense. The murderer *wasn't* one of the Forsaken.

"Yes, my Lord," Marille said. "I saw one of the knives hanging in the room of my mistress's quarters; it had belonged to her brother, who had borne it with honor until his blood turned against him."

"His family?"

"No, his blood." Marille shrank down farther.

"Tell me of them," Gawyn said urgently.

"Shrouded in the night," Marille said, "sent by the Empress's will—may she live forever—to strike down her foes and die in—"

"Yes, yes," Gawyn said. "You said that already. What methods do they use? How do they hide so well? What do you know of how this assassin will strike?"

Marille shrank down farther at each question, and began to whimper.

"Lord Trakand!" Dimana said. "Contain yourself."

"Marille doesn't know very much," the *damane* said. "Marille is sorry. Please, punish her for not listening better."

Gawyn pulled back. The Seanchan treated their *damane* worse than animals. Marille wouldn't have been told anything specific of what these Bloodknives could do. "Where did you get these *damane*?" Gawyn asked. "Were any Seanchan soldiers captured? I need to speak with one; an officer, preferably."

Dimana pursed her lips. "These were taken in Altara, and only the *damane* were sent to us."

"Dimana," the other woman said. She didn't have a Seanchan accent. "What of the *sul'dam*? Kaisea was of the low Blood."

Dimana frowned. "Kaisea is . . . unreliable."

"Please," Gawyn said. "This could save lives."

"Very well," Dimana said. "Wait here. I will return with her." She took her two charges toward the palace, leaving Gawyn to wait anxiously. A few minutes later, Dimana returned, followed by a tall woman wearing a pale gray dress without belt or embroidery. Her long black hair was woven into a braid, and she seemed determined to remain precisely one step behind Dimana—an action that bothered the Kinswoman, who seemed to be trying to keep an eye on the woman.

They reached Gawyn, and the *sul'dam*—incredibly—got down on her knees and prostrated herself on the ground, head touching the dirt. There was a smooth elegance to the bowing; for some reason, it made Gawyn feel as if he were being mocked.

"Lord Trakand," Dimana said, "this is Kaisea. Or, at least, that's what she insists that we call her now."

"Kaisea is a good servant," the woman said evenly.

"Stand up," Gawyn said. "What are you doing?"

"Kaisea has been told you are the Queen's brother; you are of the Blood of this realm, and I am a lowly *damane*."

"*Damane*? You're a *sul'dam*."

"No longer," the woman said. "I must be collared, great Lord. Will you see it done? Kaisea is dangerous."

Dimana nodded to the side, indicating they should speak privately. Gawyn withdrew with her farther down the Rose March, leaving Kaisea prostrate on the ground.

"She's a *sul'dam*?" Gawyn asked. "Or is she a *damane*?"

"All *sul'dam* can be trained to channel," Dimana explained. "Elayne thinks that fact will undermine their entire culture once revealed, so she's had us focus on teaching the *sul'dam* to access their powers. Many refuse to admit that they can see the weaves, but a few have been honest with us. To a woman, they've insisted that they should be made *damane*."

She nodded back toward Kaisea. "This one is most troubling. We think she's intentionally working to learn the weaves so that she can create an 'accident,' and use our own reasoning against us—if she does something violent with the One Power, she can claim that we were wrong to leave her free."

A woman who could be trained to kill with the One Power, who was not bound by the Three Oaths, *and* who had a determination to prove that she was dangerous? Gawyn shivered.

"We keep some forkroot in her most days," Dimana said. "I don't tell you this to worry you, but to warn you that what she says and does may not be reliable."

Gawyn nodded. "Thank you."

Dimana led him back, and the *sul'dam* remained on the ground. "How may Kaisea serve you, great Lord?" Her actions seemed a parody of Marille's subservience. What Gawyn had originally taken for mockery wasn't that at all—instead, it was the imperfect efforts of one who was highborn to imitate the lowly.

"Have you ever seen one of these before?" Gawyn asked casually, taking out the Bloodknife.

Kaisea gasped. "Where did you find that? Who gave it to

you?" She cringed almost immediately, as if realizing that she'd stepped out of her assumed role.

"An assassin tried to kill me with it," Gawyn said. "We fought, and he got away."

"That is impossible, great Lord," the Seanchan woman said, her voice more controlled.

"Why do you say that?"

"Because if you had fought one of the Bloodknives, great Lord, you would be dead. They are the most expert killers in all of the Empire. They fight the most ruthlessly, because they are already dead."

"Suicide troops." Gawyn nodded. "Do you have any information about them?"

Kaisea's face grew conflicted.

"If I see you leashed?" Gawyn asked. "Will you answer me then?"

"My Lord!" Dimana said. "The Queen would never allow it!"

"I'll ask her," Gawyn said. "I can't promise that you'll be leashed, Kaisea, but I can promise I'll intercede with the Queen for you."

"You are powerful and strong, great Lord," Kaisea said. "And wise indeed. If you will do this thing, Kaisea will answer you."

Dimana glared at Gawyn.

"Speak," Gawyn said to the *sul'dam.*

"Bloodknives do not live long," Kaisea said. "Once they are given a duty, they do not rest from it. They are granted abilities from the Empress, may she live forever, *ter'angreal* rings that make them into great warriors."

"Those blur their forms," Gawyn said. "When they are near shadow."

"Yes," Kaisea said, sounding surprised that he knew this. "They cannot be defeated. But eventually, their own blood will kill them."

"Their own blood?"

"They are poisoned by their service. Once they are given a charge, they often will not last more than a few weeks. At most, they survive a month."

Gawyn held up the knife, disturbed. "So we only need to wait them out."

Kaisea laughed. "That will not happen. Before they die, they will see their duty fulfilled."

"This one is killing people slowly," Gawyn said. "One every few days. A handful so far."

"Tests," Kaisea said. "Prodding for weaknesses and strengths, learning where they can strike without being seen. If only a few are dead, then you have not yet seen the full power of the Bloodknife. They do not leave a 'handful' of dead, but dozens."

"Unless I stop him," Gawyn said. "What are his weaknesses?"

Kaisea laughed again. "Weaknesses? Great Lord, did I not say that they are the finest warriors in Seanchan, enhanced and aided by the Empress's favor, may she live forever?"

"Fine. What about the *ter'angreal*, then? It helps the assassin when he is in shadow? How can I stop it from working? Perhaps light a large number of torches?"

"You cannot have light without shadow, great Lord," the woman said. "Create more light, and you will create more shadows."

"There has to be a way."

"Kaisea is certain that if there is one, great Lord, you will find it." The woman's response had a smug tone to it. "If Kaisea may suggest, great Lord? Count yourself fortunate to have survived fighting a Bloodknife. You must not have been his or her true target. It would be prudent to hide yourself until a month has passed. Allow the Empress—may she live forever—to accomplish her will, and bless the omens that you were given warning enough to escape and live."

"That's enough of that," Dimana said. "I trust you have what you wish, Lord Trakand?"

"Yes, thank you," Gawyn said, disturbed. He barely noticed as Kaisea rose and the Kinswoman led her charge away.

Count yourself fortunate to have survived . . . you must not truly have been his target . . .

Gawyn tested the throwing knife in his hands. The target was Egwene, obviously. Why else would the Seanchan expend such a powerful weapon? Perhaps they thought her death would bring down the White Tower.

Egwene had to be warned. If it made her angry at him, if it flew in the face of what she wanted, he had to bring her this information. It could save her life.

He was still standing there—considering how to approach Egwene—when a servant in red and white found him. She carried a plate with a sealed envelope on it. "My Lord Gawyn?"

"What's this?" Gawyn asked, taking the letter and using the Bloodknife to cut it open along the top.

"From Tar Valon," the servant said, bowing. "It came through a gateway."

Gawyn unfolded the thick sheet of paper inside. He recognized Silviana's script.

Gawyn Trakand, it read. *The Amyrlin was thoroughly displeased to discover your departure. You were never instructed to leave the city. She has asked me to send this missive, explaining that you have been given ample time to idle in Caemlyn. Your presence is required in Tar Valon, and you are to return with all haste.*

Gawyn read the letter, then read it again. Egwene screamed at him for disturbing her plans, all but threw him out of the Tower, and she was *displeased* to discover he'd left the city? What did she *expect* him to do? He almost laughed.

"My Lord?" the servant asked. "Would you like to send a reply?" There was paper and pen on the tray. "They implied that one would be expected."

"Send her this," Gawyn said, tossing the Bloodknife onto the tray. He felt so angry, suddenly, and all thoughts of returning fled his mind. Flaming woman!

"And tell her," he added after a moment's thought, "that the assassin is Seanchan, and carries a special *ter'angreal* that makes him difficult to see in shadows. Best to keep extra lights burning. The other murders were tests to gauge our defenses. *She* is the true target. Emphasize that the assassin is very, very dangerous—but not the person she thought it was. If she needs proof, she can come talk to some of the Seanchan here in Caemlyn."

The servant looked perplexed, but when he said nothing further, the woman retreated.

He tried to cool his rage. He wouldn't go back, not now.

Not when it would look as if he'd come crawling back at her command. She had her "careful plans and traps." She had said she didn't need him. She would have to do without him for a while, then.

CHAPTER
34

Judgment

I want the scouts out watching," Perrin said forcefully. "Even during the trial."

"The Maidens won't like this, Perrin Aybara," Sulin said. "Not if it makes them miss the chance to dance the spears."

"They'll do it anyway," Perrin said, walking through camp, Dannil and Gaul at his side. Behind followed Azi and Wil al'Seen, his two guards for the day.

Sulin inspected Perrin, then nodded. "It will be done." She moved off.

"Lord Perrin," Dannil asked, smelling nervous. "What's this about?"

"I don't know yet," Perrin said. "Something's wrong on the wind."

Dannil frowned, looking confused. Well, Perrin was confused, too. Confused and increasingly certain. It seemed a contradiction, but it was true.

The camp was busy, his armies gathering to meet the Whitecloaks. Not his army, his *armies*. There was so much division among them. Arganda and Gallenne jostling one another for position, the Two Rivers men resenting the newer bands of mercenaries, the former refugees mashed between them all. And, of course, the Aiel, aloof and doing as they wished.

I'm going to disband them, Perrin told himself. *What does it matter?* It bothered him nonetheless. It was a disorderly way to run a camp.

Anyway, Perrin's people had mostly recovered from this latest bubble of evil. None of them would probably look at their weapons again the same way, but the wounded had been Healed and the channelers were rested. The White-cloaks had not been pleased at the delay, which had extended longer than they had probably expected. But Perrin had needed the time, for a number of reasons.

"Dannil," he said. "My wife has you mixed up in her plots to protect me, I assume."

Dannil started. "How—"

"She needs her secrets," Perrin said. "I miss half of them, but this one was as plain as day. She's not happy about this trial. What's she got you doing? Some plan with the Asha'man to get me out of danger?"

"Something like that, my Lord," Dannil admitted.

"I'll go, if it turns bad," Perrin said. "But don't jump to it too early. I won't have this turn into a bloodbath because one of the Whitecloaks lets out a curse at the wrong time. Wait for my signal. Understood?"

"Yes, my Lord," Dannil said, smelling sheepish.

Perrin needed to be done with this. Free of it. Now. Because, over these last few days, it had begun to feel natural to him. *I'm just a . . .* He trailed off. Just a what? A blacksmith? Could he say that anymore? What *was* he?

Up ahead, Neald sat on a stump near the Traveling ground. During the last few days, the youthful Asha'man soldier and Gaul had scouted out in several directions at Perrin's orders, to see if gateways worked if one got far enough away from camp. Sure enough, it turned out they did, though one had to go for hours to escape the effect.

Neither Neald nor Gaul had noted any sort of change other than the weave for gateways working again. There was no barrier or visible indication on this side, but if Perrin guessed right, the area where gateways didn't work matched exactly the area covered by the dome in the wolf dream.

That was the dome's purpose, and that was why Slayer guarded it. It wasn't about hunting the wolves, though he surely did that with pleasure. Something was causing both the dome and the problems with the Asha'man.

"Neald," Perrin said, walking up to the Asha'man. "Latest scouting mission went well?"

"Yes, my Lord."

"When Grady and you were first telling me about the

failing weaves, you said it had happened to you before. When was that?"

"When we tried to open the gateway to retrieve the scouting group from Cairhien," Neald said. "We tried at first and the weaves fell apart. But we waited a little while and tried again. That time it worked."

That was just after the first night I saw the dome, Perrin thought. *It came up for a short time, then vanished. Slayer must have been testing it.*

"My Lord," Neald said, stepping close. He was a fop of a man, but he'd been reliable when Perrin needed him. "What's going on?"

"I think someone's setting a trap for us," Perrin said softly. "Boxing us in. I've sent some others out to look for the thing causing this; it's probably some kind of object of the One Power." He worried that it might be hidden in the wolf dream. Could something there produce an effect in the real world? "Now, you're sure you can't create gateways at all? Not even to other points nearby, inside the affected area?"

Neald shook his head.

The rules are different on this side, then, Perrin thought. *Or, at least, it works differently on Traveling than it does on shifting in the wolf dream.* "Neald, you said with the larger gateways—using a circle—you could move the entire army through in a few hours?"

Neald nodded. "We've been practicing."

"We need to be ready for that," Perrin said, looking at the sky. He could still smell that *oddity* in the air. A faint staleness.

"My Lord," Neald said. "We'll be ready, but if we can't create gateways, then it doesn't matter. We could march the army out to that point beyond the effect, though, and escape from there."

Unfortunately, Perrin suspected that wouldn't do. Hopper had called this a thing of the deep past. That meant there was a good chance Slayer was working with the Forsaken. Or he *was* one of the Forsaken himself. Perrin had never considered that. Either way, the ones planning this trap would be watching. If his army tried to escape, the enemy would spring its trap or they'd move the dome.

The Forsaken had been fooling the Shaido with those boxes and had placed them here. And there was his picture, being distributed. Was it all part of this trap, whatever it was? Dangers. So many dangers hunting him.

Well, what did you expect, he thought. *It's Tarmon Gai'don.*

"I wish Elyas would return," he said. He'd sent the man on a special scouting mission of his own. "Just be ready, Neald. Dannil, it'd be best if you'd go pass my cautions on to your men. I don't want any accidents."

Dannil and Neald went their separate ways, and Perrin walked to the horse pickets to find Stepper. Gaul, quiet as the wind, fell in beside him.

Someone's pulling a snare tight, Perrin thought, *slowly, inch by inch, around my leg.* Probably waiting for him to fight the Whitecloaks. Afterward, his army would be weakened and wounded. Easy pickings. It gave him a chill to realize that if he'd gone to battle with Damodred earlier, the trap might have been sprung right then. The trial suddenly took on enormous import.

Perrin *had* to find a way to forestall a battle until he could get to the wolf dream one more time. In it, perhaps he could find a way to destroy the dome and free his people.

"You change, Perrin Aybara," Gaul said.

"What's that?" Perrin said, taking Stepper from a groom.

"This is a good thing," Gaul replied. "It is good to see you stop protesting about being chief. It is better to see you enjoy command."

"I've stopped protesting because I have better things to do," Perrin said. "And I *don't* enjoy being in command. I do it because I have to."

Gaul nodded, as if he thought Perrin were agreeing with him.

Aiel. Perrin swung into the saddle. "Let's go on, then. The column is starting to march."

"Off with you," Faile said to Aravine. "The army is moving out."

Aravine curtsied and moved to pass the orders to the refugees. Faile wasn't certain what this day would bring, but she wanted those who stayed behind to break camp and be ready to march, just in case.

As Aravine left, Faile noticed Aldin the bookkeeper joining her. He did seem to be visiting Aravine quite often lately. Perhaps he'd finally given up on Arrela.

She hastened toward the tent. On her way, she passed Flann Barstere, Jon Gaelin and Marek Cormer checking over their bowstrings and arrow fletchings. All three looked up at her and waved. There seemed to be a sense of relief in their eyes, which was a good sign. Once, these men had looked ashamed when they'd seen her, as if they felt bad for the way Perrin had seemingly dallied with Berelain during Faile's absence.

Faile spending time with Berelain, mixed with the formal denunciation of the rumors, was working to convince the camp that nothing inappropriate had happened. Interestingly, it seemed that Faile saving Berelain's life during the bubble of evil had had the strongest effect in changing people's minds. They assumed because of that event that there was no grudge between the two women.

Of course, Faile *hadn't* saved the woman's life, just helped her. But that wasn't what the rumors said, and Faile was pleased to see them working in her and Perrin's favor for once.

She reached the tent and hurriedly washed up with a damp cloth at their basin. She put on some perfume, then dressed in her nicest gown—a deep gray-green with embroidered vine patterns across the bodice and around the hem. Finally, she checked herself in the mirror. Good. She was hiding her anxiety. Perrin would be all right. He *would* be.

She slipped a few knives into her belt and up her sleeves anyway. Outside, a groom had brought Daylight for her. She climbed up—missing Swallow, who had been killed by the Shaido. Even her finest dress had skirts divided for riding; she wouldn't carry anything else on the road. Her mother had taught her that nothing destroyed a woman's credibility with soldiers more quickly than riding sidesaddle. And, should the unthinkable happen and Perrin fall, Faile might need to take command of their forces.

She trotted up to the front of the gathering army. Perrin sat in his saddle there. How dare he look so patient!

Faile didn't let her annoyance show. There was a time to be a tempest, and a time to be a tender breeze. She had already let Perrin know, in no uncertain terms, what she thought of this trial. For the moment, she needed to be seen supporting him.

She rode up beside Perrin as the Aes Sedai gathered behind, walking like the Wise Ones. No Maidens. Where were they? It must be important to keep them from the trial. To Sulin and the others, protecting Perrin was a duty given them by their *Car'a'carn*, and it would be a grave matter of *toh* to them if he fell.

Scanning the camp, she noted two *gai'shain* in hooded white robes hurrying to the front of the line. Gaul, who stood beside Perrin's horse, scowled. One of the figures bowed to him, holding forth a collection of spears wrapped in cloth. "Freshly sharpened," Chiad said.

"And newly fletched arrows," Bain added.

"I have arrows and spears already," Gaul said.

"Yes," the women said, kneeling before him, still holding their offerings.

"What?" he asked.

"We were simply worried for your safety," Bain said. "You prepared those weapons yourself, after all." She said it earnestly, no hint of mockery or insincerity. Yet the words themselves were close to patronizing.

Gaul started laughing. He took the weapons offered and gave the women his own. Despite the troubles of the day, Faile found herself smiling. There was a devious complexity to Aiel interactions. What should have pleased Gaul regarding his *gai'shain* often seemed to frustrate him, and yet that which should have been insulting was met with amusement.

As Bain and Chiad retreated, Faile looked over the gathering army. Everyone was coming, not just captains or token forces. Most wouldn't be able to watch the trial, but they needed to be there. In case.

Faile pulled up beside her husband. "Something worries you," she said to him.

"The world holds its breath, Faile," he said.

"What do you mean?"

He shook his head. "The Last Hunt is here. Rand is in

danger. More than any of us, he is in danger. And I can't go to him, not yet."

"Perrin, you're not making any sense. How can you know Rand is in danger?"

"I can see him. Any time I mention his name or think on him, a vision of him opens to my eyes."

She blinked.

He turned toward her, his yellow eyes thoughtful. "I'm connected to him. He . . . pulls at me, you see. Anyway, I told myself I was going to be open with you about things like this." He hesitated. "My armies here, they're being herded, Faile. Like sheep being driven to the butcher.

"I had a vision in the wolf dream. There were sheep running in front of wolves. I thought I was one of the wolves. But maybe I was wrong.

"Light! I was wrong about that! I know what it means, now. I can feel it on the wind," he said. "The problem with gateways, it's related to something happening in the wolf dream. Somebody wants us to be unable to escape this place."

A cold breeze, odd in the noonday heat, washed over them. "Are you certain?" Faile asked.

"Yes," Perrin said. "Oddly, I am."

"That's where the Maidens are? Scouting?"

"Someone wants to trap us and attack. Makes most sense to let us clash with the Whitecloaks, then kill whoever survives. But that would require an army, of which there is no sign. Just us and the Whitecloaks. I have Elyas hunting out signs of a Waygate in the area, but he hasn't found anything yet. So maybe there's nothing, and I'm just jumping at shadows."

"Lately, husband, it's become likely that those shadows can bite. I trust your instincts."

He looked to her, then smiled deeply. "Thank you."

"So what do we do?"

"We ride to this trial," Perrin said. "And do whatever we can to keep from going to battle with the Whitecloaks. Then tonight, I see if I can stop the thing that is preventing the gateways. We can't just ride far enough away to escape it; the thing can be moved. I saw it in two places. I'll have to destroy it, somehow. After that, we escape."

She nodded, and Perrin gave the call to march. Though the force behind still seemed chaotic—like a rope that had been tangled—the army began to move. The various groups sorted themselves out, unraveling.

They made the short trip down the Jehannah Road, approaching the field with the pavilion. The Whitecloaks had already arrived; they were in formation. It looked as if they'd brought their entire army as well.

This was going to be a tense afternoon.

Gaul ran beside Perrin's horse, and he didn't seem worried, nor did he have his face veiled. Faile knew he thought it honorable for Perrin to go to trial. Perrin either had to defend himself or admit *toh* and accept judgment. Aiel had walked freely to their own executions to meet *toh*.

They rode down to the pavilion. A chair had been set on a low platform at the northern end, its back to the distant forest of leatherleaf. Morgase sat in the elevated chair, looking every inch a monarch, wearing a gown of red and gold that Galad must have found for her. How had Faile *ever* mistaken this woman for a simple lady's maid?

Chairs had been placed in front of Morgase, and Whitecloaks filled half of them. Galad stood beside her makeshift throne of judgment. His every lock of hair was in place, his uniform without blemish, his cloak falling behind him. Faile glanced to the side and caught Berelain staring at Galad and blushing, looking almost *hungry*. She had not given up on her attempts to persuade Perrin to let her go make peace with the Whitecloaks.

"Galad Damodred," Perrin called, dismounting before the pavilion. Faile dismounted and walked beside him. "I want you to promise me something before this begins."

"And what would that be?" the young commander called from the open-sided tent.

"Vow not to let this turn to battle," Perrin said.

"I could promise that," Galad said. "But, of course, you'd have to promise *me* that you're not going to run if the judgment falls against you."

Perrin fell silent. Then he rested his hand upon his hammer.

"Not willing to promise it, I see," Galad said. "I give you this chance because my mother has persuaded me that you should be allowed to speak in your defense. But I would sooner die than allow a man who has murdered Children to walk away unchallenged. If you do not wish this to turn to battle, Perrin Aybara, then present your defense well. Either that, or accept punishment."

Faile glanced at her husband; he was frowning. He looked as if he wanted to speak the requested promise. She laid a hand on his arm.

"I should do it," he said quietly. "How can any man be above the law, Faile? I killed those men in Andor when Morgase was Queen. I should abide by her judgment."

"And your duty to the people of your army?" she asked. "Your duty to Rand, and to the Last Battle?" *And to me?*

Perrin hesitated, then nodded. "You're right." Then, louder, he continued, "Let's be on with this."

Perrin strode into the pavilion, joined immediately by Neald, Dannil and Grady. Their presence made Perrin feel like a coward; the way they stood made it obvious that they had no intention of letting Perrin be taken.

What was a trial, if Perrin would not abide by its determination? Nothing more than a sham.

The Whitecloaks watched tensely, their officers standing in the shade of the pavilion, their army at parade rest. They looked as if they had no intention of standing down during the proceedings. Perrin's own forces—larger, but less orderly—responded by standing at the ready opposite the Whitecloaks.

Perrin nodded, and Rowan Hurn moved off to make certain Galad had released the captives. Perrin walked to the front of the pavilion, stopping just before Morgase's elevated seat. Faile stayed by his side. There were chairs for him here, and he sat. Several steps to his left was Morgase's stand. To his right, the people sat to watch the trial. His back was toward his army.

Faile—smelling wary—sat next to him. Others filed in. Berelain and Alliandre sat with their guards near him; the Aes Sedai and Wise Ones stood at the back, refusing seats. The last few seats were taken by a few of the Two Rivers men and some of the senior former refugees.

The Whitecloak officers sat down opposite them, facing Faile and Perrin, Bornhald and Byar at the front. There were about thirty chairs, likely taken from Perrin's supplies that the Whitecloaks had appropriated.

"Perrin," Morgase said from her seat. "Are you certain you want to go through with this?"

"I am," he said.

"Very well," she said, her face impassive, though she smelled hesitant. "I formally begin this trial. The accused is Perrin Aybara, known as Perrin Goldeneyes." She hesitated. "Lord of the Two Rivers," she added. "Galad, you will present the charges."

"There are three," Galad said, standing. "The first two are the unlawful murder of Child Lathin and the unlawful murder of Child Yamwick. Aybara is also accused of being a Darkfriend and of bringing Trollocs into the Two Rivers."

There were angry murmurs from the Two Rivers men at that last charge. Those Trollocs had killed Perrin's own family.

Galad continued, "The last charge cannot be substantiated yet, as my men were forced out of the Two Rivers before they could gather proof. As to the first two charges, Aybara has already admitted his guilt."

"Is this so, Lord Aybara?" Morgase asked.

"I killed those men, sure enough," Perrin said. "But it wasn't murder."

"Then this is what the court will determine," Morgase said formally. "And this is the dispute."

Morgase seemed a completely different person from Maighdin. Was this how people expected Perrin to act when they came to him for judgment? He had to admit, she did lend the proceedings a measure of needed formality. After all, the trial was happening in a tent on a field with the judge's chair elevated by what appeared to be a small stack of boxes with a rug thrown over them.

"Galad," Morgase said. "Your men may tell their side of the story."

Galad nodded to Byar. He stood, and another Whitecloak—a young man with a completely bald head—stepped forward to join him. Bornhald remained seated.

"Your Grace," Byar said, "it happened about two years ago. During the spring. An unnaturally cold spring, I remember. We were on our way back from important business at the command of the Lord Captain Commander, and we were passing through the wilderness of central Andor. We were going to camp for the night at an abandoned Ogier *stedding*, at the base of what was once an enormous statue. The kind of place you assume will be safe."

Perrin remembered that night. A chill east wind blowing across him, ruffling his cloak as he stood by a pool of fresh water. He remembered the sun dying silently in the west. He remembered staring at the pool in the waning light, watching the wind ruffle its surface, holding the axe in his hands.

That blasted axe. He should have thrown it away right then. Elyas had persuaded him to keep it.

"When we arrived," Byar continued, "we found that the campsite had been used recently. That concerned us; few people knew of the *stedding*. We determined, from the single firepit, that there were not many of these mysterious wayfarers."

His voice was precise, his description methodical. That wasn't how Perrin remembered the night. No, he remembered the hiss of the flames, sparks fluttering angrily into the air as Elyas dumped the teapot's contents into the firepit. He remembered a hasty sending from the wolves flooding his mind, confusing him.

The wolves' wariness had made it hard to separate himself from them. He remembered the smell of fear on Egwene, the way he fumbled with Bela's saddle as he cinched it. And he remembered hundreds of men who smelled wrong. Like the Whitecloaks in the pavilion. They smelled like sick wolves who snapped at anything that got too close.

"The Lord Captain was worried," Byar continued. He was obviously not mentioning the captain's name, perhaps to spare Bornhald. The young Whitecloak captain sat perfectly still, staring at Byar as if he didn't trust himself to look at Perrin. "He thought that maybe the camp had been used by brigands. Who else would douse their fire and vanish the moment someone else approached? That's when we saw the first wolf."

Hiding, breath coming in quick short gasps, Egwene

huddled beside him in the dark. The scent of campfire smoke rising from her clothing and from his. Bela breathing in the darkness. The sheltering confines of an enormous stone hand, the hand of Artur Hawkwing's statue, which had broken free long before.

Dapple, angry and worried. Images of men in white with flaming torches. Wind, darting between the trees.

"The Lord Captain thought the wolves were a bad sign. Everyone knows they serve the Dark One. He sent us to scout. My team searched to the east, looking through the rock formations and shards of the enormous broken statue."

Pain. Men shouting. *Perrin? Will you dance with me at Sunday? If we're home by then. . . .*

"The wolves started to attack us," Byar said, voice growing hard. "It was obvious that they were no ordinary creatures. There was too much coordination to their assaults. There seemed to be dozens of them, moving through the shadows. There were men among them, striking and killing our mounts."

Perrin had watched it with two sets of eyes. His own, from the vantage of the hand. And the eyes of the wolves, who only wanted to be left alone. They had been wounded earlier by an enormous flock of ravens. They'd tried to drive the men away. Scare them.

So much fear. Both the fear of the men and the fear of the wolves. It had ruled that night, controlling both sides. He could remember fighting to remain himself, bewildered by the sendings.

"That night stretched long," Byar said, voice growing softer, yet full of anger. "We passed a hillside with a massive flat rock at the top, and Child Lathin said he thought he saw something in the shadows there. We stopped, holding forward our lights, and saw the legs of a horse beneath the overhang. I gave Lathin a nod, and he stepped forward to order whoever was in there down to identify themselves.

"Well, that man—Aybara—came out of the darkness with a young woman. He was carrying a wicked axe, and he walked calmly right up to Lathin, ignoring the lance pointed at his chest. And then. . . ."

And then the wolves took over. It was the first time it had happened to Perrin. Their sendings had been so strong that Perrin had lost himself. He could remember crushing Lathin's neck with his teeth, the warm blood bursting into his mouth as if he'd bitten into a fruit. That memory had been Hopper's, but Perrin couldn't separate himself from the wolf for the moments of that fight.

"And then?" Morgase prompted.

"And then there was a fight," Byar said. "Wolves leaped from the shadow and Aybara attacked us. He didn't move like a man, but like a beast, growling. We subdued him and killed one of the wolves, but not before Aybara had managed to kill two of the Children."

Byar sat down. Morgase asked no questions. She turned to the other Whitecloak who had stood with Byar.

"I have little to lend," the man said. "I was there, and I remember it exactly the same way. I want to point out that when we took Aybara into custody, he was already judged guilty. We were going to—"

"That judgment is of no concern to this trial," Morgase said coldly.

"Well, then, allow my voice to be the testimony of a second witness. I saw it all, too." The bald Whitecloak sat down.

Morgase turned to Perrin. "You may speak."

Perrin stood up slowly. "Those two spoke truly, Morgase. That's about how it happened."

"About?" Morgase asked.

"He's nearly right."

"Your guilt or innocence hangs on his 'nearly,' Lord Aybara. It is the measure by which you will be judged."

Perrin nodded. "That it does. Tell me something, Your Grace. When you judge someone like this, do you try to understand their different pieces?"

She frowned. "What?"

"My master, the man who trained me as a blacksmith, taught me an important lesson. To create something, you have to understand it. And to understand something, you have to know what it is made of." A cool breeze blew through the pavilion, ruffling cloaks. That matched the quiet sounds from the plains outside—men shifting in ar-

mor and horses stamping, coughs and occasional whispers
as his words were passed through the ranks.

"I've come to see something lately," Perrin said. "Men
are made up of a lot of different pieces. Who they are depends on what situation you put them in. I had a hand in
killing those two men. But to understand, you have to see
the pieces of me."

He met Galad's eyes. The young Whitecloak captain
stood with a straight back, hands clasped behind his back.
Perrin wished he could catch the man's scent.

Perrin turned back to Morgase. "I can speak with
wolves. I hear their voices in my mind. I know that sounds
like the admission of a madman, but I suspect that many
in my camp who hear it won't be surprised. Given time, I
could prove it to you, with the cooperation of some local
wolves."

"That won't be necessary," Morgase said. She smelled of
fear. The whispers from the armies grew louder. He caught
Faile's scent. Worry.

"This thing I can do," Perrin said. "It's a piece of me,
just as forging iron is. Just as leading men is. If you're
going to pass judgment on me because of it, you should
understand it."

"You dig your own grave, Aybara," Bornhald said, rising
and pointing. "Our Lord Captain Commander said he could
not prove you were a Darkfriend, and yet here you make the
case for us!"

"This doesn't make me a Darkfriend," Perrin said.

"The purpose of this court," Morgase said firmly, "is *not*
to judge that allegation. We will determine Aybara's cul-
pability for the deaths of those two men, and nothing else.
You may sit, Child Bornhald."

Bornhald sat angrily.

"I have yet to hear your defense, Lord Aybara," Morgase
said.

"The reason I told you what I am—what I do—is to show
you that the wolves were my friends." He took a deep breath.
"That night in Andor . . . it was terrible, as Byar said. We
were scared, all of us. The Whitecloaks were scared of the
wolves, the wolves were scared of the fire and the threatening motions the men made, and I was plain scared of the

world around me. I'd never been out of the Two Rivers before, and didn't understand why I heard wolves in my head.

"Well, none of that is an excuse, and I don't mean it to be one. I killed those men, but they attacked my friends. When the men went hunting for wolf pelts, the wolves fought back." He stopped. They needed the whole truth. "To be honest, Your Grace, I wasn't in control of myself. I was ready to surrender. But with the wolves in my head. . . . I felt their pain. Then the Whitecloaks killed a dear friend of mine, and I *had* to fight. I'd do the same thing to protect a farmer being harassed by soldiers."

"You're a creature of the Shadow!" Bornhald said, rising again. "Your lies insult the dead!"

Perrin turned toward the man, holding his eyes. The tent fell silent, and Perrin could smell the tension hanging in the air. "Have you never realized that some men are different from you, Bornhald?" Perrin asked. "Have you ever *tried* to think what it must be like to be someone else? If you could see through these golden eyes of mine, you'd find the world a different place."

Bornhald opened his mouth as if to spit out another insult, but licked his lips, as if they had grown dry. "You murdered my father," he finally said.

"The Horn of Valere had been blown," Perrin said, "the Dragon Reborn fought Ishamael in the sky. Artur Hawkwing's armies had returned to these shores to dominate. Yes, I was in Falme. I rode to battle alongside the heroes of the Horn, alongside Hawkwing himself, fighting *against* the Seanchan. I fought on the same side as your father, Bornhald. I've said that he was a good man, and he was. He charged bravely. He died bravely."

The audience was so still they seemed statues. Not a one moved. Bornhald opened his mouth to object again, but then closed it.

"I swear to you," Perrin said, "under the Light and by my hope of salvation and rebirth, that I did *not* kill your father. Nor had I anything to do with his death."

Bornhald searched Perrin's eyes, and looked troubled.

"Don't listen to him, Dain," Byar said. The scent of him was strong, stronger than any other in the pavilion. Frenzied, like rotten meat. "He *did* kill your father."

Galad still stood, watching the exchange. "I've never understood how you know this, Child Byar. What did you see? Perhaps *this* should be the trial we hold."

"It is not what I saw, Lord Captain," Byar said. "But what I know. How else can you explain how *he* survived, yet the legion did not! Your father was a valiant warrior, Bornhald. He would never have fallen to the Seanchan!"

"That's foolishness," Galad said. "The Seanchan have beaten us over and over again. Even a good man can fall in battle."

"I *saw* Goldeneyes there," Byar said, gesturing toward Perrin. "Fighting alongside ghostly apparitions! Creatures of evil!"

"The Heroes of the Horn, Byar," Perrin said. "Couldn't you see that we were fighting alongside the Whitecloaks?"

"You *seemed* to be," Byar said wildly. "Just as you *seemed* to be defending the people in the Two Rivers. But I saw through you, Shadowspawn! I saw through you the moment I met you!"

"Is that why you told me to escape?" Perrin said softly. "When I was confined in the elder Lord Bornhald's tent, following my capture. You gave me a sharp rock to cut my bonds and told me that if I ran, nobody would chase me."

Byar froze. He seemed to have forgotten that until this moment.

"You wanted me to try to get away," Perrin said, "so that you could kill me. You wanted Egwene and me dead very badly."

"Is this true, Child Byar?" Galad asked.

Byar stumbled. "Of course . . . of course not. I. . . ." Suddenly, he spun and turned to Morgase atop her simple throne of judgment. "This trial is about me, but him! You have heard both sides. What is your answer? Judge, woman!"

"You should not speak to my mother so," Galad said quietly. His face was impassive, but Perrin smelled danger on him. Bornhald, looking very troubled, had sat back down and was holding his head with his hand.

"No, it is all right," Morgase said. "He is right. This trial *is* about Perrin Aybara." She turned from Byar to regard Perrin. He looked back calmly. She smelled . . . as if she were curious about something. "Lord Aybara. Do you feel you have spoken adequately for yourself?"

"I was protecting myself and my friends," Perrin said. "The Whitecloaks had no authority to do as they did, ordering us out, threatening us. You know their reputation as well as any, I suspect. We had good reason to be wary of them and disobey their orders. It wasn't murder. I was just defending myself."

Morgase nodded. "I will make my decision, then."

"What of having others speak for Perrin?" Faile demanded, standing.

"That won't be needed, Lady Faile," Morgase said. "So far as I can tell, the only other person we could interview would be Egwene al'Vere, which doesn't seem within the reasonable bounds of this trial."

"But—"

"It is enough," Morgase interrupted, voice growing cold. "We could have a dozen Children name him Darkfriend and two dozen of his followers laud his virtues. Neither would serve this trial. We are speaking of specific events, on a specific day."

Faile fell silent, though she smelled furious. She took Perrin's arm, not sitting back down. Perrin felt . . . regretful. He had presented the truth. But he wasn't satisfied.

He hadn't wanted to kill those Whitecloaks, but he had. And he'd done it in a frenzy, without control. He could blame the wolves, he could blame the Whitecloaks, but the honest truth was that he *had* lost control. When he'd awoken, he'd barely remembered what he had done.

"You know my answer, Perrin," Morgase said. "I can see it in your eyes."

"Do what you must," Perrin said.

"Perrin Aybara, I pronounce you guilty."

"No!" Faile screamed. "How dare you! He took you in!"

Perrin put a hand on her shoulder. She'd been reaching for her sleeve by reflex, aiming for the knives there.

"This has nothing to do with how I personally feel about Perrin," Morgase said. "This is a trial by Andoran law. Well, the law is very clear. Perrin may feel that the wolves were his friends, but the law states that a man's hound or livestock is worth a certain price. Slaying them is unlawful, but killing a man in retribution is even more so. I can quote the very statutes to you if you wish."

The pavilion was silent. Neald had risen halfway from

his chair, but Perrin met his eyes and shook his head. The Aes Sedai and Wise Ones wore faces that betrayed nothing. Berelain looked resigned, and dark-haired Alliandre had one hand to her mouth.

Dannil and Azi al'Thone moved up to Perrin and Faile, and Perrin did not force them to back down.

"What does this matter?" Byar demanded. "He's not going to abide by the judgment!"

Other Whitecloaks stood, and this time Perrin couldn't stare down all those on his side who did likewise.

"I have not passed sentence yet," Morgase said, voice crisp.

"What other sentence could there be?" Byar asked. "You said he's guilty."

"Yes," Morgase said. "Though I believe there are further circumstances relevant to the sentencing." Her face was still hard, and she smelled determined. What was she doing?

"The Whitecloaks were an unauthorized military group within the confines of my realm," Morgase said. "By this light, while I do rule Perrin guilty of killing your men, I rule the incident subject to the Kainec protocol."

"Is that the law that governs mercenaries?" Galad asked.

"Indeed."

"What is this?" Perrin asked.

Galad turned to him. "She has ruled that our altercation was a brawl between unemployed mercenary groups. Essentially, the ruling states there were no innocents in the clash—you are not, therefore, charged with murder. Instead, you have killed illegally."

"There's a difference?" Dannil asked, frowning.

"One of semantics," Galad said, hands still clasped behind his back. Perrin caught his scent; it was curious. "Yes, this is a good ruling, Mother. But the punishment is still death, I believe."

"It can be," Morgase said. "The code is much more lenient, depending on the circumstances."

"Then what do you rule?" Perrin asked.

"I do not," Morgase said. "Galad, you are the one responsible for the men killed, or the closest we have. I will pass sentencing on to you. I have given the ruling and the legal definitions. You decide the punishment."

Galad and Perrin locked eyes across the pavilion. "I see,"

Galad said. "A strange choice, Your Grace. Aybara, it must be asked again. Will you abide by the decisions of this trial that you yourself suggested? Or must this be settled with conflict?"

Faile tensed at his side. Perrin could hear his army moving behind him, men loosening swords in their sheaths, muttering. The word passed through them as a low hum. *Lord Perrin, named guilty. They're going to try to take him. We won't let it happen, will we?*

The bitter scents of fear and anger mixed in the pavilion, both sides glowering at one another. Above it all, Perrin could smell that *wrongness* to the air.

Can I continue to run? he thought. *Hounded by that day?* There were no coincidences with *ta'veren*. Why had the Pattern brought him here to confront these nightmares from his past?

"I *will* abide by it, Damodred," Perrin said.

"What?" Faile gasped.

"But," Perrin said, raising a finger, "only so long as you promise to delay execution of this punishment until after I have done my duty at the Last Battle."

"You'll accept judgment after the Last Battle?" Bornhald asked, sounding befuddled. "After what may be the end of the world itself? After you've had time to escape, perhaps betray us? What kind of promise is that?"

"The only kind I can make," Perrin said. "I don't know what the future will bring, or if we'll reach it. But we're fighting for survival. Maybe the world itself. Before that, all other concerns are secondary. This is the only way I can submit."

"How do we know you'll keep your word?" Galad asked. "My men name you Shadowspawn."

"I came here, didn't I?" Perrin asked.

"Because we had your people captive."

"And would Shadowspawn give one hair's worry about that?" Perrin asked.

Galad hesitated.

"I swear it," Perrin said. "By the Light and by my hope of salvation and rebirth. By my love of Faile and on the name of my father. You'll have your chance, Galad Damodred. If you and I both survive until the end of this, I'll submit to your authority."

Galad studied him, then nodded. "Very well."

"No!" Byar cried. "This is foolishness!"

"We leave, Child Byar," Galad said, walking to the side of the pavilion. "My decision has been made. Mother, will you attend me?"

"I'm sorry, Galad," Morgase said. "But no. Aybara is making his way back to Andor, and I must go with him."

"Very well." Galad continued on.

"Wait," Perrin called. "You didn't tell me what my punishment will be, once I submit."

"No," Galad said, still walking. "I didn't."

CHAPTER
35

The Right Thing

You understand what you are to do?" Egwene asked, walking toward her rooms in the White Tower.

Siuan nodded.

"If they do appear," Egwene said, "you will *not* let yourself be drawn into a fight."

"We're not children, Mother," Siuan said dryly.

"No, you're Aes Sedai—nearly as bad at following directions."

Siuan gave her a flat look, and Egwene regretted her words. They had been uncalled-for; she was on edge. She calmed herself.

She had tried several forms of bait to lure Mesaana out, but so far, there hadn't been any nibbles. Egwene swore she could almost *feel* the woman watching her in *Tel'aran'rhiod.* Yukiri and her group were at a standstill.

Her best hope was the meeting tonight. It *had* to draw her. Egwene didn't have any time left—the monarchs she'd persuaded were already beginning to move, and Rand's forces were gathering.

Tonight. It must happen tonight.

"Go," Egwene said. "Speak with the others. I don't want there to be any foolish mistakes."

"Yes, Mother," Siuan grumbled, turning away.

"And Siuan," Egwene called after her.

The former Amyrlin hesitated.

"See to your safety tonight," Egwene said. "I would not lose you."

Siuan often gave such concern a crusty reply, but tonight

he smiled. Egwene shook her head and hurried on to her
ooms, where she found Silviana waiting.

"Gawyn?" Egwene asked.

"There has been no news of him," Silviana replied. "I
ent a messenger for him this afternoon, but the messenger
asn't returned. I suspect that Gawyn is delaying his reply
o be difficult."

"He's nothing if not stubborn," Egwene said. She felt ex-
osed without him. That was surprising, since she'd point-
dly ordered him to stay away from her door. Now she
vorried about him not being there?

"Double my guard, and make certain to have soldiers
osted nearby. If my wards go off, they will raise a clatter."

"Yes, Mother," Silviana said.

"And send Gawyn another messenger," she said. "One
vith a more politely worded letter. Ask him to return; don't
rder him." Knowing Silviana's opinion of Gawyn, Egwene
vas sure the original letter had been brusque.

With that, Egwene took a deep breath, then went into her
ooms, checked on her wards, and prepared to go to sleep.

shouldn't feel so exhausted, Perrin thought as he climbed
lown from Stepper. *I didn't do anything but talk.*

The trial weighed on him. It seemed to weigh upon the
ntire army. Perrin looked at them as they rode back into
amp. Morgase was there, off on her own. Faile had watched
er the whole way back, smelling of anger, but not speaking
 word. Alliandre and Berelain had kept their distance.

Morgase had condemned him, but in truth, he didn't much
are. He had deflected the Whitecloaks; now he needed
o lead his people to safety. Morgase rode through camp,
eeking out Lini and Master Gill. They'd arrived safely,
ogether with all the other captives, as Galad Damodred
ad promised. Surprisingly, he'd sent the supplies and carts
vith them.

The trial was a victory, then. Perrin's men didn't seem to
ee it that way. The soldiers split into groups as they slunk
ack into camp. There was little talking.

Beside Perrin, Gaul shook his head. "Two silver points."

"What's that?" Perrin asked, handing Stepper to a groom.

"A saying," Gaul said, glancing up at the sky. "Two silver points. Twice we have run to battle and found no foe. Once more, and we lose honor."

"Better to find no foe, Gaul," Perrin said. "Better no blood be shed."

Gaul laughed. "I do not say I wish to end the dream, Perrin Aybara. But look at your men. They can feel what I say. You should not dance the spears without purpose, but neither should you too often demand that men prepare themselves to kill, then give them nobody to fight."

"I'll do it as often as I like," Perrin said gruffly, "if it means avoiding a battle. I—"

A horse's hooves thumped the ground, and the wind brought him Faile's scent as he turned to face her.

"A battle avoided indeed, Perrin Aybara," Gaul said, "and another invited. May you find water and shade." He trotted away as Faile dismounted.

Perrin took a deep breath.

"All right, husband," she said, striding up to him. "You will explain to me just *what* you thought you were doing. You let him pass judgment on you? You *promised* to deliver yourself to him? I wasn't under the impression that I'd married a fool!"

"I'm no fool, woman," he roared back. "You keep telling me I need to lead. Well, today I took your advice!"

"You took it and made the wrong decision."

"There was no *right* decision!"

"You could have let us fight them."

"They intend to fight at the Last Battle," Perrin said. "Every Whitecloak we killed would be one less man to face the Dark One. Me, my men, the Whitecloaks—none of us matter compared to what is coming! They had to live, and so did we. And this was the only way!"

Light, but it felt wrong to yell at her. Yet it actually softened her temper. Remarkably, the soldiers nearby him started to nod, as if they hadn't been able to see the truth until he'd bellowed it out.

"I want you to take command of the retreat," Perrin said to Faile. "The trap hasn't sprung yet, but I find myself itching more each minute. Something's watching us; they have taken away our gateways, and they intend to see us dead. They now know we won't fight the Whitecloaks, which

neans they'll attack soon. Maybe this evening; if we're
ucky, they'll delay until tomorrow morning."

"We aren't done with this argument," she warned.

"What's done is done, Faile. Look forward."

"Very well." She still smelled angry, those beautiful dark
eyes of hers fierce, but she contained it.

"I'm going to the wolf dream," Perrin said, glancing
oward the edge of camp, where their tent lay. "I'll either
lestroy that dome, or I'll find a way to force Slayer to tell
ne how to make Traveling work again. Get the people
eady to march, and have the Asha'man try to make a gate-
vay on every count of a hundred. The moment it works, get
)ur people out of here."

"Where?" Faile asked. "Jehannah?"

Perrin shook his head. "Too close. The enemy might be
vatching there. Andor. Take them to Caemlyn. Actually,
10. Whitebridge. Let's stay away from anywhere they might
:xpect. Besides, I don't want to show up with an army on
Ilayne's doorstep until I've warned her."

"A good plan," Faile said. "If you fear attack, we should
nove the camp followers first, rather than moving the
irmies through and leaving us undefended."

Perrin nodded. "But get them moving as *soon* as the
;ateways work again."

"And if you don't succeed?" Faile had begun to sound
letermined. Frightened, but determined.

"If I haven't restored gateways in one hour, start them
narching toward the perimeter where Neald discovered
:hat he can make gateways. I don't think that will work;
think Slayer will just move the dome, always keeping us
inderneath it. But it's something."

Faile nodded, but her scent became hesitant. "That will
ilso put us marching, rather than in camp. Much easier to
imbush that way."

"I know," Perrin said. "That is why I must not fail."

She took him into her arms, head against his chest. She
:melled so wonderful. Like Faile. That was the definition of
vonderful to him. "You've said he's stronger than you are,"
,he whispered.

"He is."

"Can I do anything to help you face him?" she asked
.oftly.

"If you watch over them while I'm gone, that *will* help."

"What happens if he kills you while you're there?"

Perrin didn't reply.

"There's no other way?" she asked.

He pulled back from her. "Faile, I'm fairly certain tha he's Lord Luc. They smell different, but there's something similar about them, too. And when I wounded Slayer in the wolf dream before, Luc bore the wound."

"Is that supposed to help me feel better?" she asked, gri macing.

"It's all coming back around. We finish with Malden and find ourselves within a stone's toss of the remnants of the Whitecloaks, Byar and Bornhald with them. Slayer appear: in the wolf dream again. That man I told you of, Noam, the one who was in the cage. Do you remember where I found him?"

"You said you were chasing Rand. Through . . ."

"Ghealdan," Perrin said. "It happened not one week' ride from here."

"An odd coincidence, but—"

"No coincidences, Faile. Not with me. I'm here for a rea son. He's here for a reason. I must face this."

She nodded. He turned to walk toward their tent, he hand slipping free of his. The Wise Ones had given him a tea that would let him sleep so he could enter the wol dream.

It was time.

"How could you let him go?" Byar said, knuckles clenched on the pommel of his sword, white cloak flapping behind him. He, Bornhald and Galad walked through the middle of their camp.

"I did what was right," Galad said.

"Letting him go free was *not* right!" Byar said. "You can't believe—"

"Child Byar," Galad said softly, "I find your attitude increasingly insubordinate. That troubles me. It should trouble you as well."

Byar closed his mouth and said no more, though Galad could see that it was difficult for him to hold his tongue Behind Byar, Bornhald walked silently, looking very upset

"I believe that Aybara will keep his oath," Galad said. "And if he does not, I now have the legal grounds to hunt him and exact punishment. It is not ideal, but there was wisdom to his words. I *do* believe the Last Battle is coming, and if so, it is time to unite against the Shadow."

"My Lord Captain Commander," Byar said, managing his tone, "with all respect, that man *is* of the Shadow. He will not be fighting beside us, but against us."

"If that is true," Galad said, "we will still have a chance to face him on the field of battle. I have made my decision, Child Byar." Harnesh strode up to join them and saluted. Galad nodded. "Child Harnesh, strike camp."

"My Lord Captain Commander? This late in the day?"

"Yes," Galad said. "We will march into the night and put some distance between us and Aybara, just in case. Leave scouts, make certain he doesn't try to follow us. We'll make for Lugard. We can recruit and resupply, then continue on toward Andor."

"Yes, my Lord Captain Commander," Harnesh said.

Galad turned to Byar as Harnesh left. The skeletal man gave a salute, sunken eyes dangerously resentful, then stalked off. Galad stopped on the field, between white tents, hands behind his back as he watched messengers relay his orders through camp.

"You are quiet, Child Bornhald," Galad said after a few moments. "Are you as displeased with my actions as Child Byar is?"

"I don't know," Bornhald said. "I've believed for so long that Aybara killed my father. And yet, seeing how Jaret acts, remembering his description . . . There is no evidence. It frustrates me to admit it, Galad, but I have no proof. He did kill Lathin and Yamwick, however. He killed Children, so he *is* a Darkfriend."

"I killed one of the Children, too," Galad said. "And was named Darkfriend for it."

"That was different." Something seemed to be troubling Bornhald, something he wasn't saying.

"Well, that is true," Galad said. "I do not disagree that Aybara should be punished, but the day's events leave me strangely troubled."

He shook his head. Finding answers should be easy. The right thing always came to him. However, whenever he thought he'd seized upon the right course of action regarding Aybara, he found distasteful worries cropping up inside of him.

Life is not so easy as the toss of a coin, his mother had said. *One side or the other . . . your simple illusions . . .*

He did not like the feeling. Not at all.

Perrin inhaled deeply. Flowers bloomed in the wolf dream, even as the sky raged silver, black and gold. The scents were so incongruous. Baking cherry pie. Horse dung. Oil and grease. Soap. A wood fire. Arrath. Thyme. Catfern. A hundred other herbs he couldn't name.

Very few of them fit the meadow where he had appeared. He'd made certain not to appear where his camp was in the wolf dream; that would have put him too near Slayer.

The scents were fleeting. Vanishing too quickly, as if they'd never really been there.

Hopper, he sent.

I am here, Young Bull. The wolf appeared beside him. "It smells strange."

Scents blend, Hopper sent. *Like the waters of a thousand streams. It is not natural. It is not good. This place begins to break.*

Perrin nodded. He *shifted*, appearing knee deep in brown cockleburrs just outside of the violet dome. Hopper appeared to his right, weeds crackling as he moved among them.

The dome rose, ominous and unnatural. A wind blew, shuffling the weeds and shaking tree limbs. Lightning flashed silently in the sky.

He is there, Hopper sent. *Always.*

Perrin nodded. Did Slayer come to the wolf dream the way Perrin did? And did spending time in it leave him still tired, as it did Perrin? The man never seemed to leave this area.

He was guarding something. There had to be a way in the wolf dream to disable the dome.

Young Bull, we come. The sending was from Oak Dancer. Her pack was approaching, now only three strong. Sparks, Boundless, Oak Dancer herself. They had chosen to come here, rather than join the wolves running northward.

The three appeared behind Hopper. Perrin looked to them, and sent concern. *This will be dangerous. Wolves may die.*

Their sending back was insistent. *Slayer must fall for what he has done. Together we are strong. Young Bull should not hunt such dangerous prey alone.*

He nodded in agreement, letting his hammer appear in his hand. Together, they approached the dome. Perrin walked into it with a slow, determined stride. He refused to feel weakness. He *was* strong. The dome was nothing but air. He believed the world to be as he wished it.

He stumbled, but pulled through into the inside of the dome. The landscape felt faintly darker here. Elder trees more dim of bark, the dying dogfennel a deeper green or brown. Hopper and the pack moved through the dome around him.

We make for the center, Perrin sent. *If there is a secret to discover, it will probably be there.*

They moved slowly through the brush and stands of trees. Perrin imposed his will upon the area around him, and the leaves stopped crackling, weeds remaining silent when he brushed against them. That was natural. It was the way things *should* be. So it was.

It would be a long distance to the center, so Perrin began hopping forward. Not jumps or steps; he simply stopped being in one place, appearing in a different location. He masked his scent, though Slayer was not a wolf.

That has to become my advantage, Perrin thought as they grew closer and closer to the center. *He is more experienced than I. But I have the wolf within me. This place is our dream. He is the invader. However skilled he may be, he is not one of us.*

And that is why I will win.

Perrin smelled something; an increasing wrongness in the air. He and the wolves crept up to a large hillside, then peered around a cleft in the land there. A small stand of elder trees stood just ahead, perhaps fifty paces away. Looking up, he judged this to be very near the center of the dome. Using the shifting way of wolves, they'd traveled several hours' worth of walking in a few minutes.

That is it, Perrin sent. He looked at Hopper. The wolf's scent was masked, but he was coming to know wolves well enough to read concern in Hopper's stare and the way he stood with forelegs bent just a fraction.

Something changed.

Perrin heard nothing. He smelled nothing. But he *felt* something, a small tremble in the ground.

Go! he sent, vanishing. He appeared ten paces away to see an arrow hit the hillside where he'd been standing. The shaft split a large stone, embedding itself in the rock and earth up to its black fletching.

Slayer stood from a crouch, turning to look at Perrin across the short expanse of ground. His eyes seemed black, his square face shadowed, his tall body muscular and dangerous. As he often did, he wore a smile. Really a sneer. He wore leather breeches and a shirt of deep green, forearms exposed, hand holding his wicked bow of dark wood. He wore no quiver; he created arrows as he needed them.

Perrin held his eyes, stepping forward as if in challenge. That was enough of a distraction for the wolves to attack from behind.

Slayer yelled, spinning as Boundless slammed into him. Perrin was there in an eyeblink, bringing his hammer down. Slayer vanished, and Perrin struck only earth, but he caught a whiff of where Slayer had gone.

Here? That scent was of the same place that Perrin was. Alarmed, he looked up to see Slayer hovering in the air just above, drawing an arrow.

The wind, Perrin thought. *It is so strong!*

The arrow loosed, but a sudden gust blew it sideways. It sank into the earth just beside Perrin. He did not flinch, raising his hands, his own bow appearing in them. Already drawn, arrow in place.

Slayer's eyes opened wider as Perrin loosed. Slayer vanished, appearing on the ground a short distance away— and Hopper leaped on him from above, pulling him to the ground. Slayer cursed with a guttural sound, then vanished.

Here, Hopper sent, showing a hillside.

Perrin was there in an instant, hammer in his hands, the pack with him. Slayer raised a sword in one hand and a knife in the other as Perrin and the four wolves attacked.

Perrin hit first, swinging his hammer with a roar. Slayer actually *sank* into the ground, as if it were liquid, dropping beneath the hammer blow. He rammed his knife forward—

piercing Oak Dancer's breast with a splash of scarlet blood as he swung to the side, slashing across Sparks' face.

Oak Dancer didn't get time to howl; she collapsed to the ground, and Slayer vanished as Perrin brought his hammer back around. Whimpering, Sparks sent agony and panic and vanished. He would live. But Oak Dancer was dead.

Slayer's scent was in this place again. Perrin turned to smash his hammer into Slayer's sword as it sought to pierce him from behind. Again a look of surprise from Slayer. The man bared his teeth, pulling back, keeping a wary eye on the two remaining wolves, Hopper and Boundless. Slayer's forearm was bleeding where Hopper had bitten him.

"How is the dome created, Luc?" Perrin said. "Show me and leave. I will let you depart."

"Bold words, cub," Slayer snarled back. "For one who just watched me kill one of your pack."

Boundless howled in anger, leaping forward. Perrin attacked at the same time, but the ground beneath them trembled, shaking.

No, Perrin thought. His own footing became firm as Boundless was knocked to the ground.

Slayer lunged, and Perrin raised his hammer to block— but Slayer's weapon turned into smoke and passed right through it, solidifying on the other side. With a yelp, Perrin tried to pull back, but the blade scored him across the chest, cutting through his shirt and leaving a gash from one arm to the other. It flared with pain.

Perrin gasped, stumbling backward. Slayer drove forward, but something crashed into him from above. Hopper. Once again the grizzled wolf bore Slayer to the ground, growling, fangs flashing.

Slayer cursed and kicked the wolf free. Hopper went flying with a whimper of pain, tossed some twenty feet. To the side, Boundless had caused the earth to stop rumbling, but had hurt his paw.

Perrin shook himself free of his pain. Slayer was *strong* in control over this world. Perrin's hammer felt sluggish whenever he swung, as if the air itself were thicker.

Slayer had smiled when he'd killed Oak Dancer. Perrin moved forward, enraged. Slayer was on his feet and retreating back down the hillside, toward the trees. Perrin chased after him, ignoring his wound. It wasn't bad enough to stop him, though he did imagine a bandage in place on it, his clothing mended and tight against his chest to stanch the blood.

He entered the trees just behind Slayer. The branches closed overhead, and vines whipped from the darkened shadows. Perrin didn't bother fighting them off. Vines didn't move like that. They couldn't touch him. Sure enough, as soon as they grew close, they withered and fell still.

Slayer cursed, then began to move in bursting steps, leaving a blur behind him. Perrin followed, enhancing his own speed.

Perrin didn't consciously make the decision to drop to four legs, but in a heartbeat he had done so, chasing after Slayer as he'd hunted the white stag.

Slayer was fast, but he was merely a man. Young Bull was part of the land itself, the trees, the brush, the stones, the rivers. He moved through the forest like a breeze blowing through a hollow, keeping pace with Slayer, gaining on him. Each log in Slayer's way was an obstruction, but to Young Bull each was just a part of the pathway.

Young Bull leaped to the side, paws against the tree trunks pushing him when he turned. He soared, over stones and rocks, leaping from one to the next, leaving a blur in the air behind him.

Slayer smelled afraid for the first time. He vanished, but Young Bull followed, appearing in the field where the army camped, beneath the shadow of the large stone sword. Slayer looked over his shoulder and cursed, vanishing again.

Young Bull followed. The place where the Whitecloaks had made camp.

The top of a small plateau.

A cavern burrowed into a hillside.

The middle of a small lake. Young Bull ran upon the surface with ease.

Each place Slayer went, he followed, each moment growing closer. There was no time for swords, hammers, or bows. This was a chase, and Young Bull was the hunter this time. He—

He leaped into the middle of a field, and Slayer wasn't there. He smelled where the man had gone, however. He followed him, and appeared in another place on the same field. There were scents of places all around. What?

Perrin came to a stop, booted feet grinding into the ground. He spun, bewildered. Slayer must have hopped quickly through several different places in the same field, confusing his trail. Perrin tried to determine which one to follow, but they all faded and intermixed.

"Burn him!" he said.

Young Bull, a sending came. Sparks. The wolf had been wounded, but he hadn't fled as Perrin had assumed. He sent an image of a thin silver rod, two handspans high, sprouting from the ground in the middle of a stand of dogfennel.

Perrin smiled and sent himself there. The wounded wolf, still trailing blood, lay beside the object. It was obviously some sort of *ter'angreal.* It appeared to be made of dozens upon dozens of fine, wirelike bits of metal woven together like a braid. It was about two handspans long, and was driven point first into the soft earth.

Perrin pulled it from the ground. The dome didn't vanish. He turned the spike over in his hand, but had no idea how to make the dome stop. He willed the spike to change into something else, a stick, and was shocked when he was rebuffed. The object actually seemed to *push* his mind away.

It is here in its reality, Sparks sent. The sending tried to convey something, that the item was somehow more real than most things in the dream world.

Perrin didn't have time to wonder about it. First priority was to move the dome, if he could, away from where his people camped. He sent himself to the edge where he'd entered the dome.

As he'd hoped, the center of the dome moved with him. He was at the place where he'd entered, but the edge of the dome had changed positions, the center falling wherever Perrin was standing. The dome still dominated the sky, extending far in every direction.

Young Bull, Sparks sent. *I am free. The wrongness is gone.*

Go, Perrin sent. *I'll take this and get rid of it. Each of you, go a different direction and howl. Confuse Slayer.*

The wolves responded. A part of Perrin, the hunter inside of him, was frustrated at not having been able to defeat Slayer directly. But this was more important.

He tried to *shift* to someplace distant, but it didn't work.

It appeared that even though he was holding the *ter'angreal*, he was still bound by the dome's rules.

So, instead, he shifted as far as he could. Neald had said it was about four leagues from their camp to the perimeter, so Perrin shifted that far to the north, then did so again, and again. The enormous dome moved with him, its center always appearing directly over his head.

He would take the spike someplace safe, someplace where Slayer couldn't find it.

CHAPTER
36

An Invitation

Egwene appeared in *Tel'aran'rhiod* wearing a pure white gown sewn with golden thread at the seams and in the embroidery, tiny bits of obsidian—polished but unshaped—sewn in gold along the trim of the bodice. A terribly impractical dress to own, but that didn't matter here.

She was in her chambers, where she'd wanted to appear. She sent herself to the hallway outside the Yellow Ajah's quarters. Nynaeve was there, arms folded, her dress a far more sensible tan and brown.

"I want you to be *very* careful," Egwene said. "You're the only one here who has faced one of the Forsaken directly, and you also have more experience with *Tel'aran'rhiod* than the others. If Mesaana arrives, you are to lead the attack."

"I think I can manage that," Nynaeve said, the corners of her mouth rising. Yes, she could manage it. Holding Nynaeve back from attacking, *that* would have been the difficult task.

Egwene nodded, and Nynaeve vanished. She'd remain hidden near the Hall of the Tower, watching for Mesaana or Black sisters coming to spy on the decoy meeting happening there. Egwene sent herself to another place in the city, a hall where the true meeting would take place between herself, the Wise Ones and the Windfinders.

Tar Valon had several meeting halls used for musical performances or for gatherings. This one, known as the Musician's Way, was perfect for her needs. It was precisely decorated with leatherleaf wood paneling carved to look like a forest of trees lining the walls. The chairs were of a matching wood, sung by Ogier, each one a thing of beauty. They were arranged in the round, facing a central podium. The domed ceiling was inset with marble carved to look like stars in the sky. The ornamentation was remarkable; beautiful without being gaudy.

The Wise Ones had already arrived—Amys, Bair and Melaine, whose belly was great with the later stages of pregnancy. This amphitheater had a raised platform along one side where the Wise Ones could sit comfortably on the floor, yet those seated in the chairs would not look down at them.

Leane, Yukiri and Seaine sat in chairs facing the Wise Ones, each wearing one of Elayne's copied dream *ter'angreal*, looking shadowy and insubstantial. Elayne was supposed to be there, too, but she had warned she might have trouble channeling enough to enter *Tel'aran'rhiod*.

The Aes Sedai and Wise Ones inspected one another with a nearly palpable air of hostility. The Aes Sedai considered the Wise Ones to be poorly trained wilders; the Wise Ones, in turn, thought the Aes Sedai full of themselves.

As Egwene arrived, a group of women with dark skin and black hair appeared in the very center of the room. The Windfinders glanced about suspiciously. Siuan had said, from her time teaching them, that the Sea Folk had legends about *Tel'aran'rhiod* and its dangers. That hadn't stopped the Windfinders from learning everything they could about the World of Dreams the moment they discovered that it was real.

At the head of the Windfinders was a tall, slender woman with narrow eyes and a long neck, numerous medallions on the fine chain connecting her nose to her left ear. That would be Shielyn, one of those Nynaeve had told Egwene about. The three other Windfinders included a dignified woman with white locks of hair woven among her black. That would be Renaile, according to the letters they'd sent and Nynaeve's instruction. Egwene had been led to believe she'd be foremost among them, but she seemed subservient to the others. Had she lost her place as Windfinder to the Mistress of the Ships?

"Welcome," Egwene said to them. "Please, sit."

"We will stand," Shielyn said. Her voice was tense.

"Who are these ones, Egwene al'Vere?" Amys asked. "Children should not be visiting *Tel'aran'rhiod*. It is not an abandoned sand-badger's den to be explored."

"Children?" Shielyn asked.

"You are children here, wetlander."

"Amys, please," Egwene cut in. "I lent them *ter'angreal* to come here. It was necessary."

"We could have met outside the World of Dreams," Bair said. "Choosing the middle of a battlefield might have been safer."

Indeed, the Windfinders were *very* unfamiliar with the workings of *Tel'aran'rhiod*. Their bright clothing periodically changed colors—in fact, as Egwene watched, Renaile's blouse vanished entirely. Egwene found herself blushing, though Elayne had mentioned that when on the waves, Sea Folk men and women both worked wearing not a stitch above the waist. The blouse was back a moment later. Their jewelry also seemed in almost constant flux.

"There are reasons I have done what I have done, Amys," Egwene said, striding forward and seating herself. "Shielyn din Sabura Night Waters and her sisters have been told of the dangers of this place, and have accepted responsibility for their own safety."

"A little like giving a firebrand and a cask of oil to a child," Melaine muttered, "and claiming you've given *him* responsibility for his own safety."

"Must we endure this squabbling, Mother?" Yukiri asked.

Egwene took a calming breath. "Please, you are leaders of your separate peoples, women with reputations for great wisdom and acuity. Can we not at least be civil with one another?" Egwene turned to the Sea Folk. "Windfinder Shielyn, you have accepted my invitation. Surely you will not now reject my hospitality by standing through the entire meeting?"

The woman hesitated. She had a proud air to her; recent interaction between the Aes Sedai and the Sea Folk had made her bold. Egwene shoved down a stab of anger; she did *not* like the details of the bargain regarding the Bowl of Winds. Nynaeve and Elayne should have known better. They—

No. Elayne and Nynaeve had done their best, and had been under unusual strain. Besides, bargaining with the Sea

Folk was said to be only one step safer than bargaining with the Dark One himself.

Shielyn finally gave a curt nod, though her blouse changed colors several times while she considered, settling on crimson, and her jewelry kept vanishing and reappearing. "Very well. We are indebted to you for the gift of this place, and will agree to your hospitality." She sat down in a chair apart from Egwene and the other Aes Sedai, and those with her did as well.

Egwene released a soft breath of relief and summoned several small tables with cups of warm, fragrant tea. The Windfinders jumped, though the Wise Ones didn't bat an eye. Amys did, however, reach for her cup and change the rose-blossom tea to something with a much darker cast.

"Perhaps you will tell us the purpose of this meeting," Bair said, sipping her tea. The Sea Folk did not pick up theirs, though the Aes Sedai did begin to drink.

"We have guessed it already," Shielyn said. "This confrontation is inevitable, though I wish to the winds that it were not so."

"Well, speak up, then," Yukiri said. "What is it about?"

Shielyn focused on Egwene. "For many seasons and tides we hid the nature of our Windfinding from the Aes Sedai. The White Tower inhales, but does not exhale—that which is brought in is never allowed to leave. Now that you know of us, you want us, for you cannot stand the thought of women channeling outside of your grasp."

The Aes Sedai frowned. Egwene caught Melaine nodding in agreement. The words were true enough, though only one side of the issue. If they'd known how useful White Tower training would be, and how important it was for the people to know that channelers were being cared for and trained . . .

However, that thinking felt hollow to her. The Sea Folk had their own traditions, and made fine use of their channelers without regulation from the White Tower. Egwene hadn't spent as much time with the Sea Folk as Nynaeve or Elayne, but she'd had detailed reports. The Windfinders were unskilled with many weaves, but their abilities with specific weaves—particularly those focusing on Air—were far more advanced than those practiced by Aes Sedai.

These women deserved the truth. Was that not what the

White Tower, and the Three Oaths, stood for? "You are correct, Shielyn din Sabura Night Waters," Egwene said. "And your people may have been wise to keep their abilities hidden from the Aes Sedai."

Yukiri gasped, a quite un-Aes Sedai reaction. Shielyn froze, chain from her ear to nose tinkling softly as the medallions on it hit together. Her blouse changed to blue. "What?"

"You may have been wise," Egwene said. "I would not presume to second-guess the Amyrlins who came before me, but there is an argument to be made. Perhaps we have been overly zealous to control women who can wield the One Power. It is obvious that the Windfinders have done well in training themselves. I should think that the White Tower could learn much from you."

Shielyn settled back, scanning Egwene's face. Egwene met the woman's eyes and kept her expression calm. *See that I am resolute,* she thought. *See that I mean what I say. That is not flattery. I am Aes Sedai. I speak the truth.*

"Well," Shielyn said. "Perhaps we could make a bargain that would allow us to train your women."

Egwene smiled. "I was hoping that you would see the advantage in that." To the side, the three other Aes Sedai regarded Egwene with measured hostility. Well, they would see. The best way to gain the upper hand was to shake expectations like rindwater beetles in a jar.

"And yet," Egwene said, "you acknowledge that there are things the White Tower knows that you do not. Otherwise you would not have striven to bargain for our women to train your Windfinders."

"We will not rescind that agreement," Shielyn said quickly. Her blouse turned pale yellow.

"Oh, I expect nothing of the sort," Egwene said. "It is well that you now have Aes Sedai teachers. Those who bargained with you achieved something unexpected."

True words, every one. However, the way she said them implied something more—that Egwene had *wanted* the Aes Sedai to be sent to the Sea Folk ships. Shielyn's frown deepened, and she sat back in her chair. Egwene hoped she was considering whether her people's grand victory over the Bowl of the Winds had been a setup from the start.

"If anything," Egwene continued, "I feel that the previous

agreement was not ambitious enough." She turned to the Wise Ones. "Amys, would you agree that the Aes Sedai have knowledge of weaves that the Wise Ones do not?"

"It would be foolish not to admit Aes Sedai expertise in these areas," Amys said carefully. "They spend much time practicing their weaves. But there are things we know that they do not."

"Yes," Egwene said. "During my time training beneath the Wise Ones, I learned more about leadership than I did during my time in the White Tower. You also gave me very helpful training in *Tel'aran'rhiod* and Dreaming."

"All right," Bair said, "out with it. We've been chasing a three-legged lizard this entire conversation, poking it with a stick to see if it will move any further."

"We need to share what we know with one another," Egwene said. "We three groups—women who can channel—need to form an alliance."

"With the White Tower in control, I assume," Shielyn said.

"All I am saying," Egwene replied, "is that there is wisdom in sharing and learning from others. Wise Ones, I would have Accepted from the White Tower be sent to train with you. It would be particularly useful to have you train them to master *Tel'aran'rhiod*."

It was unlikely that another Dreamer, such as Egwene, would be discovered among the Aes Sedai, though she could hope. The Talent was very rare. Still, it would be advantageous to have some sisters trained in *Tel'aran'rhiod*, even if they did have to enter with *ter'angreal*.

"Windfinders," Egwene continued. "I would send women to you as well, particularly those skilled in Air, to learn to call the winds as you do."

"Life for an apprentice Windfinder is not easy," Shielyn said. "I think your women would find it very different from the soft life in the White Tower."

Egwene's backside still remembered the pain of her "soft" life in the White Tower. "I do not doubt that it will be challenging," she said, "but I do not doubt that it would be very helpful for that very reason."

"Well, I suspect this could be arranged," Shielyn said, leaning forward, sounding eager. "There would have to be payment, of course."

"An equal one," Egwene said. "In allowing you to send
ome of your apprentices to the White Tower to train with us."

"We already send women to you."

Egwene sniffed. "Token sacrifices sent so we will not be-
ome suspicious of your Windfinders. Your women often
eclude themselves, or come reluctantly. I would have that
ractice stop—there is no reason to deny potential Wind-
inders to your people."

"Well, what would be the difference?" Shielyn asked.

"The women you send would be allowed to return to you
fter their training," Egwene said. "Wise Ones, I would
ave Aiel apprentices sent to us as well. Not reluctantly, and
ot to become Aes Sedai, but to train and learn our ways.
hey, too, would be allowed to return, should they desire it,
nce they are finished."

"It would have to be more than that," Amys said. "I worry
vhat would happen to women who become too accustomed
o soft wetlander ways."

"Surely you wouldn't want to compel them—" Egwene
egan.

Bair cut in. "They'd still be apprentice Wise Ones, Egwene
l'Vere. Children who need to complete their training. And
hat is assuming we agree to this plan; something about it
nsettles my stomach, like too much food after a day of
asting."

"If we let the Aes Sedai set hooks into our apprentices,"
Melaine said, "they will not soon be pulled free."

"Do you want them to be?" Egwene said. "Do you see
vhat you have in me, Melaine? An Amyrlin Seat who was
rained by the Aiel? What sacrifice would it be worth to
our people to have more like me? Aes Sedai who under-
tand ji'e'toh and the Three-fold Land, who respect Wise
)nes rather than seeing them as rivals or wilders?"

The three Aiel settled back at that, looking at one an-
ther, troubled.

"And what of you, Shielyn?" Egwene said. "What would
t be worth to your people to have an Amyrlin Seat who,
aving trained with you, regards you as friends and who
espects your ways?"

"That could be valuable," Shielyn admitted. "Assuming
he women you send to us have a better temperament than
hose whom we have seen so far. I have yet to meet an Aes

Sedai who could not benefit from a few days hanging from the high mast."

"That is because you insisted on getting Aes Sedai," Egwene said, "who are set in their ways. If we were to send you Accepted instead, they would be much more pliable."

"Instead?" Shielyn said immediately. "This is not the bargain we were discussing."

"It could be," Egwene replied. "If we allow Sea Folk channelers to return to you instead of requiring that they stay in the Tower, you will no longer have such a strong need of the Aes Sedai teachers."

"This must be a different agreement." Shielyn shook her head. "And it will not be a bargain to make lightly. Aes Sedai are serpents, like those rings you wear."

"What if I offer to include the dream *ter'angreal* you were loaned?" Egwene asked.

Shielyn glanced at her hand where, in the real world, she would be holding the small plate that—with a channeled bit of Spirit—let a woman enter *Tel'aran'rhiod*. Egwene hadn't given them the *ter'angreal* that Elayne had finally perfected that let one enter without needing to channel, of course. Those were more versatile, and therefore more powerful. Best to keep those a secret.

"In *Tel'aran'rhiod*," Egwene said, leaning forward, "you can go anywhere. You can meet those who are distant without needing to Travel there, can learn what is hidden, and can confer in secret."

"This is a dangerous thing you suggest, Egwene al'Vere," Amys said sternly. "To let them loose would be like letting a group of wetlander children run wild in the Three-fold Land."

"You cannot keep this place for yourself, Amys," Egwene said.

"We are not so selfish," the Wise One said. "It is their safety I speak of."

"Then perhaps," Egwene said, "it would be best if the Sea Folk sent some of their apprentices to train with you Wise Ones—and perhaps you could send some back."

"To live on *ships*?" Melaine said, aghast.

"What better way to conquer your fears of the water?"

"We aren't afraid of it," Amys snapped. "We respect

it. You wetlanders . . ." She always spoke of ships as one spoke of a caged lion.

"Regardless." Egwene turned back to the Sea Folk. "The *ter'angreal* could be yours, should we have a bargain."

"You already gave these to us," Shielyn said.

"They were *lent* to you, Shielyn, as was made very clear by the women who delivered them."

"And you would give them to us permanently?" Shielyn asked. "With none of this nonsense about all *ter'angreal* belonging to the White Tower?"

"It is important that there be a rule to prevent *ter'angreal* from being kept by those who discover them," Egwene said. "That way, we can remove a potentially dangerous item from a foolish merchant or farmer. But I would be willing to make a formal exception for the Windfinders and Wise Ones."

"So the glass pillars . . ." Amys said. "I have wondered if the Aes Sedai would ever try to lay claim to them."

"I doubt that would happen," Egwene said. "But I also suspect that it would ease Aiel minds if we were to proclaim it officially, that those *ter'angreal*—and others you possess—belong to you, and that sisters cannot claim them."

That gave the Wise Ones serious thought.

"I still find this agreement odd," Bair said. "Aiel, training in the White Tower, but not becoming Aes Sedai? It is not the way things have been."

"The world is changing, Bair," Egwene said softly. "Back in Emond's Field, there was a patch of fine, cultivated Emond's Glory flowers near a brook. My father liked to walk there, and loved their beauty. But then when the new bridge was built, people began traipsing across the patch to get to it.

"My father tried for years to keep them off the patch. Small fences, signs. Nothing worked. And then he thought to build a neat path of river stones through the patch, cultivating the flowers to the sides. After that, people stopped walking on them.

"When change comes, you can scream and try to force things to stay the same. But you'll usually end up getting trampled. However, if you can *direct* the changes, they can serve you. Just as the Power serves us, but only after we surrender to it."

Egwene looked at each woman in turn. "Our three groups should have begun working together long ago. The Last Battle is upon us, and the Dragon Reborn threatens to free the Dark One. If that weren't enough, we have another common foe—one who would see Aes Sedai, Windfinders and Wise Ones alike destroyed."

"The Seanchan," Melaine said.

Renaile, sitting at the back of the Windfinders, let out a soft hiss at the word. Her clothing changed, and she was wearing armor, holding a sword. It was gone in a moment.

"Yes," Egwene said. "Together, we can be strong enough to fight them. Apart . . ."

"We must consider this bargain," Shielyn said. Egwene noticed a wind blowing through the room, likely created by one of the Sea Folk by accident. "We will meet again and perhaps make a promise. If we make it, the terms will be this: We will send you two apprentices a year, and you will send two to us."

"Not your weakest," Egwene said. "I want your most promising."

"And you will send the same?" Shielyn said.

"Yes," Egwene said. Two was a start. They would probably wish to move to larger numbers once the plan was proven effective. But she would not push for that at the start.

"And us?" Amys said. "We are part of this 'bargain' as you put it?"

"Two Accepted," Egwene said, "in return for two apprentices. They train for a period of no less than six months, but no more than two years. Once our women are among you, they are to be considered your apprentices, and must follow your rules." She hesitated. "At the end of their training, all apprentices and Accepted must return to their people for at least one year. After that, if yours decide they want to be Aes Sedai, they can return to be considered. The same goes for women among us, should they decide to join with you instead."

Bair nodded thoughtfully. "Perhaps there will be women like yourself who, seeing our ways, will know them superior. It is still a shame we lost you."

"My place was elsewhere," Egwene said.

"Will you accept this between us as well?" Shielyn said

to the Wise Ones. "Should we agree to this bargain, two for two, in a similar manner?"

"If the bargain is agreed to," Bair said, looking to the other Wise Ones, "we will make it with you as well. But we must speak with the other Wise Ones about it."

"And what of the *ter'angreal*?" Shielyn said, turning back to Egwene.

"Yours," Egwene said. "In exchange, you will release us from our promise to send sisters to train you, and we will let any Sea Folk currently among us return to their people. All of this is subject to the approval of your people, and I will have to bring this before the Hall of the Tower."

Of course, as Amyrlin, her decrees were law. If the Hall balked, however, those laws could end up being ignored. In this, she would need to get their support—and she wanted to, particularly considering her stance that the Hall should work together with her more and meet in secret less.

She was reasonably certain she could get approval for this proposal, however. The Aes Sedai wouldn't like giving up *ter'angreal*, but they also did *not* like the bargain that had been made with the Sea Folk over the Bowl of the Winds. To be rid of that, they would give almost anything.

"I knew you would try to end the sisters training us," Shielyn said, sounding self-satisfied.

"Which would you rather have?" Egwene asked. "Women who are among our weakest members, and who see their service as a punishment? Or instead, your own Sea Folk, who have learned the best we can offer and return happily to share?" Egwene had been half-tempted to simply send Sea Folk Aes Sedai to them to fulfill the bargain anyway; it seemed a proper twisting of the situation.

Hopefully, however, this new bargain would supplant the old one. She had a feeling she'd lose the Sea Folk sisters anyway, at least the ones who longed to be back with their people. The world *was* changing, and now that the Wind-finders were no longer a secret, the old ways need not be maintained.

"We will discuss," Shielyn said. She nodded to the others, and they vanished from the room. They certainly did learn quickly.

"This dance is a dangerous one, Egwene al'Vere," Amys

said, standing and adjusting her shawl. "There was a time when the Aiel would have taken pride to have served the Aes Sedai. That time has passed."

"The women you thought you would find are nothing more than a dream, Amys," Egwene said. "Real life is often more disappointing than dreams, but at least when you find honor in the real world, you know it to be more than a fancy."

The Wise One nodded. "We will likely agree to this bargain. We have need to learn what the Aes Sedai can teach."

"We will pick our strongest women," Bair added. "Those who will not be corrupted by wetlander softness." There was no condemnation in those words. Calling wetlanders soft was not an insult, in Bair's mind.

Amys nodded. "This work you do is a good one so long as you do not presume to tie us in steel bands."

No, Amys, Egwene thought. *I will not tie you in bands of steel. I'll use lace instead.*

"Now," Bair said. "You still have need of us this day? You indicated a battle . . . ?"

"Yes," Egwene said. "Or so I hope." No word had come. That meant Nynaeve and Siuan hadn't discovered anyone listening. Had her ploy failed?

The Wise Ones nodded to her, then walked to the side, conferring quietly. Egwene trailed over to the Aes Sedai.

Yukiri stood. "I don't like this, Mother," Yukiri said, speaking softly and eyeing the Wise Ones. "I don't think the Hall will agree to this. Many are adamant that all objects of the One Power should belong to us."

"The Hall will see reason," Egwene said. "We've already returned the Bowl of the Winds to the Sea Folk, and now that Elayne has rediscovered the method of crafting *ter'angreal*, it is only a matter of time before there are so many we cannot keep track of them all."

"But Elayne is an Aes Sedai, Mother," Seaine said, rising, face troubled. "Surely you can keep her in line."

"Perhaps," Egwene said, speaking softly. "But doesn't it strike you odd that—after all of these years—so many Talents are returning, so many discoveries being made? My Dreaming, Elayne's *ter'angreal*, Foretelling. Rare Talents seem in abundance. An Age is ending, and the

world is changing. I doubt that Elayne's Talent will remain unique. What if one of the Wise Ones or Sea Folk
manifest it?"

The other three sat quietly, troubled.

"It still isn't right to give up, Mother," Yukiri finally said.
"With effort, we *could* bring the Wise Ones and Windfinders
under control."

"And the Asha'man?" Egwene said softly, unable to keep
a hint of discomfort out of her voice. "Will we insist that
all *angreal* and *sa'angreal* created for men belong to us,
though we cannot use them? What if there are Asha'man
who learn to create objects of Power? Will we force them
to give up everything they create to us? *Could* we enforce
that?"

"I . . ." Yukiri said.

Leane shook her head. "She's right, Yukiri. Light, but
she is."

"The world as it was cannot be ours any longer," Egwene
said softly, not wanting the Wise Ones to overhear. "Was it
ever? The Black Tower bonds Aes Sedai, the Aiel no longer revere us, the Windfinders have hidden their best channelers from us for centuries and are becoming increasingly
belligerent. If we try to hold too tightly to all of this, we
will either become tyrants or fools, depending upon how
successful we are. I accept neither title.

"We will *lead* them, Yukiri. We must become a source
that women look to, all women. We achieve that by not holding too tightly, by bringing their channelers to train with
us and by sending our most talented Accepted to become
experts in the things they are best at."

"And if they are saying the same thing right now?"
Leane asked softly, looking over at the Wise Ones, who
were speaking in hushed tones on the far side of the room.
"If they try to play us as we play them?"

"Then we have to play the best," Egwene said. "All of this
is secondary, for now. We need unity against the Shadow
and the Seanchan. We have to—"

A frazzled-looking Siuan appeared in the room, her dress
singed on one side. "Mother! We need you!"

"The battle has begun?" Egwene said, urgent. To the
side, the Wise Ones perked up.

"It has," Siuan said, panting. "It happened right off. Mother, they didn't come to eavesdrop! They *attacked*."

Perrin streaked across the land, covering leagues with each step. He needed to take the spike someplace away from Slayer. Perhaps the ocean? He could—

An arrow hissed through the air, slicing his shoulder. Perrin cursed and spun. They were on a high rocky hillside. Slayer stood downhill from him, bow raised to his angular face, dark eyes alight with anger. He released another arrow.

A wall, Perrin thought, summoning a wall of bricks in front of him. The arrow punched several inches into the bricks, but stopped. Perrin immediately sent himself away. He couldn't go far, though, not while carrying the dome.

Perrin changed so that he wasn't going straight north any longer, but moving toward the east. He doubted that would throw off Slayer—he could probably see the dome moving and judge its direction.

What to do? He'd planned to toss the spike into the ocean, but if Slayer was following, he'd just recover it. Perrin concentrated on moving as quickly as he could, covering leagues with each heartbeat. Could he outrun his foe? The landscape passed him in a blur. Mountains, forests, lakes, meadows.

Just as he thought he might have gotten ahead, a figure appeared just beside him, swinging a sword at his neck. Perrin ducked, barely dodging the attack. He growled, raising his hammer, but Slayer vanished.

Perrin stopped in place, frustrated. Slayer could move faster than Perrin, and could get under the dome by jumping ahead of it, then waiting for Perrin to move it on top of him. From there, he could jump directly to Perrin and attack.

I can't outrun him, Perrin realized. The only way to be certain, the only way to protect Faile and the others, was to kill Slayer. Otherwise the man would recover the spike from wherever Perrin put it, then return it to trap his people.

Perrin glanced around, getting his bearings. He was on a lightly forested slope, and could see Dragonmount to the north of him. He glanced eastward, and saw the tip of a large structure peeking out over the treetops. The White

Tower. The city might give Perrin an advantage, make it easier to hide in one of the many buildings or alleys.

Perrin leaped off in that direction, carrying the spike with him, the dome it created traveling with him as he moved. It would come down to a fight after all.

CHAPTER
37

Darkness in the Tower

Gawyn sat on a bench in the Caemlyn Palace gardens. It had been several hours since he'd sent Egwene's messenger away. A gibbous moon hung fat in the sky. Servants occasionally passed by to see if he needed anything. They seemed worried about him.

He just wanted to watch the sky. It had been weeks since he'd been able to do that. The air was cooling, but he left his coat off, hung over the back of the bench. The open air felt good—different, somehow, from the same air beneath a cloudy sky.

With the last light of dusk fading, the stars shone like hesitant children, peeking out now that the uproar of day had died down. It felt so good to finally see them again. Gawyn breathed in deeply.

Elayne was right. Much of Gawyn's hatred of al'Thor came from frustration. Maybe jealousy. Al'Thor was playing a role closer to what Gawyn would have chosen for himself. Ruling nations, leading armies. Looking at their lives, who had taken on the role of a prince, and who the role of a lost sheepherder?

Perhaps Gawyn resisted Egwene's demands because he wanted to lead, to be the one who accomplished the heroic acts. If he became her Warder, he would have to step aside and help *her* change the world. There was honor in keeping someone great alive. A deep honor. What was the point of great acts? The recognition they brought, or the better lives they created?

To step aside. He'd admired men like Sleete for their willingness to do this, but had never understood them. Not truly. *I can't leave her to do it alone,* he thought. *I have to help her. From within her shadow.*

Because he loved her. But also because it was for the best. If two bards tried to play different songs at the same time, they both made noise. But if one stepped back to give harmony to the other's melody, then the beauty could be greater than either made alone.

And in that moment, finally, he understood. He stood up. He couldn't go to Egwene as a prince. He had to go to her as a Warder. He had to watch over her, to serve her. See her wishes done.

It was time to return.

Slinging his coat on, he strode down the path toward the Palace. The opening serenades of various pond frogs cut short—followed by splashes—as he passed them and entered the building. It wasn't a long walk to his sister's rooms. She would be up; she had trouble sleeping lately. During the past few days, they had often enjoyed conversation and a cup of warm tea before bed. At her doors, however, he was stopped by Birgitte.

She gave him another glare. Yes, she did *not* like being forced to act as Captain-General in his stead. He could see that now. He felt a little awkward stepping up to her. The woman held up a hand. "Not tonight, princeling."

"I'm leaving for the White Tower," he said. "I'd like to say farewell."

He moved to step forward, but Birgitte held a hand against his chest, gently pushing him back. "You can leave in the morning."

He almost reached for his sword, but stopped himself. Light! There had been a time when he hadn't reacted that way to everything. He *had* become a fool. "Ask if she'll see me," he said politely. "Please."

"I have my orders," Birgitte said. "Besides, she couldn't talk to you. She's asleep."

"I'm sure she'd like to be awakened."

"It's not that kind of sleep," Birgitte said. She sighed. "It has to do with Aes Sedai matters. Go to bed. In the morning, your sister will probably have word from Egwene for you."

Gawyn frowned. How would . . .

The dreams, he realized. *This is what the Aes Sedai meant, about Egwene training them to walk in their dreams.* "So Egwene's sleeping as well?"

Birgitte eyed him. "Bloody ashes, I've probably said too much already. Off to your rooms."

Gawyn stepped away, but not to go to his rooms. *He'll wait for a time of weakness,* he thought, remembering the sul'dam's words. *And when he strikes, he'll leave such desolation as you wouldn't believe a single man could create . . .*

A time of weakness.

He dashed away from Elayne's rooms, sprinting through the palace hallways to the Traveling room that Elayne had set up. Blessedly, a Kinswoman was on duty here—bleary-eyed, but waiting in case emergency messages needed to be sent. Gawyn didn't recognize the dark-haired woman, but she seemed to recognize him.

She yawned and opened a gateway at his request. He ran through and onto the Traveling ground of the White Tower. The gateway vanished right behind him. Gawyn started, spinning with a curse. That had nearly closed right on him! Why had the Kinswoman let it vanish so abruptly, and so dangerously? A split second sooner, and it would have taken his foot off, or worse.

There was no time. He turned and continued running.

Egwene, Leane and the Wise Ones appeared in a room at the base of the Tower, where a group of anxious women waited. This was a guard post that Egwene had stipulated as a fallback position.

"Report!" Egwene demanded.

"Shevan and Carlinya are dead, Mother," Saerin said grimly. The brusque Brown was panting.

Egwene cursed. "What happened?"

"We were in the middle of our ploy, having a discussion about a fake plot to bring peace to Arad Doman, as you'd ordered. And then . . ."

"Fire," Morvrin said, shivering. "Blasting through the walls. Women channeling, several with incredible Power. I saw Alviarin there. Others, too."

"Nynaeve is still up there," Brendas added.

"Stubborn woman," Egwene said, looking at the three Wise Ones. They nodded. "Send Brendas out," she said, pointing at the cool-eyed White. "When you wake, go and wake the others here so they will be out of danger. Leave Nynaeve, Siuan, Leane and myself."

"Yes, Mother," Brendas said.

Amys did something that made her form fade away.

"The rest of you," Egwene said, "go someplace safe. Away from the city."

"Very well, Mother," Saerin said. She stayed in place, however.

"What?" Egwene said.

"I . . ." Saerin frowned. "I can't go. Something is odd."

"Nonsense," Bair snapped. "It—"

"Bair," Amys said. "I can't leave. Something is very wrong."

"The sky is violet," Yukiri said, looking out a small window. "Light! It looks like a dome, covering the Tower and the city. When did that happen?"

"Something is very wrong here," Bair said. "We should awaken."

Amys suddenly vanished, causing Egwene to start. She was back in a moment. "I was able to go to the place where we were before, but I cannot leave the city. I do not like this, Egwene al'Vere."

Egwene tried sending herself to Cairhien. It didn't work. She looked out the window, feeling worried, but resolute. Yes, there was violet above.

"Wake if you must," she said to the Wise Ones. "I will fight. One of the Shadowsouled is here."

The Wise Ones fell silent. "We will go with you," Melaine finally said.

"Good. You others, be away from this place. Go to the Musician's Way and stay there until awakened. Melaine, Amys, Bair, Leane, we are going to a place higher in the Tower, a room with wood paneling and a four-poster bed, gauze drapings around it. It is my bedroom."

The Wise Ones nodded, and Egwene sent herself there. A lamp sat on her nightstand; it didn't burn here in *Tel'aran'rhiod*, though she'd left it burning in the real world. The Wise Ones and Leane appeared around her. The gauze draping Egwene's bed ruffled in the breeze of their appearance.

The Tower shook. The fighting continued.

"Be careful," Egwene said. "We hunt dangerous foes, and they know this terrain better than you."

"We will be careful," Bair replied. "I have heard that the Shadowsouled think themselves masters of this place. Well, we shall see."

"Leane," Egwene said, "can you handle yourself?" Egwene had been tempted to send her away, but she and Siuan had spent some measure of time in *Tel'aran'rhiod*. Certainly, she was more experienced than most.

"I'll keep my head low, Mother," she promised. "But there are bound to be more of them than us. You need me."

"Agreed," Egwene said.

The four women winked away. Why couldn't they leave the Tower? It was troubling, but also useful. It would mean she was trapped here.

But hopefully so was Mesaana.

Five doves rose into the air, scattering from the ledge of the rooftop. Perrin spun. Slayer stood behind him, smelling like stone.

The hard-eyed man glanced up at the fleeing birds. "Yours?"

"For warning," Perrin replied. "I figured you'd see through walnut shells on the ground."

"Clever," Slayer said.

Behind him spread a magnificent city. Perrin hadn't believed that any city could be as magnificent as Caemlyn. But if there was such a thing, Tar Valon was it. The entire city was a work of art, almost every building decked with archways, spires, engravings and ornamentation. Even the *cobblestones* seemed to be arranged artistically.

Slayer's eyes flickered down to Perrin's belt. There, affixed in a pouch Perrin had created to hold it, was the *ter'angreal*. The tip stuck out the top, silvery bits wrapping around one another in a complex knotted braid. Perrin had tried again to destroy the thing by thinking of it, but had been rebuffed. Attacking it with his hammer hadn't so much as bent it. Whatever this thing was, it had been built to resist such attacks.

"You've grown skilled," Slayer said. "I should have killed you months ago."

"I believe you tried," Perrin said, raising his hammer, resting it on his shoulder. "Who are you really?"

"A man of two worlds, Perrin Aybara. And one owned by both. I'll need the dreamspike back."

"Step closer, and I'll destroy it," Perrin said.

Slayer snorted, walking forward. "You don't have the strength for that, boy. I don't even have the strength to manage that." His eyes flickered unconsciously over Perrin's shoulder. Toward what?

Dragonmount, Perrin thought. *He must have worried I was coming this way to toss it in.* Was that, then, an indication of a way Perrin could destroy the *ter'angreal*? Or was Slayer trying to mislead him?

"Don't press me, boy," Slayer said, sword and knife appearing in his hands as he walked forward. "I've already killed four wolves today. Give me the spike."

Four? But he'd killed only one that Perrin had seen. *He's trying to goad me.*

"You think I'll believe that you won't kill me if I give it to you?" Perrin said. "If I gave this to you, you'd have to go put it back in Ghealdan. You know I'd just follow you there." Perrin shook his head. "One of us has to die, and that's that."

Slayer hesitated, then smiled. "Luc hates you, you know. Hates you deeply."

"And you don't?" Perrin asked, frowning.

"No more than the wolf hates the stag."

"You are *not* a wolf," Perrin said, growling softly.

Slayer shrugged. "Let us be done with this, then." He dashed forward.

Gawyn charged into the White Tower; the men on guard barely had time to salute. He dashed past mirrored stand-lamps. Only one in every two was lit, to conserve oil. As he reached a ramp upward, he heard feet behind him.

His sword hissed as he pulled it free, spinning. Mazone and Celark pulled to a halt. The former Younglings wore Tower Guard uniforms now. Would they try to stop him? Who knew what kind of orders Egwene had left?

They saluted.

"Men?" Gawyn said. "What are you doing?"

"Sir," Celark said, lean face shadowed in the patchy lamplight. "When an officer runs by with a look like that on his face, you don't ask if he needs help. You just follow!"

Gawyn smiled. "Come on." He dashed up the ramps, the two men following, swords at the ready.

Egwene's quarters were some way up, and Gawyn's pulse was racing—his breathing forced—by the time they reached her level. They hurried down three hallways; then Gawyn held up his hand. He glanced at the nearby shadowed recesses. Were any of them deep enough to hide a Bloodknife?

You cannot have light without shadow . . .

He peeked around the corner toward Egwene's door; he stood in virtually the same position he had when he had ruined her plans before. Was he doing the same thing now? His two guardsmen stood up close behind him, waiting on his command.

Yes. He was doing the same thing as before. And yet, something had changed. He *would* see her protected so that she could do great things. He would stand in her shadow and be proud. He would do as she asked—but would see her safe no matter what.

Because that was what a Warder did.

He slipped forward, waving his men to follow. The darkness in that shadowy alcove from before didn't seem to *repel* his attention as it had last time. A good sign. He stopped at the door and tried it carefully. It was unlocked. He took a deep breath, then slipped inside.

No alarms went off; no traps caught him and flung him about. A few lamps shone on the walls. At a faint noise, he looked upward. A Tower maid hung there, struggling, with wide eyes, mouth gagged by an invisible flow of Air.

Gawyn cursed, dashing across the room, and threw open the door to Egwene's sleeping chamber. Her bed, one side against the far wall, was draped with white gauze curtains, and a lamp burned on the stand beside it. Gawyn crossed the room to her, pushing the gauze aside. Was she sleeping? Or was she . . .

He reached a hand toward her neck, but at a faint thump behind, Gawyn whipped his sword around and blocked the strike coming at his back. Not one, but *two* blurs of darkness leaped from the shadows. He spared a glance for

Egwene; there was no blood, but he couldn't tell if she was breathing or not. Had his entrance interrupted the assassins in time?

There was no time to check. He fell into Apple Blossoms in the Wind and began to shout. His men stepped up to the doorway, then froze there, stunned.

"Get more help!" Gawyn said. "Go!"

Dark-skinned Mazone turned to obey while Celark, looking determined, leaped into the fight.

The Bloodknives shifted and undulated. Gawyn managed to slip into Cat on Hot Sand to test them, but each strike hit only air. His eyes were already hurting from trying to follow the figures.

Celark attacked from behind, but was as ineffective as Gawyn. Gawyn gritted his teeth, fighting with his back against the bed. He had to keep them away from Egwene, long enough for help to come. If he could—

Both figures twisted suddenly, striking in tandem at Celark. The man barely had time to curse before a sword took him in the neck, and bright blood spurted out. Gawyn yelled again, falling into Lizard in the Thornbush, striking at the backs of the assassins.

Again, his attacks missed. It seemed he was off by only a few hairs. Celark stumbled to the floor with a gurgle, his blood reflecting lanternlight, and Gawyn couldn't step forward to defend him. Not without exposing Egwene.

One of the assassins turned back to Gawyn while the other beheaded Celark, with a slash that—despite the shadows—looked a lot like The River Undercuts the Bank. Gawyn stepped back, trying to keep his eyes off the fallen man. Defend. He only had to defend until help came! He edged to the side.

The Seanchan were wary; they knew he'd fought one of them off before. But they had such a strong advantage. Gawyn wasn't certain he could stand against two of them.

Yes you will, he told himself sternly. *If you fall, Egwene dies.*

Was that a flicker of movement from the other room? Could help have come? Gawyn felt a surge of hope, and edged to the side. From there, he could see Mazone's body on the floor, bleeding.

A third shadowed figure glided into the room and shut

the door behind, locking it. That was why the other two
had been hesitating. They'd wanted to wait until their ally
arrived.

The three of them attacked together.

Perrin let the wolf free.

For once, he didn't worry about what it would do to him.
He let himself *be*, and as he fought, the world seemed to
become right around him.

Perhaps that was because it bent to his will.

Young Bull leaped from a rooftop in Tar Valon, powerful hind legs springing him into the air, *ter'angreal* pouch
fastened to his back. He soared over a street and landed on
a white marble roof with groups of statues on its edges. He
rolled, coming up as a man—*ter'angreal* tied at his waist—
with hammer swinging.

Slayer vanished right before the hammer hit, then appeared beside Perrin. Perrin vanished as Slayer swung, then
appeared just to the left. Back and forth they went, spinning around one another, each disappearing then appearing
again, struggling to land a blow.

Perrin threw himself out of the cycle, sending himself to
a place beside one of the roof's large statues, a pompous-
looking general. He swung, smashing his hammer into it,
magnifying the power of the blow. Chunks of statue exploded toward Slayer. The wolf-killer appeared, expecting
to find Perrin beside him. Instead, a storm of stone and dust
crashed into him.

Slayer bellowed, stone chips slicing his skin. His cloak
immediately became as strong as steel, deflecting chunks
of stone. He whipped it back and the entire building started
to shake. Perrin cursed and leaped free as the roof fell in.

Perrin soared, becoming a wolf before landing on a nearby
rooftop. Slayer appeared in front of him, bow drawn. Young
Bull growled, imagining the wind blowing, but Slayer didn't
fire. He just stood there, as if—

As if he were just a statue.

Perrin cursed, spinning as an arrow shot past him, narrowly missing him at the waist. The real Slayer stood a
short distance off; he vanished, leaving the remarkably detailed statue he'd created to distract Perrin.

Perrin took a deep breath and made the sweat leave his brow. Slayer could come at him from any direction. He put a wall at his back and stood carefully, scanning the roof-top. The dome shook overhead. He'd grown used to that—it moved with him.

But he *wasn't moving*.

He looked down with a panic. The pouch was gone—the arrow Slayer had fired at his waist had sliced it free. Perrin dashed forward to the edge of the roof. Below, Slayer ran through the street, the pouch in his hand.

A wolf leaped from an alley, crashing into Slayer, tossing him to the ground. Hopper.

Perrin was there in a moment, attacking. Slayer cursed, vanishing from underneath Hopper and appearing at the end of the street. He began to flee, leaving a blur behind him.

Perrin followed, Hopper joining him. *How did you find me?* Perrin sent.

You are two foolish cubs, Hopper sent. *Very loud. Like snarling cats. Easy to find.*

He'd deliberately not shown Hopper where he was. After seeing Oak Dancer die . . . well, this was Perrin's fight. Now that the *ter'angreal* was away from Ghealdan and his people were escaping, he didn't want to risk the lives of other wolves.

Not that Hopper would go if he told him to. Growling again, Perrin barreled after Slayer, wolf at his side.

Egwene crouched beside the wall of the hallway, panting, sweat dripping from her brow. Across from her, molten drops of rock cooled from a blast of fire.

The Tower hallway fell still. A few lamps flickered on the wall. Through a window, she could see the purple sky above, between the Tower and the dark clouds. She'd been fighting for what seemed like hours, though it had prob-ably been only fifteen minutes. She'd lost track of the Wise Ones.

She began to creep forward, using the anti-eavesdropping weave to make her footfalls silent until she reached a corner and peered around it. Darkness in both directions. Egwene crept forward, moving carefully, resolutely. The Tower was her domain. She felt invaded, as surely as when the Seanchan had come. However, this fight was proving very different from fighting off the Seanchan. Then, the enemy had been bold, easy to spot.

Faint light appeared under a doorway ahead. She shifted herself into the room, preparing weaves. Two women were there, speaking in whispers, one holding a globe of light. Evanellein and Mestra, two of the Black sisters who had fled the White Tower.

Egwene let loose with a ball of fire that destroyed Mestra in an inferno. Evanellein yelped, and Egwene used a trick Nynaeve had taught her—she *imagined* Evanellein being stupid, unable to think, unable to react.

The woman's eyes glazed over, and her mouth opened. Thought was faster than weaves. Egwene hesitated. Now what? Kill her, while defenseless? Her stomach turned at that thought. *I could take her captive. Go and—*

Someone appeared in the room with her. The newcomer wore black, a magnificent gown with silver trim. Darkness swirled about her, made of spinning ribbons of cloth, her skirt rippling. The effect was unnatural and impressive; possible only here in *Tel'aran'rhiod.*

Egwene looked into the woman's eyes. Large and blue, set in an angular face with chin-length black hair. There was a power to those eyes, and Egwene immediately knew what she was facing. Why fight? She couldn't—

Egwene felt her mind change, become accepting. She fought it with a burst of panic, and in a moment of clarity, she sent herself away.

Egwene appeared in her rooms, then raised her hand to her head, sitting down on the bed. Light, but that woman had been strong.

Something sounded behind her; someone appearing in the room. Egwene leaped to her feet, preparing weaves. Nynaeve stood there, eyes wide with fury. The woman thrust her hands forward, weaves forming, but she froze.

"To the gardens," Egwene said, not trusting her quarters. She shouldn't have come here; Mesaana would know this place.

Nynaeve nodded, and Egwene vanished, appearing in the lower Tower garden. The strange violet dome extended above. What *was* that, and how had Mesaana brought it here? Nynaeve appeared a moment later.

"They're still up there," Nynaeve whispered. "I just saw Alviarin."

"I saw Mesaana," Egwene said. "She nearly took me."

"Light! Are you all right?"

Egwene nodded. "Mestra is dead. I saw Evanellein, too."

"It's black as a tomb up there," Nynaeve whispered. "I think they made it that way. They shouldn't be able to channel this well with those imperfect copies. Siuan and Leane are all right; I saw them a little bit ago, sticking together. Just before that, I managed to hit Notori with a blast of fire. She's dead."

"Good. The Black Ajah stole nineteen *ter'angreal*. That might give us an estimate of how many Black Ajah we have to contend with. Or since they are able to channel so strongly, perhaps not." She, Siuan, Nynaeve, Leane and the three Wise Ones were outnumbered—but the Black Ajah didn't seem to have much experience with *Tel'aran'rhiod*.

"Have you seen the Wise Ones?"

"They're up there." Nynaeve grimaced. "They seem to be enjoying this."

"They would," Egwene said. "I want you and me to go together. We will appear in intersections, back to back, and quickly scan for light or people. If you see a Black, strike. If someone sees you, say 'Go' and we'll jump back here."

Nynaeve nodded.

"First intersection is the one outside my room," Egwene said. "Hallway on the south side. I'll flood it with light; you be ready. From there, we'll jump down one hallway, by the door into the servants' ramp. Then on down the line."

Nynaeve nodded sharply.

The world winked around Egwene. She appeared in the hallway, and immediately thought of the place lit, imposing her will upon it. Light flooded the entire space. A round-faced woman crouched near the side of the wall, wearing white. Sedore, one of the Black sisters.

Sedore spun, looking angry, weaves springing up around her. Egwene worked faster, creating a column of fire right before Sedore would have released her own. No weaves on Egwene's part. Just the fire.

Egwene saw the Black's eyes open wider as the fire roared around her. Sedore screeched, but that cut off as the heat consumed her. Her burned corpse collapsed to the floor, smoldering.

Egwene let out a relieved breath. "Anyone on your side?"

"No," Nynaeve said. "Who was that you hit?"

"Sedore."

"Really?" Nynaeve said, turning. She had been a Sitter for the Yellow.

Egwene smiled. "Next hallway."

They jumped, and repeated their strategy, flooding the hallway with light. There was nobody there, so they moved on. The next two hallways were empty. Egwene was about to leave when a voice hissed, "Foolish child! Your pattern is obvious."

Egwene spun. "Where . . ."

She cut off as she saw Bair. The aged Wise One had changed her clothing and even her *skin itself* to match the white walls and floor tiles. She was practically invisible, crouching in an alcove.

"You shouldn't—" Bair began.

A wall beside them exploded outward, throwing up chunks of rock. Six women stood beyond, and they released weaves of Fire.

It appeared that the time for sneaking had ended.

Perrin crested the wall surrounding the White Tower grounds, coming down with a thump. The strangeness of the wolf dream continued; he now not only smelled odd scents, but heard odd sounds as well. Rumblings from inside the Tower.

He leaped after Slayer, who crossed the grounds, then ran up the outside of the Tower itself. Perrin followed, running up into the air. Slayer stayed just ahead, *ter'angreal* pouch tied at his waist.

Perrin created a longbow. He pulled it back, freezing in place, standing on the side of the Tower. He loosed, but the wolf-killer leaped up, then fell into the Tower through a window. The arrow passed overhead.

Perrin leaped to the window, then ducked inside, Hopper

leaping in after him, leaving a blur behind. They entered a bedroom hung with brocades of blue. The door slammed, and Perrin charged after Slayer. He didn't bother to open the door; he smashed it with his hammer.

Slayer charged down a hallway.

Follow, Perrin sent to Hopper. *I'll cut him off.*

The wolf raced forward, after Slayer. Perrin ran to the right, then cut down a hallway. He moved quickly, the walls speeding past.

He passed a hallway that appeared to be full of people. He was so surprised that he froze, the hall lurching around him.

They were *Aes Sedai*, and they were fighting. The hallway was alight, trails of fire flying from one end to the other. The sounds he'd heard before hadn't been phantoms. And, he thought, yes . . .

"Egwene?" Perrin asked.

She stood pressed against the wall nearby, intently looking down the hallway. When he spoke, she spun on him, hands going up. He felt something grab him. His mind instantly reacted, however, pushing the air away.

Egwene started as she failed to snatch him.

He stepped forward. "Egwene, you shouldn't be here. This place is dangerous."

"Perrin?"

"I don't know how you got here," Perrin said. "But you need to go. Please."

"How did you stop me?" she demanded. "What are you doing here? Have you been with Rand? Tell me where he is."

She spoke with such authority now. She almost seemed a different person, decades older than the girl he'd known. Perrin opened his mouth to reply, but Egwene cut him off.

"I don't have time for this," she said. "I'm sorry, Perrin. I'll be back for you." She raised a hand, and he felt things change around him. Ropes appeared, binding him.

He looked down, amused. The ropes slipped free the moment he thought of them being too loose.

Egwene blinked, watching them drop to the ground. "How—"

Someone burst out of a room nearby, a tall, slender-necked

woman with raven hair, wearing a sleek white dress. She smiled, raising her hands, and a light appeared before her.

Perrin didn't need to know what she was doing. He was a wolf; *he* was the ruler of this place. Weaves were meaningless. He imagined the woman's attack missing him; he *knew* it would be so.

A bar of white-hot light shot from the woman. Perrin raised a hand before himself and Egwene. The light vanished, as if stopped by his palm.

Egwene turned, and the wall above the woman burst, rock showering down. A chunk smashed the woman on the head brutally, knocking her to the ground. Light, she was probably dead, after a blow like that.

Egwene smelled amazed. She spun on him. "Balefire? You stopped *balefire*? *Nothing* should be able to do that."

"It's just a weave," Perrin said, reaching out for Hopper. Where was Slayer?

"It's not *just* a weave, Perrin, it's—"

"I'm sorry, Egwene," he said. "I will speak to you later. Be careful in this place. You probably already know that you need to be, but still. It's more dangerous than you know."

He turned and ran, leaving Egwene sputtering. It seemed she'd managed to become an Aes Sedai. That was good; she deserved it.

Hopper? he sent. *Where are you?*

His only reply was a sudden, terrifying, sending of pain.

Gawyn fought for his life against three living shadows of darkness and steel.

They pressed him to the utmost of his ability, leaving him bloodied half a dozen times over on arms and legs. He used The Cyclone Rages, and it defended his vitals. Barely.

Drops of his blood stained the gauze draping Egwene's bed. If his opponents had already killed Egwene, then they made a good show of continuing to threaten her.

He was growing weak and tired. His boots left bloody prints when he stepped. He couldn't feel the pain. His parries were becoming sluggish. They'd have him in another moment or two.

No help came, although his voice was hoarse from yelling. *Fool!* he thought. *You need to spend more time thinking and less time running straight into danger!* He should have alerted the entire Tower.

The only reason he was alive was because the three were being careful, wearing him down. Once he fell, that *sul'dam* had indicated they would go on a rampage through the White Tower. It would take the Aes Sedai completely by surprise. This night could be a disaster greater than the original Seanchan strike had been.

The three moved forward.

No! Gawyn thought as one of them tried The River Undercuts the Bank. He leaped forward, dodging between two blades, swinging his weapon. Amazingly, he actually struck, and a voice cried out in the room. Blood sprayed across the ground, one shadowy form falling.

The two others muttered curses, and all pretense of wearing him down vanished. They struck at him, weapons flashing amid dark mist. Exhausted, Gawyn took another hit on the shoulder, blood trickling down his arm beneath his coat.

Shadows. How could a man be expected to fight against shadows? It was impossible!

Where there is light, there must be shadow . . .

A last, desperate thought occurred to him. With a cry, he leaped to the side and yanked a pillow from Egwene's bed. Blades cut the air around him as he spun and slammed the pillow on the lantern, smothering it.

Plunging the room into darkness. No light. No shadows.

Equality.

The darkness evened out everything, and in the night, you couldn't see color. He couldn't see the blood on his arms, couldn't see the black shadows of his enemies or the whiteness of Egwene's bed. But he could hear the men move.

He raised his blade for a desperate strike, using Hummingbird Kisses the Honeyrose, predicting where the Bloodknives would move. He was no longer distracted by their misted figures, and his strike hit true, sinking into flesh.

He twisted, yanking his blade free. The room fell silent save for the fall of the man he'd hit. Gawyn held his breath, heartbeat thumping in his ears. Where was the last assassin?

No light came in from the room next door; Celark had fallen beside the doorway, blocking the light underneath.

Gawyn was feeling shaky now. He'd lost too much blood. If he had something to throw to create a distraction . . . but no. Moving would rustle clothing, would give him away.

So, gritting his teeth, he tapped his foot and raised his blade to protect his neck, praying to the Light that the attack came low.

It did, cutting deeply into his side. He took it with a grunt, but immediately lashed out with all he had. His sword hissed, and with a brief tug it sliced true. A thump followed; a decapitated head bouncing off the wall, followed by the noise of a corpse hitting the ground.

Gawyn slumped against the bed, blood gushing from his side. He was blacking out, although it was hard to tell in the unlit room.

He reached for where he remembered Egwene's hand being, but was too weak to find it.

He hit the floor a moment later. His last thought was that he still didn't know whether or not she was dead.

"Great Mistress," Katerine said, kneeling before Mesaana, "we cannot find the thing you describe. Half of our women search for it while the other half fight the worms who resist. But it is nowhere!"

Mesaana folded her arms beneath her breasts as she considered the situation. With an offhanded thought, she strapped Katerine's back with lines of Air. Failure needed always to be punished. Consistency was the key in all forms of training.

The White Tower rumbled above her, though she was safe here. She'd imposed her will on this area, creating a new room beneath the basements, carved as a pocket in the stone. The children who fought above obviously thought themselves practiced in this place, but children they were. *She* had been coming to *Tel'aran'rhiod* for a century before her imprisonment.

The Tower rumbled again. Carefully, she considered her situation. Somehow, the Aes Sedai had found a dreamspike. How had they located such a treasure? Mesaana was nearly as interested in gaining control of it as she was in dominating the child Amyrlin, Egwene al'Vere. The ability to forbid gateways into your places of refuge . . . Well, it was a vital tool, particularly when she decided to move against the other Chosen. It was more effective than wards, protecting one's dreams from any intrusion, and it stopped all forms of Traveling in or out of the area except for those allowed.

However, with the dreamspike in place, she *also* could not move this battle with the children above to a more suitable, carefully selected location. Aggravating. But no, she would not allow herself to become emotional about the situation.

"Return above and concentrate everything on capturing the woman Egwene al'Vere," Mesaana said. "She will know where the device is." Yes, that was clear to her now. She would achieve two victories with a single act.

"Yes . . . Mistress . . ." Katerine was still cowering, straps of Air beating against her back. Ah, yes. Mesaana waved curtly, dispelling the weave. As she did so, a thought occurred to her.

"Wait here, a moment," she said to Katerine. "I'm going to place a weave upon you. . . ."

Perrin appeared on the very top of the White Tower.

Slayer held Hopper by the scruff of his neck. The wolf had an arrow through his side; blood ran down his paw. Wind blew across the rock, catching the blood and spraying it across the stones.

"Hopper!" Perrin took a step forward. He could still sense Hopper's mind, though it was weak.

Slayer held the wolf up, lifting him easily. He raised a knife.

"No," Perrin said. "You have what you want. Just go."

"And what was it you said earlier?" Slayer asked. "That you know where I would go, and you'd follow? The dreamspike is too easy to locate on this side."

He casually tossed the wolf off the side of the Tower.

"NO!" Perrin screamed. He leaped for the side, but Slayer appeared beside him, grabbing him, raising his dagger. The leap knocked them both off the side of the Tower, Perrin's stomach lurching as they fell.

He tried to send himself away, but Slayer had hold of him, and *he* tried very hard to keep them in place. They shook for a moment, but kept falling.

Slayer was so *strong*. He smelled wrong, like staleness and wolf's blood. His knife sought Perrin's throat, and the best Perrin could do was raise his arm to block, thinking of his shirt being as hard as steel.

Slayer pressed harder. Perrin felt a moment of weakness, the wound across his chest throbbing as he and Slayer tumbled. The knife split Perrin's sleeve and rammed into his forearm.

Perrin screamed. The wind was so loud. It had been mere seconds. Slayer pulled the knife free.

Hopper!

Perrin roared and kicked at Slayer, pushing him away, breaking his grip. Arm aflame, Perrin twisted in the air. The ground rushed at them. He *willed* himself to another place, and he appeared just below Hopper, catching the wolf and crashing into the ground. His knees buckled; the ground around him shattered. But he lowered Hopper safely.

A black-fletched arrow zipped from the sky and pierced Hopper's back, passing all the way through the wolf and hitting Perrin in his thigh, which was bent at the knee just beneath the wolf.

Perrin yelled, feeling his own pain mix with a sudden wash of agony from Hopper. The wolf's mind was fading.

"No!" Perrin sent, eyes wet with tears.

Young Bull . . . Hopper sent.

Perrin tried to send himself away, but his mind was fuzzy. Another arrow would soon fall. He knew it. He managed to roll out of the way as it struck the ground, but his leg no longer worked, and Hopper was so heavy. Perrin pitched to the ground, dropping the wolf, rolling.

Slayer landed a short distance away, long, wicked black bow in hand. "Goodbye, Aybara." Slayer raised his bow. "Looks like I kill *five* wolves today."

Perrin stared up at the arrow. Everything was blurry.

I can't leave Faile. I can't leave Hopper.

I won't*!*

As Slayer released, Perrin desperately imagined himself strong, not faint. He felt his heart become hale again, his veins filling with energy. He yelled, head clearing enough to make himself vanish and appear standing behind Slayer.

He swung his hammer.

Slayer turned casually and blocked it with his arm, which was enormously strong. Perrin fell to one knee, the pain in his leg still there. He gasped.

"You can't heal yourself," Slayer said. "There are ways, but simply imagining yourself well does not work. You do seem to have figured out how to replenish your blood, however, which is useful."

Perrin smelled something. Terror. Was it his own?

No. No, *there*. Behind Slayer was a doorway open into the White Tower. Inside was blackness. Not just shadow, *blackness*. Perrin had done enough practice with Hopper to recognize what it was.

A nightmare.

As Slayer opened his mouth to say something, Perrin growled and threw all of his weight forward, ramming into Slayer. His leg screamed in pain.

They tumbled directly into the blackness of the nightmare.

CHAPTER 38

Wounds

S purts of fire flashed through the dark hallways of the White Tower, leaving trails of smoke that curled in the air, thick and pungent. People screamed and yelled and cursed. The walls shook as blasts took them; chips and chunks of rock sprayed off weaves of Air crafted for protection.

There. Egwene noted a place where several Black sisters were lobbing fire down the hallway. Evanellein was there.

Egwene sent herself into the room next to the one where they were standing; she could hear them on the other side of the wall. She opened her hands and released a powerful blast of Earth and Fire directly at the wall, blowing it outward.

The women beyond stumbled and fell, Evanellein collapsing, bloodied. The other woman was quick enough to send herself away.

Egwene checked to see that Evanellein was dead. She was. Egwene nodded with satisfaction; Evanellein was one of those that she'd been most eager to find. Now if she could only track down Katerine or Alviarin.

Channeling. Behind her. Egwene threw herself to the ground as a blast of Fire sprayed over her head. Mesaana, black cloth swirling about her. Egwene gritted her teeth and sent herself away. She didn't dare face the woman directly.

Egwene appeared in a storage room not far away, then stumbled as a blast shook the area. She waved a hand, making a window in the door, and saw Amys charging past. The Wise One wore *cadin'sor* and carried spears. Her shoulder was bleeding and blackened. Another blast hit near her, but she vanished. That blast made the air outside swelter, melting Egwene's window and forcing her to step back.

Saerin's research had been correct. Despite the open battle, Mesaana had not fled or hidden, as Moghedien might have. Perhaps she was confident. Perhaps she was frightened; likely, she needed Egwene's death to prove a victory before the Dark One.

Egwene took a deep breath and prepared to return to the fighting. She hesitated, however, thinking of Perrin's appearance. He'd acted as if she were a novice. How had he grown so confident, so strong? She hadn't been surprised by the things he'd done so much as by the fact that *he* had been the one doing them.

His appearance was a lesson. Egwene had to be very careful not to rely on her weaves. Bair couldn't channel, but she was as effective as the others. However, it did seem that for some things, weaves were better. Blowing the wall outward, for instance, had seemed easier with a weave than by imagining it, where imposing her will against so large and thick a surface might have been difficult.

She was Aes Sedai and she was a Dreamer. She had to use both. Egwene cautiously sent herself back to the room where she'd seen Mesaana. It was empty, though the wall was still rubble. Blasts sounded from the right, and Egwene peeked around. Balls of fire shot back and forth in that direction, weaves flying in the air.

Egwene sent herself behind one of the fighting groups and created a thick cylinder of glass around her for protection. The Tower was broken and scarred here, the walls smoldering. Egwene caught sight of one figure stooping beside a section of rubble, wearing a blue dress.

Nicola? Egwene thought with anger. *How did she get here? I thought I could trust her now!* The fool girl must have gotten a dream *ter'angreal* from one of the others who had awakened.

Egwene prepared to jump over and send the girl away, but the ground suddenly ripped up beneath Nicola, fire blazing. Nicola screamed as she was tossed into the air, bits of molten rock spraying around her.

Egwene yelled, sending herself there, imagining a strong

wall of stone beneath Nicola. The girl fell and landed on it, bloodied, eyes unseeing. Egwene cursed, kneeling. The girl wasn't breathing.

"No!" Egwene said.

"Egwene al'Vere! Beware!" Melaine's voice.

Egwene turned with alarm as a wall appeared beside her, made of thick granite, blocking several blasts of fire that had come from behind. Melaine appeared next to Egwene, dressed in all black, her very skin colored dark. She'd been hiding in the shadows beside the hallway.

"This place grows too dangerous for you," Melaine said. "Leave it to us."

Egwene looked down. Nicola's corpse faded away. *Foolish child!* She peeked around the wall to see two Black sisters—Alviarin and Ramola—standing back-to-back and sending destructive weaves in different directions. There was a room behind them. Egwene could do as she had several times before, jumping into the room, destroying the wall and hitting the two of them . . .

Foolish child, Bair had said, *your pattern is obvious.*

That was what Mesaana wanted her to do. The two Black sisters were bait.

Egwene jumped into the room, but put her back to the wall. She emptied her mind, waiting, tense.

Mesaana appeared as she had before. That swirling black cloth was impressive, but it was also foolish. It took thought to maintain. Egwene stared into the woman's surprised eyes and saw the weaves the woman had prepared.

Those will not hit me, Egwene thought, confident. The White Tower was hers. Mesaana and her minions had invaded, killing Nicola, Shevan and Carlinya.

Weaves shot forward, but they bent around Egwene. In a moment Egwene was wearing the clothing of a Wise One. White blouse, brown skirt, shawl on her shoulders. She imagined a spear in her hand, an Aiel spear, and she threw it with a precise motion.

The spear pierced the weaves of Fire and Air, blasting them away, then hit something thick. A wall of Air before Mesaana. Egwene refused to allow it. That wall didn't belong here. It did *not* exist.

The spear stopped slowing and shot forward, taking Mesaana in the neck. The woman's eyes opened wide and she slumped backward, blood spurting from the wound. The black strips swirling around her vanished completely, as did the dress. So it had been a weave. Mesaana's darkened face turned into that of . . .

Katerine? Egwene frowned. Mesaana had been Katerine all along? But she'd been Black, and fled the Tower. She hadn't remained, and that meant—

No, Egwene thought, *I've been had. She's a—*

At that moment, Egwene felt something snap around her neck. Something cold and metallic, something familiar and terrifying. The Source fled her in a moment, for she was no longer authorized to hold it.

She spun in terror. A woman with chin-length dark hair and deep blue eyes stood beside her. She did not look very imposing, but she was very strong in the Power. And her wrist held a bracelet, connected by a leash to the band around Egwene's neck.

An *a'dam.*

"Excellent," Mesaana said. "Such unruly children you are." She clicked her tongue in disapproval. In a moment, she *shifted* somewhere else, taking Egwene with her. A chamber with no windows, looking as if it were cut directly from stone. There wasn't even a doorway.

Alviarin waited here, wearing a dress of white and red. The woman immediately knelt before Mesaana, though she spared a satisfied glance for Egwene.

Egwene barely noticed. She stood, stiff, a tide of panicked thoughts flooding her mind. She was trapped again! She could not stand it. She would *die* before she allowed this to happen. Images flashed in her head. Trapped in a room, unable to move more than a few feet without being overcome by the *a'dam.* Treated like an animal, a creeping sense that she would eventually break, would eventually become exactly what they wanted her to be.

Oh, Light. She could not suffer this again. *Not this.*

"Tell those above to withdraw," Mesaana was saying to Alviarin, her voice calm. Egwene barely registered the words. "Fools they are, and their showing here was pathetic. Punishments will be administered."

This was how Moghedien had been captured by Nynaeve and Elayne. She was kept captive, forced to do as they demanded. Egwene would suffer the same! Indeed, Mesaana would probably use Compulsion on her. The White Tower would be fully in the hands of the Forsaken.

The emotions welled up. Egwene found herself clawing at the collar, which got a look of amusement from Mesaana as Alviarin vanished to relay her order.

This could not be happening. It was a nightmare. A—

You are Aes Sedai. A quiet piece of her whispered the words, yet for all their softness, they were strong. And they were deep within her. The voice was deeper than the terror and fear.

"Now," Mesaana said. "We will speak of the dreamspike. Where might I find it?"

An Aes Sedai is calmness, an Aes Sedai is control, regardless of the situation. Egwene lowered her hands from the collar. She had not gone through the testing, and she had not planned to. But if she had, what if she had been forced to face a situation like this? Would she have broken? Proven herself unworthy of the mantle she claimed to carry?

"Not speaking, I see," Mesaana said. "Well, that can be changed. These *a'dam.* Such lovely devices. Semirhage was so delightfully wonderful in bringing them to my attention, even if she did so accidentally. Pity she died before I could place one on her neck."

Pain shot through Egwene's body, like fire beneath her skin. Her eyes watered from it.

But she had suffered pain before, and laughed while being beaten. She had been captive before, in the White Tower itself, and captivity had not stopped her.

But this is different! The larger part of her was terrified. *This is the* a'dam*! I cannot withstand it!*

An Aes Sedai must, the quiet piece of her replied. *An Aes Sedai can suffer all things, for only then can she be truly a servant of all.*

"Now," Mesaana said. "Tell me where you have hidden the device."

Egwene controlled her fear. It was not easy. Light, but it was hard! But she did it. Her face became calm. She defied the *a'dam* by not giving it power over her.

Mesaana hesitated, frowning. She shook the leash, and more pain flooded Egwene.

She made it vanish. "It occurs to me, Mesaana," Egwene

said calmly, "that Moghedien made a mistake. She accepted the *a'dam*."

"What are you—"

"In this place, an *a'dam* is as meaningless as the weaves it prevents," Egwene said. "It is only a piece of metal. And it only will stop you if you accept that it will." The *a'dam* unlocked and fell free of her neck.

Mesaana glanced at it as it dropped to the ground with a metallic ring. Her face grew still, then cold as she looked up at Egwene. Impressively, she did not panic. She folded her arms, eyes impassive. "So, you have practiced here."

Egwene met her gaze.

"You are still a child," Mesaana said. "You think that you can best me? I have walked in *Tel'aran'rhiod* longer than you can imagine. You are what, twenty years old?"

"I am the Amyrlin," Egwene said.

"An Amyrlin to children."

"An Amyrlin to a Tower that has stood for thousands of years," Egwene said. "Thousands of years of trouble and chaos. Yet most of your life, you lived in a time of peace, not strife. Curious, that you should think yourself so strong when much of your life was so easy."

"Easy?" Mesaana said. "You know nothing."

Neither broke her gaze. Egwene felt something press against her, as it had before. Mesaana's will, demanding her subservience, her supplication. An attempt to use *Tel'aran'rhiod* to change the very way that Egwene thought.

Mesaana *was* strong. But strength in this place was a matter of perspective. Mesaana's will pressed against her. But Egwene had defeated the *a'dam*. She could resist this.

"You *will* bend," Mesaana said quietly.

"You are mistaken," Egwene replied, voice tense. "This is not about *me*. Egwene al'Vere is a child. But the Amyrlin is not. I may be young, but the Seat is ancient."

Neither woman looked away. Egwene began to push back, to *demand* that Mesaana bow before her, before the Amyrlin. The air began to feel heavy around them, and when Egwene breathed it in, it seemed *thick* somehow.

"Age is irrelevant," Egwene said. "To an extent, even experience is irrelevant. This place is about what a person is. The Amyrlin is the White Tower, and the White Tower will not bend. It defies you, Mesaana, and your lies."

Two women. Gazes matched. Egwene stopped breathing. She did not need to breathe. All was focused on Mesaana. Sweat trickled down Egwene's temples, every muscle in her body tense as she pushed back against Mesaana's will.

And Egwene knew that this woman, this creature, was an insignificant insect shoving against an enormous mountain. That mountain would not move. Indeed, shove against it too hard, and . . .

Something snapped, softly, in the room.

Egwene breathed in with a gasp as the air returned to normal. Mesaana dropped like a doll made of strips of cloth. She hit the ground with her eyes still open, and a little bit of spittle dribbled from the corner of her mouth.

Egwene sat down, dazed, breathing in and out in gasps. She looked to the side, where the *a'dam* lay discarded. It vanished. Then she looked back at Mesaana, who lay in a heap. Her chest was still rising and lowering, but she stared with sightless eyes.

Egwene lay for a long moment recovering before standing and embracing the Source. She wove lines of Air to lift the unresponsive Forsaken, then *shifted* both herself and the woman back to the upper floors of the Tower.

Women turned toward her with a start. The hallway here was strewn with rubble, but everyone Egwene saw was one of hers. The Wise Ones, spinning on her. Nynaeve picking through some rubble. Siuan and Leane, the latter bearing several blackened cuts on her face, but looking strong.

"Mother," Siuan said with relief. "We had feared . . ."

"Who is that?" Melaine asked, walking up to Mesaana, hanging limply in the weaves of Air and staring at the ground. The woman cooed suddenly, like a child, eyes watching a bit of burning fire on the remnants of a tapestry.

"It is her," Egwene said, tired. "Mesaana."

Melaine turned to Egwene, eyes wide with surprise.

"Light!" Leane exclaimed. "What have you done?"

"I have seen this before," Bair said, inspecting the woman. "Sammana, a Wise One Dreamer from my youth. She encountered something in the dream that broke her mind." She hesitated. "She spent the rest of her days in the waking world drooling, and needing her linen changed. She never spoke again, at least nothing more than the words of a babe who can barely walk."

"Perhaps it is time to stop thinking of you as an apprentice, Egwene al'Vere," Amys said.

Nynaeve stood with hands on hips, looking impressed but still clinging to the Source. Her braid was full length again in the dream. "The others have gone," she said.

"Mesaana ordered them to flee," Egwene said.

"They couldn't have gone far," Siuan said. "That dome is still there."

"Yes," Bair said. "But it is time for this battle to end. The enemy has been defeated. We will speak again, Egwene al'Vere."

Egwene nodded. "I agree on both points. Bair, Amys, Melaine, thank you for your much-needed aid. You have gained much *ji* in this, and I am in your debt."

Melaine eyed the Forsaken as Egwene sent herself out of the dream. "I believe it is us, and the world itself, who are in your debt, Egwene al'Vere."

The others nodded, and as Egwene faded from *Tel'aran'rhiod*, she heard Bair muttering, "Such a *shame* she didn't return to us."

Perrin ran through crowds of terrified people, in a burning city. Tar Valon. Aflame! The very stones burned, the sky a deep red. The ground trembled, like a wounded buck kicking as a leopard bled its neck. Perrin stumbled as a chasm opened before him, flames blazing upward, singeing the hairs on his arms.

People screamed as some fell into the terrible rift, burning away into nothing. Bodies suddenly littered the ground. To his right, a beautiful building with arched windows began to melt, the rock turning liquid, lava bleeding from between stones and out of openings.

Perrin climbed to his feet. *It's not real.*

"Tarmon Gai'don!" people yelled. "The Last Battle has come! It ends! Light, it ends!"

Perrin stumbled, pulling himself up against a chunk of rock, trying to stand. His arm hurt, and his fingers wouldn't grip, but the worst wound was in his leg, where the arrow had hit. His trousers and coat were wet with blood, and the scent of his own terror was powerful in his nose.

He knew this nightmare was not real. And yet, how could

one not feel the horror of it? To the west, Dragonmount was erupting, plumes of angry smoke billowing into the sky. The entire mountain seemed aflame, rivers of red surging down its sides. Perrin could feel it shaking, dying. Buildings cracked, trembled, melted, shattered. People died, crushed by stones or burned to death.

No. He would not be drawn in. The ground around him changed from broken cobbles to neat tiles; the servants' entrance to the White Tower. Perrin forced himself to his feet, creating a staff to use in limping.

He didn't destroy the nightmare; he had to find Slayer. In this terrible place, Perrin might be able to gain an advantage. Slayer was very practiced in *Tel'aran'rhiod*, but perhaps—if Perrin had luck on his side—the man was skilled enough to have avoided nightmares in the past. Perhaps he would be startled by this one, taken in.

Reluctantly, Perrin weakened his resolve, letting himself be drawn into the nightmare. Slayer would be close. Perrin stumbled across the street, staying far from the building with the lava boiling from its windows. It was hard to keep himself from giving in to the screams of horror and pain. The calls for help.

There, Perrin thought, reaching an alley. Slayer stood inside, head bowed, a hand up against one wall. The ground beside the man ended in a rift, boiling magma at the bottom. People clung to the edge of the gap, screaming. Slayer ignored them. Where his hand touched the wall, it started to change from whitewashed brick to the gray stone of the White Tower's interior.

The *ter'angreal* still hung at Slayer's waist. Perrin had to move quickly.

The wall is melting from the heat, Perrin thought, focusing on the wall beside Slayer. It was easier, here, to change things like that—it was playing into the world the nightmare created.

Slayer cursed, pulling his hand back as the wall grew red-hot. The ground beneath him rumbled, and his eyes opened wide in alarm. He spun as a rift opened beside him, projected there by Perrin. In that moment, Perrin saw that Slayer believed—for just a fraction of a second—that the nightmare was real. Slayer stepped away from the rift, raising a hand against its heat, believing it real.

Slayer vanished in the blink of an eye, appearing beside those hanging above the rift. The nightmare incorporated him, sucking him into its whims, making him play a role in its terrors. It nearly took Perrin, too. He felt himself waver, nearly responding to the heat. But no. Hopper was dying. He would not fail!

Perrin imagined himself as someone else. Azi al'Thone, one of the Two Rivers men. Perrin put himself in clothing like that he'd seen on the street, a vest and a white shirt, finer trousers than any man would wear while working in Emond's Field. This step was almost too much for him. His heart beat faster, and he stumbled as the ground rumbled. If he let himself be caught up completely in the nightmare, he'd end up like Slayer.

No, Perrin thought, forcing himself to hold to his memory of Faile in his heart. His home. His face might change, the world might shake, but that was still home.

He ran to the edge of the rift, above the heat, acting as if he were just another part of the nightmare. He screamed in terror, reaching down to help those who were falling. Though he reached for someone else, Slayer cursed and grabbed his arm, using it to heave himself upward.

And as he passed, Perrin grabbed the *ter'angreal.* Slayer crawled over him, reaching the relative safety of the alley. Covertly, Perrin made a knife in his other hand.

"Burn me," Slayer growled. "I hate these things." The area around them suddenly changed to tiles.

Perrin stood up, holding a staff to steady himself and trying to appear terrified—it wasn't hard. He began to stumble past Slayer. In that moment, the hard-faced man looked down and saw the *ter'angreal* in Perrin's fingers.

His eyes opened wide. Perrin rammed his hand forward, plunging the knife into Slayer's stomach. The man screamed, lurching backward, hand to his belly. Blood soaked his fingers.

Slayer clenched his teeth. The nightmare bent around him. It would burst soon. Slayer righted himself, lowering his bloodied hand, eyes alight with anger.

Perrin felt unsteady on his feet, even with the staff. He'd been wounded so badly. The ground trembled. A rift opened in the ground next to him, steaming with heat and lava, like . . .

Perrin started. *Like Dragonmount.* He looked down at the *ter'angreal* in his fingers. *The fear-dreams of people are strong.* Hopper's voice whispered in Perrin's mind. *So very strong. . . .*

As Slayer advanced on him, Perrin gritted his teeth and hurled the *ter'angreal* into the river of lava.

"No!" Slayer screamed, reality returning around him. The nightmare burst, its last vestiges vanishing. Perrin was left kneeling on the cold tiled floor of a small hallway.

A short distance to his right, a melted lump of metal lay on the ground. Perrin smiled.

Like Slayer, the *ter'angreal* was here from the real world. And like a person, it could be broken and destroyed here. Above them, the violet dome had vanished.

Slayer growled, then stepped forward and kicked Perrin in the stomach. His chest wound flared. Another kick followed. Perrin was growing dizzy.

Go, Young Bull, Hopper sent, his voice so weak. *Flee.*

I can't leave you!

And yet . . . I must leave you.

No!

You have found your answer. Seek Boundless. He will . . . explain . . . that answer.

Perrin blinked through tears as another kick landed. He screamed, raggedly, as Hopper's sending—so comforting, so familiar—faded from his mind.

Gone.

Perrin screamed in anguish. Voice ragged, eyes stained with tears, Perrin willed himself out of the wolf dream and away. Fleeing like an utter coward.

Egwene awoke with a sigh. Eyes still closed, she breathed in. The battle with Mesaana had left her mind feeling strained—indeed, she had a splitting headache. She had quite nearly been defeated there. Her plans had worked, but the weight of what had happened left her feeling contemplative, even a little overwhelmed.

Still, it had been a great victory. She would have to do a search of the White Tower and find the woman who, when awakened, now had the mind of a child. She knew, somehow, that this was not something Mesaana would recover from. She'd known it even before Bair had spoken her words.

Egwene opened her eyes to a comfortably dark room, making plans to gather the Hall and explain why Shevan and Carlinya would never awaken. She spared a moment to mourn for them as she sat up. She'd explained to them the dangers, but still she felt as if she'd failed them. And Nicola, always trying to go faster than she should. She shouldn't have been there. It—

Egwene hesitated. What was that smell? Hadn't she left a lamp burning? It must have gone out. Egwene embraced the Source and wove a ball of light to hang above her hand. She was stunned by the scene it revealed.

The translucent curtains of her bed had been sprayed red with blood, and five bodies littered the floor. Three were in black. One was an unfamiliar young man in the tabard of the Tower Guard. The last wore a fine white and red coat and trousers.

Gawyn!

Egwene threw herself from the bed and knelt beside him, ignoring the pain of her headache. He was breathing shallowly, and had a gaping wound in his side. She wove Water, Spirit and Air into a Healing, but she was far from talented in this area. She worked on, in a panic. Some of his color returned and the wounds began to close, but she couldn't do nearly enough.

"Help!" she yelled. "The Amyrlin needs help!"

Gawyn stirred. "Egwene," he whispered, his eyes fluttering open.

"Hush, Gawyn. You're going to be fine. Aid! To the Amyrlin!"

"You . . . didn't leave enough lights on," he whispered.

"What?"

"The message I sent. . . ."

"We never got a message," she said. "Be still. Help!"

"Nobody is near. I yelled. The lamps . . . it is good . . . you didn't . . ." He smiled dazedly. "I love you."

"Lie still," she said. Light! She was crying.

"The assassins *weren't* your Forsaken, though," he said, words slurring. "I was right."

And he had been; what were those unfamiliar black uniforms? Seanchan?

I should be dead, she realized. If Gawyn hadn't stopped these assassins, she'd have been murdered in her sleep and would have vanished from *Tel'aran'rhiod.* She'd never have defeated Mesaana.

Suddenly, she felt a fool, any sense of victory completely evaporating.

"I'm sorry," Gawyn said closing his eyes, "for disobeying you." He was slipping.

"It's all right, Gawyn," she said, blinking away tears. "I'm going to bond you now. It's the only way."

His grip on her arm became slightly more firm. "No. Not unless . . . you want . . ."

"Fool," she said, preparing the weaves. "Of course I want you as my Warder. I always have."

"Swear it."

"I swear it. I swear that I want you as my Warder, and as my husband." She rested her hand on his forehead and laid the weave on him. "I love you."

He gasped. Suddenly, she could feel his emotions, and his pain, as if they were her own. And, in return, she knew that he could feel the truth of her words.

Perrin opened his eyes and took a deep breath. He was crying. Did people cry in their sleep when they dreamed normal dreams?

"Light be praised," Faile said. He opened his eyes and found that she knelt next to him, as did someone else. Masuri?

The Aes Sedai grabbed Perrin's head in her hands, and Perrin felt the icy cold of a Healing wash across him. The wounds in his leg and across his chest closed.

"We tried to Heal you while you slept," Faile said, cradling Perrin's head in her lap. "But Edarra stopped us."

"It is not to be done. Wouldn't work anyway." That was the Wise One's voice. Perrin could hear her in the tent somewhere. He blinked his eyes. He lay on his pallet. It was dim outside.

"It's been longer than an hour," he said. "You should have left by now."

"Hush," Faile said. "Gateways are working again, and almost everyone is through. Only a few thousand soldiers remain—Aiel and Two Rivers men, mostly. You think they'd leave, you think *I'd* leave, without you?"

He sat up, wiping his brow. It was damp with sweat. He tried to make it vanish, as he had in the wolf dream. He failed, of course. Edarra stood by the far wall, behind him. She watched him with a measuring gaze.

He turned to Faile. "We have to get away," he said, voice ragged. "Slayer will not be working alone. There will be a trap, probably an army. Someone with an army. They might try to strike at any moment."

"Can you stand?" Faile asked.

"Yes." He felt weak, but he managed, with Faile's help. The flap rustled and Chiad entered with a waterskin. Perrin took it gratefully, drinking. It slaked his thirst, but pain still burned inside of him.

Hopper . . . He lowered the waterskin. In the wolf dream, death was final. Where would Hopper's soul go?

I must keep going, Perrin thought. *See my people to safety.* He walked to the tent flaps. His legs were already more steady.

"I see your sorrow, my husband," Faile said, walking beside him, hand on his arm. "What happened?"

"I lost a friend," Perrin said softly. "For the second time."

"Hopper?" She smelled fearful.

"Yes."

"Oh, Perrin, I'm sorry." Her voice was tender as they stepped out of the tent. It stood, alone, on the meadow that had once held his forces. The brown and yellow grass still bore the impressions of tents, paths worn down to the mud in a large crisscross pattern. It looked like a layout for a town, sections stamped down for buildings, lines cut to become roadways. But it was nearly empty of people now.

The rumbling sky was dark. Chiad held a lantern up to illuminate the grass in front of them. Several groups of soldiers waited. Maidens raised their spears high when they saw him, then banged them on their shields. A sign of approval.

The Two Rivers men were there as well, gathering around as word spread. How much could they guess of what he'd done tonight? Two Rivers men cheered, and Perrin nodded to them, though he felt on edge. The wrongness was still there, in the air. He'd assumed that the dreamspike was causing it, but he had apparently been wrong. The air smelled like the Blight.

The Asha'man stood where the center of the camp had once stood. They turned when Perrin approached, saluting, hands to chests. They looked to be in good shape, despite just having moved almost the entire camp.

"Get us out of here, men," Perrin said to them. "I don't want to spend another minute in this place."

"Yes, my Lord," Grady said, sounding eager. He got a look of concentration on his face, and a small gateway opened beside him.

"Through," Perrin said, waving to the Two Rivers men. They crossed with a quick step. The Maidens and Gaul waited with Perrin, as did Elyas.

Light, Perrin thought, scanning the field where they'd camped. *I feel like a mouse being eyed by a hawk.*

"I don't suppose you could give us some light," Perrin said to Neald, standing beside the gateway.

The Asha'man cocked his head, and a group of glowing globes appeared around him. They zipped up into the air around the meadow.

They illuminated nothing. Just the abandoned campsite. The last of the troops finally filed through. Perrin and Faile crossed, Gaul, Elyas and the Maidens going after him. Finally, the channelers passed through, walking in a cluster.

The air on the other side of the gateway was cool, and smelled refreshingly clean. Perrin hadn't realized how much the evil smell had been bothering him. He inhaled deeply. They were on a rise, some distance from a splash of lights beside the river that was probably Whitebridge.

His troops cheered as he stepped through. The great camp was already mostly set up, guard posts in place. The gateway had been opened into a large area, marked off with posts, near the back.

They'd escaped. The cost had been great, but they'd escaped.

Graendal sat back in her chair. The leather cushions were stuffed with the down of the fledgling kallir, which during this Age lived only in Shara. She barely noticed the luxury.

The servant—one Moridin had loaned her—was on one

knee before her. His eyes were tempestuous, and only half-lowered. This one was under control, but barely. He knew he was unique.

He also seemed to know that his failure would fall upon her shoulders. Graendal did *not* sweat. She was too controlled for that. The shutters on the window in the wide, red-tiled room burst open suddenly, a cold sea wind blowing through the chamber and putting out several of the lamps. Tendrils of smoke wove up from their wicks.

She would *not* fail.

"Prepare to spring the trap anyway," she commanded.

"But—" the servant said.

"Do it, and do *not* speak back to one of the Chosen, dog."

The servant lowered his eyes, though there was still a rebellious spark to them.

Never mind. She still had one tool left to her, one she had positioned so very carefully. One she had prepared for a moment such as this.

It had to be done carefully. Aybara was *ta'veren*, and so strongly one as to be frightening. Arrows fired from afar would miss, and in a time of peaceful contemplation, he would be alerted and escape.

She needed a tempest with him at the center of it. And then, the blade would fall. *This is not done yet, Fallen Blacksmith. Not by an inch or by a league.*

CHAPTER
39

In the Three-fold Land

A viendha felt right again.

There was a calming perfection to the Three-fold Land. Wetlanders thought the landscape's uniform colors drab, but Aviendha found them beautiful. Simple browns and tans. They were familiar and dependable, not like the wetlands, where both the landscape and the weather were different every time you turned around.

Aviendha ran forward in the darkening night, each foot falling on dusty ground. For the first time in many months, she felt alone. In the wetlands, she always felt as if she was being watched by some enemy she could not see or attack.

Not that the Three-fold Land was safer. Far from it. That shadowed patch beneath the *nadra*-scrub was the den of a lethal snake. If one brushed the spindly branches, the snake would strike; she had seen five men die from those bites. The den was merely one of the many hazards she passed during her run to Rhuidean. But those dangers were understandable. She could see them, measure them and avoid them. If she died from the snake's bite or fell to the land's heat, the fault would be her own.

It was *always* preferable to face the enemy or the danger you could see than to fear the one that hid behind the faces of lying wetlanders.

She continued running, despite the dimming light. It was good to sweat again. People didn't sweat enough in the wetlands; perhaps that was what made them so unusual. Instead of letting the sun warm them, they sought refreshment. Instead of going to a proper sweat tent to get clean, they submersed themselves in water. That couldn't be healthy.

She would not lie to herself. Aviendha herself had partaken of those luxuries, and she *had* come to enjoy those baths and the fine dresses Elayne forced upon her. One had to acknowledge one's weaknesses before one could defeat them. Now, as she ran across the gently sloping earth of the Three-fold Land, Aviendha's perspective was restored.

Finally, she slowed. As tempting as it was to travel in the dark and sleep through the day's heat, it was not wise. A misstep in the dark could end your life. She quickly collected some dead *tak*-brush and some *ina'ta* bark, then made herself a camp at the side of a tremendous stone.

Soon she had a fire burning, the orange light reflecting off the rock that towered over her. She'd slain a small shellback earlier, and she unwrapped it, skinned it, then set it up on a spit. Not the most delicate of meals, but satisfactory.

Aviendha settled down, watching the fire crackle, smelling the meat. Yes, she was glad she hadn't Traveled directly to Rhuidean, instead taking the time—precious though that time was—to run in the Three-fold Land. It helped her see what she had been, and what she had become. Aviendha the Maiden was gone. She had embraced her path as a Wise One, and that brought her honor back. She had purpose again. As a Wise One, she could help lead her people through their most trying time.

Once this was through, her people would need to return to the Three-fold Land. Each day in the wetlands made them weaker; she herself was an excellent example. She had grown soft there. How could one *not* grow soft in that place? It would have to be abandoned. Soon.

She smiled, settling back and closing her eyes for a moment, letting the day's fatigue melt away. Her future seemed so much more clear. She was to visit Rhuidean, pass through the crystal columns, then return and claim her share of Rand's heart. She would fight at the Last Battle. She would help preserve the remnant of the Aiel who survived, then bring them home where they belonged.

A sound came from outside her camp.

Aviendha opened her eyes and jumped up, embracing the Source. A piece of her was pleased that she now instinctively looked to the One Power, rather than spears that were not there. She wove a globe of light.

A woman stood in the darkness nearby, wearing Aiel

garb. Not *cadin'sor*, but normal clothing: a dark skirt and a tan blouse and shawl, a kerchief on her graying hair. She was middle-aged, and she carried no weapons. She was still.

Aviendha glanced to the sides. Was this an ambush? Or was this woman a specter? One of the dead walking? Why hadn't Aviendha heard her approach?

"Greetings, Wise One," the woman said, bowing her head. "Might I share water with you? I am traveling far, and saw your fire." The woman had furrowed skin, and she could not channel—Aviendha could sense that easily.

"I am not yet a Wise One," Aviendha said, wary. "I currently take my second path into Rhuidean."

"Then you will soon find much honor," the woman said. "I am Nakomi. I promise that I mean you no harm, child."

Suddenly, Aviendha felt foolish. The woman had approached without weapons drawn. Aviendha had been distracted by her thoughts; that was why she hadn't heard Nakomi approach. "Of course, please."

"Thank you," Nakomi said, stepping into the light and setting down her pack beside the small fire. She clicked her tongue, then drew some small branches out of her pack to build up the flames. She removed a pot for tea. "Might I have some of that water?"

Aviendha got out a waterskin. She could hardly spare a drop—she was still several days from Rhuidean—but it would give offense not to respond to the request after offering to share shade.

Nakomi took the waterskin and filled her teapot, which she then set beside the fire to warm. "It is an unexpected pleasure," Nakomi said, rifling through her pack, "to cross the path of one on her way to Rhuidean. Tell me, was your apprenticeship long?"

"Too long," Aviendha said. "Though primarily because of my own stubbornness."

"Ah," Nakomi said. "You have the air of a warrior about you, child. Tell me, are you from among those who went west? The ones who joined the one named the *Car'a'carn*?"

"He *is* the *Car'a'carn*," Aviendha said.

"I did not say that he was not," Nakomi said, sounding amused. She got out some tea leaves and herbs.

No. She hadn't said so. Aviendha turned her shellback,

and her stomach rumbled. She'd need to share her meal with Nakomi as well.

"May I ask," Nakomi said. "What do you think of the *Car'a'carn*?"

I love him, Aviendha thought immediately. But she couldn't say that. "I think he has much honor. And though he is ignorant of the proper ways, he is learning."

"You have spent time with him, then?"

"Some," Aviendha said. Then, to be more honest, she added, "More than most."

"He is a wetlander," Nakomi said, thoughtful. "And *Car'a'carn*. Tell me, are the wetlands as glorious as so many say? Rivers so wide you cannot see the other side, plants so full of water they burst when squeezed?"

"The wetlands are not glorious," Aviendha said. "They are dangerous. They make us weak."

Nakomi frowned.

Who is this woman? It was not unusual to find Aiel traveling the Three-fold Land; even children learned to protect themselves. But should Nakomi not be traveling with friends, family? She did not wear the clothing of a Wise One, but there was something about her . . .

Nakomi stirred the tea, then repositioned Aviendha's shellback, placing it over the coals to cook it more evenly. From inside her pack, she drew forth several deepearth roots. Aviendha's mother had always cooked those. Nakomi placed them in a small ceramic baking box, then slid this into the coals. Aviendha hadn't realized the fire had grown so warm. Where had all those coals come from?

"You seem troubled," Nakomi said. "Far be it from me to question an apprentice Wise One. But I do see worry in your eyes."

Aviendha stifled a grimace. She would have preferred to be left alone. And yet, she *had* invited this woman to share her water and shade. "I am worried about our people. Dangerous times come."

"The Last Battle," Nakomi said softly. "The thing the wetlanders speak of."

"Yes. I worry about something beyond that. The wetlands, corrupting our people. Making them soft."

"But the wetlands are part of our destiny, are they not? The things the *Car'a'carn* is said to have revealed . . . they link us to the wetlands in curious ways. Assuming what he said was true."

"He would not lie about this," Aviendha said.

A small wake of buzzards cawed and flapped past in the dark night air. Aviendha's people's history—the things Rand al'Thor had revealed—still caused many of the Aiel grief. In Rhuidean, Aviendha would soon see this history for herself: that the Aiel had broken their vows. Aviendha's people had once followed, then abandoned, the Way of the Leaf.

"Interesting thoughts you raise, apprentice," Nakomi said, pouring the tea. "Our land here is called the Threefold Land. Three-fold, for the three things it did to us. It punished us for sin. It tested our courage. It formed an anvil to shape us."

"The Three-fold Land makes us strong. So, by leaving it, we become weak."

"But if we had to come here to be forged into something of strength," Nakomi said, "does that not suggest that the tests we were to face—in the wetlands—were as dangerous as the Three-fold Land itself? So dangerous and difficult that we had to come here to prepare for them?" She shook her head. "Ah, but I should not argue with a Wise One, not even an apprentice. I have *toh.*"

"There is never *toh* for speaking wise words," Aviendha said. "Tell me, Nakomi, where is it you travel? Which sept is your own?"

"I am far from my roof," the woman said, wistful, "yet not far at all. Perhaps *it* is far from *me.* I cannot answer your question, apprentice, for it is not my place to give this truth."

Aviendha frowned. What kind of answer was that?

"It seems to me," Nakomi said, "that by breaking our ancient oaths to do no violence, our people have gained great *toh.*"

"Yes," Aviendha said. What did you do when your entire people had done something so awful? This realization was what had caused so many of the Aiel to be taken by the bleakness. They had thrown down their spears, or refused to remove the white of *gai'shain*, implying that their people had such great *toh*, it could never be met.

But they were wrong. The Aiel *toh* could be met—it had

to be met. That was the purpose of serving the *Car'a'carn*, the representative of the ones to whom the Aiel had originally sworn their oaths.

"We will meet our *toh*," Aviendha said. "By fighting in the Last Battle."

The Aiel would therefore regain their honor. Once you paid *toh*, you forgot it. To remember a fault that had been repaid was arrogant. They would be finished. They could return and no longer feel shame for what had happened in the past. Aviendha nodded to herself.

"And so," Nakomi said, handing over a cup of tea, "the Three-fold Land was our punishment. We came here to grow so that we could meet our *toh*."

"Yes," Aviendha said. It felt clear to her.

"So, once we have fought for the *Car'a'carn*, we will have met that *toh*. And therefore will have no reason to be punished further. If that is the case, why would we return to this land? Would that not be like seeking more punishment, once *toh* is met?"

Aviendha froze. But no, that was silly. She did not want to argue with Nakomi on the point, but the Aiel *belonged* in the Three-fold Land.

"People of the Dragon," Nakomi said, sipping her tea. "That is what we are. Serving the Dragon was the point behind everything we did. Our customs, our raids on each other, our harsh training . . . our very *way of life*."

"Yes," Aviendha said.

"And so," Nakomi said softly, "once Sightblinder is defeated, what is left for us? Perhaps this is why so many refused to follow the *Car'a'carn*. Because they worried at what it meant. Why continue the old ways? How do we find honor in raiding, in killing one another, if we are no longer preparing for such an important task? Why grow harder? For the sake of being hard itself?"

"I . . ."

"I'm sorry," Nakomi said. "I've let myself ramble again. I am prone to it, I fear. Here, let us eat."

Aviendha started. Surely the roots weren't done yet. However, Nakomi pulled them out, and they smelled wonderful. She cut the shellback, fishing a pair of tin plates from her pack. She seasoned the meat and roots, then passed a plate to Aviendha.

She tasted hesitantly. The food was delicious. Wonderful, even. Better than many a feast she'd had in fine palaces back in the wetlands. She stared at the plate, amazed.

"If you'll excuse me," Nakomi said. "I need to see to nature." She smiled, rising, then shuffled off into the darkness.

Aviendha ate quietly, disturbed by what had been said. Was not a wonderful meal like this, cooked over a fire and made from humble ingredients, proof that the luxury of the wetlands wasn't needed?

But what *was* the purpose of the Aiel now? If they did not wait for the *Car'a'carn*, what did they do? Fight, yes. And then? Continue to kill one another on raids? To what end?

She finished her meal, then thought for a long time. Too long. Nakomi did not return. Worried, Aviendha went to search for her, but found no trace of the woman.

Upon returning to the fire, Aviendha saw that Nakomi's pack and plate were gone. She waited up for a time, but the woman did not return.

Eventually, Aviendha went to sleep, feeling troubled.

CHAPTER
40

A Making

Perrin sat alone on a tree stump, eyes closed and face to the dark sky. The camp was situated, the gateway closed, and reports taken. Perrin finally had time to rest.

That was dangerous. Resting let him think. Thinking brought him memories. Memories brought pain.

He could smell the world on the wind. Layers of scents, swirling together. The camp around him: sweaty people, spices for cooking, soaps for cleaning, horse dung, emotions. The hills around them: dried pine needles, mud from a stream, the carcass of a dead animal. The world beyond: hints of dust from the distant road, a stand of lavender that somehow survived in the dying world.

There was no pollen. There were no wolves. Both seemed terrible signs to him.

He felt sick. Physically ill, as if his stomach were filled with muddy swamp water, rotting moss and bits of dead beetles. He wanted to scream. He wanted to find Slayer and kill him, pound fists on the man's face until the blood engulfed it.

Footsteps approached. Faile. "Perrin? Do you want to talk?"

He opened his eyes. He should be crying, screaming. But he felt so cold. Cold and furious. Those two didn't go together for him.

His tent had been set up nearby; its flaps fluttered in the wind. Nearby, Gaul reclined against a leatherleaf sapling. In the distance, one of the farriers worked late. Soft peals in the night.

"I failed, Faile," Perrin whispered.

"You got the *ter'angreal*," she said, kneeling beside him. "You saved the people."

"And still Slayer beat us," he said bitterly. "A pack of five of us together weren't enough to fight him."

Perrin had felt this way when he'd found his family dead, killed by Trollocs. How many was the Shadow going to take from him by the time this was done? Hopper should have been *safe* in the wolf dream.

Foolish cub, foolish cub.

Had there even really been a trap for Perrin's army? Slayer's dreamspike could have been meant for another purpose entirely. Just a coincidence.

There are no coincidences for ta'veren . . .

He needed to find something to do with his anger and his pain. He stood, turning, and was surprised to see how many lights still shone in camp. A group of people waited nearby, far enough away from him that he hadn't made out their scents specifically. Alliandre in a golden gown. Berelain in blue. Both sat on chairs beside a small wooden travel table, set with a lantern. Elyas sat on a rock beside them, sharpening his knife. A dozen of the Two Rivers men—Wil al'Seen, Jon Ayellin and Grayor Frenn among them—huddled around a firepit, glancing at him. Even Arganda and Gallenne were there, speaking softly.

"They should be sleeping," Perrin said.

"They're worried about you," Faile said. She smelled worried as well. "And they're worried you will send them away, now that gateways work again."

"Fools," Perrin whispered. "Fools to follow me. Fools not to hide."

"You'd really have them do that?" Faile said, angry. "Cower someplace while the Last Battle happens? Didn't you say every man would be needed?"

She was right. Every man would be needed. He realized that part of his frustration was that he didn't know what he'd escaped. He'd gotten away, but from what? For what had Hopper died? Not knowing the enemy's plan made Perrin feel blind.

He walked away from the stump, over to where Arganda and Gallenne were talking. "Bring me our map," he said. "Of the Jehannah Road."

Arganda called over Hirshanin and told him where

to find one. Hirshanin ran off, and Perrin began to walk through camp. Toward the sound of metal hitting metal, the farrier working. Perrin seemed drawn to it. The scents of camp swirled around him, the sky rumbling above him.

The others trailed after him. Faile, Berelain and Alliandre, the Two Rivers men, Elyas, Gaul. The group grew, other Two Rivers men joining it. Nobody spoke, and Perrin ignored them, until he came to Aemin working at an anvil, one of the camp's horse-pulled forges set up beside him and burning with a red light.

Hirshanin caught up to Perrin as he arrived, carrying the map. Perrin unrolled it, holding it before him as Aemin stopped his work, smelling curious. "Arganda, Gallenne," Perrin said. "Tell me. If you were going to set up the best ambush for a large group moving along this road toward Lugard, where would you place it?"

"Here," Arganda said without hesitation, pointing to a location several hours from where they'd been camping. "See here? The road turns to follow an old, dried-out streambed. An army passing through there would be totally exposed to an ambush; you'd be able to attack them from the heights here and here."

Gallenne nodded. "Yes. This is marked as an excellent place for a large group to camp. At the base of that hill where the road bends. But if someone's on the heights above with a mind to do you harm, you might not wake up in the morning."

Arganda nodded.

The heights rose flat-topped to the north of the road; the old riverbed had cut a wide, level pathway that was washed out to the south and west. You could fit an army on those heights.

"What are these?" Perrin asked, pointing to some marks south of the road.

"Old ruins," Arganda said. "Nothing of relevance; they've degraded too far to provide cover. They're really just a few moss-covered boulders."

Perrin nodded. Something was coming together for him. "Are Grady and Neald asleep?" he asked.

"No," Berelain said. "They said they wanted to stay awake, just in case. I think your mood gave them a fright."

"Send for them," Perrin said to nobody in particular.

"One of them needs to check on the Whitecloak army. I remember someone telling me they had broken camp." He didn't wait to see if the order was followed. He stepped up to the forge, laying a hand on Aemin's shoulder. "Get some sleep, Aemin. I need something to work on. Horseshoes, is it?"

The man nodded, looking perplexed. Perrin took the man's apron and gloves, and Aemin departed. Perrin got out his own hammer. The hammer he'd been given in Tear, a hammer that had been used to kill, but hadn't been used to create in such a long time.

The hammer could be either a weapon or a tool. Perrin had a choice, just as everyone who followed him had a choice. Hopper had had a choice. The wolf had made that choice, risking more in defense of the Light than any human—save Perrin—would ever understand.

Perrin used the tongs to pull a small length of metal from the coals, then placed it on the anvil. He raised his arm and began to pound.

It had been a long time since he'd found his way to a forge. In fact, the last he could remember doing any substantial work at one was back in Tear, on that peaceful day when he'd left his responsibilities for a short time and worked at that smithy.

You are like a wolf, husband. Faile had told him that, referring to how focused he became. That was a thing of wolves; they could know the past and the future, yet keep their attention on the hunt. Could he do the same? Allow himself to be consumed when needed, yet keep balance in other parts of his life?

The work began to absorb him. The rhythmic beating of hammer on metal. He flattened the length of iron, occasionally returning it to the coals and getting out another one, working on several shoes at once. He had the measurements nearby for the sizes of what was needed. He slowly bent the metal against the side of the anvil, shaping it. His arms began to sweat, his face warmed by the fire and the work.

Neald and Grady arrived, along with the Wise Ones and Masuri. As Perrin worked, he noticed them sending Sulin through a gateway to check on the Whitecloaks. She returned a short time later, but delayed her report, since Perrin was busy with his work.

Perrin held up a horseshoe, then frowned. This wasn't difficult enough work. It was soothing, yes, but today he wanted something more challenging. He felt a *need* to create, as if to balance the destruction he'd seen in the world, the destruction he'd helped create. There were several lengths of unworked steel stacked beside the forge, finer material than what was used for shoes. They were probably waiting to be turned into swords for the former refugees.

Perrin took several of those lengths of steel and set them into coals. This forge wasn't as nice as what he was accustomed to; though he had a bellows and three barrels for quenching, the wind cooled the metal, and the coals didn't get as hot as he'd like. He watched with dissatisfaction.

"I can help you with that, Lord Perrin," Neald said from the side. "Heat the metal up, if you want."

Perrin eyed him, then nodded. He plucked out a length of steel, holding it up with his tongs. "I want it a nice yellow-red. Not so hot it goes white, mind you."

Neald nodded. Perrin set the bar on the anvil, took out his hammer, and began to pound again. Neald stood at the side, concentrating.

Perrin lost himself in the work. Forge the steel. All else faded. The rhythmic pounding of hammer on metal, like the beating of his heart. That shimmering metal, warm and dangerous. In that focus, he found clarity. The world was cracking, breaking further each day. It needed help, right now. Once a thing shattered, you couldn't put it back together.

"Neald," Grady's voice said. It was urgent, but distant to Perrin. "Neald, what are you doing?"

"I don't know," Neald replied. "It feels right."

Perrin continued to pound, harder and harder. He folded the metal, flattening pieces against one another. It was wonderful the way the Asha'man kept it at exactly the right temperature. That freed Perrin from needing to rely on only a few moments of perfect temperature between heatings.

The metal seemed to flow, almost as if shaped by his will alone. What was he making? He took the other two lengths out of the flames, then began to switch between the three. The first—and largest—he folded upon itself, molding it, using a process known as shrinking where he increased its girth. He made it into a large ball, then added more steel to it until it was nearly as large as a man's head. The second he drew, making it long and thin, then folded it into a narrow rod. The final, smallest piece he flattened.

He breathed in and out, his lungs working like bellows. His sweat was like the quenching waters. His arms were like the anvil. He *was* the forge.

"Wise Ones, I need a circle," Neald said urgently. "*Now.* Don't argue! I need it!"

Sparks began to fly as Perrin pounded. Larger showers with each blow. He felt something *leaking* from him, as if each blow infused the metal with his own strength, and also his own feelings. Both worries and hopes. These flowed from him into the three unwrought pieces.

The world *was* dying. He couldn't save it. That was Rand's job. Perrin just wanted to go back to his simple life, didn't he?

No. No, he wanted Faile, he wanted complexity. He wanted *life.* He couldn't hide, any more than the people who followed him could hide.

He didn't want their allegiance. But he had it. How would he feel if someone else took command, and then got them killed?

Blow after blow. Sprays of sparks. Too many, as if he were pounding against a bucket of molten liquid. Sparks splashed in the air, exploding from his hammer, flying as high as treetops and spreading tens of paces. The people watching withdrew, all save the Asha'man and Wise Ones, who stood gathered around Neald.

I don't want to lead them, Perrin thought. *But if I don't, who will? If I abandon them, and they fall, then it will be my fault.*

Perrin saw now what he was making, what he'd been trying to make all along. He worked the largest lump into a brick shape. The long piece became a rod, thick as three fingers. The flat piece became a capping bracket, a piece of metal to wrap around the head and join it to the shaft.

A hammer. He was making a hammer. These were the parts.

He understood now.

He grew to his task. Blow after blow. Those beats were so loud. Each blow seemed to *shake* the ground around

him, rattling tents. Perrin exulted. He knew what he was
making. He *finally* knew what he was making.

He hadn't asked to become a leader, but did that ab-
solve him of responsibility? People needed him. The world
needed him. And, with an understanding that cooled in him
like molten rock forming into a shape, he realized that he
wanted to lead.

If someone had to be lord of these people, he wanted to
do it himself. Because doing it yourself was the only way to
see that it was done right.

He used his chisel and rod, shaping a hole through the
center of the hammer's head, then grabbed the haft and—
raising it far over his head—slammed it down into place.
He took the bracket and laid the hammer on it, then shaped
it. Mere moments ago, this process had fed off his anger.
But now it seemed to draw forth his resolution, his determination.

Metal was something alive. Every blacksmith knew this.
Once you heated it, while you worked it, it *lived*. He took
his hammer and chisel and began to shape patterns, ridges,
modifications. Waves of sparks flew from him, the ringing
of his hammer ever stronger, ever louder, pealing like bells.
He used his chisel on a small chunk of steel to form a shape,
then placed it down on top of the hammer.

With a roar, he raised his old hammer one last time over
his head and beat it down on the new one, imprinting the ornamentation upon the side of the hammer. A leaping wolf.

Perrin lowered his tools. On the anvil—still glowing
with an inner heat—was a beautiful hammer. A work beyond anything he'd ever created, or thought that he might
create. It had a thick, powerful head, like a maul or sledge,
but the back was formed cross-face and flattened. Like a
blacksmith's tool. It was four feet from bottom to top,
maybe longer, an enormous size for a hammer of this type.

The haft was all of steel, something he'd never seen on
a hammer before. Perrin picked it up; he was able to lift it
with one hand, but barely. It was heavy. Solid.

The ornamentation was of a crosshatch pattern with the
leaping wolf stamped on one side. It looked like Hopper.
Perrin touched it with a callused thumb, and the metal quieted. It still felt warm to the touch, but did not burn him.

He turned to look, and was amazed at the size of the

crowd watching him. The Two Rivers men stood at the front, Jori Congar, Azi al'Thone, Wil al'Seen and hundreds more. Ghealdanin, Cairhienin, Andorans, Mayeners. Watching, quiet. The ground around Perrin was blackened from the falling sparks; drops of silvery metal spread out from him like a sunburst.

Neald fell to his knees, panting, his face coated with sweat. Grady and the women of the circle sat down, looking exhausted. All six Wise Ones had joined in. What had they done?

Perrin felt exhausted, as if all of his strength and emotion had been forged into the metal. But he could not rest. "Wil. Weeks ago, I gave you an order. Burn the banners that bore the wolfhead. Did you obey? Did you burn every one?"

Wil al'Seen met his eyes, then looked down, ashamed. "Lord Perrin, I tried. But . . . Light, I couldn't do it. I kept one. The one I'd helped sew."

"Fetch it, Wil," Perrin said. His own voice sounded like steel.

Wil ran, smelling frightened. He returned shortly, bearing a folded cloth, white with a red border. Perrin took it, then held it in a reverent hand, hammer in the other. He looked at the crowd. Faile was there, hands clasped before her. She smelled hopeful. She could see into him. She knew.

"I have tried to send you away," Perrin announced to the crowd. "You would not go. I have failings. You must know this. If we march to war, I will not be able to protect you all. I will make mistakes."

He looked across the crowd, meeting the eyes of those who stood there. Each man or woman he looked at nodded silently. No regrets, no hesitations. They nodded.

Perrin took a deep breath. "If you wish this, I *will* accept your oaths. I *will* lead you."

They cheered him. An enormous roar of excitement. "Goldeneyes! Goldeneyes the wolf! To the Last Battle! *Tai'shar Manetheren!*"

"Wil!" Perrin bellowed, holding up the banner. "Raise this banner high. Don't take it down again until the Last Battle has been won. I march beneath the sign of the wolf. The rest of you, rouse the camp. Get every soldier ready to fight. We have another task tonight!"

The young man took the banner and unfurled it, Jori and Azi joining him and holding it so it didn't touch the ground. They raised it high, running to get a pole. The group broke up, men running this way and that, shouting the summons.

Perrin took Faile by the hand as she walked up to him. She smelled satisfied. "That's it, then?"

"No more complaining," he promised. "I don't like it. But I don't like killing, either. I'll do what must be done." He looked down at the anvil, blackened from his work. His old hammer, now worn and dented, lay across it. He felt sad to leave it, but he had made his decision.

"What did you do, Neald?" he asked as the Asha'man— still looking pale—stumbled up to his feet. Perrin raised the new hammer, showing the magnificent work.

"I don't know, my Lord," Neald said. "It just . . . well, it was like I said. It felt right. I saw what to do, how to put the weaves into the metal itself. It seemed to draw them in, like an ocean drinking in the water of a stream." He blushed, as if he thought it a foolish figure of speech.

"That sounds right," Perrin said. "It needs a name, this hammer. Do you know much of the Old Tongue?"

"No, my Lord."

Perrin looked at the wolf imprinted on the side. "Does anyone know how you say 'He who soars'?"

"I . . . I don't . . ."

"*Mah'alleinir*," Berelain said, stepping up from where she'd been watching.

"*Mah'alleinir*," Perrin repeated. "It feels right. Sulin? What of the Whitecloaks?"

"They have made camp, Perrin Aybara," the Maiden replied.

"Show me," he said, gesturing to Arganda's map.

She pointed out the location: a piece of land on the side of a hill, heights running to the north of it, roadway coming in from the northeast, wrapping around the south of the heights—following the ancient riverbed—and then bending southward when it hit the campsite by the hill. From there, the road headed toward Lugard, but the campsite was protected from wind on two sides. It was a perfect campsite, but also a perfect place for an ambush. The one Arganda and Gallenne had pointed out.

He looked at that passageway and campsite, thinking of what had happened the last few weeks. *We met travelers. . . . said that the muds to the north were almost completely impassable with wagons or carts . . .*

A flock of sheep, running before the pack into the jaws of a beast. Faile and the others, walking toward a cliff. Light!

"Grady, Neald," Perrin said. "I'm going to need another gateway. Can you manage?"

"I think so," Neald said. "Just give us a few minutes to catch our breath."

"Very well. Position it here." Perrin pointed to the heights above the Whitecloaks' camp. "Gaul!" As usual, the Aiel man waited nearby. He loped up. "I want you to go speak with Dannil, Arganda, Gallenne. I want the entire army to cross through as quickly as possible, but they are to keep *quiet*. We move with as much stealth as an army this size can manage."

Gaul nodded, running off. Gallenne was still nearby; Gaul started by speaking with him.

Faile watched Perrin, smelling curious and a little anxious. "What are you planning, husband?"

"It's time for me to lead," Perrin said. He looked one last time at his old hammer, and laid fingers on its haft. Then he hefted *Mah'alleinir* to his shoulder and strode away, feet crackling on drops of hardened steel.

The tool he left behind was the hammer of a simple blacksmith. That person would always be part of Perrin, but he could no longer afford to let him lead.

From now on, he would carry the hammer of a king.

Faile ran her fingers across the anvil as Perrin strode away, calling further orders to prepare the army.

Did he realize how he'd looked, standing amid those showers of sparks, each blow of his hammer causing the steel before him to pulse and flare to life? His golden eyes had blazed as brightly as the steel; each peal of the hammer had been nearly deafening.

"It has been many centuries since this land has seen the creation of a Power-wrought weapon," Berelain said. Most others had left to follow Perrin's orders, and the two were alone, save for Gallenne standing nearby and studying the map while rubbing his chin. "It is a strong Talent the young man just displayed. This will be of use. Perrin's army will have Power-wrought blades to strengthen them."

"The process seemed very draining," Faile said. "Even if Neald can repeat what he did, I doubt we will have time to make many weapons."

"Every small advantage helps," Berelain said. "This army your husband has forged, it will be something incredible. *Ta'veren* is at work here. He gathers men, and they learn with amazing speed and skill."

"Perhaps," Faile said, walking around the anvil slowly, keeping her eyes on Berelain, who strolled around it opposite her. What was Berelain's game, here?

"Then we must speak with him," Berelain said. "Turn him from this course of action."

"This course of action?" Faile asked, genuinely confused.

Berelain stopped, her eyes alight with something. She seemed tense. *She's worried,* Faile thought. *Worried deeply about something.*

"Lord Perrin must *not* attack the Whitecloaks," Berelain said. "Please, you must help me persuade him."

"He's not going to attack them," Faile said. She was reasonably certain of that.

"He's setting up a perfect ambush," Berelain said. "Asha'man to use the One Power, Two Rivers bowmen to shoot from the heights down on the camp of the Children. Cavalry to ride down and sweep up after." She hesitated, seeming pained. "He's set them up perfectly. He told them that if he and Damodred both survived the Last Battle, he'd submit to punishment. But Perrin is going to make certain the Whitecloaks don't *reach* the Last Battle. He can keep his oath that way, but also avoid turning himself in."

Faile shook her head. "He'd never do that, Berelain."

"Can you be certain?" Berelain asked. "Absolutely certain?"

Faile hesitated. Perrin had been changing lately. Most of the changes were good ones, such as his decision to finally accept leadership. And the ambush Berelain spoke of *would* make a kind of perfect, ruthless sense.

But it was also wrong. Terribly wrong. Perrin wouldn't do that, no matter how much he'd changed. Of that, Faile could be certain.

"Yes," she said. "Giving a promise to Galad, then slaughtering the Whitecloaks in this way, it would rip Perrin apart. He doesn't think that way. It won't happen."

"I hope that you are right," Berelain said. "I had hoped some sort of accommodation could be reached with their commander before we left . . ."

A Whitecloak. Light! Couldn't she have picked one of the noblemen in camp to give her attentions to? One who *wasn't* married? "You aren't very good at picking men, are you, Berelain?" The words just slipped out.

Berelain turned back to Faile, eyes widening in either shock or anger. "And what of Perrin?"

"A terrible match for you," Faile said with a sniff. "You've shown that tonight, by what you think he is capable of."

"How good a match he was is irrelevant. I was promised him."

"By whom?"

"The Lord Dragon," Berelain said.

"What?"

"I came to the Dragon Reborn in the Stone of Tear," she said. "But he would not have me—he even grew angry with my advances. I realized that he, the Dragon Reborn, intended to marry a much higher lady, probably Elayne Trakand. It makes sense—he cannot take every realm by the sword; some will have to come to him through alliances. Andor is very powerful, is ruled by a woman, and would be advantageous to hold through marriage."

"Perrin says Rand doesn't think like that, Berelain," Faile said. "Not so calculating. It's my inclination, too, from what I know of him."

"And you say the same thing about Perrin. You'd have me believe they're all so simple. Without a wit in their heads."

"I didn't say that."

"And yet you use the same old protests. Tiring. Well, I realized what the Lord Dragon was implying, so I turned my attentions toward one of his close attendants. Perhaps he did not 'promise' them to me. That was a poor choice of words. But I knew he would be pleased if I made a union with one of his close allies and friends. Indeed, I suspect that he wished me to do it—after all, the Lord Dragon *did* place me and Perrin together for this mission. He could not

e frank about what he desired, however, so as to not offend
Perrin."

Faile hesitated. On one hand, what Berelain said was
purely foolish . . . but on the other, she could see what the
woman might have seen. Or, perhaps, what she wished to
see. To her, breaking apart a husband and wife was nothing
immoral. This was politics. And, logically, Rand probably
should have wanted to tie nations to him through bonds of
marriage to those closest to him.

That didn't change the fact that neither he, nor Perrin,
regarded matters of the heart in such a way.

"I have given up on Perrin," Berelain said. "I hold to my
promise there. But it leaves me in a difficult situation. I
have long thought that a connection to the Dragon Reborn
is Mayene's only hope in maintaining independence in the
coming years."

"Marriage isn't only about claiming political advantages," Faile said.

"And yet the advantages are so obvious that they cannot
be ignored."

"And this Whitecloak?" Faile asked.

"Half-brother of the Queen of Andor," Berelain said,
blushing slightly. "If the Lord Dragon does intend to marry
Elayne Trakand, this will give me a link to him."

It was much more than that; Faile could see it in the way
Berelain acted, in the way she looked when she spoke of
Galad Damodred. But if she wanted to rationalize a political motivation for it, Faile had no reason to dissuade her, so
long as it helped distract her from Perrin.

"I have done as you asked," Berelain said. "And so now,
I ask your aid. If it appears that he *is* going to attack them,
please join me in trying to dissuade him. Together, perhaps
we can manage it."

"Very well," Faile said.

Perrin rode at the head of an army that felt unified for the
first time. The flag of Mayene, the flag of Ghealdan, the
banners of noble Houses from among the refugees. Even a
few banners the lads had made up representing the parts of
the Two Rivers. Above them all flapped the wolfhead.

Lord Perrin. He would never get used to that, but maybe that was a good thing.

He trotted Stepper over to the side of the open gateway as the troops marched past, saluting. They were lit by torches for now. Hopefully the channelers would be able to light the battlefield later.

A man came up beside Stepper, and Perrin smelled animal pelts, loam and rabbit's blood. Elyas had gone hunting while he waited for the army to gather. It took quite a keen hunter to catch rabbits at night. Elyas said it was a better challenge.

"You said something to me once, Elyas," Perrin said. "You told me that if I ever grew to like the axe, I should throw it away."

"That I did."

"I think it applies to leadership, too. The men who don't want titles should be the ones who get them, it seems. So long as I keep that in mind, I think I might do all right."

Elyas chuckled. "The banner looks good, hanging up there."

"It fits me. Always has. I just haven't always fit it."

"Deep thoughts, for a blacksmith."

"Perhaps." Perrin pulled the blacksmith's puzzle from his pocket, the one he'd found in Malden. He still hadn't managed to get the thing apart. "Has it ever struck you as odd that blacksmiths seem like such simple folk, yet they're the ones who make all of these blasted puzzles that are so hard to figure out?"

"Never thought of it like that. So you're one of us, finally?"

"No," Perrin said, putting the puzzle away. "I am who I am. Finally." He wasn't certain what had changed within him. But perhaps trying to think it through too much had been the problem in the first place.

He knew that he'd found his balance. He would never become like Noam, the man who had lost himself to the wolf. And that was enough.

Perrin and Elyas waited for a time, watching the army pass. These larger gateways made it much easier to Travel; they'd have all of the fighting men and women through in under an hour. Men raised hands to Perrin, smelling proud. His connection to the wolves did not frighten them; in fact, they actually seemed less worried now that they knew the specifics of it. Before, there had been speculation. Questions. Now, they could begin to grow comfortable with the truth. And proud of it. Their lord was no ordinary man. He was something special.

"I need to leave, Perrin," Elyas said. "Tonight, if I can."

"I know. The Last Hunt has begun. Go with them, Elyas. We will meet in the north."

The aging Warder laid a hand on Perrin's shoulder. "If we don't see one another there, perhaps we'll meet in the dream, my friend."

"This is the dream," Perrin said, smiling. "And we *will* meet again. I will find you, if you are with the wolves. Hunt well, Long Tooth."

"Hunt well, Young Bull."

Elyas vanished into the darkness with barely a rustle.

Perrin reached down to the warm hammer at his side. He had thought that responsibility would be another weight upon him. And yet, now that he had accepted it, he actually felt lighter.

Perrin Aybara was just a man, but Perrin Goldeneyes was a symbol created by the people who followed him. Perrin didn't have a choice about that; all he could do was lead the best he could. If he didn't, the symbol wouldn't vanish. The people would just lose faith in it. As poor Aram had.

I'm sorry, my friend, he thought. *You I failed most of all.* There was no point in looking backward at that. He would simply have to continue forward and do better. "I'm Perrin Goldeneyes," he said, "the man who can speak to wolves. And I guess that's a good person to be."

He kicked Stepper through the gateway. Unfortunately, Perrin Goldeneyes had some killing to do tonight.

Galad awoke as soon as his tent flap rustled. He drove away the vestiges of his dream—a silly thing, of him dining with a dark-haired beauty with perfect lips and cunning eyes—and reached for his sword.

"Galad!" a voice hissed. It was Trom.

"What's wrong?" Galad asked, hand still on his sword.

"You were right," Trom said.

"About what?"

"Aybara's army is back. Galad, they're on the heights just above us! We only caught sight of them by accident; our men were watching along the road, as you told us."

Galad cursed, sat up and reached for his smallclothes. "How did they get up there without us seeing?"

"Dark powers, Galad. Byar was right. You saw how fast their camp emptied."

Their scouts had returned an hour before. They'd found Aybara's campsite eerily empty, as if it had been populated by ghosts. Nobody had seen them leave along the road.

Now this. Galad dressed quickly. "Rouse the men. See if you can do it quietly. You were wise to bring no light; that might have alerted the enemy. Have the men put on their armor inside their tents."

"Yes, my Lord Captain Commander," Trom said. A rustling accompanied his departure.

Galad hurried to dress. *What have I done?* Every step of the way, he'd been confident in his choices, yet this was where they had led him. Aybara, positioned to attack, Galad's men asleep. Ever since Morgase had returned, Galad had felt his world crumbling. What was right was no longer clear to him, not as it had once been. The way ahead seemed clouded.

We should surrender, he thought, affixing his cloak in place over his mail. *But no. Children of the Light never give in to Darkfriends. How could I think that?*

They had to die fighting. But what would that accomplish? The end of the Children, dead before the Last Battle began?

His tent flaps rustled again, and he had his sword out, ready to strike.

"Galad," Byar said. "You've killed us." All respect was gone from his voice.

The accusation set Galad on edge. "Those who walk in the Light must take no responsibility for the actions of those who follow the Shadow." A quote from Lothair Mantelar. "I have acted with honor."

"You should have attacked instead of going through that ridiculous 'trial.'"

"We would have been slaughtered. He had Aes Sedai, Aiel, men who can channel, more soldiers than us, and powers we don't understand."

"The Light would have protected us!"

"And if that is true, it will protect us now," Galad said, confidence strengthening.

"No," Byar said, voice an angry whisper. "We have led ourselves to this. If we fall, it will be deserved." He left with a rustle of the flaps.

Galad stood for a moment, then buckled on his sword. Recrimination and repentance would wait. He had to find a way to survive this day. If there was a way.

Counter their ambush, with one of our own, he thought. *Have the men stay in their tents until the attack starts, then surprise Aybara by rushing out in force, and . . .*

No. Aybara would start with arrows, raining death on the tents. It would be the best way to take advantage of his high ground and his longbowmen.

The best thing to do was get the men armored, then have them break from their tents together on a signal and run for their horses. The Amadicians could form a pikewall at the base of the heights. Aybara might risk running cavalry down the steep slope leading up to the rise, but pikemen could upset that maneuver.

Archers would still be a problem. Shields would help. A little. He took a deep breath, then strode into the night to give the orders.

"Once the battle begins," Perrin said, "I want you three to retreat to safety. I won't try to send you back to Andor; I know you wouldn't go. But you're not to participate in the battle. Stay behind the battle lines and with the rear guard."

Faile glanced at him. He sat his mount, eyes forward. They stood atop the heights, the last of his army emerging from the gateways positioned behind. Jori Congar held a shielded lantern for Perrin. It gave the area a very faint light.

"Of course, my Lord," Berelain said smoothly.

"I'll have your oaths on it, then," Perrin said, eyes still forward. "You and Alliandre, Berelain. Faile, I'll simply ask and hope."

"You have my oath, my Lord," Alliandre said.

Perrin's voice was so *firm,* and that worried Faile. Could Berelain be right? Was he going to attack the Whitecloaks?

They were an unpredictable element, for all their professions of wanting to fight in the Last Battle. They could cause more harm than help. Beyond that, Alliandre was Perrin's liegewoman, and the Whitecloaks were in her realm. Who knew what damage they would cause before they left? Beyond that, there was the future sword of Galad's judgment.

"My Lord," Berelain said, sounding worried. "Please don't do this."

"I'm only doing what I must," Perrin said, looking along the roadway that ran toward Jehannah. That wasn't the direction of the Whitecloaks. They were just south of Perrin's position.

"Perrin," Faile said, glancing at Berelain. "What are you—"

A man suddenly emerged from the shadows, making no sound, despite the dried underbrush. "Perrin Aybara," Gaul said. "The Whitecloaks know we're here."

"Are you certain?" Perrin asked. He didn't seem alarmed.

"They are trying not to let us know," Gaul said, "but I can see it. The Maidens agree. They are preparing for battle, the grooms unhobbling the horses, guards moving from tent to tent."

Perrin nodded. He nudged Stepper forward through the brush, riding right up to the edge of the heights. Faile moved Daylight up behind him, Berelain staying close to her.

The land sloped steeply down to the ancient riverbed that flanked the roadway below. The road ran from the direction of Jehannah, until it passed the base of these heights and took a turn in the direction of Lugard. Right at the bend was the hollow, sheltered against the hill, where the Whitecloaks had arranged their circles of tents.

The clouds were thin, allowing pale moonlight to coat the land in silvery white. A low fog was rolling in, staying mainly in the riverbed, deep and thick. Perrin scanned the scene; he had a clear view of the road in both directions. Suddenly, shouts rang out below, men bursting from the Whitecloak tents and sprinting toward horselines. Torches flared to life.

"Archers forward!" Perrin bellowed.

The Two Rivers men scrambled to the edge of their elevated position.

"Infantry, ready behind the archers!" Perrin yelled. "Ar-

ganda, on the left flank. Gallenne, on the right! I'll call if I
need you to sweep for us." He turned to the foot soldiers—
mainly former refugees. "Keep in a tight formation, boys.
Keep your shields up and your spear arms flexed. Archers,
arrows to bow!"

Faile felt herself start to sweat. This was wrong. Surely
Perrin wasn't going to . . .

He still wasn't looking at the Whitecloaks below them.
He was staring at the riverbed on the other side, perhaps a
hundred yards or so beyond the heights, which ended in a
steep drop-off because of the ancient river's washing. Perrin looked as if seeing something the rest of them weren't.
And with those golden eyes of his, perhaps he was doing
just that.

"My Lord," Berelain said, moving her horse up beside
him, sounding desperate. "If you must attack, could you
spare the commander of the Whitecloaks? He might be useful for political reasons."

"What are you talking about?" Perrin said. "The whole
reason I'm *here* is to keep Damodred alive."

"You . . . what?" Berelain asked.

"My Lord!" Grady suddenly exclaimed, riding nearby. "I
sense *channeling*!"

"What's that, there!" Jori Congar yelled, pointing.
"Something in the fog. It's . . ."

Faile squinted. There, just below the army in the former
riverbed, figures began to rise as if from the ground. Misshapen creatures with animal heads and bodies, half again
as tall as Perrin, bearing brutish weapons. Moving among
them were sleek, eyeless figures in black.

Fog streamed around them as they strode forward, trailing wisps. The creatures continued to appear. Dozens of
them. Hundreds. Thousands.

An entire army of Trollocs and Myrddraal.

"Grady, Neald!" Perrin bellowed. "Light!"

Brilliant white globes appeared in the air and hung there.
More and more Trollocs were rising from the fog, as if it
were spawning them, but they seemed bewildered by the
lights. They looked up, squinting and shielding their eyes.

Perrin grunted. "How about that? They weren't ready
for us; they thought they'd have an easy shot at the Whitecloaks." He turned, looking down the lines of surprised

soldiers. "Well, men, you wanted to follow me to the Last Battle? We're going to get a taste of it right here! Archers, loose! Let's send those Shadowspawn back to the pit that birthed them!"

He raised his newly forged hammer, and the battle began.

CHAPTER
41

An Unexpected Ally

Galad ran with his shield raised high. Bornhald
joined him, also holding a shield and tossing aside
his lantern as those unnatural lights flared in the
air. Neither spoke. The hail of arrows would begin momentarily.

They reached the horse pickets, where a pair of nervous
grooms handed over their horses. Galad lowered his shield,
feeling terribly exposed as he swung onto Stout's back. He
turned the horse and got the shield back up. He could hear
the familiar twang of bows, distant, arrows snapping as
they rained down.

None fell near him.

He hesitated. The lights hanging in the air made it bright
as a night with a full moon, maybe brighter.

"What's going on?" Bornhald said, horse dancing nervously beneath him. "They missed? Those arrows are falling well outside of camp."

"Trollocs!" A shout from camp. "There are thousands of
them coming down the roadway!"

"Monsters!" a terrified Amadician yelled. "Monsters of
the Shadow! Light, they're *real*?"

Galad glanced at Bornhald. They galloped their horses to
the edge of camp, white cloaks streaming behind them, and
looked up the road.

At a slaughter.

Waves of arrows fell from the heights, crashing into the
mob of Shadowspawn. The creatures howled and screeched,
some trying to run for Galad's camp, others to climb toward
the archers. Trollocs exploded suddenly into the air, the

ground heaving beneath them, and fire fell from above. Aybara's channelers had joined the fight.

Galad took it in. "Foot, form a shieldwall on this side of the camp," he bellowed. "Crossbowmen, to those ruins there. Split the legions into eight cavalry companies, and prepare to sally! Bowmen, get ready!" The Children were primarily a cavalry force. His men would ride out, hit the Trollocs in waves, one company at a time, then retreat back behind the foot's defensive shieldwall. Crossbowmen to weaken the Trolloc lines before the heavy cavalry hit them with lances, archers to cover them as they returned behind their defenses.

The orders were passed quickly, the Children moving more efficiently than the Amadicians. Bornhald nodded. This was a mostly defensive posture, but that made the most sense, at least until Galad could sort through what was happening.

Hoofbeats announced Byar galloping up. He reared his horse, then turned, eyes wide. "Trollocs? How . . . It's Aybara. He's brought an army of Shadowspawn!"

"If he did," Galad said, "he's treating them to a slaughter."

Byar edged closer. "It's *exactly* like the Two Rivers. Dain, you remember what he did? Trollocs attack. Aybara rallies a defense, and therefore earns support."

"What would be the point?" Bornhald said.

"To trick us."

"By killing as many Trollocs as it gains him in followers?" Bornhald frowned. "It . . . it makes no sense. If Aybara can command thousands of Trollocs, why would he need us?"

"His mind is sick, twisted," Byar said. "If he didn't have something to do with the appearance of the Trollocs, then how did both show up right now, at the same time?"

Well, there was a grain a truth in that, Galad had to admit. "For now," he said, "it gains us the time we need to form up. Bornhald, Byar, help pass my orders. I want the riders ready to sally as soon as the crossbowmen finish." He hesitated. "But let the men know that we are *not* to expose our flanks to Aybara. Keep some foot with pikes at the base of those heights. Just in case."

* * *

Trollocs fell screaming under the arrows. Still more continued to appear, and many of the beasts didn't fall until they had multiple arrows in them. The Shadowspawn were preparing for a rush up the incline toward Perrin's forces. If they did, he'd have his foot hold for a time—then pull them back and run the cavalry sweep along in front of them.

"How did you know?" Faile asked softly.

He glanced at her. "It's time for you three to retreat behind to the rear guard." He glanced at Berelain, white-faced on her horse, as if seeing the Trollocs had unhinged her. He knew her to be of stronger steel than that, however. Why did she smell so worried?

"I will go," Faile said. "But I have to know."

"It made sense," Perrin said. "That dome was meant to keep us from fleeing by gateway. But it was also to encourage us along the road, to keep us from Traveling directly to Andor. It seemed odd to us that Master Gill would turn along the road, disobeying orders—but it happened because he was convinced by people coming from the north that the way was impassable. Plants by our enemies, I suspect, to lure us this direction.

"We were being herded all along. They weren't waiting for us to engage the Whitecloaks, they were waiting for us to make for Lugard as fast as we could. If we'd tried to go cross-country, I'll bet something would have happened to turn us back. They desperately wanted us to walk into their ambush. Galad's force probably wasn't part of it—he was a burr that got under their saddle."

"But the Trollocs. Where—"

"I think it must be a Portal Stone," Perrin said. "I knew some kind of attack was going to come here. Didn't know how. I half thought it would be Draghkar from the sky or a Waygate we'd missed. But those ruins Arganda pointed out seem like they might be a good place for a Portal Stone. It must be buried, having fallen under the river when it changed its course. The Trollocs aren't coming out of the ground; I think they're appearing from the stone.

"This was the trap. They probably would have attacked us much earlier, but the Whitecloaks were in the way. They *had* to wait for us to deal with them. And then we left. So . . ."

"So they attacked Damodred and his men," Faile said.

"After setting up the trap, they at least wanted to do some damage to those who might fight later on."

"I suspect one of the Forsaken is behind this," Perrin said, turning toward Grady.

"One of the Forsaken?" Alliandre said, voice rising. "We can't fight one of the *Forsaken*!"

Perrin glanced at her. "What did you think you were signing up to do, Alliandre, when you joined me? You fight for the Dragon Reborn in *Tarmon Gai'don* itself. We'll have to face the Forsaken sooner or later."

She paled, but to her credit, she nodded.

"Grady!" Perrin called to the Asha'man, who was firing blasts down at the Trollocs. "You still sense channeling?"

"Only off and on, my Lord," Grady called back. "Whoever it is, they're strong, but not terribly so. And they're not joining the battle. I think they must be doing something to bring the Trollocs, jumping in with fists of them, then jumping away immediately to fetch more."

"Watch for him," Perrin said. "See if you can take him down."

"Yes, my Lord," Grady said, saluting.

So it wasn't one of the Forsaken bringing the Trollocs directly. That didn't mean this wasn't the work of one of them, just that they hadn't decided to commit themselves directly. "Back with you three," Perrin said to Faile, Berelain and Alliandre, hefting his hammer. The Trollocs had begun charging up the rise, many dropping to arrows, but there were enough that some would reach the top soon. It was time to fight.

"You don't know how many of them there are, my husband," Faile said softly. "They keep coming. What if they overwhelm us?"

"We'll retreat through a gateway if things turn poor for us. But I'm not letting them have the Whitecloaks without a fight—I won't leave any man to the Trollocs, not even their lot. They ignored the Two Rivers when we were attacked. Well, I won't do the same. And that's that."

Faile, suddenly, leaned over to kiss him. "Thank you."

"For what?"

"For being the man that you are," she said, turning her mount and leading the other two away.

Perrin shook his head. He had been worrying that he'd

need to have Grady wrap her up in Air and tow her away. He turned back to the approaching Trollocs. The Two Rivers men weren't making it easy for them to get up the incline. The men were running out of arrows, though.

Perrin hefted *Mah'alleinir*. A part of him felt sorry to bathe the weapon in blood so soon after its birth, but the greater part of him was pleased. These Trollocs, and those who led them, had caused Hopper's death.

A fist of Trollocs crested the hilltop, a Fade moving in behind them, led by another Fade with a black sword. Perrin let out a roar and charged forward, hammer held high.

Galad cursed, turning Stout and chopping his sword down into the neck of a Trolloc with the head of a bear. Dark, thick blood spurted out in a noisome gush, but the beasts were terribly difficult to kill. Galad had heard the stories, had trained with men who had fought Shadowspawn. Still, their resilience surprised him.

He had to hack at the creature three more times before it dropped. Already, Galad's arm was aching. There was no finesse to fighting monsters like this. He used horseback sword forms, but often the most direct and brutal of them. Woodsman Strips the Branch. Arc of the Moon. Striking the Spark.

His men weren't faring well. They were boxed in, and there was no longer room for lances. The sallying attacks had worked for a time, but the heavy cavalry had been forced to retreat back to the foot lines, and his whole force was being pushed east. The Amadicians were being overwhelmed, and the force of the attack was too great to allow further cavalry charges. All the Children on horseback could do was swing their weapons wildly in an attempt to stay alive.

Galad turned Stout, but two snarling Trollocs leaped for him. He quickly took one across the neck with Heron Snatches the Silverfish, but the creature fell forward onto Stout, causing the horse to lurch away. Another brute slashed a catchpole at the horse's neck. The horse fell.

Galad barely managed to throw himself free, hitting the ground in a heap as Stout collapsed, legs jerking, neck spurting blood across his white shoulder. Galad rolled,

sword twisted to the side, but he had landed wrong. His
ankle wrenched in pain.

Ignoring the pain, he brought his sword up in time to de-
flect the hook of a brown-furred monster, nine feet tall, that
stank of death. Galad's parry sent him off balance again.

"Galad!"

Figures in white crashed into the Trollocs. Reeking blood
sprayed in the air. White figures tumbled to the ground,
but the Trollocs were driven back. Bornhald stood panting,
sword out, shield dented and sprayed with dark blood. He
had four men with him. Two others had fallen.

"Thank you," Galad said. "Your mounts?"

"Cut down," Bornhald said. "They must have orders to
go after the horses."

"Don't want us escaping," Galad said. "Or rallying a
charge." He glanced down the line of beleaguered soldiers.
Twenty thousand had seemed a grand army, but the battle
lines were a mess. And the Trollocs continued to come,
wave after wave. The northern section of the Children's line
was breaking, and the Trollocs were pushing forward there
with a pincer movement to surround Galad's force. They'd
cut them off on the north and south, then ram them against
the hill. Light!

"Rally to the northern foot line!" Galad yelled. He ran in
that direction as quickly as he could, his ankle protesting,
but still functioning. Men joined with him. Their clothing
was no longer white.

Galad knew that most generals, like Gareth Bryne, didn't
fight on the front lines. They were too important for that,
and their minds were needed for organizing the fight. Perhaps that was what Galad should have done. It was falling
apart.

His men were good. Solid. But they were inexperienced
with Trollocs. Only now—charging across muddy ground
on a dark night, lit by globes hanging in the air—did he see
how inexperienced many of them were. He had some veter-
ans, but the larger group had fought mostly against unruly
bandits or city militias.

The Trollocs were different. The howling, grunting,
snarling monsters were in a frenzy. What they lacked in
military discipline they made up for in strength and ferocity. And hunger. The Myrddraal amid them were terrible

enough to break a formation all on their own. Galad's soldiers were buckling.

"Hold!" Galad bellowed, reaching the breaking section of the line. He had Bornhald and about fifty men. Not nearly enough. "We are the Children of the Light! We do not give before the Shadow!"

It didn't work. Watching the disaster play out, his entire framework of understanding started to crack. The Children of the Light were not protected by their goodness; they were falling in swaths, like grain before the scythe. Worse than that, some did not fight valiantly or hold with resolve. Too many yelled in terror, running. The Amadicians he could understand, but a lot of the Children themselves were little better.

They weren't cowards. They weren't poor fighters. They were just men. Average. That wasn't how it was supposed to be.

Thunder sounded as Gallenne brought his horsemen around in another charge. They hammered into the Trolloc line and forced many of them off the edge, tumbling them back down the incline.

Perrin slammed *Mah'alleinir* into a Trolloc's head. The force of the blow tossed the creature to the side, and—oddly—its skin sizzled and smoked where the hammer had hit. This happened with each blow, as if the touch of *Mah'alleinir* burned them, though Perrin felt only a comfortable warmth from the hammer.

Gallenne's charge punched through the Trolloc ranks, separating them into two cohorts, but there were so many carcasses it was getting difficult for his lancers to charge. Gallenne withdrew and a contingent of Two Rivers men moved in and shot arrows at the Trollocs, cutting them down in a wave of screaming, howling, reeking death.

Perrin pulled Stepper back, foot soldiers forming around him. Very few of his men had fallen among the Trollocs. Of course, even one was too many.

Arganda trotted up on his horse. He'd lost his helmet's plumes somewhere, but was smiling broadly. "I've rarely had such a pleasing battle, Aybara," he said. "Enemies to fell that you need not feel a sting of pity for, a perfect staging area and defensible position. Archers to dream of and Asha'man to stop the gaps! I've laid down over two dozen of the beasts myself. For this day alone, I'm glad we followed you!"

Perrin nodded. He didn't point out that one of the reasons they were having an easy time of it was that most of the Trollocs were focused on the Whitecloaks. Trollocs were nasty, monstrous things, and they had a fiercely selfish streak. Charge up the hillside at balls of fire and longbowmen, only to try and seize ground from two full contingents of cavalry? Better to seek the easier foe, and it made tactical sense, too. Focus on the easier battle first, when you had two fronts to fight on.

They were trying to crush the Whitecloaks back against the hillside as quickly as possible, and had swarmed them, not leaving them room to ride their cavalry in charges, separating groups of them. The person leading this understood tactics; this wasn't the work of Trolloc minds.

"Lord Perrin!" Jori Congar's voice rose above the din of howling Trollocs. He scrambled up to Stepper's side. "You asked me to watch and tell you how they were doing. Well, you'll want to look, maybe."

Perrin nodded, raising his fist, then making a chopping motion. Grady and Neald stood behind him, on a rock formation that could look down toward the roadway. Their main orders were to take down any Myrddraal they spotted. Perrin wanted to keep as many of those things as possible off the heights; it could cost dozens of lives to kill a single Myrddraal with the sword or axe. Best to kill with Fire, from a distance. Besides, sometimes killing one of the Fades would mean killing a complement of Trollocs linked to it.

The Asha'man, Aes Sedai and Wise Ones saw Perrin's signal. They began a full assault on the Trollocs, fire flying from hands, lightning blasting from the sky, pushing the Trollocs back down the incline. Perrin's foot soldiers pulled back for a few moments' rest.

Perrin nudged Stepper to the edge, looking down the slope to the south, holding *Mah'alleinir* down by his leg. Below, Damodred's force was doing even worse than Perrin had worried. The Trollocs had drilled forward, nearly dividing the Whitecloaks into two sections. The monsters were surging around the sides, entrapping Galad, making the Whitecloaks fight on three fronts. Their backs were to the hillside, and many groups of cavalry had been cut off from the main body of fighting.

Gallenne trotted up beside Perrin. "The Trollocs are still appearing. I'd guess fifty thousand of the beasts so far. The Asha'man say they've only sensed the one channeler, and he isn't engaging."

"The one leading the Shadowspawn won't want to commit their channelers," Perrin guessed. "Not with us having the high ground. They'll leave the Trollocs to do what damage they can, and see if they gain the upper hand. If they do, we will see channelers come out."

Gallenne nodded.

"Damodred's force is in trouble."

"Yes," Gallenne said. "You positioned us well to help them, but it appears we weren't enough."

"I'm going down for them," Perrin decided. He pointed. "The Trollocs are surrounding him, boxing him in against the hillside. We could sweep down and surprise the beasts with a broadside, breaking through and freeing Damodred's men to get themselves up on the plateau here."

Gallenne frowned. "Pardon, Lord Perrin, but I must ask. What is it that you feel you owe them? I would have sorrowed if, indeed, we'd come here to attack them—though I would have seen its logic. But I see no reason to help them."

Perrin grunted. "It's just the right thing to do."

"That is a subject of debate," Gallenne said, shaking his helmeted head. "Fighting the Trollocs and Fades is excellent, for every one that falls is one fewer to face at the Last Battle. Our men get practice fighting them, and can learn to control their fears. But that slope is steep and treacherous; if you try to ride down to Damodred, you could destroy our advantage."

"I'm going anyway," Perrin said. "Jori, go get the Two Rivers men and the Asha'man. I'll need them to soften the Trollocs for my charge." He looked down again. Memories of the Two Rivers flooded his mind. Blood. Death. *Mah'alleinir* grew warmer in his fist. "I won't leave them to it, Gallenne. Not even them. Will you join me?"

"You are a strange man, Aybara." Gallenne hesitated. "And one of true honor. Yes, I will."

"Good. Jori, get moving. We must reach Damodred before his lines break."

A shock rippled through the mass of Trollocs. Galad hesitated, sword gripped in sweaty fingers. His entire body ached. Moans came from all around him, some guttural and snarling—Trollocs dying—some piteous from fallen men. The Children near him were holding. Barely.

The night was dim, even with those lights. It felt like fighting nightmares. But if the Children of the Light could not stand against darkness, who could?

The Trollocs began howling more loudly. Those in front of him turned, speaking to one another in a crude, snarling tongue that caused him to pull back in revulsion. Trollocs could speak? He hadn't known that. What had drawn their attention?

And then he saw it. A hail of arrows, falling from above, ripped into ranks of the nearby Trollocs. The Two Rivers bowmen lived up to their reputation. Galad wouldn't have trusted most archers to shoot like that, not without stray arrows falling on the Whitecloaks. These archers were precise, however.

The Trollocs screamed and howled. Then, from the top of the rise, a thousand horsemen charged. Lights flashed around them; fires fell from above, arcing down like red-golden lances. They illuminated the horsemen in silver.

It was an incredible maneuver. The incline was steep enough that horses could have tripped, fallen, tumbled the entire force into a useless mass of bodies. But they didn't fall. They galloped sure-footed, lances gleaming. And at their front rode a bearded monster of a man with a large hammer held high. Perrin Aybara himself, above his head a banner flapping, carried by a man riding just behind. The crimson wolfhead.

Despite himself, Galad lowered his shield at the sight. Aybara almost seemed aflame from the tongues of fire that surrounded him. Galad could see those wide, golden eyes. Like fires themselves.

The horsemen crashed into the Trollocs that had surrounded Galad's force. Aybara let out a roar over the din, then began to lay about him with the hammer. The attack forced the Trollocs back.

"Assault!" Galad yelled. "Press the attack! Force them into the cavalry!" He charged northward, toward the face of the heights, Bornhald at his side. Nearby, Trom rallied what was left of his legion and brought it around to attack the Trollocs opposite Aybara.

The fray grew increasingly chaotic. Galad fought furiously. Above, incredibly, Aybara's entire army poured down the incline, giving up the high ground. They fell upon the Trollocs, tens of thousands of men yelling, "Goldeneyes! Goldeneyes!"

The attack put Galad and Bornhald into the Trollocs' ranks. The creatures tried to pull back from Aybara, surging in all directions. The men near Galad and Bornhald were soon fighting desperately to stay alive. Galad finished off a Trolloc with Ribbon in the Air, but spun and immediately found himself facing a ram-faced behemoth ten feet tall. Horns curled around the sides of its enormous square face, but the eyes were human, and the lower jaw as well.

Galad ducked when it swung its catchpole, then rammed his sword up into its gut. The creature screamed, and Bornhald hamstrung it from the side.

Galad yelled and leaped backward, but his twisted ankle finally failed him. It got caught in a cleft in the ground, and Galad heard a terrible *snap* as he fell.

The dying monster crashed down on him, pinning him to the ground. Pain shot up his leg, but he ignored it. He dropped his sword, trying to shove the carcass free. Bornhald, swearing, fended off a Trolloc that had the snout of a boar. It made a horrid grunting sound.

Galad heaved off the stinking carcass. To the side, he could see men in white—Trom, with Byar at his side, fighting desperately to reach Galad. There were so many Trollocs, and those Children immediately nearby had mostly fallen.

Galad reached for his sword just as a mounted figure burst through the shadows and Trollocs just to the north. Aybara. He rode up and pounded that massive hammer of his into a boar Trolloc, sending it crashing to the ground. Aybara leaped off his horse as Bornhald scrambled over to help Galad to his feet.

"You are wounded?" Aybara asked.

"My ankle," Galad said.

"On my horse," Aybara said.

Galad didn't protest; it made sense. He did, however, feel embarrassed as Bornhald helped him up. Aybara's men filled in around them, pushing the Trollocs back. Now that Aybara's army had joined the fray, Galad's men were rallying.

Rushing down the slope had been a dangerous gamble, but as soon as Galad was astride Aybara's horse, he could see that the gamble had worked. The massive charge had broken the Trollocs apart, and some groups started fleeing. Tongues of flame fell from above, burning Myrddraal and dropping entire fists of Trollocs linked to them.

There was still a great deal of fighting to do, but the tide was turning. Aybara's forces carved out a section around their leader, giving him—and by extension Galad—some breathing room to consider the next stage of the attack.

Galad turned to Aybara, who was studying the Trollocs with keen eyes. "I assume you think that saving me will influence my decision about your judgment," Galad said.

"It had better," Aybara muttered.

Galad raised an eyebrow. It wasn't the response he'd been expecting. "My men find it suspicious that you appeared so soon before the Trollocs."

"Well, they can think that if they want," Aybara said. "I doubt anything I say will change their minds. In a way, this is my fault. The Trollocs were here to kill me; I just got away before they could spring their trap. Be glad I didn't leave you to them. You Whitecloaks have caused me nearly as much grief as they have."

Oddly, Galad found himself smiling. There was a straightforward air about this Perrin Aybara. A man could ask for little more in an ally.

Are we allies, then? Galad thought, nodding to Trom and Byar as they approached. *Perhaps for now.* He did trust Aybara. Yes, perhaps there were men in the world who would put together an intricate plot like this one, all to trick his way into Galad's favor. Valda had been like that.

Aybara wasn't. He really *was* straightforward. If he'd wanted the Children out of his way, he'd have killed them and moved on.

"Then so be it, Perrin Aybara," Galad said. "I name your punishment here, this night, at this moment."

Perrin frowned, turning away from his contemplation of the battle lines. "What? *Now?*"

"I deem, as punishment, that you pay blood price to the families of the dead Children in the amount of five hundred crowns. I also order you to fight in the Last Battle with all the strength you can muster. Do these things, and I pronounce you cleansed of guilt."

It was an odd time for him to give this proclamation, but he had made his decision. They would still fight, and perhaps one would fall. Galad wanted Aybara to know the judgment, in case.

Aybara studied him, then nodded. "I name that fair, Galad Damodred." He held up his hand.

"Creature of darkness!" Someone moved behind Aybara. A figure, pulling free his sword. A hiss, a flash of metal. Byar's eyes, alight with anger. He'd positioned himself right where he could strike Aybara in the back.

Aybara spun; Galad raised his sword. Both were too slow.

But Jaret Byar's blow did not fall. He stood with his weapon upraised, frozen, blood dribbling from his lips. He fell to his knees, then flopped onto the ground right at Aybara's feet.

Bornhald stood behind him, eyes wide with horror. He looked down at his sword. "I . . . It wasn't right, to strike a man in the back after he saved us. It . . ." He dropped his sword, stumbling back from Byar's corpse.

"You did the right thing, Child Bornhald," Galad said with regret. He shook his head. "He was a fine officer. Unpleasant at times, perhaps, but also brave. I am sorry to lose him."

Aybara glanced to the sides, as if looking for other Children who might strike him. "From the beginning, that one was looking for an excuse to see me dead."

Bornhald looked at Aybara, eyes still hateful, then cleaned his sword and rammed it into its sheath. He walked away, toward the area where the wounded had been taken. The area around Galad and Aybara was increasingly safe, the Trollocs pushed back, more solid battle lines forming, made of Aybara's men and the remaining Children.

"That one still thinks I killed his father," Aybara said.

"No," Galad replied. "I think he believes that you did not. But he has hated you for very long, Lord Aybara, and has loved Byar longer." He shook his head. "Killing a friend. It is sometimes painful to do what is right."

Aybara grunted. "You should get to the wounded," he said, hefting his hammer and looking toward where the fighting was still thick.

"I am well enough to fight if I have your mount."

"Well then, let's be on with it." Aybara eyed him. "I'll stay by you, though, just in case it looks like you might fall."

"Thank you."

"I'm fond of the horse."

Smiling, Galad joined him, and they waded back into the melee.

CHAPTER
42

Stronger than Blood

Once again, Gawyn sat in the small, unadorned room of Egwene's quarters. He was exhausted, which wasn't surprising, considering what he'd been through, Healings included.

His attention was consumed by the new awareness inside of him. That wonderful blossoming in the back of his mind, that link to Egwene and her emotions. The connection was a wonder, and a comfort. Sensing her let him know she was alive.

Able to anticipate her approach, he stood up as the door opened. "Gawyn," she said as she stepped in, "you shouldn't be standing up in your condition. Please, sit."

"I'm fine," he said, but did as commanded.

She pulled over the other stool, sitting down in front of him. She was calm and serene, but he could sense that she was overwhelmed by events during the night. Servants were still dealing with the bloodstains and the bodies while Chubain was holding the entire Tower at alert, checking on each and every sister. One other assassin had turned up. They'd lost two soldiers and a Warder killing her.

Yes, he could feel her emotional tempest behind that calm face. During the past few months, Gawyn had begun to think that maybe Aes Sedai learned not to feel anything at all. The bond gave him proof otherwise. Egwene *did* feel; she merely didn't let her emotions touch her features.

Looking at her face and feeling the storm inside, Gawyn was given—for the first time—another perspective on the Warder and Aes Sedai relationship. Warders weren't just bodyguards; they were the ones—the only ones—who saw the truth of what happened within the Aes Sedai. No matter how proficient the Aes Sedai became at hiding emotions, her Warder knew there was more than the mask.

"You found Mesaana?" he asked.

"Yes, though it took some time. She was impersonating an Aes Sedai named Danelle, of the Brown Ajah. We found her in her room, babbling like a child. She had already soiled herself. I'm not sure what we will do with her."

"Danelle. I didn't know her."

"She kept to herself," Egwene said. "Which is probably why Mesaana picked her."

They sat in silence for a few moments longer. "So," Egwene finally said, "how do you feel?"

"You know how I feel," Gawyn said honestly.

"It was simply a means of beginning the conversation."

He smiled. "I feel wonderful. Amazing. At peace. And concerned, and worried, anxious. Like you."

"Something must be done about the Seanchan."

"I agree. But that's not what is worrying you. You're bothered by how I disobeyed you, and yet you know it was the right thing to do."

"You didn't disobey," Egwene said. "I *did* tell you to return."

"The moratorium on guarding your room had not been lifted. I could have unhinged plans, caused a disturbance, and scared off the assassins."

"Yes," she said. Her emotions grew more troubled. "But instead, you saved my life."

"How did they get in?" Gawyn asked. "Shouldn't you have awakened when the maid tripped your alarms?"

She shook her head. "I was deep within the dream, fighting Mesaana. Tower Guards were within range to hear the alarms," Egwene said. "They have all been found dead. It sounds like the assassins were expecting me to come running. They had one of their members hiding in the entry room to kill me after I captured the other two." She grimaced. "It might have worked. I was anticipating the Black Ajah, or maybe a Gray Man."

"I sent warning."

"The messenger has been found dead as well." She eyed him. "You did the right thing tonight, but it still has me worried."

"We'll work it out," Gawyn said. "You let me protect you, Egwene, and I'll obey you in anything else. I promise it."

Egwene hesitated, then nodded. "Well, I'll need to go speak with the Hall. They'll be ready to break down my door and demand answers, by now." He could tell that on the inside, she was grimacing.

"It may help," he said, "if you imply that my return was always part of the plan."

"It was," Egwene said. "Though the timing wasn't anticipated." She hesitated. "When I realized how Silviana had phrased my request that you return, I was worried that you wouldn't come back at all."

"I nearly didn't."

"What made the difference?"

"I had to learn how to surrender. It's something I've never been good at."

Egwene nodded, as if understanding. "I'll leave orders for a bed to be brought into this room. I was always planning this to be my Warder's station."

Gawyn smiled. Sleep in another room? Underneath it all, there was still some of the conservative innkeeper's daughter remaining. Egwene blushed as she sensed his thoughts.

"Why don't we get married?" Gawyn said. "Right here, today. Light, Egwene, you're Amyrlin—your word is as good as law in Tar Valon. Speak the words, and we'd be wedded."

She paled; odd, how that would unsettle her this night. Gawyn felt a stab of anxiety. She'd said she loved him. Didn't she want to—

But no, he could feel her emotions. She did love him. Then why?

Egwene sounded aghast when she spoke. "You think I could face my parents if I got married without them knowing about it? Light, Gawyn, we'll at least have to *send* for them! And what about Elayne? You'd marry without telling her?"

He smiled. "You're right, of course. I'll contact them."

"I can—"

"Egwene, you're the *Amyrlin Seat*. The weight of the world itself is on your shoulders. Let me make arrangements."

"Very well," she said. She stepped outside, where Silviana waited—she had one of her glowers for Gawyn. Egwene sent some servants for a bed for him, then she and her Keeper moved off, a pair of Chubain's soldiers following.

Gawyn would have liked to go with her. There might still be assassins about. Unfortunately, she was right to send him to sleep. He was having trouble remaining upright. He stood on unsteady legs, then noticed a line of sheet-covered bodies outside. They wouldn't be removed until sisters had a chance to look them over. Right now, finding Mesaana—and looking for other assassins—had been more pressing.

Gritting his teeth, he forced himself to walk over and pull back the sheet, revealing Celark's and Mazone's lifeless faces—Celark's, unfortunately, sitting beside his body, separated from it at the neck.

"You did well, men," he said. "I'll see that your families know that you saved the life of the Amyrlin." It made him angry to lose such good men.

Burn those Seanchan, he thought. *Egwene is right about them. Something needs to be done.*

He glanced to the side, to where the three assassins lay beneath sheets of their own, black-slippered feet sticking out the bottom. Two women and a man.

I wonder . . . he thought, then crossed to where they lay. Guards glanced at him as he pulled back the sheet, but nobody forbade him.

The *ter'angreal* were easy to pick out, though only because he'd been told what to look for. Identical black stone rings, worn on the middle fingers of their right hands. The rings were carved in the shape of a vine with thorns. Apparently none of the Aes Sedai had recognized them for what they were, at least not yet.

Gawyn slipped all three rings off, then tucked them into his pocket.

Lan could feel something, a distinct difference to the emotions in the back of his mind. He'd grown accustomed to ignoring those, and the woman they represented.

Lately, those emotions had changed. More and more, he was certain that Nynaeve had taken his bond. He could identify her by the way she felt. How could one not know her, that sense of passion and kindness? It felt . . . remarkable.

He stared down the roadway. It twisted around the side of a hill before turning straight toward a distinctive fortress ahead. The border between Kandor and Arafel was marked by the Silverwall Keeps, a large fortification built on two sides of Firchon Pass. It was an extremely impressive fortress—really two of them, each one built up the straight wall of the narrow canyonlike pass. Like two sides of an enormous doorway.

Getting through the pass required traveling a considerable distance between large stone walls pocked with arrowslits, and it would be effective at stopping armies moving in either direction.

They were all allies, the Borderlanders were. But that didn't stop the Arafellin from wanting a nice fortress blocking the way up to Shol Arbela. Camped in front of that fortress was a gathering of thousands of people, clustered in smaller groups. The flag of Malkier—the Golden Crane— flew over some of the groups. Others flew flags of Kandor or Arafel.

"Which of you broke your oath?" Lan asked, looking back at the caravan.

The men there shook their heads.

"Nobody needed to break his oath," Andere said. "What else would you do? Cut through the Broken Lands? The Uncapped Hills? It is here or nowhere. They know this. And so they wait for you."

Lan growled. It was probably true. "We are a caravan," he said loudly. "Remember, if any ask, you may admit that we are Malkieri. You may say you wait for your king. That is truth. You may not mention that you have found him."

The others seemed troubled, but they made no objection. Lan led the way down the slope, their caravan of twenty wagons, warhorses and attendants following.

This was what he'd always worried would happen. Reclaiming Malkier was impossible. They would die, no matter how large their force. An assault? On the Blight? Ridiculous.

He could not ask that of them. He could not *allow* that of them. As he continued down the road, he became more resolute. Those brave men, flying those flags . . . they should join with the Shienaran forces and fight in a battle that meant something. He would not take their lives.

Death is lighter than a feather . . . Rakim had thrown that at him several times during their ride. He had followed Lan decades ago, during the Aiel War. *Duty is heavier than a mountain.*

Lan was *not* running from duty. He was running toward it. Still, sight of the camps stirred his heart as he reached the bottom of the slope, then rode forward. The waiting men wore simple warrior's garb, *hadori* in place, women marked with a *ki'sain* on their foreheads. Some of the men wore coats with the Golden Crown on the shoulders— the mark of the royal guard of Malkier. They would have donned those only if their fathers or grandfathers had served in that guard.

It was a sight that would have made Bukama cry. He had thought the Malkieri gone as a people, broken, shattered, absorbed by other nations. Yet here they were, gathering at the faintest whisper of a call to arms. Many were older— Lan had been but a babe when his kingdom fell, and those who remembered that day as men would now be in their seventh or eighth decade. They had gray hair, but they were still warriors, and they'd brought their sons and grandsons.

"*Tai'shar Malkier!*" a man cried as Lan's group passed. The call went up a dozen, two dozen times as they saw his *hadori*. None seemed to recognize him for who he was. They assumed that he had come for the reason they had come.

The Last Battle comes, Lan thought. *Must I deny them the right to fight alongside me?*

Yes, he must. Best he passed unnoticed and unrecognized. He kept his eyes forward, his hand on his sword, his mouth closed. But each call of *Tai'shar Malkier* made him want to sit up straighter. Each seemed to strengthen him, push him forward.

The gates between the two fortress keeps were open, though soldiers checked every man who went through. Lan halted Mandarb, and his people stopped behind him. Could the Arafellin have orders to watch for him? What other choice did he have but to go forward? Going around would take weeks. His caravan waited its turn, then stepped up to the guard post.

"Purpose?" asked the uniformed Arafellin, hair in braids.

"Traveling to Fal Moran," Lan said. "Because of the Last Battle."

"You're not going to wait here like the rest?" the guard said, waving a gauntleted hand at the gathered Malkieri. "For your king?"

"I have no king," Lan said softly.

The soldier nodded slowly, rubbing his chin. Then he waved for some soldiers to inspect the goods in the wagons. "There will be a tariff on that."

"I plan to give it to Shienarans to fight in the Last Battle," Lan said. "No price asked."

The guard raised an eyebrow.

"You have my oath on it," Lan said softly, meeting the man's eyes.

"No tariff, then. *Tai'shar Malkier,* friend."

"*Tai'shar Arafel.*" Lan kicked his horse forward. He hated riding through the Silverwalls; they made him feel as though a thousand archers were drawing on him. The Trollocs would not easily get through *here*, if the Arafellin were forced to retreat back this far. There were times that had happened, and they had held here each time, as in the days of Yakobin the Undaunted.

Lan practically held his breath the entire way. He reached the other side gratefully, and urged Mandarb out onto the roadway to the northeast.

"Al'Lan Mandragoran?" a voice yelled, sounding distant.

Lan froze. That call had come from above. He turned, looking back at the leftmost keep. A head was sticking from a window there.

"Light be praised, it *is* you!" the voice called. The head ducked back inside.

Lan felt like bolting. But if he did, this person would surely call back to the others. He waited. The figure came running out of one of the fortress doorways. Lan recognized him: a boy not yet grown into a man wearing red, with a rich blue cloak. Kaisel Noramaga, grandson of the Queen of Kandor.

"Lord Mandragoran," the youth said, trotting up. "You came! When I heard that the Golden Crane was raised—"

"I have not raised it, Prince Kaisel. My plan was to ride alone."

"Of course. I would like to ride alone with you. May I?"

"This is not a wise choice, Your Highness," Lan said. "Your grandmother is in the South; I assume your father rules in Kandor. You should be with him. What are you doing here?"

"Prince Kendral invited me," Kaisel said. "And my father bade me come. We both plan to ride with you!"

"Kendral, too?" Lan asked, aghast. The grandson of the Arafellin king? "Your places are with your people!"

"Our ancestors swore an oath," the young man said. "An oath to protect, to defend. That oath is stronger than blood, Lord Mandragoran. It is stronger than will or choice. Your wife told us to wait here for you; she said that you might try to pass without greeting us."

"How did you notice me?" Lan asked, containing his anger.

"The horse," Kaisel said, nodding to Mandarb. "She said you might disguise yourself. But you would never leave the horse."

Burn that woman, Lan thought as he heard a call being raised through the fortress. He'd been outmaneuvered. *Curse Nynaeve. And bless her, too.* He tried to send a sense of love and frustration through the bond to her.

And then, with a deep sigh, he gave in. "The Golden Crane flies for Tarmon Gai'don," Lan said softly. "Let any man or woman who wishes to follow join it and fight."

He closed his eyes as the call went up. It soon became a cheer. Then a roar.

CHAPTER

43

Some Tea

A nd these Asha'man claim they are free of the taint?"
Galad asked, as he and Perrin Aybara picked their
way through the aftermath of the battle.

"They do," Perrin said. "And I've a mind to trust them.
Why would they lie?"

Galad raised an eyebrow. "Insanity?"

Perrin nodded at that. This Perrin Aybara was an interesting man. Others often responded with anger when Galad
said what he thought, but he was coming to realize that he
didn't need to hold himself back with Perrin. This man responded well to honesty. If he *was* a Darkfriend or Shadowspawn, he was a very odd sort.

The horizon was starting to grow brighter. Light, had
night already passed? Bodies littered the ground, most of
them Trollocs. The stench was of burned flesh and fur, nauseating as it mixed with that of blood and mud. Galad felt
exhausted.

He'd allowed an Aes Sedai to Heal him. "Once you've
committed your reserves, there's no use holding back your
scouts," Gareth Bryne was fond of saying. If he was going
to let Aes Sedai save his men, then he might as well accept
their Healing. Once, accepting Aes Sedai Healing hadn't
bothered him nearly so much.

"Perhaps," Perrin said. "Perhaps the Asha'man are mad,
and the taint isn't cleansed. But they've served me well,
and I figure they've earned the right to be trusted until they
show me otherwise. You and your men might owe your
lives to Grady and Neald."

"And they have my thanks," Galad said, stepping over

the hulking body of a Trolloc with a bear's snout. "Though few of my men will express that emotion. They aren't certain what to think of your intervention here, Aybara."

"Still think I set them up somehow?"

"Perhaps," Galad said. "Either you are a Darkfriend of unsurpassed cunning, or you really did as you said—coming to save my men despite your treatment at our hands. In that case, you are a man of honor. Letting us die would have made your life much easier, I believe."

"No," Perrin said. "Every sword is needed at the Last Battle, Galad. Every one."

Galad grunted, kneeling beside a soldier with a red cloak and turning him over. It wasn't a red cloak; it was a white one soaked in blood. Ranun Sinah would not see the Last Battle. Galad closed the young man's eyes, breathing a prayer to the Light in his name.

"So what now for you and yours?" Perrin asked.

"We continue on," Galad said, rising. "North, to my estates in Andor to prepare."

"You could—" Perrin froze. Then he turned, trotting across the battlefield.

Galad hurried after him. Perrin reached a heap of Trollocs, then began pushing bodies aside. Galad heard a very faint sound. Moaning. He helped move a dead hawk-headed beast, its too-human eyes staring lifelessly.

Beneath it, a young man looked up, blinking. It was Jerum Nus, one of the Children.

"Oh, Light," the young man croaked. "It hurts. I thought I was dead. Dead . . ."

His side was cut open. Perrin knelt hastily, lifting the boy's head, giving him a drink of water as Galad took a bandage from the bag he carried and used it to wrap the wound. That cut was bad. The unfortunate youth would die for certain. He—

No, Galad realized. *We have Aes Sedai.* It was hard to get used to thinking that way.

Jerum was crying with joy, holding to Perrin's arm. The boy looked delusional. He didn't seem to care one bit about those golden eyes.

"Drink, son," Perrin said, voice soothing. Kindly. "It's all right. We found you. You're going to be fine."

"It seemed like I yelled for hours," the youth said. "But I

was so weak, and they were on top of me. How . . . how did you find me?"

"I have good ears," Perrin said. He nodded to Galad, and together they lifted the youth, Perrin beneath the arms, Galad taking the legs. They carefully carried him across the battlefield. The youth continued mumbling, consciousness slipping.

At the side of the battlefield, the Aes Sedai and Aiel Wise Ones were Healing the wounded. As Galad and Perrin arrived, a light-haired Wise One—a woman who looked not a day older than Galad, but spoke with the authority of an aged matron—hustled over. She began chastising them for moving the lad as she reached out to touch his head.

"Do you give permission, Galad Damodred?" she asked. "This one is too far gone to speak for himself."

Galad had insisted that each Child be given the choice to refuse Healing, regardless of the nature of their wound. The Aes Sedai and Wise Ones hadn't liked it, but Perrin had repeated the order. They seemed to listen to him. Odd. Galad had rarely met Aes Sedai who would listen to the orders, or even opinions, of a man.

"Yes," Galad said. "Heal him."

The Wise One turned to her work. Most Children had refused Healing, though some had changed their minds once Galad himself accepted it. The youth's breathing steadied, his wound closing. The Wise One didn't Heal him completely—only far enough that he'd survive the day. When she opened her eyes, she looked haggard, even more tired than Galad felt.

The channelers had fought all night, followed by performing Healings. Galad and Perrin moved back onto the field. They weren't the only ones searching for wounded, of course. Perrin himself could have gone back to camp to rest. But he hadn't.

"I can offer you another option," Perrin said as they walked. "As opposed to staying here, in Ghealdan, weeks from your destination. I could have you in Andor tonight."

"My men would not trust this Traveling."

"They'd go if you ordered them," Perrin said. "You've said that you'll fight alongside Aes Sedai. Well, I don't see anything different between that and this. Come with me."

"You'd let us join you, then?"

Perrin nodded. "I'd need an oath from you, though."

"What manner of oath?"

"I'll be frank with you, Galad. I don't think we have much time left. A few weeks, maybe. Well, I fancy we'll need you, but Rand won't like the idea of Whitecloaks in the battle lines unsupervised. So, I want you to swear you'll accept me as your commander until the battle is through."

Galad hesitated. Dawn was close now; in fact, it might have arrived, behind those clouds. "Do you realize what an audacious suggestion you make? The Lord Captain Commander of the Children of the Light obeying the orders of any man would be remarkable. But to you, a man I just recently saw judged a killer? A man most of the Children are convinced is a Darkfriend?"

Perrin turned to him. "You come with me now, and I'll get you to the Last Battle. Without me, who knows what will happen?"

"You said every sword was needed," Galad replied. "You'd leave us?"

"Yes. If I don't have that oath, I will. Rand may come back for you himself, though. In me, you know what you're getting. I'll be fair to you. All I'll ask is that your men stay in line, then fight where they're told when the battle comes. Rand . . . well, you can say no to me. You'll find it much harder to say it to him. And I doubt you'll like the result half as much, either, once you end up saying yes."

Galad frowned. "You're an oddly compelling man, Perrin Aybara."

"We have a bargain?" Perrin held out a hand.

Galad took it. It wasn't the threat that did it; it was remembering Perrin's voice when he'd found Jerum wounded. That compassion. No Darkfriend could feign that.

"You have my oath," Galad said. "To accept you as my military commander until the end of the Last Battle." He suddenly felt weaker than he had before, and he released a breath, then sat on a nearby rock.

"And you have my oath," Perrin said. "I'll see your men cared for like the others. Sit here and rest a spell; I'll search that patch over there. The weakness will pass soon."

"Weakness?"

Perrin nodded. "I know what it's like to be caught up in the needs of a *ta'veren*. Light, but I do." He eyed Galad.

"You ever wonder why we ended up here, in this same place?"

"My men and I assumed it was because the Light had placed you before us," Galad said. "So we could punish you."

Perrin shook his head. "That's not it at all. Truth is, Galad, I apparently needed you. And that's why you ended up here." With that, he headed off.

Alliandre carefully folded the bandage, then passed it to a waiting *gai'shain*. His fingers were thick and callused, his face hidden beneath the hood of his robe. She thought it might be Niagen, the Brotherless that Lacile had been taking after. That still irked Faile, but Alliandre couldn't fathom why. An Aiel man would probably match Lacile well.

Alliandre began rolling another bandage. She sat with other women in a small clearing near the battlefield, surrounded by scraggly scatterhead and stands of leatherleaf. The cool air was quiet save for the nearby groans of the wounded.

She cut another length of cloth in the morning light. The cloth had been a shirt. Now it was bandages. Not a great loss; it hadn't been a very good shirt, by the looks of it.

"The battle is through?" Berelain said softly. She and Faile worked nearby, sitting on stools across from one another as they cut.

"Yes, it appears that it is," Faile replied.

Both fell silent. Alliandre raised an eyebrow, but did not say anything. Something was going on between those two. Why suddenly start pretending they were the greatest of friends? The act seemed to fool many of the men in camp, but Alliandre could see the truth in the way their lips tightened when they saw one another. It had lessened after Faile had saved Berelain's life, but not vanished entirely.

"You were right about him," Berelain said.

"You sound surprised."

"I am not often wrong when it comes to men."

"My husband is not like other men. It—" Faile cut off. She looked toward Alliandre, eyes narrowing.

Bloody ashes, Alliandre thought. She'd sat too far away,

which made her strain, turning to eavesdrop. That was suspicious.

The two of them fell silent again, and Alliandre held up a hand, as if inspecting her nails. *Yes,* she thought. *Ignore me. I don't matter, I'm just a woman in over her head and struggling to keep up.* Faile and Berelain didn't think that, of course, any more than the Two Rivers men had ever thought Perrin had been unfaithful. If you sat them down and asked them—really made them think about it—they'd come to the conclusion that something else must have happened.

But things like superstition and bias ran deeper than mere thoughts. What the other two *thought* about Alliandre and what they instinctively *felt* were different. Besides, Alliandre really *was* a woman who was in over her head and struggling to keep up.

Best to know what your strengths were.

Alliandre turned back to cutting bandages. Faile and Berelain had insisted on staying to help; Alliandre couldn't go. Not with the two of them acting so bloody *fascinating* lately. Besides, she didn't mind the work. Compared to their captivity by the Aiel, this was really quite pleasant. Unfortunately, the two didn't go back to their conversation. In fact, Berelain rose, looking frustrated, and walked toward the other side of the clearing.

Alliandre could practically *feel* the frost coming off the woman. Berelain stopped over where others were rolling the strips of cloth. Alliandre stood up, carrying her stool, scissors and cloths over to Faile. "I don't believe I've ever seen her this unsettled," Alliandre said.

"She's not fond of being wrong," Faile noted. She took a deep breath, then shook her head. "She sees the world as a network of half-truths and inferences, ascribing complex motivations to the simplest of men. I suspect it makes her very good at court politics. But I wouldn't want to live that way."

"She's very wise," Alliandre said. "She *does* see things, Faile. She understands the world; she merely has a few blind spots, like most of us."

Faile nodded absently. "The thing I pity most is the fact that, despite all of this, I don't believe she was ever in love with Perrin. She chased him for sport, for political advan-

tage, and for Mayene. In the end, it was more the challenge
than anything else. She may be fond of him, but nothing
more. I could, perhaps, understand her if it had been for
love."

Alliandre kept her tongue after that, cutting bandages.
She ran across a fine blue silk shirt in the pile. Surely there
could be something better done with that! She stuffed it between two others and set those beside her, as if in a pile she
intended to cut.

Perrin eventually tramped into the clearing, followed by
some workers in bloodied clothing. He made instantly for
Faile, sitting down on Berelain's stool, setting his marvelous hammer down in the weeds beside him. He looked exhausted. Faile got him something to drink and then rubbed
his shoulder.

Alliandre excused herself, leaving Perrin and his wife.
She made her way over to where Berelain stood at the edge
of the clearing, sipping a cup of tea taken from the pot on
the fire. Berelain eyed her.

Alliandre poured herself a cup of tea, then blew on it for
a moment. "They *are* good for one another, Berelain," she
said. "I cannot say I'm sorry to see this result."

"Every relationship deserves to be challenged," Berelain
replied. "And if she had fallen in Malden—an outcome
all too possible—he would have needed someone. It is
not a great loss to me, however, to take my eyes off Perrin Aybara. I would have liked to make a connection to the
Dragon Reborn through him, but there will be other opportunities." She seemed far less frustrated now than she had
moments ago. In fact, she seemed to have returned to her
calculating self.

Alliandre smiled. *Clever woman.* Faile needed to see her
rival completely beaten down, so that she would consider
the threat passed. This was why Berelain let some of her
frustration show, more than she normally would have.

Alliandre sipped her tea. "Marriage seems nothing to you
other than a calculation, then? The advantages gained?"

"There's also the joy of the hunt, the thrill of the game."

"And what of love?"

"Love is for those who do not rule," Berelain said. "A
woman is worth *far* more than her ability to make a match,
but I must care for Mayene. If we enter the Last Battle

without my having secured a husband, that puts the succession in danger. And when Mayene has a succession crisis, Tear is all too quick to assert itself. Romance is an unaffordable distraction I . . ."

She trailed off suddenly, her expression changing. What was going on? Alliandre turned to the side, frowning until she saw the cause.

Galad Damodred had entered the clearing.

He had blood on his white uniform, and he looked exhausted. Yet he stood upright, straight-backed, and his face was clean. He almost seemed too beautiful to be human, with that perfectly masculine face and graceful, lean figure. And those eyes! Like deep, dark pools. He practically seemed to *glow*.

"I . . . What was I saying?" Berelain asked, eyes on Damodred.

"That there is no place for romance in a leader's life?"

"Yes," Berelain said, sounding distracted. "It's just not reasonable at all."

"Not at all."

"I—" Berelain began, but Damodred turned toward them. She cut off as their eyes met.

Alliandre suppressed a smile as Damodred crossed the clearing. He executed another set of perfect bows, one for each of them, though he barely seemed to notice Alliandre.

"My . . . Lady First," he said. "Lord Aybara says that, when he first approached this battle, you pled to him on my behalf."

"Foolishly," Berelain said. "I feared he would attack you."

"If fearing that makes one a fool," Damodred said, "then we two are fools together in it. I was certain that my men would soon fall to Aybara."

She smiled at him. That quickly, she seemed to have forgotten everything she'd been saying previously.

"Would you like some tea?" Damodred said, speaking a little abruptly as he reached for the teacups, which sat on a cloth away from the fire.

"I'm drinking some," she noted.

"Some more then?" he asked, hastily kneeling and pouring a cup.

"Er."

He stood up, holding the cup, then seeing that she already had one in her hands.

"There are still bandages to cut," Berelain said. "Perhaps you could help."

"Perhaps," he said. He handed the cup he'd poured over to Alliandre. Berelain—her eyes still holding his—handed hers over as well, seeming oblivious to what she was doing.

Alliandre smiled deeply—now holding three teacups—as the two of them walked over to the stack of cloths to be cut. This might turn out well indeed. At the very least, it would get those blasted Whitecloaks out of her kingdom.

She walked back toward Faile and Perrin. As she did so, she slipped the blue silk shirt from the pile of cloth she'd set aside to cut.

It really would make a nice sash.

CHAPTER

44

A Backhanded Request

Morgase stepped out of her hillside tent and looked out at Andor. Whitebridge lay below, blessedly familiar, although she could see that it had grown. The farms were failing, the last of the winter stores spoiling, so people made for the cities.

The landscape should have been green. Instead, even the yellowed grass was dying off, leaving scars of brown. It wouldn't be long before the entire land was like the Waste. She longed to take action. This was her nation. Or it had once been.

She left her tent, looking for Master Gill. On the way, she passed Faile, who was speaking with the quartermaster again. Morgase nodded, showing deference. Faile nodded back. There was a rift between the two of them now. Morgase wished it could be otherwise. She and the others had shared a sliver of their lives when hope had been weaker than a candle's flame. It had been Faile who had encouraged Morgase to use the One Power—squeezing every last drop from her pathetic ability—to signal for help while they were trapped.

The camp was already well set up, and amazingly the Whitecloaks had joined them, but Perrin hadn't yet decided what to do. Or at least if he *had* decided, he wasn't sharing that decision with Morgase.

She walked to the wagon lines, past farriers and grooms looking for the best pasture, people arguing in the supply dump, soldiers grudgingly digging trenches for waste. Everyone had their place except Morgase. Servants backed away, half-bowing, uncertain how to treat her. She wasn't a queen, but neither was she simply another noblewoman. She certainly wasn't a servant anymore.

Though her time with Galad had reminded her what it was to be a queen, she was thankful for what she had learned as Maighdin. That hadn't been as bad as she had feared; there had been advantages to being a lady's maid. The camaraderie of the other servants, the freedom from the burdens of leadership, the time spent with Tallanvor. . . .

That life was not hers. It was time to be done with pretending.

She eventually found Basel Gill packing the cart, Lini supervising, Lamgwin and Breane helping. Faile had released Breane and Lamgwin from her service so they could serve Morgase. Morgase had kept silent about Faile so graciously granting her back her servants.

Tallanvor wasn't there. Well, she couldn't moon over him like a girl any longer. She had to get back to Caemlyn and help Elayne.

"Your Majes—" Master Gill said, bowing. He hesitated. "I mean, my Lady. Pardon me."

"Don't mind it, Master Gill. I have trouble remembering myself."

"You sure you want to go forward with this?" Lini folded her thin arms.

"Yes," Morgase said. "It is our duty to return to Caemlyn and offer Elayne what assistance we can."

"If you say so," Lini said. "Me, I think that anyone who allows two roosters in the same barnyard deserves the ruckus they get."

Morgase raised an eyebrow. "Noted. But I think you'll find that I am quite capable of helping without usurping authority from Elayne."

Lini shrugged.

She had a point; Morgase had to be careful. Staying in the capital for too long could throw a shadow across Elayne. But if there was one thing Morgase had learned from her months as Maighdin it was that people needed to be doing something productive, even if it was something as simple as learning to serve tea. Morgase had skills that Elayne could use for the dangerous times ahead. If she began to overshadow her daughter, however, she would move out of Caemlyn to her holdings in the west.

The others worked quickly loading up, and Morgase had to fold her arms to keep from helping. There was a certain fulfillment to caring for oneself. As she waited, she noticed someone riding up the path from Whitebridge. Tallanvor. What had he been doing in the city? He saw her and approached, then bowed, his lean, square face a model of deference. "My Lady."

"You visited the city? Did you get Lord Aybara's permission?" Perrin hadn't wanted a sudden flood of soldiers and refugees going into the city, causing trouble.

"My Lady, I have family there," Tallanvor said, climbing from the saddle. His voice was stiff and formal. "I felt it wise to investigate the information discovered by Lord Aybara's scouts."

"Is that so, Guardsman-Lieutenant Tallanvor?" Morgase said. If he could act in such a formal way, then so could she. Lini, passing with an armload of linens to pack, gave a quiet snort at Morgase's tone.

"Yes, my Lady," Tallanvor replied. "My Lady . . . if I may make a suggestion?"

"Speak."

"By reports, your daughter still assumes you dead. I'm certain if we speak to Lord Aybara, he will command his Asha'man to make a gateway for us to return to Caemlyn."

"An interesting suggestion," Morgase said carefully, ignoring the smirk on Lini's face as she walked back by in the other direction.

"My Lady," Tallanvor said, eyeing Lini, "might we speak in private?"

Morgase nodded, stepping off to the side of the camp. Tallanvor followed. A short distance away, she turned to look at him. "Well?"

"My Lady," he continued in a softer voice. "The Andoran court is certain to hear that you still live, now that Aybara's entire camp knows. If you don't present yourself and explain that you've renounced the throne, the rumors of your survival could erode Elayne's authority."

Morgase didn't reply.

"If the Last Battle truly is coming," Tallanvor said, "we can't afford—"

"Oh, hush," she said curtly. "I've already given Lini and

the others the order to pack up. Didn't you notice what they were doing?"

Tallanvor flushed as he noticed Gill hauling a chest over and setting it on the cart.

"I apologize for my forwardness. With your leave, my Lady." Tallanvor nodded to her and turned to go.

"Must we be so formal with one another, Tallanvor?"

"The illusion has ended, my Lady." He walked away.

Morgase watched him go, and felt her heart twist. Curse her stubbornness! Curse Galad! His arrival had reminded her of her pride, of her royal duty.

It was bad for her to have a husband. She'd learned that from Taringail. For all of the stability her marriage to him had brought, each and every advantage had come with a threat to her throne. That was why she'd never made Bryne or Thom her official consort, and Gaebril only proved that she had been right to worry.

Any man who married her could, potentially, be a threat to Elayne as well as Andor. Her children, if she had any more, would be rivals to Elayne's. Morgase couldn't afford to love.

Tallanvor stopped a short distance away, and her breath caught. He turned, then walked back to her. He drew his sword and bent down, placing it reverently at her feet as she stood in weeds and scrub.

"I was wrong to threaten to leave, before," he said softly. "I was hurt, and pain makes a man stupid. You know that I will always be here, Morgase. I've promised it to you before, and I mean it. These days, I feel like a biteme in a world of eagles. But I have my sword and my heart, and both are yours. Forever."

He stood to go.

"Tallanvor," she said, almost in a whisper. "You've never asked me, you know. If I would have you."

"I can't put you into that position. It wouldn't be right to force you to do what we both know you must, now that you have been exposed."

"And what must I do?"

"Turn me down," he spat, obviously growing angry. "For the good of Andor."

"Must I?" she asked. "I keep telling myself that, Tallanvor, but still I question it."

"What good am I to you?" he asked. "At the very least, you should marry to help Elayne secure the loyalty of one of the factions you offended."

"And so I go to marriage without love," she said. "Again. How many times must I sacrifice my heart for Andor?"

"As many times as required, I suppose." He sounded so bitter, clenching his fists. Not angry at her, but at the situation. He always had been a man of such passion.

She hesitated, then shook her head. "No," she said. "Not again. Tallanvor, look at that sky above. You've seen the things that walk the world, felt the Dark One's curses strike us. This is not a time to be without hope. Without love."

"But what of duty?"

"Duty can bloody get in line. It's had its share of me. Everyone's had their share of me, Tallanvor. Everyone but the man I want." She stepped over his sword, still lying in the cockleburrs, then couldn't stop herself. In a blink, she was kissing him.

"All right, you two," a stern voice said from behind. "We're going to see Lord Aybara right now."

Morgase pulled away. It was Lini.

"What?" Morgase tried to regain some composure.

"You're getting married," Lini declared. "If I have to pull you to it by the ears."

"I will make my own choice," Morgase said. "Perrin tried to get me to—"

"*I'm* not him," Lini said. "This is best done before we return to Elayne. Once you're in Caemlyn there will be complications." She turned her eyes on Gill, who had the trunk stowed. "And you! Unpack my Lady's things."

"But Lini," Morgase protested, "we're going to Caemlyn."

"Tomorrow will be soon enough, child. Tonight, you celebrate." She eyed them. "And until the marriage is done, I don't think it's safe to trust you two alone."

Morgase flushed. "Lini," she hissed. "I'm not eighteen anymore!"

"No, when you were eighteen, you were married proper. Do I need to seize your ears?"

"I—" Morgase said.

"We're coming, Lini," Tallanvor said.

Morgase glared at him.

He frowned. "What?"

"You haven't asked."

He smiled, then held her close. "Morgase Trakand, will you be my wife?"

"Yes," she replied. "*Now* let's find Perrin."

Perrin tugged on the oak branch. It broke off, powdery wood dust puffing out. As he held the branch up, sawdust streamed out of the end onto the brown grass.

"Happened last night, my Lord," Kevlyn Torr said, holding his gloves. "The entire stand of hardwood over there, dead and dried in one night. Nearly a hundred trees, I'd guess."

Perrin dropped the branch, then dusted off his hands. "It's no worse than what we've seen before."

"But—"

"Don't worry about this," Perrin said. "Send some men to harvest this wood for fires; looks as if it will burn really well."

Kevlyn nodded, then hurried off. Other woodsmen were poking through the trees, looking disturbed. Oak, ash, elm and hickory trees dying overnight was bad enough. But dying, then drying out as though dead for years? That was downright unsettling. Best to take it in stride, though, not let the men grow afraid.

Perrin walked back toward camp. In the distance, anvils rang. They'd bought up raw materials, every bit of iron or steel they could get from Whitebridge. The people had been eager to trade for food, and Perrin had obtained five forges, with men to move them and set them up, along with hammers, tools and coal.

He might just have saved some in the city from starving. For a little while at least.

Smiths continued to pound. Hopefully he wasn't working Neald and the others too hard. Power-wrought weapons would give his people a critical advantage. Neald hadn't been able to figure out exactly what he'd done in helping forge *Mah'alleinir*, but Perrin hadn't been surprised. That night had been unique. He rested a hand on the weapon, feeling its faint warmth, thinking of Hopper.

Now, Neald *had* figured out how to make blades that

wouldn't dull or break. The more he practiced, the sharper edges he was able to create. The Aiel had already begun to demand those edges for their spears, and Perrin had given Neald the order to see to them first. It was the least he owed them.

On the Traveling ground at the edge of the large, increasingly entrenched camp, Grady stood in a circle with Annoura and Masuri, holding open a gateway. This was the last group of noncombatants who wanted to leave him, the group traveling to Caemlyn. Among them, he'd sent a messenger to Elayne. He'd need to meet with her soon; he wasn't certain if he should be worried or not. Time would tell.

Some others were coming back through the gateway, bringing a few carts of food purchased in Caemlyn, where supplies were still available. Eventually he caught sight of Faile picking her way through the camp toward him. He raised a hand, drawing her over.

"Everything all right with Bavin?" Perrin asked. She'd been at the quartermaster's tent.

"All is well."

Perrin rubbed his chin. "I've been meaning to tell you for some time—I don't think he's particularly honest."

"I'll keep special watch on him," she said, smelling amused.

"Berelain's been spending more time with the Whitecloaks," Perrin said. "Seems she has eyes for Damodred. She's been leaving me alone entirely."

"Is that so?"

"Yes. And she published that proclamation, condemning the rumors about me and her. Light, but people actually seem to believe it. I was worried they'd see it is a sign of desperation!"

Faile smelled satisfied.

He laid a hand on her shoulder. "I don't know what you did, but thank you."

"Do you know the difference between a hawk and a falcon, Perrin?"

"Size, mostly," he said. "Wing shape, too. The falcon has a more arrowlike look to it."

"The falcon," Faile said, "is a better flyer. It kills with the beak, and can fly fast and quick. The hawk is slower and stronger; it excels at getting prey that is moving along the ground. It likes to kill with the claw, attacking from above."

"All right," Perrin said. "But doesn't that mean that if both see a rabbit below, the hawk will be better at snatching it?"

"That's exactly what it means." She smiled. "The hawk is better at hunting the rabbit. But, you see, the falcon is better at hunting the *hawk*. You sent the messenger to Elayne?"

Women. He'd never make sense of them. For once, though, that seemed a good thing. "I did. Hopefully we'll be able to meet with her soon."

"There is already talk in camp of whom you might bring with you."

"Why would there be talk?" Perrin said. "It'll be you. You'll be best at knowing how to deal with Elayne, though having Alliandre along probably won't hurt."

"And Berelain?"

"She can stay in camp," Perrin said. "Watch over things here. She got to go last time."

Faile smelled even more satisfied. "We should—" She cut off, frowning. "Well, it looks like the last leaf finally fell."

"What?" Perrin said, turning. She was looking toward a group coming at them. Aged Lini, and trailing behind her Morgase and Tallanvor, gazing at one another like a couple just back from their first Bel Tine together. "I thought she didn't like him," he said. "Or, if she did, she wasn't going to marry him anyway."

"Minds change," Faile said, "much more quickly than hearts." Her scent was faintly angry, though she smothered it. She hadn't completely forgiven Morgase, but she was no longer outright hostile.

"Perrin Aybara," Morgase said. "You are the closest thing to a lord this camp has, other than my stepson. But it wouldn't be right for a son to marry his mother, so I suppose you will do. This man has asked my hand in marriage. Will you perform the ceremony for us?"

"You've a backhanded way of asking for my help, Morgase," he said.

The woman narrowed her eyes at him. And Faile looked at him and smelled angry as well. Perrin sighed. Fight among themselves though they might, they were always eager to pounce on a man who said the wrong thing, even if it was the truth.

However, Morgase calmed down. "I'm sorry. I did not mean to insult your authority."

"It's all right," he said. "I suppose you have reason to question."

"No," Morgase said, standing up taller. Light, but she could look like a queen when she wanted. How had they missed it before? "You *are* a lord, Perrin Aybara. Your actions show it. The Two Rivers is blessed because of you, and perhaps Andor as well. So long as you remain part of her."

"I intend to," Perrin promised.

"Well, if you would do this thing for me," she said, looking to Tallanvor, "then I would be willing to speak on your behalf with Elayne. Arrangements can be made, and titles—proper titles—can be bestowed."

"We will take your offer of speaking for us," Faile said, speaking quickly before Perrin could. "But we will decide, with Her Majesty, whether bestowing titles is the . . . proper course at this point."

Perrin eyed her. She wasn't still considering splitting the Two Rivers off into its own kingdom, was she? They'd never discussed it in such frank terms, but she'd encouraged him to use the flag of Manetheren. Well, they'd have to see about that.

Nearby, he could see Galad Damodred walking toward them, Berelain—as always lately—at his side. It appeared that Morgase had sent a messenger for him. Galad was tucking something into his pocket. A small letter, it appeared, with a red seal. Where had he gotten that? He looked troubled, though his expression lightened as he arrived. He didn't seem surprised by the news of the marriage; he had a nod for Perrin and a hug for his mother, then a stern-eyed—but cordial—greeting for Tallanvor.

"What kind of ceremony would you like?" Perrin asked Morgase. "I only know the Two Rivers way."

"I believe simple oaths before you will suffice," Morgase said. "I'm old enough to be tired of ceremony."

"Sounds appropriate to me," Perrin said.

Galad stepped to the side and Morgase and Tallanvor clasped hands. "Martyn Tallanvor," she said. "I've had

nore from you than I deserve, for longer than I've known
hat I've had it. You've claimed that the love of a simple
soldier is nothing before the mantle of a queen, but I say the
measure of a man is not in his title, but in his soul.

"I've seen from you bravery, dedication, loyalty, and
ove. I've seen the heart of a prince inside of you, the heart
of a man who would remain true when hundreds around
him failed. I swear that I love you. And before the Light, I
swear not to leave you. I swear to cherish you forever and
have you as my husband."

Berelain took out a kerchief and dabbed the corners of
her eyes. Well, women always wept at things like weddings.
Though Perrin . . . well, he felt a little water in his eyes, too.
Might have been the sunlight.

"Morgase Trakand," Tallanvor said, "I fell in love with
you for the way you treated those around you as Queen. I
saw a woman who took duty with not just a sense of responsibility, but with a *passion*. Even when you didn't know me
from any other guard, you treated me with kindness and
respect. You treated all of your subjects that way.

"I love you for your goodness, your cleverness, your
strength of mind and will. One of the Forsaken couldn't
break you; you escaped him when he thought you completely under control. The most terrible of tyrants couldn't
break you, even when he held you in his palm. The Shaido
couldn't break you. Another would be hateful in your place,
if they had been through what you had. But you . . . you
have grown, increasingly, into someone to admire, cherish,
and respect.

"I swear that I love you. And before the Light, I swear
that I will never, *never* leave you. I swear to cherish you
forever and have you as my wife. I swear it, Morgase,
though part of me fails to believe that this could really be
happening."

And then they stood like that, staring into one another's
eyes, as if Perrin weren't even there.

He coughed. "Well, so be it, then. You're married."
Should he give advice? How did one give advice to Morgase Trakand, a queen with children his own age? He just
shrugged. "Off with you, then."

Beside him, Faile smelled amused and faintly dissatisfied.
Lini snorted at Perrin's performance, but ushered Morgase

and Tallanvor away. Galad nodded to him, and Berelain curtsied. They walked away, Berelain remarking on the suddenness of it.

Faile smiled at him. "You'll have to get better at that."

"They wanted it simple."

"Everyone *says* that," Faile replied. "But you can have an air of authority while keeping things brief. We'll talk about it. Next time you'll do a much better job."

Next time? He shook his head as Faile turned and walked toward the camp.

"Where are you going?" Perrin asked.

"To Bavin. I need to requisition some casks of ale."

"For what?"

"The festivities," Faile said, looking over her shoulder. "Ceremony can be skimped if needed. But the *celebration* should not be skimped." She glanced upward. "Particularly at times like this."

Perrin watched her go, disappearing into the enormous camp. Soldiers, farmers, craftsmen, Aiel, Whitecloaks, refugees. Almost seventy thousand strong, despite those who had left or fallen in battle. How had he ended up with such a force? Before leaving the Two Rivers, he'd never seen more than a thousand people gathered in one place.

The largest portion was the group of former mercenaries and refugees who had been training under Tam and Dannil. The Wolf Guard, they were calling themselves, whatever that was supposed to mean. Perrin began walking to check on the supply carts, but something small struck him softly on the back of the head.

He froze, turning, scanning the forest behind him. To the right, it stood brown and dead; to his left, the tree cover dwindled. He couldn't see anyone.

Have I been pushing myself too hard? he wondered, rubbing his head as he turned to continue walking. *Imagining things that—*

Another little strike on the back of his head. He spun and caught sight of something dropping to the grass. Frowning, he knelt down and picked it up. An acorn. Another one smacked him in the forehead. It had come from the forest.

Perrin growled and strode into the trees. One of the camp's few children, perhaps? Ahead was a large oak tree; the trunk thick and wide enough to hide someone. Once he grew close, he hesitated. Was this some kind of trap? He laid his hand on his hammer and inched forward. The tree was downwind, and he couldn't catch the scent of—

A hand suddenly jutted out from behind the trunk, holding a brown sack. "I caught a badger," a familiar voice said. "Want to let it go on the village green?"

Perrin froze, then let out a bellowing laugh. He rounded the tree's trunk and found a figure in a high-collared red coat—trimmed with gold—and fine brown trousers sitting on the tree's exposed roots, the sack squirming near his ankles. Mat was chewing idly on a long length of jerky, and wore a broad-brimmed black hat. A black polearm with a broad blade at the top leaned against the tree beside him. Where had he gotten such fine clothing? Hadn't he once complained about Rand wearing outfits like that?

"Mat?" Perrin asked, nearly too stunned to speak. "What are you doing here?"

"Catching badgers," Mat said, shaking the sack. "Bloody hard to do, you know, particularly on short notice."

The sack rustled and Perrin heard a faint growl from inside. He could smell that there was, indeed, something alive in that sack. "You actually caught one?"

"Call me nostalgic."

Perrin didn't know whether to chastise Mat or laugh at him—that particular mix of emotions was common when Mat was around. No colors, fortunately, spun in Perrin's eyes now that they were near one another. Light, that would have been confusing. Perrin did feel a . . . rightness, however.

The long-limbed man smiled, setting the sack down and standing, offering a hand. Perrin took it, but pulled Mat into a hearty hug.

"Light, Mat," Perrin said. "It seems like it's been forever!"

"A lifetime," Mat said. "Maybe two. I lose count. Anyway, Caemlyn already is buzzing with news of your arrival. Figured the only way to get in a word of welcome was to slip through that gateway and find you before everyone else." Mat picked up his spear and rested it on his shoulder, blade to the back.

"What have you been doing? Where have you been? Is Thom with you? What about Nynaeve?"

"So many questions," Mat said. "How safe is this camp
of yours?"

"Safe as any place."

"Not safe enough," Mat grew solemn. "Look, Perrin,
we've got some mighty dangerous folks after us. I came
because I wanted to warn you to take extra care. Assassins will find you soon enough, and you'd best be ready for
them. We need to catch up. But I don't want to do it here."

"Where, then?"

"Meet me in an inn called The Happy Throng, in Caemlyn. Oh, and if you don't mind, I'll be wanting to borrow
one of those black-coated fellows of yours for a few shakes.
Need a gateway."

"For what purpose?"

"I'll explain. But later." Mat tipped his hat, turning to jog
back toward the still-open gateway to Caemlyn. "Really,"
he said, turning and jogging backward for a moment. "Be
careful, Perrin."

With that, he ducked past a few refugees and through
the gateway. How had he gotten past Grady? Light! Perrin
shook his head to himself, then bent to untie the sack and
ease the poor badger Mat had captured.

CHAPTER

45

A Reunion

E layne woke in her bed, bleary-eyed. "Egwene?" she said, disoriented. "What?"

The last memories of the dream were dissolving like honey consumed by warm tea, but Egwene's words remained firm in Elayne's mind. *The serpent has fallen,* Egwene had sent. *Your brother's return was timely.*

Elayne sat up, feeling a surge of relief. She had spent the entire night trying to channel enough to make her dream *ter'angreal* work, to no avail. When she'd found out that Birgitte had turned away Gawyn—while Elayne sat inside, furious but unable to attend the meeting with Egwene—she'd been livid.

Well, Mesaana had been defeated, it seemed. And what was that about her brother? She smiled. Perhaps he and Egwene had worked out their problems.

Morning light peeked through the drapes. Elayne sat back, feeling the powerful warmth through the bond with Rand that had appeared there. Light, but that was a wonderful sensation. The moment she'd begun feeling it, the cloud cover around Andor had broken.

It had been about a week since the testing of the dragons, and she'd put all of the bellfounders in her nation to work on creating them. These days, one could hear a steady sound in Caemlyn, repeating booms as members of the Band trained with the weapons in the hills outside of the city. So far, she had let only a few of the weapons be used for training; the different teams rotated practicing on them. She'd gathered the larger number in a secret warehouse inside Caemlyn for safekeeping.

She thought about the dream sending again. She hungered for specifics. Well, Egwene would probably send a messenger by gateway eventually.

The door cracked, and Melfane looked in. "Your Majesty?" the short, round-faced woman asked. "Is everything all right? I thought I heard a cry of pain." Ever since lifting her ban on Elayne remaining in bed, the midwife had decided to sleep in the antechamber outside Elayne's bedroom to keep a careful watch on her.

"That was an exclamation of joy, Melfane," Elayne said. "A greeting for the wonderful morning that has come to us."

Melfane frowned. Elayne tried to act cheerful around the woman, to persuade her that more bed rest wasn't needed, but perhaps that last part had been a little much. Elayne couldn't afford to appear as if she were forcing herself to be happy. Even if she was. Insufferable woman.

Melfane walked in and pulled open the drapes—sunlight was good for a woman with child, she'd explained. Part of Elayne's treatment lately had been to sit in her bed with the covers drawn back, letting the spring sunlight bake her skin. As Melfane moved, Elayne felt a little tremble from inside. "Oh! There was another. They're kicking, Melfane! Come feel!"

"I won't be able to feel it yet, Your Majesty. Not until they're stronger." She began the normal daily routine. Listen to Elayne's heartbeat, then listen for the babe's. Melfane still wouldn't believe there were twins. After that, she inspected and prodded Elayne, performing all of the tests in her secretive list of annoying and embarrassing things to do to women.

Finally, Melfane placed hands on hips, regarding Elayne, who was doing up her nightgown. "I think you've been straining yourself too much lately. I want you to be certain to take proper rest. My cousin Tess's daughter had a child not two years ago who was birthed barely breathing. Light be thanked that the child survived, but *she* had been working the fields late through the day before and not taking proper meals. Imagine! Take care of yourself, my Queen. Your babies will be thankful for it."

Elayne nodded, relaxing. "Wait!" she said, sitting up. "*Babies?*"

"Yes," Melfane said, walking to the door. "There are two

heartbeats in your womb, sure as I have two arms. Don't know how you knew it."

"You heard the heartbeats!" Elayne exclaimed, elated.

"Yes, they're there, sure as the sun." Melfane shook her head and left, sending in Naris and Sephanie to dress her and brush her hair.

Elayne endured the process in a state of amazement. Melfane believed! She couldn't stop herself from smiling.

An hour later, she settled into her small sitting room, windows all thrown open to let in the sunlight, sipping warm goat's milk. Master Norry entered on long spindly legs, tufts of hair sticking up behind the backs of his ears, face long and peaked, leather folder under his arm. He was accompanied by Dyelin, who didn't usually attend the morning meeting. Elayne raised an eyebrow at the woman.

"I have the information you requested, Elayne," Dyelin said, pouring herself some morning tea. Today it was cloudberry. "I hear Melfane heard heartbeats?"

"She did indeed."

"My congratulations, Your Majesty," Master Norry said. He opened his folder and began arranging his papers on the tall, narrow table beside her chair. He rarely sat down in Elayne's company. Dyelin took one of the other comfortable chairs beside the hearth.

What information had Elayne requested of the woman? She didn't recall asking for anything specific. The question distracted her as Norry went over the daily reports on the various armies in the area. There was a list of altercations between sell-sword groups.

He also talked of food problems. Despite the Kinswomen making gateways to Rand's lands to the south for supply—and despite the caches of unexpected food stores that had been discovered in the city—Caemlyn was running low.

"Finally, as for our, um, guests," Norry said. "Messengers have arrived with the anticipated responses."

None of the three Houses whose nobility had been captured could afford to pay ransom. Once the Arawn, Sarand and Marne estates had been among the most productive and extensive in Andor—and now they were destitute, their coffers dry, their fields barren. And Elayne had left two of them without leadership. Light, what a mess!

Norry moved on. She had a letter from Talmanes, agreeing to move several companies of soldiers from the Band of the Red Hand to Cairhien. She ordered Norry to send him a writ with her seal, authorizing the soldiers to "lend aid restoring order." That was, of course, nonsense. No order needed to be restored. But if Elayne was ever going to move for the Sun Throne, she'd need to make some preliminary moves in that direction.

"This is what I wanted to discuss, Elayne," Dyelin said as Norry began to pack up his papers, arranging each one with meticulous care. Light help them if one of those precious pages tore or got a stain on it.

"The situation in Cairhien is . . . complex," Dyelin said.

"When is it not?" Elayne asked with a sigh. "You've information on the political climate there?"

"It's a mess," Dyelin said simply. "We need to talk about how you're going to manage the maintenance of two nations, one in absence."

"We have gateways," Elayne said.

"True. But you *must* find a way to take the Sun Throne without letting it look as if Andor is subsuming Cairhien. The nobility there might accept you as their queen, but only if they see themselves as equals to the Andorans. Otherwise, the moment they're out of your sight, the schemes will grow like yeast in a warm bowl of water."

"They *will* be the equals of the Andorans," Elayne said.

"They won't see it that way if you go in with your armies," Dyelin said. "The Cairhienin are a proud people. To think of themselves living conquered beneath Andor's Crown. . . ."

"They lived beneath Rand's power."

"With all due respect, Elayne," Dyelin said. "He is the Dragon Reborn. You are not."

Elayne frowned, but how did one argue with that?

Master Norry cleared his throat. "Your Majesty, Lady Dyelin's advice is not born of idle speculation. I, um, have heard things. Knowing of your interests in Cairhien. . . ."

He'd been growing better at gathering informants. She'd turn him into a regular spymaster yet!

"Your Majesty," Norry continued, voice lower. "Rumors are claiming that you'll soon come to seize the Sun Throne.

There is already talk of rebellion against you. Idle speculation, I'm certain, but . . ."

"The Cairhienin could see Rand al'Thor as an emperor," Dyelin said. "Not a foreign king. That is a different thing."

"Well, we don't need to move armies to take the Sun Throne," Elayne said thoughtfully.

"I . . . am not certain of that, Your Majesty," Norry said. "The rumors are quite pervasive. It seems that as soon as the Lord Dragon announced the throne was to be yours, some elements in the nation began working—very subtly—to prevent it from happening. Because of these rumors, many people worry that you will seize the titles of the Cairhienin nobility and give them to Andorans instead. Others claim you will relegate any Cairhienin to a secondary state of citizenship."

"Nonsense," Elayne said. "That's plain ridiculous!"

"Obviously," Norry said. "But there are many rumors. They do tend to, um, grow like chokevines. The sentiment is strong."

Elayne gritted her teeth. The world was fast coming to be a place for those with strong alliances, knit together with bonds of both blood and paper. She had the best chance of uniting Cairhien and Andor that any queen had had in generations. "Do we know who has been starting the rumors?"

"That has been very difficult to ascertain, my Lady," Norry said.

"Who stands to benefit most?" Elayne asked. "That's the first place we should look for the source."

Norry glanced at Dyelin.

"Any number of people *could* benefit," Dyelin said, stirring her tea. "I would guess that those with the greatest chance of taking the throne themselves would benefit the most."

"Those who resisted Rand," Elayne guessed.

"Perhaps," Dyelin said. "Or perhaps not. The strongest of the rebellious elements received great attention from the Dragon, and many of them were either converted or broken. So his allies—those he trusted most, or who professed greatest allegiance to him—are the ones we should probably suspect. This *is* Cairhien, after all."

Daes Dae'mar. Yes, it would make sense for Rand's allies to resist her ascent to the throne. Those who had been favored by Rand would be favored for the throne, should Elayne prove incapable. However, those people would also have undermined their chances by professing allegiance to a foreign leader.

"I should think," Elayne said thoughtfully, "that those in the *best* position for the throne would be those in the middle. Anyone who didn't oppose Rand, and so didn't earn his ire. But also someone who didn't support him too wholeheartedly—someone who can be viewed as a patriot who can reluctantly step in and take power once I've failed." She eyed the other two. "Get me the names of anyone who has risen sharply in influence recently, a nobleman or woman who fits those criteria."

Dyelin and Master Norry nodded. Eventually, she would probably have to build a stronger network of eyes-and-ears, as neither of these two was perfectly suited to leading them. Norry was too obvious, and he already had enough to do with his other duties. Dyelin was . . . well, Elayne wasn't certain what Dyelin was.

She owed much to Dyelin, who seemed to have taken it upon herself to act as a surrogate mother to Elayne. A voice of experience and wisdom. But eventually, Dyelin would have to take a few steps back. Neither of them could afford to encourage the notion that Dyelin was the real power behind the throne.

But Light! What would she have done without the woman? Elayne had to steel herself against the sudden surge of feeling. Blood and bloody ashes, *when* was she going to get over these mood swings? A queen couldn't afford to be seen crying on a whim!

Elayne dabbed her eyes. Dyelin wisely said nothing.

"This will be for the best," Elayne said firmly, to distract attention from her treacherous eyes. "I'm still worried about the invasion."

Dyelin said nothing to that. She didn't believe that Chesmal had been talking of a specific invasion of Andor; she thought that the Black sister had been speaking of the Trolloc invasion of the Borderlands. Birgitte took the news more seriously, beefing up soldiers on the Andoran borders. Still, Elayne would very much like to have control of Cairhien; if

Trollocs were to march on Andor, her sister realm would be one of the avenues they might use.

Before the conversation could go further, the door to the hallway opened, and Elayne would have jumped in alarm had she not felt that it was Birgitte. The Warder never knocked. She strode in, wearing a sword—reluctantly—and her knee-high black boots over trousers. Oddly, she was followed by two cloaked figures, their faces hidden by hoods. Norry stepped back, raising a hand to his breast at the irregularity of it. Everyone knew that Elayne didn't like to see visitors in the small sitting room. If Birgitte was bringing people here. . . .

"Mat?" Elayne guessed.

"Hardly," a familiar voice said, firm and clear. The larger of the figures lowered his hood, revealing a perfectly beautiful masculine face. He had a square jaw and a set of focused eyes that Elayne remembered well from her childhood—mostly when he had noticed her doing something wrong.

"Galad," Elayne said, surprised at the warmth she felt for her half-brother. She rose, holding out her hands toward him. She'd spent most of their childhood frustrated with him for one reason or another, but it *was* good to see him alive and well. "Where have you been?"

"I have been seeking truth," Galad said, bowing with an expert bow, but he did not approach to take her hands. He rose and glanced to the side. "I found that which I did not expect. Steel yourself, sister."

Elayne frowned as the second, shorter figure lowered her hood. Elayne's mother.

Elayne gasped. It *was* her! That face, that golden hair. Those eyes that had so often looked at Elayne as a child, judging her, measuring her—not merely as a parent measured her daughter, but as a queen measured her successor. Elayne felt her heart beating in her chest. Her mother. Her *mother* was alive.

Morgase was alive. The Queen still lived.

Morgase locked eyes with Elayne, then—oddly—Morgase looked down. "Your Majesty," she said with a curtsy, still remaining beside the door.

Elayne controlled her thoughts, controlled her panic. She was Queen, or she *would* have been Queen, or . . . Light! She'd taken the throne, and she was at *least* the

Daughter-Heir. But now her own mother came back from the bloody *dead*?

"Please, sit," Elayne found herself saying, gesturing Morgase toward the seat beside Dyelin. It did Elayne good to see that Dyelin wasn't dealing with the shock any better than Elayne. She sat with her hand gripping her cup of tea, knuckles white, eyes bulging.

"Thank you, Your Majesty," Morgase said, walking forward, Galad joining her and resting a hand on Elayne's shoulder in a comforting way. He then fetched himself a seat from the other side of the room.

Morgase's tone was more reserved than Elayne remembered. And why did she continue to call Elayne that title? The Queen had come in secret, with hood drawn. Elayne regarded her mother, putting the pieces together as she sat. "You renounced the throne, didn't you?"

Morgase gave a stately nod.

"Oh, thank the Light," Dyelin said, letting out a loud breath, hand raised to her breast. "No offense, Morgase. But for a moment there, I imagined a war between Trakand and Trakand!"

"It wouldn't have come to that," Elayne said, virtually at the same time that her mother said something similar. Their eyes met, and Elayne allowed herself to smile. "We would have found a . . . reasonable accommodation. This will do, though I certainly wonder at the circumstances of the event."

"I was being held by the Children of the Light, Elayne," Morgase said. "Old Pedron Niall was a gentleman in most respects, but his successor was not. I would *not* let myself be used against Andor."

"Bloody Whitecloaks," Elayne muttered under her breath. Light, they'd actually been telling the *truth* when they'd written, claiming to have Morgase in their possession?

Galad eyed her, raising an eyebrow. He placed the chair he'd brought over, then undid his cloak, revealing the brilliant white uniform underneath, with the sunburst on the breast.

"Oh, that's *right*," Elayne said, exasperated. "I almost forgot that. Intentionally."

"The Children had answers, Elayne," he said, sitting.

Light, but he was frustrating. It was good to see him, but he *was* frustrating!

"I don't wish to discuss it," Elayne said. "How many Whitecloaks have come with you?"

"The entire force of *Children* accompanied me to Andor," Galad said. "I am their Lord Captain Commander."

Elayne blinked, then glanced at Morgase. The elder Trakand nodded. "Well," Elayne said, "I see we have much to catch up on."

Galad took that as a request—he could be very literal—and began explaining how he'd come by his station. He was quite detailed about it, and Elayne occasionally glanced at her mother. Morgase's expression was unreadable.

Once Galad was done, he asked after the Succession war. Conversing with Galad was often like this: an exchange, more formal than familiar. Once, it had frustrated her, but this time she found that—against her better wishes—she'd actually been missing him. So she listened with fondness.

Eventually, the conversation wound down. There was more to talk about with him, but Elayne was dying for a chance to speak just with her mother. "Galad," Elayne said, "I'd like to talk further. Would you be amenable to an early dinner this evening? You may take refreshment in your old quarters until then."

He nodded, standing. "That would be well."

"Dyelin, Master Norry," Elayne said. "My mother's survival will lead to some . . . delicate issues of state. We will need to publish her abdication officially, and quickly. Master Norry, I'll leave the formal document to you. Dyelin, please inform my closest allies of this news so that they will not be taken by surprise."

Dyelin nodded. She glanced at Morgase—Dyelin wasn't one of those whom the former Queen had embarrassed during the days of Rahvin's influence, but she had undoubtedly heard the stories. Then Dyelin withdrew with Galad and Master Norry. Morgase glanced at Birgitte as soon as the door closed; the Warder was the only other one in the room.

"I trust her like a sister, Mother," Elayne said. "An insufferable older sister, sometimes, but a sister nonetheless."

Morgase smiled, then rose and took Elayne by the hands, pulling her up into an embrace. "Ah, my daughter," she said, tears in her eyes. "Look at what you've done! Queen in your own right!"

"You trained me well, Mother," Elayne said. She pulled back. "And you're a grandmother! Or soon will be!"

Morgase frowned, looking down at her. "Yes, I thought as much from looking at you. Who . . . ?"

"Rand," Elayne said, blushing, "though it's not widely known, and I'd rather it stay that way."

"Rand al'Thor . . ." Morgase said, her mood darkening. "That—"

"Mother," Elayne said, raising a hand to grasp hers. "He's a good man, and I love him. What you have heard is exaggeration or bitter rumor."

"But he's . . . Elayne, a man who can channel, the Dragon Reborn!"

"And still a man," Elayne said, feeling his knot of emotions in the back of her mind, so warm. "Just a man, for all that is demanded of him."

Morgase drew her lips into a thin line. "I shall withhold judgment. Though in a way I still feel that I should have thrown that boy in the Palace dungeons the moment we found him skulking in the gardens. I didn't like how he looked at you even then, mind you."

Elayne smiled, then gestured back to the seats. Morgase sat, and this time Elayne took the seat directly beside her, still clutching her mother's hands. She sensed amusement from Birgitte, who stood with her back against the far wall, one knee bent so that the sole of her boot rested against the wood paneling.

"What?" Elayne asked.

"Nothing," Birgitte said. "It's good to see you two acting like mother and child, or at least woman and woman, rather than staring at each other like two posts."

"Elayne is Queen," Morgase said stiffly. "Her life belongs to her people, and my arrival threatened to upset her Succession."

"It still *might* muddy things, Mother," Elayne said. "Your appearance could open old wounds."

"I will have to apologize," Morgase said. "Perhaps offer reparations." She hesitated. "I had intended to stay away, daughter. It would be best if those who hated me still thought me dead. But—"

"No," Elayne said quickly, squeezing her hands. "This *is* for the best. We simply will have to approach it with skill and care."

Morgase smiled. "You make me proud. You will be a wonderful queen."

Elayne had to force herself to stop beaming. Her mother had never been free with compliments.

"But tell me, before we go further," Morgase said, voice growing more hesitant. "I have heard reports that Gaebril was . . ."

"Rahvin," Elayne said, nodding. "It's true, Mother."

"I hate him for what he did. I can see him, using me, driving spikes through the hearts and loyalty of my dearest friends. And yet there is a part of me that longs to see him, irrationally."

"He used Compulsion on you," Elayne said softly. "There is no other explanation. We will have to see if any from the White Tower can Heal it."

Morgase shook her head. "Whatever it was, it is faint now, and manageable. I have found another to give my affection."

Elayne frowned.

"I will explain that at another point," Morgase said. "I'm not certain *I* understand it yet. First we must decide what to do about my return."

"That is easy," Elayne said. "We celebrate!"

"Yes, but—"

"But nothing, Mother," Elayne said. "You have returned to us! The city, the entire nation, will celebrate." She hesitated. "And after that, we will find an important function for you."

"Something that takes me away from the capital, so I cast no unfortunate shadows."

"But a duty that *is* important, so that you are not thought of as having been put out to pasture." Elayne grimaced. "Perhaps we can give you charge of the western quarter of the realm. I have little pleasure in the reports of what is happening there."

"The Two Rivers?" Morgase asked. "And Lord Perrin Aybara?"

Elayne nodded.

"He is an interesting one, Perrin is," Morgase said

thoughtfully. "Yes, perhaps I could be of some use there. We have something of an understanding already."

Elayne raised an eyebrow.

"He was behind my safe return to you," Morgase said. "He is an honest man, and honorable as well. But also a rebel, despite his good intentions. You will not have an easy time of it if you come to blows with that one."

"I'd rather avoid it." She grimaced. The easiest way to deal with it would be to find him and execute him, but of course she wasn't going to do that. Even if reports had her fuming enough to almost wish that she could.

"Well, we shall begin working on a way." Morgase smiled. "It will help you to hear of what happened to me. Oh, and Lini is safe. I don't know if you've worried over her or not."

"To be honest, I didn't," Elayne said, grimacing, feeling a spike of shame. "It seems that the collapse of Dragonmount itself couldn't harm Lini."

Morgase smiled, then began her story. Elayne listened with awe, and not a little excitement. Her mother lived. Light be blessed, so many things had gone wrong recently, but at least one had gone right.

The Three-fold Land at night was peaceful and quiet. Most animals were active near dusk and dawn, when it was neither sweltering nor freezing.

Aviendha sat on a small rock outcropping, legs folded beneath her, looking down upon Rhuidean, in the lands of the Jenn Aiel, the clan that was not. Once Rhuidean had been shrouded in protective mists. That was before Rand had come. He'd broken the city in three very important, very discomforting ways.

The first was the simplest. Rand had taken away the mist. The city had shed its dome like an *algai'd'siswai* unveiling his face. She didn't know how Rand had caused the transformation; she doubted that he knew himself. But in exposing the city, he had changed it forever.

The second way Rand had broken Rhuidean was by bringing it water. A grand lake lay beside the city, and phantom moonlight, filtered through clouds above, made the waters

hine. The people were calling the lake Tsodrelle'Aman.
'ears of the Dragon, though the lake *should* be called Tears
f the Aiel. Rand al'Thor had not known how much pain
e would cause in what he revealed. Such was the way with
im. His actions were often so innocent.

The third way Rand had broken the city was the most
rofound. Aviendha was slowly coming to understand this
ne. Nakomi's words worried her, unnerved her. They had
wakened in her shadows of memories, things from poten-
ial futures that Aviendha had seen in the rings during her
rst visit to Rhuidean, but that her mind could not quite
ecall, at least not directly.

She worried that Rhuidean would stop mattering very
oon. Once, the city's ultimate purpose had been to show
Vise Ones and clan chiefs their people's secret past. To
repare them for the day when they'd serve the Dragon.
hat day had come. So who should come to Rhuidean now?
ending the Aiel leaders through the glass columns would
e reminding them of *toh* they had begun to meet.

This bothered Aviendha in ways that itched beneath her
kin. She didn't want to acknowledge these questions. She
vanted to continue with tradition. But she could not get
hem out of her head.

Rand caused so many problems. Still, she loved him. She
oved him *for* his ignorance, in a way. It allowed him to
earn. And she loved him for the foolish way he tried to
rotect those who did not want to be protected.

Most of all, she loved him for his desire to be strong.
Aviendha had *always* wanted to be strong. Learn the spear.
'ight and earn *ji*. Be the best. She could feel him now, dis-
ant from her. They were so alike in this way.

Her feet ached from running. She'd rubbed them with the
ap of a *segade* plant, but she could still feel them throb-
ing. Her boots sat on the stone beside her, along with the
ine woolen stockings that Elayne had given her.

She was tired and thirsty—she would fast this night, con-
emplating, then refill her waterskin at the lake before go-
ng into Rhuidean tomorrow. Tonight, she sat and thought,
reparing.

The lives of the Aiel were changing. It was strength to
ccept change when it could not be avoided. If a hold was

damaged during a raid and you rebuilt it, you never made
it exactly the same way. You took the chance to fix the
problems—the door that creaked in the wind, the uneven
section of floor. To make it exactly as it had been would be
foolishness.

Perhaps traditions—such as coming to Rhuidean, and
even living in the Three-fold Land itself—would need to be
reexamined eventually. But for now, the Aiel couldn't leave
the wetlands. There was the Last Battle. And then the Seanchan had captured many Aiel and made Wise Ones into *da
mane*; that could not be allowed. And the White Tower still
assumed that all Aiel Wise Ones who could channel were
wilders. Something would have to be done about that.

And herself? The more she thought of it, she realized
that she couldn't go back to her old life. She had to be with
Rand. If he survived the Last Battle—and she intended to
fight hard to make certain he did—he would still be a wetlander king. And then there was Elayne. Aviendha and she
were going to be sister-wives, but Elayne would never leave
Andor. Would she expect Rand to stay with her? Would that
mean Aviendha would need to as well?

So troubling, both for herself and her people. Tradition
should not be maintained just because they were traditions. Strength was not strength if it had no purpose or
direction.

She studied Rhuidean, such a grand place of stone and
majesty. Most cities disgusted her with their corrupt filth,
but Rhuidean was different. Domed roofs, half-finished
monoliths and towers, carefully planned sections with
dwellings. The fountains flowed now, though a large section
still bore the scars of when Rand had fought there. Much of
that had been cleaned up by the families who lived here, Aiel
who had not gone to war.

There would be no shops. No arguments in streets, no
murderers in alleys. Rhuidean might have been deprived of
meaning, but it would remain a place of peace.

I will go on, she decided. *Pass through the glass columns.* Perhaps her worries were true, and the passage was
now far less meaningful, but she was genuinely curious to
see what the others had seen. Besides, knowing one's past
was important in order to understand the future.

Wise Ones and clan chiefs had been visiting this location for centuries. They returned with knowledge. Maybe the city would show her what to do about her people, and about her own heart.

CHAPTER
46

Working Leather

A ndrol carefully took the oval piece of leather from the steaming water; it had darkened and curled. He moved quickly, picking it up in his callused fingers. The leather was springy and flexible now.

He quickly sat down at his bench, a square of sunlight coming in through the window on his right side. He wrapped the leather around a thick wooden rod about two inches across, then poked holes around the edges.

From there, he began stitching the leather to another piece he'd prepared earlier. A good stitching around the outside would keep it from fraying. A lot of leatherworkers were casual about stitching. Not Androl. The stitching was what people saw first; it stood out, like paint on a wall.

As he worked, the leather dried and lost some of its springiness, but it was still flexible enough. He made the stitches neat and even. He pulled the last few tight and used them to tie the leather around the wooden rod; he'd cut those last once the leather dried.

Stitching done, he added some ornaments. A name across the top, pounded into place using his small mallet and letter-topped pins. The symbols of the Sword and Dragon came next; he'd made those plates himself, based on the pins the Asha'man wore.

At the bottom, using his smaller letter pins, he stamped the words, "Defend. Guard. Protect." As the leather continued to dry, he got out his stain and gauze to carefully color the letters and the designs for contrast.

There was a tranquility to this kind of work; so much of his life was about destruction these days. He knew that had to be. He'd come to the Black Tower in the first place because he understood what was to come. Still, it was nice to create something.

He left his current piece, letting it dry while working on some saddle straps. He measured the straps with the marks on his table, then reached for his shears in the tool pouch that hung from the side of the table—he'd made that himself. He was annoyed to discover that they weren't in their place.

Burn the day word got out that I had good shears in here, he thought. Despite Taim's supposedly strict rules for the Black Tower, there was a distressing amount of chaos. Large infractions were punished with harsh measures, but the little things—like wandering into a man's workshop and "borrowing" his shears—were ignored. Particularly if the borrower was one of the M'Hael's favorites.

Androl sighed. His belt knife was waiting at Cuellar's place for sharpening. *Well,* he thought, *Taim* does *keep telling us to look for excuses to channel* . . . Androl emptied himself of emotion, then seized the Source. It had been months since he'd had trouble doing that—at first, he'd been able to channel only when he was holding a strap of leather. The M'Hael had beaten that out of him. It had not been a pleasant process.

Saidin flooded into him, sweet, powerful, beautiful. He sat for a long moment, enjoying it. The taint was gone. What a wonder that was. He closed his eyes and breathed in deeply.

What would it be like to draw in as much of the One Power as the others could? At times, he thirsted for that. He knew he was weak—weakest of the Dedicated in the Black Tower. Perhaps so weak he should never have been promoted from soldier. Logain had gone to the Lord Dragon about it, and made the promotion happen, against Taim's express wishes.

Androl opened his eyes, then held up the strap and wove a tiny gateway, only an inch across. It burst alive in front of him, slicing the strap in two. He smiled, then let it vanish and repeated the process.

Some said that Logain had forced Androl's promotion only as a dig against Taim's authority. But Logain had said that it was Androl's incredible Talent with gateways that had earned him the title of Dedicated. Logain was a hard man, broken around the edges, like an old scabbard that hadn't been properly lacquered. But that scabbard still held a deadly sword. Logain was honest. A good man, beneath the scuff marks.

Androl eventually finished with the straps. He walked over and snipped the string holding the oval piece of leather in place. It retained its shape, and he held it up to the sunlight, inspecting the stitching. The leather was stiff without being brittle. He fit it onto his forearm. Yes, the molding was good.

He nodded to himself. One of the tricks to life was paying attention to the small details. Focus, make the small things right. If each stitch was secure on an armguard, then it wouldn't fray or snap. That could mean the difference between an archer lasting through a barrage or having to put away his bow.

One archer wouldn't make a battle. But the small things piled up, one atop another, until they became large things. He finished the armguard by affixing a few permanent ties to its back, so one could bind it in place on the arm.

He took his black coat off the back of his chair. The silver sword pin on the high collar glimmered in the window's sunlight as he did up the buttons. He glanced at himself in the glass's reflection, making certain the coat was straight. Small things were important. Seconds were small things, and if you heaped enough of those on top of one another, they became a man's life.

He put the armguard on his arm, then pushed open the door to his small workshop and entered the outskirts of the Black Tower's village. Here, clusters of two-storied buildings were arranged much like any small town in Andor. Peaked roofs, thatched, with straight wooden walls, some stone and brick as well. A double line of them ran down the center of the village. Looking only at those, one might have thought he was strolling through New Braem or Grafendale.

Of course, that required ignoring the men in black coats. They were everywhere, running errands for the M'Hael, going to practice, working on the foundations of the Black Tower structure itself. This place was still a work in progress. A group of soldiers—bearing neither the sword pin

nor the red-and-gold Dragon—used the Power to blast a
long trough in the ground beside the road. It had been decided that the village needed a canal.

Androl could see the weaves—mostly Earth—spinning
around the soldiers. In the Black Tower, you did as much
with the Power as you could. Always training, like men lifting stones to build their strength. Light, how Logain and
Taim pushed those lads.

Androl moved out onto the newly graveled roadway.
Much of that gravel bore melted edges from where it had
been blasted. They had brought in boulders—through gateways, on weaves of Air—then shattered them with explosive weaves. It had been like a war zone, rocks shattering,
spraying chips. With Power—and training—like that, the
Asha'man would be able to reduce city walls to rubble.

Androl continued on his way. The Black Tower was a
place of strange sights, and melted gravel wasn't nearly
the strangest of them. Neither were the soldiers tearing up
ground, following Androl's own careful surveying. Lately,
the strangest sight to him was the children. They ran and
played, jumping into the trough left behind by the working soldiers, sliding down its earthen sides, then scrambling
back up.

Children. Playing in the holes created by *saidin* blasts.
The world was changing. Androl's own gramma—so ancient she'd lost every tooth in her mouth—had used stories
of men channeling to frighten him into bed on nights when
he tried to slip outside and count the stars. The darkness
outside hadn't frightened him, nor had stories of Trollocs
and Fades. But men who could channel . . . that had terrified him.

Now he found himself here, grown into his middle years,
suddenly afraid of the dark but completely at peace with
men who could channel. He walked down the road, gravel
crunching beneath his boots. The children came scrambling up out of the ditch and flocked around him. He idly
brought out a handful of candies, purchased on the last
scouting mission.

"Two each," he said sternly as dirty hands reached for
the candies. "And no shoving, mind you." Hands went to
mouths, and the children gave him bobbed heads in thanks,
calling him "Master Genhald," before racing away. They

didn't go back to the trench, but invented a new game, running off toward the fields to the east.

Androl brushed off his hands, smiling. Children were so adaptable. Before them, centuries of tradition, terror and superstition could melt away like butter left too long in the sun. But it was good that they'd chosen to leave the trench. The One Power could be unpredictable.

No. That wasn't right. *Saidin* was very predictable. The men who wielded it, however . . . well, they were a different story.

The soldiers halted their work and turned to meet him. He wasn't a full Asha'man, and didn't merit a salute, but they showed him respect. Too much. He wasn't sure why they deferred to him. He was no great man, particularly not here, in the Black Tower.

Still, they nodded to him as he passed. Most of these were among the men who had been recruited from the Two Rivers. Sturdy lads and men, eager, though many were on the young side. Half of them didn't need to shave but once a week. Androl walked up to them, then inspected their work, eyeing the line of string he'd tied to small stakes. He nodded in approval. "Angle is good, lads," he said. "But keep the sides steeper, if you can."

"Yes, Master Genhald," said the one leading the team. Jaim Torfinn was his name, a spindly young man with dusty brown hair. He still held the Power. That raging river of strength was so enticing. Rare was the man who could release it without a sense of loss.

The M'Hael encouraged them to keep hold of it, said that holding it taught them to control it. But Androl had known seductive sensations somewhat like *saidin* before—the exhilaration of battle, the intoxication of rare drinks from the Isles of the Sea Folk, the heady feeling of victory. A man could be swept up in those feelings and lose control of himself, forgetting who he was. And *saidin* was more seductive than anything else he'd experienced.

He said nothing to Taim about his reservations. He had no business lecturing the M'Hael.

"Here," Androl said, "let me show you what I mean by straight." He took a deep breath, then emptied himself of feeling. He used the old soldier's trick to do that—he'd been taught it by his first instructor in the sword, old one-armed

Garfin, whose heavy rural Illianer accent had been virtually incomprehensible. Of course, Androl himself had a
faint Taraboner accent, he was told. It had faded over the
years since he'd last been home.

Within the nothing—the void—Androl could feel
the raging force that was *saidin*. He grabbed it as a man
grabbed the neck of a horse running wild, hoping to steer in
some small way but mostly just trying to hold on.

Saidin was wonderful. Yes, it was more powerful than
any intoxicant. It made the world more beautiful, more
lush. Holding that terrible Power, Androl felt as if he'd
come to life, leaving the dry husk of his former self behind.
It threatened to carry him away in its swift currents.

He worked quickly, weaving a tiny trickle of Earth—
the best he could manage, for Earth was where he was
weakest—and carefully shaved the sides of the canal. "If
you leave too much jutting out," he explained as he worked,
"then the canal flow will stay muddy as it washes away the
earth on the sides. The straighter and more firm the sides,
the better. You see?"

The soldiers nodded. Sweat had beaded on their brows,
flakes of dirt sticking to their foreheads and cheeks. But
their black coats were clean, particularly the sleeves. You
could judge a man's respect for his uniform by whether or
not he used the sleeve to wipe his brow on a day like this.
The Two Rivers lads used handkerchiefs.

The more senior Asha'man, of course, rarely sweated at
all. It would take these lads more practice to get that down
while concentrating so much.

"Good men," Androl said, standing up and glancing over
them. Androl laid a hand on Jaim's shoulder. "You lads are
doing a fine job here. The Two Rivers, it grows men right."

The lads beamed. It was good to have them, particularly
compared to the quality of men Taim had been recruiting
lately. The M'Hael's scouts claimed they took whoever they
could find, yet why was it that most they brought back had
such angry, unsettling dispositions?

"Master Genhald?" asked one of the soldiers.

"Yes, Trost?" Androl asked.

"Have you . . . Have you heard anything of Master
Logain?"

The others looked hopeful.

Androl shook his head. "He hasn't returned from his scouting mission. I'm sure he'll be back soon."

The lads nodded, though he could see that they were beginning to worry. They had a right to. Androl had been worrying for weeks now. Ever since Logain had left in the night. Where had he gone? Why had he taken Donalo, Mezar and Welyn—three of the most powerful Dedicated loyal to him—along?

And now there were those Aes Sedai camped outside, supposedly sent with authority from the Dragon to bond Asha'man. Taim had given one of his half-smiles at that, the kind that never reached his eyes, and told them the group from the White Tower had first pick, since they'd come first. The others waited, impatiently.

"The M'Hael," one of the Two Rivers men said, expression growing dark. "He—"

"Keep your heads on your shoulders," Androl interrupted, "and don't make waves. Not yet. We wait for Logain."

The men sighed, but nodded. Distracted by the conversation, Androl almost didn't notice when the shadows nearby began creeping toward him. Shadows of men, lengthening in the sunlight. Shadows within the trough. Shadows of rocks and clefts in the earth. Slowly, deviously, they turned toward Androl. Androl steeled himself, but couldn't dispel the panic. This one terror he could feel despite the void.

They came whenever he held *saidin* for too long. He released it immediately, and the shadows reluctantly crept back to their places.

The Two Rivers lads watched him, discomfort in their faces. Could they see the wild cast to Androl's eyes? Nobody spoke of the . . . irregularities that afflicted men of the Black Tower. It just wasn't done. Like whispering dirty family secrets.

The taint was cleansed. These lads would never have to feel the things that Androl did. Eventually, he and the others who had been in the Tower before the cleansing would become rarities. Light, but he couldn't understand why anyone would listen to him. Weak in the Power and insane to boot?

And the worst part was, he *knew*—deeply, down to his very center—that those shadows were real. Not just some madness concocted by his mind. They were real, and they would destroy him if they reached him. They *were* real. They had to be.

Oh, Light, he thought, gritting his teeth. *Either option is terrifying. Either I'm insane or the darkness itself wants to destroy me.*

That was why he could no longer sleep at nights without huddling in fear. Sometimes he could go hours holding the Source without seeing the shadows. Sometimes only minutes. He took a deep breath.

"All right," he said, satisfied that his voice—at least— sounded in control. "You best get back to work. Keep that slope moving the right direction, mind you. We'll have a mess and a half to deal with if the water overflows and floods this area."

As they obeyed, Androl left them, cutting back through the village. Near the center stood the barracks, five large, thick-stoned buildings for the soldiers, a dozen smaller buildings for the Dedicated. Right now, this little village *was* the Black Tower. That would change. A tower proper was being built nearby, the foundation already dug.

He could visualize what the place might someday look like. He'd once worked with a master architect—one of a dozen different apprenticeships he'd held in a life that sometimes seemed to have lasted too long. Yes, he could see it in his mind's eye. A domineering black stone tower, Power-built. Strong, sturdy. At its base would be blockish square structures with crenelated tops.

This village would grow to become a town, then a large city, as vast as Tar Valon. The streets had been built to allow the passing of several wagons at a time. New sections were surveyed and laid. It bespoke vision and planning. The streets themselves whispered of the Black Tower's destiny.

Androl followed a worn pathway through the scrub grass. Distant *boom*s and *snap*s echoed across the plains like the sounds of a whip being cracked. Each man had his own reasons for coming. Revenge, curiosity, desperation, lust for power. Which was Androl's reason? All four, perhaps?

He left the village, and eventually rounded a line of trees and came to the practice range—a small canyon between two hills. A line of men stood channeling Fire and Earth. The hills needed to be leveled to make land for farming. An opportunity to practice.

These men were mostly Dedicated. Weaves spun in the air, much more skillful and powerful than those the Two Rivers lads had used. These were streamlined, like hissing vipers or striking arrows. Rocks exploded, and bursts of dirt sprayed into the air. The blasting was done in an unpredictable pattern to confuse and disorient foes. Androl could imagine a group of cavalry thundering down that slope, only to be surprised by exploding Earth. A single Dedicated could wipe out dozens of riders in moments.

Androl noted with dissatisfaction that the working men stood in two groups. The Tower was beginning to split and divide, those loyal to Logain shunned and ostracized. On the right, Canler, Emarin and Nalaam worked with focus and dedication, joined by Jonneth Dowtry—the most skilled soldier among the Two Rivers lads. On the left, a group of Taim's cronies were laughing among themselves. Their weaves were more wild, but also much more destructive. Coteren lounged at the back, leaning against a leafy hardgum tree and overseeing the work.

The workers took a break and called for a village boy to bring water. Androl walked up, and Arlen Nalaam saw him first, waving with a broad smile. The Domani man wore a thin mustache. He was just shy of his thirtieth year, though he sometimes acted much younger. Androl was still smarting from the time Nalaam had put tree sap in his boots.

"Androl!" Nalaam called. "Come tell these uncultured louts what a Retashen Dazer is!"

"A Retashen Dazer?" Androl said. "It's a drink. Mix of mead and ewe's milk. Foul stuff."

Nalaam looked at the others proudly. He had no pins on his coat. He was only a soldier, but he should have been advanced by now.

"You bragging about your travels again, Nalaam?" Androl asked, unlacing the leather armguard.

"We Domani get around," Nalaam said. "You know, the kind of work my father does, spying for the Crown. . . ."

"Last week you said your father was a merchant," Canler said. The sturdy man was the oldest of the group, his hair graying, his square face worn from many years in the sun.

"He is," Nalaam said. "That's his front for being a spy!"

"Aren't women the merchants in Arad Doman?" Jonneth asked, rubbing his chin. He was a large, quiet man with a round face. His entire family—his siblings, his parents, and his grandfather Buel—had relocated to the village rather than letting him come alone.

"Well, they're the best," Nalaam said, "and my mother is no exception. We men know a thing or two, though. Besides, since my mother was busy infiltrating the Tuatha'an, my father had to take over the business."

"Oh, now that's just ridiculous," Canler said with a scowl. "Who would ever want to infiltrate a bunch of Tinkers?"

"To learn their secret recipes," Nalaam said. "It's said that a Tinker can cook a pot of stew so fine that it will make you leave house and home to travel with them. It's true, I've tasted it myself, and I had to be tied in a shed for three days before the effect wore off."

Canler sniffed. However, after a moment, the farmer added, "So . . . did she find the recipe or not?"

Nalaam launched into another story, Canler and Jonneth listening intently. Emarin stood to the side, looking on with amusement—he was the other soldier in the group, bearing no pins. He was an older man, with thin hair and wrinkles at his eyes. His short white beard was trimmed to a point.

The distinguished man was something of an enigma; he'd arrived with Logain one day, and had said nothing of his past. He had a poised bearing and a delicate way of speaking. He was a nobleman, that was certain. But unlike most other noblemen in the Black Tower, Emarin made no attempt at asserting his presumed authority. Many noblemen took weeks to learn that once you joined the Black Tower, your outside rank was meaningless. That made them sullen and snappish, but Emarin had taken to life in the Tower immediately.

It took a nobleman with true dignity to follow the orders of a commoner half his age without complaint. Emarin took a sip of water from the serving boy, thanking the lad, then stepped up to Androl. He nodded toward Nalaam, who was still talking to the others. "That one has the heart of a gleeman."

Androl grunted. "Maybe he can use it to earn some extra coin. He still owes me a new pair of socks."

"And you, my friend, have the soul of a scribe!" Emarin laughed. "You never forget a thing, do you?"

Androl shrugged.

"How did you know what a Retashen Dazer was? I consider myself quite educated in these matters, yet I'd heard not a word of it."

"I had one once," Androl said. "Drank it on a bet."

"Yes, but where?"

"Retash, of course."

"But that's leagues off shore, in a cluster of islands not even the Sea Folk often visit!"

Androl shrugged again. He glanced over at Taim's lackeys. A village boy had brought them a basket of food from Taim, though the M'Hael claimed not to play favorites. If Androl asked, he'd find that a boy was supposed to have been sent with food for the others, too. But that lad would have become lost, or had forgotten, or made some other innocent mistake. Taim would have someone whipped, and nothing would change.

"This division is troubling, my friend," Emarin said softly. "How can we fight for the Lord Dragon if we cannot make peace among ourselves?"

Androl shook his head.

Emarin continued. "They say that no man favored of Logain has had the Dragon pin in weeks. There are many, like Nalaam there, who should have had the sword pin long ago—but are denied repeatedly by the M'Hael. A House whose members squabble for authority will never present a threat to other Houses."

"Wise words," Androl said. "But what should we do? What *can* we do? Taim is M'Hael, and Logain hasn't returned yet."

"Perhaps we could send someone for him," Emarin said. "Or maybe you could calm the others. I fear that some of them are near to snapping, and if a fight breaks out, I have little doubt who would see the rough side of Taim's punishments."

Androl frowned. "True. But why me? You're far better with words than I am, Emarin."

Emarin chuckled. "Yes, but Logain trusts you, Androl. The other men look to you."

They shouldn't, Androl thought. "I'll see what I can think of." Nalaam was winding up for another story, but before he could begin, Androl gestured to Jonneth, holding up the armguard. "I saw your old one had cracked. Try this."

Jonneth's face brightened as he took the armguard. "You're amazing, Androl! I didn't think anyone had noticed. It's a silly thing, I know, but . . ." His smile broadened and he hurried to a nearby tree, beside which sat some of the men's equipment, including Jonneth's bow. These Two Rivers men liked to have them handy.

Jonneth returned, stringing the bow. He put on the armguard. "Fits like a dream!" he said, and Androl felt himself smiling. Small things. They could mean so much.

Jonneth took aim and launched an arrow, the shaft streaking into the air, bowstring snapping against the armguard. The arrow soared far, striking a tree on a hill better than two hundred paces away.

Canler whistled. "Ain't ever seen anything like those bows of yours, Jonneth. Never in my life." They were fellow Andorans, though Canler had come from a town much closer to Caemlyn.

Jonneth looked at his shot critically, then drew again—fletching to cheek—and loosed. The shaft fell true and hit the very same tree. Androl would guess that the shafts were less than two handspans apart.

Canler whistled again.

"My father trained on one of those," Nalaam noted. "Learned the art from a Two Rivers man whom he rescued from drowning in Illian. Has the bowstring as a memento."

Canler raised an eyebrow, but he seemed taken with the tale at the same time. Androl just chuckled, shaking his head. "Mind if I have a go, Jonneth? I'm a pretty dead shot with a Tairen bow, and they're a little longer than most."

"Surely," the lanky man said, unstrapping the armguard and handing over the bow.

Androl donned the armguard and lifted the bow. It was of black yew, and there wasn't as much spring to the string as he was used to. Jonneth handed him an arrow and Androl mimicked the man's pull, drawing to his cheek.

"Light!" he said at the weight of the pull. "Those arms of yours are deceptively small, Jonneth. How do you manage to aim? I can barely keep it steady!"

Jonneth laughed as Androl's arms trembled, and he finally loosed, unable to keep the bow drawn for a breath longer. The arrow hit the ground far off target. He handed the bow to Jonneth.

"That was fairly good, Androl," Jonneth said. "A lot of men can't even get the string back. Give me ten years, and I could have you shooting like one born in the Two Rivers!"

"I'll stick to shortbows for now," Androl said. "You'd never be able to shoot a monster like that from horseback."

"I wouldn't need to!" Jonneth said.

"What if you were being chased?"

"If there were fewer than five of them," Jonneth said, "I'd take them all down with this before they got to me. If there were more than five, then what am I doing shooting at them? I should be running like the Dark One himself was after me."

The other men chuckled, though Androl caught Emarin eyeing him. Probably wondering how Androl knew to shoot a bow from horseback. He was a keen one, that nobleman. Androl would have to watch himself.

"And what is this?" a voice asked. "You do be trying to learn to shoot a bow, pageboy? Is this so you can actually defend yourself?"

Androl gritted his teeth, turning as Coteren sauntered up. He was a bulky man, his black, oily hair kept long and loose. It hung around a blunt face with pudgy cheeks. His eyes were focused, dangerous. He smiled. The smile of a cat that had found a rodent to play with.

Androl quietly undid the armguard, handing it to Jonneth. Coteren was full Asha'man, a personal friend of the M'Hael. He outranked everyone here by a long stride.

"The M'Hael will hear of this," Coteren said. "You do be ignoring your lessons. You have no need for arrows or bows—not when you can kill with the Power!"

"We aren't ignoring anything," Nalaam said stubbornly.

"Quiet, lad," Androl said. "Mind your tongue."

Coteren laughed. "Listen to the pageboy, you lot. The M'Hael will hear of your impudence also." He focused on Androl. "Seize the Source."

Androl obliged reluctantly. The sweetness of *saidin* flowed into him, and he glanced nervously to the side. There was no sign of the shadows.

"So pathetic," Coteren said. "Destroy that stone over there."

It was far too large for him. But he'd dealt with bullies before, and Coteren was a bully of the most dangerous type—one with power and authority. The best thing to do was to mind. Embarrassment was a small punishment. That was something few bullies seemed to understand.

Androl wove the requisite weave of Fire and Earth, striking at the large stone. The thin weave held almost all of the Power he could manage, but it only flaked a few chips off the large stone.

Coteren laughed heartily, as did the group of Dedicated eating beneath the nearby tree. "Bloody ashes, but you're useless!" Coteren said. "Forget what I said earlier, pageboy! You *need* that bow!"

Androl released the One Power. Coteren had had his laugh; he would be satisfied. Unfortunately, Androl felt men seize the Source behind him. Jonneth, Canler and Nalaam stepped up beside Androl, each of them filled with the One Power and bristling with anger.

The men who had been eating stood up, each holding the Source as well. There were twice as many of them as there were of Androl's friends. Coteren smirked.

Androl eyed Canler and the others. "Now lads," he said, raising a hand, "Asha'man Coteren was just doing what the M'Hael ordered him. He's trying to make me mad so I'll push myself."

The two groups hesitated. The intensity of their locked gazes rivaled that of the Power within them. Then Jonneth released the Source. This caused Nalaam to do likewise, and finally gruff Canler turned away. Coteren laughed.

"I don't like this," Canler muttered as the group of them walked off. He shot a glance over his shoulder. "Don't like it at all. Why'd you stop us, Androl?"

"Because they'd have made rubble of us faster than you can curse, Canler," Androl snapped. "Light, man! I can barely channel worth a bean, and Emarin hasn't been here a month yet. Jonneth's learning fast, but we all know he's never actually fought with the Power before, and half of Coteren's men saw battle beneath the Lord Dragon! You really think you and Nalaam could handle ten men, virtually on your own?"

Canler continued to bristle, muttering, but let the argument drop.

"Makashak Na famalashten morkase," Nalaam mumbled, "delf takaksaki mere!" He laughed to himself, eyes wild. It wasn't a language Androl knew—it wasn't the Old Tongue, that was for certain. It probably wasn't even a language at all.

None of the others said anything. Nalaam occasionally cackled to himself in gibberish. If asked about it, he'd claim he'd spoken in plain ordinary words. The outburst seemed to discomfit Emarin and Jonneth a great deal. They hadn't ever seen friends go mad and kill those around them. Light send that they'd never *have* to see it, now. Whatever else Androl thought of the Lord Dragon for leaving them alone, the cleansing earned al'Thor redemption. Channeling was safe now.

Or, at least, it was *safer*. Channeling would never be safe, particularly now with Taim pushing them.

"More and more people are taking those burning personal lessons from Taim," Nalaam muttered as they walked to the shade of the trees. "Nensen's success has the men eager. We've lost a good dozen to Taim's side in the last few weeks. Soon there won't be anyone left besides us here. I'm afraid to talk to half the men I used to trust."

"Norley is trustworthy," Canler said. "Evin and Hardlin, too."

"That's a small list," Nalaam said. "Too small."

"The Two Rivers men are with us," Jonneth said. "To a man."

"Still a small list," Nalaam said. "And not a full Asha'man among us."

They all looked to Androl. He glanced back at Taim's lackeys, laughing among themselves again.

"What, Androl?" Nalaam asked. "Not going to chastise us for talking like that?"

"Like what?" Androl asked, looking back at them.

"Like it's us against them."

"I didn't want you lads to get yourselves killed or imprisoned, but that doesn't mean I don't see a problem." He glanced back at them. "Aye, there's trouble here, brewing like a storm."

"The men who take Taim's private lessons learn too quickly," Nalaam said. "Nensen was barely powerful enough to be considered for Dedicated just a short time ago. Now he's full Asha'man. Something very strange is going on. And those Aes Sedai. Why did Taim agree to let them bond us? You know he's protected all of his favorites by stopping the Aes Sedai from choosing any man with the Dragon pin. Burn me, but I don't know what I'll do if one chooses me. I'm not going to be put on some Aes Sedai's string."

There were several mutters about that.

"Taim's men spread rumors among the newcomers," Jonneth said softly. "They talk about the Lord Dragon, and how he drove good men to turn traitor. They say he's abandoned us, and that he's gone mad. The M'Hael doesn't want those rumors pointing back to him, but burn me if he isn't the source of them all."

"Maybe he's right," Canler said. The others looked at him sharply, and the leathery man scowled. "I'm not saying that I'm going to go jump into Taim's camp. But the Lord Dragon? What has *he* done for us? Seems like he's forgotten about this place. Maybe he *is* mad."

"He's not," Emarin said, shaking his head. "I met him just before I came here."

The others looked at him, surprised.

"He impressed me," Emarin said. "Young, but with a powerful will. I trust him. Light! I barely spoke with him a half-dozen times, but I trust him."

The others slowly nodded.

"Burn me," Canler said, "I suppose that's good enough for me. But I wish he'd listen! I heard Logain cursing that the Lord Dragon won't hear him when he gives warnings about Taim."

"And if we gave him evidence?" Jonneth asked. "What if we could find something that *proves* that Taim is up to no good?"

"Something *is* strange about Nensen," Nalaam repeated. "And that Kash. Where did he even come from, and how did he grow so powerful so quickly? What if, when Logain returned, we had information for him. Or if we could take it to the Lord Dragon directly . . ."

The group turned to Androl. Why did they look to him, the weakest of them? All he could do was create gateways. That was where Coteren's nickname for Androl had come from. Pageboy. The only thing he was good for was delivering messages, taking people places.

But the others looked to him. For one reason or another, they looked to him.

"All right," Androl said. "Let's see what we can find. Bring Evin, Hardlin and Norley into this but don't tell anyone else, not even the other Two Rivers lads. Don't rile Taim or his men . . . but if you *do* find something, bring it to me. And I'll see if I can find a way to contact Logain, or at least find where he went."

Each man nodded, somber. *Light help us if we're wrong,* Androl thought, looking back at Taim's favorites. *And Light help us more if we're right.*

CHAPTER
47

A Teaching Chamber

Faile sat impatiently atop Daylight, trying to keep herself from twitching as the gateway split the air. A browning meadow lay on the other side; Gaul and the Maidens immediately slipped through to scout.

"Are you certain you don't want to come?" Perrin asked Galad, who stood nearby, watching the procession with arms clasped behind his back.

"No," Galad said. "My meal with Elayne was sufficient for us to catch up."

"Suit yourself," Perrin said. He turned to Faile and gestured to the gateway.

She kicked Daylight into motion. It was time, at long last, to face the Queen of Andor, and she had to work to contain her nervousness. Perrin passed through the gateway with her; on the other side, Caemlyn was close, the grand city topped by peaked towers and banners of red and white, palace rising in the center. Low Caemlyn, which sprawled outside the city walls, was a growing city of its own.

Perrin's procession followed them out of the gateway; it had been carefully planned to look impressive, but not hostile. Alliandre with a hundred guardsmen. A hundred Two Rivers archers with unstrung longbows carried like staves. A hundred representatives of the Wolf Guard, including a large contingent of minor Cairhien nobility, the colored slashes on their uniforms created from cloth purchased in Whitebridge. And, of course, Gaul and the Maidens.

Grady came last. The man wore a neatly pressed black coat, his Dedicated pin polished and gleaming on the high collar. He immediately looked westward, toward the Black

Tower. He'd tried to make a gateway there earlier in the day, when Perrin had given him permission. It hadn't worked. Perrin was disturbed by that. He intended to investigate soon, tonight or tomorrow night at the latest.

Gaul and the Maidens formed up around Perrin and Faile, and the procession moved down onto the road, Arganda and a squad of Perrin's Wolf Guards riding ahead to announce them. The rest of them moved along the road at a regal pace. Caemlyn's sprawling growth was even worse than that of Whitebridge. Several armies camped near Low Caemlyn. Probably supported by the various lords who had supported Elayne's ascent to the throne.

There was a distinct irregularity here. The clouds broke around Caemlyn. The cloud cover had been so universal elsewhere that Faile started upon seeing this. The clouds formed an open circle above the city, eerily even.

Arganda and the Wolf Guards returned. "They will receive us, my Lord, my Lady," he announced.

Faile and Perrin rode in silence as the group made its way down the road. They had discussed the coming meeting dozens of times over; there wasn't anything more to say. Perrin had wisely given her the lead in the diplomatic negotiations. The world could not afford war between Andor and the Two Rivers. Not now.

As they passed through the city gates, Perrin and the Aiel grew more alert. She suffered their overprotectiveness in silence. How long would her capture by the Shaido loom over her life? At times, it seemed Perrin was loath to let her use the privy without four dozen guards.

Inside the walls, the streets teemed with people, the buildings and markets packed. Refuse was beginning to pile up, and a frightening number of urchins moved through the crowds. Criers yelled about the dangerous times, some perhaps in the employ of the merchants, encouraging people to hoard. Perrin's people had bought food here, but it was expensive; soon, Elayne would need to subsidize it, if she hadn't already. How good were the royal stores?

They passed through the New City, then entered the Inner City, climbing the hill to the Palace itself. The Queen's Guards stood at attention in their red-and-white tabards and burnished plate-and-mail outside the Palace gates in the pristine white Palace walls.

Once past the gates, they dismounted. A force of one hundred continued on with Perrin and Faile into the Palace. All of the Aiel, and a smaller honor guard from each contingent. The Palace hallways were wide, but that many people still made Faile feel crowded. The path she and Perrin were led along was a different way to the throne room than she'd taken before. Why not use the direct way?

It seemed that little had changed about the Palace since Rand's time ruling it. There were no Aiel now—save for the ones Perrin had brought. The same narrow red rug ran down the middle of the hallway, the same urns at the corners, the same mirrors on the walls to give an illusion of greater size.

A structure like this could stand unaltered over the centuries, paying little attention to whose feet trod the rugs and whose backside warmed the throne. In one year's time, this palace had known Morgase, one of the Forsaken, the Dragon Reborn and finally Elayne.

In fact, Faile half-expected—as they rounded the corner to the throne room—to find Rand lounging on his Dragon Throne, that strange half-spear held in the crook of his arm, a glimmer of madness in his eyes. However, the Dragon Throne had been removed, and the Lion Throne again held its queen. Rand had set that throne aside and protected it, like a flower he intended to present to a future love.

The Queen was a younger version of her mother. True, Elayne's face had angles that were more delicate than Morgase's. But she had that same red-gold hair and that same stunning beauty. She was tall, and was showing her pregnancy at the belly and through the chest.

The throne room was suitably ornate, with gilded wood trim and narrow pillars in the corners, probably ornamental. Elayne kept the room better lit than Rand had, stand-lamps burning brightly. Morgase herself stood at the base of the throne on the right side, and eight members of the Queen's Guard stood on the left. Some lesser nobles lined the sides of the room, watching with keen attention.

Elayne leaned forward on her throne as Perrin, Faile and the others entered. Faile curtsied, of course, and Perrin bowed. Not a low bow, but a bow nonetheless. By arrangement, Alliandre curtsied deeper than Faile had. That would immediately set Elayne thinking.

The official purpose of this visit was a commendation by the Crown, a thanks to Perrin and Faile for bringing back Morgase. That was just an affectation, of course. Their real reason for meeting was to discuss the future of the Two Rivers. But that was the sort of delicate goal that neither could speak of outright, at least not at first. Merely stating the objective would reveal too much to the other side.

"Let it be known," Elayne said with a musical voice, "that the throne welcomes you, Lady Zarine ni Bashere t'Aybara. Queen Alliandre Maritha Kigarin. Perrin Aybara." No use of title for him. "Let it be proclaimed in person our gratitude to you for returning our mother. Your diligence in this matter earns you the Crown's deepest appreciation."

"Thank you, Your Majesty," Perrin said with his usual gruffness. Faile had spoken to him at length about not trying to dispense with the formality or ceremony.

"We will declare a day of celebration for my mother's safe return," Elayne continued. "And for her . . . restoration to proper status."

Well, that pause meant Elayne was displeased to know that her mother had been treated as a servant. She had to realize that Perrin and Faile hadn't known what they were doing, but a queen could still claim indignation for such an event. It was an edge that, perhaps, she planned to use.

Perhaps Faile was reading too much into the comments, but she couldn't help it. In many ways, being a lady was much like being a merchant, and she had been trained well for both roles.

"Finally," Elayne said, "we come to the purpose of our meeting. Lady Bashere, Master Aybara. Is there a boon you would ask in return for the gift you have given to Andor?"

Perrin rested his hand on his hammer, then looked to Faile questioningly. Obviously, Elayne expected them to ask for him to be named formally a lord. Or, perhaps, to ask forbearance for impersonating one, along with a formal pardon. Either direction could be a result of this conversation.

Faile was tempted to demand the first. It would be a simple answer. But perhaps too simple; there were things Faile had to know before they could proceed. "Your Majesty," Faile said, carefully, "might we discuss this boon in a more intimate setting?"

Elayne gave that some thought—at least thirty seconds'

worth, which seemed an infinity. "Very well. My sitting room is prepared."

Faile nodded, and a servant opened a small door on the left-hand wall of the throne room. Perrin walked toward it, then held up a hand to Gaul, Sulin and Arganda. "Wait here." He hesitated, glancing at Grady. "You, too."

None of them seemed to like that, but they obeyed. They'd been warned this might happen.

Faile contained her nervousness—she didn't like leaving the Asha'man, their best means of escape. Particularly since Elayne undoubtedly had spies and Guards hidden inside the sitting room, ready to spring out should matters turn dangerous. Faile would have liked a similar protection, but bringing a male channeler in to speak with the Queen . . . well, this was how it would have to be. They were in Elayne's domain.

Faile took a deep breath, joining Perrin, Alliandre and Morgase in the small side room. Chairs had been arranged; Elayne had foreseen this possibility. They waited for Elayne to enter before sitting. Faile couldn't see any place for Guards to be hiding.

Elayne entered and waved a hand. The Great Serpent ring on her finger glittered in the lamplight. Faile had nearly forgotten that she was Aes Sedai. Perhaps there weren't any Guardsmen lurking around to help—a woman who could channel was as dangerous as a dozen soldiers.

Which of the rumors regarding the father of Elayne's child were to be believed? Surely not the ones about that fool of a man in her Guard—that was most likely obfuscation. Could it possibly be Rand himself?

Morgase entered after Elayne. She wore a subdued gown of deep red. She sat down beside her daughter, watching carefully, remaining silent.

"So," Elayne said, "explain to me why I shouldn't just execute you both as traitors."

Faile blinked in surprise. Perrin, however, snorted. "I don't think Rand would think very highly of that move."

"I'm not beholden to him," Elayne said. "You expect me to believe that *he* was behind you seducing my citizens and naming yourself a king?"

"You have a few of your facts backward, Your Majesty," Faile said testily. "Perrin never named himself king."

"Oh, and did he raise the flag of Manetheren, as my informants tell me he did?" Elayne asked.

"I did that," Perrin said. "But I put it away of my own choice."

"Well, that's something," Elayne replied. "You may not have called yourself a king, but holding up that banner was essentially the same thing. Oh, sit down, all of you." She waved a hand. A tray lifted off the far table and floated over to her. It bore goblets and a pitcher of wine, as well as a teapot and cups.

Fetching it with the One Power, Faile thought. *It's a reminder of her strength.* A rather unsubtle one.

"Still," Elayne said, "I will do the best for my realm, regardless of the cost."

"I doubt that upsetting the Two Rivers," Alliandre said hesitantly, "would be best for your realm. Executing their leader would undoubtedly throw the region into rebellion."

"So far as I'm concerned," Elayne said, pouring several cups of tea, "they're already in rebellion."

"We came to you peacefully," Faile said. "Hardly the action of rebels."

Elayne took a sip of the tea first, as was the custom, to prove it wasn't poisoned. "My envoys to the Two Rivers have been refused, and your people there gave me a message—and I quote—'The lands of Lord Perrin Goldeneyes refuse your Andoran taxes. *Tai'shar Manetheren!*'"

Alliandre paled. Perrin groaned softly, a sound that came out faintly like a growl. Faile took her cup and sipped her tea—mint, with cloudberries; it was good. The Two Rivers folk had pluck, that was certain.

"These are passionate times, Your Majesty," Faile said. "Surely you can see that the people might be concerned; the Two Rivers has not often been a priority for your throne."

"That's putting it mildly," Perrin added with a snort. "Most of us grew up not knowing we were part of Andor. You ignored us."

"That was because the area wasn't rising in rebellion." Elayne sipped her tea.

"Rebellion isn't the only reason men might need the attention of the queen who claims them," Perrin said. "I don't know if you've heard, but last year we faced Trollocs on our own, and without a whisker of help from the Crown. You'd have helped if you'd known, but the fact that there were no troops nearby—none *capable* of knowing our danger—says something."

Elayne hesitated.

"The Two Rivers has rediscovered its history," Faile said carefully. "It couldn't rest forever, not with Tarmon Gai'don looming. Not after sheltering the Dragon Reborn during his childhood. Part of me wonders if Manetheren had to fall, if the Two Rivers had to rise, to provide a place for Rand al'Thor to be raised. Among farmers with the blood—and obstinacy—of kings."

"Which makes it all the more important that I quiet things *now*," Elayne said. "I offered you a boon so that you could ask for forgiveness. I'd pardon you, and I'll be certain to send troops so that your people are protected. Accept this, and we can all go back to life the way it should be."

"That isn't going to happen," Perrin said softly. "The Two Rivers will have lords, now. I fought it for a time. You may, too, but it won't change anything."

"Perhaps," Elayne said. "But recognizing *you* would be to agree that a man can just claim a title within my nation, then keep it by stubbornly gathering an army. It makes for a terrible precedent, Perrin. I don't think you realize the predicament you've put me in."

"We'll muddle through," Perrin said in that stubborn tone he used when he wasn't going to budge. "I'm not stepping down."

"You're doing a poor job of persuading me you will accept my authority," Elayne snapped.

Not good, Faile thought, opening her mouth to jump in. A clash here would *not* serve them well.

Before she could speak, however, another voice cut in. "Daughter," Morgase said softly, drinking her tea. "If you plan to dance with *ta'veren*, be sure that you know the proper steps. I've traveled with this man. I've seen the world bend around him; I've seen bitter enemies become his allies. To fight the Pattern itself is to try to move a mountain with a spoon."

Elayne hesitated, looking at her mother.

"Please forgive me if I overstep myself," Morgase continued. "But Elayne, I promised these two that I would speak for them. I told you I would. Andor is strong, but I fear it

could break itself against this man. He does not want your
throne, I promise it, and the Two Rivers *does* need supervi-
sion. Would it be such a terrible thing to let them have the
man they themselves have chosen?"

The small room fell silent. Elayne eyed Perrin, sizing
him up. Faile held her breath.

"All right," Elayne said. "I assume you've come with demands. Let's hear them so we can discover if there's anything that can be done."

"No demands," Faile said. "An offer."

Elayne raised an eyebrow.

"Your mother is right," Faile said. "Perrin does not want
your throne."

"What you two want may be irrelevant once your people
get an idea in their minds."

Faile shook her head. "They love him, Your Majesty.
They respect him. They'll do what he says. We *can* and *will*
put down ideas of Manetheren rising again."

"And why would you do that?" Elayne asked. "I know
how fast the Two Rivers is growing with those refugees
coming in over the mountains. Nations could rise and fall
with the coming of the Last Battle. You have no reason to
give up the chance to form your own kingdom."

"Actually," Faile said, "we have good reason. Andor is a
strong nation, and prosperous. The towns in the Two Rivers
may be growing rapidly, but the people have barely begun
to want a lord. They're still farmers at heart. They don't
want glory; they want their crops to survive." Faile paused.
"Perhaps you're right, perhaps there will be another Breaking, but that's only more reason to have allies. Nobody
wants civil war in Andor, least of all the Two Rivers folk."

"What do you propose, then?" Elayne said.

"Nothing, really, that doesn't exist already," Faile said.
"Give Perrin an official title and make him High Lord over
the Two Rivers."

"And what do you mean by 'High Lord'?" Elayne asked.

"He'd rank higher than other noble Houses in Andor, but
beneath the Queen."

"I doubt the others would like that," Elayne said. "What
of taxes?"

"The Two Rivers is exempt," Faile said. As Elayne's expression soured, she continued quickly. "Your Majesty, the

throne ignored the Two Rivers for generations, not protecting them from bandits or sending workers to improve their roads, not giving them anything in the way of magistrates or justices."

"They didn't need it," Elayne said. "They governed themselves fine." She left unsaid that the Two Rivers folk would probably have tossed out tax collectors, magistrates or justices sent by the Queen—but she seemed to know it.

"Well," Faile said, "nothing needs change, then. The Two Rivers governs itself."

"You could have tariff-free trade with them," Alliandre said.

"Something I already have," Elayne said.

"So nothing changes," Faile said again. "Except that you gain a powerful province to the west. Perrin, as your ally and subject lord, will agree to marshal troops in your defense. He will also call up his sworn monarchs to your allegiance."

Elayne glanced at Alliandre. She'd probably heard of Alliandre's swearing from Morgase, but also would want to hear it for herself.

"I swore fealty to Lord Perrin," Alliandre said. "Ghealdan had long lacked strong allies. I meant to change that."

"Your Majesty," Faile said, leaning forward, tea cupped in her hands before her. "Perrin spent several weeks with some Seanchan officers. They have created a great pact of nations allied beneath one banner. Rand al'Thor, though you may trust him as a friend, has done the same. Tear, Illian, and maybe now Arad Doman are beneath his rule. Nations *join* rather than split, these days. Andor looks smaller by the hour."

"That's why I did what I did," Alliandre said.

Well, in Faile's view, Alliandre had been caught up by Perrin as a *ta'veren*. There hadn't been much planning. But Alliandre might see it otherwise.

"Your Majesty," Faile continued, "there is much to gain here. Through my marriage to Perrin, you gain a tie to Saldaea. Through Alliandre's oaths, you gain Ghealdan. Berelain also follows Perrin and has often mentioned her desire to find strong allies for Mayene. If we were to speak with her, I suspect she might be willing to make an alliance with us. We could create our own pact. Five nations, if you count the Two Rivers as one—six, if you do take the Sun Throne, as rumor claims you will. We are not the most powerful nations, but the many are stronger than the one. And you would be at our head."

Elayne's face had lost almost all of its hostility. "Saldaea. What are you in its line of succession?"

"I'm second," Faile admitted, which Elayne probably already knew. Perrin shifted in his chair. She knew he was still uncomfortable with that fact; well, he would simply have to get used to it.

"Second is too close," Elayne replied. "What if you end up with the throne of Saldaea? I could lose the Two Rivers to another country that way."

"This is easy to fix," Alliandre said. "If Faile were to ascend, one of her and Perrin's children could continue as Lord of the Two Rivers. Another could take the throne of Saldaea. Put it in writing, and you will be protected."

"I could accept such an arrangement," Elayne said.

"I don't have problems with it," Faile replied, looking at Perrin.

"I suppose."

"I should like one of them myself," Elayne said thoughtfully. "One of your children, I mean, to marry into the Andoran royal line. If the Two Rivers is to be ruled by a lord with as much power as this treaty would give him, then I would love to have blood connections to the throne."

"I won't promise that," Perrin said. "My children will make their own choices."

"It is sometimes the way of nobility," Elayne said. "It would be unusual, but not unheard of, for children like ours to be engaged from birth."

"We won't do it that way in the Two Rivers," Perrin said stubbornly. "Ever."

Faile shrugged. "We could offer encouragement, Your Majesty."

Elayne hesitated, then nodded. "That will be fine. But the other Houses won't like this 'High Lord' business. There'd need to be a way around it . . ."

"Give the Two Rivers to the Dragon Reborn," Morgase said.

Elayne's eyes lit up. "Yes. That would work. If I gave the area to him to be his seat in Andor . . ."

Faile opened her mouth, but Elayne cut her off with a

wave of the hand. "This isn't negotiable. I'll need *some* way to convince the other lords and ladies that I'm right to give the Two Rivers so much autonomy. If the lands are granted to the Dragon Reborn, giving him a title in Andor and making the Two Rivers his seat, then it will make sense for your home to be treated differently.

"The noble Houses of Andor will accept this, since the Two Rivers is where Rand came from, and Andor *does* owe him a debt. We'll have him appoint Perrin's line as his stewards. Instead of capitulating to rebels within my borders, I'll be seen allowing the Dragon Reborn, the man I love, to elevate his good friend. It might also give us some ground against the Illian-Tear pact you mentioned, who are bound to claim that their ties to Rand give them the right of conquest." She grew thoughtful, tapping the side of her cup.

"That seems reasonable," Perrin said, nodding. "Steward of the Two Rivers. I like the sound of that."

"Yes, well," Faile said. "I guess it's settled, then."

"The taxes," Elayne said, as if she hadn't heard. "You put them into a trust to be administered by Perrin and his line, with the understanding that if the Dragon ever returns, he can call upon them. Yes. That gives us a legal excuse for your exemption. Of course, Perrin will have authority to dip into those funds to improve the Two Rivers. Roads, food stores, defenses."

Elayne looked at Faile, then smiled, taking a long drink of tea. "I'm beginning to think it was a good idea not to execute you."

"That's certainly a relief," Alliandre said, smiling. As the least powerful one in the union, she stood to gain a lot from the alliances.

"Your Majesty—" Faile said.

"Call me Elayne," she said, pouring a goblet of wine for Faile.

"Very well, Elayne," Faile said, smiling and putting aside her tea, then accepting the wine. "I need to ask. Do you know what is happening with the Dragon Reborn?"

"Ox-brained lummox," Elayne said, shaking her head. "The bloody man's got Egwene all riled up."

"Egwene?" Perrin asked.

"She's Amyrlin, finally," Elayne said, as if the fact had been inevitable. Perrin nodded, though Faile found herself amazed. How had *that* happened, and why wasn't Perrin surprised by it?

"What's he gone and done?" Perrin asked.

"He says he's going to break the remaining seals of the Dark One's prison," Elayne said, frowning. "We'll need to stop him, of course. Foolish plan. You could help with that. Egwene's gathering a force to persuade him."

"I think I could be of help," Perrin said.

"Do you know where he is currently?" Faile asked. Perrin had a good idea, from his visions, but she wanted to know what Elayne knew.

"I don't know," Elayne said. "But I do know where he *will* be . . ."

Fortuona Athaem Devi Paendrag, ruler of the Glorious Seanchan Empire, marched into her Teaching Chamber. She wore a magnificent gown of golden cloth, cut after the highest Imperial fashion. The skirt split at the front to just above the knees, and was so long that it took five *da'covale* to carry the sides and train.

She wore an ornate headdress, of gold and crimson silk with beautiful silken wings shaped like those of an owl taking flight, and her arms glittered with thirteen bracelets, each of a different gemstone combination. She wore crystal at her throat in a long strand. She had heard an owl above her window the last night, and it had not flown away when she looked out. An omen indicating great care should be taken, that the next days would be ones of important decisions. The proper response was to wear jewelry with powerful symbolism.

When she entered the chamber, those inside prostrated themselves. Only the Deathwatch Guard—men in armor of blood red and deep green—was exempt; they bowed, but kept their eyes up, watching for danger.

The large chamber was windowless. Lines of stacked pottery stood at one end, a place for *damane* to practice weaves of destruction. The floor was covered in woven mats where stubborn *damane* were sent to the ground, writhing in pain. It would not do for them to be harmed physically. *Damane* were among the most important tools the Empire had, more valuable than horses or *raken*. You did not de-

stroy a beast because it was slow to learn; you punished it
until it learned.

Fortuona crossed the chamber to where a proper Imperial Throne had been set up. She commonly came here, to
watch the *damane* being worked or broken. It soothed her.
The throne was atop a small dais; she climbed the steps,
train rustling as her *da'covale* carried it. She turned to face
the room, allowing the servants to arrange her dress. They
took her by her arms and lifted her back into the throne,
draping her long golden skirts down the front of the dais
like a tapestry.

Those skirts were sewn with the writings of Imperial
power. *The Empress IS Seanchan. The Empress WILL live
forever. The Empress MUST be obeyed.* She sat as a living
banner to the might of the Empire.

Selucia took her position on the lower steps of the dais.
This done, the courtiers raised themselves. The *damane*, of
course, remained kneeling. There were ten of them, with
heads bowed, their *sul'dam* holding their leashes and—in a
few cases—patting them affectionately on the heads.

King Beslan entered. He'd shaved most of his head, leaving only a dark strip on the top, and seven of his fingernails
had been lacquered. One more fingernail than anyone on
this side of the ocean, excepting Fortuona herself. He still
wore Altaran clothing—a uniform of green and white—
rather than Seanchan robes. She had not pressed him on
this.

So far as she knew, since his raising, Beslan hadn't
made any plans to have her assassinated. Remarkable. Any
Seanchan would have immediately begun scheming. Some
would have tried an assassination; others would have decided to make only plans, but remain supportive. But all
would have *considered* killing her.

Many on this side of the ocean thought differently. She'd
never have believed it, if not for her time with Matrim. That
was obviously one reason why Fortuona had been required
to go with him. She just wished she'd interpreted the omens
earlier.

Beslan was joined by Captain-General Lunal Galgan
and a few members of the low Blood. Galgan was a wide-
shouldered fellow with a crest of white hair atop his head.
The other members of the Blood deferred to him; they knew

he had her favor. If things went well here and with the rec-
lamation of Seanchan, there was a good chance she'd raise
him to the Imperial family. The ranks of the family would
need to be refilled, after all, once Fortuona returned and restored order. Undoubtedly, many had been assassinated or
executed. Galgan was a valuable ally. He'd not only worked
openly against Suroth, but had suggested the assault on the
White Tower, which had gone well. Extremely well.

Melitene, Fortuona's *der'sul'dam*, stepped forward and
bowed again. The stout, graying woman led a *damane* with
dark brown hair and bloodshot eyes. Apparently this one
wept often.

Melitene had the presence to look embarrassed at the
weeping, and bowed extra low. Fortuona chose not to notice
that the *damane* was acting so displeasingly. This one was a
fine catch, despite her petulance.

Fortuona made a series of gestures to Selucia, instructing
her in what to say. The woman watched with keen eyes, half
of her head covered in cloth while she waited for the hair to
grow there, the other half shaved. Fortuona would eventually have to choose another Voice, as Selucia was now her
Truthspeaker.

"Show us what this woman can do," Selucia said, Voicing
the words Fortuona had signed to her.

Melitene patted the *damane* on the head. "Suffa will show
the Empress—may she live forever—the Power of slicing the
air."

"Please," Suffa said, looking pleadingly toward Fortuona. "Please, listen to me. I am the *Amyrlin Seat*."

Melitene hissed, and Suffa's eyes opened wide, obviously
feeling a blast of pain through the *a'dam*. The *damane*
continued anyway. "I can offer great bounty, powerful Empress! If I am returned, I will give you ten women to take
my place. Twenty! The most powerful the White Tower has.
I—" She broke off, moaning, and collapsed to the ground.

Melitene was sweating. She looked to Selucia, speaking
quickly, nervously. "Please explain to the Empress of us
all—may she live forever—that my eyes are lowered for not
having trained this one properly. Suffa is amazingly stubborn, despite how quick she is to weep and offer others in
her place."

Fortuona sat for a moment, letting Melitene sweat. Eventually, she signed for Selucia to speak.

"The Empress is not displeased with you," Selucia Voiced. "These *marath'damane* who call themselves Aes Sedai have all proven stubborn."

"Please express my gratitude to the Greatest One," Melitene said, relaxing. "If it pleases She Whose Eyes Look Upward, I *can* make Suffa perform. But there may be further outbursts."

"You may continue," Selucia Voiced.

Melitene knelt beside Suffa, speaking sharply at first, then consolingly. She was very skilled at working with former *marath'damane*. Of course, Fortuona considered herself good with *damane* as well. She enjoyed breaking *marath'damane* as much as her brother Halvate had enjoyed training wild *grolm*. She'd always found it a pity that he had been assassinated. He was the only one of her brothers who she'd ever been fond of.

Suffa finally got back onto her knees. Fortuona leaned forward, curious. Suffa bowed her head, and a line of light—brilliant and pure—cut the air in front of her. That line turned sideways along a central axis, opening a hole directly in front of Fortuona's throne. Trees rustled beyond, and Fortuona's breath caught as she saw a hawk with a white head streak away from the portal. An omen of great power. The normally unflappable Selucia gasped, though whether it was at the portal or the omen, Fortuona did not know.

Fortuona covered her own surprise. So it was true. Traveling wasn't a myth or a rumor. It was real. This changed everything about the war.

Beslan walked forward, bowing to her, looking hesitant. She waved for him and Galgan to come to where they could see the forest glade through the opening. Beslan stared, mouth hanging open.

Galgan clasped his hands behind his back. He was a curious one. He'd met with assassins in the city, and had inquired about the cost for having Fortuona killed. Then, he'd had each of the men who quoted him a price executed. A very subtle maneuver—it was meant to show that she should consider him a threat, as he was not afraid of meeting with assassins. However, it was also a visible sign of loyalty. *I follow you for now,* the move said, *but I am watching, and I am ambitious.*

In many ways, his careful maneuvering was more comforting to her than Beslan's apparently unwavering loyalty. The first, she could anticipate. The second . . . well, she wasn't certain what to make of it yet. Would Matrim be equally loyal? What would it be like, to have a Prince of the Ravens whom she did not have to plot against? It seemed almost a fantasy, the type of tale told to common children to make them dream of an impossible marriage.

"This is incredible!" Beslan said. "Greatest One, with this ability . . ." His station made him one of the only people able to speak directly to her.

"The Empress wishes to know," Selucia Voiced, reading Fortuona's fingers, "if any of the captured *marath'damane* spoke of the weapon."

"Tell the highest Empress—may she live forever—that they did not," Melitene said, sounding worried. "And, if I may be so bold, I believe that they are not lying. It seems that the explosion outside the city was an isolated accident— the result of some unknown *ter'angreal*, used imprudently. Perhaps there *is* no weapon."

It was possible. Fortuona had already begun to doubt the validity of those rumors. The explosion had happened before Fortuona had arrived in Ebou Dar, and the details were confusing. Perhaps this had all been a ploy by Suroth or her enemies.

"Captain-General," Selucia Voiced. "The Greatest One wishes to know what you would do with a Power such as this Traveling ability."

"That depends," Galgan said, rubbing his chin. "What is its range? How large can she make it? Can all *damane* do this? Are there limitations on where a hole can be opened? If it pleases the Greatest One, I will speak with the *damane* and get these answers."

"It does please the Empress," Selucia Voiced.

"This is troubling," Beslan said. "They could attack behind our battle lines. They could open a portal like this into the Empress's own chambers, may she live forever. With this . . . everything we know about war will change."

The members of the Deathwatch Guard shuffled—a sign of great discomfort. Only Furyk Karede did not move. If

anything, his expression grew harder. Fortuona knew that
he would soon be suggesting a new, rotating location of her
sleeping quarters.

Fortuona thought for a moment, staring at that rent in the
air. That rent in reality itself. Then, contrary to tradition,
she stood up on her dais. Fortunately, Beslan was there,
one she could address directly—and let the others hear her
commands.

"Reports say," Fortuona announced, "that there are still
hundreds of *marath'damane* in the place called the White
Tower. They are the key to recapturing Seanchan, the key
to holding this land, and the key to preparing for the Last
Battle. The Dragon Reborn *will* serve the Crystal Throne.

"We have been provided with a way to strike. Let it be
said to the Captain-General that he should gather his finest soldiers. I want each and every *damane* we control to
be brought back to the city. We will train them in this
method of Traveling. And then we will go, in force, to
the White Tower. Before, we struck them with a pinprick.
Now, we will let them know the full weight of our sword.
All of the *marath'damane* must be leashed."

She sat back down, letting the room fall still. It was rare
that the Empress made such announcements personally.
But this was a time for boldness.

"You should not allow word of this to spread," Selucia
said to her, voice firm. She was now speaking in her role
as Truthspeaker. Yes, another would have to be chosen to
be Fortuona's Voice. "You would be a fool to let the enemy
know for certain we have this Traveling."

Fortuona took a deep breath. Yes, that was true. She
would make certain each in this room was held to secrecy.
But once the White Tower was captured, they would talk of
her proclamation, and would read the omens of her victory
upon the skies and world around them.

We will need to strike soon, Selucia signed.

Yes, Fortuona signed back. *Our previous attack will have
them gathering arms.*

Our next move will have to be decisive, then, Selucia
signed. *But think. Delivering thousands of soldiers into the
White Tower through a hidden basement room. Striking
with the force of a thousand hammers against a thousand
anvils!*

Fortuona nodded.

The White Tower was doomed.

"Don't know that there's much more to say, Perrin," Thom said, leaning back in his chair, tabac smoke curling out of his long-stemmed pipe. It was a warm night, and they didn't have a fire in the hearth. Just a few candles on the table, with some bread, cheeses and a pitcher of ale.

Perrin puffed on his own pipe. Only he, Thom and Mat were in the room. Gaul and Grady waited out in the common room. Mat had cursed Perrin for bringing those two—an Aiel and an Asha'man were rather conspicuous. But Perrin felt safer with those two than with an entire company of soldiers.

He'd shared his story with Mat and Thom first, speaking of Malden, the Prophet, Alliandre, and Galad. Then they had filled him in on their experiences. It stunned Perrin, how much had happened to the three of them since their parting.

"Empress of the Seanchan, eh?" Perrin said, watching the smoke twist above him in the dim room.

"Daughter of the Nine Moons," Mat said. "It's different."

"And you're married." Perrin grinned. "Matrim Cauthon. Married."

"You didn't have to share that part, you know," Mat said to Thom.

"Oh, I assure you, I did indeed."

"For a gleeman, you seem to leave out most of the heroic parts of the things I do," Mat said. "At least you mentioned the hat."

Perrin smiled, contented. He hadn't realized how much he'd missed sitting with friends to spend the evening chatting. A carved wooden sign hung outside the window, dripping with rainwater. It depicted faces wearing strange hats and exaggerated smiles. The Happy Throng. There was probably a story behind the name.

The three of them were in a private dining chamber, paid for by Mat. They'd brought in three of the inn's large hearth chairs. They didn't fit the table, but they were comfortable. Mat leaned back, putting his feet up on the table. He took up a hunk of ewe's milk cheese and bit off a piece, then balanced the rest on his chair arm.

"You know, Mat," Perrin said, "your wife is probably going to expect you to be taught table manners."

"Oh, I've been taught," Mat said. "I just never learned."

"I'd like to meet her," Perrin said.

"She's something interesting," Thom replied.

"Interesting," Mat said. "Yeah." He looked wistful. "Anyway, you've heard the lot of it now, Perrin. That bloody Brown brought us here. Haven't seen her in over two weeks, now."

"Can I see the note?" Perrin asked.

Mat patted a few pockets, then fished out a small white piece of paper, folded closed and sealed with red wax. He tossed it onto the table. The corners were bent, the paper smudged, but it hadn't been opened. Matrim Cauthon was a man of his word, at least when you could pry an oath out of him.

Perrin lifted the note. It smelled faintly of perfume. He turned it over, then held it up to a candle.

"Doesn't work," Mat said.

Perrin grunted. "So what do you think it says?"

"Don't know," Mat said. "Bloody insane Aes Sedai. I mean, they're all odd. But Verin's fallen completely off her stone. Don't suppose you've heard from her?"

"I haven't."

"Hope she's all right," Mat said. "She sounded worried something might happen to her." He took the note back, then tapped it on the table.

"You going to open it?"

Mat shook his head. "I'll open it when I get back. I—"

A knock came at the door, then it creaked open, revealing the innkeeper, a younger man named Denezel. He was tall, with a lean face and a head he kept shaved. The man was all but Dragonsworn, from what Perrin had seen, even going so far as to have a portrait of Rand commissioned and hung in the common room. It wasn't a bad likeness.

"I apologize, Master Crimson," Denezel said, "but Master Golden's man insisted on speaking with him."

"It's all right," Perrin said.

Grady poked his weathered face into the room and Denezel retreated.

"Ho, Grady," Mat said, waving. "Blown up anyone interesting lately?"

The tanned Asha'man frowned, looking to Perrin. "My Lord. Lady Faile asked me to remind you when midnight arrived."

Mat whistled. "See, this is why I left my wife in another kingdom."

Grady's frown deepened.

"Thank you, Grady," Perrin said with a sigh. "I hadn't realized the time. We'll be going soon."

The Asha'man nodded, then withdrew.

"Burn him," Mat said. "Can't the man at least smile? Flaming sky is depressing enough without people like him trying to imitate it."

"Well, son," Thom said, pouring some ale, "some just don't find the world particularly humorous lately."

"Nonsense," Mat said. "The world's plenty humorous. The whole bloody place has been laughing at me, lately. I'm telling you, Perrin. With those drawings of us about, you need to keep your head low."

"I don't see how I can," Perrin said. "I've got an army to lead, people to care for."

"I don't think you're taking Verin's warning seriously enough, lad," Thom said, shaking his head. "You ever heard of the Banath people?"

"No," Perrin said, looking at Mat.

"They were a group of savages who roamed what is now Almoth Plain," Thom said. "I know a couple fine songs about them. See, their various tribes always painted the skin of their leader red to make him stand out."

Mat took another bite of his cheese. "Bloody fools. Painted their leader red? That would make him a target for every soldier on the field!"

"That was the point," Thom said. "It was a challenge, you see. How else would their enemies be able find him and test their skill against him?"

Mat snorted. "I'd have painted a few decoy soldiers red to distract them from me, then had my archers feather their leader with arrows while everyone was trying to hunt down the fellows they thought were leading my army."

"Actually," Thom said, taking a sip of his ale, "that's exactly what Villiam Bloodletter did during his first, and last, battle with them. 'The Song of a Hundred Days' talks about it. Brilliant maneuver. I'm surprised you've heard of that song—it's very obscure, and the battle happened so long ago, most history books don't even remember it."

For some reason, the comment made Mat smell nervous.

"You're saying that we're making ourselves targets," Perrin said.

"I'm saying," Thom replied, "that you boys are getting harder and harder to hide. Everywhere you go, banners proclaim your arrival. People talk about you. I'm half-convinced you have only survived this long because the Forsaken didn't know where to find you."

Perrin nodded, thinking of the trap his army had nearly fallen into. Assassins in the night *would* come. "So what should I do?"

"Mat's been sleeping in a different tent each night," Thom said. "And sometimes in the city. You should try something like that. Grady can make gateways, right? Why not have him make one for you into the middle of your tent each night? Sneak out and sleep someplace else, then Travel back in the morning. Everyone will assume you're in your tent. If assassins strike, you won't be there."

Perrin nodded thoughtfully. "Even better, I could leave five or six Aiel inside, on alert, waiting."

"Perrin," Mat said, "that's downright devious." He smiled. "You've changed for the better, my friend."

"From you, I'll try to accept that as a compliment," Perrin said. He paused, then added, "It will be difficult."

Thom chuckled. "He's right, though. You've changed. What happened to the soft-spoken, unsure boy I helped escape the Two Rivers?"

"He passed through the blacksmith's fire," Perrin said softly.

Thom nodded, seeming to understand.

"And you, Mat?" Perrin said. "Can I do something to help you? Maybe let you Travel between tents?"

"No. I'll be fine."

"How are you going to protect yourself?"

"With my wits."

"Planning to find some of those, then?" Perrin said. "About time."

Mat snorted. "What is it with everyone and my wits

lately? I'll be fine, trust me. Remind me to tell you about the night when I first figured out I could win whatever dice game I wanted to. It's a good story. Involves falling off bridges. One bridge, at least."

"Well . . . you could tell us now," Perrin said.

"Not the right time. Anyway, it doesn't matter. See, I'm leaving soon."

Thom smelled excited.

"Perrin, you will lend us a gateway, won't you?" Mat asked. "Hate to leave the Band. They'll be inconsolable without me. At least they have those dragons to blow things up."

"But where are you going?" Perrin asked.

"Suppose I should explain it," Mat said. "That *was* the reason for meeting with you, aside from the amiable discourse and all." He leaned in. "Perrin, Moiraine is alive."

"What?"

"It's true," Mat said. "Or, well, we think it is. She sent Thom a letter, claiming she'd foreseen the battle with Lanfear, and knew that she would . . . Well, anyway, there's this tower west of here on the River Arinelle. It's made all of metal. It—"

"The Tower of Ghenjei," Perrin said softly. "Yes, I know of it."

Mat blinked. "You do? Burn me. When did you get to be a scholar?"

"I've merely heard some things. Mat, that place is evil."

"Well, Moiraine is inside," Mat said. "Captured. I mean to get her back. I have to beat the snakes and the foxes. Bloody cheats."

"Snakes and foxes?" Perrin said.

Thom nodded. "The children's game is named after the things that live in the tower. So we think."

"I've seen them," Mat said. "And . . . well, there's really not time for that now."

"If you're going to rescue her," Perrin said, "perhaps I could come. Or at least send one of the Asha'man."

"I'll take a gateway gladly," Mat said. "But you can't come, Perrin. Moiraine explained it in her letter. Only three can come, and I know already who they have to be." He hesitated. "Olver is going to bloody kill me for not taking him, you know."

"Mat," Perrin said, shaking his head. "You're not making any sense."

Mat sighed. "Let me tell you the whole story, then." He eyed the pitcher of ale. "We're going to need more of that, and you'd better tell Grady you'll be some time yet . . ."

CHAPTER
48

Near Avendesora

Aviendha took one final step and was out of the forest of glass pillars. She took a deep breath, then glanced back at the path she had taken.

The central plaza of Rhuidean was an awe-inspiring sight. Smooth white flagstones carpeted the entire square save for the absolute center. There stood an enormous tree, branches spread wide like arms reaching to embrace the sun. The massive tree had a perfection she could not explain. It had a natural symmetry—no missing branches, no gaping holes in its leafy upper reaches. It was particularly impressive since, when she'd last seen it, it had been blackened and burned.

In a world where other plants were dying without explanation, this one healed and flourished faster than ever should have been possible. Its leaves rustled soothingly in the wind, and its gnarled roots poked through the ground like the aged fingers of a wise elder. The tree made her want to sit and bask in the simple peace of the moment.

It was as if this tree were the ideal, the one after which all other trees were patterned. In legend it was called *Avendesora*. The Tree of Life.

To the side sat the glass columns. There were dozens of them, perhaps hundreds, forming concentric rings. Spindly and thin, they reached high into the sky. As purely—even superlatively—natural as *Avendesora* was, these columns were equally *un*natural. They were so thin and tall, logic said that the first gust of wind should have toppled them. It wasn't that they were aberrant, merely artificial.

When she had first entered days before, there had been

gai'shain in white carefully picking up fallen leaves and twigs. They had retreated as soon as they had seen her. Was she the first to go through the glass pillars since Rhuidean's transformation? Her own clan had sent no one, and she was certain she would have heard of it if the others had.

That left only the Shaido, but they had rejected Rand's claims about the Aiel past. Aviendha suspected that if any Shaido had come, they would not have been able to bear what was shown here. They would have passed into the center of the glass columns and never returned.

That had not been the case for Aviendha. She had survived. Indeed, everything she'd seen had been expected. Almost disappointingly so.

She sighed, walking over to *Avendesora*'s trunk, then looking up through its web of branches.

Once, this plaza had been cluttered with other *ter'angreal*; this was where Rand had first discovered the access keys he had used to cleanse *saidin*. That wealth of *ter'angreal* was gone now; Moiraine had claimed many pieces for the White Tower, and the Aiel who lived here must have taken the others away. That left only the tree, the columns and the three rings that women went through on their first trip here, the trip that made them apprentice Wise Ones.

She remembered some of her trip through those rings, which had showed her life—her many possible lives—to her. Really, only bits and pieces remained in her memory. Her knowledge that she would love Rand, that she would have sister-wives. Included in that knowledge was the impression that she'd return here, to Rhuidean. She had known, though only stepping into this courtyard again had sparked some of those memories to life in her mind.

She sat down cross-legged between two of the great tree's roots. The soft wind was soothing, the air dry and familiar, the dusty scent of the Three-fold Land reminding her of her childhood.

Her trip through the columns had certainly been immersive. She had expected to see the origins of the Aiel, perhaps witness the day when they had—as a people—decided to take up the spears and fight. She'd anticipated a noble decision, where honor overcame the inferior lifestyle dictated by the Way of the Leaf.

She had been surprised to see how mundane—almost

accidental—the true event had been. No grand decision; only a man who had been unwilling to let his family be murdered. There was honor in wanting to defend others, but he had not approached his decision with honor.

She rested her head back against the trunk of the tree. The Aiel *did* deserve their punishment in the Three-fold Land, and they did have *toh*—as a people—to the Aes Sedai. She had seen everything she had expected. But many of the things she had been *hoping* to learn had been absent. Aiel would continue to visit this place for centuries, as they had for centuries. And each of them would learn something that was now common knowledge.

That bothered her deeply.

She looked upward, watching branches quiver in the breeze, several leaves falling and drifting down toward her. One passed her face, brushing her cheek before alighting on her shawl.

Passing through the glass columns was no longer a *challenge*. Originally, this *ter'angreal* had provided a test. Could the potential leader face and accept the Aiel's darkest secret? As a Maiden, Aviendha had been tested in body and strength. Becoming a Wise One tested a person emotionally and mentally. Rhuidean was to be the capstone of that process, the final test of mental endurance. But that test was gone now.

More and more, she was coming to believe that tradition for the sake of tradition was *foolishness*. Good traditions—strong, Aiel traditions—taught the ways of *ji'e'toh*, methods of survival.

Aviendha sighed, standing. The forest of columns looked like the strange lines of frozen water she had seen during winter in the wetlands. Icicles, Elayne had called them. These grew up from the ground, pointing toward the sky, things of beauty and Power. It was sad to witness their lapse into irrelevance.

Something occurred to her. Before she had left Caemlyn, she and Elayne had made a remarkable discovery. Aviendha had manifested a Talent in the One Power: the ability to identify *ter'angreal*. Could she determine, exactly, what the glass pillars did? They couldn't have been created specifically for the Aiel, could they? Most things of great Power like this hailed from very ancient days. The pillars would have been created during the Age of Legends, then adapted to the purpose of showing the Aiel their true past.

There was so much they didn't know about *ter'angreal*. Had the ancient Aes Sedai really understood them, the same way Aviendha understood exactly how a bow or spear worked? Or had they themselves been mystified by the things they created? The One Power was so wondrous, so mysterious, that even working practiced weaves often made Aviendha feel like a child.

She stepped up to the nearest glass pillar, careful not to pass inside the ring. If she touched one of the rods, perhaps her Talent would let her read something about them. It was dangerous to experiment with *ter'angreal*, but she had already passed their challenge and was unscathed.

Hesitantly, she reached out and laid fingers on the slick, glassy surface. It was about a foot thick. She closed her eyes, trying to read the pillar's function.

She sensed the powerful aura of the pillar. It was far more potent than any of the *ter'angreal* she had handled with Elayne. Indeed, the pillars seemed . . . alive, somehow. It was almost as if she could sense an awareness from them.

That gave her a chill. Was she touching the pillar, or was it touching her?

She tried to read the *ter'angreal* as she had done before, but this one was vast. Incomprehensible, like the One Power itself. She inhaled sharply, disoriented by the *weight* of what she felt. It was as if she had suddenly fallen into a deep, dark pit.

She snapped her eyes open, pulling her hand away, palm quivering. This was beyond her. She was an insect, trying to grasp the size and mass of a mountain. She took a breath to steady herself, then shook her head. There was nothing more to be done here.

She turned from the glass pillars and took a step.

She was Malidra, eighteen but scrawny enough to appear much younger. She crawled in the darkness. Careful. Quiet. It was dangerous to get this close to the Lightmakers. Hunger drove her forward. It always did.

The night was cold, the landscape barren. Malidra had heard stories of a place beyond the distant mountains, where the land was green and food grew everywhere. She didn't believe those lies. The mountains were just lines in the sky, jagged teeth. Who could climb something so tall?

Maybe the Lightmakers could. They did come from that direction, usually. Their camp was ahead of her, glowing in the darkness. That glow was too steady to be fire. It came from the balls they carried with them. She inched closer, crouching, bare feet and hands dusty. There were a few men and women of the Folk with her. Grimy faces, stringy hair. Ragged beards on the men.

A mishmash of clothing. Tattered trousers, garments that might once have been shirts. Anything to keep the sun off during the day, because the sun could kill. And did. Malidra was the last of four sisters, two dead by the sun and hunger, one dead from the bite of a snake.

But Malidra survived. Anxiously, she survived. The best way was to follow the Lightmakers. It was dangerous, but her mind barely noticed danger anymore. That was what happened when virtually anything could kill you.

Malidra passed a bush, watching the Lightmaker guards. Two sentries, carrying their long, rodlike weapons. Malidra had found one on a dead man once, but she hadn't been able to make it do anything. The Lightmakers had magics, the same magics that created their food and their lights. Magics that kept them warm in the bitter cold at night.

The two men wore strange clothing. Trousers that fit too well, coats covered with pockets and glistening bits of metal. Both had hats, though one wore his back, held around his neck by a thin leather strap. The men chatted. They didn't have beards like the Folk did. Their hair was darker.

One of the other Folk got too close, and Malidra hissed at her. The woman shot back a glare, but moved away. Malidra stayed at the edge of the light. The Lightmakers wouldn't see her. Their strange glowing orbs ruined their night vision.

She rounded their massive wagon. There were no horses. Only the wagon, large enough to house a dozen people. It moved magically during the daylight, rolling on wheels nearly as wide as Malidra was tall. She had heard—in the hushed, broken communication of Folk—that in the east, the Lightmakers were creating a massive roadway. It would pass directly through the Waste. It was made by laying down strange pieces of metal. They were too big to pry up, though Jorshem had shown her a large nail he had found. He used it to scrape meat off bones.

It had been quite a while since she had eaten well—not since they'd managed to kill that merchant in his sleep two years ago. She could still remember that feast, digging into his stores, eating until her stomach ached. Such an odd feeling. Wondrous and painful.

Most Lightmakers were too careful for her to kill them in their sleep. She didn't dare face them when they were awake. They could make one such as her vanish with a stare.

Nervously, trailed by a couple of other Folk, she rounded the wagon and approached it from the back. Sure enough, here the Lightmakers had tossed some of the leavings from their earlier meal. She scuttled forward and began to dig through the trash. There were some cuttings of meat, strips of fat. She snatched these up eagerly—holding them close before the others could see—and stuffed them into her mouth. She felt dirt grind against her teeth, but meat was *food*. She hurriedly picked through the waste some more.

A bright light shone on her. She froze, hand halfway to her mouth. The other two Folk screamed, scrambling away. She tried to do likewise but tripped. There was a hiss of sound—one of the Lightmaker weapons—and something popped against her back. It felt like she'd been hit with a small rock.

She collapsed, the pain sudden and sharp. The light faded slightly. She blinked, eyes adjusting even as she felt her life seeping out and around her hands.

"I told you," a voice said. Two shadows moved in front of the light. She had to run! She tried to rise, but only managed to thrash weakly.

"Blood and char, Flern," a second voice said. A silhouette knelt beside her. "Poor thing. Almost a child. She wasn't doing any harm."

Flern snorted. "No harm? I've seen these creatures try to slit a sleeping man's throat. All for his trash. Bloody pests."

The other shadow looked at her, and she caught sight of

a grim face. Twinkling eyes. Like stars. The man sighed, rising. "Next time we bury the trash." He retreated back toward the light.

The second man, Flern, stood watching her. Was that her blood? All over her hands, warm, like water that had been sitting in the sun for too long?

Death did not surprise her. In a way, she'd been expecting it for most of her eighteen years.

"Bloody Aiel," Flern said as her sight faded.

Aviendha's foot hit the flagstone in Rhuidean's square, and she blinked in shock. The sun had changed in the sky above. Hours had passed.

What had happened? The vision had been so real, like her viewings of the early days of her people. But she could make no sense of it. Had she gone even farther back into history? That seemed like the Age of Legends. The strange machines, clothing, and weapons. But that *had* been the Three-fold Land.

She could remember distinctly being Malidra. She could remember years of hunger, of scavenging, of hatred—and fear—of the Lightmakers. She remembered her death. The terror, trapped and bleeding. That warm blood on her hands. . . .

She raised a hand to her head, sick and unsettled. Not by the death. Everyone woke from the dream, and while she did not welcome it, she would not fear it. No, the horrible thing about the vision had been the complete lack of honor she'd seen. Killing men in the night for their food? Scavenging for half-chewed meat in the dirt? Wearing scraps? She'd been more an animal than a person!

Better to die. Surely the Aiel *couldn't* have come from roots like those, long ago. The Aiel in the Age of Legends had been peaceful servants, respected. How could they have started as scavengers?

Perhaps this was merely one tiny group of Aiel. Or maybe the man had been mistaken. There was little way to tell from this single vision. Why had she been shown it?

She took a hesitant step away from the glass columns, and nothing happened. No further visions. Disturbed, she began to walk from the plaza.

Then she slowed.

Hesitantly she turned back. The columns stood in the dimming light, quiet and alone, seeming to buzz with an unseen energy.

Was there more?

That one vision seemed so disconnected from the others she'd seen. If she passed into the columns' midst again, would she repeat what she'd been given before? Or . . . had she, perhaps, changed something with her Talent?

In the centuries since Rhuidean's founding, those columns had shown the Aiel what they *needed* to know about themselves. The Aes Sedai had set that up, hadn't they? Or had they simply placed the *ter'angreal* and allowed it to do what it pleased, knowing it would grant wisdom?

Aviendha listened to the tree's leaves rustle. Those pillars were a challenge, as sure as an enemy warrior with his spear in hand. If she passed into their midst again, she might never come out; nobody visited this *ter'angreal* a second time. It was forbidden. One trip through the rings, one through the columns.

But she had come seeking knowledge. She would not leave without it. She turned and—taking a deep breath—walked up to the pillars.

Then took a step.

She was Norlesh. She held her youngest child close to her bosom. A dry wind tugged at her shawl. Her baby, Garlvan, started to whimper, but she quieted him as her husband spoke with the outlanders.

An outlander village stood in the near distance, built of shacks against the foothills of the mountains. They wore dyed clothing and strangely cut trousers with buttoning shirts. They had come for the ore. How could rocks be so valuable that they would live on this side of the mountains, away from their fabled land of water and food? Away from their buildings where light shone without candles and their carts that moved without horses?

Her shawl slipped and she pulled it up. She needed a new one; this one was ragged, and she didn't have any more thread left for patching. Garlvan whimpered in her arms, and her only other living child—Meise—held to her skirts.

Meise hadn't spoken for months, now. Not since her older brother had died from exposure.

"Please," said her husband—Metalan—to the outlanders. There were three of them, two men and a woman, all wearing trousers. Rugged folk, not like the other foreigners, with their delicate features and too-fine silks. Illuminated Ones, those others sometimes called themselves. These three were more ordinary.

"Please," Metalan repeated. "My family . . ."

He was a good man. Or he had been once, back when he'd been strong and fit. Now he seemed a shell of that man, his cheeks sunken. His once-vibrant blue eyes stared absently much of the time. Haunted. That look came from watching three of his children die in eighteen months' time. Though Metalan was a head taller than any of the outlanders, he seemed to grovel before them.

The lead outlander—a man with a bushy beard and wide, honest eyes—shook his head. He returned to Metalan the sack full of stones. "The Raven Empress, may she always draw breath, forbids it. No trading with Aiel. We could be stripped of our charter for talking to you."

"We have no food," Metalan said. "My children are starving. These stones contain ore. I *know* that it is the type for which you search. I spent weeks gathering it. Give us a bit of food. Something. Please."

"Sorry, friend," the lead outlander said. "It isn't worth trouble with the Ravens. Go on your way. We don't want an incident." Several outlanders approached from behind, one carrying an axe, two others with hiss-staves.

Her husband slumped. Days of travel, weeks of searching for the stones. For nothing. He turned and walked back to her. In the distance, the sun was setting. Once he reached her, she and Meise joined him, walking away from the outlander camp.

Meise began to sniffle, but neither of them had the will or strength to carry her. About an hour away from the outlander camp, her husband found a hollow in a rock shelf. They settled in, not making a fire. There was nothing to burn.

Norlesh wanted to cry. But . . . feeling anything seemed difficult. "I'm so hungry," she whispered.

"I will trap something in the morning," her husband said, staring up at the stars.

"We haven't caught anything in days," she said.

He didn't reply.

"What are we going to do?" she whispered. "We haven't been able to keep a home for our people since my great-mother Tava's day. If we gather, they attack us. If we wander the Waste, we die off. They won't trade with us. They won't let us cross the mountains. What are we going to *do*?"

His response was to lie down, turning away from her.

Her tears did come then, quiet, weak. They rolled down her cheeks as she undid her shirt to nurse Garlvan, though she had no suck for him.

He didn't move. He didn't latch on. She lifted his small form and realized that he was no longer breathing. Somewhere along the walk to the hollow, he had died without her realizing it.

The most frightening part was how difficult she found it to summon any sorrow at the death.

Aviendha's foot hit the flagstones. Around her, the forest of glass columns shimmered with prismatic color. It was like standing in the middle of an Illuminator's firework. The sun was high in the sky, cloud cover remarkably gone.

She wanted to leave the square forever. She had been prepared for the knowledge that the Aiel had once followed the Way of the Leaf. That knowledge wasn't very disturbing. They would soon fulfill their *toh*.

But *this*? These scattered and broken wretches? People who didn't stand up for themselves, who begged, who didn't know how to survive off the land? To know that these were her ancestors was a shame she nearly could not bear. It was good that Rand al'Thor had not revealed *this* past to the Aiel.

Could she flee? Run from the plaza and see no more? If it grew any worse, the shame would overwhelm her. Unfortunately, she knew that there was only one way out, now that she'd begun.

Gritting her teeth, she took a step forward.

* * *

She was Tava, fourteen years old and screaming in the night as she ran from her burning house. The entire valley— really a canyon, with steep sides—was in flames. Every building in the fledgling hold had been set afire. Nightmarish creatures, with sinuous necks and wide wings, flapped in the night above, bearing riders with bows, spears, and strange new weapons that made a hissing sound when they fired.

Tava cried, searching for her family, but the hold was a mass of chaos and confusion. Some few Aiel warriors resisted, but anyone who raised a spear fell moments later, killed by arrow or by one of the invisible shots from the new weapons.

An Aiel man fell before her, corpse rolling on the ground. Tadvishm had been his name, a Stone Dog. It was one of the few societies which still maintained an identity. Most warriors no longer held to a society; they made brothers and sisters of those with whom they camped. All too often, those camps were scattered anyway.

This hold was to have been different, secret, deep within the Waste. How had their enemies found them?

A child of only two years was crying. She dashed to him, snatching him from where he lay near the flames. Their homes burned. The wood had been scavenged with difficulty from the mountains on the eastern edge of the Waste.

She held the child close and ran toward the deeper recesses of the canyon. Where was her father? With a sudden whoosh of sound, one of the nightmarish creatures landed before her, the burst of wind making her skirt flap. A fearsome warrior sat upon the creature's back, helmet like that of an insect, mandibles sharp and jagged. He lowered his hissing staff toward her. She cried out in terror, huddling around the crying child and closing her eyes.

The hissing sound never came. At a grunt and a sudden screech from the serpentine beast, she looked up and saw a figure struggling with the outlander. The firelight showed the face of her father, clean-shaven as the old traditions dictated. The beast beneath the two men lurched, throwing both to the ground.

A few moments later, her father rose, holding the invader's sword in his hands, its length stained dark. The invader did not move, and behind them the beast leaped into the air, howling. Tava looked up, and saw that it was following the rest of the pack. The invaders were withdrawing, leaving a broken people with burning homes.

She looked down again. The scene horrified her; so many bodies, dozens, lay bleeding on the ground. The invader that her father had killed appeared to be the only enemy that had fallen.

"Gather sand!" her father—Rowahn—roared. "Quench the flames!"

Tall—even for an Aiel—with striking red hair, he wore the old clothing of brown and tan, boots tied high to his knees. That clothing marked one as Aiel, therefore many had abandoned it. Being known as Aiel meant death.

Her father had inherited his clothing from his grandfather, along with a charge. *Follow the old ways. Remember* ji'e'toh. *Fight and maintain honor.* Though he had been in the hold for only a few days, the others listened when he yelled for them to put out the fires. Tava returned the child to a grateful mother and then helped gather sand and dirt.

A few hours later, a tired and bloodied people gathered in the center of the canyon, regarding with dull eyes what they had worked for months to build. It had been wiped out in a single night. Her father still carried the sword. He used it to direct the people. Some of the old ones said that a sword was bad luck, but why would they say that? It was only a weapon.

"We must rebuild," her father said, surveying the wreckage.

"Rebuild?" said a soot-stained man. "The granary was the first to burn! There is no food!"

"We will survive," her father said. "We can move deeper into the Waste."

"There is nowhere else to go!" another man said. "The Raven Empire has sent word to the Far Ones, and they hunt us at the eastern border!"

"They find us whenever we gather!" another cried.

"It is a punishment!" her father said. "But we must endure!"

The people looked at him. Then, in pairs or small groups, they began to walk away.

"Wait," her father said, raising his hand. "We must stay together, keep fighting! The clan—"

"We are *not* a clan," an ashen man said. "I can survive better on my own. No more fighting. They beat us when we fight."

Her father lowered the sword, its tip hitting the ground. Tava moved up beside him, worried as she watched the others walk their ways into the night. The air was still thick with smoke. The departing Aiel were shadows, melting into darkness, like swirls of dust blown on the wind. They didn't pause to bury their dead.

Her father bowed his head and dropped the sword to the ash-covered ground.

There were tears in Aviendha's eyes. There was no shame at crying over this tragedy. She had feared the truth, and she could no longer deny it.

Those had been *Seanchan* raiders, riding atop *raken*. The Raven Empire, the Lightmakers from her first vision, were the Seanchan—and they hadn't existed until the middle of the current Age, when Artur Hawkwing's armies had crossed the oceans.

She was not seeing the deep past of her people. She was seeing their future.

Her first time through the pillars, each step had taken her backward, moving her through time toward the Age of Legends. It appeared that this time, the visions had started at a distant point in the future, and were working back toward her day, each vision jumping back a generation or two.

Tears streaking her face, she took the next step.

CHAPTER
49

Court of the Sun

S he was Ladalin, Wise One of the Taardad Aiel. How she wished that she had been able to learn to channel. That was a shameful thought, wishing for a talent one did not have, but she could not deny it.

She sat in the tent, feeling regretful. If she'd been able to work with the One Power, perhaps she could have done more to help the wounded. She could have remained young to lead her clan, and perhaps her bones would not ache so. Old age was a frustration when there was so much to do.

The tent walls rustled as the remaining clan chiefs settled down. There was only one other Wise One in the room, Mora of the Goshien Aiel. She could not channel either. The Seanchan were particularly determined when it came to killing or capturing all Aiel—male or female—who showed any talent with the One Power.

It was a sorry group gathered in the tent. A one-armed young soldier entered with a warm brazier and set it in the middle of them, then retreated. Ladalin's mother had spoken of the days when there had still been *gai'shain* to do such work. Had there really been Aiel, man or Maiden, who had not been needed for the war against the Seanchan?

Ladalin reached forward to warm her hands at the brazier, fingers knotted with age. She'd held a spear as a young woman; most women did, before they married. How could a woman remain behind when the Seanchan used female soldiers and their *damane* with such effectiveness?

She'd heard stories about her mother and greatmother's

days, but they seemed incredible. The war was all Ladalin had ever known. Her first memories as a little girl were of the Almoth strikes. Her youth had been spent training. She had fought in the battles focused around the land that had been known as Tear.

Ladalin had married and raised children, but had focused every breath on the conflict. Aiel or Seanchan. Both knew that, eventually, only one of the two would remain.

It was looking more and more like the Aiel would be the ones forced out. That was another difference between her day and her mother's day. Her mother had not spoken of failure; Ladalin's lifetime was filled with milestones of withdrawal and retreat.

The others seemed absorbed in their thoughts. Three clan chiefs and two Wise Ones. They were all that remained of the Council of Twenty-Two. Highland winds seeped through the tent flaps, chilling her back. Tamaav was the last to arrive. He looked as old as she felt, his face scarred and his left eye lost in battle. He sat down on the rock. The Aiel no longer carried rugs or cushions. Only the essentials could be transported.

"The White Tower has fallen," he said. "My scouts informed me not an hour ago. I trust their information." He had always been a blunt man, and a good friend to her husband, who had fallen last year.

"Then with it goes our last hope," said Takai, the youngest of the clan chiefs. He was the third chief of the Miagoma in as many years.

"Speak not so," Ladalin said. "There is always hope."

"They have pushed us all the way to these cursed mountains," Takai said. "The Shiande and the Daryne are no more. That leaves only five clans, and one of those is broken and scattered. We are beaten, Ladalin."

Tamaav sighed. She'd have lain a bridal wreath at his feet, had the years been earlier and the times different. Her clan needed a chief. Her son still thought to become the one, but with the recent Seanchan capture of Rhuidean, the clans were uncertain how to choose new leaders.

"We must retreat into the Three-fold Land," Mora said in her soft, matronly voice. "And seek penance for our sins."

"What sins?" Takai snapped.

"The Dragon wanted peace," she replied.

"The Dragon left us!" Takai said. "I refuse to follow the memory of a man my greatfathers barely knew. We made no oaths to follow his foolish pact. We—"

"Peace, Takai," Jorshem said. The last of the three clan chiefs was a small, hawk-faced man with some Andoran blood in him from his greatfather. "Only the Three-fold Land holds any hope for us, now. The war against the Ravens has been lost."

The tent fell still.

"They said they'd hunt us," Takai said. "When they demanded surrender, they warned us against retreat. You know that. They said they would destroy any place where three Aiel gathered."

"We will *not* surrender," Ladalin said firmly. More firmly than she felt, to be honest.

"Surrender would make us *gai'shain*," Tamaav said. They used the word to mean one without honor, though that was not the way Ladalin's mother had used it. "Ladalin. What is your advice?"

The other four looked at her. She was of the lineage of the Dragon, one of the last living. The other three lines had been killed off.

"If we become slaves to the Seanchan, the Aiel as a people will be no more," she said. "We cannot win, so we must retreat. We will return to the Three-fold Land and build up our strength. Perhaps our children can fight where we cannot."

Silence again. They all knew her words to be optimistic at best. After decades of war, the Aiel were a bare fraction of the number they had once been.

Seanchan channelers were brutal in their effectiveness. Though the Wise Ones and Dragon Blooded used the One Power in battle, it was not enough. Those cursed *a'dam*! Each channeler the Aiel lost to capture was eventually turned against them.

The real turning point in the war had been the entry of the other nations. After that, the Seanchan had been able to seize wetlander peoples and cull more channelers from their ranks. The Ravens were unstoppable; now that Tar

Valon had fallen, every realm in the wetlands was subject
to the Seanchan. Only the Black Tower still fought, though
the Asha'man did so in secret, as their fortress had fallen
years before.

Aiel could not fight in secret. There was no honor to
that. Of course, what did honor matter now? After deaths
numbering in the hundreds of thousands? After the burning
of Cairhien and the scouring of Illian? It had been twenty
years since the Seanchan had gained the Andoran war machines. The Aiel had been tumbling toward defeat for decades; it was a testament to their tenacious nature that they
had lasted so long.

"This is *his* fault," Takai said, still looking sullen. "The
Car'a'carn could have led us to glory, but he abandoned us."

"His fault?" Ladalin said, understanding—perhaps for
the first time—why that statement was wrong. "No. Aiel
take responsibility for themselves. This is *our* fault, and not
that of my distant greatfather. We have forgotten who we
are. We are without honor."

"Our honor was taken from us," Takai said, sighing as he
stood. "People of the Dragon indeed. What is the good of
being *his* people? We were crafted to be a spear, the legends
say, forged in the Three-fold Land. *He* used us, then cast us
away. What is a discarded spear to do, but go to war?"

What indeed, Ladalin thought. The Dragon had demanded
peace, thinking that it would bring happiness to the Aiel.
But how could they be happy, when the Light-cursed Seanchan were in the land? Her hatred of the invaders ran deep.

Perhaps that hatred had destroyed the Aiel. She listened
to the wind howl as Takai stalked from the tent. On the
morrow the Aiel would return to the Three-fold Land. If
they would not accept peace themselves, it seemed they
would have to have it forced upon them.

Aviendha took another step forward. She'd nearly reached
the very center of the columns, and shards of light sparkled
around her.

Her tears flowed freely now. She felt like a child. Being
Ladalin had been worse than the others, for in her, Aviendha had seen hints of true Aiel ways, but corrupted, as

if to make mockery. The woman had thought of war and associated it with honor, but hadn't understood what honor was. No *gai'shain*? Retreat? There had been no mention of *toh*. This was battle stripped completely of point or reason.

Why fight? For Ladalin, it had been about hatred of the Seanchan. There was war because there had always been war.

How? How had this happened to the Aiel?

Aviendha took a step forward.

She was Oncala, Maiden of the Spear. She would eventually give the spear up and marry, just as her mother had and her mother's mother before her. But now was the time to fight.

She strode through the streets of Caemlyn, her near-sister carrying the banner of the Dragon to announce her lineage. Next to Oncala was the man for whom she would likely give up her spears. Hehyal, Dawn Runner, had killed more Seanchan than any of his society, gaining much *ji*. He had been granted permission to travel to Rhuidean last year to become clan chief.

Rhuidean. The city was besieged by Seanchan. Oncala sneered. Seanchan had no honor. They had been *told* that Rhuidean was a place for peace. The Aiel did not assault the palace in Ebou Dar. The Seanchan should not attack Rhuidean.

They were lizards. It was a source of constant frustration that, after decades of war, the battle lines remained nearly the same as they had been after her greatfather went to Shayol Ghul.

She and Hehyal were accompanied by two thousand spears as a guard of honor. Queen Talana knew to expect them, and so the white Andoran palace gates were open. Hehyal waved for fifty spears, preselected, to walk with them through the fine halls. Lushness abounded here in the palace. Each tapestry, each vase, each golden frame seemed an insult to Oncala. Forty years of war, and Andor had not been touched. It lay safe, basking in the protection the Aiel defense gave them.

Well, Andor would see. The Aiel had grown stronger

through their fighting. Once, their prowess had been legendary. Now it was greater! When the Aiel had destroyed the Seanchan, the world would see what the Aiel had learned. The wetland rulers would wish they had been more generous.

The throne room doors were open; Oncala and Hehyal entered, leaving their escort. The banner of the Dragon flew here, too, a reminder that the Andoran royal line *also* carried the lineage of the *Car'a'carn*. One more reason for Oncala to hate them. The Andoran nobility thought themselves her equals.

Queen Talana was a middle-aged woman with deep, lustrous red hair. Not very pretty, but very regal. She was speaking quietly with one of her advisors, and she waved for the Aiel to wait. An insult, deliberate. Oncala fumed.

Finally, they were summoned to approach the Lion Throne. Talana's brother, her protector, stood behind her in court clothing—a vest and coat—hand on his sword. Oncala could have killed him while barely breaking a sweat.

"Ah," Queen Talana said. "The Taardad Aiel again. You still carry the spear, Oncala?"

Oncala folded her arms, but said nothing. She knew she was not good with people. When she spoke, insults were too common. Better to let the clan chief take the lead.

"I assume you're here to beg for aid again," Talana said.

Hehyal flushed, and Oncala wished—for a moment—she hadn't left her spear outside.

"We have something for you," Hehyal said, taking out a leather pouch and handing it to one of the Queen's Guards. The man opened it, inspecting the papers inside. Another insult. Must they be treated like assassins? Oncala did not like the Queen, true, but her family and Talana's were sworn to allegiance because of their greatmothers, who had been first-sisters.

The soldier handed the Queen the papers. Talana perused them, face growing concerned and thoughtful.

Talana, like most of the rulers beneath the Dragon's Peace, worried about the Seanchan. The Raven Empire's techniques and skill with shaping the One Power were growing. The Aiel had them held at a stalemate, for now. What would happen if the Seanchan won? Would they hold to their oaths?

How much could the Seanchan be trusted? Hehyal's agents had spent a great deal of time over the last decade seeding that very question among the great courts of the world. He was a wise man. Even before he had become chief, he had realized that this war could not be won by the Aiel alone. They needed these soft wetlanders.

And that was the final reason Oncala hated them.

"Where did you get these?" Talana asked.

"From the Seanchan palace," Hehyal said. "They should not have struck at Rhuidean. By honor, that allowed us to reciprocate—though our attack was done quietly to recover these. I had long suspected where they were located, and only my honor in not breaching the Seanchan sacred palace held me back."

Talana's face grew hard. "You're certain these are authentic?"

"You question me?" Hehyal asked.

Queen Talana shook her head, looking troubled. She knew that the Aiel did not lie.

"We have been patient with you," Hehyal said. "We have come to you and explained what will happen if we cannot hold off the Seanchan."

"The Dragon's Peace—"

"What care do *they* have for the Dragon?" Hehyal asked. "They are invaders who forced *him* to bow to *their* Empress. She is considered above him. They will not keep promises they made to an inferior."

Queen Talana looked down again. The documents were Seanchan plans for attacking Andor, along with a detailed plot for the assassination of the Queen. Underneath that were similar plans for dealing with the rulers of Tear, the Two Rivers, and Illian.

"I must have time to consult with my advisors," Talana said.

We have her, Oncala thought, smiling. Oncala already knew what the Queen's answer would be. The trick had been to get her to consider action.

Hehyal nodded, and the two of them withdrew. Oncala had to keep herself from yelling in victory. If Andor entered the war, the other nations would as well, particularly those in the Pact of the Griffin and those in the Court of the Sun.

They looked to the Andoran Queen much as the other Aiel clans looked to Oncala. The blood of Rand al'Thor held much weight.

"Is this right?" Hehyal asked as they walked, their spears surrounding them to keep away prying ears.

Oncala started. "It was your plan."

He nodded, frowning.

Nothing he had said to the Queen had been untrue. Their honor was unsoiled. However, Hehyal *had* left out one of the sheets they'd discovered. That one had explained that the other sheets were contingency plans.

The descriptions of Andor's military forces, suggestions on how to use gateways and dragons to attack Caemlyn, the very plot to assassinate Queen Talana—these had been drawn up only in case Andor entered the war. They were meant as a preemptive study on a potential enemy, not an actual plan to attack.

It was virtually the same thing. The Seanchan were snakes. They would seize Andor eventually, and by then the Aiel might be unable to help. If this war went badly, her people would go to the Three-fold Land and leave the foolish wetlanders to be conquered. The Seanchan would find it impossible to fight the Aiel in their homeland.

Much better for Queen Talana to enter the war now. For her own good, it was best she never saw that other sheet.

"It is done," Hehyal said. "There is no room for question now."

Oncala nodded. The Seanchan would fall, and the Aiel would take their rightful place. The blood of the Dragon Reborn was in her veins. She deserved to rule.

It would not be the Raven Empire that rose at the end of this all, but the Dragon Empire.

"I don't want to go on," Aviendha said to the empty forest of glass.

The breeze had fallen still. Her comment was met with silence. Her tears had marked the dust by her feet, like fallen drops of rain.

"That . . . *creature* had no honor," she said. "She has ruined us."

The worst part was, the woman—Oncala—had thought

of her mother's mother. Her greatmother. Inside Oncala's head, there had been a face attached to that title. Aviendha had recognized it.

As her own.

Cringing, closing her eyes, she stepped forward into the very center of the radiant columns.

She was Padra, daughter of the Dragon Reborn, proud Maiden of the Spear. She yanked her weapon from the neck of a dying Seanchan, then watched the rest flee through their gateway.

Light curse the one who taught the Seanchan Traveling, Padra thought. *Even if their weaves aren't very elegant.*

She was convinced that no living person understood the One Power as she and her siblings did. She'd been able to weave since she'd been a child, and her brothers and sister were the same. To them, it was natural, and all others who channeled seemed awkward by comparison.

She was careful not to speak that way. Aes Sedai and Wise Ones didn't like being reminded of their shortcomings. It was true nonetheless.

Padra joined her spear-sisters. They left one of their number dead on the grass, and Padra mourned for her. Tarra, of the Taardad Aiel. She would be remembered. But honor was theirs, for they had slain eight Seanchan soldiers.

She wove a gateway—for her, it happened as fast as she could think. She held the One Power perpetually, even while she slept. She'd never known what it was like not to have that comforting, surging Power in the back of her mind. Others said they feared being consumed by it, but how was that possible? *Saidar* was a piece of her, like her arm or her leg. How could one be consumed by one's own flesh, bone and blood?

The gateway led to the Aiel camp in the land called Arad Doman. The camp wasn't a city; Aiel didn't have cities. But it *was* a very large camp, and it had not moved in almost a decade. Padra strode across the grass, and Aiel in *cadin'sor* showed her deference. Padra and her siblings, as children of the Dragon, had become . . . something to the Aiel.

Not lords—that concept made her sick. But she was more than an ordinary *algai'd'siswai*. The clan chiefs looked to

her and her siblings for advice, and the Wise Ones took special interest in them. They allowed her to channel, though
she was not one of them. She could no sooner stop channeling than she could stop breathing.

She dismissed her spear-sisters, then made her way directly to Ronam's tent. The clan chief—son of Rhuarc—
would need to hear her report. She entered and was
surprised to see that Ronam was not alone. A group of men
sat on the rug, clan chiefs every one. Her siblings were sitting there as well.

"Ah, Padra," Ronam said. "You have returned."

"I can come back another time, Ronam," she said.

"No, you were wanted for this meeting. Sit and share my
shade."

Padra bowed her head at the honor he showed her. She
sat between Alarch and Janduin, her brothers. Though the
four siblings were quadruplets, they looked very dissimilar.
Alarch took more after their wetlander side, and had dark
hair. Janduin was blond and tall. Beside him sat Marinna,
their sister, small of build with a round face.

"I should report," Padra said to Ronam, "that the Seanchan patrol was where we thought. We engaged them."

There were uncomfortable mumbles about that.

"It is not against the Dragon's Peace for them to enter Arad Doman," said Tavalad, clan chief of the Goshien
Aiel.

"Nor is it wrong for us to kill them for getting too close,
clan chief," Padra replied. "The Aiel are not bound by the
Dragon's Peace. If the Seanchan wish to risk inspecting our
camp, then they need to know that it *is* a risk."

Several of the others—more than she would have
expected—nodded at that comment. She glanced at Janduin, and he raised an eyebrow. She covertly raised two
fingers. Two Seanchan, dead by her spear. She would have
liked to take them captive, but the Seanchan did not deserve
to become *gai'shain*. They also made terrible prisoners.
Better to spare them the shame and let them die.

"We should speak what we came to say," said Alalved,
chief of the Tomanelle Aiel. Padra did a quick count. All
eleven chiefs were accounted for, including those who had
blood oaths against one another. A meeting like this hadn't

been seen in years, not since her father had been preparing for the Last Battle.

"And what did we come to say?" asked one of the others.

Alalved shook his head. "The spears grow restless. The Aiel are not meant to grow fat in lush lands, tending crops. We are warriors."

"The Dragon asked for peace," Tavalad said.

"The Dragon asked others for peace," Alalved replied. "He excluded the Aiel."

"That is true," said Darvin, chief of the Reyn.

"Do we return to raiding one another after all of these years of holding our blood feuds in abeyance?" Ronam asked softly. He was an excellent clan chief, much as Rhuarc had been. Wise, yet not afraid of battle.

"What would be the point?" asked Shedren, chief of the Daryne Aiel.

Others nodded. But that raised a larger problem, one her mother had often spoken of. What was it to be Aiel, now that their duty to the past had been fulfilled, their *toh* as a people cleansed?

"How long can we wait," Alalved said, "knowing that they have Aiel women captive with those bracelets of theirs? It has been years, and they still continue to refuse all offers of payment and barter! They return our civility with rudeness and insults."

"We are not meant to beg," said aged Bruan. "The Aiel will soon become milk-fed wetlanders."

All nodded at his words. Wise Bruan had lived through the Last Battle.

"If only the Seanchan Empress . . ." Ronam shook his head, and she knew what he was thinking. The old empress, the one who had ruled during the days of the Last Battle, had been considered a woman of honor by Ronam's father. An understanding had nearly been reached with her, so it was said. But many years had passed since her rule.

"Regardless," Ronam continued, "the spears clash; our people fight when they meet. It is our nature. If the Seanchan won't listen to reason, then what cause do we have to leave them be?"

"This peace of the Dragon's will not last long, anyway,"

Alalved said. "Skirmishes between the nations are common, though none speak of them. The *Car'a'carn* required promises of the monarchs, but there is no enforcement. Many wetlanders cannot be held at their word, and I worry that the Seanchan will devour them while they squabble."

There were many nods. Only Darvin and Tavalad did not seem convinced.

Padra held her breath. They had known this was coming. The skirmishes with the Seanchan, the restlessness of the clans. She had dreamed of this day, but feared it as well. Her mother had gained great *ji* in battle. Padra had had few chances to prove herself.

A war with the Seanchan . . . the prospect invigorated her. But it would also mean much death.

"What say the Dragon's children?" Ronam asked, looking at the four of them.

It still seemed strange that these elders looked to her. She checked on *saidar*, comfortable in the back of her mind, and drew strength from it. What would she do without it?

"I say that we must reclaim our own who are held by the Seanchan," said Marinna. She was training to become a Wise One.

Alarch seemed uncertain, and he glanced at Janduin. Alarch often deferred to his brother.

"The Aiel must have a purpose," Janduin said, nodding. "We are useless as we are, and we made no promise not to attack. It is a testament to our patience and respect for my father that we have waited this long."

Eyes turned to Padra. "They are our enemies," she said.

One by one, the men in the room nodded. It seemed such a simple event to end years of waiting.

"Go to your clans." Ronam stood up. "Prepare them."

Padra remained seated as the others said their farewells, some somber, others excited. Seventeen years was too long for the Aiel to be without battle.

Soon, the tent was empty save for Padra. She waited, staring at the rug before her. War. She was excited, but another part of her was somber. She felt as if she had set the clans on a path that would change them forever.

"Padra?" a voice asked.

She turned to see Ronam standing in the entryway to the tent. She blushed and stood. Though he was ten years her senior, he was quite handsome. She'd never give up the spear, of course, but if she did. . . .

"You seem worried," he said.

"I was simply thinking."

"About the Seanchan?"

"About my father," she replied.

"Ah." Ronam nodded. "I remember when he first came to Cold Rocks Hold. I was very young."

"What was your impression of him?"

"He was an impressive man," Ronam said.

"Nothing else?"

He shook his head. "I'm sorry, Padra, but I did not spend much time with him. My path led me elsewhere. I . . . heard things, from my father, though."

She cocked her head.

Ronam turned and looked out the open tent flaps, toward the green grass beyond. "My father called Rand al'Thor a clever man and great leader, but one who did not know what to do with the Aiel. I remember him saying that when the *Car'a'carn* was among us, he did not *feel* like one of us. As if we made him uncomfortable." Ronam shook his head. "Everyone else was planned for, but the Aiel were left adrift."

"Some say we should have returned to the Three-fold Land," she said.

"No," Ronam said. "No, that would have destroyed us. Our fathers knew nothing of steamhorses or dragon tubes. Were the Aiel to return to the Waste, we would have become irrelevant. The world would pass us by, and we would vanish as a people."

"But war?" Padra said. "Is it right?"

"I do not know," Ronam said softly. "We are Aiel. It is what we know how to do."

Padra nodded, feeling more certain.

The Aiel would run to war again. And there would be much honor in it.

Aviendha blinked. The sky was dark.

She was exhausted. Her mind was drained, her heart opened—as if bleeding out strength with every beat. She sat down in the midst of the dimming columns. Her . . . children.

She remembered their faces from her first visit to Rhuidean. She had not seen this. Not that she remembered, at least.

"Is it destined?" she asked. "Can we change it?"

There was no answer, of course.

Her tears were dry. How did one react to seeing the utter destruction—no, the utter *decay*—of one's people? Each step had seemed logical to the people who took it. But each had taken the Aiel toward their end.

Should anyone have to see such terrible visions? She wished she'd never stepped back into the forest of pillars. Was she to blame for what was to happen? It was her line that would doom her people.

This was not like the events she had seen when passing into the rings during her first visit to Rhuidean. Those had been possibilities. This day's visions seemed more *real*. She felt almost certain that what she had experienced was not simply one of many possibilities. What she had seen *would* occur. Step by step, honor drained from her people. Step by step, the Aiel turned from proud to wretched.

There had to be more. Angry, she stood up and took another step. Nothing happened. She walked all the way to the edge of the pillars, then turned, furious.

"Show me more," she demanded. "Show me what I did to cause this! It is my lineage that brought us ruin! What is my part in it?"

She walked into the pillars again.

Nothing. They seemed dead. She reached out and touched one, but there was no life. No hum, no sense of Power. She closed her eyes, squeezing one more tear from the corner of each eye. The tears trailed down her face, leaving a line of cold wetness on her cheeks.

"Can I change it?" she asked.

If I can't, she thought, *will that stop me from trying?*

The answer was simple. No. She could not *live* without doing something to avert that fate. She had come to Rhuidean seeking knowledge. Well, she had received it. In more abundance than she had wanted.

She opened her eyes and gritted her teeth. Aiel took responsibility. Aiel fought. Aiel stood for honor. If she was the only one who knew the terrors of their future, then it was her duty—as a Wise One—to act. She *would* save her people.

She walked from the pillars, then broke into a run. She needed to return, to consult with the other Wise Ones. But first she needed quiet, out in the Three-fold Land. Time to think.

CHAPTER
50

Choosing Enemies

Elayne sat anxiously, hands in her lap, listening to the distant booms. She'd intentionally chosen the throne room, rather than a less formal audience chamber. Today, she needed to be seen as a queen.

The throne room was imposing, with its majestic pillars and lavish ornamentation. Golden stand-lamps burned in a long double row on either side of the room, breaking only for the pillars. Guardsmen in white and red stood in front of them, burnished breastplates gleaming. The marble columns were matched by the thick crimson rug, woven with the Lion of Andor in gold at its center. It led toward Elayne, wearing the Rose Crown. Her gown was after a traditional fashion rather than those favored in court right now; the sleeves were wide, with the cuffs designed to droop down to a gold-embroidered point beneath her hand.

That pattern was echoed by the bodice, which was high enough to be modest, but low enough to remind all that Elayne was a woman. One still unmarried. Her mother had married a man from Cairhien early in her reign. Others might wonder if Elayne would do the same to cement her hold there.

Another distant boom sounded. The noise of the dragons firing was growing familiar. Not quite a clap of thunder—lower, more regular.

Elayne had been taught to conceal her nervousness. First by her tutors, and then by the Aes Sedai. Whatever some people thought, Elayne Trakand *could* control her temper when she needed to. She kept her hands in her lap and forced her tongue to be still. Showing nervousness would be far worse than anger.

Dyelin sat in a chair near the throne. The stately woman wore her golden hair unbound around her shoulders, and she was working quietly at a hoop of embroidery. Dyelin said it relaxed her, providing something for the hands to do while the mind was busy. Elayne's mother was not in attendance. Today, she might be too much of a distraction.

Elayne couldn't afford herself Dyelin's same luxury. She needed to be seen leading. Unfortunately, "leading" often took the form of sitting on her throne, eyes forward, projecting determination and control while she waited. Surely the demonstration was done by now?

Another boom. Perhaps not.

She could hear soft chat in the sitting chamber to the side of the throne room. Those High Seats still in Caemlyn had received a royal invitation to meet with the Queen in a discussion of sanitation requirements for those staying outside the city. That meeting would happen at the strike of five, but the invitations had hinted the High Seats were to arrive two hours early.

The wording of the message should have been obvious. Elayne was going to do something important today, and she was inviting the High Seats early so that they could enjoy some sanctioned eavesdropping. They were kept well supplied with drinks and small dishes of meats and fruits in the sitting room. Likely, the chat she overheard was speculation about what she was going to reveal.

If they only knew. Elayne kept her hands in her lap. Dyelin continued her needlework, clicking her tongue to herself as she pulled out a wrong stitch.

After a nearly insufferable wait, the dragons stopped sounding and Elayne felt Birgitte returning to the palace. Sending her with the group was the best way to know when it was returning. The timing today needed to be handled with absolute care. Elayne breathed in and out to still her nerves. There. Birgitte was surely in the palace now.

Elayne nodded to Captain Guybon. It was time to bring in the prisoners.

A group of Guards entered a moment later, leading three individuals. Sniffling Arymilla was still plump, despite her captivity. The older woman was pretty, or might have been, had she been wearing more than rags. Her large brown eyes were wide with fright. As if she thought Elayne might still execute her.

Elenia was far more in control. She, like the others, had been stripped of her fine dress and wore a tattered gown instead, but she had cleaned her face and dressed her gold hair in a neat bun. Elayne didn't starve or abuse her prisoners. Her enemies though they were, they *weren't* traitors to Andor.

. Elenia regarded Elayne. That vulpine face of hers was thoughtful, calculating. Did she know where her husband's army had vanished to? That force felt like a hidden knife, pressed to Elayne's back. None of her scouts had been able to discover its location. Light! Problems atop problems.

The third woman was Naean Arawn, a slim, pale woman whose black hair had lost much of its luster during her captivity. This one had seemed broken before Elayne had taken her captive, and she kept back from the other two women.

The three were prodded to the foot of the throne's dais, then forced down on their knees. In the hallway, the Cairhienin nobles were returning noisily from the demonstration of the dragons. They would assume that they'd happened upon Elayne's display by accident.

"The Crown acknowledges Naean Arawn, Elenia Sarand and Arymilla Marne," Elayne said in a loud voice. That stilled the outside conversations—both those of the Andoran nobles in the sitting room and the Cairhienin outside in the hallway.

Of the three, only Elenia dared glance up. Elayne met the gaze with one as hard as stone, and the woman blushed before looking down again. Dyelin had put away her needlework and was watching closely.

"The Crown has given much thought to you three," Elayne pronounced. "Your misguided war against Trakand has left you destitute, and requests for ransom have been turned away by your heirs and scions. Your own Houses have abandoned you."

Her words rang in the grand throne room. The women before her bowed down further.

"This leaves the Crown with a conundrum," Elayne said. "You vex us with your troubling existences. Perhaps some queens would have left you to prison, but I find that reeks of indecision. You would drain my resources and make men whisper of ways to free you."

The hall fell silent save for the husky breathing of the prisoners.

"*This* Crown is not prone to indecisiveness," Elayne pronounced. "On this day, Houses Sarand, Marne and Arawn are stripped of title and estate, their lands forfeit to the Crown in retribution for their crimes."

Elenia gasped, looking up. Arymilla groaned, slouching down on the lion-centered rug. Naean did not respond. She seemed numb.

Murmuring rose immediately from the sitting room. This was worse than an execution. When nobles were executed, they were at least executed with their titles—in a way, an execution was an acknowledgment of a worthy foe. The title and lands passed on to the heir, and the House survived.

But this . . . this was something few queens would ever attempt. If Elayne were seen as seizing land and money for the throne, the other nobles would unite against her. She could guess the conversations in the other room. Her power base was shaky. Her allies, who had stood with her before the siege and faced the possibility of execution themselves, might very well now begin to question.

Best to move on quickly. Elayne gestured, and the Guards pulled the three prisoners to their feet and then led them to the side of the room. Even defiant Elenia seemed stunned. In essence, this proclamation was a proclamation of death. As soon as possible, they would commit suicide rather than face their Houses.

Birgitte knew her cue. She entered, leading the group of Cairhienin nobles. They had been invited to a display of Andor's new weapon for "defending against the Shadow," and were a mixed band. The most important in the group was probably either Bertome Saighan or Lorstrum Aesnan.

Bertome was a short man with a kind of handsomeness, though Elayne was not fond of the way the Cairhienin shaved and powdered their foreheads. He wore a large knife at his belt—swords had been forbidden in the Queen's presence—and seemed disturbed by Elayne's treatment of the prisoners. As well he should have been. His cousin, Colavaere, had received a similar punishment from Rand, though that had not affected her entire House. She'd hanged herself rather than face the shame.

Her death had elevated Bertome, and while he'd been very careful not to make public waves against Rand's rule, Elayne's sources picked him out as one of the major private critics of Rand in Cairhien.

Lorstrum Aesnan was a quiet, thin man who walked with his hands behind his back, and tended to look down his nose. Like the others in the group, he wore dark clothing after the Cairhienin fashion, his coat striped with the colors of his House. He had risen to prominence following Rand's disappearance from Cairhien. Desperate times made for quick advances, and this man had not moved against Rand too quickly, yet also hadn't allied with him. That middle ground gave him power, and some whispered that he was considering seizing the throne.

Other than those two, the Cairhienin here were a smattering of other nobility. Ailil Riatin was not the head of her House, but since the disappearance of her brother—a disappearance that was looking more and more like death—she had assumed power. Riatin was a powerful House. The slim, middle-aged woman was tall for a Cairhienin, and wore a dark blue dress slashed with colors, her dress shaped by hoops through the skirts. Her family had held the Sun Throne recently, if only for a relatively short time, and she was known to be a vocal supporter of Elayne.

Lord and Lady Osiellin, Lord and Lady Chuliandred, Lord and Lady Hamarashle, and Lord Mavabwin had gathered behind those of more importance. All were of middling power, and all—for one reason or another—were likely roadblocks to Elayne. They were a cluster of carefully done hair and powdered foreheads, wide dresses on the women, coats and trousers on the men, lace at the cuffs.

"My Lords and Ladies," Elayne said, naming each House in turn. "You have enjoyed Andor's demonstration?"

"Indeed we have, Your Majesty," lanky Lorstrum said, bowing his head graciously. "Those weapons are quite . . . intriguing."

He was obviously digging for information. Elayne blessed her tutors for their insistence that she understand the Game of Houses. "We all know that the Last Battle quickly approaches," Elayne said. "I thought that Cairhien should best be apprised of the strength of its greatest and closest ally. There will be times in the near future when we will need to rely upon one another."

"Indeed, Your Majesty," Lorstrum said.

"Your Majesty," Bertome said, stepping forward. The short man folded his arms. "I assure you, Cairhien exults in Andor's strength and stability."

Elayne eyed him. Was he offering her support? No, it seemed he was also digging, wondering if Elayne would declare herself a candidate for the Sun Throne. Her intentions should have been obvious by now—sending some of the Band to the city had been an obvious move, nearly too obvious for the subtle Cairhienin.

"Would that Cairhien had similar stability," Elayne said carefully.

Several of them nodded, no doubt hoping she intended to offer one of *them* the throne. If she threw Andor's support behind one of these, it would guarantee him or her victory. And it would give her a sympathizer as King or Queen.

Another might have made that ploy. Not she. That throne *would* be hers.

"The taking of a throne is a very delicate business," Lorstrum said. "It has proven . . . dangerous in the past. And so many are hesitant."

"Indeed," Elayne said. "I do not envy Cairhien the uncertainty that it has known these last months." And now the moment. Elayne took a deep breath. "Faced with the strength in Andor, one might think this would be an obvious time to have strong alliances. In fact, the throne recently acquired several estates of no small means. It occurs to me that these estates have no stewards."

All grew quiet. The whispers in the other room stopped. Had they heard correctly? Had Elayne offered estates in Andor to *foreign* nobility?

She hid her smile. Slowly, some of them got it. Lorstrum gave a sly smile, and he nodded to her ever so slightly.

"Cairhien and Andor have long shared fellowship," Elayne continued, as if the idea were only now occurring to her. "Our lords have married your ladies, our ladies your lords, and we share many common bonds of blood and affection. I should think the wisdom of a few Cairhienin lords would be a great addition to my court, and perhaps educate me upon my heritage on my father's side."

She locked eyes with Lorstrum. Would he bite? His lands in Cairhien were small, and his influence great for a time—but that could tip. The estates she'd seized from the three prisoners were among the most enviable in her country.

He *had* to see it. If she took the throne of Cairhien by force, the people and the nobility would rebel against her. That was partially Lorstrum's fault, if her suspicions were true.

But what if she gave lands within Andor to some of the Cairhienin nobility? What if she created multiple bonds between their countries? What if she proved that she would not steal their titles—but would instead be willing to give some of them greater holdings? Would that be enough to prove that she didn't intend to steal the lands of the Cairhien nobility and give them to her own people? Would that ease their worries?

Lorstrum met her eyes. "I see great potential for alliances."

Bertome was nodding in appreciation. "I too, think this could be arranged." Neither would give up their lands, of course. They simply planned to gain estates in Andor. Wealthy ones.

The others shared glances. Lady Osiellin and Lord Mavabwin were the first two to figure it out. They spoke at the same time, offering alliances.

Elayne stilled her anxious heart, sitting back in the throne. "I have but one more estate to give," she said. "But I believe it could be divided." She would give some to Ailil also, to curry favor and reward her support. Now for the second part of the ploy. "Lady Sarand," Elayne called toward the back of the room.

Elenia stepped forward, wearing her rags.

"The Crown is not without mercy," Elayne said. "Andor cannot forgive you for the pain and suffering you caused. But other countries have no such memories. Tell me, if the Crown were to provide you with an opportunity for new lands, would that opportunity be taken?"

"New lands, Your Majesty?" Elenia asked. "Of which lands do you speak?"

"A unification between Andor and Cairhien would offer many opportunities," Elayne said. "Perhaps you have heard

of the Crown's alliance with Gheáldan. Perhaps you have
heard of the newly revitalized lands in the west of the realm.
This is a time of great opportunity. If I were to find you and
your husband a place to form a new seat in Cairhien, would
you take what is given?"

"I . . . would certainly consider it, Your Majesty," Elenia
said, showing a glimmer of hope.

Elayne turned to the Cairhienin lords. "For any of this to
take effect," she said, "I would need authority to speak for
both Andor *and* Cairhien. How long, do you suspect, might
it take for such a situation to be arranged?"

"Return me to my homeland through one of those strange
portals," Lorstrum said, "and give me one hour."

"I need only a half an hour, Your Majesty," Bertome put
in, glancing at Lorstrum.

"One hour," Elayne said, holding up her hands. "Prepare
well."

"All right," Birgitte said as the door to the smaller chamber
closed. "What in the name of the Dark One's *bloody* left
hand just happened?"

Elayne sat down. It had worked! Or it seemed as if it
would. The plush chair was a comfort after the stiffness of
the Lion Throne. Dyelin took a seat to her right; Morgase
sat to her left.

"What happened," Morgase said, "is that my daughter is
brilliant."

Elayne smiled in gratitude. Birgitte, however, frowned.
Elayne could feel the woman's confusion. She was the only
one in the room with them; they had to wait one hour to see
the true results of Elayne's plotting.

"All right," Birgitte said. "So you gave up a bunch of Andor's land to Cairhienin nobility."

"As a bribe," Dyelin said. She didn't seem as convinced
as Morgase. "A clever maneuver, Your Majesty, but dangerous."

"Dangerous?" Birgitte said. "Blood and ashes, will
someone please explain to the idiot over here *why* bribery
is brilliant or clever? It's hardly Elayne who *discovered* it."

"This was more than a gift," Morgase said. Incongru-
ously, she took to pouring tea for those in the room. Elayne

couldn't ever recall seeing her mother pour tea before. "The major obstacle blocking Elayne from Cairhien was that she would be viewed as a conqueror."

"Yes, so?" Birgitte asked.

"So she made bonds between the two nations," Dyelin said, accepting a cup of Tremalking black from Morgase. "By giving that group some land in Andor, she shows that she's not going to ignore or impoverish the Cairhienin nobility."

"Beyond that," Morgase said, "she makes herself less of an oddity. If she'd taken the throne, she'd have gained its lands—and become the only person to have holdings in both countries. Now she'll be one of many."

"But it's dangerous," Dyelin repeated. "Lorstrum didn't give in because of the bribe."

"He didn't?" Birgitte said, frowning. "But—"

"She's right," Elayne said, sipping her tea. "He gave in because he saw that I was handing him the chance for both thrones."

The room fell silent.

"Bloody ashes," Birgitte finally swore.

Dyelin nodded. "You have created enemies who could overthrow you, Elayne. If something were to happen to you, there is a good chance that either Lorstrum or Bertome could make a play for both countries."

"I'm counting on it," Elayne said. "They're the two most powerful noblemen in Cairhien right now, particularly since Dobraine hasn't returned from wherever Rand took him. With them actively supporting the idea of a common monarch, we actually have a chance at this."

"They'll only be supporting you because they see a chance of taking both thrones for themselves!" Dyelin said.

"Better to choose your enemies than remain in ignorance," Elayne said. "I've essentially limited my competition. They saw the dragons, and those made them envious. Then I offered them the chance not only to gain access to those weapons, but to double their wealth. And on top of that, I gave them the seed of possibility that one day, they might be named king."

"So they'll try to kill you," Birgitte said flatly.

"Perhaps," Elayne said. "Or, perhaps they'll try to undermine me. But not for many years—a decade, I'd guess.

To strike now would be to risk the nations dividing again. No, first they'll establish themselves and enjoy their wealth. Only once they're certain that things are secure—and that I've grown lax—will they move. Fortunately, there are two of them, and that will let me play them against one another. And for now, we have gained two staunch allies—men who keenly want my bid for the Sun Throne to succeed. They will hand the crown right to me."

"And the prisoners?" Dyelin said. "Elenia and the other two? Do you really intend to find them lands?"

"Yes," Elayne said. "What I've done for them is actually very kind. The Crown will assume their debts, then give them a fresh start in Cairhien, if this all works. It will be good to have Andoran nobility taking lands there, though I will probably have to give them land out of my own Cairhienin holdings."

"You'll leave yourself surrounded by enemies," Birgitte said, shaking her head.

"As usual," Elayne said. "Fortunately, I have you to watch over me, don't I?"

She smiled at the Warder, but knew that Birgitte could sense her nervousness. This was going to be a long hour's wait.

CHAPTER
51

A Testing

The hair on Min's neck rose as she held the crystal sword. *Callandor*. She'd heard stories of this weapon since she was a child, wild tales of distant Tear and the strange Sword That Is Not a Sword. Now she held it in her own fingers.

It was lighter than she'd expected. Its crystalline length caught and played with the lamplight. It seemed to shimmer too much, the light inside changing even when she didn't move. The crystal was smooth, but warm. It almost felt alive.

Rand stood in front of her, looking down at the weapon. They were in their rooms inside the Stone of Tear, accompanied by Cadsuane, Narishma, Merise, Naeff and two Maidens.

Rand reached out, touching the weapon. She glanced at him, and a viewing sprang to life above him. A glowing sword, *Callandor*, being gripped in a black hand. She gasped.

"What did you see?" Rand asked softly.

"*Callandor*, held in a fist. The hand looks to be made of onyx."

"Any idea what it means?"

She shook her head.

"We should hide it away again," Cadsuane said. She wore brown and green today, earthy colors lightened by her golden hair ornaments. She stood with arms folded, back straight. "Phaw! Getting the object out now is foolhardy, boy."

"Your objection is noted," Rand said. He took the

sa'angreal from Min, then slid it over his shoulder into a sheath on his back. At his side, he once again wore the ancient sword with the red-and-gold dragons painted on the sheath. He'd said before that he considered that to be a kind of symbol. It represented the past to him, and *Callandor*—somehow—represented the future.

"Rand," Min said, taking his arm. "My research . . . remember, *Callandor* seems to have a deeper flaw than we've discovered. This viewing only reinforces what I said before. I worry it may be used against you."

"I suspect that it will," Rand said. "Everything else in this world has been used against me. Narishma, a gateway, please. We've kept the Borderlanders waiting long enough."

The Asha'man nodded, bells in his hair tinkling.

Rand turned to Naeff. "Naeff, there has still been no word from the Black Tower?"

"No, my Lord," the tall Asha'man said.

"I have been unable to Travel there," Rand said. "That implies great trouble, worse than I had feared. Use this weave. It can disguise you. Travel to a place a day's ride outside, and ride in, hiding yourself. See what you can discover. Help if you can, and when you find Logain and those loyal to him, deliver him a message for me."

"What message, my Lord?"

Rand looked distant. "Tell them that I was wrong. Tell them that we're not weapons. We're men. Perhaps it will help. Take care. This could be dangerous. Bring me word. I will need to fix things there, but I could easily stumble into a trap more dangerous than any I've avoided so far. Problems . . . so many problems that need fixing. And only one of me. Go in my place, Naeff, for now. I need information."

"I . . . Yes, my Lord." He seemed confused, but he ducked out of the room to obey.

Rand took a deep breath, then rubbed the stump of his left arm. "Let's go."

"Are you certain you don't want to bring more people?" Min asked.

"Yes," Rand said. "Cadsuane, be ready to open a gateway and get us out if needed."

"We're going into Far Madding, boy," Cadsuane said. "Surely you haven't forgotten that we are prevented from touching the Source while there."

Rand smiled. "And you're wearing a full paralis-net in your hair, which includes a Well. I'm certain you keep it full, and that should be enough to create a single gateway."

Cadsuane's face grew expressionless. "I've never heard of a paralis-net."

"Cadsuane Sedai," Rand said softly. "Your net has a few ornaments I don't recognize—I suspect it is a Breaking-era creation. But I was there when the first ones were designed, and I wore the original male version."

The room fell still.

"Well, boy," Cadsuane finally said. "You—"

"Are you ever going to give up that affectation, Cadsuane Sedai?" Rand asked. "Calling me boy? I no longer mind, though it does feel odd. I was four hundred years old on the day I died during the Age of Legends. I suspect that would make you my junior by several decades at the least. I show you respect. Perhaps it would be appropriate for you to return it. If you wish, you may call me Rand Sedai. I am, so far as I know, the only male Aes Sedai still alive who was properly raised but who never turned to the Shadow."

Cadsuane paled visibly.

Rand's smile turned kindly. "You wished to come in and dance with the Dragon Reborn, Cadsuane. I am what I need to be. Be comforted—you face the Forsaken, but have one as ancient as they at your side." He turned away from her, eyes growing distant. "Now, if only great age really *were* an indication of great wisdom. As easy to wish that the Dark One would simply let us be."

He took Min by the arm, and together they walked through Narishma's gateway. Beyond, a small cluster of Maidens waited inside a wooded clearing, guarding a group of horses. Min climbed into her saddle, noting how reserved Cadsuane looked. As well she should. When Rand spoke like that, it troubled Min more than she wanted to admit.

They rode out of the small thicket, down toward Far Madding, an impressive city set on an island in the middle of a lake. A large army—flying hundreds of banners—spread out around the lake.

"It's always been a city of importance, you know," Rand said from beside Min, his eyes distant. "The Guardians are newer, but the city was here long ago. Aren Deshar, Aren Mador, Far Madding. Always a thorn in our side, Aren

Deshar was. The enclave of the Incastar—those afraid of progress, afraid of wonder. Turns out they had a right to be afraid. How I wish I had listened to Gilgame . . ."

"Rand?" Min said softly.

It drew him out of his reverie. "Yes?"

"Is it really as you said? Are you *four centuries* old?"

"I'm nearly four and a half, I suppose. Do my years in this Age add to those I had before?" He looked at her. "You're worried, aren't you? That I'm no longer me, the man you knew, the foolish sheepherder?"

"You've got all of this in your mind, so much *past*."

"Memories, only," Rand said.

"But you're him, too. You talk like *you* were the one who tried to seal the Bore. Like you knew the Forsaken personally."

Rand rode in silence for a time. "I suppose I am him. But Min, what you're missing is this: I may be him now, but he was *always* me as well. I was always him. I'm not going to change just because I remember—I was the same. I'm *me*. And I always have been me."

"Lews Therin was mad."

"At the end," Rand said. "And yes, he made mistakes. *I* made mistakes. I grew arrogant, desperate. But there's a difference this time. A great one."

"What difference?"

He smiled. "This time, I was raised better."

Min found herself smiling as well.

"You know me, Min. Well, I promise you, I feel more like myself now than I have in months. I feel more like myself than I ever did as Lews Therin, if *that* makes any kind of sense. It's because of Tam, because of the people around me. You, Perrin, Nynaeve, Mat, Aviendha, Elayne, Moiraine. *He* tried very hard to break me. I think if I'd been the same as I was so long ago, he would have succeeded."

They rode across the meadow surrounding Far Madding. As everywhere else, the green here had departed, leaving yellow and brown. It was getting worse and worse.

Pretend that it slumbers, Min told herself. *The land isn't dead. It's waiting through the winter.* A winter of storms and war.

Narishma hissed softly, riding behind. Min glanced at him. The Asha'man's face had gone hard. Apparently, they'd passed inside the bubble of the Guardian's influence. Rand gave no indication he'd noticed. He didn't seem to be having the trouble with sickness when he channeled any longer, which relieved her. Or was he just covering it?

She turned her mind to the task at hand. The Borderlander armies had never explained why they'd defied custom and logic by marching south to find Rand. They were needed desperately. Rand's intervention at Maradon had saved what was left of the city, but if that sort of thing was happening all across the border with the Blight. . . .

Twenty soldiers—lances upheld with narrow, blood-red banners flapping from them like streamers—intercepted Rand's group long before it reached the army. Rand stopped and let them approach.

"Rand al'Thor," one of the men announced. "We are representatives of the Unity of the Border. We will provide escort."

Rand nodded, and the procession started forward again, this time with guards.

"They didn't call you Lord Dragon," Min whispered to Rand. He nodded thoughtfully. Perhaps the Borderlanders did not believe he *was* the Dragon Reborn.

"Do not be arrogant here, Rand al'Thor," Cadsuane said, trotting up to ride beside him. "But do *not* back down. Most Borderlanders will respond to strength when they see it."

So. Cadsuane called Rand by name, instead of naming him "boy." It seemed a victory, and it made Min smile.

"I will have that gateway ready," Cadsuane continued more softly. "But it will be very small. The Well will only give me enough to make one we'd have to crawl through. We shouldn't need it. These people will fight for you. They will *want* to fight for you. Only bumbling foolishness could keep them from it."

"There is more to it than that, Cadsuane Sedai," Rand replied, his voice hushed. "Something drove them southward. This is a challenge, one I am uncertain how to meet. But your advice is appreciated."

Cadsuane nodded. Eventually, Min picked out a line of people waiting at the forefront of the army. There were thousands of soldiers behind, standing in rows. Saldaeans, with their bowed legs. Shienarans in topknots. Arafellin, each soldier with two swords strapped to his back. Kandori, with forked beards.

The group at the head stood on the ground, without mounts. They wore fine clothing. Two women and two men, all with what were obviously Aes Sedai at their sides, some with an attendant or two behind.

"The one at the front is Queen Ethenielle," Cadsuane whispered. "She is a stern woman, but fair. She is known for meddling in the affairs of the southern nations, and I suspect the others will let her take the lead today. The handsome man beside her is Paitar Nachiman, King of Arafel."

"Handsome?" Min asked, inspecting the balding older Arafellin. "Him?"

"It depends on one's perspective, child," Cadsuane said without missing a beat. "He was once known widely for his face, and he is still known for his sword. Beside him is King Easar Togita of Shienar."

"So sad," Rand said softly. "Who did he lose?"

Min frowned. Easar didn't look particularly sad to her. Solemn, perhaps.

"He's a Borderlander," Cadsuane said. "He's fought the Trollocs all his life; I'd suspect he's lost many a person dear to him. His wife did die some years back. He's said to have the soul of a poet, but he is an austere man. If you could earn his respect, it would mean much."

"The last one is Tenobia, then," Rand said, rubbing his chin. "Still wish I had Bashere with us." Bashere had said that his face might fuel Tenobia's anger, and Rand had listened to reason on that count.

"Tenobia," Cadsuane said, "is a wildfire. Young, impertinent and reckless. Don't let her draw you into an argument."

Rand nodded. "Min?"

"Tenobia has a spear hovering over her head," Min said. "Bloody, but shining in the light. Ethenielle will soon be wed—I see that by white doves. She plans to do something dangerous today, so be careful. The other two have various swords, shields and arrows hovering about them. Both will fight soon."

"In the Last Battle?" Rand asked.

"I don't know," she admitted. "It could be here, today."

Their escort led them up to the four monarchs. Rand slid out of the saddle, patting Tai'daishar on the neck as the horse snorted. Min moved to dismount, as did Narishma, but Rand held up a hand to stop them.

"Blasted fool," Cadsuane muttered from beside Min, low enough that nobody else could hear. "He asks me to be ready to get him out, then leaves us?"

"He likely meant that you should get me away," Min said softly. "Knowing him, he's more worried about me than himself." She paused. "Blasted fool."

Cadsuane shot her a glance, then smiled slightly before turning back to watch Rand.

He stepped up to the four monarchs and stopped, raising his arms to the sides, as if to ask, "What is it you wish of me?"

Ethenielle took the lead, as Cadsuane had guessed. She was a plump woman, her dark hair pulled away from her face and tied at the back. She strode up to Rand, a man walking beside her and carrying a sheathed sword in his arm, hilt pointed toward her.

Nearby, the Maidens rustled. They stepped up beside Rand. As usual, they assumed that commands to stay back didn't include them.

Ethenielle raised a hand and slapped Rand across the face.

Narishma cursed. The Maidens raised their veils and drew spears. Min nudged her horse forward, breaking through the line of guards.

"Stop!" Rand said, raising his hand. He turned, looking at the Maidens.

Min stilled her mare, patting her on the neck. She was skittish, as might be expected. The Maidens reluctantly backed down, though Cadsuane did take the opportunity to move her horse up beside Min's.

Rand turned back to Ethenielle and rubbed his face. "I hope that's some traditional Kandori greeting, Your Majesty."

She raised an eyebrow, then gestured to the side, and King Easar of Shienar stepped up to Rand. The man backhanded Rand across the mouth, the force of it causing Rand to stumble.

Rand righted himself, again waving the Maidens down. He met Easar's eyes. A trickle of blood ran down Rand's chin. The Shienaran studied him for a moment, then nodded and stepped back.

Tenobia came next. She slapped Rand with her left hand, a strong blow that cracked in the air. Min felt a flash of pain from Rand. Tenobia shook her hand afterward.

King Paitar came last. The aging Arafellin with only a fringe of hair walked with his hands behind his back, contemplative. He stepped up to Rand and reached over and dabbed at the blood on Rand's cheek. Then he backhanded Rand with a blow that sent him to his knees, a spray of blood flying from his mouth.

Min couldn't sit by any longer. "Rand!" she said, jumping down from her saddle and running to him. She reached his side, steadying him while glaring at the monarchs. "How *dare* you! He came to you peacefully."

"Peacefully?" Paitar said. "No, young woman, he did not come to this world in peace. He has consumed the land with terror, chaos and destruction."

"As the prophecies said that he would," Cadsuane said, walking up as Min helped Rand back to his feet. "You lay before him the burdens of an entire Age. You cannot hire a man to rebuild your house, then reproach him when he must knock down a wall to do the job."

"That presumes that he *is* the Dragon Reborn," Tenobia said, folding her arms. "We—"

She cut off as Rand stood, then carefully slid *Callandor* from its sheath, glittering blade rasping. He held it forth. "Do you deny this, Queen Tenobia, Shield of the North and Sword of the Blightborder, High Seat of House Kazadi? Will you look upon this weapon and call me a false Dragon?"

That quieted her. To the side, Easar nodded. Behind them, ranks of silent troops watched with lances, pikes and shields held high. As if in salute. Or as if in preparation to attack. Min looked up, and could faintly make out people lining the walls of Far Madding to watch.

"Let us proceed," Easar said. "Ethenielle?"

"Very well," the woman said. "I will say this, Rand al'Thor. Even if you *do* prove to be the Dragon Reborn, you have much to answer for."

"You may take your price from my skin, Ethenielle," Rand said softly, sliding *Callandor* back into its sheath. "But only once the Dark One has had his day with me."

"Rand al'Thor," Paitar said. "I have a question for you. How you answer will determine the outcome of this day."

"What kind of question?" Cadsuane demanded.

"Cadsuane, please," Rand said, holding up his hand. "Lord Paitar, I see it in your eyes. You know that I am the Dragon Reborn. Is this question necessary?"

"It is vital, Lord al'Thor," Paitar replied. "It drove us here, though my allies did not know it from the start. I have always believed you to be the Dragon Reborn. That made my quest here even more vital."

Min frowned. The aging soldier reached down to his sword hilt, as if ready to draw. The Maidens grew more alert. With a start, Min realized Paitar was still standing close to Rand. Too close.

He could have that sword out and swinging for Rand's neck in an eyeblink, she realized. *Paitar placed himself there to be ready to strike.*

Rand didn't break his gaze from the monarch. "Ask your question."

"How did Tellindal Tirraso die?"

"Who?" Min asked, looking at Cadsuane. The Aes Sedai shook her head, confused.

"How do you know that name?" Rand demanded.

"Answer the question," Easar said, hand on his hilt, body tense. Around them, ranks of men prepared themselves.

"She was a clerk," Rand said. "During the Age of Legends. Demandred, when he came for me after founding the Eighty and One . . . She fell in the fighting, lightning from the sky . . . Her blood on my hands . . . *How do you know that name!*"

Ethenielle looked to Easar, then to Tenobia, then finally to Paitar. He nodded, then closed his eyes, letting out a sigh that sounded relieved. He took his hand from his sword.

"Rand al'Thor," Ethenielle said, "Dragon Reborn. Would you kindly sit down and speak with us? We will answer your questions."

"Why have I never heard of this so-called prophecy?" Cadsuane asked.

"Its nature required secrecy," King Paitar said. They all sat on cushions in a large tent in the middle of the Borderlander army. It made Cadsuane's shoulders itch, being surrounded like this, but the fool boy—he would *always* be a fool boy, no matter how old he was—looked perfectly at peace.

Thirteen Aes Sedai waited outside the tent, which wasn't large enough for them all. *Thirteen*. That hadn't made al'Thor blink. What man who could channel would sit amid thirteen Aes Sedai and not sweat?

He's changed, Cadsuane told herself. *You're just going to have to accept that.* Not that he didn't need her anymore. Men like him grew overly confident. A few little successes, and he'd trip over his own feet and land in some predicament.

But . . . well, she was proud of him. Grudgingly proud. A little.

"It was given by an Aes Sedai of my own family line," Paitar continued. The square-faced man sipped a small cup of tea. "My ancestor, Reo Myershi, was the only one who heard it. He ordered the words preserved, passed from monarch to monarch, for this day."

"Speak them to me," Rand said. "Please."

"I see him before you!" Paitar quoted. "Him, the one who lives many lives, the one who gives deaths, the one who raises mountains. He will break what he must break, but first he stands here, before our king. You will bloody him! Measure his restraint. He speaks! How was the fallen slain? Tellindal Tirraso, murdered by his hand, the darkness that came the day after the light. You *must* ask, and you *must* know your fate. If he cannot answer . . ."

He trailed off, falling silent.

"What?" Min asked.

"If he cannot answer," Paitar said, "then you will be lost. You will bring his end swiftly, so that the final days may have their storm. So that Light may not be consumed by he who was to have preserved it. I see him. And I weep."

"You came to murder him, then," Cadsuane said.

"To *test* him," Tenobia said. "Or so we decided, once Paitar told us of the prophecy."

"You don't know how close you came to doom," Rand said softly. "If I had come to you but a short time earlier, I'd have returned those slaps with balefire."

"Inside the Guardian?" Tenobia sniffed disdainfully.

"The Guardian blocks the One Power," Rand whispered. "The One Power only."

What does he mean by that? Cadsuane thought, frowning.

"We knew well the risk," Ethenielle said proudly. "I demanded the right to slap you first. Our armies had orders to attack if we fell."

"My family has analyzed the words of the prophecy a hundred times over," Paitar said. "The meaning seemed clear. It was our task to test the Dragon Reborn. To see if he could be trusted to go to the Last Battle."

"Only a month earlier," Rand said. "I wouldn't have had the memories to answer you. This was a foolish gambit. If you *had* killed me, then all would have been lost."

"A gamble," Paitar said evenly. "Perhaps another would have risen in your stead."

"No," Rand said. "This prophecy was like the others. A declaration of what might happen, not advice."

"I see it differently, Rand al'Thor," Paitar said. "And the others agreed with me."

"It should be noted," Ethenielle said, "that I didn't come south because of this prophecy. My goal was to see if I could bring some sense to the world. And then . . ." She grimaced.

"What?" Cadsuane asked, finally sipping her tea. It tasted good, as it usually did near al'Thor these days.

"The storms," Tenobia said. "The snow stopped us. And then, finding you proved more difficult than we'd assumed. These gateways. Can you teach them to our Aes Sedai?"

"I will have your Aes Sedai taught in return for a promise," Rand said. "You will swear to me. I have need of you."

"We are sovereigns," Tenobia snapped. "I'm not going to bow to you as quickly as my uncle did. We have to speak about *that*, by the way."

"Our oaths are to the lands we protect," Easar said.

"As you wish," Rand said, rising. "I once gave you an ultimatum. I phrased it poorly, and I regret that, but I remain your only path to the Last Battle. Without me, you will remain here, hundreds of leagues from those lands you swore to protect." He nodded to each of them, then helped Min to her feet. "Tomorrow, I meet with the monarchs of the world. After that, I am going to go to Shayol Ghul and break the remaining seals on the Dark One's prison. Good day."

Cadsuane didn't rise. She sat, sipping her tea. The four

seemed astounded. Well, the boy certainly had picked up an understanding of the dramatic.

"Wait!" Paitar finally sputtered, rising. "You're going to do *what*?"

Rand turned. "I'm going to shatter the seals, Lord Paitar. I'm going to 'break what he must break' as your own prophecy says I must. You cannot stop me, not when those words prove what I will do. Earlier, I stepped in to prevent Maradon from falling. It was near to it, Tenobia. The walls are shattered, your troops bloodied. With help, I was able to save it. Barely. Your countries need you. And so, you have two choices. Swear to me, or sit here and let everyone else fight in your place."

Cadsuane sipped her tea. That was going a little too far.

"I'll leave you to discuss my offer," Rand said. "I can spare one hour—though, before you start your deliberation, could you send for someone on my behalf? There is a man in your army named Hurin. I would like to apologize to him."

They still looked stunned. Cadsuane rose to go speak with the sisters waiting outside; she knew a few of them, and needed to feel out the others. She didn't worry about what the Borderlanders would decide. Al'Thor had them. *Another army beneath his banner. I didn't think he'd manage this one.*

One more day and it all began. Light, but she hoped that they were ready.

CHAPTER
52

Boots

Elayne settled herself in Glimmer's saddle. The mare was one of the prizes of the royal stable; she was of fine Saldaean stock with a brilliant white mane and coat. The saddle itself was rich, the leather trimmed with wine-red and gold. It was the sort of saddle you used when parading.

Birgitte rode Rising, a tall dun gelding, also one of the fastest in the royal stables. The Warder had chosen both horses. She expected to have to run.

Birgitte wore one of Elayne's foxhead copies, though it had a different shape, a thin silver disc with a rose on the front. Elayne carried another wrapped in cloth inside her pocket.

She'd tried making another this morning, but it had melted, nearly setting her dresser on fire. She was having a great deal of difficulty without the original to study. Her dreams of arming all of her personal Guards with medallions was looking less and less possible, unless she somehow managed to persuade Mat to give her the original again.

Her honor guard fell into mounted ranks around her and Birgitte in the Queen's Plaza. She was bringing only a hundred soldiers—seventy-five Guardsmen and an inner ring of twenty-five Guardswomen. It was a tiny force, but she'd have gone without those hundred if she'd been able to get away with it. She couldn't afford to be seen as a conqueror.

"I don't like this," Birgitte said.

"You don't like anything, lately," Elayne said. "I swear, you're becoming more irritable by the day."

"It's because you're becoming more foolhardy by the day."

"Oh, come now. This is *hardly* the most foolhardy thing I've done."

"Only because you've set a very high benchmark for yourself, Elayne."

"It will be fine," Elayne said, glancing southward.

"Why do you keep looking in that direction?"

"Rand," Elayne said, feeling that warmth again, pulsing from the knot of emotions in her mind. "He's getting ready for something. He feels troubled. And peaceful at the same time." Light, but that man could be confusing.

The meeting would happen in one day, if his original deadline still held. Egwene *was* right; breaking the seals would be foolish. But Rand would see reason.

Alise rode up to her, accompanied by three Kinswomen. Sarasia was a plump woman with a grandmotherly air; dark-skinned Kema kept her black hair in three long braids, and prim Nashia with a youthful face wore a baggy dress.

The four took up positions beside Elayne. Only two of them were strong enough for a gateway—many of the Kin were weaker than most Aes Sedai. But that would be enough, assuming Elayne had trouble embracing the Source.

"Can you do something to prevent archers from hitting her?" Birgitte asked Alise. "Some kind of weave?"

Alise cocked her head thoughtfully. "I know of one that might help," she said, "but I've never tried it."

Another Kinswoman wove a gateway up ahead. It opened to a span of rough, brown-grassed land outside of Cairhien. A much larger army waited there, wearing the cuirasses and bell-shaped helmets of Cairhienin troops. The officers were easy to spot with their dark clothing, in the colors of the Houses they served. They wore *con* rising over their backs.

Tall, narrow-faced Lorstrum sat his mount at the front of his army, which wore dark green with crimson slashes; Bertome was on the other side. Their forces looked to be about the same size. Five thousand each. The other four Houses had fielded smaller armies.

"If they wanted to take you captive," Birgitte said grimly, "you're handing them the chance."

"There's no way to do this and remain safe, not unless I want to hide in my palace and send my troops in. *That* would only lead to rebellion in Cairhien and potential collapse in Andor." She glanced at the Warder. "I'm Queen now, Birgitte. You're not going to be able to keep me from danger, no more than you could keep a lone soldier safe on the battlefield."

Birgitte nodded. "Stay close to me and Guybon."

Guybon approached, on a large dappled gelding. With Birgitte on one side of her and Guybon on the other—and with both of their horses taller than Elayne's—a would-be assassin would have great difficulty picking her off without first hitting her friends.

So it would be for the rest of her life. She nudged Glimmer into motion, and her troop made its way through the gateway and onto Cairhienin soil. The noblemen and noblewomen ahead bowed or curtsied from horseback, and those oblations were deeper this time than they had been when meeting Elayne in her throne room. The show had begun.

The city was just ahead, walls still blackened from fires during the fight with the Shaido. Elayne could sense Birgitte's tension as the gateway vanished behind them. The Kin around Elayne embraced the Source, and Alise wove an unfamiliar weave, placing it in the air around the inner ring of troops. It made a small—but swift—wind spinning in the air.

Birgitte's anxiety was contagious, and Elayne found herself holding her reins in a tight grip as Glimmer moved forward. The air was drier here in Cairhien, with a faint dusty scent to it. The sky was overcast.

The Cairhienin troops formed around her small group of Andorans in white and red. Most of the Cairhienin forces were foot, though there was some heavy cavalry, horses in shiny barding and men carrying lances pointed high into the air. All marched in perfect lines, protecting Elayne. Or keeping her captive.

Lorstrum moved his bay stallion closer to Elayne's outer ranks. Guybon glanced at her, and she nodded, so the captain allowed him to approach.

"The city is nervous, Your Majesty," Lorstrum said. Birgitte was still careful to keep her mount between his and

Elayne's. "There are . . . unfortunate rumors surrounding your ascension."

Rumors you probably initiated, Elayne thought, *before you decided to support me instead.* "Surely they won't rise against your troops?"

"I hope they will not." He eyed her from under his flat cap of forest green. He wore a black coat that went down to his knees and slashes of color across it all the way down, to denote his House. It was the type of clothing he'd wear if going to a ball. That projected a sense of confidence. His force wasn't seizing the city, it was escorting the new queen with an honorary parade. "It is unlikely that there will be armed resistance. But I wanted to warn you."

Lorstrum nodded to her with respect. He knew she was manipulating him, but he also accepted that manipulation. She would have to keep a careful watch on him in the years to come.

Cairhien was such a boxish city, all straight lines and fortified towers. Though some of its architecture was beautiful, there was no comparing the place to Caemlyn or Tar Valon. They rode directly in through the northern gates, the River Alguenya to their right.

Crowds waited inside. Lorstrum and the others had done their work well. There were cheers, probably started by carefully placed courtiers. As Elayne entered the city, the cheers grew louder. That surprised her. She had expected hostility. And yes, there was some of that—the occasional thrown piece of refuse, hurled from the back of the crowd. She caught a jeer here and there. But most seemed pleased.

As she rode down that broad passageway, lined with the rectangular buildings Cairhienin favored, she realized that perhaps these people had been *waiting* for an event like this. Talking of it, spreading tales. Some of those tales had been hostile, and those were what Norry had reported. But they now seemed to her more a sign of worry than hostility. Cairhien had been too long without a monarch, their king dead by unknown hands, the Lord Dragon seemingly abandoning them.

Her confidence grew. Cairhien was a wounded city. The burned and broken remnants of the Foregate outside. Cobbles had been torn up to be thrown from the walls. The city

had never fully recovered from the Aiel War, and the unfinished Topless Towers—symmetrical in design, but woefully
forlorn in appearance—were a lofty declaration of that fact.

That bloody Game of Houses was nearly as bad a
scourge. Could she change that? The people around her
sounded hopeful, as if they knew what a twisted mess their
nation had become. One could sooner take away an Aiel's
spears than cut the craftiness out of the Cairhienin, but perhaps she could teach them a greater loyalty to country and
throne. So long as they had a throne worth that loyalty.

The Sun Palace stood at the exact center of the city. Like
the rest of the city, it was square and angular, but here the
architecture gave a sense of imposing strength. It was a
grand building, despite the broken wing where the attempt
on Rand's life had taken place.

More nobles waited here, standing on covered steps or
in front of ornate carriages. Women in formal gowns with
wide hoops, the men in neat coats of dark colors, caps on
the heads. Many looked skeptical, and some amazed.

Elayne shot Birgitte a satisfied smile. "It's working.
Nobody expected me to ride to the palace escorted by a
Cairhienin army."

Birgitte said nothing. She was still tense—and probably
would be until Elayne returned to Caemlyn.

Two women stood at the foot of the steps, one a pretty
woman with bells in her hair, the other with curly hair and
a face that did not seem Aes Sedai, for all the fact that she
had been one for years. That was Sashalle Anderly, and the
other woman—who did have an ageless face—was Samitsu
Tamagowa. From what Elayne's sources had been able to
determine, these two were as close to "rulers" as the city
had in Rand's absence. She'd corresponded with both,
and found Sashalle remarkably keen at understanding the
Cairhienin way of thinking. She'd offered Elayne the city,
but had implied that she understood that being offered it
and taking it were two different things.

Sashalle stepped forward. "Your Majesty," she said formally, "let it be known that the Lord Dragon gives you all
rights and claim to this land. All formal control he had over
the land is ceded to you, and the position of steward over
the nation is dissolved. May you rule in wisdom and peace."

Elayne nodded to her regally from horseback, but inside

she seethed. She'd said she didn't mind Rand's help taking this throne, but it wasn't like she wanted her nose rubbed in it. Still, Sashalle seemed to take her position seriously, though from what Elayne had discovered, that position was in large measure self-created.

Elayne and her procession dismounted. Had Rand thought that it would be as easy as that to give her the throne? He'd stayed in Cairhien long enough to know how they schemed. One Aes Sedai making a proclamation would never have been enough. But having powerful nobles support her directly should be enough to do it.

Their procession made its way up the steps. They entered, and each of those supporting her brought a smaller honor guard of fifty. Elayne brought her entire force; it was crowded, but she didn't intend to leave any behind.

The inner hallways were straight, with peaked ceilings and golden trim. The symbol of the Rising Sun emblazoned each door. There were alcoves for riches to be displayed, but many were empty. The Aiel had taken their fifth from this palace.

Upon reaching the entrance to the Grand Hall of the Sun, Elayne's Andoran Guardsmen and Guardswomen arranged themselves lining the outer hallway. Elayne took a deep breath, then strode into the throne room with a group of ten. Blue-streaked marble columns rose to the ceiling at the sides of the room, and the Sun Throne sat on its blue marble dais at the back of the large hall.

The seat was of gilded wood, but was surprisingly unassuming. Perhaps that was why Laman had decided to build himself a new throne, using *Avendoraldera* itself as a material. Elayne walked up to the dais, then turned as the Cairhienin nobility entered, her supporters first, then the others, ranked according to the complicated dictates of *Daes Dae'mar*. Those rankings could change by the day, if not the hour.

Birgitte eyed each one who entered, but the Cairhienin were models of propriety. None would show anything like Ellorien's audacity in Andor. She was a patriot, if one who frustratingly continued to disagree with Elayne. In Cairhien, one did not do such things.

Once the crowd had stilled, Elayne took a deep breath. She'd considered a speech, but her mother had taught her that sometimes, decisive action made for the best speech. Elayne moved to sit down in the throne.

Birgitte caught her arm.

Elayne glanced at her questioningly, but the Warder was eyeing the throne. "Wait a moment," she said, bending down.

The nobles began murmuring one to another, and Lorstrum stepped up to Elayne. "Your Majesty?"

"Birgitte," Elayne said, blushing, "is this really necessary?"

Birgitte ignored her, prodding at the seat's cushion. Light! Was the Warder determined to embarrass her in *every* possible situation? Surely the—

"Aha!" Birgitte said, yanking something from the pillowed cushion.

Elayne started, then stepped closer, Lorstrum and Bertome at her side. Birgitte was holding up a small needle, tipped black. "Hidden in the cushion."

Elayne paled.

"It was the only place they *knew* you'd be, Elayne," Birgitte said softly. She knelt down and began prodding for more traps.

Lorstrum had grown flushed. "I will find who did this, Your Majesty," he said in a low voice. A dangerous voice. "They will know my wrath."

"Not if they know mine first," stocky Bertome said, looking over the needle.

"Obviously an assassination attempt intended for the Lord Dragon, Your Majesty," Lorstrum said in a louder voice, for the benefit of the audience. "None would dare try to kill you, our beloved sister from Andor."

"That is good to hear," Elayne said, eyeing him. That expression of hers said to everyone in the room that she would put up with this ruse, intended to save his face. As her strongest supporter, the shame of an assassination attempt fell on him.

Agreeing to let him save face would cost him. He lowered his eyes briefly in understanding. Light, she hated this game. But she would play it. And she would play it well.

"Is it safe?" she asked Birgitte.

The Warder rubbed her chin. "One way to find out," she

said, then plopped herself down in the throne with an un-
ceremonious amount of force.

Not a few of the nobles in the hall gasped, and Lorstrum
grew more pale.

"Not very comfortable," Birgitte said, leaning to the side,
then pushing her back up against the wood. "I would have
expected a monarch's throne to be more cushioned, what
with your delicate backside and all."

"Birgitte!" Elayne hissed, feeling her face grow red
again. "You can't sit in the *Sun Throne*!"

"I'm your bodyguard," Birgitte said. "I can taste your
food if I want, I can walk through doorways before you,
and I can bloody sit in your chair if I think it will protect
you." She grinned. "Besides," she added in a lower voice, "I
always wondered what one of these felt like." The Warder
stood up, still wary, but also satisfied.

Elayne turned and faced the nobility of Cairhien. "You
have waited long for this," she said. "Some of you are dissatisfied, but remember that half of my blood is Cairhienin.
This alliance will make *both* of our nations great. I do not
demand your trust, but I *do* demand your obedience." She
hesitated, then added, "Remember again, this is as the
Dragon Reborn wishes it to be."

She saw that they understood. Rand had conquered this
city once, though it had been to liberate it from the Shaido.
They would be wise not to tempt him to come back and
conquer it again. A queen used the tools that she had at
hand. She had taken Andor on her own; she would let Rand
help her with Cairhien.

She sat down. Such a simple thing, but the implications
would be far-reaching indeed. "Gather your individual
forces and House guards," she commanded to the collected
nobles. "You will be marching, with the forces of Andor,
through gateways to a place known as the Field of Merrilor.
We will be meeting the Dragon Reborn."

The nobles seemed surprised. She would come in, take
the throne, then command their armies from the city the
same day? She smiled. Best to act quickly and decisively; it
would build precedent for obeying her. And would begin to
ready them for the Last Battle.

"Also," she announced as they began to whisper, "I want

you to gather every man in this realm who can hold a sword and conscript them into the Queen's army. There won't be much time for training, but every man will be needed in the Last Battle—and those women who wish to fight may report as well. Also, send word to the bellfounders in your city. I will need to meet with them within the hour."

"But," Bertome said, "the coronation feast, Your Majesty. . . ."

"We will feast when the Last Battle has been won and Cairhien's children are safe," Elayne said. She needed to distract them from their plots, give them work to keep them busy, if possible. "Move! Pretend the Last Battle is on your doorstep, and will arrive on the morrow!"

For, indeed it might.

Mat leaned against a dead tree, looking over his camp. He breathed in and out, smiling, feeling the beautiful comfort of knowing that he was no longer being chased. He had forgotten how good that felt. Better than a pretty serving girl on each knee, that feeling was. Well, better than one serving girl, anyway.

A military camp at evening was one of the most comfortable places in all the world, even if half the camp was empty, the men there having gone to Cairhien. The sun had set, and some of those who remained had turned in. But for those who had pulled afternoon duty the next day, there was no reason to sleep just yet.

A dozen firepits smoldered through the camp, men sitting to share tales of exploits, of women left behind, or of rumors from far off. Tongues of flames flickered as men laughed, sitting on logs or rocks, someone occasionally digging into the coals with a twisted branch and stirring tiny sparks into the air as his friends sang "Come Ye Maids" or "Fallen Willows at Noon."

The men of the Band were from a dozen different nations, but this camp was their true home. Mat strode through them, hat on his head, *ashandarei* over his shoulder. He had gotten a new scarf for his neck. People knew about his scar, but there was no reason to show it off like one of Luca's bloody wagons.

The scarf he had chosen this time was red. In memory

of Tylin and the others who had fallen to the *gholam*. For a short time, he had been tempted to choose pink. A *very* short time.

Mat smiled. Though songs rang from several of the campfires, none were loud, and there was a healthy stillness about the camp. Not a *silence*. Silence was never good. He hated silence. Made him wonder who was trying so hard to sneak up on him. No, this was a stillness. Men snoring softly, fires crackling, other men singing, weeds crunching as those on watch passed by. The peaceful noises of men enjoying their lives.

Mat found his way back to his table outside his darkened tent. He sat down, looking over the papers he had stacked here. The inside of the tent had been too stuffy. Besides, he had not wanted to wake Olver.

Mat's tent rippled in the wind. His seat did look odd, the fine oak table sitting in a patch of hensfoot, Mat's chair beside it, a pitcher of mulled cider on the ground beside him. The papers on his table were weighed down with various rocks he had picked up, lit by a single flickering lamp.

He should not have to have stacks of paper. He should be able to sit at one of those fires and sing "Dance with Jak o' the Shadows." He could faintly make out the words of the song from a nearby campfire.

Papers. Well, he had agreed to Elayne's employment, and there were papers for that sort of thing. And papers about setting up the dragon crews. Papers about supplies, discipline reports, and all kinds of nonsense. And a few papers he had been able to wiggle out of her royal majesty, spy reports he had wanted to look over. Reports on the Seanchan.

Much of the news was not new to him; by courtesy of Verin's gateway, Mat had traveled to Caemlyn more quickly than most rumors. But Elayne had gateways of her own, and some of the news from Tear and Illian was fresh. There was talk of the new Seanchan Empress. So Tuon really had crowned herself, or whatever it was the Seanchan did to name a new leader.

That made him smile. Light, but they did not know what they were in for! They probably *thought* they did. But she would surprise them, sure as the sky was blue. Or, well, it had been gray lately.

There was also talk of Sea Folk in alliance with the

Seanchan. Mat dismissed that. The Seanchan had captured enough Sea Folk vessels to give that impression, but it was not the truth. He found some pages with news about Rand, too, most of it unspecific or untrustworthy.

Blasted colors. Rand was sitting around and talking with some people in a tent. Perhaps he *was* in Arad Doman, but he could not be both there *and* fighting in the Borderlands, now could he? One rumor said that Rand had killed Queen Tylin. Which bloody idiots thought that?

He turned over the reports on Rand quickly. He hated having to banish those flaming colors over and over again. At least Rand was wearing clothes this time.

The last page was curious. Wolves running in enormous packs, congregating in clearings and howling in chorus? The skies shining red at night? Livestock lining up in the fields, all facing toward the north, watching silently? The footprints of Shadowspawn armies in the middle of fields? These things smelled of simple hearsay, passed on from farmwife to farmwife until they reached the ears of Elayne's spies.

Mat looked over the sheet, then—without even thinking of it—realized he had pulled Verin's envelope out of his pocket. The still-sealed letter was looking worn and dirty, but he had not opened it. It seemed like the most difficult thing he had ever done, resisting that urge.

"Now that is a sight of some irregularity," a woman's voice said. Mat looked up to see Setalle strolling toward him. She wore a brown dress that laced over her ample bosom. Not that Mat spent any time looking at it.

"You like my den?" Mat asked. He set the envelope aside, then put the last of the spy reports on a stack, just beside a series of sketches he'd been doing on some new crossbows, based on the ones Talmanes had bought. The papers threatened to blow away. As he had no rock for this stack, he pulled off one of his boots and set it on the top.

"Your den?" Setalle asked, sounding amused.

"Sure," Mat said, scratching the bottom of his stockinged foot. "You'll have to make an appointment with my steward if you want to come in."

"Your steward?"

"The stump right over there," Mat said, nodding. "Not the little one, the big one with moss growing on the top."

She raised an eyebrow.

"He's quite good," Mat said. "Hardly ever lets anyone in I don't want to see."

"You are an interesting creature, Matrim Cauthon," Setalle said, seating herself on the larger stump. Her dress was after the Ebou Dar style, with the side pinned up to reveal petticoats colorful enough to scare away a Tinker.

"Did you want anything specific?" Mat asked. "Or did you just drop by so that you could sit on my steward's head?"

"I heard that you visited the palace again today. Is it true that you know the Queen?"

Mat shrugged. "Elayne's a nice enough girl. Pretty thing, that's for certain."

"You don't shock me anymore, Matrim Cauthon," Setalle noted. "I've realized that the things you say are often intended to do that."

They were? "I say what I'm thinking, Mistress Anan. Why does it matter to you if I know the Queen?"

"Merely another piece of the puzzle that you represent," Setalle said. "I received a letter from Joline today."

"What did she want from you?"

"She didn't ask for anything. She merely wanted to send word that they had arrived safely in Tar Valon."

"You must have read it wrong."

Setalle gave him a chiding stare. "Joline Sedai respects you, Master Cauthon. She often spoke highly of you, and the way that you rescued not only her, but the other two. She asked after you in the letter."

Mat blinked. "Really? She said things like that?"

Setalle nodded.

"Burn me," he said. "Almost makes me feel bad for painting her mouth blue. But you wouldn't have known she thought that way, considering how she treated me."

"Speaking such things to a man inflates his opinion of himself. One would think that the way she treated you would have been enough."

"She's Aes Sedai," Mat muttered. "She treats everyone like they're mud to be scraped off her boots."

Setalle glared at him. She had a stately way about her, part grandmother, part court lady, part no-nonsense inn-keeper.

"Sorry," he said. "Some Aes Sedai aren't as bad as others. I didn't mean to insult you."

"I'll take that for a compliment," Setalle said. "Though I'm *not* Aes Sedai."

Mat shrugged, finding a nice small rock at his feet. He used it to replace his boot atop the stack of paper. The rains of the last few days had passed, leaving a crisp freshness to the air. "I know you said it didn't hurt," Mat said. "But . . . what does it feel like? The thing you lost?"

She pursed her lips. "What is the most delightful food you enjoy, Master Cauthon? The one thing that you would eat above all others?"

"Ma's sweet pies," Mat said immediately.

"Well, it is like that," Setalle said. "Knowing that you used to be able to enjoy those pies every day, but now they have been denied you. Your friends, *they* can have as many of those pies as they want. You envy them, and you hurt, but at the same time you're happy. At least *someone* can enjoy what you cannot."

Mat nodded slowly.

"Why is it that you hate Aes Sedai so, Master Cauthon?" Setalle asked.

"I don't hate them," Mat said. "Burn me, but I don't. But sometimes, a man can't seem to do two things without women wanting him to do one of those things a different way and ignore the other one completely."

"You aren't *forced* to take their advice, and I warrant that much of the time, you eventually admit it is good advice."

Mat shrugged. "Sometimes, a man just likes to do what he wants, without someone telling him what's wrong with it and what's wrong with him. That's all."

"And it has nothing to do with your . . . peculiar views of nobles? Most Aes Sedai act as if they were noblewomen, after all."

"I have nothing against nobles," Mat said, straightening his coat. "I just don't fancy being one myself."

"Why is that, then?"

Mat sat for a moment. Why was it? Finally, he looked down at his foot, then replaced his boot. "It's boots."

"Boots?" Setalle looked confused.

"Boots," Mat said with a nod, tying his laces. "It's all about the boots."

"But—"

"You see," Mat said, pulling the laces tight, "a lot of men don't have to worry much about what boots to wear. They're the poorest of folks. If you ask one of them 'What boots are you going to wear today, Mop?' their answer is easy. 'Well, Mat. I only have one pair, so I guess I'm gonna wear that pair.'"

Mat hesitated. "Or, I guess they wouldn't say *that* to you, Setalle, since you're not me and all. They wouldn't call you Mat, you understand."

"I understand," she said, sounding amused.

"Anyway, for people that have a little coin, the question of which boots to wear is harder. You see, average men, men like me. . . ." He eyed her. "And I'm an average man, mind you."

"Of course you are."

"Bloody right I am," Mat said, finishing with his laces and sitting up. "An average man might have three pairs of boots. Your *third* best pair of boots, those are the boots you wear when you're working at something unpleasant. They might rub after a few paces, and they might have a few holes, but they're good enough to keep your footing. You don't mind mucking them up in the fields or the barn."

"All right," Setalle said.

"Then you have your *second* best pair of boots," Mat said. "Those are your day-to-day boots. You wear those if you are going over to dinner at the neighbors'. Or, in my case, you wear those if you're going to battle. They're nice boots, give you good footing, and you don't mind being seen in them or anything."

"And your best pair of boots?" Setalle asked. "You wear those to social events, like a ball or dining with a local dignitary?"

"Balls? *Dignitaries?* Bloody ashes, woman. I thought you were an innkeeper."

Setalle blushed faintly.

"We're not going to any balls," Mat said. "But if we had to, I suspect we'd wear our *second* best pair of boots. If they're good enough for visiting old lady Hembrew next door, then they're bloody well good enough for stepping on the toes of any woman fool enough to dance with us."

"Then what are the best boots for?"

"Walking," Mat said. "Any farmer knows the value of good boots when you go walking a distance."

Setalle looked thoughtful. "All right. But what does this have to do with being a nobleman?"

"Everything," Mat said. "Don't you see? If you're an average fellow, you know exactly when to use your boots. A man can keep track of three pairs of boots. Life is simple when you have three pairs of boots. But noblemen . . . Talmanes claims he has *forty* different pairs of boots at home. Forty pairs, can you imagine that?"

She smiled in amusement.

"Forty pairs," Mat repeated, shaking his head. "Forty *bloody* pairs. And, they aren't all the same kind of boots either. There is a pair for each outfit, and a dozen pairs in different styles that will match any number of half your outfits. You have boots for kings, boots for high lords, and boots for normal people. You have boots for winter and boots for summer, boots for rainy days and boots for dry days. You have bloody shoes that you wear *only* when you're walking to the bathing chamber. Lopin used to complain that I didn't have a pair to wear to the privy at night!"

"I see. . . . So you're using boots as a metaphor for the onus of responsibility and decision placed upon the aristocracy as they assume leadership of complex political and social positions."

"Metaphor for. . . ." Mat scowled. "Bloody ashes, woman. This isn't a metaphor for anything! It's just *boots*."

Setalle shook her head. "You're an unconventionally wise man, Matrim Cauthon."

"I try my best," he noted, reaching for the pitcher of mulled cider. "To be unconventional, I mean." He poured a cup and lifted it in her direction. She accepted graciously and drank, then stood. "I will leave you to your own amusements, then, Master Cauthon. But if you have made any progress on that gateway for me. . . ."

"Elayne said she would have one for you soon. In a day or two. Once I'm back from the errand I have to run with Thom and Noal, I'll see it done."

She nodded in understanding. If he did not return from that "errand," she would see to Olver. She turned to leave. Mat waited until she was gone before taking a slurp of the cider straight from the pitcher. He had been doing that all evening, but he figured she would probably rather not know. It was the sort of thing women were better off not thinking about.

He turned back to his reports, but soon found his mind wandering to the Tower of Ghenjei, and those bloody snakes and foxes. Birgitte's comments had been enlightening, but not particularly encouraging. Two months? Two *bloody* months spent wandering those hallways? That was a mighty, steaming bowl of worry, served up like afternoon slop. Beyond that, she had taken fire, music, and iron. Breaking the rules was not so original an idea.

He was not surprised. Likely, the day the Light made the very first man, and that man had made the first rule, someone else had thought to break it. People like Elayne made up rules to suit them. People like Mat found ways to get around the stupid rules.

Unfortunately, Birgitte—one of the legendary Heroes of the Horn—had not been able to defeat the Aelfinn and Eelfinn. That was disconcerting.

Well, Mat had something she had not had. His luck. He sat thoughtfully, leaning back in his chair. One of his soldiers passed by. Clintock saluted; the Redarm checked on Mat every half-hour. They still had not gotten over the shame of letting the *gholam* sneak into camp.

He picked up Verin's letter again, feeling it over in his fingers. The worn corners, the smudges of dirt on the once-white paper. He tapped it against the wood.

Then he tossed it onto the desk. No. No, he was not going to open it, even when he got back. That was that. He would never know what was in it, and he bloody did not care.

He stood up and went looking for Thom and Noal. Tomorrow, they would leave for the Tower of Ghenjei.

CHAPTER
53

Gateways

P evara kept her tongue as she walked through the village of the Black Tower with Javindhra and Mazrim Taim.

There was activity all through the place. There was *always* activity in the Black Tower. Soldiers felling trees nearby; Dedicated stripping the bark away, then slicing the logs into lumber with focused jets of Air. Sawdust coated the path; with a chill, Pevara realized that the stack of boards nearby had probably been cut by Asha'man.

Light! She'd known what she'd find here. It was much harder to face than she'd assumed it would be.

"And you see," Taim said, walking with one hand folded—fingers making a fist—behind his back. With his other hand, he pointed toward a distant, part-finished wall of black stone. "Guard posts spaced at fifty-foot intervals. Each with two Asha'man atop them." He smiled in satisfaction. "This place will be impregnable."

"Yes indeed," Javindhra said. "Impressive." Her tone was flat and uninterested. "But the item I wished to speak with you about. If we could choose men with the Dragon pin to—"

"This again?" Taim said. He had fire in his eyes, this Mazrim Taim. A tall, black-haired man with high, Saldaean cheekbones. He smiled. Or the closest he came to such an expression—a half-smile that did not reach his eyes. It looked . . . predatory. "I have made my will known. And yet you continue to push. No. Soldiers and Dedicated only."

"As you demand," Javindhra said. "We will continue our consideration."

"Weeks pass," Taim replied, "and still you consider? Well, far be it from *me* to question Aes Sedai. I care not what you do. But the women outside my gates claim to be from the White Tower as well. Do you not wish me to invite them in to meet with you?"

Pevara felt a chill. He always seemed to know too much, and hint that he knew too much, about internal White Tower politics.

"That won't be needed," Javindhra said coldly.

"As you wish," he said. "You should make your choices soon. They grow impatient, and al'Thor has given them permission to bond my men. They will not suffer my stalling forever."

"They are rebels. You need pay them no heed at all."

"Rebels," Taim said, "with a much larger force than you. What do you have? Six women? From the way you talk, you seem to intend to bond the entirety of the Black Tower!"

"Perhaps we might." Pevara spoke calmly. "No limit was placed upon us."

Taim glanced at her, and she had the distinct feeling she was being inspected by a wolf considering whether she'd make a good meal. She shoved that feeling aside. She was Aes Sedai, no easy meat. Still, she couldn't help remembering that they were only six. Inside a camp filled with hundreds of men who could channel.

"I once saw a skyfisher dying on the city docks of Illian," Taim said. "The bird was choking, having tried to swallow two fish at once."

"Did you help the sorry thing?" Javindhra asked.

"Fools will always choke themselves when they grasp for too much, Aes Sedai," Taim said. "What matters that to me? I had a fine meal of it that night. The flesh of the bird, *and* of the fish. I must go. But be warned, now that I have a defensible perimeter, you must give me warning if you wish to pass outside."

"You mean to keep comings and goings that tight?" Pevara asked.

"The world becomes a dangerous place," Taim said smoothly. "I must think of the needs of my men."

Pevara had noticed how he saw to the "needs" of his men. A group of young soldiers passed by, saluting Taim. Two bore bruised features, one with an eye swollen shut. Asha'man were beaten brutally for making mistakes in their training, then forbidden Healing.

The Aes Sedai were never touched. In fact, the deference they were shown bordered on mockery.

Taim nodded, then stalked off, meeting up with two of his Asha'man who waited nearby, beside the smithy. They immediately began speaking in hushed tones.

"I don't like this," Pevara said as soon as the men were away. Perhaps she said it too quickly, betraying her worries, but this place had her on edge. "This could easily turn to disaster. I'm beginning to think that we should do as I originally stated—bond a few Dedicated each and return to the White Tower. Our task was never to lock down the entire Black Tower, but to gain access to Asha'man and learn about them."

"That's what we're doing," Javindhra said. "*I've* been learning much these last few weeks. What have you been doing?"

Pevara did not rise to the other woman's tone. *Must* she be so contrary? Pevara had leadership of this team, and the others would defer to her. But it didn't mean that they would always be pleasant about it.

"This has been an interesting opportunity," Javindhra continued, scanning the Tower grounds. "And I *do* think he will yield eventually on the subject of full Asha'man."

Pevara frowned. Javindhra couldn't honestly think that, could she? After how stubborn Taim had been? Yes, Pevara had yielded to suggestions that they remain in the Black Tower a little longer, to learn of its workings and ask Taim to allow them access to the more powerful Asha'man. But it was obvious now he would not give in. Surely Javindhra saw that.

Unfortunately, Pevara was having great difficulty reading Javindhra lately. Originally, the woman had seemed against coming to the Black Tower, only agreeing to the mission because the Highest had ordered it. Yet now she offered reasons to remain here.

"Javindhra," Pevara said, stepping closer. "You heard

what he said. We now need *permission* to leave. This place is turning into a cage."

"I think, we're safe," Javindhra said, waving a hand. "He doesn't know we have gateways."

"So far as we know," Pevara said.

"If you order it, I'm sure the others will go," Javindhra said. "But I intend to continue to use the opportunity to learn."

Pevara took a deep breath. Insufferable woman! Surely she wasn't going so far as to ignore Pevara's leadership of the group? After the Highest herself had placed Pevara in charge? Light, but Javindhra was growing erratic.

They parted without another word, Pevara spinning and walking back down the path. She kept her temper with difficulty. That last statement had been close to outright defiance! Well, if she wanted to disobey and remain, so be it. It was time to be returning to the White Tower.

Men in black coats walked all around her. Many nodded with those too-obsequious grins of feigned respect. Her weeks here had not done anything to make her more comfortable around these men. She *would* make a few of them Warders. Three. She could handle three, couldn't she?

Those dark expressions, like the eyes of executioners while waiting for the next neck to line up before them. The way some of them muttered to themselves, or jumped at shadows, or held their heads and looked dazed. She stood in the very pit of madness itself, and it made her skin creep as if covered in caterpillars. She couldn't help quickening her pace. *No,* she thought. *I can't leave Javindhra here, not without trying one more time.* Pevara would explain to the others, give them the order to leave. Then she'd ask them, Tarna first, to approach Javindhra. Surely their united arguments would convince her.

Pevara reached the huts they had been given. She purposely did not look to the side, toward the line of small buildings where the bonded Aes Sedai made their homes. She'd heard what some of them were doing, trying to control their Asha'man using . . . various methods. That made her skin crawl, too. While she thought most Reds had too harsh an opinion of men, what those women did crossed the line with a heedless leap.

She stepped inside her hut, and there found Tarna at the desk writing a letter. The Aes Sedai had to share their huts, and Pevara had picked Tarna specifically. Pevara might have been made leader of this group, but Tarna was Keeper of the Chronicles. The politics of this particular expedition were very delicate, with so many influential members and so many opinions.

Last night, Tarna had agreed that it was time to leave. She'd work with Pevara on going to Javindhra.

"Taim has locked down the Black Tower," Pevara said calmly, sitting on her bed in the small, circular chamber. "We now need his permission to leave. He said it offhandedly, as if it weren't really meant to stop *us*. Just a rule he'd forgotten to give us a blanket exception to."

"Likely, that's just what it was," Tarna said. "I'm sure it's nothing."

Pevara fell still. *What?* She tried again. "Javindhra still irrationally thinks he will change his mind on letting us bond full Asha'man. It's time to bond Dedicated and leave, but she's hinted that she'll remain regardless of my intentions. I want you to speak to her."

"Actually," Tarna said, continuing to write, "I've been thinking on what we discussed last night. Perhaps I was hasty. There is much to learn here, and there is the matter of the rebels outside. If we leave, they will bond Asha'man, which should not be allowed."

The woman looked up, and Pevara froze. There was something different in Tarna's eyes, something cold. She'd always been a distant one, but this was worse.

Tarna smiled, a grimace that looked completely unnatural on her face. Like the smile on the lips of a corpse. She turned back to her writing.

Something is very, very wrong here, Pevara thought. "Well, you may be right," she found herself saying. Her mouth worked, though her mind reeled. "This expedition was your suggestion, after all. I will think on it further. If you'll excuse me."

Tarna waved ambivalently. Pevara stood, years as an Aes Sedai keeping her profound worry from showing in her posture. She stepped outside, then walked eastward, along the unfinished wall. Yes, guard stations *had* been set up regularly. Earlier this morning, those hadn't been manned.

Now they were, with men who could channel. One of those men could strike her dead before she could respond. She couldn't see their weaves, and she couldn't strike first, because of her oaths.

She turned and walked to a small stand of trees, a place that was to become a garden. Inside, she sat down on a stump, breathing deeply. The coldness—almost lifelessness—she'd seen in Tarna's eyes still chilled her.

Pevara had been ordered by the Highest not to risk gateways unless the situation were dire. This seemed like a dire situation to her. She embraced the Source and wove the proper weave.

The weave fell apart the moment she completed it. No gateway formed. Eyes wide, she tried again, but got the same result. She tried other weaves, and they worked, but gateways failed every time.

Her chill became frost within her. She was trapped.

They all were.

Perrin clasped hands with Mat. "Good luck, my friend."

Mat grinned, tugging down the broad brim of his dark hat. "Luck? I *hope* this all comes down to luck. I'm good with luck."

Mat carried a bulging pack over one shoulder, as did the bony, gnarled man that Mat had introduced as Noal. Thom had his harp on his back and a similar pack. Perrin still wasn't clear on what they were bringing. Mat only planned to be at the tower for a few days, so there was no need for a lot of supplies.

The small group stood on the Traveling ground outside Perrin's camp. Behind them, Perrin's people shouted back and forth, breaking down the camp. None had any inkling of how important this day could prove. Moiraine. Moiraine was alive. *Light, let it be so.*

"Are you certain I can't convince you to take more help?" Perrin asked.

Mat nodded. "Sorry. These things . . . well, they tend to be particular. The note was clear. Only three of us can enter, otherwise we'll fail. If we fail anyway . . . well, I guess it will be her own bloody fault then, won't it?"

Perrin frowned. "Just be careful. I'm expecting another

helping from your pouch of tabac at Master Denezel's place when you return."

"You'll have it," Thom said, taking Perrin's offered hand. He hesitated, smiling, a faint twinkle in his eyes.

"What?" Perrin asked.

Thom repositioned his pack. "Is every last farmboy I know going to transform into a nobleman by the time this is through?"

"I'm no nobleman," Mat said.

"Oh?" Thom asked. "Prince of the Ravens?"

Mat pulled his hat down. "People can call me what they want. That doesn't mean I'm one of them."

"Actually," Thom said, "it—"

"Open the gateway so we can get going," Mat said. "No more nonsense."

Perrin nodded to Grady. The air rent, a twisting beam of light opening a portal that overlooked a broad, slow-moving river. "This is as close as he can get," Perrin said. "At least, not without a better description of the place."

"It'll do," Mat said, poking his head through the gateway. "You'll open one for us to get back?"

"Each day at noon," Grady said, repeating Perrin's orders to him. "Into that exact spot." He smiled. "Take care you don't get your toes cut off when it appears, Master Cauthon."

"I'll do my best," Mat said. "I'm attached to those toes." He took a breath and stepped through the gateway. Quiet Noal followed, smelling of determination. That one was a lot tougher than he looked. Thom nodded to Perrin, mustaches wagging, then hopped through. He was spry, though he still bore the stiff leg from fighting that Fade two years ago.

Light guide you, Perrin prayed, raising a hand to the three as they trudged along the river's bank.

Moiraine. Perrin should send word to Rand. The colors appeared, showing Rand speaking with a group of Borderlanders. But . . . no. Perrin couldn't tell Rand until he was certain she lived. To do otherwise would be too cruel, and would be an invitation for Rand to meddle in Mat's mission.

Perrin turned as the portal closed. As he stepped, he felt a faint throbbing from his leg, where Slayer's arrow had hit him. He had been Healed of that wound, and from what he'd been able to tell, the Healing had been complete. There was no injury. But his leg . . . it felt like it could remember the wound anyway. It was like a shadow, very faint, almost unnoticeable.

Faile walked up to him, her face curious. Gaul was with her, and Perrin smiled at the way he kept glancing over his shoulder at Bain and Chiad. One carried his spears, the other his bow, all wrapped in cloth. So that he didn't have to, apparently.

"I missed the sendoff?" Faile asked.

"As you intended," Perrin replied.

She sniffed. "Matrim Cauthon is a bad influence. I'm surprised he didn't drag you off to another tavern before leaving."

Amusingly, the colors appeared, showing him Mat—who had just left—walking along the river. "He's not as bad as all that," Perrin said. "Are we ready?"

"Aravine has everyone organized and moving," Faile said. "We should be ready to march within the hour."

That proved a good estimate. In about a half-hour, Perrin stood to the side as an enormous gateway split the air, created by Grady and Neald linked together with the Aes Sedai and Edarra. Nobody had questioned Perrin's decision to move. If Rand was traveling to this place known as the Field of Merrilor, then that was where Perrin wanted to be. It was where he *needed* to be.

The land beyond this gateway was more rugged than southern Andor. Fewer trees, more prairie grass. Some ruins lay in the distance. The open area before them was filled with tents, banners, and camps. It looked as if Egwene's coalition was gathered.

Grady peered through, then whistled softly. "How many people *is* that?"

"Those are the Crescent Moons of Tear," Perrin noted, pointing toward a banner. "And that's Illian. Camped on opposite sides of the field." A green banner set with nine golden bees marked that army.

"A large number of Cairhienin Houses," Faile said, looking out off the rise. "Not a few Aiel . . . No Borderlander flags."

"I've never seen so many troops in one place," Grady said.

It's really happening, Perrin thought, heart thumping. *The Last Battle.*

"Do you think they'll be enough to stop Rand?" Faile asked. "To help us keep him from breaking the seals?"

"Help us?" Perrin asked.

"You told Elayne that you'd go to the Field of Merrilor," Faile said. "Because of what Egwene had asked."

"Oh, I told her I needed to be there," Perrin said. "But I never said I was going to take Egwene's side. I trust Rand, Faile, and it seems right to me that he'd need to break the seals. It's like making a sword. You usually don't want to forge one out of the pieces of a broken and ruined weapon. You get new good steel to make it. Rather than patch the old seals, he'll need to make new ones."

"Perhaps," Faile said. "But this is going to be a fine line to walk. So many armies in one place. If some side with Rand and others with the White Tower . . ."

Nobody would win if they turned against one another. Well, Perrin would have to make sure that didn't happen.

The soldiers were already gathered in lines, preparing to march. Perrin turned to them. "Rand sent us away to search for an enemy," he bellowed. "We return to him having found allies. Onward, to the Last Battle!"

Only the ones at the front could hear him, but they cheered and passed the word back. Rand or Elayne would have given a far more inspiring speech. But Perrin wasn't them. He'd have to do things his way.

"Aravine," Perrin called to the plump Amadician. "Go through and make sure that nobody fights over where to set up their camps."

"Yes, Lord Goldeneyes."

"Keep us away from the other armies for now," Perrin said, pointing. "Have Sulin and Gaul pick a good site. Pass the word to each of the armies as we set up. We're not to interact with, or look the wrong way at, any of those other forces. And don't let people go wandering off southward either! We're not in the wilderness anymore, and I don't want the local farmers complaining of mischief."

"Yes, my Lord," she said.

He'd never asked Aravine why she didn't join one of the groups that had been sent back to Amadicia. It was probably because of the Seanchan, though. She was obviously noble, but didn't say much of her past. He was glad to have her. As his camp steward, she was his liaison between the various factions that made up his army.

The Wolf Guard had drawn first lot, so they led the way through the gateway. The large column began to move. Perrin went down the line, giving orders, mostly reinforcing that he didn't want trouble with the locals or the other armies. He stopped as he met Whitecloaks waiting their turn. Berelain was riding next to Galad again; they seemed very amenably lost in conversation. Light, but the woman had spent pretty much every waking hour with Galad these last few days.

Perrin hadn't put the Whitecloaks and Mayeners together, yet they seemed to have somehow ended up that way. As they started moving, Galad's Whitecloaks rode in a perfect line, four across, their white tabards set with sunbursts. Perrin still had a gut reaction akin to panic whenever he saw them, but they'd made surprisingly little trouble since the trial.

Mayene's Winged Guards rode along the other side, Gallenne just behind Berelain, their lances held high. Red streamers came from the lances, and breastplates and helms were shined to perfection. It seemed they were ready to parade. And maybe they were. If you were going to ride to the Last Battle, you did it with lance held high and armor polished.

Perrin continued on. Alliandre's army came next, riding in a tight formation of heavy cavalry, eight men across, Arganda at their head. He called orders when he saw Perrin, and the serpentine column of soldiers turned and saluted.

Perrin returned their salute. He'd asked Alliandre, and she'd indicated that was the appropriate response. She rode with Arganda, sidesaddle, in a slim maroon gown with gold trim. An impractical outfit for riding, but they wouldn't be in the saddle very long. Three hundred paces and as many leagues.

He could see her satisfaction as he saluted her soldiers. She was pleased to see him stepping into his role as leader of the coalition. In fact, many in camp reacted the same way. Perhaps before, they'd been able to sense how much he resented leadership. How did people do that, without being able to smell emotions?

"Lord Perrin," Alliandre said, riding past him. She gave a bowing sort of sway that was the equivalent of a horseback curtsy. "Should you not be riding?"

"I like my feet," Perrin said.

"It looks more authoritative when a commander rides."

"I've decided to lead this bunch, Alliandre," Perrin said gruffly, "but I'll do it my way. That means walking when I want to." They were only going a few feet through the gateway. His feet would serve him well enough.

"Of course, my Lord."

"Once we're settled, I want you to send some men back to Jehannah. See if you can recruit anyone else, pick up whatever city guard you have. Bring them here. We're going to need everyone we can get, and I want to train them as much as possible before this war hits."

"Very well, my Lord."

"I've sent to Mayene already," Perrin said. "And Tam's been gathering what extras he can from the Two Rivers." Light, but he wished he could let them stay behind, on their farms, to live in peace while the storm raged elsewhere. But this really *was* the end. He could feel it. Lose this fight and they lost everything. The world. The Pattern itself. Facing that, he'd field boys who could barely swing a sword and grandfathers who had trouble walking. It twisted his stomach to admit it, but it was the truth.

He continued down the line and gave some orders to several other groups. As he was finishing up with the last, he noticed a handful of Two Rivers men passing by. One, Azi, held the wolfhead banner. Jori Congar hung back. He stopped, then waved the other three on before trotting up to Perrin. Was something wrong?

"Lord Perrin." Jori drew himself up, long and lanky, like a bird standing on one leg. "I. . . ."

"Well?" Perrin said. "Out with it."

"I wanted to apologize," Jori said, words coming in a rush.

"For what?"

"For some things I said," Jori said, looking away. "I mean, some foolish words. It was after you were ill, you see, and you were taken to the First's tent and . . . well, I—"

"It's all right, Jori," Perrin said. "I understand."

Jori looked up, smiling. "It's a pleasure to be here with you, Lord Perrin. A real pleasure. We'll follow you anywhere, the others and I."

With that, Jori saluted, then ran off. Perrin scratched at his beard, watching the man go. Jori was one of a good dozen Two Rivers men who had approached Perrin over the last few days to apologize. It seemed all of them felt guilty for spreading rumors about Perrin and Berelain, though none would say it straight out.

Bless Faile for what she had done there.

Everyone seen to, Perrin took a deep breath, then walked up the column and stepped through the gateway.

Come quickly, Rand, he thought, colors blossoming in his vision. *I can feel it starting.*

Mat stood with Thom at his left and Noal at his right, looking up through the trees at the spire ahead. A trickling, musical stream gurgled behind them, a tributary of the nearby Arinelle. A grassy plain spread behind them, and beyond that, the grand river itself.

Had he passed this way before? So much of his memory from that time was fragmented. And yet, this tower remained clear in his mind, viewed from a distance. Even the darkness of Shadar Logoth had not been able to excise it from his mind.

The tower looked to be of pure metal, its solid steel gleaming in the overcast sunlight. Mat felt an iciness between his shoulder blades. Many travelers along the river thought it some relic from the Age of Legends. What else did you make of a column of steel rising out of the forest, seemingly uninhabited? It was as unnatural and out of place as the twisted red doorways were. Those warped the eyes to look at them.

The forest felt too still here, quiet save for the footsteps of the three. Noal walked with a long staff, taller than he was. Where had he gotten it? It had that smooth, oiled look of wood that had spent more years as a walking staff than it originally had as a tree. Noal had also put on a dark blue— nearly black—pair of trousers and a shirt that was of an odd, unknown style. The shoulders were stiffer than the cuts Mat was familiar with, and the coat longer, going almost all the way down to Noal's knees. It buttoned to the waist, then split at the legs. Strange indeed. The old man never *would* answer questions about his past.

Thom had opted for his gleeman's clothing. It was good to see him in that again, rather than the frilly court bard apparel. The patchwork cloak, the simple shirt that tied up the front, the tight breeches tucked into boots. When Mat had asked about the choice, Thom had shrugged, saying, "It feels like what I should wear if I'm going to see her."

"Her" meant Moiraine. But what had the snakes and foxes done to her? It had been so long, but burn him if he was going to let another hour pass. He had chosen clothing of forest greens and earthy browns, along with a deep brown cloak. He carried his pack slung over one arm and his *ashandarei* in his hand. He had practiced with the new iron counterweight on the butt, and was pleased.

The Eelfinn had given him the weapon. Well, if they dared stand between him and Moiraine, then they would see what he could do with their gift. Burn him, but they would.

The three men stepped up to the tower. It did not appear to have a single opening anywhere on its two-hundred-foot-tall height. Not a window, not a seam, not a scratch. Mat looked up, feeling disoriented as he stared along its gleaming length toward the distant gray sky. Did the tower reflect *too* much light?

He shuddered and turned to Thom. Mat gave a single nod.

Hesitating only briefly, Thom slid a bronze knife from its sheath on his belt and stepped over to set the tip against the tower. He grimly slid the knife in the shape of a triangle, about a palm wide, point down. Metal scraped against metal, but left no trail. Thom finished by making a wavy line through the center, as one did at the start of any game of Snakes and Foxes.

All stood silently. Mat glanced at Thom. "Did you do it right?"

"I think so," Thom said. "But how do we know what 'right' is? That game has been passed down for—"

He cut off as a line of light appeared on the tower front. Mat jumped back, leveling his spear. The glowing lines formed a triangle matching the one that Thom had drawn, and then—quick as a single beat of a moth's wings—the steel in the center of the triangle vanished.

Noal eyed the palm-sized hole. "That's a tad small to get through." He stepped up to it and looked through. "Nothing but darkness on the other side."

Thom looked down at the knife. "Guess that triangle is actually a doorway. That's what you're drawing when you start the game. Should I try a bigger one?"

"Guess so," Mat said. "Unless the *gholam* taught you how to squeeze through holes the size of a fist."

"No need to be unpleasant," Thom said, using the knife to draw another triangle around the first, this one large enough to walk through. He finished with the wavy line.

Mat counted. It took seven heartbeats for the lines of white to appear. The steel between them faded away, opening a triangular corridor leading into the tower. The inside looked to be solid steel.

"Light burn me," Noal whispered. The corridor disappeared into darkness; the sunlight seemed hesitant to enter the opening, though it was probably just a trick of the light.

"And so we begin the game that cannot be won," Thom said, sliding the knife back into its sheath.

"Courage to strengthen," Noal whispered, stepping forward, holding up a lantern with a flickering flame. "Fire to blind. Music to dazzle. Iron to bind."

"And Matrim Cauthon," Mat added. "To bloody even the odds." He stepped through the doorway.

Light flashed, brilliant white, blinding. He cursed, squeezing his eyes shut and lowering his *ashandarei* in what he hoped was a threatening posture. He blinked and the whiteness faded. He was in the center of a wide room with a triangular opening behind him, freestanding, with the point down at the floor. It was pure black, made of twisting cords that in some places seemed metal and in other places seemed wood.

The room was black as well, shaped like an off-kilter square. Rippling white steam poured up from holes at all four corners; that mist glowed with a white light. There were four hallways extending from the room, one in each direction.

The chamber was not exactly square. Each side was a slightly different length than the others, making for an odd meeting of angles at the corners. And that steam! It gave off a sulphurous stench that made him want to breathe through his mouth. The onyx-colored walls were not stone, but were of some reflective material, like the scales of enormous fish. The steam collected at the ceiling, glowing faintly with a soft light.

Burn him! This was not like the first place he had visited, with its twisting coils and circular doorways, but nor was it like the second one, with the star-shaped rooms and lines of yellow light! Where *was* he? What had he gotten himself into? He turned about, nervous.

Thom stumbled through the doorway, blinking, dazed. Mat dropped his pack and caught the gleeman by one arm. Noal came next. The bony man kept his footing, but was obviously blinded, his lantern held forward defensively.

The two others blinked, tears streaming from Noal's eyes, but they eventually got their bearings and glanced about. The room, like the hallways extending in all four directions, was empty.

"This doesn't look like what you described, Mat," Thom said. His voice echoed faintly, though the sounds seemed eerily warped. Almost like whispers thrown back at them. It made the hair on Mat's neck rise.

"I know," Mat said, pulling a torch from his pack. "This place doesn't make sense. The stories agree about that, at least. Here, light this, Noal."

Thom got out a torch of his own and both lit from Noal's lantern. They had strikers from Aludra, but Mat wanted to save those. He had been half-afraid that in the tower, flames would go out once lit. But the lights burned steady and true. That heartened him somewhat.

"So where are they?" Thom asked, walking around the perimeter of the black room.

"They're never here when you come through," Mat said, holding up his own torch and inspecting a wall. Was that writing, carved into the not-stone? The unfamiliar script was so fine and delicate he could barely see it. "But watch yourself. They can appear behind you, faster than an inn-keeper who heard coins clink in your pouch."

Noal inspected the triangular opening they had come through. "Do you suppose we can use this to get back?" It resembled the stone *ter'angreal* Mat had stepped through before. Just a different shape.

"I hope so," Mat said.

"Maybe we should try," Noal said.

Mat nodded to him. He did not like being separated, but they *did* need to know if this was a way back or not. Noal looked determined and stepped through. He vanished.

Mat held his breath for a long moment, but the aged man did not return. Was it a trick? Had this doorway been placed here to—

Noal stumbled back into the room through the opening. Thom set his torch on the floor and dashed over to help. Noal recovered more quickly this time, blinking away the blindness. "It sealed me out," he explained. "I had to draw another triangle to get back in."

"At least we know we've got a means of escape," Thom said.

Assuming those bloody Aelfinn or Eelfinn don't move it, Mat thought, remembering his previous visit, the one that had ended with him being hanged. That time, the rooms and corridors had shifted mysteriously, in total defiance of what was right.

"Will you look at that?" Thom said.

Mat lowered his spear and Noal had an iron shortsword in his hand in a moment. Thom was pointing at his torch, which burned fitfully where he had set it on the floor beside one of the glowing steam vents.

The white steam pushed *away* from the flames, like it was being blown by a breeze. Only, no breeze ever made steam move so unnaturally. It curved around the fire in a loop. Thom stepped over and picked up the torch. He moved it toward the column of steam, and it bowed out of the way. Thom rammed the torch directly into the steam's path, and the steam split, going around the flame and meld-ing together into a single stream again above.

Thom glanced at the others.

"Don't ask me," Mat said, scowling. "I *said* this place

doesn't make sense. If that's the oddest thing we see here, I'll be a Murandian's mustache. Come on."

Mat picked one of the hallways and began to walk down it. The other two hurried to catch up. The steam glowed on the ceiling, bathing the black hallway with its milky light. The floor was made of interlocking triangular tiles that, once again, looked discomfortingly like scales. The corridor was wide and long, the other end distant and dark.

"To think," Noal said, holding up his lantern, "all of this hidden in that single tower."

"I doubt we're in the tower anymore," Mat said. Up ahead, he could see a slice out of the side of the wall, a kind of window. It was set a little too high up to feel natural.

"Then where. . . ." Noal trailed off as they reached the window, which was an off-center square. Through it, they could look out at an unnatural landscape. They were up several floors in some kind of spire, but that certainly was *not* Andor outside.

The window looked out over a canopy of dense vegetation that was too yellow. Mat recognized the wispy trees with a drooping umbrella of branches at the top, though before he had seen them from below. The fernlike trees with their spreading fans of leaves were familiar as well, though those had deep black fruits hanging from them now. The large fruits caused the leaves to droop.

"Mercy of the Winnower," Noal whispered, a phrase Mat had never heard before.

Noal had reason to be astonished; Mat remembered looking out at that forest for the first time, realizing that the twisted doorway had not brought him to another place, but another *world* entirely.

Mat looked to the side. Could he see the three spires he had noted on his first visit? They did not seem to be about, though in this place, the very next window they passed could show a different scene. They could. . . .

He paused, then glanced sharply through the window. He could make out a spire to the left. And then he knew. He was *in* one of the spires he had seen in the distance during his first visit.

He stifled a shiver and turned away. At least he knew

for certain he was in the same place. Did that mean that the worlds of the Aelfinn and the Eelfinn were the same? He hoped so. Moiraine had fallen through the *second* of the twisted red doorways, which meant she had most likely been taken by the Eelfinn, the foxes.

They were the ones who had hanged Mat; the snakes, at least, had only tossed him out of their realm without any useful answers. He bore them a grudge, but the foxes . . . *they* had refused to answer his questions, and had given him these bloody memories instead!

Mat and the others continued down the hallway, their footsteps echoing against the flooring. Soon, Mat began to get the sense that he was being watched. He had felt it before, on his other visits. He turned to the side, and caught a glimpse of faint motion far behind.

He spun, preparing to toss his torch aside and fight with his *ashandarei*, but saw nothing. The other two froze, looking about, anxious. Mat continued on sheepishly, though he felt less so after Thom did the same thing a short time later. Thom went so far as to throw a knife at a darkened patch of the wall.

The iron weapon clanked against the surface. The dull ring echoed for far too long in the hallway.

"Sorry," Thom said.

"It's all right," Mat said.

"They're watching us, aren't they?" Noal asked. His voice was soft, faintly nervous. Light! Mat felt as if he was going to jump out of his skin and run away, leaving it behind. Compared to that, Noal seemed steady.

"I suspect they are, at that," Mat said.

Within a few moments, they reached the end of the too-long hallway. Here, they entered a chamber that was identical to the first, save it had no doorway in the center. It split off in four directions, each corridor disappearing into the distant darkness.

They picked another direction, memorizing the path they were taking, unseen eyes scratching at their backs. His footsteps grew more hurried as they traversed the length of the hallway and entered another chamber. It was exactly like the previous one.

"Easy to be disoriented in a place like this," Noal said.

He opened his pack and got out a sheet of paper and a charcoal pencil. He made three dots on his paper, then connected them by lines, representing the corridors and rooms they'd gone through. "It's all a matter of keeping a good map. A good map can mean life or death; you can trust me on that."

Mat turned around, looking back the way they had come. Part of him wanted to keep going, not look backward, but he *had* to know. "Come on," he said, going back the way they had come.

Thom and Noal shared looks, but once again hurried to catch up. It took them a good half-hour to retrace their steps back to the first chamber, the one that should contain the doorway. They found it empty. Those columns of steam rose from the corners. They had in the other two rooms, too.

"Impossible!" Noal said. "We retraced our steps perfectly! The way out should be here."

In the distance—faint and almost inaudible—Mat heard laughter. A hissing, dangerous laughter. Malicious.

Mat's skin grew icy. "Thom," he said, "you ever hear a story about Birgitte Silverbow and her visit to the Tower of Ghenjei?"

"Birgitte?" Thom asked, looking up from his inspection—with Noal—of the floor. They seemed convinced that the doorway must have been pulled down into some hidden trapdoor. "No, can't say that I have."

"What about a story of a woman trapped for two months in a maze of corridors inside a fortress?"

"Two months?" Thom said. "Well, no. But there's the tale of Elmiara and the Shadoweyes. She spent a hundred days wandering in a maze, looking for the infamous healing spring of Sund to save her lover's life."

That was probably it. The story had survived; it had changed forms, the way so many of them did. "She didn't get out, did she?"

"No. She died at the end, only two steps away from the fountain, but separated from it by a wall. She could hear it bubbling; it was the last sound she heard before dying from thirst." He glanced about uncomfortably, as if uncertain he wanted to be sharing such a story in this place.

Mat shook his head, worried. Burn him, but he hated these foxes. There *had* to be a way to—

"You have broken the bargain," a soft voice said.

Mat spun and the other two cursed, standing up, hands on weapons. A figure stood in the hallway behind them. It was one of the creatures Mat remembered, perhaps the exact same one who had met him last time. Short, bright red hair sprouted from the creature's pale scalp. A pair of ears clung to the head, slightly pointed at the tips. The figure was willowy and tall, the shoulders disproportionately wide for the waist, and it wore pale leather straps across its chest—Mat *still* did not want to think about what those might have been made of—and a long black kilt below.

It was the face that was most distinctive. Large, unnatural eyes, pale with a shade of iris in the center. A narrow jaw and angular features. Like a fox. One of the Eelfinn, masters of this realm.

It had come to play with the mice.

"There is no bargain this way," Mat said, trying to keep the nervousness from his voice. "We can bloody bring what we want."

"Having no bargain is dangerous," the Eelfinn said in a smooth voice. "For you. Fortunately, I can take you where you desire."

"Well, then," Mat said. "Do it."

"Leave your iron," the Eelfinn said. "Your implements of music. Your fire."

"Never," Mat said.

The Eelfinn blinked large eyes. Slowly, deliberately. It stepped forward, footsteps soft. Mat raised his *ashandarei*, but the Eelfinn made no directly threatening moves. It glided around the three of them, speaking softly.

"Come now," it said. "Can we not speak with civility? You have come to our realm seeking. We have power to grant what you wish, what you *need*. Why not show good faith? Leave behind your implements of fire. Those only, and I promise to lead you for a time."

Its voice was hypnotic, soothing. It did make sense. What need had they of fire? It was light enough with that mist. It . . .

"Thom," Mat said. "Music."

"What?" Thom said, shaking a little bit.

"Play anything. It doesn't matter what."

Thom took out his flute, and the Eelfinn narrowed its eyes. Thom began playing. It was a familiar song, "The Wind That Shakes the Willows." Mat had intended to soothe the Eelfinn, maybe put it off guard. But the familiar tune seemed to help dispel the cloud on Mat's mind.

"This isn't needed," the Eelfinn said, glaring at Thom.

"Yes it is," Mat said. "And we're not bloody leaving our fire. Not unless you promise to take us all the way to the central chamber and give us back Moiraine."

"I cannot make that bargain," the creature said, continuing to walk around them. Mat turned to follow it, never letting his back to the thing. "I have not the authority."

"Bring someone who can."

"Impossible," the Eelfinn said. "Listen to me. Fire isn't needed. I will lead you half of the way to the central chamber, the Chamber of Bonds, should you leave behind that terrible fire. It offends us. We wish only to meet your desires."

The creature was obviously trying to lull them again, but its cadence was off, at odds with Thom's playing. Mat watched it, then began to sing along with the flute playing. He did not have the best voice among those he knew, but he was not terrible either. The Eelfinn yawned, then settled down beside the wall and closed its eyes. In moments, it was sleeping.

Thom lowered the flute from his lips, looking impressed.

"Nicely done," Noal whispered. "I had no idea you were so fluent in the Old Tongue."

Mat hesitated. He had not even realized they had been speaking in it.

"My Old Tongue is rusty," Noal said, rubbing his chin, "but I caught a lot of that. Problem is, we still don't know the way through this place. How will we make our way without one of them to guide us?"

He was right. Birgitte had wandered for months, never knowing if her goal was merely a few steps away. The chamber where Mat had met the Eelfinn leaders . . . she had said that once you were there, they had to bargain with you. That must be the Chamber of Bonds the Eelfinn had mentioned.

Poor Moiraine. She had come through one of the red doorways; she should have been protected by whatever treaty the Eelfinn had with the ancient Aes Sedai. But that doorway had been destroyed. No way back.

When Mat had come originally, they had praised him as wise for thinking to ask for a leave-taking. Though he grumbled, still, about the Eelfinn not answering his questions, he could see that was not what they did. The Aelfinn were for questions; the Eelfinn granted requests. But they twisted those requests, and took whatever price they wanted. Mat had unwittingly asked for his memory filled, for a way to be free of the Aes Sedai, and a way out of the Tower.

If Moiraine had not known this, and had not asked for passage out as he had done . . . or if she had asked for passage back to the doorway, not knowing it had been destroyed. . . .

Mat had asked for a way out. They had given it to him, but he could not *remember* what it was. Everything had gone black, and he had awakened hanging from the *ashandarei*.

Mat pulled something from his pocket, holding it tightly in his fist. "The Aelfinn and the Eelfinn get around in here somehow," his whispered. "There *has* to be a correct pathway."

"One way," Noal said. "Four choices, followed by four choices, followed by four choices . . . The odds against us are incredible!"

"Odds," Mat said, holding out his hand. He opened it, revealing a pair of dice. "What do *I* care for odds?"

The two looked at his ivory dice, then looked back up at his face. Mat could feel his luck surge. "Twelve pips. Three for each doorway. If I roll a one, a two, or a three, we go straight. Four, five, or six, we take the right path, and so on."

"But Mat," Noal whispered, glancing at the sleeping Eelfinn. "The rolls won't be equal. You *can't* roll a one, for example, and a seven is *far* more likely to—"

"You don't understand, Noal," Mat said, tossing the dice to the floor. They rattled against the scale-like tiles, clacking like teeth. "It doesn't matter what is *likely*. Not when I'm around."

The dice came to a rest. One of them caught in a rut between two tiles and froze precariously, one of the corners
to the air. The other came to rest with a single pip showing.

"How about that, Noal," Thom said. "Looks like he can
roll a one after all."

"Now that's something," Noal said, rubbing his chin.

Mat fetched his *ashandarei*, then picked up the dice and
walked straight ahead. The others followed, leaving the
sleeping Eelfinn behind.

At the next intersection, Mat rolled again, and got a
nine. "Back the way we came?" Thom asked, frowning.
"That's—"

"Just what we're going to do," Mat said, turning and going
back. In the other room, the sleeping Eelfinn was gone.

"They could have wakened him," Noal pointed out.

"Or it could be a different room," Mat said, tossing the
dice again. Another nine. He was facing the way he had
come, so a nine meant going back again. "The Aelfinn
and the Eelfinn have rules," Mat said, turning and running
down the corridor, the other two chasing after him. "And
this *place* has rules."

"Rules have to make sense, Mat," Noal said.

"They have to be consistent," Mat said. "But they don't
have to follow our logic. Why should they?"

It made sense to him. They ran for a time—this hallway
seemed much longer than the others. He was starting to feel
winded when he reached the next room. He tossed the dice
again, but suspected what he would see. Nine. Back to the
first room again.

"Look, this is foolish!" Noal said as they turned and ran
back the other way. "We're never going to get anywhere this
way!"

Mat ignored him, continuing to run. Soon they approached the first room again.

"Mat," Noal said, pleadingly. "Can we at least. . . ."

Noal trailed off as they burst into the first chamber. Only
it was *not* the first chamber. This room had a white floor,
and was enormous, with thick, black columns rising toward
an unseen ceiling far above.

The glowing white steam that pooled atop their corridor
poured into the room and fell upward into that blackness,
like a waterfall going in the wrong direction. Though the

floor and the columns looked like glass, Mat knew they would feel porous, like stone. The room was lit by a series of glowing yellow stripes that ran up each column, marking places where the carved glass-stone was fluted to a point.

Thom clapped him on the shoulder. "Mat, lad, that was insane. And effective. Somehow."

"About what you should expect from me," Mat said, pulling down the brim of his hat. "I've been in this room before. We're on track. If Moiraine still lives, then she'll be somewhere past here."

CHAPTER

54

The Light of the World

Thom held up his torch, inspecting the enormous star-shaped black columns and their glowing yellow lines. Those lines gave the entire room a sickly light, making Thom look wan and jaundiced.

Mat remembered the stink of this place, that musty staleness. Now that he knew what to look for, he could smell something else, too. The musky stink of an animal's den. A predator's lair.

There were five corridors leading out of the room, one at each inner point of the star shape. He remembered passing through one of those passageways, but had there not been only one way out before?

"Wonder how high up the pillars go," Thom said, raising his torch higher and squinting.

Mat held his *ashandarei* in a firmer grip, palms sweaty. They had entered the foxes' den. He felt at his medallion. The Eelfinn had not used the Power on him before, but they had to have some understanding of it, did they not? Of course, Ogier could not channel. Perhaps that meant Eelfinn could not either.

Rustling sounds came from the edges of the room. Shadows shifted and moved. The Eelfinn were in there, in that darkness. "Thom," Mat said. "We should play some more music."

Thom watched that darkness. He did not object; he raised his flute and began playing. The sound seemed lonely in the vast room.

"Mat," Noal said, kneeling near the center of the room. "Look at this."

"I know," Mat said. "It looks like glass but feels like stone."

"No, not that," Noal said. "There's something here."

Mat edged over to Noal. Thom joined them, watching and playing as Noal used his lantern to illuminate a melted lump of slag on the floor, perhaps the size of a small chest. It was black, but a deeper, less reflective black than the floor and the columns.

"What do you make of it?" Noal asked. "Maybe one of the trapdoors?"

"No," Mat said. "It's not that."

The other two looked at him.

"It's the doorframe," Mat said, feeling sick. "The red-stone doorframe. When I came through it before, it was in the center of a room like this. When it melted on the other side . . ."

"It melted here too," Noal said.

The three stared at it. Thom's music sounded haunting.

"Well," Mat said. "We knew it wasn't a way out in the first place. We'll have to bargain our way free." *And I'll make bloody sure not to get hanged this time.*

"Will the dice lead us?" Noal asked, rising.

Mat felt them in his coat pocket. "I don't see why not." But he did not take them out. He turned to regard the depths of the room. Thom's music seemed to have stilled some of the shadows. But others still moved. There was a restless energy to the air.

"Mat?" Thom asked.

"You knew I'd come back," Mat said loudly. His voice did not echo. Light! How large *was* the thing? "You knew I'd come marching back to your bloody realm, didn't you? You knew you'd have me eventually."

Hesitant, Thom lowered his flute.

"Show yourselves!" Mat said. "I can hear you scrambling, hear you breathing."

"Mat," Thom said, laying a hand on his shoulder. "They couldn't have known that you'd come back. Moiraine didn't know that you'd come for certain."

Mat watched the darkness. "You ever see men lead cattle to slaughter, Thom?"

The gleeman hesitated, then shook his head.

"Well, every man has his own ways," Mat said. "But

cattle, see, they'll know something is wrong. They'll smell the blood. They'll get frenzied, refuse to enter the slaughterhouse. And you know how you fix that?"

"Do we have to talk about this now, Mat?"

"You fix it," Mat said, "by taking them through the slaughterhouse a few times when it is clean, when the scents aren't so strong. You let them go through and escape, see, and they'll think the place is safe." He looked at Thom. "They knew I'd be back. They knew I'd survive that hanging. They *know* things, Thom. Burn me, but they do."

"We'll get out, Mat," Thom promised. "We can. Moiraine saw it."

Mat nodded firmly. "Bloody right we will. They're playing a game, Thom. I win games." He pulled a handful of dice from his pocket. *I win them most of the time, anyway.*

A voice whispered suddenly from behind them. "Welcome, son of battles."

Mat spun, cursing, glancing about the chamber.

"There," Noal said, pointing with his staff. There was a figure beside one of the pillars, half lit by the yellow light. Another Eelfinn. Taller, his face more angular. His eyes reflected torchlight. Orange.

"I can take you where you wish to go," the Eelfinn said, voice rough and gravelly. He raised an arm against the glow of the torches. "For a price."

"Thom, music."

Thom began playing again.

"One of you already tried to get us to leave our tools behind," Mat said. He pulled a torch from the pack over his arm, then thrust it to the side, lighting it on Noal's lantern. "It won't work."

The Eelfinn shied away from the new light, snarling softly. "You come looking to bargain, yet you purposely antagonize? We have done nothing to earn this."

Mat pulled the scarf free from his neck. "Nothing?"

The creature made no response, though it did back away, stepping into the darker area between pillars. Its too-angular face was now only barely lit by the yellow lights.

"Why do you wish to speak with us, son of battles," the whisperer said from the shadows, "if you are not willing to bargain?"

"No," Mat said. "No bargaining until we reach the great

hall, the Chamber of Bonds." That was the only place where they would be bound to the agreement. Was that not what Birgitte had said? Of course, she had seemed to be relying on stories and hearsay herself.

Thom continued playing, eyes darting from side to side, trying to watch the shadows. Noal began to play the little cymbals he had tied to the legs of his trousers, tapping them in time with Thom's music. The shadows continued to move out there, however.

"Your . . . comforts will not slow us, son of battles," a voice said from behind. Mat spun, lowering his weapon. Another Eelfinn stood there, just inside the shadows. A female, with a crest of red running down her back, the leather straps crossing her breasts in an 'X' pattern. Her red lips smiled. "We are the near ancient, the warriors of final regret, the knowers of secrets."

"Be proud, son of battles," another voice hissed. Mat spun again, sweat dampening his brow. The female vanished back into the shadows, but another Eelfinn strolled through the light. He carried a long, wicked bronze knife, with a crosswork pattern of roses along its length and thorns sticking out near the top of the crossguard. "You draw out our most skilled. You are to be . . . savored."

"What—" Mat began, but the lean, dangerous-looking Eelfinn stepped back into the shadows and vanished. Too quickly. As if the darkness had absorbed him.

Other whispers began in the shadows, speaking in low voices, overlapping each other. Faces appeared from the darkness, inhuman eyes wide, lips curled in smiles. The creatures had pointed teeth.

Light! There were dozens of Eelfinn in the room. Shifting, moving about, dancing into the light, then jumping back into the dark. Some were casual, others energetic. All looked dangerous.

"Will you bargain?" one asked.

"You come without treaty. Dangerous," said another.

"Son of battles."

"The savor!"

"Feel his fear."

"Come with us. Leave your terrible light."

"A bargain must be made. We will wait."

"Patient we are. Ever patient."

"The savor!"

"Stop it!" Mat bellowed. "No bargains! Not until we reach the center."

At his side, Thom lowered the flute. "Mat. I don't think the music is working anymore."

Mat nodded curtly. He needed Thom ready with weapons. The gleeman tucked away his flute, getting out knives. Mat ignored the whispering voices and tossed the dice onto the ground.

As they rolled, a figure scuttled from the darkness beside the nearest pillar. Mat cursed, lowering his spear and striking at the Eelfinn, which moved across the ground on all fours. But his blade passed right through it, as if it were smoke.

Was it an illusion? A trick of the eyes? Mat hesitated long enough for another creature to snatch the dice and leap back toward the shadows. Something sparkled in the air. Thom's dagger found its mark, striking the creature in the shoulder. This time the blade pierced and stayed, releasing a spray of dark blood.

Iron, Mat thought, cursing his stupidity. He spun the *ashandarei* around, using the side banded with iron. He shivered as he saw the Eelfinn's blood on the ground begin to steam. White steam, as in the other chambers, but this had shapes in it. They looked like twisted faces, appearing briefly and yelling before vanishing.

Burn them! He couldn't get distracted. He had other dice. He reached for his pocket, but an Eelfinn ducked from the shadows, as if to grab at his coat.

Mat spun his weapon, striking the side of the fox male's face with the banded iron. He crushed bone, tossing the creature to the side like a bundle of sticks.

Hisses and growls surrounded them. Eyes shifted in the darkness, reflecting torchlight. The Eelfinn moved, cloaked in blackness, surrounding Mat and the others. Mat cursed, taking a step in the direction of the Eelfinn he had struck.

"Mat!" Thom said, grabbing the cuff of his coat. "We can't wade into that."

Mat hesitated. It seemed that the stink from before was stronger, the scent of beasts. Shadows moved all about, more frantic now, their whispers angry and mixed with yipping calls.

"They control the darkness," Noal said. He stood with his back to Mat and Thom, wary. "Those yellow lights are to distract us; there are breaks in them and sheltered alcoves. It's all a trick."

Mat felt his heart beating rapidly. A trick? No, not just a trick. There was something *unnatural* about the way those creatures moved in the shadow. "Burn them," Mat said, shaking Thom's hand free but not chasing into the darkness.

"Gentlemen," Noal said. "Gather arms. . . ."

Mat glanced over his shoulder. There were Eelfinn stalking from the shadows behind them, a double wave, one group sliding on all fours before a second group. The second group carried those wicked-looking bronze knives.

The shadows from the depths of the room seemed to be extending with the Eelfinn, closing on Mat and his group. His heart beat even faster.

The Eelfinn eyes shone, and those on all fours began to lope forward. Mat swung as the Eelfinn reached his group, but they split, ducking to the sides. Distracting him.

Behind! Mat thought with alarm. Another group of Eelfinn jumped out of the darkness there.

Mat turned on them, swinging. They ducked back before he hit. Light! They were all around, seething out of the darkness, coming close enough to be dangerous, then backing away.

Thom whipped out a pair of daggers, throwing, and Noal kept his shortsword at the ready, waving his torch with his other hand, his banded staff on the floor at his feet. One of Thom's knives flashed, seeking flesh, but missed and passed into the darkness.

"Don't waste knives!" Mat said. "Bloody sons of goats, they're trying to make you waste them, Thom!"

"They're harrying us," Noal growled. "They'll overwhelm us eventually. We have to move!"

"Which way?" Thom asked, urgent. He cursed as a pair of Eelfinn appeared from the shadows carrying bronze-ended lances. They thrust forward, forcing Mat, Thom, and Noal to back away.

No time for dice. They would just snatch those anyway. Mat yanked open his pack and pulled out a nightflower. "Once this goes off, I'm going to close my eyes and spin about."

"*What?*" Thom said.

"It's worked before!" Mat said, lighting the nightflower and throwing it as hard as he could into the darkness. There was a count of five, and the boom that followed rattled the room. All three of them averted their eyes, but the colorful flash was bright enough to see through eyelids.

Eelfinn screamed in pain, and Mat distinctly heard pings as weapons were dropped. No doubt hands were raised to eyes.

"Here we go!" Mat said, spinning.

"This is flaming insane," Thom said.

Mat kept going, trying to feel for it. Where was that luck? "That way!" he said, pointing in a random direction.

He opened his eyes in time to leap over the dark form of an Eelfinn huddling on the ground. Noal and Thom followed, and Mat led them straight into the darkness. He charged ahead until his friends were barely visible. All he could see were those lines of yellow.

Oh, bloody ashes, he thought. *If my luck fails me now. . . .*

They burst into a five-sided corridor, the darkness vanishing around them. They had not been able to *see* this corridor from the other room, but here it was.

Thom let out a whoop. "Mat, you wood-headed shepherd! For this, I'll let you play my harp!"

"I don't want to play your bloody harp," Mat said, glancing over his shoulder. "But you can buy me a mug or two when we're out."

He heard screams and screeches from the dark room. That was one trick used up; they would be expecting nightflowers now. *Birgitte, you were right,* he thought. *You probably walked past the corridor you needed several times, never knowing it was only a few feet away.*

Never choose the card a man wants you to. Mat should have realized that. It was one of the oldest cons in creation. They hastened forward, passing five-sided doorways leading into large star-shaped caverns. Thom and Noal glanced into them, but Mat kept on. Straight forward. This was the way his luck had sent them.

Something was different from when he had visited before. There was no dust on the floor to make footprints. Had they known he was coming, and used the dust to confuse him? Or had they cleaned the place this time, knowing that visitors might arrive? Who knew in a realm such as this?

It had been a long walk before. Or had it been a short one? Time blended here. It seemed that they ran for many hours, yet it also felt like moments.

And then the doorway was in front of them, appearing like a striking adder. It had not been there a moment before. The rim of the opening was intricately carved wood, with an impossible pattern of weaving vines that seemed to double back on one another and make no sense.

All three pulled to a halt. "Mirrors," Noal said. "I've seen it before. That's how they do it, obscuring things with mirrors." He sounded unnerved. Where did one hide mirrors in a bloody straight tunnel?

They were in the right place; Mat could smell it. The stink of the Eelfinn was strongest here. He set his jaw and stepped through the doorway.

The room beyond was as he remembered it. No columns here, though the room was distinctly star-shaped. Eight tips and only the one doorway. Those glowing yellow strips ran up the sharp ends of the room, and eight empty pedestals stood, black and ominous, one at each point.

It was exactly the same. Except for the woman floating at its center.

She was clothed only in a fine white mist that shifted and shone around her, the details of her figure obfuscated but not hidden. Her eyes were closed, and her dark hair—curly but no longer in perfect ringlets—fluttered as if in a wind blowing up from beneath. Her hands rested atop her stomach, and there was a strange bracelet of something that looked like aged ivory on her left wrist.

Moiraine.

Mat felt a surge of emotions. Worry, frustration, concern, awe. She was the one who had started this all. He had hated her at times. He also owed her his life. She was the first one who had meddled, yanking him this way and that. Yet—looking back—he figured that she had been the most honest about it of anyone who had used him. Unapologetic, unyielding. And selfless.

She had dedicated everything to protecting three foolish boys, all ignorant of what the world would demand of them. She had determined to take them to safety. Maybe train them a little, whether they wanted it or not.

Because they *needed* it.

Light, her motives seemed clear to him now. That did not make him any less angry with her, but it *did* make him grateful. Burn her, but this was a confusing set of emotions! Those bloody foxes—how *dare* they keep her like this! Was she alive?

Thom and Noal were staring—Noal solemn, Thom disbelieving. So Mat stepped forward to pull Moiraine free. As soon as his hands touched the mist, however, he felt a blazing pain. He screamed, pulling back, shaking his hand.

"It's bloody *hot*," Mat said. "It—"

He cut off as Thom stepped forward.

"Thom . . ." Mat said warningly.

"I don't care," the gleeman said. He stepped up to the mist, reaching in, his clothing beginning to steam, his eyes watering from the pain. He did not flinch. He dug into that mist and took hold of her, then pulled her free. Her weight sank into his arms, but his aging limbs were strong, and she looked frail enough that she must not have weighed much.

Light! Mat had forgotten how small she was. A good head shorter than he was. Thom knelt, pulling off his gleeman's cloak and wrapping her in it. Her eyes were still closed.

"Is she . . ." Noal asked.

"She lives," Thom said quietly. "I felt her heartbeat." He took the bracelet off her arm. It was in the shape of a man bent backward with his wrists bound to his ankles, clothed in a strange suit of clothing. "It looks like a *ter'angreal* of some sort," Thom said, tucking it into his coat pocket. "I—"

"It is an *angreal*," a voice proclaimed. "Strong enough to be nearly *sa'angreal*. It can be part of her price, should you wish to pay it."

Mat spun. The pedestals were now occupied by Eelfinn, four males, four females. All eight wore white instead of black—white skirts with straps across the chests for the males and blouses for the females, made from that disturbing pale substance that looked like skin.

"Mark your tongues," Mat said to Thom and Noal, trying to contain his worry. "Speak amiss, and they'll have you strung up, claiming it was your own desire. Ask nothing of them."

The other two fell silent, Thom holding Moiraine close, Noal carrying his torch and staff warily, pack over his shoulder.

"This is the great hall," Mat said to the Eelfinn. "The place called the Chamber of Bonds. You must abide by the pacts you make here."

"The bargain has been arranged," one of the Eelfinn males said, smiling, showing pointed teeth.

The other Eelfinn leaned in, breathing deeply, as if smelling something. Or . . . as if *drawing* something from Mat and the others. Birgitte had said that they fed off emotion.

"What bargain?" Mat snapped, glancing around at the pedestals. "Burn you, *what bargain?*"

"A price must be paid," one said.

"The demands must be met," said another.

"A sacrifice must be given." This from one of the females. She smiled more broadly than the others. Her teeth were pointed, too.

"I want the way out restored as part of the bargain," Mat said. "I want it back where it was and open again. And I'm not bloody done negotiating, so don't assume that *this* is my only request, burn you."

"It will be restored," an Eelfinn said. The others leaned forward. They could sense his desperation. Several of them seemed dissatisfied. *They didn't expect us to make it here,* Mat thought. *They don't like to risk losing us.*

"I want you to leave that way out open until we get through," Mat continued. "No blocking it up or making it bloody vanish when we arrive. And I want the way to be direct, no changing rooms about. A straight pathway. And you bloody foxes can't knock us unconscious or try to kill us or anything like that."

They did not like that. Mat caught several of them frowning. Good. They would see they were not negotiating with a child.

"We take her," Mat said. "We get out."

"These demands are expensive," one of the Eelfinn said. "What will you pay for these boons?"

"The price has been set," another whispered from behind.

And it had been. Somehow, Mat knew. A part of him had known from the first time he had read that note. If he had never spoken to the Aelfinn that first time, would any of this have happened? Likely, he would have died. They had to tell the truth.

They had warned him of a payment to come. For life. For Moiraine. And he would have to pay it. In that moment, he knew that he would. For he knew that if he did not, the cost would be too great. Not just to Thom, not just to Moiraine, and not just to Mat himself. By what he'd been told, the fate of the world itself depended on this moment.

Well burn me for a fool, Mat thought. *Maybe I am a hero after all.* Didn't that beat all?

"I'll pay it," Mat announced. "Half the light of the world." *To save the world.*

"Done!" one of the male Eelfinn announced.

The eight creatures leaped—as if one—from their pedestals. They enclosed him in a tightening circle, like a noose. Quick, supple and predatory.

"Mat!" Thom cried, struggling to hold the unconscious Moiraine while reaching for one of his knives.

Mat held up a hand toward Thom and Noal. "This must be done," he said, taking a few steps away from his friends. The Eelfinn passed them without sparing a glance. The gold studs on the straps crossing the male Eelfinn's chests glittered in the yellow light. All eight creatures were smiling wide.

Noal raised his sword.

"No!" Mat yelled. "Don't break this agreement. If you do, we all will die here!"

The Eelfinn stepped up in a tight circle around Mat. He tried to look at them all at once, heart thudding louder and louder in his chest. They were sniffing at him again, drawing in deep breaths, enjoying whatever it was they drew from him.

"Do it, burn you," Mat growled. "But know this is the last you'll get of me. I'll escape your tower, and I'll find a way to free my mind from you forever. You won't have me. Matrim Cauthon is not your bloody puppet."

"We shall see," an Eelfinn male growled, eyes lustful. The creature's hand snapped forward, too-sharp nails glittering in the dim light. He drove them directly into the socket around Mat's left eye, then ripped the eye out with a snap.

Mat screamed. Light, but it hurt! More than any wound taken in battle, more than any insult or barb. It was as if the creature had pressed its deceitful claws into his mind and soul.

Mat fell to his knees, spear clattering to the ground as he raised hands to his face. He felt slickness on his cheek, and he screamed again as his fingers felt the empty hole where his eye had been.

He threw his head back and yelled into the room, bellowing in agony.

Eelfinn watched with their horrid, almost-human faces, eyes narrowed in ecstasy as they fed on something rising from Mat. An almost invisible vapor of red and white.

"The savor!" one Eelfinn exclaimed.

"So long!" cried another.

"How it twists around him!" said the one who had taken his eye. "How it spins! Scents of blood in the air! And the gambler becomes the center of all! I can taste *fate* itself!"

Mat howled, his hat falling back as he looked through a single, tear-muddled eye toward the darkness above. His eye socket seemed to be on fire! Blazing! He felt the blood and sera dry on his face, then flake away as he screamed. The Eelfinn drew in deeper breaths, looking drunk.

Mat let out one final scream. Then he clenched his fists and shut his jaw, though he could not stop a low groan—a growl of anger and pain—from sounding deep within his throat. One of the Eelfinn males collapsed, as if overwhelmed. He was the one who had taken Mat's eye. He clutched it in his hands, curling around it. The others stumbled away, finding their way to pillars or the sides of the room, resting against them for support.

Noal dashed to Mat's side, Thom following more carefully, still cradling Moiraine.

"Mat?" Noal asked.

Teeth still clenched against the pain, Mat forced himself to reach back and snatch his hat off the white floor. He was not leaving his hat, burn him. It was a bloody good hat.

He stumbled to his feet.

"Your eye, Mat . . ." Thom said.

"Doesn't matter," Mat said. *Burn me for a fool. A bloody, goat-headed fool.* He could barely think through the agony.

His other eye blinked tears of pain. It really *did* seem

he had lost half of the light of the world. It was like look-ing through a window with one half blackened. Despite the blazing pain in his left socket, he felt as he should be able to open his eye.

But he could not. It was gone. And no Aes Sedai channel-ing could replace that.

He pulled on his hat, defiantly ignoring the pain. He pulled the brim down on the left, shading the empty socket, then bent down and picked up his *ashandarei*, stumbling but managing it.

"I should have been the one to pay," Thom said, voice bitter. "Not you, Mat. You didn't even want to come."

"It was my choice," Mat said. "And I had to do it, any-way. It's one of the answers I was told by the Aelfinn when I first came. I'd have to give up half the light of the world to save the world. Bloody snakes."

"To save the world?" Thom asked, looking down at Moi-raine's peaceful face, her body wrapped in the patchwork cloak. He had left his pack on the floor.

"She has something yet to do," Mat said. The pain was retreating somewhat. "We need her, Thom. Burn me, but it's probably something to do with Rand. Anyway, this had to happen."

"And if it hadn't?" Thom asked. "She said she saw . . ."

"It doesn't matter," Mat said, turning toward the door-way. The Eelfinn were still overwhelmed. One would think *they* had been the ones to lose an eye, looking at those ex-pressions! Mat set his pack on his shoulder, leaving Thom's where it sat. He could not carry two, not and be able to fight.

"Now I've seen something," Noal said, looking over the room and its occupants. "Something no man has ever seen, I warrant. Should we kill them?"

Mat shook his head. "Might break our bargain."

"Will they keep it?" Thom asked.

"Not if they can wiggle out of it," Mat said, then winced again. Light, but his head hurt! Well, he could not sit around and cry like he had lost his favorite foal. "Let's go."

They made their way out of the grand hall. Noal carried a torch, though he had reluctantly left his staff behind, favor-ing his shortsword.

There were no openings in the hallway this time, and Mat

heard Noal muttering at that. It felt right. He had demanded a straight pathway back. The Eelfinn were liars and cheats, but they seemed to be liars and cheats like the Aes Sedai. Mat had made his demands carefully this time, rather than spouting out whatever occurred to him.

The hallway went on for a long while. Noal was growing more and more nervous; Mat kept on forward, footsteps in time with his throbbing skull. How would missing an eye change how he fought? He would have to be more careful of that left side. And he would have trouble judging distance now. In fact, he had that trouble now—walls and floor were disturbingly hard to judge.

Thom clutched Moiraine close to his chest, like a miser holding his gold. What was she to him, anyway? Mat had assumed that Thom was along for the same reason that Mat was—because it felt as if it needed to be done. That tenderness in Thom's face was *not* what Mat had expected to see.

The hallway ended abruptly in a five-sided arch. The room beyond appeared to be the one with the melted slag on the floor. No signs of the fight before were visible, no blood on the floor.

Mat took a deep breath and led the way through. He tensed as he saw Eelfinn here, crouching or standing in the shadows, hissing and growling. They did not move, did not strike, though some yipped quietly. Shadows made them seem even more like foxes. If Mat looked right at one, he could almost mistake them for ordinary men and women, but the way they moved in darkness, sometimes on all fours . . . No man walked like that, with the anxious tension of a chained predator. Like an angry hound, separated from you by a fence and fiercely eager to get to your throat.

But they held to their bargain. None attacked, and Mat began to feel right good about himself once they reached the other side of the room. He had *beaten* them. Last time, they had gotten the better end, but that was only because they had fought like cowards, punching a man who did not know the fight had started.

This time he had been ready. He had shown them that Matrim Cauthon was no fool.

They entered a corridor with the faintly glowing white steam at the top. The floor was of those black, interlocking triangles, curved on the sides like scales. Mat began to breathe easier as they entered one of the rooms with the twisting steam rising from the corners, though his eye socket still hurt like the nethers of a freshly gelded stallion.

He stopped in the center of the room, but then continued forward. He had demanded a straight pathway. That was what he would get. No doubling back and forth this time. "Blood and bloody ashes!" Mat said, realizing something as he walked.

"What?" Thom asked, looking up from Moiraine with alarm.

"My dice," Mat said. "I should have included getting my dice back in the bargain."

"But we discovered you don't need them to guide us."

"It's not about that," Mat grumbled. "I like those dice." He pulled his hat down again, looking down the hallway ahead. Was that motion he saw? All the way in the distance, a good dozen rooms away? No, it must be a trick of the shadows and the shifting steam.

"Mat," Noal said. "I've mentioned that my Old Tongue isn't what it once was. But I think I understood what you said. The bargain you made."

"Yes?" Mat said, only half-listening. Had he been speaking in the Old Tongue again? Burn him. And what *was* that down the hallway?

"Well," Noal said, "you said—as part of the bargain— something like 'you foxes can't knock us down or try to kill us or anything.'"

"Sure did," Mat said.

"You said foxes, Mat," Noal said. "The foxes can't hurt us."

"And they let us pass."

"But what about the others?" Noal asked. "The Aelfinn? If the Eelfinn can't hurt us, are the Aelfinn required to leave us be as well?"

The shadows in the far-distant corridor resolved into figures carrying long, sinuous bronze swords with curving blades. Tall figures, wearing layers of yellow cloth, the hair on their heads straight and black. Dozens of them, who moved with an unnatural grace, eyes staring forward. Eyes with pupils that were vertical slits.

Bloody and bloody ashes!

"Run!" Mat yelled.

"Which direction?" Noal asked, alarmed.

"Any direction!" Mat yelled. "So long as it's away from them!"

CHAPTER

55

The One Left Behind

A loud boom shook the hallways, making the entire structure rumble. Mat stumbled, leaning against the wall for support as smoke and chips of rock sprayed out of the opening behind them.

He ducked his head around and looked down the hallway as Thom and Noal ran onward, Thom clutching Moiraine. Noal had tossed his torch aside and gotten out a drum to try to soothe the Aelfinn. That had not worked, and so Mat had turned to the exploding cylinders and nightflowers.

Light, but the cylinders were deadly! He saw corpses of Aelfinn lying scattered through the hallway, their glistening skin ripped and torn, evil-looking smoke steaming from their blood. Others slid out of doorways and alcoves, pushing through the smoke. They walked on two legs, but they seemed to slither as they walked, waving back and forth through the hallway, their hissing growing angrier and angrier.

Heart pounding, Mat charged after Thom and Noal. "They still following?" Noal called.

"What do you think?" Mat said, catching up to the other two. "Light, but those snakes are *fast*!"

Mat and the other two burst into another room, identical to all of the others. Vaguely off-scale square walls, steam rising from the corners, black triangle-pattern floor tiles. There was no triangular opening at the center to get them out. Blood and bloody ashes.

Mat glanced at the three ways out, holding his *ashandarei* in sweaty hands. They could not do the same trick as before, bouncing back and forth between the same two rooms.

Not with the Aelfinn behind them. He needed to invoke his luck. He prepared to spin, and—

"We have to keep moving!" Noal yelled. He had stopped by the doorway, dancing from one toe to the next in anxiety. "Mat! If those snakes catch us . . ."

Mat could hear them behind, hissing. Like the rush of a river. He picked a direction and ran.

"Throw another cylinder!" Thom said.

"That was the last one!" Mat said. "And we've only got three nightflowers." His pack was feeling light.

"Music doesn't work on them," Noal said, throwing aside his drum. "They're too angry."

Mat cursed and lit a nightflower with a striker, then tossed it over his shoulder. The three of them barreled into another room, then continued on directly through the doorway on the other side.

"I don't know what way to go, lad," Thom said. He sounded so winded! "We're lost."

"I've been picking directions at random!" Mat said.

"Only you can't go backward," Thom said. "That's probably the direction the luck wants us to go!"

The nightflower boomed, the explosion echoing through the corridors. It was not nearly as great as that of the cylinders. Mat risked a glance over his shoulder, seeing smoke and sparks fly through the tunnel. The fire slowed the Aelfinn, but soon the more daring members of the band slithered through the smoke.

"Maybe we can negotiate!" Thom panted.

"They look too angry!" Noal said.

"Mat," Thom said, "you mentioned that they knew about your eye. They answered a question about it."

"They told me I'd bloody give up half the light of the world," Mat said, skull still throbbing. "I didn't want to know, but they told me anyway."

"What else did they say?" Thom asked. "Anything that can be a clue? How did you get out last time?"

"They threw me out," Mat said.

He and the others burst into another room—no doorway—then dashed out the left-hand exit. What Thom had said before was correct. They probably needed to double back. But they could not, not with that nest of vipers following so closely!

"They threw me out of the doorframe in the Aelfinn realm," Mat said, feeling winded. "It leads to the basement of the Stone of Tear."

"Then maybe we can find that!" Thom said. "Your luck, Mat. Have it take us to the Aelfinn realm."

It might work. "All right," he said, closing his eye and spinning about.

Mat pointed in a direction and opened his eye. He was pointing directly toward the gang of Aelfinn, weaving up the corridor toward them.

"Bloody ashes!" Mat cursed, turning and running away from them, picking another corridor at random.

Thom joined him, but was looking *very* wearied. Mat could take Moiraine from him for a while, but Thom would be so tired he would not be able to fight. The Aelfinn were going to run them ragged, as they had Birgitte centuries ago.

In the next room, Thom stumbled to a halt, drooping, though he still held Moiraine. Like all of the chambers, this one had four ways out. But the only way that mattered was one directly toward the Aelfinn. The one they couldn't take.

"There's no winning this game," Thom said, panting. "Even if we cheat, there's no winning."

"Thom . . ." Mat said urgently. He handed Thom his *ashandarei*, then picked up Moiraine. She was so light. A good thing, too, otherwise Thom would never have lasted as long as he had.

Noal glanced at them, then down the corridor. The Aelfinn would be on them in moments. Noal met Mat's eye. "Give me your pack. I need those nightflowers."

"But—"

"No arguing!" Noal said. He dashed over and snagged one of the nightflowers. It had a very short fuse. He lit it and tossed it into the corridor. The Aelfinn were close enough that Mat could hear them scream and hiss as they saw the firework.

The boom came, sparks spurting out of the corridor and lighting the dark room. Where sparks came close to one of the rising columns of steam, that steam shied back, dancing away from the flames. The air smelled strongly of smoke and sulphur. Light, his socket was throbbing again.

"Now, Mat," Noal said, Mat's ears still ringing from the blast, "give me the pack."

"What are you doing?" Mat said warily as Noal took the pack, then fished out the last nightflower.

"You can see it, Mat," Noal said. "We need more time. You have to get far enough ahead of those vipers that you can double back a few times, let your luck work you out of this."

Noal nodded to one of the corridors. "These corridors are narrow. Good choke points. A man could stand there and only have to fight one or two at a time. He'd last maybe a few minutes."

"Noal!" Thom said, wheezing, standing with his hands on his knees, near Mat's *ashandarei* leaning against the wall. "You can't do this."

"Yes I can," Noal said. He stepped up to the corridor, beyond which the Aelfinn gathered. "Thom, you're in no shape to fight. Mat, you're the one whose luck can find the way out. Neither of you can stay. But I can."

"There will be no coming back for you," Mat said grimly. "As soon as we double back, this flaming place will take us somewhere else."

Noal met his eye, that weathered face determined. "I know. A price, Mat. We knew this place would demand a price. Well, I've seen a lot of things, done a lot of things. I've been used, Mat, one too many times. This is as good a place as any to meet the end."

Mat stood up, lifting Moiraine, then nodded in respect to Noal. "Come on, Thom."

"But—"

"Come *on*!" Mat barked, dashing to one of the other doorways. Thom hesitated, then cursed and joined him, carrying Mat's torch in one hand and his *ashandarei* in the other. Noal stepped into the corridor behind, hefting his shortsword. Shapes moved in the smoke beyond him.

"Mat," Noal called, glancing over his shoulder.

Mat waved Thom on, but hesitated, looking back.

"If you ever meet a Malkieri," Noal said, "you tell him Jain Farstrider died clean."

"I will, Jain," Mat said. "May the Light hold you."

Noal turned back to face the Aelfinn and Mat left him.

There was another boom as a nightflower went off. Then Mat heard Noal's voice echo down the corridor as he screamed a battlecry. It was not in any tongue Mat had ever heard.

He and Thom entered another chamber. Thom was weeping, but Mat held his tears. Noal would die with honor. Once, Mat would have thought that kind of thinking foolish—what good was honor if you were dead? But he had too many memories of soldiers, had spent too much time with men who fought and bled for that honor, to discredit such notions now.

He closed his eye and spun, Moiraine's weight almost unbalancing him. He picked a direction and found himself pointing back the way they had come. He charged down the corridor, Thom following.

When they reached the end of the corridor, it did not open into the room where they had left Noal. This room was round and was filled with yellow columns, made in the shape of enormous vines twisting around one another with an open cylinder of space at the center. Coiled lamp stands held globes of white that gave the room a soft light, and the floor was tiled in the pattern of white and yellow strips, spiraling out from the center. It smelled pungently of dry snakeskin.

Matrim Cauthon, you're no hero, he thought, glancing over his shoulder. *That man you left behind,* he's *the hero. Light illumine you, Noal.*

"Now what?" Thom asked. He seemed to have recovered some of his strength, so Mat handed back Moiraine and took his spear. There were only two doorways in this room, the one behind and one directly across the chamber. But Mat spun with his eye closed anyway. The luck pointed them to the doorway opposite the one they had entered.

They took it. The windows in this hallway looked out at the jungle, and they were now down in the thick of it. Mat occasionally spotted those three spires. The place where they had been moments ago, the place where Noal bled.

"This is where you got your answers, isn't it?" Thom asked.

Mat nodded.

"You think I could get some of those myself?" Thom asked. "Three questions. Any answers you like. . . ."

"You don't want them," Mat said, tugging down the brim of his hat. "Trust me, you don't. They aren't answers. They're threats. Promises. We—"

Thom stopped beside him. In Thom's arms, Moiraine was beginning to stir. She let out a soft groan, eyes still closed. But that was not what made Mat freeze.

He could see another circular yellow room up ahead. Sitting in the middle of that room was a redstone doorway. Or what was left of it.

Mat cursed, running forward. The floor was strewn with chunks of red rock rubble. Mat groaned, dropping his spear and taking a few of the chunks, holding them up. The doorway had been shattered by something, a blow of awesome force.

Near the entrance to the room, Thom sank down, holding the stirring Moiraine. He looked exhausted. Neither of them had a pack anymore; Mat had given his to Noal, and Thom had left his behind. And this room was a dead end, with no other doorways.

"Burn this place!" Mat shouted, ripping off his hat, staring up into the expansive, endless darkness above. "Burn you all, snakes and foxes! Dark One take the lot of you. You have my eye, you have Noal. That's enough of a price for you! That's *too much* of a price! Isn't the life of Jain bloody Farstrider enough to appease you, you monsters!"

His words rang and vanished, with no reply. The old gleeman squeezed his eyes shut, holding Moiraine. He looked beaten, ground down to nothing. His hands were red and blistered from pulling her free, his coat sleeves burned.

Mat looked about, desperate. He tried spinning about with eye closed, pointing. When he opened his eye, he was pointing at the center of the room. The broken doorway.

It was then that he felt hope start to die inside of him.

"It was a good try, lad," Thom said. "We did well. Better than we should have expected."

"I won't give up," Mat said, trying to defy the crushing sense inside of him. "We'll . . . we'll retrace our steps, find a way back to the place between the Aelfinn and Eelfinn. The bargain said they had to leave that portal open. We'll take it and get out of here, Thom. I'll be burned if I'm going to die in here. You still owe me a couple of mugs."

Thom opened his eyes and smiled, but did not stand up.

He shook his head, those drooping mustaches wagging, and looked down at Moiraine.

Her eyes fluttered open. "Thom," she whispered, smiling. "I thought I heard your voice."

Light, but her voice took Mat back. To other times. Ages ago.

She glanced at him. "And Mat. Dear Matrim. I knew you would come for me. Both of you. I wish you hadn't, but I knew you would. . . ."

"Rest, Moiraine," Thom said softly. "We'll be out of here in two strums of a harp."

Mat looked at her, lying there, helpless. "Burn me. I'm not going to let it end like this!"

"They're coming, lad," Thom said. "I can hear them."

Mat turned to look through the opening. He could see what Thom had heard. The Aelfinn crept through the corridor, sinuous and deadly. They smiled, and he could see fanglike incisors at the forefront of those smiles. They could have been human, save for those fangs. And those eyes. Those unnatural, slitted eyes. They moved sleekly. Terrible, eager.

"No," Mat whispered. "There *has* to be a way." *Think,* he told himself. *Mat, you fool. There has to be a way out. How did you escape the last time?* Noal had asked. That was no help.

Thom, looking desperate, unhooked his harp from his back. He began to play it. Mat recognized the tune, "Sweet Whispers of Tomorrow." A mournful sound, played for the fallen dead. It was beautiful.

Remarkably, the music did seem to soothe the Aelfinn. They slowed, the ones at the front beginning to sway to the beat of the melody as they walked. They knew. Thom played for his own funeral.

"I don't know how I got out last time," Mat whispered. "I was unconscious. I woke up being hanged. Rand cut me down."

He raised a hand to his scar. His original Aelfinn answers revealed nothing. He knew about the Daughter of the Nine Moons, he knew about giving up half the light of the world. He knew about Rhuidean. It all made sense. No holes. No questions.

Except. . . .

What did the Eelfinn give you?

"If I had my way," Mat whispered, staring at the oncoming Aelfinn, "I would want those holes filled."

The Aelfinn slithered forward, wearing those cloths of yellow wrapping their bodies. Thom's music spun in the air, echoing. The creatures approached with steady, slow steps. They knew they had their prey now.

The two Aelfinn at the front carried swords of gleaming bronze, dripping red. Poor Noal.

Thom began to sing. "Oh, how long were the days of a man. When he strode upon a broken land."

Mat listened, memories blossoming in his mind. Thom's voice carried him to days long ago. Days in his own memories, days of the memories of others. Days when he had died, days when he had lived, days when he had fought and when he had won.

"I want those holes filled . . ." Mat whispered to himself. "That's what I said. The Eelfinn obliged, giving me memories that were not my own."

Moiraine's eyes had closed again, but she smiled as she listened to Thom's music. Mat had thought Thom was playing for the Aelfinn, but now he wondered if he was playing for Moiraine. A last, melancholy song for a failed rescue.

"He sailed as far as a man could steer," Thom sang, voice sonorous, beautiful. "And he never wished to lose his fear."

"I want those holes filled," Mat repeated, "so they gave me memories. That was my first boon."

"For the fear of man is a thing untold. It keeps him safe, and it proves him bold!"

"I asked something else, not knowing it," Mat said. "I said I wanted to be free of Aes Sedai and the Power. They gave me the medallion for that. Another gift."

"Don't let fear make you cease to strive, for that fear it proves you remain alive!"

"And . . . and I asked for one more thing. I said I wanted to be away from them and back to Rhuidean. The Eelfinn gave me everything I asked for. The memories to fill my holes. The medallion to keep me free from the Power. . . ."

And what? They sent him back to Rhuidean to hang. But hanging was a price, not an answer to his demands.

"I will walk this broken road," Thom sang, voice growing louder, "and I will carry a heavy load!"

"They did give me something else," Mat whispered, looking down at the *ashandarei* in his hands as the Aelfinn began to hiss more loudly.

Thus is our treaty written; thus is agreement made.

It was carved on the weapon. The blade had two ravens, the shaft inscribed with words in the Old Tongue.

Thought is the arrow of time; memory never fades.

Why had they given it to him? He had never questioned it. But he had not asked for a weapon.

What was asked is given. The price is paid.

No, I didn't ask for a weapon. I asked for a way out.

And they gave me this.

"So come at me with your awful lies," Thom bellowed the final line of the song. "I'm a man of truth, and I'll *meet your eyes!*"

Mat spun the *ashandarei* and thrust it into the wall. The point sank into the not-stone. Light sprayed out around it, spilling free like blood gushing from a split vein. Mat screamed, ramming it in farther. Powerful waves of light erupted from the wall.

He drew the *ashandarei* down at an angle, making a slit. He pulled the weapon up the other side, cutting out a large inverse triangle of light. The light seemed to *thrum* as it washed across him. The Aelfinn had reached the doorway by Thom, but they hissed, shying back from the powerful radiance.

Mat finished by drawing a wavy line down the middle of the triangle. He could barely see, the light was so bright. The section of the wall in front of him fell away, revealing a glowing white passage that seemed to be cut out of steel.

"Well I'll . . ." Thom whispered, standing up.

The Aelfinn screamed with high-pitched anger. They entered the room, arms raised to shield their eyes, wicked swords gripped in opposing hands.

"Get her out!" Mat bellowed, spinning to face the creatures. He lifted the *ashandarei*, using the butt end to smash the face of the first Aelfinn. "Go!"

Thom grabbed Moiraine, then spared a glance at Mat.

"*Go!*" Mat repeated, smashing the arm of another Aelfinn.

Thom leaped into the doorway and vanished. Mat smiled, spinning among the Aelfinn with his *ashandarei*, laying into legs, arms, heads. There were a lot of them, but they seemed dazed by the light, frenzied to get to him. As he tripped the first few, the others stumbled. The creatures became a squirming mass of sinuous arms and legs, hissing and spitting in anger, several of those in back trying to crawl over the pile to reach him.

Mat stepped back and tipped his hat to the creatures. "Looks like the game can be won after all," he said. "Tell the foxes I'm mighty pleased with this key they gave me. Also, you can all go rot in a flaming pit of fire and ashes, you unwashed lumps on a pig's backside. Have a grand bloody day."

He held his hat and leaped through the opening.

All flashed white.

CHAPTER
56

Something Wrong

A soft knock came at the post outside Egwene's tent. "Come," she said, shuffling through the papers on her desk.

Gawyn slipped in. He'd given up his fine clothing, choosing trousers of brown and a slightly lighter shirt. A Warder's color-shifting cloak hung around his shoulders, making him blend into his surroundings. Egwene herself was wearing a regal dress of green and blue.

His cloak rustled as he took a seat beside her desk. "Elayne's army is crossing. She sent word that she's on her way to come visit our camp."

"Excellent," Egwene said.

Gawyn nodded, but he was troubled. Such a useful thing, that ball of emotions caused by the bond. If she'd known earlier the depth of his devotion to her, she'd have bonded him weeks ago.

"What?" Egwene asked, setting aside her papers.

"Aybara," he said. "He hasn't agreed to meet with you."

"Elayne said he might be difficult."

"I think he's going to take al'Thor's side," Gawyn said. "You can see it in the way he set up camp, apart from everyone else. He sent messengers immediately to the Aiel and to the Tairens. He's got a good army, Egwene. A huge one. With Whitecloaks in it."

"That doesn't sound likely to make him side with Rand," Egwene said.

"Doesn't seem like it makes him likely to side with us either," Gawyn said. "Egwene . . . Galad leads the Whitecloaks."

"Your *brother*?"

"Yes." Gawyn shook his head. "This many armies, this many loyalties, all rubbing against one another. Aybara and his force could be a spark that sends us all up like a firework."

"It will be better when Elayne settles in," Egwene said.

"Egwene, what if al'Thor isn't coming? What if he did this to distract everyone from whatever else he's doing?"

"Why would he do that?" Egwene said. "He's already proven that he can avoid being found, if he wants to." She shook her head. "Gawyn, he *knows* he shouldn't break those seals. A part of him does, at least. Perhaps that's why he told me—so I could gather resistance, so I could talk him out of it."

Gawyn nodded. No further complaint or argument. It was a wonder how he'd changed. He was as intense as ever, yet less abrasive. Ever since that night with the assassins, he had started doing as she asked. Not as a servant. As a partner dedicated to seeing her will done.

It was a wonderful thing. It was also important, since the Hall of the Tower seemed determined to overturn their agreement to let her take charge of dealings with Rand. She looked down at her stack of papers, not a few of which were letters of "advice" from Sitters.

But they came to her, rather than circumventing her. That was good, and she couldn't ignore them. She had to make them continue to believe that working *with* her was for the best. At the same time, she couldn't let them assume that she'd be blown over by a few good shouts.

Such a delicate balance. "Well, let's go meet your sister, then."

Gawyn rose, moving smoothly. The three rings he wore on a chain around his neck rattled as he moved; she'd have to ask him again where he'd gotten those. He had been oddly closemouthed about them. He held open the tent flaps for her, and she stepped out.

Outside, the late-afternoon sun was hidden by gray clouds. Bryne's soldiers worked busily on a palisade. His army had swelled during the last few weeks, and they dominated the eastern side of the wide, forest-rimmed grassland that had once been known as Merrilor. The ruins of the tower fortress that had stood here were strewn across the northern side of the field, moss-covered, nearly hidden by chokevine.

Egwene's tent was on a rise, and she could overlook the many armies encamped here. "Is that one new?" she asked, gesturing toward a smaller force that had taken up a position just below the ruins.

"They came on their own," Gawyn said. "Farmers, mostly. Not really a true army; most don't have swords. Pitchforks, wood axes, quarterstaffs. I assume al'Thor sent them. They started wandering in yesterday."

"Curious," Egwene said. They seemed a varied bunch, with mismatched tents and little understanding of how to set up an army camp. But there did seem to be some five or ten thousand of them. "Have some scouts keep an eye on them."

Gawyn nodded.

Egwene turned and noted a procession moving through several gateways nearby, setting up camp. The Lion of Andor flew high above them, and the soldiers marched in orderly rows. A procession in red and white had left them and was marching toward Egwene's camp, the banner of the Queen flying above them.

Gawyn accompanied Egwene across the yellowed grass to meet Elayne. The Andoran Queen had certainly taken her time. Only one day until the time specified by Rand. Still, she had come, as had others. Aiel had accompanied Darlin from Tear, and her persuasion had been enough to bring a large contingent of Illianers, who camped on the western side of the grass.

The Cairhienin were Elayne's now, by reports, and were coming through with the Andorans and a large number of men from the Band of the Red Hand. Egwene had sent an offer, and a woman to offer Traveling, to King Roedran of Murandy, but she was uncertain if he would come. Even without him, however, a considerable number of the world's nations were represented here, particularly since the flags of Ghealdan and Mayene could be seen among Perrin's armies. She would have to contact their two rulers and see if she could sway them to her way of thinking. But even if not, surely what she had gathered would be enough to convince Rand to change his plans. Light send it was enough.

She didn't want to think of what would happen if he forced her hand.

She walked down the pathway, nodding back to sisters who nodded and Accepted who curtsied, soldiers who saluted and servants who bowed. Rand would—

"It *can't* be," Gawyn said suddenly, freezing in place.

"Gawyn?" she said, frowning. "Are you—"

He took off at a run across the weed-strewn hill. Egwene looked after him with dissatisfaction. He still had an impulsive streak. Why was he so upset, suddenly? It wasn't worry; she could feel that. It was confusion. She hastened after him with as much speed as decorum would allow. Elayne's envoy had stopped in the dead grass.

Gawyn was on his knees there, before someone. An older woman with red-gold hair, standing beside a smiling Elayne, who still sat her horse.

Ah, Egwene thought. Her spies had delivered word of this rumor just last night, but she'd wanted to confirm it before speaking to Gawyn.

Morgase Trakand lived.

Egwene stood back, for now. Once she stepped forward, Elayne would have to kiss her ring and the entire procession would bow; that would spoil Gawyn's moment. As she waited, the clouds above grew thinner.

Suddenly they split, the dark thunderheads pulling back. The sky became an open field of blue, a deep, pure expanse. Elayne's eyes opened wide, and she turned on her horse, looking at Perrin's section of camp.

He's come, then, Egwene thought. *And the calm is here. The brief moment of peace before the storm that destroys.*

"You give it a try, Emarin," Androl said, standing with a small group inside a stand of trees near the border of the Black Tower grounds.

The stately nobleman concentrated, holding the One Power. Weaves sprang up around him. He was remarkably skillful, considering his short time practicing, and expertly crafted the weave for a gateway.

Instead of opening a hole in the air, the weave unraveled and vanished. Emarin turned to the rest of them, sweat streaming down his face. "Forming those weaves seemed harder than before," he said.

"Why won't they work?" Evin said. The young man's youthful face flushed with anger—as if the problem with gateways was an insult.

Androl shook his head, arms folded. The trees rustled, leaves shivering, many falling to the ground. Brown, as if it were autumn. That unnerved him. He'd spent some time working the ground during his journeys in life, and had acquired a farmer's sense for right and wrong regarding the land.

"You try it again, Androl," Evin said. "You're always so good with gateways."

He glanced at the other three. Canler was the other one there; the aging Andoran farmer wore a deep frown. Of course, Canler often scowled at one thing or another.

Androl closed his eyes, emptying himself of all passions, embracing the void. *Saidin* shone in there, life and Power. He seized it, drinking it in. He opened his eyes to a world that was more vibrant. Could dead plants look both sickly and vibrant at the same time? A strange juxtaposition made possible by *saidin*.

He focused. Making gateways came so much easier to him than other weaves did; he'd never understood why. Though he couldn't break even a small rock apart by channeling, he could make a gateway large enough for a wagon to drive through. Logain had called it impressive; Taim had called it impossible.

This time, Androl pushed all of the Power he had into his weave. He understood gateways. They made sense. Maybe it was the innate fondness he had for traveling, for discovering new places and new arts.

The weaves came together. He didn't notice any of the difficulty that Emarin had mentioned. However, when the familiar slash of light should have come, the weave began to unravel instead. Androl tried to hold to it, pulling it together. For a moment, it looked like that would work. Then the threads slid from his grip, evaporating. The gateway never formed.

"The other weaves I've tried all work," Evin said, making a globe of light. "Every one of them."

"Only gateways," Canler said with a grunt.

"It's like . . ." Emarin said. "It's as if something wants to keep us here. In the Black Tower."

"Try them in other places inside the perimeter," Androl said. "But try not to let any of Taim's loyalists see what you're doing. Pretend to be surveying, as Taim ordered."

The men nodded, the three of them hiking toward the east. Androl left the glade. Norley was standing beside the road, looking about for him. The short, thick-waisted Cairhienin man waved and approached. Androl met him halfway. Norley had an open, inviting smile. Nobody ever suspected him of spying on them, something Androl had put to good use.

"You spoke with Mezar?" Androl asked.

"Sure did," Norley replied. "Shared a lunch with him." Norley waved at Mishraile as they passed him supervising a group of soldiers practicing their weaves. The golden-haired man turned away dismissively.

"And?" Androl asked, tense.

"It's not really Mezar," Norley said. "Oh, it has Mezar's face, right enough. But it's not him. I can see it in his eyes. Trouble is, whatever the thing is, it has Mezar's memories. Talks right like him. But the smile is wrong. All wrong."

Androl shivered. "It has to be him, Norley."

"It ain't. I promise you that."

"But—"

"It just *ain't*," the stout man said.

Androl took a deep breath. When Mezar had returned a few days back—explaining that Logain was well and that all would soon be resolved with Taim—Androl had begun to hope that there was a way out of this mess. But something had seemed off about the man. Beyond that, the M'Hael had made a great show of accepting Mezar as a full Asha'man; the Dragon had raised him. And now Mezar—once fiercely loyal to Logain—was spending his time with Coteren and Taim's other lackeys.

"This is getting bad, Androl," Norley said softly, smiling and waving toward another group of practicing men. "I'd say it's time for us to leave here, whether or not it's against orders."

"We'd never get past those guard posts," Androl said.

"Taim won't even let those Aes Sedai leave; you heard the fit that plump one threw at the gates the other day. Taim doubles the guard at night, and gateways don't work."

"Well, we have to do something, don't we? I mean . . . what if they've got Logain? What then?"

"I . . ." *I don't know.* "Go talk to the others who are loyal to Logain. I'm going to move us to a shared barrack. Them and their families. We'll tell the M'Hael that we want to give more space for his new recruits. Then we'll post a guard at nights."

"That's going to be a little obvious."

"The division is already obvious," Androl said. "Go do it."

"Sure thing. But what are you going to do?"

Androl took a deep breath. "I'm going to find us some allies."

Norley moved off to the left, but Androl continued down the path, through the village. It seemed that fewer and fewer people were showing him respect these days. Either they were afraid to do so, or they'd thrown their lot in with Taim.

Packs of black-coated men stood, with arms folded, watching him. Androl tried not to feel a chill. As he walked, he noted Mezar—hair graying at the sides, skin a Domani copper—standing with a group of lackeys. The man smiled at him. Mezar hadn't ever been one who smiled easily. Androl nodded to him, meeting his eyes.

And he saw what Norley had seen. Something was deeply wrong, something not-quite-alive inside those eyes. This didn't seem to be a man, but a parody of one. A shadow stuffed inside human skin.

Light help us all, Androl thought, hurrying by. He made his way to the southern side of the village, to a group of small huts with bleached white wood walls and thatched roofs that needed to be replaced.

Androl hesitated outside. What was he doing? This was where the women of the *Red Ajah* were staying. They said they'd come to bond the Asha'man, but they hadn't done it so far. That was obviously some kind of ruse. Perhaps they'd come here to try to find a way to gentle the entire lot.

But if that were the case, then at least he could count on them not siding with Taim. When you stared down the gullet of a lionfish, a pirate's brig didn't seem so bad. Androl had heard the saying once while working a fisher's boat in the south.

Taking a deep breath, he knocked. The plump Red answered the door. She had the ageless face of an Aes Sedai—not young, really, but also not old. She eyed him.

"I hear you want to leave the Black Tower," Androl said, hoping he was doing the right thing.

"Has your M'Hael changed his mind?" she asked, sounding hopeful. She actually smiled. A rare action for an Aes Sedai.

"No," Androl said, "so far as I know, he still forbids you to leave."

She frowned. "Then—"

Androl lowered his voice. "You're not the only one who would like to leave this place, Aes Sedai."

She looked at him, her face becoming perfectly calm. *She doesn't trust me,* he thought. Odd, how the mere lack of emotion could itself convey meaning.

Desperate, he took a step forward, laying a hand on the frame of the door. "Something's wrong in this place. Something worse than you understand. Once, long ago, men and women who worked the Power strove together. They were stronger for it. Please. Hear me out."

She stood for a moment longer, then pulled the door open. "Come in, quickly. Tarna—the woman I share this hut with—is away. We must be done before she returns."

Androl stepped up into the building. He didn't know whether he was stepping into the pirate's brig or the lionfish's mouth. But it would have to do.

CHAPTER

57

A Rabbit for Supper

Mat hit uneven ground, blinded by the flash of light. Cursing, he used the *ashandarei* to steady himself on the springy earth. He smelled foliage, dirt and rotting wood. Insects buzzed in the shade.

The whiteness faded, and he found himself standing outside the Tower of Ghenjei. He had half-expected to reappear in Rhuidean. It seemed that the spear returned him to his world in the place where he had entered. Thom sat on the ground, propping up Moiraine, who was blinking and looking about her.

Mat spun on the tower and pointed upward. "I know you're watching!" he said, thrilled. He had made it. He had *bloody* made it out alive! "I beat you, you crusty boot-leavings! I, Matrim Cauthon, survived your traps! Ha!" He raised the *ashandarei* over his head. "And *you* gave me the way out! Chew on that bitterness for lunch, you flaming, burning, misbegotten liars!"

Mat beamed, slamming the spear down butt first onto the ground beside him. He nodded. Nobody got the better of Matrim Cauthon. They had lied to him, told him vague prophecies and threatened him, and then they had hanged him. But Mat came out ahead in the end.

"Who was the other?" Moiraine's soft voice asked from behind. "The one I saw, but did not know?"

"He didn't make it out," Thom said somberly.

That dampened Mat's spirits. Their victory had come at a price, a terrible one. Mat had been traveling with a legend all this time?

"He was a friend," Thom said softly.

"He was a great man," Mat said, turning and pulling his *ashandarei* from where he had planted it in the dirt. "When you write the ballad of all this, Thom, make sure you point out that he was the hero."

Thom glanced at Mat, then nodded knowingly. "The world will want to know what happened to that man." Light. As Mat thought about it, Thom had not been at all surprised to hear Noal was Jain Farstrider. He had *known*. When had he figured it out? Why had he said nothing to Mat? Some friend Thom was.

Mat just shook his head. "Well, we're out, one way or another. But Thom, next time I want to do the bloody negotiating, sneak up behind and hit me on the head with something large, heavy and blunt. Then take over."

"Your request is noted."

"Let's move on a little way. I don't like that bloody tower looming over me."

"Yes," Moiraine said, "you could say that they feed off emotion. Though I wouldn't call it 'feeding off' so much as 'delighting in' emotion. They don't *need* it to survive, but it pleases them greatly."

They sat in a wooded hollow a short walk from the tower, next to the meadow beside the Arinelle. The thick tree canopy cooled the air and obscured their view of the tower.

Mat sat on a small, mossy boulder as Thom made a fire. He had a few of Aludra's strikers in his pocket as well as some packets of tea, though there was nothing to warm the water in.

Moiraine sat on the ground, still wrapped in Thom's cloak, leaning back against a fallen log. She held the cloak closed from the inside, letting it envelop her completely, save for her face and those dark curls. She looked more a woman than Mat remembered—in his memories, she was like a statue. Always expressionless, face like polished stone, eyes like dark brown topaz.

Now she sat with pale skin, flushed cheeks, hair curled and falling naturally around her face. She was fetching, save for that ageless Aes Sedai face. Yet that face showed far more emotion than Mat remembered, a look of fondness when she glanced at Thom, a faint shiver when she spoke of her time in the tower.

She glanced at Mat, and her eyes were still appraising. Yes, this was the same Moiraine. Humbled, cast down. That made her seem *stronger* to him for some reason.

Thom blew at a hesitant flame that curled a lock of smoke into the air before flickering out. The wood was probably too wet. Thom cursed.

"It's all right, Thom," Moiraine said softly. "I will be well."

"I won't have you catching cold the moment we free you from that *place*," Thom said. He got out a striker, but suddenly the wood sparked, and then fire sputtered to life as it consumed the too-wet tinder.

Mat glanced at Moiraine, who had a look of concentration on her face.

"Oh," Thom said, then chuckled. "I'd forgotten about that, nearly. . . ."

"It's all I can manage now on my own," Moiraine said, grimacing. Light, had Moiraine *grimaced* before? She had been too high-and-mighty for that, had she not? Or was Mat remembering her wrong?

Moiraine. He was talking to flaming *Moiraine*! Though he had gone into the tower with the distinct purpose of rescuing her, it seemed incredible that he was speaking with her. It was like talking to . . .

Well, like talking to Birgitte Silverbow or Jain Farstrider. Mat smiled, shaking his head. What a world this was, and what a strange place he had in it.

"What did you mean by that, Moiraine?" Thom asked, nurturing the fire with some sticks. "It's all you can manage?"

"The Aelfinn and Eelfinn," she explained, voice calm. "They savor and relish powerful emotions. For some reason the effects of a *ta'veren* are even more intoxicating to them. There are other things that they enjoy."

Thom glanced at her, frowning.

"My Power, Thom," she explained. "I could hear them barking and hissing to one another as they fed on me, both Aelfinn and Eelfinn in turn. They have not often had an Aes Sedai to themselves, it seems. While draining my ability to channel, they were fed twofold—my sorrow at what I was losing and the Power itself. My capacity has been greatly reduced.

"They claimed to have killed Lanfear by draining her too quickly, though I think they may have been trying to make me afraid. A man was there once, when they woke me. He said I was not the one he wanted." She hesitated, then shivered. "Sometimes I wished that they would drain me quickly and end my life."

The small camp grew silent save for the popping of the fire. Thom looked toward Moiraine, seeming helpless.

"Do not show me such sorrow, Thom Merrilin," Moiraine said, smiling. "I have felt terrible things, but all people know such moments of despair. I believed that you would come." She removed her hand from the cloak—revealing a slender, pale shoulder and collarbone—and reached toward him. He hesitated, then took the hand and squeezed it.

Moiraine looked to Mat. "And you, Matrim Cauthon. Not a simple farm lad any longer. Does your eye pain you much?"

Mat shrugged.

"I would Heal the wound if I could," Moiraine said. "But even were I still as strong as I once was, I couldn't restore your eye." She looked down, releasing Thom's hand and holding up her arm. "Do you have the *angreal*?"

"Oh, yes," Thom said, fishing the strange bracelet out of his pocket. He put it on her arm.

"With this," Moiraine said. "I will be strong enough to at least take the pain away. They placed it on me to let me draw more of the Power, to make their feeding more succulent. I asked for it, actually, as one of my three demands. I did not realize they would end up using it against me."

"They gave you your three demands?" Mat asked, frowning.

"I passed through the *ter'angreal*," she said. "The ancient treaty held for both of us, though with the doorway destroyed, there was no simple return. I knew from . . . previous events that I would not escape unless you came for me, no matter what my demands were or how carefully I worded them. So I used them for the best."

"What did you ask for?" Mat asked. "Beyond the *angreal*?"

She smiled. "I shall keep that to myself, for now. You do have my thanks, young Matrim. For my life."

"Then I guess we're equal," he said. "You saved me from life in the Two Rivers. Burn me if I haven't had a nice gallop of it since then."

"And your wound?"

"Doesn't hurt so much." Actually, it throbbed. Really, really badly. "No need for you to waste strength on it."

"Still afraid of the One Power, I see."

He bristled. "Afraid?"

"I should think you have good reason for that wariness." She looked away from him. "But take care. The most displeasing of events in our lives are sometimes for our good."

Yes, she was still Moiraine. Quick with a moral and advice. But perhaps she had a right—after what she had been through—to lecture on suffering. Light! She had *known* what she would have to go through, and yet she had still pulled Lanfear into that *ter'angreal*? Maybe Mat was not the hero here, and maybe Noal was not either.

"So what now?" Thom said, settling back on a stump. The warmth of the fire did feel good.

"I must find Rand," Moiraine said. "He will need my help. I trust he has done well in my absence?"

"I don't know about that," Mat said. "He's half mad and the whole bloody world is at one another's throats." Colors swirled. Rand eating a meal with Min. Mat dispelled the image.

She raised an eyebrow.

"But," Mat acknowledged, "he's got most everybody pointed toward the Last Battle. And Verin says he managed to clean the taint from *saidin*."

"Blessed Light," Moiraine whispered. "How?"

"I don't know."

"This changes everything," she said, smile deepening. "He has fixed what he once set wrong. 'By the Dragon came our pain, and by the Dragon was the wound repaired.'"

"Mat keeps saying we should be having a festival or something to celebrate," Thom noted. "Though maybe he only wants a good excuse to get drunk."

"I'd say that's a certainty," Mat added. "Anyway, Rand's been busy. Elayne says he's got some kind of meeting arranged with the monarchs under him coming up soon."

"Elayne is Queen, then?"

"Sure is. Everyone thought her mother was killed by Rahvin, but she had run away," Mat said.

"Yes, you told me Rahvin had killed Morgase."

"I did? When?"

"A lifetime ago, Matrim," she replied, smiling.

"Oh. Well, Rand finished him off. So that's good."

"And the other Forsaken?" Moiraine asked.

"Don't know," Mat said.

"Mat's been too busy to keep track," Thom added. "He's been spending his time marrying the Empress of the Seanchan."

Moiraine blinked in surprise. "You did *what*?"

"It was an accident," Mat said lamely, hunching down.

"You *accidentally* married the Seanchan Empress?"

"They've got some odd customs," Mat said, pulling his hat down. "Strange folk." He forced out a chuckle.

"*Ta'veren*," Moiraine said.

Somehow, he had known she would say that. Light. Well, it was good to have her back. Mat was surprised at how strongly he felt that. Who would have thought it? Affection for an Aes Sedai, from him?

"Well," she said, "I can see there are many tales I need to be told. But for now, we will need to seek out Rand."

He had also known that she would try to take charge. "You find him, Moiraine, but I've got things to do in Caemlyn. Don't mean to argue and all, but that's the fact of it. You should come there, too. Elayne's more likely than anyone else to be able to help you with Rand."

Bloody colors. As if having one eye were not bad enough, he had those flaming visions bunching up his sight every time he so much as thought of Ran—

Burn those visions!

Moiraine raised an eyebrow as he shook his head, then blushed. He probably looked like he was having a fit.

"We shall see, Matrim," she said, then glanced at Thom, who stood holding the packets of tea. Mat half thought he would try to boil water in his own hands, if only to get some warm tea for Moiraine. Thom looked at her, and she held out her hand again.

"Dearest Thom," she said. "I would have you for a husband, if you'll have me for a wife."

"*What?*" Mat said, standing up. He raised a hand to his forehead, nearly knocking his hat free. "What did you say?"

"Hush, Mat," Thom said. He did not take Moiraine's offered hand. "You know I've never much liked women who can channel the One Power, Moiraine. You know it held me back in the past."

"I don't have much of the Power now, dearest Thom. Without this *angreal*, I wouldn't be strong enough to be raised Accepted in the White Tower. I will throw it away, if you wish it of me." She lifted out her other hand, barely staying modest. She pulled off the *angreal*.

"I don't think so, Moiraine," Thom said, kneeling down, taking her hands. "No, I won't rob you of anything."

"But with it I'll be very strong, stronger in the Power than before I was taken."

"So be it, then," he said. He put the bracelet back on her wrist. "I'll marry you now, if you wish it."

She smiled deeply.

Mat stared, stunned. "And who's going to bloody marry you?" he blurted out. "It sure as thunder isn't going to be me, I'll tell you that."

The two glanced at him, Thom with a flat stare, Moiraine with a hint of a smile. "I can see why the Seanchan woman had to have you, Mat," she noted. "You certainly have a mind for romance."

"I just . . ." He pulled off his hat, holding it awkwardly, looking back and forth between them. "I just—burn me! How did I miss *this*? I was with the two of you most of the time you were together! When did you become affectionate?"

"You weren't watching very closely," Thom said. He turned back to Moiraine. "I assume you'll want me as a Warder, too."

She smiled. "My previous Gaidin has been appropriated by another by now, I hope."

"I'll take the job," Thom said, "though you'll have to explain to Elayne why her court-bard is someone's Warder." He hesitated. "You think they can make one of those color-changing cloaks with some patches on it?"

"Well, you two have gone bloody insane, I see," Mat said. "Thom, didn't you once tell me that the two most painful places for you to be were Tar Valon and Caemlyn? Now you're running headlong down the hillside that will end with you living in one or the other!"

Thom shrugged. "Times change."

"I never have spent much of my time in Tar Valon," Moiraine said. "I think we shall enjoy traveling together, Thom Merrilin. Should we survive the months to come." She looked at Mat. "You should not spurn the Warder bond so easily, Mat. The blessings it provides will be of great use to men in these days."

Mat pulled his hat back on. "That may be true, but you'll never see me bloody trapped by one. No offense, Moiraine. I like you well enough. But to be *bonded* to a woman? Isn't going to happen to Matrim Cauthon."

"Is that so?" Thom asked, amused. "Didn't we determine that your Tuon would be capable of channeling, should she decide to learn?"

Mat froze. Bloody ashes. Thom was right. But channeling would make her *marath'damane*. She would not do such a thing. He did not have to worry.

Did he?

He must have made a face at the thought, for Thom chuckled and Moiraine smiled again. The two of them soon lost interest in sporting with Mat, however, and turned to a soft discussion. That affection in their eyes was true. They *did* love each other. Light! How had Mat missed it? He felt like a man who had brought a hog to a horse race.

He decided to make himself scarce, leaving the two of them alone. He went to scout the area where their gateway was supposed to appear. It had better. They had no supplies, and Mat did not fancy flagging down a ship and riding the long way back to Caemlyn.

It was a short hike across the meadow to the banks of the Arinelle. Once there, he made a small cairn for Noal, then tipped his hat to it and sat down to wait and think.

Moiraine was safe. Mat had survived, though that bloody socket throbbed like nothing else. He still was not certain if the Aelfinn and Eelfinn had strings around him or not, but he had gone into their den and come out unscathed. Mostly, anyway.

One eye lost. What would that do to his ability to fight? That worried him more than anything. He had put on a brave front, but inside he trembled. What would Tuon think of a husband missing an eye? A husband who might not be able to defend himself?

He pulled out a knife, flipping it. Then, on a whim, he tossed it behind him without looking. He heard a soft screech, then turned to see a rabbit slump to the ground, speared by the idly thrown knife.

He smiled, then turned back to the river. There, he noticed something caught between two large river stones along the shore. It was an overturned cooking pot, with a copper bottom, barely used, only dinged on the sides a couple of times. It must have been dropped by a traveler walking up the river.

Yes, he might not be able to judge distance, and he might not be able to see as well. But luck worked better when you were not looking anyway.

He smiled wider, then fetched the rabbit—he would skin that for supper—and plucked the pot out of the river.

Moiraine would get her tea after all.

EPILOGUE

And After

Graendal hurriedly gathered what she needed from her new palace. From her desk, she took a small *angreal* Mesaana had traded her in exchange for information. It was in the shape of a small, carved ivory knife; she'd lost her gold ring in al'Thor's attack.

Graendal tossed it in her pack, then snatched a sheaf of papers from her bed. Names of contacts, eyes-and-ears—everything she'd managed to remember from what had been destroyed at Natrin's Barrow.

Waves surged against the rocks outside. It was still dark. Only moments had passed since her last tool had failed her, Aybara surviving the battlefield. That was supposed to have *worked*!

She was in her elegant manor house a few leagues from Ebou Dar. Now that Semirhage was gone, Graendal had begun placing some strings around their new, childlike Empress. She'd have to abandon those schemes now.

Perrin Aybara had escaped. She felt stunned. Plan after perfect plan had fallen in place. And then . . . he'd escaped. How? The prophecy . . . it had said . . .

That fool Isam, Graendal thought, stuffing the papers in her pack. *And that idiot Whitecloak!* She was sweating. She shouldn't be sweating.

She tossed a few *ter'angreal* from her desk into the pack, then rifled her closet for changes of clothing. He could find her anywhere in the world. But perhaps one of the mirror realms of the Portal Stones. Yes. There, his connections were not—

She turned, arms full of silk, and froze. A figure stood in

the room. Tall, like a pillar dressed in black robes. Eyeless. Smiling lips the color of death.

Graendal dropped to her knees, throwing aside the clothing. Sweat ran down her temple onto her cheek.

"Graendal," said the tall Myrddraal. His voice was terrible, like the last whispers of a dying man. "You have failed, Graendal."

Shaidar Haran. Very bad. "I . . ." she said, licking her dry lips. How to twist this to a victory? "It is according to plan. It is merely a—"

"I know your heart, Graendal. I can taste your *terror*."

She squeezed her eyes shut.

"Mesaana has fallen," Shaidar Haran whispered. "Three Chosen, destroyed by your actions. The design builds, a lattice of failure, a framework of incompetence."

"I had nothing to do with Mesaana's fall!"

"Nothing? Graendal, the dreamspike was there. Those who fought with Mesaana said that they tried to move, to draw the Aes Sedai to a location where their trap could be sprung. They were not meant to fight in the White Tower. They could not leave. Because of you."

"Isam—"

"A tool given you. The failure is yours, Graendal."

She licked her lips again. Her entire mouth had gone dry. There *had* to be a way out. "I have a better plan, more bold. You will be impressed. Al'Thor thinks I am dead, and so I can—"

"No." Such a quiet voice, but so horrible. Graendal found she could not speak. Something had taken her voice. "No," Shaidar Haran continued. "This opportunity has been given to another. But Graendal, you shall not be forgotten."

She looked up, feeling a surge of hope. Those dead lips were smiling widely, that eyeless gaze fixed on her. She felt a horrible sinking feeling.

"No," Shaidar Haran said, "I shall not forget you, and you shall not forget that which comes next."

She opened her eyes wide, then howled as he reached for her.

* * *

The sky rumbled; the grass around Perrin shivered. That grass was spotted black, just as in the real world. Even the wolf dream was dying.

The air was full of scents that did not belong. A fire burning. Blood drying. The dead flesh of a beast he didn't recognize. Eggs rotting.

No, he thought. *No it will* not *be.*

He gathered his will. Those scents *would* vanish. They did, replaced with the scents of summer. Grass, hedgehogs, beetles, moss, mice, blue-winged doves, purple finches. They appeared, bursting to life in a circle around him.

He gritted his teeth. The reality spread from him like a wave, blackness fading from the plants. Above him, the clouds undulated, then parted. Sunlight streamed down. The thunder calmed.

And Hopper lives, Perrin thought. *He does! I can smell his coat, hear him loping in the grass.*

A wolf appeared before him, forming as if from mist. Silvery gray, grizzled from years of life. Perrin thrilled in his power. It *was* real.

And then he saw the wolf's eyes. Lifeless.

The scent turned stale and wrong.

Perrin was sweating from the strain of concentrating so hard. Something within him became disjointed. He was coming into the wolf dream too strongly; to try to control this place absolutely was like trying to contain a wolf in a box.

He cried out, falling to his knees. The misty not-Hopper vanished in a puff and the clouds crashed back into place. Lightning exploded above him and the black spots flooded the grass. The wrong scents returned.

Perrin knelt, sweat dripping from his brow, one hand on the prickly brown and black grass. Too stiff.

Perrin thought of Faile in their tent back in the Field of Merrilor. *She* was his home. There was much to do. Rand had come, as promised. Tomorrow, he would face Egwene. Thought of the real world grounded Perrin, keeping him from entering the wolf dream too strongly.

Perrin stood. He could do many things in this place, but there were limits. There were always limits.

Seek Boundless. He will explain.

Hopper's last sending to him. What did it mean? Hopper had said that Perrin had found the answer. And yet, Boundless would explain that answer? The sending had been awash with pain, loss, satisfaction at seeing Perrin accept the wolf within him. One final image of a wolf leaping proudly into the darkness, coat shining, scent determined.

Perrin sent himself to the Jehannah Road. Boundless was often there, with the remnants of the pack. Perrin reached out and found him: a youthful male with brown fur and a lean build. Boundless teased him, sending the image of Perrin as a bull trampling a stag. The others had left that image alone, but Boundless continued to remember.

Boundless, Perrin sent. *Hopper told me I needed you.*

The wolf vanished.

Perrin started, then jumped to the place the wolf had been—a cliff top several leagues from the road. He caught the faintest scent of the wolf's destination, and then went there. An open field with a distant barn, looking rotted.

Boundless? Perrin sent. The wolf crouched in a pile of brush nearby.

No. No. Boundless sent fright and anger.

What did I do?

The wolf streaked away, leaving a blur. Perrin growled, and went down on all fours, becoming a wolf. Young Bull followed, wind roaring in his ears. He forced it to part before him, increasing his speed further.

Boundless tried to vanish, but Young Bull followed, appearing in the middle of the ocean. He hit the waves, water firm beneath his paws, and continued after Boundless without breaking stride.

Boundless's sendings flashed with images. Forests. Cities. Fields. An image of Perrin, looking down at him, standing outside a cage.

Perrin froze, becoming human again. He stood upon the surging waves, rising slowly into the air. *What?* That sending had been of a younger Perrin. And *Moiraine* had been with him. How could Boundless have . . .

And suddenly, Perrin knew. Boundless was always found in Ghealdan in the wolf dream.

Noam, he sent to the wolf, now distant.

There was a start of surprise, and then the mind vanished. Perrin moved to where Boundless had been, and there smelled a small village. A barn. A cage.

Perrin appeared there. Boundless lay on the ground between two houses, looking up at Perrin. Boundless was indistinguishable from the other wolves, for all that Perrin now suspected the truth. This was not a wolf. He was a man.

"Boundless," Perrin said, kneeling down on one knee to look the wolf in the eyes. "Noam. Do you remember me?"

Of course. You are Young Bull.

"I mean, do you remember me from before, when we met in the waking world? You sent an image of it."

Noam opened his jaws, and a bone appeared in them. A large femur with some meat still on it. He lay on his side, chewing the bone. *You are Young Bull,* he sent, stubborn.

"Do you remember the cage, Noam?" Perrin asked softly, sending the image. The image of a man, his filthy clothing half ripped off, locked in a makeshift wooden cell by his family.

Noam froze, and his image wavered momentarily, becoming that of a man. The wolf image returned immediately, and he growled a low, dangerous growl.

"I do not bring up bad times to make you angry, Noam," Perrin said. "I. . . . Well, I'm like you."

I am a wolf.

"Yes," Perrin said. "But not always."

Always.

"No," Perrin said firmly. "Once you were like me. Thinking it differently doesn't make it so."

Here it does, Young Bull, Noam sent. *Here it does.*

That was true. Why was Perrin pressing this issue? Hopper had sent him here, though. Why should Boundless have the answer? Seeing him, knowing who he was, brought back all of Perrin's fears. He'd made peace with himself, yet here was a man who had lost himself completely to the wolf.

This was what Perrin had been terrified of. This was what had driven the wedge between him and the wolves. Now that he'd overcome that, why would Hopper send him here? Boundless scented his confusion. The bone vanished and Boundless set his head on his paws, looking up at Perrin.

Noam—his mind almost gone—had thought only of
breaking free and of killing; he'd been a danger to everyone around him. There was none of that now. Boundless
seemed at peace. When they'd freed Noam, Perrin had worried that the man would die quickly, but he seemed alive
and well. Alive, at least—Perrin couldn't judge much about
his wellness from how the man looked in the wolf dream.

Still, Boundless's mind was far better now. Perrin
frowned to himself. Moiraine had said there was nothing
left of the man Noam in the mind of the creature.

"Boundless," Perrin said. "What do you think of the
world of men?"

Perrin was immediately hit with a rapid succession of
images. Pain. Sadness. Dying crops. Pain. A large, stout
man, half-drunk, beating a pretty woman. Pain. A fire. Fear,
sorrow. *Pain.*

Perrin stumbled back. Boundless kept sending the images. One after another. A grave. A smaller grave beside
it, as if for a child. The fire getting larger. A man—Noam's
brother; Perrin recognized him, though the man had not
seemed dangerous at the time—enraged.

It was a flood, too much. Perrin howled. A lament for
the life that Noam had led, a dirge of sorrow and pain. No
wonder this man preferred the life of a wolf.

The images stopped, and Boundless turned his head
away. Perrin found himself gasping for breath.

A gift, Boundless sent.

"By the Light," Perrin whispered. "This was a choice,
wasn't it? You picked the wolf intentionally."

Boundless closed his eyes.

"I always thought it would take me, if I weren't careful,"
Perrin said.

The wolf is peace, Boundless sent.

"Yes," Perrin said, laying a hand on the wolf's head. "I
understand."

This was the balance for Boundless. Different from the
balance for Elyas. And different from what Perrin had
found. He understood. This did not mean that the way he let
himself lose control was not a danger. But it was the final
piece he needed to understand. The final piece of himself.

Thank you, Perrin sent. The image of Young Bull the
wolf and Perrin the man standing beside one another, atop

a hill, their scents the same. He sent that image outward, as powerfully as he could. To Boundless, to the wolves nearby. To any who would listen.

Thank you.

"*Dovie'andi se tovya sagain,*" Olver said, throwing the dice. They rolled across the canvas floor of the tent. Olver smiled as they came up. All black dots, no wavy lines or triangles. A lucky roll indeed.

Olver moved his piece along the cloth board of the Snakes and Foxes game his father had made for him. Seeing that board made Olver hurt every time. It reminded him of his father. But he kept his lip stiff and did not let anyone know. Warriors did not cry. And besides, someday he would find that Shaido who had killed his father. Then Olver would get his vengeance.

That was the sort of thing a man did, when he was a warrior. He figured Mat would help, once he was done with all of this business at the Last Battle. He would owe Olver by then, and not just for all the time Olver had spent being Mat's personal messenger. For the information he had given him about the snakes and the foxes.

Talmanes sat in a chair beside Olver. The stoic man was reading a book, only paying mild attention to the game. He was not nearly as good to play with as Noal or Thom. But then, Talmanes had not been sent to play with Olver so much as watch over him.

Mat did not want Olver to know that he had gone to the Tower of Ghenjei, leaving Olver behind. Well, Olver was not a fool, and he knew what was going on. He was not mad, not really. Noal was a good one to take, and if Mat could only take three, well . . . Noal could fight better than Olver. So it made sense for him to go.

But *next* time, Olver would do the choosing. And then Mat had better be nice, or *he* would be left behind.

"Your roll, Talmanes," Olver said.

Talmanes mumbled something, reaching over and tossing the handful of dice without losing his place in the book. He was an all-right fellow, though a little stiff. Olver would not choose to have a man like him on a good night of drinking and hunting serving girls. As soon as Olver was old enough to go drinking and hunting serving girls. He figured he would be ready in another year or so.

Olver moved the snakes and foxes, then picked up the dice for his next throw. He had figured it all out. There were a *lot* of Shaido out there, and he had no idea how to find the one who had killed his parents. But the Aelfinn, they could answer questions. He had heard Mat talking about it. So Olver would go get his answers, then track the man down. Easy as riding a horse. He just had to train with the Band beforehand, so he could fight well enough to see done what needed to be done.

He threw his dice. Another full run. Olver smiled, moving his piece back toward the center of the board, half lost in thought and dreaming of the day when he would finally get his revenge, like was proper.

He moved his piece across one more line, then froze.

His piece was on the center spot.

"I *won*!" he exclaimed.

Talmanes looked up, pipe lowering in his lips. He cocked his head, staring at the board. "Burn me," he muttered. "We must have counted wrong, or . . ."

"Counted wrong?"

"I mean . . ." Talmanes looked stunned. "You can't win. The game can't be won. It just can't."

That was nonsense. Why would Olver play if it could not be won? He smiled, looking over the board. The snakes and the foxes were within one toss of getting to his piece and making him lose. But this time, he'd gotten all the way to the outside ring and back. He had *won*.

Good thing, too. He had started to think he would never manage it!

Olver stood up, stretching his legs. Talmanes climbed off his chair, squatting down beside the game board and scratching his head, smoke idly curling from the end of his pipe.

"I hope Mat will be back soon," Olver said.

"I'm sure he will be," Talmanes said. "His task for Her Majesty shouldn't take much longer." That was the lie they had told Olver—that Mat, Thom and Noal had gone off on some secret errand for the Queen. Well, that was just another reason that Mat would owe him. Honestly, Mat could be so *prim* sometimes, acting as if Olver could not take care of himself.

Olver shook his head, strolling over to the side of the tent, where a stack of Mat's papers sat awaiting his return. There, peeking from between two of them, Olver noticed something interesting. A bit of red, like blood. He reached up, sliding a worn letter from between two of the sheets. It was sealed closed with a dollop of wax.

Olver frowned, turning the small letter over. He had seen Mat carrying it about. Why had he not opened it? That was downright rude. Setalle had worked hard to explain propriety to Olver, and while most of what she said made no sense—he just nodded his head so she would let him snuggle up to her—he was sure you were supposed to open letters people sent you, then respond kindly.

He turned the letter over again, then shrugged and broke the seal. Olver was Mat's personal messenger, all official and everything. It was no wonder Mat sometimes forgot things, but it was Olver's job to take care of him. Now that Lopin was gone, Mat would need extra taking care of. It was one of the reasons Olver stayed with the Band. He was not sure what Mat would do without him.

He unfolded the letter and removed a small, stiff piece of paper inside. He frowned, trying to make out the words. He was getting pretty good with reading, mostly because of Setalle, but some words gave him trouble. He scratched his head. "Talmanes," he said. "You should probably read this."

"What's that?" the man looked up from the game. "Here, now! Olver, what are you doing? That wasn't to be opened!" The man rose, striding over to snatch the paper from Olver's fingers.

"But—" Olver began.

"Lord Mat didn't open it," Talmanes said. "He knew that it would get us tied up in White Tower politics. He waited all those weeks! Now look what you've done. I wonder if we can stuff it back inside . . ."

"Talmanes," Olver said insistently. "I think it's *important*."

Talmanes hesitated. He seemed torn for a moment, then held the letter so that the light shone better on it. He read it quickly, with the air of a boy stealing food from a street vendor's cart and stuffing it into his mouth before he could be discovered.

Talmanes whispered a curse under his breath. He read

the letter again, then cursed more loudly. He grabbed his sword from the side of the room and dashed out of the tent. He left the letter on the floor.

Olver looked it over again, sounding out the words he had not understood the first time.

Matrim,

If you are opening this, then I am dead. I had planned to return and release you of your oath in a single day. There are many potential complications to my next task, however, and a large chance that I will not survive. I needed to know that I'd left someone behind who could see this work done.

Fortunately, if there's one thing I believe I can rely upon, it is your curiosity. I suspect you lasted a few days before opening this letter, which is long enough for me to have returned if I were going to. Therefore, this task falls upon you.

There is a Waygate in Caemlyn. It is guarded, barricaded, and thought secure. It is not.

An enormous force of Shadowspawn moves through the Ways toward Caemlyn. I do not know when they left exactly, but there should be time to stop them. You must reach the Queen and persuade her to destroy the Waygate. It can be done; walling it up will not suffice. If you cannot destroy it, the Queen must bring all of her forces to bear upon guarding the location.

If you fail in this, I fear Caemlyn will be lost before the month is out.

Sincerely,
Verin Mathwin

Olver rubbed his chin. What was a Waygate? He thought he had heard Mat and Thom talking about them. He took the letter and walked out of the tent.

Talmanes stood just outside the tent, looking eastward. Toward Caemlyn. A reddish haze hung on the horizon, a glow over the city. One larger than had been there on other nights.

"Light preserve us," Talmanes whispered. "It's burning. The city is burning." He shook his head, as if clearing it, then raised a call. "To arms! Trollocs in Caemlyn! The city is at war! To arms, men! Burn me, we have to get into the city and salvage those dragons! If those fall into the Shadow's hands, we're all dead men!"

Olver lowered the letter in his fingers, eyes wide. Trollocs in Caemlyn? It would be like the Shaido in Cairhien, only worse.

He hurried into Mat's tent, stumbling over the rug, and threw himself to his knees beside his sleeping pallet. He hurriedly pulled at the stitchings on the side. The wool stuffed inside bulged out through the opening. He reached in, fishing about, and pulled free the large knife he had hidden there. It was wrapped in a leather sheath. He had taken it from one of the Band's quartermasters, Bergevin, when he had not been looking.

After Cairhien, Olver had sworn to himself that he would never prove himself a coward again. He gripped the large knife in two hands, knuckles white, then dashed out of the tent.

It was time to fight.

Barriga stumbled as he crawled past the stump of a fallen tree. Blood from his brow dripped onto the ground, and the dark-speckled nettles seemed to soak it in, feeding upon his life. He raised a trembling hand to his brow. The bandage was soaked through.

No time to stop. No time! He forced himself to his feet and hastily scrambled through the brown sawleaf. He tried not to look at the black spots on the plants. The Blight, he'd entered the *Blight*. But what else was he to do? The Trollocs rampaged to the south; the towers had all fallen. *Kandor itself* had fallen.

Barriga tripped and fell to the earth. He groaned, rolling over, gasping. He was in a trough between two hills north of Heeth Tower. His once fine clothing—coat and vest of rich velvet—was ragged and stained with blood. He stank of smoke, and when he closed his eyes, he saw the Trollocs. Washing over his caravan, slaughtering his servants and soldiers.

They'd all fallen. Thum, Yang . . . both dead. Light, they were *all dead*.

Barriga shuddered. How had he come to this? He was just a merchant. *I should have listened to Rebek,* he thought. Smoke rose from Heeth Tower behind. That was where his caravan had been going. How could this be happening?

He needed to keep moving. East. He'd make for Arafel. The other Borderlands couldn't have fallen, could they?

He climbed up a hillside, hands pulling against short, coiling chokevine. Like worms between his fingers. He was growing woozy. He reached the hilltop; the world was spinning. He fell there, blood seeping from his bandage.

Something moved in front of him. He blinked. Those clouds above were a tempest. In front of him, three figures wearing black and brown approached with a sleek grace. Myrddraal!

No. He blinked the tears and blood from his eyes. No, those *weren't* Myrddraal. They were men, wearing red veils over their faces. They walked at a crouch, scanning the terrain, short spears worn on their backs.

"Light be praised," he whispered. "Aiel." He'd been in Andor when Rand al'Thor had come. Everyone knew the Aiel followed the Dragon Reborn. He had tamed them.

I'm safe!

One of the Aiel stepped up to Barriga. Why was the man's veil red? That was unusual. The Aiel's dark eyes were glassy and hard. The Aiel man undid his veil, and revealed a smiling face.

The man's teeth had been filed to points. His smile broadened, and he slipped a knife from his belt.

Barriga stuttered, looking at that horrific maw and the glee in this man's eyes as he reached in for the kill. These weren't Aiel. They were something else.

Something terrible.

Rand al'Thor, the Dragon Reborn, sat quietly in his dream. He breathed in the cool, chill air. White clouds floated gently around him, kissing his skin with their condensation.

His throne for the night was a flat boulder on a mountain slope; he looked down through the clouds at a narrow valley. This wasn't the real location. It wasn't even the World of Dreams, that place where he'd fought Forsaken, the place he'd been told was so dangerous.

No, this was one of his own ordinary dreams. He controlled them now. They were a place he could find peace to think, protected by wards while his body slept beside Min in their new camp, surrounded by Borderlanders, set up on the Field of Merrilor. Egwene was there, with armies marshaled. He was ready for that. He'd counted on it.

On the morrow, they'd hear his demands. Not what he would demand to keep him from breaking the seals—he was going to do that, regardless of what Egwene said. No, these would be the demands he made on the monarchs of the world in exchange for going to Shayol Ghul to face the Dark One.

He wasn't certain what he'd do if they refused him. They'd find it very difficult to do so. Sometimes, it could be useful to have a reputation for being irrational.

He breathed in deeply, peaceful. Here, in his dreams, the hills grew green. As he remembered them. In that nameless valley below, sheltered in the Mountains of Mist, he'd begun a journey. Not his first, and not his last, but perhaps the most important. One of the most painful, for certain.

"And now I come back," he whispered. "I've changed again. A man is always changing."

He felt a unity in returning here, to the place where he'd first confronted the killer inside him. The place where he'd first tried to flee from those whom he should have kept near. He closed his eyes, enjoying tranquility. Calmness. Harmony.

In the distance, he heard screams of pain.

Rand opened his eyes. What had that been? He stood up, spinning. This place was created of his own mind, protected and safe. It couldn't—

The scream came again. Distant. He frowned and raised a hand. The scene around him vanished, puffing away into mist. He stood in blackness.

There, he thought. He was in a long corridor of dark wood paneling. He walked down it, boots thumping. That screaming. It shook his peace. Someone was in *pain*. They needed him.

Rand began to run. He reached a doorway at the end of the hall. The door's russet wood was knobbed and ridged, like the thick roots of an ancient tree. Rand seized the handle—just another root—and wrenched the door open.

The vast room beyond was pure black, lightless, like a cavern deep beneath the ground. The room seemed to suck in the light and extinguish it. The screaming voice was inside. It was weak, as if it were being smothered by the darkness.

Rand entered. The darkness swallowed him. It seemed to pull the life out of him, like a hundred leeches sucking blood from his veins. He pressed onward. He couldn't distinguish the direction of the cries, so he moved along the walls; they felt like bone, smooth but occasionally cracked.

The room was round. As if he stood inside the bowl of an enormous skull.

There! A faint light ahead, a single candle on the ground, illuminating a floor of black marble. Rand hurried toward it. Yes, there was a figure there. Huddled against the bone-white wall. It was a woman with silvery hair, wearing a thin white shift.

She was weeping now, her figure shaking and trembling. Rand knelt beside her, the candle flickering from his motion. How had this woman gotten into his dream? Was she someone real, or was this a creation of his mind? He laid a hand on her shoulder.

She glanced toward him, eyes red, face a mask of pain, tears dripping from her chin. "Please," she pled. "*Please.* He has me."

"Who are you?"

"You know me," she whispered, taking his hand, clinging to it. "I'm sorry. I'm *so* sorry. He has me. He flays my soul anew each eve. Oh, please! Let it stop." The tears flowed more freely.

"I don't know you," Rand said. "I . . ."

Those eyes. Those beautiful, terrible eyes. Rand gasped, releasing her hand. The face was different. But he *did* know that soul. "Mierin? You're dead. I saw you die!"

She shook her head. "I wish I were dead. I wish it. Please! He grinds my bones and snaps them like twigs, then leaves me to die before Healing me just enough to keep me alive. He—" She cut off, jerking.

"What?"

Her eyes opened wide and she spun toward the wall. "No!" she screamed. "He comes! The Shadow in every man's mind, the murderer of truth. No!" She spun, reach-

ing for Rand, but something towed her backward. The wall
broke away, and she tumbled into the darkness.

Rand jumped forward, reaching for her, but he was too
late. He caught a glimpse of her before she vanished into
the blackness below.

Rand froze, staring into that pit. He sought calmness, but
he could not find it. Instead, he felt hatred, concern, and—
like a seething viper within him—desire. That *had* been
Mierin Eronaile, a woman he had once called the Lady Se-
lene.

A woman most people knew by the name she'd taken
upon herself. Lanfear.

A cruel, dry wind blew across Lan's face as he looked down
at a corrupt landscape. Tarwin's Gap was a wide pass, rocky,
speckled with Blighted knifegrass. This had once been part
of Malkier. He was home again. For the last time.

Masses of Trollocs clustered on the other side of the Gap.
Thousands. Tens of thousands. Probably hundreds of thousands. Easily ten times the number of men Lan had gathered
during his march across the Borderlands. Normally, men
held at their side of the Gap, but Lan could not do that.

He had come to attack, to ride for Malkier. Andere rode
up beside him on his left, young Kaisel of Kandor on his
right. He could feel something, distant, that had given him
strength recently. The bond had changed. The emotions had
changed.

He could still feel Nynaeve, so wonderful, caring, and
passionate in the back of his mind. He should have been
pained to know that now she would suffer when he died,
instead of another. However, that closeness to her—a final
closeness—brought him strength.

The hot wind seemed too dry; it smelled of dust and dirt,
and drew the moisture from his eyes, forcing him to blink.

"It is fitting," Kaisel said.

"What?" Lan asked.

"That we should strike here."

"Yes," Lan said.

"It is bold," Kaisel said. "It shows the Shadow that we
will not be beaten down, that we will not cower. This is
your land, Lord Mandragoran."

My land, he thought. Yes, it was. He nudged Mandarb forward.

"I am al'Lan Mandragoran," Lan bellowed. "Lord of the Seven Towers, Defender of the Wall of First Fires, Bearer of the Sword of the Thousand Lakes! I was once named *Aan'allein,* but I reject that title, for I am alone no more. Fear me, Shadow! Fear me and know. I have returned for what is mine. I may be a king without a land. But I am *still a king!*"

He roared, raising his sword. A cheer rose from behind him. He sent a final, powerful sensation of love to Nynaeve as he kicked Mandarb into a gallop.

His army charged behind him, each man mounted—a charge of Kandori, Arafellin, Shienarans, and Saldaeans. But most of all Malkieri. Lan wouldn't be surprised if he'd drawn every living man from his former kingdom who could still hold a weapon.

They rode, cheering, brandishing swords and leveling lances. Their hooves were thunder, their voices a crash of waves, their pride stronger than the blazing sun. They were twelve thousand strong. And they charged a force of at least one hundred and fifty thousand.

This day will be remembered in honor, Lan thought, galloping forward. *The Last Charge of the Golden Crane. The fall of the Malkieri.*

The end had come. They would meet it with swords raised.

The End
of the Thirteenth Book of
The Wheel of Time

Lo, it shall come upon the world that the prison of the Greatest One shall grow weak, like the limbs of those who crafted it. Once again, His glorious cloak shall smother the Pattern of all things, and the Great Lord shall stretch forth His hand to claim what is His. The rebellious nations shall be laid barren, their children caused to weep. There shall be none but Him, and those who have turned their eyes to His majesty.

In that day, when the One-Eyed Fool travels the halls of mourning, and the First Among Vermin lifts his hand to bring freedom to Him who will Destroy, the last days of the Fallen Blacksmith's pride shall come. Yea, and the Broken Wolf, the one whom Death has known, shall fall and be consumed by the Midnight Towers. And his destruction shall bring fear and sorrow to the hearts of men, and shall shake their very will itself.

And then, shall the Lord of the Evening come. And He shall take our eyes, for our souls shall bow before Him, and He shall take our skin, for our flesh shall serve Him, and He shall take our lips, for only Him will we praise. And the Lord of the Evening shall face the Broken Champion, and shall spill his blood and bring us the Darkness so beautiful. Let the screams begin, O followers of the Shadow. Beg for your destruction!

—from *The Prophecies of the Shadow*

GLOSSARY

A Note on Dates in This Glossary. The Toman Calendar (devised by Toma dur Ahmid) was adopted approximately two centuries after the death of the last male Aes Sedai, recording years After the Breaking of the World (AB). So many records were destroyed in the Trolloc Wars that at their end there was argument about the exact year under the old system. A new calendar, proposed by Tiam of Gazar, celebrated freedom from the Trolloc threat and recorded each year as a Free Year (FY). The Gazaran Calendar gained wide acceptance within twenty years after the Wars' end. Artur Hawkwing attempted to establish a new calendar based on the founding of his empire (FF, From the Founding), but only historians now refer to it. After the death and destruction of the War of the Hundred Years, a third calendar was devised by Uren din Jubai Soaring Gull, a scholar of the Sea Folk, and promulgated by the Panarch Farede of Tarabon. The Farede Calendar, dating from the arbitrarily decided end of the War of the Hundred Years and recording years of the New Era (NE), is currently in use.

Aelfinn: A race of beings, largely human in appearance but with snake-like characteristics, who will give true answers to three questions. Whatever the question, their answers are always correct, if frequently given in forms that are not clear, but questions concerning the Shadow can be extremely dangerous. Their true location is unknown, but they can be visited by passing through a *ter'angreal*, once a possession of Mayene but in recent years held in the Stone of Tear. They can also be reached by entering the Tower of Ghenjei. They speak the Old Tongue, mention treaties and agreements, and ask if those entering carry iron, instruments of music, or devices that can make fire. *See also* Eelfinn, Snakes and Foxes.

Arad Doman: A nation on the Aryth Ocean, currently racked by civil war and by wars against those who have declared for the Dragon Reborn. Its capital is Bandar Eban, where many of its people have come for refuge. Food is scarce. In Arad Doman, those who are descended from the nobility at the time of the founding of the nation, as opposed to those raised later, are known as the bloodborn. The ruler (king or queen) is elected by a council of the heads of merchant guilds (the Council of Merchants), who are almost always women. He or she must be from the noble class, not the merchant, and is elected for life. Legally the king or queen has absolute authority, except that he or she can be deposed by a three-quarter vote of the Council. The current ruler is King Alsalam Saeed Almadar, Lord of Almadar, High Seat of House Almadar.

area, units of: (1) Land: 1 ribbon = 20 paces × 10 paces (200 square paces); 1 cord = 20 paces × 50 paces (1000 square paces); 1 hide = 100 paces × 100 paces (10,000 square paces); 1 rope = 100 paces × 1000 paces (100,000 square paces); 1 march = 1000 paces × 1000 paces (¼ square mile). (2) Cloth: 1 pace = 1 pace plus 1 hand × 1 pace plus 1 hand.

Asha'man: (1) In the Old Tongue, "Guardian" or "Guardians," but always a guardian of justice and truth. (2) The name given, both collectively and as a rank, to the men who have come to the Black Tower, near Caemlyn in Andor, in order to learn to channel. Their training largely concentrates on the ways in which the One Power can be used as a weapon, and in another departure from the usages of the White Tower, once they learn to seize *saidin*, the male half of the Power, they are required to perform all chores and labors with the Power. When newly enrolled, a man is termed a soldier; he wears a plain black coat with a high collar, in the Andoran fashion. Being raised to Dedicated brings the right to wear a silver pin, called the Sword, on the collar of his coat. Promotion to Asha'man brings the right to wear a Dragon pin, in gold and red enamel, on the collar opposite the Sword. Although many women, including wives, flee when they learn that their men actually can channel, a fair number of men at the Black Tower are married, and they use a version of the Warder bond to create a link with their wives. This same bond, altered to compel obedience, has been used to bond captured Aes Sedai as well. Some Asha'man have been bonded by Aes Sedai, although the traditional Warder bond is used. The Asha'man are led by Mazrim Taim, who has styled himself the M'Hael, Old Tongue for "leader."

Avendesora: In the Old Tongue, "the Tree of Life." It is located in Rhuidean.

Balwer, Sebban: Formerly Pedron Niall's secretary, in public, and secretly Niall's spymaster. He aided Morgase's escape from the Seanchan in Amador for his own reasons, and now is employed as secretary to Perrin t'Bashere Aybara and Faile ni Bashere t'Aybara. His duties expanded, however, and he now directs *Cha Faile* in their activities, acting as a spymaster for Perrin, though Perrin doesn't think of him so. *See also Cha Faile.*

Band of the Red Hand: *See Shen an Calhar.*

Bloodknives: An elite division of Seanchan soldiers. Each is equipped with a *ter'angreal* that increases his strength and speed and shrouds him in darkness. The *ter'angreal* is activated by touching a drop of the Bloodknife's blood to the ring, and once activated, it slowly leaches the life from its host. Death occurs within a matter of days.

Brown Ajah Council: The Brown Ajah is headed by a council instead of an individual Aes Sedai. The current head of the council is Jesse Bilal; the other members are unknown.

Captain-General: (1) The military rank of the leader of the Queen's Guard of Andor. This position is currently held by Lady Birgitte Trahelion. (2) The title given to the head of the Green Ajah. This position is currently held by Adelorna Bastine.

calendar: There are 10 days to the week, 28 days to the month and 13 months to the year. Several feast days are not part of any month; these include Sunday (the longest day of the year), the Feast of Thanksgiving (once every four years at the spring equinox) and the Feast of All Souls Salvation, also called All Souls Day (once every ten years at the autumn equinox). While the months have names (Taisham, Jumara, Saban, Aine, Adar, Saven, Amadaine, Tammaz, Maigdhal, Choren, Shaldine, Nesan and Danu), these are seldom used except in official documents and by officials. For most people, using the seasons is good enough.

Callandor: The Sword That Is Not a Sword, the Sword That Cannot Be Touched. A crystal sword once held in the Stone of Tear, it is a powerful *sa'angreal* for use by male channelers. It has known flaws: It lacks the buffer that makes *sa'angreal* safe to use, and magnified the taint. Other flaws are suspected.

Cha Faile: (1) In the Old Tongue, "the Falcon's Talon." (2) Name taken by the young Cairhienin and Tairens, attempted followers of *ji'e'toh*, who have sworn fealty to Faile ni Bashere t'Aybara. In secret, they act as her personal scouts and spies. During her captivity with the Shaido, they continued their activities under the guidance of Sebban Balwer. *See also* Balwer, Sebban.

Charin, Jain: *See* Farstrider, Jain.

Children of the Light: Society of strict ascetic beliefs, owing allegiance to no nation and dedicated to the defeat of the Dark One and the destruction of all Darkfriends. Founded during the War of the Hundred Years by Lothair Mantelar to proselytize against an increase in Darkfriends, they evolved during the war into a completely military society. They are extremely rigid in their beliefs, and certain that only they know the truth and the right. They consider Aes Sedai and any who support them to be Darkfriends. Known disparagingly as Whitecloaks, a name they themselves despise, they were formerly headquartered in Amador, Amadicia, but were forced out when the Seanchan conquered the city. Galad Damodred became Lord Captain Commander after he killed Eamon Valda in a duel for assaulting his stepmother, Morgase. Valda's death produced a schism in the organization, with Galad leading one faction, and Rhadam Asunawa, High Inquisitor of the Hand of the Light, leading the other. Their sign is a golden sunburst on a field of white. *See also* Questioners.

Consolidation, the: When the armies sent by Artur Hawkwing under his son Luthair landed in Seanchan, they discovered a shifting quilt of nations often at war with one another, where Aes Sedai often reigned. Without any equivalent of the White Tower, Aes Sedai worked for their own individual interests, using the Power. Forming small groups, they schemed against one another constantly. In large part it was this constant scheming for personal advantage and the resulting wars among the myriad nations that allowed the armies from east of the Aryth Ocean to begin the conquest of an entire continent, and for their descendants to complete it. This conquest, during which the descendants of the original armies became Seanchan as much as they conquered Seanchan, took centuries and is called the Consolidation. *See also* Towers of Midnight.

cuendillar: A supposedly indestructible substance created during the Age of Legends. Any known force used in an attempt to break it, including the One Power, is absorbed, making *cuendillar* stronger. Although the making of *cuendillar* was thought lost forever, new objects made from it have surfaced. It is also known as heartstone.

currency: After many centuries of trade, the standard terms for coins are the same in every land: crowns (the largest coin in size), marks and pennies. Crowns and marks can be minted of gold or silver, while pennies can be silver or copper, the last often called simply a copper. In different lands, however, these coins are of different sizes and weights. Even in one nation, coins of different sizes and weights have been minted by different rulers. Because of trade, the coins of many nations can be found almost anywhere, and for that reason, bankers, money-lenders and merchants all use scales to determine the value of any given coin. Even large numbers of coins are weighed.

The heaviest coins come from Andor and Tar Valon, and in those two places the relative values are: 10 copper pennies = 1 silver penny; 100 silver pennies = 1 silver mark; 10 silver marks = 1 silver crown; 10 silver crowns = 1 gold mark; 10 gold marks = 1 gold crown. By contrast, in Altara, where the larger coins contain less gold or silver, the relative values are: 10 copper pennies = 1 silver penny; 21 silver pennies = 1 silver mark; 20 silver marks = 1 silver crown; 20 silver crowns = 1 gold mark; 20 gold marks = 1 gold crown.

The only paper currency is "letters-of-rights," which are issued by bankers, guaranteeing to present a certain amount of gold or silver when the letter-of-rights is presented. Because of the long distances between cities, the length of time needed to travel from one to another, and the difficulties of transactions at long distance, a letter-of-rights may be accepted at full value in a city near to the bank which issued it, but it may only be accepted at a lower value in a city farther away. Generally, someone intending to be traveling for a long time will carry one or more letters-of-rights to exchange for coin when needed. Letters-of-rights are usually accepted only by bankers or merchants, and would never be used in shops.

da'covale: (1) In the Old Tongue, "one who is owned," or "person who is property." (2) Among the Seanchan, the term often used, along with "property," for slaves. Slavery has a long and unusual history among the Seanchan, with slaves having the ability to rise to positions of great power and open authority, including authority over those who are free. It is also possible for those in positions of great power to be reduced to *da'covale. See also so'jhin.*

Deathwatch Guards, the: The elite military formation of the Seanchan Empire, including both humans and Ogier. The human members of the Deathwatch Guard are all *da'covale,* born as property and chosen while young to serve the Empress, whose personal property they are. Fanatically loyal and fiercely proud, they often display the ravens tattooed on their shoulders, the mark of a *da'covale* of the Empress. The Ogier members are known as Gardeners, and they are not *da'covale.* The Gardeners are as fiercely loyal as the human Deathwatch Guards, though, and are even more feared. Human or Ogier, the Deathwatch Guards not only are ready to die for the Empress and the Imperial family, but believe that their lives are the property of the Empress, to be disposed of as she wishes. Their helmets and armor are lacquered in dark green (so dark that it is often mistakenly called black) and blood red, their shields are lacquered black, and their swords, spears, axes and halberds carry black tassels. *See also da'covale.*

Delving: (1) Using the One Power to diagnose physical condition and illness. (2) Finding deposits of metal ores with the One Power. That this has long been a lost ability among Aes Sedai may account for the name becoming attached to another ability.

der'morat-: (1) In the Old Tongue, "master handler." (2) Among the Seanchan, the prefix applied to indicate a senior and highly skilled handler of one of the exotics, one who trains others, as in *der'morat'raken.* *Der'morat* can have a fairly high social status, the highest of all held by *der'sul'dam*, the trainers of *sul'dam*, who rank with fairly high military officers. *See also morat-.*

dragon: A powerful new weapon capable of firing explosive charges over large distances, causing extensive damage to the enemy.

dragons' eggs: The name given to the explosive charges fired by dragons.

Eelfinn: A race of beings, largely human in appearance but with fox-like characteristics, who will grant three wishes, although they ask for a price in return. If the person asking does not negotiate a price, the Eelfinn choose it. The most common price in such circumstances is death, but they still fulfill their part of the bargain, although the manner in which they fulfill it is seldom the manner the one asking expects. Their true location is unknown, but it was possible to visit them by means of a *ter'angreal* that was located in Rhuidean. That *ter'angreal* was taken by Moiraine Damodred to Cairhien, where it was destroyed. They may also be reached by entering the Tower of Ghenjei. They ask the same questions as the Aelfinn regarding fire, iron, and musical instruments. *See also* Aelfinn, Snakes and Foxes.

Farstrider, Jain: A hero of the northern lands who journeyed to many lands and had many adventures; he captured Cowin Fairheart and brought him to the king's justice. He was the author of several books, as well as the subject of books and stories. He vanished in 981 NE, after returning from a trip into the Great Blight which some said had taken him all the way to Shayol Ghul.

Fel, Herid: The author of *Reason and Unreason* and other books. Fel was a student (and teacher) of history and philosophy at the Academy of Cairhien. He was discovered in his study torn limb from limb.

First Reasoner: The title given to the head of the White Ajah. This position is currently held by Ferane Neheran.

First Selector: The title given to the head of the Blue Ajah. The First Selector is currently unknown, although it is suspected that Lelaine Akashi fills this position.

First Weaver: The title given to the head of the Yellow Ajah. This position is currently held by Suana Dragand.

Forsaken, the: The name given to thirteen powerful Aes Sedai, men and women both, who went over to the Shadow during the Age of Legends and were trapped in the sealing of the Bore into the Dark One's prison. While it has long been believed that they alone abandoned the Light during the War of the Shadow, in fact others did as well; these thirteen were only the highest-ranking among them. The Forsaken (who call themselves the Chosen) are somewhat reduced in number since their awakening in the present day. Some of those killed were reincarnated in new bodies.

Golden Crane, the: The banner of the lost Borderland nation of Malkier.

Graendal: One of the Forsaken. Once known as Kamarile Maradim Nindar, a noted ascetic, she was the second of the Forsaken to decide to serve the Dark One. A ruthless killer, she was responsible for the deaths of Aran'gar and Asmodean and for the destruction of Mesaana. Her present circumstances are uncertain.

hadori: The braided leather cord that a Malkieri man tied around his temples to hold his hair back. Until after Malkier fell to the Blight, every adult Malkieri male wore his hair to the shoulders and tied back with a *hadori*. Like the presentation of his sword, being allowed to wear the *hadori* marked the move from childhood to adulthood for Malkieri males. The *hadori* symbolized the duties and obligations that bound him as an adult, and also his connection to Malkier. *See also ki'sain.*

Hanlon, Daved: A Darkfriend, also known as Doilin Mellar, who was captured with Lady Shiaine, Chesmal Emry, Eldrith Jhondar, Temaile Kinderode, Falion Bhoda and Marillin Gemalphin.

Head Clerk: The title given to the head of the Gray Ajah. This position is currently held by Serancha Colvine.

Head of the Great Council of Thirteen: The title given to the head of the Black Ajah. This position is currently held by Alviarin Freidhen.

heart: The basic unit of organization in the Black Ajah. In effect, a cell. A heart consists of three sisters who know each other, with each member of the heart knowing one additional sister of the Black who is unknown to the other two of her heart.

Highest: The title given to the head of the Red Ajah. This position is currently held by Tsutama Rath.

Illuminators, Guild of: A society that held the secret of making fireworks. It guarded this secret very closely, even to the extent of doing murder to protect it. The Guild gained its name from the grand displays, called Illuminations, that it provided for rulers and sometimes for greater lords. Lesser fireworks were sold for use by others, but with dire warnings of the disaster that could result from attempting to learn what was inside them. The Guild once had chapter houses in Cairhien and Tanchico, but both are now destroyed. In addition, the members of the Guild in Tanchico resisted the invasion by the Seanchan and were made *da'covale*, and the Guild as such no longer exists. However, individual Illuminators still exist outside of Seanchan rule and work to make sure that the Guild will be remembered. *See also da'covale.*

Imfaral: The sixth-largest city of Seanchan. It is located northwest of Seandar, and is home to the Towers of Midnight. *See also* Towers of Midnight.

ki'sain: A small mark, a dot, which an adult Malkieri woman painted on her forehead each morning in pledge that she would swear (or had sworn) her sons to fight the

Shadow. This pledge was not necessarily that they would be warriors, but that they would oppose the Shadow every day in every way that they could. Like the *hadori*, the *ki'sain* was also considered a symbol of connection to Malkier, and of the bonds that united her with other Malkieri. Also like the *hadori*, the *ki'sain* was a sign of adulthood. The *ki'sain* also gave information about the woman who wore it. A blue mark was worn by a woman who had not married, a red mark by a married woman and a white mark by a widow. In death, she would be marked with all three, one of each color, whether she had ever married or not. *See also hadori.*

Legion of the Dragon, the: A large military formation, all infantry, giving allegiance to the Dragon Reborn, trained by Davram Bashere along lines worked out by himself and Mat Cauthon, lines which depart sharply from the usual employment of foot. While many men simply walk in to volunteer, large numbers of the Legion are scooped up by recruiting parties from the Black Tower, who first gather all of the men in an area who were willing to follow the Dragon Reborn, and only after taking them through gateways near Caemlyn winnow out those who can be taught to channel. The remainder, by far the greater number, are sent to Bashere's training camps. The Legion of the Dragon is at present training for the Last Battle.

length, units of: 10 inches = 1 foot; 3 feet = 1 pace; 2 paces = 1 span; 1000 spans = 1 mile; 4 miles = 1 league.

Listeners: A Seanchan spy organization. Almost anyone in the household of a Seanchan noble, merchant or banker may be a Listener, including *da'covale* occasionally, though seldom *so'jhin*. They take no active role, merely watching, listening and reporting. Their reports are sent to Lesser Hands who control both them and the Seekers and decide what should be passed on to the Seekers for further action. *See also* Seekers.

marath'damane: In the Old Tongue, "those who must be leashed," and also "one who must be leashed." The term applied by the Seanchan to any woman capable of channeling who has not been collared as a *damane*.

march: *See* area, units of.

Mellar, Doilin: *See* Hanlon, Daved.

Mera'din: In the Old Tongue, "the Brotherless." The name adopted, as a society, by those Aiel who abandoned clan and sept and went to the Shaido because they could not accept Rand al'Thor, a wetlander, as the *Car'a'carn*, or because they refused to accept his revelations concerning the history and origins of the Aiel. Deserting clan and sept for any reason is anathema among the Aiel, therefore their own warrior societies among the Shaido were unwilling to take them in, and they formed this society, the Brotherless.

Moiraine Damodred: A Cairhienin Aes Sedai of the Blue Ajah. Long presumed dead. Thom Merrilin has, however, revealed the receipt of a letter purporting to be from her. It is reproduced here:

My dearest Thom,

There are many words I would like to write to you, words from my heart, but I have put this off because I knew that I must, and now there is little time. There are many things I cannot tell you lest I bring disaster, but what I can, I will. Heed carefully what I say. In a short while I will go down to the docks, and there I will confront Lanfear. How can I know that? That secret belongs to others. Suffice it that I know, and let that foreknowledge stand as proof for the rest of what I say.

When you receive this, you will be told that I am dead. All will believe that. I am not dead, and it may be that I shall live to my appointed years. It also may be that you and Mat Cauthon and another, a man I do not know, will try to rescue me. May, I say because it may be that you will not or cannot, or because Mat may refuse. He does not hold me in the affection you seem to, and he has his reasons which he no doubt thinks are good. If you try, it must be only you and Mat and one other. More will mean death for all. Fewer will mean death for all.

Even if you come only with Mat and one other, death also may come. I have seen you try and die, one or two or all three. I have seen myself die in the attempt.

I have seen all of us live and die as captives. Should you decide to make the attempt anyway, young Mat knows the way to find me, yet you must not show him this letter until he asks about it. That is of the utmost importance. He must know nothing that is in this letter until he asks. Events must play out in certain ways, whatever the costs.

If you see Lan again, tell him that all of this is for the best. His destiny follows a different path from mine. I wish him all happiness with Nynaeve.

A final point. Remember what you know about the game of Snakes and Foxes. Remember, and heed.

It is time, and I must do what must be done.

May the Light illumine you and give you joy, my dearest Thom, whether or not we ever see one another again.

Moiraine

morat-: In the Old Tongue, "handler." Among the Seanchan, it is used for those who handle exotics, such as *morat'raken*, a *raken* handler or rider, also informally called a flier. *See also der'morat-.*

Prophet, the: More formally, the Prophet of the Lord Dragon. Once known as Masema Dagar, a Shienaran soldier, he underwent a revelation and decided that he had been called to spread the word of the Dragon's Rebirth. He believed that nothing—nothing!—was more important than acknowledging the Dragon Reborn as the Light made flesh and being ready when the Dragon Reborn called, and he and his followers would use any means to force others to sing the glories of the Dragon Reborn. Those who refused were marked for death, and those who were slow might find their homes and shops burned and themselves flogged. Forsaking any name but "the Prophet," he brought chaos to much of Ghealdan and Amadicia, large parts of which he controlled, although with him gone, the Seanchan are reestablishing order in Amadicia and the Crown High Council in Ghealdan. He joined with Perrin Aybara, who was sent to bring him to Rand, and, for reasons unknown, stayed with him even though this delayed his going to the Dragon Reborn. He was followed by men and women of the lowest sort; if they were not so when they were pulled in by his charisma, they became so under his influence. He died under mysterious circumstances.

Queen's Guards, the: The elite military formation in Andor. In peacetime the Guard is responsible for upholding the Queen's law and keeping the peace across Andor. The uniform of the Queen's Guard include a red undercoat, gleaming mail and plate armor, a brilliant red cloak, and a conical helmet with a barred visor. High-ranking officers wear knots of rank on their shoulder and golden lion-head spurs. A recent addition to the Queen's Guards is the Queen's personal bodyguard, which is composed entirely of women since the arrest of its former captain, Doilin Mellar. These Guardswomen wear much more elaborate uniforms than their male counterparts, including broad-brimmed hats with white plumes, red-lacquered breastplates and helmets trimmed in white, and lace-edged sashes bearing the White Lion of Andor.

Questioners, the: An order within the Children of the Light. They refer to themselves as the Hand of the Light—they intensely dislike being called Questioners—and their avowed purposes are to discover the truth in disputations and uncover Darkfriends. In the search for truth and the Light, their normal method of inquiry is torture; their normal manner is that they know the truth already and must only make their victim confess to it. At times they act as if they are entirely separate from the Children and the Council of the Anointed, which commands the Children. Their sign is a blood-red shepherd's crook.

Redarms: Soldiers of the Band of the Red Hand, who have been chosen out for temporary police duty to make sure that other soldiers of the Band cause no trouble or damage in a town or village where the Band has stopped. So named because, while on duty, they wear very broad red armbands that reach from cuff to elbow. Usually chosen from among the most experienced and reliable men. Since any damages must be paid for by the men serving as Redarms, they work hard to make sure all is quiet and peaceful. *See also Shen an Calhar.*

Saldaea: A nation in the Borderlands. Its capital is Maradon, and its royal palace is known as the Cordamora (from the Old Tongue for "Heart of the People"). It is ruled by a king or queen, and is a hereditary monarchy. The Crown High Council, also known as the Council of Lords, advises and assists the monarch in administering the nation. The husband or wife of a Saldaean ruler is not simply a consort, but an almost co-equal ruler. Saldaea is currently ruled by Her Most Illumined Majesty, Tenobia si Bashere Kazadi, Queen of Saldaea, Defender of the Light, Sword of the Blightborder, High Seat of House Kazadi and Lady of Shahanyi, Asnelle, Kunwar and Ganai; her Marshal-General and the leader of her army is her uncle and heir, Davram Bashere, although he has been missing from his post for some time.

Seandar: The Imperial capital of Seanchan, located in the northeast of the Seanchan continent. It is also the largest city in the Empire. After the death of Empress Radhanan, it descended into chaos.

Seekers: More formally, Seekers for Truth, they are a police/spy organization of the Seanchan Imperial Throne. Although most Seekers are *da'covale* and the property of the Imperial family, they have wide-ranging powers. Even one of the Blood can be arrested for failure to answer any question put by a Seeker, or for failure to cooperate fully with a Seeker, this last defined by the Seekers themselves, subject only to review by the Empress. Their reports are sent to Lesser Hands, who control both them and the Listeners. Most Seekers feel that the Hands do not pass on as much information as they should. Unlike the Listeners', the Seekers' role is active. Those Seekers who are *da'covale* are marked on either shoulder with a raven and a tower. Unlike the Deathwatch Guards, Seekers are seldom eager to show their ravens, in part because it necessitates revealing who and what they are. *See also* Listeners.

Shara: A mysterious land to the east of the Aiel Waste which is the source of silk and ivory, among other trade goods. The land is protected both by inhospitable natural features and by man-made walls. Little is known about Shara, as the people of that land work to keep their culture secret. The Sharans deny that the Trolloc Wars touched them, despite Aiel statements to the contrary. They deny knowledge of Artur Hawkwing's attempted invasion, despite the accounts of eyewitnesses from the Sea Folk. The little information that has leaked out reveals that the Sharans are ruled by a single absolute monarch, a Sh'boan if a woman and a Sh'botay if a man. That monarch rules for exactly seven years, then dies. The rule then passes to the mate of that ruler, who rules for seven years and then dies. This pattern has repeated itself since the time of the Breaking of the World. The Sharans believe that the deaths are the "Will of the Pattern."

There are channelers in Shara, known as the Ayyad, who are tattooed on their faces at birth. The women of the Ayyad enforce the Ayyad laws stringently. A sexual relationship between Ayyad and non-Ayyad is punishable by death for the non-Ayyad, and the Ayyad is also executed if force on his or her part can be proven. If a child is born of the union, it is left exposed to the elements, and dies. Male Ayyad are used as breeding stock only. They are not educated in any fashion, not even how to read or write, and when they reach their twenty-first year or begin to channel, whichever comes first, they are killed and the body cremated. Supposedly, the Ayyad channel the One Power only at the command of the Sh'boan or Sh'botay, who is always surrounded by Ayyad women.

Even the name of the land is in doubt. The natives have been known to call it many different names, including Shamara, Co'dansin, Tomaka, Kigali and Shibouya.

Shen an Calhar: In the Old Tongue, "the Band of the Red Hand." (1) A legendary group of heroes who had many exploits, finally dying in the defense of Manetheren when that land was destroyed during the Trolloc Wars. (2) A military formation put together almost by accident by Mat Cauthon and organized along the lines of military forces during what is considered the height of the military arts, the days of Artur Hawkwing and the centuries immediately preceding.

Sisnera, Darlin: A High Lord in Tear, he was formerly in rebellion against the Dragon Reborn. After serving for a short period as Steward of the Dragon Reborn in Tear, he was chosen to be the first king of Tear.

Snakes and Foxes: A game that is much loved by children until they mature enough to realize that it can never be won without breaking the rules. It is played with a board that has a web of lines with arrows indicating direction. There are ten discs inked with triangles to represent the foxes, and ten discs inked with wavy lines to represent the snakes. The game is begun by saying "Courage to strengthen, fire to blind, music to dazzle, iron to bind," while describing a triangle with a wavy line through it with one's hand. Dice are rolled to determine moves for the players and the snakes and foxes. If a snake or fox lands on a player's piece, he is out of the game, and as long as the rules are followed, this always happens. *See also* Aelfinn, Eelfinn.

so'jhin: The closest translation from the Old Tongue would be "a height among lowness," though some translate it as meaning "both sky and valley" among several other possibilities. *So'jhin* is the term applied by the Seanchan to hereditary upper servants. They are *da'covale*, property, yet occupy positions of considerable authority and often power. Even the Blood step carefully around *so'jhin* of the Imperial family, and speak to *so'jhin* of the Empress herself as to equals. *See also da'covale.*

Stump: A public meeting among the Ogier. It is presided over by the Council of Elders of a *stedding*, but any adult Ogier may speak, or may choose an advocate to speak for him. A Stump is often held at the largest tree stump in a *stedding*, and may last for several years. When a question arises that affects all Ogier, a Great Stump is held, and Ogier from all *stedding* meet to address the question. The various *stedding* take turns hosting the Great Stump.

Succession: In general, when one House succeeds another on the throne. In Andor, the term is widely used for the struggle for the throne that arose upon Mordrellen's death. Tigraine's disappearance had left Mantear without a Daughter-Heir, and two years passed before Morgase, of House Trakand, took the throne. Outside of Andor, this conflict was known as the Third War of Andoran Succession.

Tarabon: A nation on the Aryth Ocean. Once a great trading nation, a source of rugs, dyes and the Guild of Illuminators' fireworks among other things, Tarabon has fallen on hard times. Racked by anarchy and civil war compounded by simultaneous wars against Arad Doman and the Dragonsworn, it was ripe for the picking when the Seanchan arrived. It is now firmly under Seanchan control, the chapter house of the Guild of Illuminators has been destroyed and the Illuminators themselves have been made *da'covale*. Most Taraboners appear grateful that the Seanchan have restored order, and since the Seanchan allow them to continue living their lives with minimal interference, they have no desire to bring on more warfare by trying to chase the Seanchan out. There are, however, some lords and soldiers who remain outside the Seanchan sphere of influence and are fighting to reclaim their land.

Tower of Ravens, the: The central Imperial prison of Seanchan. It is located in the capital of Seandar and serves as the headquarters for the Seekers for Truth. Members of the Blood are imprisoned, questioned and executed within it. The questioning and execution must be accomplished without spilling a drop of blood. *See also* Seekers.

Towers of Midnight, the: Thirteen fortresses of unpolished black marble located in Imfaral, Seanchan. At the time of the Consolidation of Seanchan, it was the center of military might. The final battle of the Consolidation took place there, leaving Hawkwing's descendants in power. Since that time, it has been unoccupied. Legend has it that in time of dire need, the Imperial family will return to the Towers of Midnight and "right that which is wrong." *See also* Consolidation.

weight, units of: 10 ounces = 1 pound; 10 pounds = 1 stone; 10 stone = 1 hundredweight; 10 hundredweight = 1 ton.

Winged Guards, the: The personal bodyguards of the First of Mayene, and the elite military formation of Mayene. Members of the Winged Guards wear red-painted breastplates and helmets shaped like rimmed pots that come down to the nape of the necks in the back, and carry red-streamered lances. Officers have wings worked on the sides of their helmets, and rank is denoted by slender plumes.

PROLOGUE

A preview of
A Memory of Light

Book Fourteen of
The Wheel of Time

By Grace and Banners Fallen

Bayrd pressed the coin between his thumb and forefinger. It was thoroughly unnerving to feel the metal *squish*.

He removed his thumb. The hard copper now clearly bore its print, reflecting the uncertain torchlight. He felt chilled, as if he'd spent an entire night in a cellar.

His stomach growled. Again.

The north wind picked up, making torches sputter. Bayrd sat with his back to a large rock near the center of the war camp. Hungry men muttered as they warmed their hands around firepits; the rations had spoiled long ago. Other soldiers nearby began laying all of their metal—swords, armor clasps, mail—on the ground, like linen to be dried. Perhaps they hoped that when the sun rose, it would change the material back to normal.

Bayrd rolled the once-coin into a ball between his fingers. *Light preserve us,* he thought. *Light . . .* He dropped the ball to the grass, then reached over and picked up the stones he'd been working with.

"I want to know what happened here, Karam," Lord Jarid snapped. Jarid and his advisors stood nearby in front of a table draped with maps. "I want to know how they

drew so close, and I want that bloody Darkfriend Aes
Sedai queen's head!" Jarid pounded his fist down on the
table. Once, his eyes hadn't displayed such a crazed fervor.
The pressure of it all—the lost rations, the strange things
in the nights—was changing him.

Behind Jarid, the command tent lay in a heap. Jarid's
hair—grown long during their exile—blew free, face bathed
in ragged torchlight. Bits of dead grass still clung to his
coat from when he'd crawled out of the tent.

Baffled servants picked at the iron tent spikes, which—
like all metal in the camp—had become soft to the touch.
The tent's mounting rings had stretched and snapped like
warm wax.

The night smelled wrong. Of staleness, of rooms that
hadn't been entered in years. The air of a forest clearing
should not smell like ancient dust. Bayrd's stomach growled
again. Light, but he would've liked to have something to
eat. He set his attention on his work, slapping one of his
stones down against the other.

He held the stones as his old pappil had taught him as a
boy. The feeling of stone striking stone helped push away
the hunger and coldness. At least something was still solid in
this world.

Lord Jarid glanced at him, scowling. Bayrd was one of
ten men Jarid had insisted guard him this night. "I *will* have
Elayne's head, Karam," Jarid said, turning back to his captains. "This unnatural night is the work of her witches."

"Her head?" Eri's skeptical voice came from the side.
"And how, precisely, is someone going to bring you her
head?"

Lord Jarid turned, as did the others around the torchlit
table. Eri stared at the sky; on his shoulder, he wore the
mark of the golden boar charging before a red spear. It was
the mark of Lord Jarid's personal guard, but Eri's voice
bore little respect. "What's he going to use to cut that head
free, Jarid? His teeth?"

The camp stilled at the horribly insubordinate line.
Bayrd stopped his stones, hesitating. Yes, there had been
talk about how unhinged Lord Jarid had become. But this?

Jarid sputtered, face growing red with rage. "You dare
use such a tone with me? One of my own *guards*?"

Eri continued inspecting the cloud-filled sky.

"You're docked two months' pay," Jarid snapped, but his voice trembled. "Stripped of rank and put on latrine duty until further notice. If you speak back to me again, I'll cut out your tongue."

Bayrd shivered in the cold wind. Eri was the best they had in what was left of their rebel army. The other guards shuffled, looking down.

Eri looked toward the lord and smiled. He didn't say a word, but somehow, he didn't have to. Cut out his tongue? Every scrap of metal in the camp had gone soft as lard. Jarid's own knife lay on the table, twisted and warped—it had stretched thin as he pulled it from his sheath. Jarid's coat flapped, open; it had had silver buttons.

"Jarid . . ." Karam said. A young lord of a minor house loyal to Sarand, he had a lean face and large lips. "Do you really think . . . really think this was the work of Aes Sedai? All of the metal in the camp?"

"Of course," Jarid barked. "What else would it be? Don't tell me you believe those campfire tales. The Last Battle? Phaw." He looked back at the table. Unrolled there, with pebbles weighting the corners, was a map of Andor.

Bayrd turned back to his stones. *Snap, snap, snap.* Slate and granite. It had taken work to find suitable sections of each, but Pappil had taught Bayrd to recognize all kinds of stone. The old man had felt betrayed when Bayrd's father had gone off and become a butcher in the city, instead of keeping to the family trade.

Soft, smooth slate. Bumpy, ridged granite. Yes, some things in the world were still solid. Some few things. These days, you couldn't rely on much. Once immovable lords were now soft as . . . well, soft as metal. The sky churned with blackness, and brave men—men Bayrd had long looked up to—trembled and whimpered in the night.

"I'm worried, Jarid," Davies said. An older man, Lord Davies was as close as anyone was to being Jarid's confidant. "We haven't seen anyone in days. Not farmer, not queen's soldier. Something is happening. Something wrong."

"She cleared the people out," Jarid snarled. "She's preparing to pounce."

"I think she's ignoring us, Jarid," Karam said, looking at the sky. Clouds still churned there. It seemed like months since Bayrd had seen a clear sky. "Why would she bother?

Our men are starving. The food continues to spoil. The
signs—"

"She's trying to squeeze us," Jarid said, eyes wide with
fervor. "This is the work of the Aes Sedai."

Stillness came suddenly to the camp. Silence, save for
Bayrd's stones. He'd never felt right as a butcher, but he'd
found a home in his lord's guard. Cutting up cows or cutting
up men, the two were strikingly similar. It bothered him
how easily he'd shifted from one to the other.

Snap, snap, snap.

Eri turned. Jarid eyed the guard suspiciously, as if ready
to scream out harsher punishment.

He wasn't always this bad, was he? Bayrd thought. *He
wanted the throne for his wife, but what lord wouldn't?* It
was hard to look past the name. Bayrd's family had followed the Sarand family with reverence for generations.

Eri strode away from the command post.

"Where do you think you're going?" Jarid howled.

Eri reached to his shoulder and ripped free the badge
of the Sarand house guard. He tossed it aside and left the
torchlight, heading into the night toward the winds from
the north.

Most men in the camp hadn't gone to sleep. They sat
around firepits, wanting to be near warmth and light. A few
with clay pots tried boiling cuts of grass, leaves, or strips of
leather as something, anything, to eat.

They stood up to watch Eri go.

"Deserter," Jarid spat. "After all we've been through,
now he leaves. Just because things are difficult."

"The men are *starving*, Jarid," Davies repeated.

"I'm aware. Thank you so much for telling me about the
problems with every *bloody breath you have*." Jarid wiped
his brow with his trembling palm, then slammed it on his
map. "We'll have to strike one of the cities; there's no
running from her, not now that she knows where we are.
Whitebridge. We'll take it and resupply. Her Aes Sedai
must be weakened after the stunt they pulled tonight, otherwise she'd have attacked."

Bayrd squinted into the darkness. Other men were standing, lifting quarterstaffs or cudgels. Some went without
weapons. They gathered sleeping rolls, hoisted packs of
clothing to their shoulders. Then they began to trail out of

the camp, their passage silent, like the movement of ghosts. No rattling of chain mail or buckles on armor. The metal was all gone. As if the soul had been stripped from it.

"Elayne doesn't dare move against us in strength," Jarid said, perhaps convincing himself. "There must be strife in Caemlyn. All of those mercenaries you reported, Shiv. Riots, maybe. Elenia will be working against Elayne, of course. Whitebridge. Yes, Whitebridge will be perfect.

"We hold it, you see, and cut the nation in half. We recruit there, press the men in western Andor to our banner. Go to . . . what's the place called? The Two Rivers. We should find able hands there." Jarid sniffed. "I hear they haven't seen a lord for decades. Give me four months, and I'll have an army to be reckoned with. Enough that she won't dare strike at us with her witches . . ."

Bayrd held his stone up to the torchlight. The trick to creating a good spearhead was to start outward and work your way in. He'd drawn the proper shape with chalk on the slate, then had worked toward the center to finish the shape. From there, you turned from hitting to tapping, shaving off smaller bits.

He'd finished one side earlier; this second half was almost done. He could almost hear his pappil whispering to him. *We're of the stone, Bayrd. No matter what your father says. Deep down, we're of the stone.*

More soldiers left the camp. Strange, how few of them spoke. Jarid finally noticed. He stood up straight and grabbed one of the torches, holding it high. "What are they doing? Hunting? We've seen no game in weeks. Setting snares, perhaps?"

Nobody replied.

"Maybe they've seen something," Jarid muttered. "Or maybe they think they have. I'll stand no more talk of spirits or other foolery; the witches are creating apparitions to unnerve us. That's . . . that's what it has to be."

Rustling came from nearby. Karam was digging in his fallen tent. He came up with a small bundle.

"Karam?" Jarid said.

Karam glanced at Lord Jarid, then lowered his eyes and began to tie a coin pouch at his waist. He stopped and laughed, then emptied it. The gold coins inside had melted into a single lump, like pigs' ears in a jar. Karam pocketed this lump. He fished in the pouch and brought out a ring. The blood-red gemstone at the center was still good. "Probably won't be enough to buy an apple, these days," he muttered.

"I *demand* to know what you are doing," Jarid snarled. "Is this your doing?" He waved toward the departing soldiers. "You're staging a mutiny, is that it?"

"This isn't my doing," Karam said, looking ashamed. "And it's not really yours, either. I'm . . . I'm sorry."

Karam walked away from the torchlight. Bayrd found himself surprised. Lord Karam and Lord Jarid had been friends from childhood.

Lord Davies went next, running after Karam. Was he going to try to hold the younger man back? No, he fell into step beside Karam. They vanished into the darkness.

"I'll have you hunted down for this!" Jarid yelled after them, voice shrill. Frantic. "I will be consort to the Queen! No man will give you, or any member of your Houses, shelter or succor for ten generations!"

Bayrd looked back at the stone in his hand. Only one step left, the smoothing. A good spearhead needed some smoothing to be dangerous. He brought out another piece of granite he'd picked up for the purpose and carefully began scraping it along the side of the slate.

Seems I remember this better than I'd expected, he thought as Lord Jarid continued to rant.

There was something powerful about crafting the spearhead. The simple act seemed to push back the gloom. There had been a *shadow* on Bayrd, and the rest of the camp, lately. As if . . . as if he couldn't stand in the light no matter how he tried. He woke each morning feeling as if someone he'd loved had died the day before.

It could crush you, that despair. But the act of creating something—anything—fought back. That was one way to challenge . . . *him.* The one none of them spoke of. The one that they all knew was behind it, no matter what Lord Jarid said.

Bayrd stood up. He'd want to do more smoothing later, but the spearhead actually looked good. He raised his wooden spear haft—the metal blade had fallen free when evil had struck the camp—and lashed the new spearhead in place, just as his pappil had taught him all those years ago.

The other guards were looking at him. "We'll need more of those," Morear said. "If you're willing."

Bayrd nodded. "On our way out, we can stop by the hillside where I found the slate."

Jarid finally stopped yelling, his eyes wide in the torchlight. "No. You are my personal guard. You will not defy me!"

Jarid jumped for Bayrd, murder in his eyes, but Morear and Rosse caught the lord from behind. Rosse looked aghast at his own mutinous act. He didn't let go, though.

Bayrd fished a few things out from beside his bedroll. After that, he nodded to the others, and they joined him— eight men of Lord Jarid's personal guard, dragging the sputtering lord himself through the remnants of camp. They passed smoldering fires and fallen tents, abandoned by men who were trailing out into the darkness in greater numbers now, heading north. Into the wind.

At the edge of camp, Bayrd selected a nice, stout tree. He waved to the others, and they took the rope he'd fetched and tied Lord Jarid to the tree. The man sputtered until Morear gagged him with a handkerchief.

Bayrd stepped in close. He tucked a waterskin into the crook of Jarid's arm. "Don't struggle too much or you'll drop that, my Lord. You should be able to push the gag off—it doesn't look too tight—and angle the waterskin up to drink. Here, I'll take out the cork."

Jarid stared thunder at Bayrd.

"It's not about you, my Lord," Bayrd said. "You always treated my family well. But, here, we can't have you following along and making life difficult. There's just something that we need to do, and you're stopping everyone from doing it. Maybe someone should have said something earlier. Well, that's done. Sometimes, you let the meat hang too long, and the entire haunch has to go."

He nodded to the others, who ran off to gather bedrolls. He pointed Rosse toward the slate outcropping nearby and told him what to look for in good spearhead stone.

Bayrd turned back to the struggling Lord Jarid. "This isn't witches, my Lord. This isn't Elayne . . . I suppose I should call her the Queen. Funny, thinking of a pretty young thing like that as queen. I'd rather have bounced her on my knee at an inn than bow to her, but Andor will need a ruler to follow to the Last Battle, and it isn't your wife. I'm sorry."

Jarid sagged in his bonds, the anger seeming to bleed from him. He was weeping now. Odd thing to see, that.

"I'll tell people we pass—if we pass any—where you are," Bayrd promised, "and that you probably have some jewels on you. They might come for you. They might." He hesitated. "You shouldn't have stood in the way. Everyone seems to know what is coming but you. The Dragon is reborn, old bonds are broken, old oaths done away with . . . and I'll be *hanged* before I let Andor march to the Last Battle without me."

Bayrd left, walking into the night, raising his new spear onto his shoulder. *I have an oath older than the one to your family, anyway. An oath the Dragon himself couldn't undo.* It was an oath to the land. The stones were in his blood, and his blood in the stones of this Andor.

Bayrd gathered the others and they left for the north. Behind them in the night, their lord whimpered, alone, as the ghosts began to move through camp.

Talmanes tugged on Selfar's reins, making the horse dance and shake his head. The roan seemed eager. Perhaps Selfar sensed his master's anxious mood.

The night air was thick with smoke. Smoke and screams. Talmanes marched the Band alongside a road clogged with refugees smudged with soot. They moved like flotsam in a muddy river.

The men of the Band eyed the refugees with worry. "Steady!" Talmanes shouted to them. "We can't sprint all the way to Caemlyn. Steady!" He marched the men as quickly as he dared, nearly at a jog. Their armor clanked. Elayne had taken half of the Band with her to the Field of Merrilor, including Estean and most of the cavalry. Perhaps she had anticipated needing to withdraw quickly.

Well, Talmanes wouldn't have much use for cavalry in the streets, which were no doubt as clogged as this roadway. Selfar snorted and shook his head. They were close now; the city walls just ahead—black in the night—held in an angry light. It was as if the city were a firepit.

By grace and banners fallen, Talmanes thought with a shiver. Enormous clouds of smoke billowed over the city.

This was bad. Far worse than when the Aiel had come for Cairhien.

Talmanes finally gave Selfar his head. The roan galloped along the side of the road for a time; then Talmanes reluctantly forced his way across, ignoring pleas for help. Time he'd spent with Mat made him wish there were more he could offer these people. It was downright strange, the effect Matrim Cauthon had on a person. Talmanes looked at common folk in a very different light now. Perhaps it was because he still didn't rightly know whether to think of Mat as a lord or not.

On the other side of the road, he surveyed the burning city, waiting for his men to catch up. He could have mounted all of them—though they weren't trained cavalry, every man in the Band had a horse for long-distance travel. Tonight, he didn't dare. With Trollocs and Myrddraal lurking in the streets, Talmanes needed his men in immediate fighting shape. Crossbowmen marched with loaded weapons at the flanks of deep columns of pikemen. He would not leave his soldiers open to a Trolloc charge, no matter how urgent their mission.

But if they lost those dragons . . .

Light illumine us, Talmanes thought. The city seemed to be boiling, with all that smoke churning above. Yet some parts of the Inner City—rising high on the hill and visible over the walls—were not yet aflame. The Palace wasn't on fire yet. Could the soldiers there be holding?

No word had come from the Queen, and from what Talmanes could see, no help had arrived for the city. The Queen must still be unaware, and that was bad.

Very, *very* bad.

Ahead, Talmanes spotted Sandip with some of the Band's scouts. The slender man was trying to extricate himself from a group of refugees.

"Please, good master," one young woman was crying. "My child, my daughter, in the heights of the northern march . . ."

"I must reach my shop!" a stout man bellowed. "My glasswares—"

"My good people," Talmanes said, forcing his horse among them, "I should think that if you want us to help, you might wish to back away and allow us to reach the bloody city."

The refugees reluctantly pulled back, and Sandip nodded to Talmanes in thanks. Tan-skinned and dark-haired, Sandip was one of the Band's commanders and an accomplished hedge-doctor. The affable man wore a grim expression today, however.

"Sandip," Talmanes said, pointing, "there."

In the near distance, a large group of fighting men clustered, looking at the city.

"Mercenaries," Sandip said with a grunt. "We've passed several batches of them. Not a one seemed inclined to lift a finger."

"We shall see about that," Talmanes said. People still flooded out through the city gates, coughing, clutching meager possessions, leading crying children. That flow would not soon slacken. Caemlyn was as full as an inn on market day; the ones lucky enough to be escaping would be only a small fraction compared to those still inside.

"Talmanes," Sandip said quietly, "that city's going to become a death trap soon. There aren't enough ways out. If we let the Band become pinned inside . . ."

"I know. But—"

At the gates a wave of feeling surged through the refugees. It was almost a physical thing, a shudder. The screams grew more intense. Talmanes spun; hulking figures moved in the shadows inside the gate.

"Light!" Sandip said. "What is it?"

"Trollocs," Talmanes said, turning Selfar. "Light! They're going to try to seize the gate, stop the refugees." There were five gates out of the city; if the Trollocs held all of them . . .

This was already a slaughter. If the Trollocs could stop the frightened people from fleeing, it would grow far worse.

"Hurry the ranks!" Talmanes yelled. "All men to the city gates!" He spurred Selfar into a gallop.

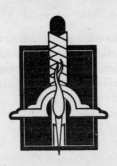

About the Authors

Robert Jordan was born in 1948 in Charleston, South Carolina. He taught himself to read when he was four with the incidental aid of a twelve-years-older brother, and was tackling Mark Twain and Jules Verne by five. He was a graduate of the Citadel, the Military college of South Carolina, with a degree in physics. He served two tours in Vietnam with the U.S. Army; among his decorations are the Distinguished Flying Cross with bronze oak leaf cluster, the Bronze Star with "V" and bronze oak leaf cluster, and two Vietnamese Gallantry Crosses with Palm. A history buff, he also wrote dance and theater criticism. He enjoyed the outdoor sports of hunting, fishing, and sailing, and the indoor sports of poker, chess, pool, and pipe collecting. He began writing in 1977 and continued until his death on September 16, 2007.

Brandon Sanderson was born in 1975 in Lincoln, Nebraska. After a semester as a biochem major, Brandon came to his senses and recognized writing as his true vocation. He switched to English, graduating from Brigham Young University, then returning for a master's in creative writing. During this time Brandon wrote thirteen novels, finally publishing his sixth, *Elantris,* in 2005. He has since released books for both adults and young readers, including the Mistborn trilogy, *Warbreaker,* and the Alcatraz series. He lives with his wife and children in Utah, where he often plays *Magic: The Gathering*, regularly eats mac-and-cheese, and occasionally teaches writing at BYU. Find more at www .brandonsanderson.com.